Case Studies in Contemporary Criticism

W9-BXN-346

JANE AUSTEN

Emma

Case Studies in Contemporary Criticism
SERIES EDITOR: Ross C Murfin

Case Studies in Contemporary Criticism

SERIES EDITOR: Ross C Murfin, *Southern Methodist University*

JANE AUSTEN
Emma

Complete, Authoritative Text with
Biographical, Historical, and Cultural Contexts,
Critical History, and Essays from
Contemporary Critical Perspectives

EDITED BY
Alistair M. Duckworth
University of Florida

Bedford/St. Martin's
BOSTON ◆ NEW YORK

For Bedford/St. Martin's

Executive Editor: Stephen A. Scipione
Editorial Assistant: Emily Goodall
Senior Production Supervisor: Dennis J. Conroy
Project Management: Stratford Publishing Services, Inc.
Marketing Manager: Richard Cadman
Text Design: Sandra Rigney, The Book Department
Cover Design: Claire Jarvis
Cover Art: John Constable, *Malvern Hall, Warwickshire,* 1809. Tate Gallery, London/Art Resource, NY.
Composition: Stratford Publishing Services, Inc.
Printing and Binding: Haddon Craftsmen, an RR Donnelley & Sons Company

President: Charles H. Christensen
Editorial Director: Joan E. Feinberg
Editor in Chief: Karen S. Henry
Director of Marketing: Karen R. Melton
Director of Editing, Design, and Production: Marcia Cohen
Manager, Publishing Services: Emily Berleth

Acknowledgments

Acknowledgments and copyrights can be found at the back of the book on page 638, which constitutes an extension of the copyright page.

About the Series

Volumes in the *Case Studies in Contemporary Criticism* series introduce college students to the current critical and theoretical ferment in literary studies. Each volume reprints the complete text of a significant literary work, together with critical essays that approach the work from different theoretical perspectives and editorial matter that introduces both the literary work and the critics' theoretical perspectives.

The volume editor of each *Case Study* has selected and prepared an authoritative text of a classic work, written introductions (sometimes supplemented by cultural documents) that place the work in biographical and historical context, and surveyed the critical responses to the work since its original publication. Thus situated biographically, historically, and critically, the work is subsequently examined in several critical essays that have been prepared especially for students. The essays show theory in practice; whether written by established scholars or exceptional young critics, they demonstrate how current theoretical approaches can generate compelling readings of great literature.

As series editor, I have prepared introductions to the critical essays and to the theoretical approaches they entail. The introductions, accompanied by bibliographies, explain and historicize the principal concepts, major figures, and key works of particular theoretical approaches as a prelude to discussing how they pertain to the critical essays that follow. It is my hope that the introductions will reveal to students that effective criticism — including their own — is informed by a set of coherent assumptions that can be not only articulated but also modified and extended through comparison of different theoretical approaches. Finally, I have included a glossary of key terms that recur in these volumes and in the discourse of contemporary theory and criticism. I hope that the *Case Studies in Contemporary Criticism* series will reaffirm the richness of its literary works, even as it presents invigorating new ways to mine their apparently inexhaustible wealth.

I would like to thank Supryia M. Ray, with whom I wrote *The Bedford Glossary of Critical and Literary Terms,* for her invaluable help in revising the introductions to the critical approaches represented in this volume.

Ross C Murfin
Provost, Southern Methodist University
Series Editor

About This Volume

The authoritative text of *Emma* printed in this volume is a corrected and annotated version of the three-volume first edition published in London in late December 1815. The editorial rationale is explained in "About the Text" (p. xi), as is the policy regarding annotations of terms and references that may prove obscure to modern readers. In Part One, the text of the novel is preceded by a historical and biographical introduction and followed by a selection of contextual documents and illustrations intended to help the reader place *Emma* in Jane Austen's cultural milieu. Part Two of this volume comprises, in addition to my critical history of the novel and Ross C Murfin's theoretical introductions and bibliographies, six critical essays on *Emma*. Five appear under the rubric of a contemporary mode of reading (respectively gender studies, Marxism, cultural criticism, new historicism, feminism), but none is restricted to the orthodoxy of a single "school" of interpretation. Though not to the extent of the final "combined approaches" essay, each makes strategic use of more than one method of criticism. All six essays have the merit of being anchored in a close reading of the novel, and the further merit of being written lucidly.

The essays on *Emma* open with Claudia Johnson's gender approach and close with Marilyn Butler's "combined" approach. No more appropriate "bookends" could be found, for Austen criticism in the last generation has typically found its bearings by reference to the markedly different perspectives taken on Austen's politics in Butler's ground-breaking *Jane Austen and the War of Ideas* (1975) and Johnson's revisionist *Jane Austen: Women, Politics, and the Novel* (1988). The essays reprinted here represent new directions for each critic, however. Both read the novel positively and progressively. Johnson is interested not only in Austen's refusal to condemn Emma's transgressions against femininity but in the redefinitions of masculinity that occur in the characterization of Mr. Woodhouse and Mr. Knightley. Even less "Emma-centric" is Butler's attention to secondary characters such as Mrs. Elton and, especially, Miss Bates, whose gossip suggests the democratizing tendency of oral speech even as it registers subtle shifts in social power in the community.

Beth Tobin's Marxist essay sees *Emma* as resisting rather than registering social change. In her view, Miss Bates as an impoverished gentlewoman exists as a rebuke to Emma, whose cruel remark on Box Hill is not only a personal slight but a threat to a paternalist system that depends upon the gentry's willingness to fulfil its charitable obligations. For Tobin, Mr. Knightley is the novel's exemplary figure, and in Emma's marriage to him, Austen reassures her readers that the traditional social structure is sound; in the process, however, she has turned a general social problem (the predicament of impoverished women) into a particular personal problem (Emma's thoughtlessness) and, in correcting Emma, has effected a fictional rather than a real solution.

Like Tobin, Paul Delany, in his essay in cultural criticism, also sees Mr. Knightley as exemplary. Unlike Tobin, he does not consider Austen an apologist for the landed classes. Invoking the support of the sociologist Max Weber, Delany is interested in status as well as class, and in the interaction of the social realities signified by these two terms, rather than in the novel's concern with gender roles, he locates the central drama of *Emma*. Only Mr. Knightley, at the top of the social hierarchy, is free from status anxiety; others in Highbury, and especially Emma, who tries to regulate the boundaries of her social world, seek in various ways to achieve "distinction" (a term Delany borrows from the contemporary French sociologist Pierre Bourdieu).

Casey Finch and Peter Bowen's new historicist essay shares with Butler's essay an interest in the role of gossip in dispersing authority in a community and providing an alternative mode of communication for women excluded from the legal and political discourses of power. Influenced by Foucault, however, they emphasize the regulatory rather than the democratic function of gossip. Like Tobin, they are interested in the way Emma's concluding marriage to Mr. Knightley confirms an existing social structure, but they view that structure less in neofeudal than in bourgeois terms. Emma's marriage is politically inevitable because it accords with the wishes of a community that, through gossip, maps out the social and gender roles it imposes upon the individual.

Devoney Looser's feminist essay, written especially for this volume, contributes to critical debates on Austen's treatment of women's friendships by setting Emma's patronage of Harriet, and Mrs. Elton's of Jane, in the context of a history of companionate relations between wealthy and dependent women, which all too often mirrored relations between powerful husbands and powerless wives. Like Delany, then, she explores the possibility that class and status, more than gender, determined the nature of female relations in Austen's world. Her conclusion, however, is that Austen, though she may not show sisterhood across, or even within, social levels in *Emma*, does expose the evils of female patronage, achieving thereby a liberal feminist position.

Taken as whole, these fine essays hardly reach a consensus about Austen's novel. Basic disagreements, common in critical responses to *Emma* over the years, recur. Is Emma, Austen's only financially independent heroine, to be commended or condemned for her self-assertive actions, praised or pitied for her acceptance of Mr. Knightley's proposal? Is Mr. Knightley, as his name implies, the very figure of traditional English manhood, with all the limitations and virtues that such a description entails? Or is he a new man, with traits that even women might wish to emulate? How villainous or charming is Frank Churchill? How odious is Mrs. Elton? Perhaps only the last of these questions will elicit agreement, as the reader joins Emma, Mr. Knightley, and Frank Churchill in finding Mrs. Elton very odious indeed. And yet Mrs. Elton, as several essays show, also needs a second look; her insufferable vulgarity has its causes and its contexts; she is intrinsic to the transitional social world that Austen represents with incomparable subtlety and skill. The authors in this *Case Study* edition may not always agree on Austen's meanings, but they do agree in their high assessments of her powers of social analysis. Using different theoretical approaches, but anchoring their readings in an understanding of Austen's historical period, they describe an author as far different from "gentle Jane," the soothing recorder of gentry life, as can be imagined.

Acknowledgments

I am grateful to all six authors for their permission to reprint their work and for their tolerance of editorial cuts and changes made to fit

the essays to the series format. To Jeffrey Barr, curator of Rare Books in
the George A. Smathers Libraries of the University of Florida, I owe
thanks for allowing me to use the copy of the first edition of *Emma*
owned by the University of Florida, and for his advice. To Steven Knox,
undergraduate university scholar, I am very grateful for help in the
preparation of the text for submission to the press. For aid with annotations, I am grateful to C. J. Nicholson for information on carriages
(including Mrs. Elton's famous barouche-landau) and to Victor Knight
for helpful comments on square pianos and "Robin Adair." To Debbie
Coutavas at the Pierpont Morgan Library; Aubrey Hall at the Walker
Art Gallery, Liverpool; Martin Hinman at The Russell Collection of
Early Keyboard Instruments, Edinburgh; Tom Carpenter of The Jane
Austen Memorial Trust, Chawton; and Alison Miles and Sarah Munday
at the Tate Gallery, London; I owe thanks for their kind responses to
my questions, and for their provision of illustrations. To Claudia Johnson and Jan Fergus, who kindly responded to textual queries, I am very
grateful; neither has any responsibility for the text's final form. To Ross
Murfin, the general editor of this series and a swift and peerless reader
of essays, I am much indebted; among other things, he sought to cure
me of my penchant for semicolons. At Bedford/St. Martin's Steve Scipione once more provided kind and patient editorial support, and Emily
Berleth, Leslie Connor, and Cathy Jewell were of great help in bringing
the book into production. I wish to thank also Charles Christensen, Joan
Feinberg, and especially Emily Goodall, for her work in assembling the
manuscript. Special thanks are due to Sears Jayne, who was willing to
give generously of his time to help with library research. My greatest
indebtedness, as always, is to Emily Jayne Duckworth, whose support
for the project was, from the beginning, uplifting and unstinting.

                                             Alistair M. Duckworth
                                             University of Florida

About the Text

Emma was published late in 1815 (probably on December 23), though the date on the title page is 1816. The publisher was John Murray, who ordered a sizeable press run of 2,000. The retail price for the three volumes was twenty-one shillings. By October 1816 some 1,200 copies had been sold; they earned Jane Austen a profit of £221.6.4, though as David Gilson points out in his *Bibliography of Jane Austen* (Oxford: Clarendon, 1982), most of this profit was used to off-set the loss on the second edition of *Mansfield Park,* also published by Murray. Why Austen should dedicate *Emma* to the Prince Regent, a man whom she disliked for, among other failings, his ill-treatment of his estranged wife Caroline, is a fascinating story told in all biographies of Austen. The Prince Regent, who admired her novels, learned from his physician (who was also at the time treating Austen's seriously ill brother Henry) that she was in London, and he arranged for his librarian, James Stanier Clarke, to meet with her. Clarke — a superlatively silly man whose attempts to have Austen write novels to his specifications prompted her satirical *Plan of a Novel* — let it be known that she was at liberty to dedicate her next novel to the prince. She was soon made aware that such an invitation was tantamount to a royal command. The dedication she planned did not suit Murray, who was probably responsible for the dedication — terse by the standards of the time — that we see.

No manuscript of *Emma* survives, and no other edition appeared in Jane Austen's lifetime. The three-volume first edition therefore has a special authority, and an editor's main task is to correct printer's errors. In this I have been greatly aided by the work of R. W. Chapman, whose edition of *Emma*, published as volume four of *The Novels of Jane Austen*, 3rd edition (Oxford: Oxford UP, 1933), and revised in 1966 by Mary Lascelles, is an indispensable reference for all scholars of the novel. Of a dozen significant emendations in the Oxford text I have accepted, and silently retained, all but three: Chapman's corrections of *cara sposo* and *cara sposa* (discussed below); the substitution of "when" for "where" in the phrase "where, all of a sudden, who should come in" (p. 151 in this volume); and the substitution of "indifference" for "indifferent" in the first paragraph of Chapter VII in Volume II (p. 171). I have also benefited from the 1996 Penguin edition of *Emma*, edited by Fiona Stafford, which is independently based on the 1816 edition. In common with these editions, this text retains the three-volume format and begins each volume with chapter one. It retains period spellings — e.g., recal, born (for borne), atchieved, waves (for waives), shew (for show), headachs; and it observes variant spellings of common words — e.g., anybody/any body, good-natured/goodnatured, connection/connexion, surprize/surprise, pianoforté/piano forté. Variant spellings of place-names are also observed — e.g., Brunswick-square/Brunswick Square, Abbey-Mill-Farm/Abbey-Mill Farm, King's-Weston/Kings Weston, Box Hill/Box-Hill. An exception is made for the name of Mr. Weston's estate; the printer of the third volume gives Randall's, but I regularize this to the spelling adopted by the printer of the first two volumes: Randalls. As Stafford points out, the William Coxe of Volume I, Chapter XVI of the first edition is the same person as the William Cox, mentioned twice elsewhere, who is a member of the Cox family, which is also referred to on several occasions; the extra *e* is therefore dropped.

Period grammar (e.g., "has drank his tea," "was all eat up") is retained, though, as several notes indicate, period grammar may be distinguished from substandard usages (in the speeches of Harriet Smith and Mrs. Elton). Period punctuation is generally observed, but where Austen's innovative style seems to have taxed the conventions of the time, chiefly regarding the use of quotation marks, I have on some few occasions changed the punctuation; these changes are noted. Where corrections are to obvious typographical errors (an extra period, missed-out letters, a wrong chapter number, truncated words, dropped quotation marks), they are made silently.

One textual crux of long standing concerns Mrs. Elton's pet name for her husband, which appears in the first edition as *cara sposo* on two occasions, *cara sposa* on one, and *caro sposo* on one. Chapman regularizes the phrase to the correct *caro sposo*; but it is likely that Austen intended the variations as yet another sign of Mrs. Elton's invincible ignorance (evident, for example, in her assertion that Surrey, and only Surrey, is "the garden of England"); the variant spellings of the phrase in the first edition have therefore been retained.

The annotations at the bottom of the page are intended to locate geographical, historical, and literary references, identify figures and events, and explain words and phrases that may no longer be widely understood. I have tried to be succinct, and where I have failed, I claim the support of *Emma* herself who tells Harriet that "A Hartfield edition of Shakespeare would have a long note on that passage." While keeping interpretation out of the annotations, I occasionally refer interested readers to books and articles that provide a fuller discussion of particular references or to pertinent illustrations and contextual documents contained in this edition. Where my indebtedness to other scholars is specific I so indicate in the notes. To the multivolume *Oxford English Dictionary* (*OED*), that great repository of historical meanings of words, I am especially indebted.

Contents

PART TWO
Emma:
A Case Study in Contemporary Criticism

PART ONE

Emma:
The Complete Text
in Cultural Context

Introduction:
Biographical and
Historical Contexts

Jane Austen was born on December 16, 1775, in the year before
the American Declaration of Independence, and she died on July 18,
1817, two years after the defeat of Napoleon by the allied armies at
Waterloo. She was thirteen when the Bastille was stormed on July 14,
1789 and seventeen when Britain, reacting to the execution of Louis
XVI in January 1793 and the policy of expansion undertaken by the
revolutionary government, went to war with France. Even in the rural
security of her rectory home in Hampshire, she must have been aware
of the dangers of the time. In 1794 the Comte de Feuillide, husband of
her cousin Eliza, was guillotined for attempting to bribe an official not
to proceed against an elderly marquise accused of conspiring against the
Republic. In 1795 her brother Henry, an officer in the Militia, witnessed the execution by firing squad of soldiers in his own regiment,
who had joined with the poor in rioting for food (Tomalin 104). During the Revolutionary and Napoleonic wars that stretched though most
of her adult life, her brothers Francis and Charles were often in peril on
the sea.

Despite living through one of the most perilous periods in English
history, Austen seemed to generations of readers not to have engaged
the major events of her time. Austen's supposed quietism was promoted as early as the "Biographical Notice" that her brother Henry

appended to the posthumous publication of *Northanger Abbey* and *Persuasion* (1818). Henry described his sister's life as one of "usefulness, literature, and religion . . . not by any means a life of event" (3). This pious perspective prevailed in the *Memoir* published by her nephew James Edward Austen-Leigh in 1870, which painted a picture of a sweet-natured, family-loving woman whose fictional subject was the uneventful life of the rural gentry. With the memoir began a "Janeite" cult that sought to make Austen's novels the preserve of an especially discriminating and genteel readership. William and Richard Austen-Leigh (son and grandson of the author of the *Memoir*) in their *Family Record* of 1913 disputed views of Austen's limited existence but failed to correct the picture. And although dissonant voices arose to contradict "gentle Janeism" (Farrer 1917; Harding 1940; Mudrick 1952), their representations of an ironical, even "subversive" author paid scant attention to her engagement with history.

Only in recent years have scholars argued that Austen responded significantly to her historical moment. In 1975 Marilyn Butler proposed that Austen, who began writing her novels in the revolutionary decade of the 1790s, engaged in "a war of ideas." While her subject matter was domestic, she wrote as a politically committed "anti-Jacobin" novelist, critical of the sensibility and individualism promoted in radical novels, and affirming instead the Tory and Anglican values of her family. Though Butler's book proved to be controversial, the effect of its emphasis on Austen's political engagement was wide-ranging. Biographers such as Park Honan (1987) and Claire Tomalin (1997) provided detailed analyses of her social milieu, while others, such as David Spring (1983), Jan Fergus (1991) and Edward Copeland (1995) uncovered the financial exigencies of her life. Far from being a haven of domestic peace, the rural society in which Jane Austen grew up was now seen to be fluid, uncertain, and riven by economic pressures. Moreover, it was a world in which — as feminist scholars were particularly aware — the plight of single women without financial resources could be bleak indeed.

In his influential article, Spring placed Austen's family in the sociologists' category of the "pseudo gentry," by which he referred to a group on the fringe of the gentry, including small landowners (with less than a hundred acres), professional and rentier families, Anglican clergymen, lawyers, and officers in the army and navy (59). Though "pseudo-gentry," in its suggestion of fraudulence, is an unfortunate term (Fergus 46), Spring showed in detail how Austen's family situation provided the incentive for her incisive analysis of "positional competition" in her society (60). Her father, George Austen (1731–1805), was a modest clergyman who was often forced to borrow large sums of money from his relations (Honan 17). He was a descendant of the Austens of Kent, clothiers who had become prosperous and landed. George, however, came from an impoverished generation and his claim to gentry status rested on his connections to rich kinsmen. His uncle Francis Austen paid George's fees at Tonbridge School, and from there George went on a fellowship to St. John's College, Oxford. Another rich kinsman, Thomas Knight II, presented him with a church living at Steventon in Hampshire, which George took up shortly after marriage. His uncle Francis bought a second living for him at nearby Deane, and when this became vacant in 1773 (two years before Jane's birth), it proved a welcome addition to his income. Despite his combined livings, however, George Austen was not well-off. Steventon was valued at £100 a year, and Deane at £110, and though tithes increased his income, he found it necessary to run a small farm and take in pupils. All the while, in a parish whose principal landowner was absent, he played the part of squire as well as parson, maintaining in this way a status that his income barely warranted.

The Austens' claim to gentry status was, in fact, stronger on her mother's side, though, again, adequate financial provision was lacking. Cassandra Austen (1739–1827) was a Leigh of the Leighs of Adlestrop. Stoneleigh Abbey in Warwickshire — a huge country house comprising the remains of a Cistercian Abbey, an Elizabeth mansion, and a classic range added in the years after 1714 — belonged to a younger, ennobled branch of the family. The Leighs were known for their Tory and Jacobite sympathies. The family at Stoneleigh had made their house available to Charles I during the Civil War when he was denied entry to Coventry; a century later, during the second Highland rebellion of 1745, they were just as willing to accommodate Bonnie Prince Charlie, until the failure of his futile quest to restore the Stuarts to the throne made their treasonous gesture unnecessary. From her mother's antecedents the young Jane gained a romantic sense of connection with an aristocratic past. The sympathy she extends to the Catholic Mary Queen of Scots in her burlesque *History of England,* written when she was fifteen, along with her tongue-in-cheek attack on the Protestant Elizabeth I there and in *Catharine, or the Bower,* written a year later, carries a measure of genuine preference for an older Tory — even Jacobite — world.

Austen's traditional roots account for the conservatism that characterizes much of her life and fiction. It is not by chance that her most admirable male character should be named Mr. Knightley. To be sure, from her earliest writings her conservatism is qualified by the discontent she feels as a woman and, especially in her mature novels, her respect for traditional moral and social principles accommodates a new respect for professional dedication and commitment. But the Tory and Anglican values she learned in the Steventon rectory remain a central strand in her conception of a good society, and they disqualify critical attempts to equate her political position with that of a radical thinker like Mary Wollstonecraft (Duckworth, *Improvement* x–xi).

Austen's conservatism is most obvious in the fiction when she takes what Nigel Everett has termed a "Tory view of landscape" — when, that is, she views changes in houses and grounds as threats to a traditional social order. John Dashwood in *Sense and Sensibility* encloses Norland common, engrosses a neighboring farm, and to his sister Elinor's dismay cuts down old walnut trees behind the house to make way for a greenhouse and flower garden for his wife (225–26). Henry Crawford in *Mansfield Park* proposes radical changes to Edmund's future parsonage, Thornton Lacey. Like Mr. Knightley's Donwell Abbey in *Emma* and Colonel Brandon's Delaford in *Sense and Sensibility*, Thornton Lacey has escaped the attentions of eighteenth-century improvers. The *unimproved* condition of these estates signifies their value as neighborhoods that have evolved naturally over the centuries.

Crawford's plans at Thornton Lacey resemble those of the leading landscape architect of the period, Humphry Repton, at Harlestone Hall (Duckworth, *Improvement* 50–53). Austen may have had personal reasons to be suspicious of Repton. He had improved the grounds of the rectory and big house at Adlestrop, homes of her mother's cousin Thomas Leigh and his nephew respectively. Removing an old-fashioned garden, Repton created a large park in its place, formed a waterfall that ran through a flower garden, and enclosed the village common. Soon after, he "improved" Stoneleigh Abbey, removing walls, opening views, and altering the course of the River Avon. Jane Austen and her mother were staying at Adlestrop in 1806 when Dr. Leigh learned of the death of Stoneleigh's owner, and they accompanied him as he hastened to take possession of the estate whose legal heir was in doubt; their visit is a probable source for the debate over improvements in chapter six of *Mansfield Park*, a chapter that reveals Austen's dislike of radical changes — in landscape, politics, or religion. But it is in *Emma* that Austen's traditional "English" values are most eloquently conveyed. A visit to Donwell Abbey allows Emma to view Mr. Knightley's house (pp. 286–88 in this volume). All the notations in this description — the low and sheltered situation of the Abbey, the "ample gardens," the "abundance of timber in rows and avenues, which neither fashion nor extravagance had rooted up" (p. 286) — imply respect for an organic society, rooted in the soil of the past. Emma's ensuing view of the Abbey-Mill farm — a view that expresses "English verdure, English culture, English comfort" (p. 288) — is a celebrated instance of scenic chauvinism.

Austen's regard for an idealized England was constant through her life, but her experience of an actual England was not so positive. As the seventh of eight children, she found herself watching (and for the most part cheering) as her brothers advanced in their careers. In her own life, she came to realize, as well as in that of her beloved elder sister Cassandra, no such rise through enterprise was possible. Austen's bitter assessments of a society in which marriage was the only means of preferment available to genteel women have their origins in her early life. It is therefore worth looking briefly at the careers of her brothers, all but one older than Jane. One of the brothers, George, seems to have been mentally retarded, and is never a part of the family success story (he was sent away to be cared for); the other five brothers had remarkable lives.

The two eldest, like their father, were beneficiaries of rich kinsmen. James, who became a clergyman, was the prospective heir of Mrs. Austen's rich brother, James Leigh Perrott, and his formidable wife; Edward was adopted in his teens by the Knights, another rich family, who eventually bequeathed to him three estates in Kent and Hampshire. Edward thus became a great gentry landowner with an income comparable to that of Rushworth in *Mansfield Park* who, with £12,000 a year, is the richest of Austen's characters. The other three brothers had to make their own way in life. Henry had a checkered career, serving as an officer in the militia, army agent, Receiver-General of Taxes for Oxfordshire, and banker with branches in Alton and London; after his bank failed in late 1815, Henry became a clergyman. The two youngest brothers, Francis and Charles, joined the Royal Navy at early ages, served with distinction in the wars, and earned considerable sums from prize money and (in Frank's instance) from the clandestine shipment of silver in Royal Navy ships for the East India Company (Honan 68–69). Both became admirals.

Critics are divided on the nature of Austen's relations to her brothers. My sense is that she loved her sailor brothers best. To the charming but unsteady Henry — usually considered her favorite — she extends an amused tolerance in her letters to Cassandra. Of Edward's hypochondria she is faintly critical. James she seems to like least, partly because he was ill-tempered, partly because his second wife was "in the main not a liberal-minded Woman" (*Letters* 341). What may be said about her brothers in general is that they gave her access to an extraordinary range of behaviors among landed, clerical, and professional circles. She knew the ways of Bath, where her family visited and for a time settled, and where Edward sought a cure for gout. She measured the distance between her frugal life at Steventon — and later at Chawton — and the luxury of well-appointed country houses such as Edward's at Godmersham in Kent. In London, on visits to Henry, she went to exhibitions, attended the theatre, and in spring 1811 met French emigrés at a party put on by Henry's wife Eliza — the same Eliza whose first husband had been guillotined in the French Revolution. A quarter of a century earlier, Eliza had descended like an exotic bird on the Steventon rectory, bringing the manners of Marie Antoinette's court to rural Hampshire and joining the Austen children in the theatricals they performed in the barn.

The Jane Austen of the early years at Steventon seems to have been a fun-loving and alarmingly frank young girl. Between the ages of twelve and eighteen she wrote twenty-seven literary pieces (commonly called her *Juvenilia*), which she later transcribed into three notebooks entitled *Volume the First, Volume the Second,* and *Volume the Third.* Not published (for the most part) until the twentieth century, these works have proved of extraordinary interest in recent years, (they supply, for example, many of the heroine's speeches in Patricia Rozema's film of *Mansfield Park* [1999]). Because the juvenilia represent the unfettered freedom of their youthful heroines, some readers have preferred them to the published novels, in which the heroines are (supposedly) tamed by the concluding marriages. The early pieces *are* anarchic — delightfully so; many of the heroines are quite without moral or religious scruples. Several get drunk, others steal, one commits suicide, and one is a mass murderer. Few show any sense of obligation to parents or guardians. Most are single-mindedly intent on fulfilling their appetites for food, or money, or men. The sixteen-year-old heroine of "The Beautiful Cassandra" is typical. Leaving her mother's shop one day to make her fortune, "she proceeded to a Pastry-cooks where she devoured six ices, refused to pay for them, knocked down the pastry Cook & walked away" (*Minor Works* 45).

More than burlesques of sentimental fiction, the early works contain a strong measure of social criticism. Everywhere in the three volumes we encounter a world in which husband hunting is the norm. Like Wollstonecraft in her *A Vindication of the Rights of Woman* (1792), Austen attacks the acquisition of superficial "accomplishments" by young women; repeatedly she satirizes those who use their money and position as social weapons. "In Lady Williams," one of her narrators writes, "every virtue met. She was a widow with a handsome Jointure & the remains of a very handsome face" (13). In such characters are the seeds for later portraits of Mrs. Ferrars in *Sense and Sensibility* and Lady Catherine in *Pride and Prejudice*. The young Austen expresses and for the most part allays her own youthful anxieties regarding her social position and marriage possibilities, but the anxieties are there, as in the following dialogue from "The Three Sisters" (1792): "Yet how can I hope that my Sister may accept a Man, who cannot make her happy," one sister asks. "He cannot it is true but his Fortune, his Name, his House, his Carriage will," a second sister replies. "He" is Mr. Watts, and his income of £3,000 a year is, as one sister says, "but six times as much as my Mother's income" (62). Or, we might add, but six times as much as Mr. Austen's probable income at the time of the story (Duckworth, "Accommodations" 172–73).

The predicament of single women without dowries is never far from her mind. The most substantial of these early works, *Catharine, or the Bower* (1792), contains, within its story of an orphaned heroine subjected to the moral surveillance of an aunt, another story of a young woman, also an orphan, who is forced to "embrace the only possibility that was offered to her . . . of a Maintenance"; she accepts an offer to pay her voyage to India, where "her personal Attractions . . . gained her a husband as soon as she arrived at Bengal" (*Minor Works* 194). Her husband is twice her age, his manners are displeasing, and the woman is unhappy. The story reflects the experiences of George Austen's sister Philadelphia Hancock, who had been obliged to travel alone to India and marry an older man, not for love, but in a commercial exchange — her body for his money. Aunt Philadelphia had died only a few months before *Catharine* was written (Tomalin 80–81). Moreover, there is reason to believe (though not all biographers do) that Philadelphia was the mistress of Warren Hastings, the Governor General of Bengal, and that Hastings was the father of her daughter Eliza (the Eliza who would later marry the Comte de Feuillide, and still later, Henry Austen). Reading *Catharine*, Austen's family may have wondered, and not for the first time, how far the ripples would extend from the stones thrown into her fictional pools.

The years at Steventon (1775–1801) may be viewed as composing the first of three phases in Austen's life. Steventon seems to have been a happy home, offering her the pleasures of reading, family theatricals at Christmas, visits to friends and neighbors, balls, and — in the winter of 1795–96, when she was twenty — romance, in the form of a brief but intense relationship with Tom Lefroy, a young Irish gentleman visiting the neighborhood on his way to study law in London. More than the flirtation she pretends it to be in the first of her extant letters (*Letters* 1–2), this relationship might have developed into an engagement, for every indication is that each was in love with the other (Honan 105–111). The relationship was nipped in the bud by Tom's aunt — and Jane Austen's friend — Madam Lefroy, on the prudent grounds that he had professional ambitions (he eventually became the Lord Chief Justice of Ireland) and she lacked money. Tomalin is persuasive in proposing that in January 1796 Austen "might quite cheerfully have exchanged her genius for the prospect of being married to Tom Lefroy" (117).

Marriage was not to be her role in life, however; writing was. Between 1795 and 1798 she was extraordinarily active as an author, writing early versions of three of her published novels: *Sense and Sensibility,* begun as the epistolary *Elinor and Marianne* in 1795; *Pride and Prejudice,* then named *First Impressions,* in 1796; and *Susan,* later titled *Northanger Abbey,* in 1798. Her father offered *First Impressions* to the publisher Cadell in 1797, who declined by return of post. She had more luck with *Susan* in 1803, the manuscript being bought for £10 by Crosby, but then allowed to languish on the shelf. No manuscripts of these early versions survive, and thus there is no way of knowing exactly how much revision occurred before their subsequent publication as *Sense and Sensibility* (1811), *Pride and Prejudice* (1813), and *Northanger Abbey* (1818). Even so, these three novels are usually referred to as the "Steventon" novels.

Pride and Prejudice and *Northanger Abbey* are comedies, and the former is, as Austen conceded, almost "too light & bright & sparkling" (*Letters* 203). Though it is close to home in its representation of the Bennet sisters, whose future lives as genteel women depend upon advantageous marriages, the novel overcomes social obstacles through the wit and intelligence of its principals, Elizabeth and Darcy. *Sense and Sensibility,* however, is quite another kind of novel. Once interpreted as a satire on the novel of sensibility, with Marianne the representative of a cult as selfish as it is self-defeating for women, the novel is more often read now as a critique of a misogynistic economy (Copeland 89–116). The second chapter, in which John Dashwood, abetted by his wife, progressively diminishes the amount he will give his half-sisters now that their father is dead is a masterpiece in the literature of greed and hypocrisy. Only in her unfinished *The Watsons* is the economic calculus in human motivation as bitterly exposed.

The Watsons was written in 1804–05, when Austen's fate as a distressed gentlewoman (she was now twenty-nine) was clearly manifest. She had had the opportunity of an advantageous marriage in December 1802 when, on a visit from Bath to Manydown in her beloved Hampshire, she had accepted the proposal of Harris Bigg-Wither, the heir of a substantial landed estate, and a man six years younger. Unlike Charlotte Lucas in *Pride and Prejudice,* however, who married a fool to gain an "establishment," Austen recanted her acceptance the next morning. Like Cassandra (whose fiancé had died in 1797 of yellow fever while serving as a military chaplain in the West Indies), she would remain unmarried, and with Cassandra and her mother she would face the challenge of maintaining a genteel level of existence. Her father died in January 1805, leaving his widow and daughters to survive on a mere £210 a year. Unlike John Dashwood in *Sense and Sensibility,* the Austen brothers came to the aid of their mother and sisters: James, Henry, and Frank each provided £50 a year, and the very rich Edward £100, a sum that seems stingy in the circumstances. The Austen women's income was now a little more than £460 a year, just enough to provide for a fairly comfortable life and a servant.

Sense and Sensibility may well reflect Austen's mood in the unhappy second phase of her life, the period she spent in Bath (1801–06) and Southampton (1806–09). Especially after her father's death in 1805 she was dependent on the charity of her brothers as well as on occasional "fees" from the dowager Mrs. Knight. At Godmersham, the hairdresser gave her special rates. That she resented her subordinate status is evident in the letters. In Bath, as early as the summer of 1799, for example, she notes that Edward has purchased a pair of coach horses for sixty guineas (*Letters* 47); a year later James goes to Winchester to buy a new horse, and his wife Mary takes on a new maid — "two great acquisitions," Austen sardonically notes (50). By December 1808, as the result of a "donation" from his aunt Leigh Perrot of £100 per annum, James is planning to keep three horses (157–58). The increase to

James's income was a further sign that the Leigh Perrot wealth would go to him and not to his mother, who was to be continually disappointed in her hopes of a legacy. Austen writes: "We have now pretty well ascertained James's income to be Eleven Hundred Pounds, curate paid, which makes us very happy — the ascertainment as well as the Income" (*Letters* 160).

The "ascertainment" of incomes is one measure of Austen's achievement as a novelist. With the skills of an actuary or property lawyer, she commands an exact knowledge of finance; she knows the law of entail, how to calculate the value of livings, what income one needs to set up a carriage, what fortune a woman must possess to marry the eldest son of a baronet or the younger son of an earl. Dispossessed herself, she possesses her world in the mode of fiction, distributing incomes and fortunes among her characters on a scale that matches the realities of her time and displaying in the process an unmatched power of social discrimination (Duckworth, "Accommodations" 171–74). Unlike Wollstonecraft, who urged women in her *Rights of Woman* (1792) to aspire to become physicians or businesswomen, Austen never presents wage-earning employment as a positive possibility for women, and while in *Sense and Sensibility* she has Elinor make fun of Marianne's unrealistic estimate of £2,000 a year as a "competence" (91), her own financial expectations were those of a gentry woman. When Colonel Brandon makes his gift of the Delaford living to Edward, that income, when joined to Edward's and Elinor's, will bring in £350 a year, but "neither of them [were] quite enough in love to think that three hundred and fifty pounds a year would supply them with the comforts of life" (369). All her novels show that survival is never merely a financial question. Social rank and status determine needs. Adam Smith's "necessaries" (as distinct from "luxuries") have symbolic as well as economic meaning: servants, fashionable dress and furniture, a carriage, a set of china, a pianoforte are only some of the possessions by means of which a family asserts its claim to social prominence (Copeland 8–9).

Austen deployed manners in the novels not only on her own behalf as a marginal woman but on her family's behalf as well. Despite the success that came to the brothers, none escaped financial anxiety. James's expectations from his father-in law General Mathew were frustrated when the General was dunned by the Treasury for money he claimed was rightfully given him as salary for his services as Governor of Grenada; despite all efforts, a huge repayment (with interest it came to £24,000) had to be made on the general's death in 1805 (Honan 90–92). In 1814, Edward's claim to the Chawton estate was contested by the Hinton/Baverstock family and he had to settle the dispute with a large sum; a year later he lost £20,000 when Henry's bank failed. The Leigh-Perrots from 1806 were engaged in a suit over the title of Stoneleigh Abbey and had to settle for what Austen termed "a vile compromise" (*Letters* 316). The compromise hardly seems "vile" (it gave the Leigh-Perrots a lump sum of £20,000 and £2,000 a year), but later they too were burned by Henry's bank's failure. Reading the letters, we get the sense of a family continually required to defend their title to property and status. Wills, inheritances, legacies, and litigation all testify to the Austens' participation in a highly competitive capitalist culture. In such a world, would it be unusual if Austen were to use manners as litigation by other means?

In *Emma*, in particular, the role of manners in the maintenance of status is evident. The heroine shows herself culpably snobbish not only in her dismissal of the worthy tenant farmer Robert Martin but in her attitude to the Coles, a family whose origins are in trade. The Coles' rise in Highbury is subtly registered; they own a carriage, for example, and, unlike Mr. Knightley, have their own carriage horses. The Coles are respectful, however, and Emma apart, the "best families" in the village welcome them into the circle of gentility, even though they still have much to learn — including how to play the grand piano that graces their drawing room. Mrs. Elton is a much more objectionable *arriviste;* her rise in Highbury is resented not only by Emma, whose preeminence she challenges, but also by Frank Churchill, Mr. Knightley, and most readers. Mrs. Elton's skin is as thick as her incivility is irremissive. Her idea of a strawberry party at Donwell is "a sort of gipsy party. . . . out of doors — a table spread in the shade. . . . Every thing as natural and simple as possible." But Mr. Knightley's idea of the natural is different: "The nature and the simplicity of gentlemen and ladies, with their servants and furniture . . . is best observed by meals within doors. When you are tired of eating strawberries in the garden, there shall be cold meat in the house" (p. 284). The exchange is richly comic and I suspect that most readers delight that a vulgarian has received her comeuppance. And yet if we judge against Mrs. Elton, are we not assenting to Mr. Knightley's idea of the "natural," an idea that comprehends "gentlemen and ladies, with their servants"? Edward Copeland suggest that Austen's "most surprising triumph may be . . . the preeminent place in posterity that she achieves for her own social rank" (87).

Though it is not always possible to separate Austen's values from the social pressures that helped to form them, in her three mature novels she goes beyond the mediation of personal and family anxieties to engage questions of national importance. In 1809 Edward offered his mother and sisters a choice of houses on his estates in Kent and Hampshire, and they chose to return to the village of Chawton in Hampshire. Now settled in the third — and mainly happy — phase of her life (1809–17), Austen prepared her early novels for publication and, in a second period of great creativity, wrote *Mansfield Park* (published 1814), *Emma* (1816), and *Persuasion* (1818). The national import of the Chawton novels is suggested by Butler when she proposes that they may be compared to Robert Southey's contemporary essays in *The Quarterly Review* and Samuel Taylor Coleridge's *Lay Sermons*, both writers called on the landed orders to behave responsibly on behalf of the nation as a whole (*War of Ideas* xliii–xliv). Distinct from Southey and Coleridge, Austen approached serious issues not in essays or sermons but in novels that focused on women. Her protests against the devaluation of women is not absent from these novels. Sir Thomas Bertram's cruel treatment of his niece Fanny in *Mansfield Park* is chillingly exposed. But her satire now works to different ends. From her depreciated position, Fanny upholds the values that her uncle and cousin profess — and then betray. Likewise, Anne Elliot in *Persuasion* maintains her belief in the obligations of the gentry even as her father neglects them, and when his vanity proves irremediable she finds another cause to support. Through her marriage to Wentworth, she joins "a profession which is, if possible, more distinguished in its domestic virtues than in its national importance" (252). With a nod to her sailor brothers, Austen in her last novel brings to completion what is at best implicit in the "Steventon" novels, namely, a respect for triumph over hardship, professional commitment, and a life of work in which women may be partners.

As Butler notes ("History, Politics, and Religion") the three "Chawton" novels provide more or less ideal versions of her brothers' professions: clergyman (*Mansfield Park*), landowner (*Emma*), and naval officer (*Mansfield Park* and *Persuasion*). In these novels the Tory principles the young Jane had imbibed in the Steventon rectory are supplemented by a new respect for hard work. In *Mansfield Park* Edmund Bertram differs from her earlier clergymen: he has a vocation. Mr. Collins in *Pride and Prejudice* is a sycophantic fool, and Henry Tilney in *Northanger Abbey* is more at home in the Bath Assembly Rooms than in his country parsonage. Edward Ferrars in *Sense and Sensibility* prefers the profession of clergyman to the more lucrative profession of law and the more fashionable professions of the army and navy (102–03); but he shows little vocation. Neither, of course, does Mr. Elton in *Emma*, as several of those providing Austen with "opinions" (see "Contextual Documents," pp. 392–94) noted with disapproval; but at least Mr. Elton attends to the poor and confers with Mr. Knightley and Mr Cole on village matters.

How far can this new concern with vocation be attributed to such evangelical writers as Hannah More, Thomas Gisborne, and Thomas Clarkson, who had a marked effect on the religious life of the landed order in the first decade of the nineteenth century? Austen's sister Cassandra, her brother Frank (known as the officer who knelt in church), and her brother Henry (who became an evangelical clergyman after his failure as a banker) were all influenced by the evangelical movement. Austen's responses in the letters are inconsistent (*Letters* 170, 280), and some scholars deny any deep involvement, or see her attitude as subversive of evangelical ideals. Yet it is not difficult to see evangelical emphases, particularly in *Mansfield Park*, where residency and the importance of pulpit delivery are enjoined on clergyman and where the evangelical distrust of private theatricals informs the episode in which the Bertrams and the Crawfords rehearse Kotzebue's *Lovers' Vows* — with its opportunities for the acting out of passionate scenes and politically radical dialogues. As a father, Sir Thomas is deeply flawed, but the lessons he realizes he has failed to give his children — the need for active principle, duty, practical religion, self-denial, and the irrelevance of female accomplishments to the moral life — are the lessons of More and Gisborne. Edmund too is flawed, but before his fall, in an earnest speech to Mary Crawford, he distinguishes between a nineteenth-century evangelical definition of manners ("conduct . . . the result of good principles") and an eighteenth-century view of the kind held by Lord Chesterfield, which stresses good breeding, refinement, courtesy, and the ceremonies of life (93).

In all three "Chawton" novels a battle is fought between Hannah More and the Earl of Chesterfield. In *Emma* Mr. Knightley places the contrast in terms of English versus French values, the manners of an "amiable" person as opposed to an "aimable" one (p. 131) (see Chesterfield's letter in "Contextual Documents," p. 389). In *Persuasion* Lady Russell must learn to appreciate the blunt manners of Captain Wentworth and suspect the "general politeness and suavity" of Mr. Elliot's manners (249). Mr. Elliot's faults are those that Hannah More points to in a "An Estimate of the Religion of the Fashionable World" (1788): Anne "saw that there had been bad habits; that Sunday travelling had been a common thing" (161).

Anne Elliot's sanctimony is an aesthetic lapse in *Persuasion,* and *Mansfield Park,* a novel indebted not only to More but to Thomas Gisborne's evangelical *Duties of the Female Sex* (1798), continues to arouse hostility in readers. Gisborne can make for dispiriting reading. With his doctrine of separate spheres of activity on sexual lines, opposition to theaters, masquerades, and amusements generally, and stress on women as superintendents of the domestic economy, who must at all costs resist the temptation to roam free or engage in intellectual or political pursuits, he represents a repressive evangelicalism. Austen's relation to conduct books such as Gisborne's was never simple, however. She was certainly a critic of the female manners proposed by such pontifical patriarchs as James Fordyce (*Character and Conduct of the Female Sex*) and John Gregory (*A Father's Legacy to His Daughters*). But it is not hard to see why she appreciated Gisborne's *Duties,* a book she was at first determined not to read (*Letters* 112). His critique of sensibility (34–35), censure of accomplishments (82–83), advocacy of exercise for young women (94–95), and opposition to blood sports (208–09) would all have met with her approval. Gisborne's sympathy for unmarried older women may not be the source of Mr. Knightley's speech to Emma following her cruel treatment of Miss Bates on Box Hill (pp. 299–300), but it is at least an interesting parallel text (97–98).

Of all the abuses that the evangelicals preached against, the one that has proved of most recent interest to Austen scholars is slavery. Though slavery is barely touched on in *Mansfield Park* — when Fanny's question about the slave trade is met with "such a dead silence" (198) — scholars such as B. C. Southam and Ruth Perry have argued for its importance to the novel. "Mansfield" recalls Lord Mansfield, author of a landmark legal decision in 1772 declaring all persons of whatever race free so long as they were on English soil; and the vicious Mrs. Norris in the novel has the same name as a slave captain (Perry 98–99). The abolition of the slave trade had been debated in Parliament for decades before a bill was passed into law in two stages in 1807–08. Austen's family had good reason to feel involved in the question (Southam, "Silence of the Bertrams"; Tomalin, Appendix iii). Her father had been the trustee of a plantation in Antigua. Her sister's fiancé died off Santo Domingo while serving on an expedition against the French, who were encouraging the slaves to revolt against their English masters. Her brother James's first wife was the daughter of General Mathew, governor of Grenada. Her naval brothers knew the West Indian possessions well; the evangelical Frank in particular was a critic of slavery.

That Austen was in favor of abolition cannot be doubted. She was in love, she joked to Cassandra, with Thomas Clarkson, author of *The History of . . . the Abolition of the African Slave-Trade* (1808) (*Letters* 198); and beyond her humanitarianism she more than once implies a connection between the slavery of Africans in the colonies and the slavery of women (like Fanny Price) at home. In *Emma*, when Jane Fairfax, fearing her future as a governess, speaks bitterly of "Offices for the sale — not quite of human flesh — but of human intellect" Mrs. Elton, from the slave port of Bristol, sees this as "a fling at the slave-trade," and protests defensively that her friend Mr. Suckling "was always rather a friend to the abolition" (p. 242).

The evangelical influence on the late novels seems incontestable, then, though it is worth observing that evangelical themes enter the fiction for dramatic as much as for didactic purposes. The fashionable London manners of the Crawfords, for example, exhibit what More describes as "modern scepticism," which, in order to gain proselytes, "must show itself under the bewitching form of the profane bon-mot, must be . . . written with . . . the point and glitter of an epigram . . . must embellish the ample margin with some offensive anecdote of impure allusion. . . ." (1. 277). Here, surely, is a recipe for Mary's offensive remarks. Asked if she knows William Price's captain, Mary tells Edward that her uncle, the Admiral, only associated with other admirals: "Of *Rears*, and *Vices*, I saw enough. Now, do not be suspecting me of a pun, I entreat" (60). Her brother is no less capable of the salacious double entendre.

Austen's strategy of condemning the Crawfords for their puns and epigrams poses a paradox in *Mansfield Park*. The paradox is that Austen condemns at one level what she creates at another. The novel's verbal brilliance is hers, after all, not the Crawfords'. As the author of an evangelical novel, she impersonates characters who live in a Restoration comedy. Not Hannah More but John Keats seems the appropriate reference here. Four years after *Mansfield Park*, Keats answered those who worried about the immoral influence of literature. "What shocks the virtuous philosopher, delights the camelion poet," he wrote to Richard Woodhouse (October 27, 1818). Taking Shakespeare as his model, Keats believed the poet took "as much delight in conceiving an Iago as an Imogen" (172). Henry Crawford could almost be Keats's poet: "I really believe," he says when the theatricals are proposed, "I could . . . undertake any character that ever was written, from Shylock or Richard III. down to the singing hero of a farce" (123). But in another sense, Keats's poet could be Austen herself, who could conceive a Lady Susan — the evil but superbly articulate widow of her epistolary novel from 1793–94 — as easily as an Anne Elliot, her picture of perfection in her last novel. In the mimetic representation of hypocrisy, Austen vies with Molière; and the best response to a Lady Susan or a Mary Crawford may be to admire the brilliance of the characterization rather than deplore the immorality of the character.

In winter 1816, at the height of her success following the publication of *Emma,* Austen fell ill, and despite periods of remission never fully recovered her health. Her illness, then unidentified, was probably "Addison's disease of the suprarenal capsules"; its symptoms were weight loss, weakness, back pain, severe gastrointestinal disturbance, and the black and white appearance of the skin as death approached (Cope). *Persuasion,* begun in the summer or autumn of 1815 and completed in August 1816, was not adversely affected; but her "last work," now known as *Sanditon,* which was begun on January 17, 1817, had to be abandoned two months later. The fragment describes a rootless, fashion-seeking Regency world. Far from reflecting illness, it makes hypochondria a target of satire. Sanditon is a seaside village which the resident landowner is intent on turning to a profit by attracting invalids and convalescents. As the setting differs from those in earlier novels, so the heroine, Charlotte Heywood, differs from previous heroines. Viewing the commercial debasement of traditional ideas of stewardship, she remains curiously detached: the scene is "very striking — and very amusing — or very melancholy, just as Satire or Melancholy might prevail" (*Minor Works* 396). It is difficult to imagine how the fragment would have ended, but one thing is clear: had Austen lived longer, she would have continued to respond to the shifting social currents of her world.

On May 24, 1817, she was taken to Winchester, not far from Chawton, to receive the attention of a physician. Less than two months later she died, and on July 24 she was buried in the cathedral. Her epitaph says nothing about her novels but praises her virtues in words that seem too good to be true ("The benevolence of her heart, the sweetness of her temper, and the extraordinary endowments of her mind obtained the regard of all who knew her . . ."). But then her epitaph was probably written (and certainly approved) by her brother James, a poet of tepid moral verse, long considered the writer in the family, and a critic of novels. Here began the process of canonization that James's brother, Henry, and son, James Edward, would carry on. Recent biographies have shown us that Jane Austen was no saint; she was something better: one of the greatest novelists in the history of English fiction.

WORKS CITED

Austen, Jane. *Jane Austen's Letters*. Ed. Deirdre Le Faye. 3rd ed. Oxford: Oxford UP, 1995.

———. *Minor Works*. Ed. R. W. Chapman. Rev. B. C. Southam. Oxford: Oxford UP, 1982. Vol. 6 of *The Works of Jane Austen*.

———. *The Novels of Jane Austen*. Ed. R. W. Chapman. 3rd ed. 5 vols. Oxford: Oxford UP, 1982.

Austen-Leigh, J. E. *A Memoir of Jane Austen*. London: Richard Bentley, 1870.

Austen-Leigh, William, and Richard Arthur Austen-Leigh. *Jane Austen: A Family Record*. Rev. and enl. by Deirdre Le Faye. London: The British Library, 1989.

Butler, Marilyn. "History, Politics, and Religion." *The Jane Austen Companion*. Ed. J. David Grey et al. New York: Macmillan, 1986. 190–208.

———. *Jane Austen and the War of Ideas*. 1975; reissued in paperback with new introduction. Oxford: Oxford UP, 1987.

Cope, Zachary. "Jane Austen's Last Illness." *British Medical Journal* (July 18, 1964): 182–83.

Copeland, Edward. *Women Writing About Money: Women's Fiction in England, 1790–1820*. Cambridge: Cambridge UP, 1995.

Duckworth, Alistair M. *The Improvement of the Estate: A Study of Jane Austen's Novels*. 1971; reissued in paperback with new preface. Baltimore: Johns Hopkins UP, 1994.

———. "Jane Austen's Accommodations." *The First English Novelists: Essays in Understanding*. Ed. J. M. Armistead. Knoxville: U of Tennessee P, 1985. 225–67.

Everett, Nigel. *The Tory View of Landscape*. New Haven: Yale UP, 1994.

Farrer, Reginald. "Jane Austen, ob. July 18, 1817." 1917. Southam, *Critical Heritage* 245–72.

Fergus, Jan. *Jane Austen: A Literary Life*. New York: St. Martin's, 1991.

Fordyce, James. *Character and Conduct of the Female Sex*. Dublin, 1776.

Gisborne, Thomas. *The Duties of the Female Sex*. London, 1798.

Gregory, John. *A Father's Legacy to his Daughters.* In *Principles of Politeness . . . By the Late Lord Chesterfield. Methodised . . . by the Rev. Dr. Trusler.* Boston, 1794.

Harding, D. W. "Regulated Hatred: An Aspect of the Work of Jane Austen." 1940. Watt 166–79.

Honan, Park. *Jane Austen: Her Life.* 1987. New York: St. Martin's Griffin, 1996.

Keats, John. *Letters of John Keats.* Ed. Frederick Page. London: Oxford UP, 1965.

More, Hannah. "An Estimate of the Religion of the Fashionable World." *The Complete Works of Hannah More.* 2 vols. New York: Harper, 1835.

Mudrick, Marvin. *Jane Austen: Irony as Defense and Discovery.* Princeton: Princeton UP, 1952.

Perry, Ruth. "Austen and Empire: A Thinking Woman's Guide to British Imperialism." *Persuasions* 16 (1994): 95–106.

Southam, B. C., ed. *Jane Austen: The Critical Heritage 1870–1940.* Vol. 2. London and New York: Routledge, 1987.

———. "The Silence of the Bertrams." *Times Literary Supplement* 17 Feb. 1995: 13–14.

Spring, David A. "Interpreters of Jane Austen's Social World: Literary Critics and Historians." *Jane Austen: New Perspectives.* Ed. Janet Todd. New York: Holmes & Meier, 1983. 53–72.

Tomalin, Claire. *Jane Austen: A Life.* New York: Knopf, 1997.

Watt, Ian., ed. *Jane Austen: A Collection of Critical Essays.* Englewood Cliffs, NJ: Prentice Hall, 1963.

EMMA:

A NOVEL.

IN THREE VOLUMES.

———◆———

BY THE

AUTHOR OF "PRIDE AND PREJUDICE,"

&c. &c.

———◆———

VOL. I.

═══════

LONDON:

PRINTED FOR JOHN MURRAY.

1816.

TO

HIS ROYAL HIGHNESS

THE PRINCE REGENT,

THIS WORK IS,

BY HIS ROYAL HIGHNESS'S PERMISSION,

MOST RESPECTFULLY

DEDICATED,

BY HIS ROYAL HIGHNESS'S

DUTIFUL

AND OBEDIENT

HUMBLE SERVANT,

THE AUTHOR.

Volume I

CHAPTER I.

EMMA Woodhouse, handsome, clever, and rich, with a comfortable home and happy disposition, seemed to unite some of the best blessings of existence; and had lived nearly twenty-one years in the world with very little to distress or vex her.

She was the youngest of the two daughters of a most affectionate, indulgent father, and had, in consequence of her sister's marriage, been mistress of his house from a very early period. Her mother had died too long ago for her to have more than an indistinct remembrance of her caresses, and her place had been supplied by an excellent woman as governess, who had fallen little short of a mother in affection.

Sixteen years had Miss Taylor been in Mr. Woodhouse's family, less as a governess than a friend, very fond of both daughters, but particularly of Emma. Between *them* it was more the intimacy of sisters. Even before Miss Taylor had ceased to hold the nominal office of governess, the mildness of her temper had hardly allowed her to impose any restraint; and the shadow of authority being now long passed away, they had been living together as friend and friend very mutually attached, and Emma doing just what she liked; highly esteeming Miss Taylor's judgment, but directed chiefly by her own.

The real evils indeed of Emma's situation were the power of having rather too much her own way, and a disposition to think a little too well of herself; these were the disadvantages which threatened alloy to her many enjoyments. The danger, however, was at present so unperceived, that they did not by any means rank as misfortunes with her.

Sorrow came — a gentle sorrow — but not at all in the shape of any disagreeable consciousness. — Miss Taylor married. It was Miss Taylor's loss which first brought grief. It was on the wedding-day of this beloved friend that Emma first sat in mournful thought of any continuance. The wedding over and the bride-people gone, her father and herself were left to dine together, with no prospect of a third to cheer a long evening. Her father composed himself to sleep after dinner, as usual, and she had then only to sit and think of what she had lost.

The event had every promise of happiness for her friend. Mr. Weston was a man of unexceptionable character, easy fortune, suitable age and pleasant manners; and there was some satisfaction in considering with what self-denying, generous friendship she had always wished and promoted the match; but it was a black morning's work for her. The want of Miss Taylor would be felt every hour of every day. She recalled her past kindness — the kindness, the affection of sixteen years — how she had taught and how she had played with her from five years old — how she had devoted all her powers to attach and amuse her in health — and how nursed her through the various illnesses of childhood. A large debt of gratitude was owing here; but the intercourse of the last seven years, the equal footing and perfect unreserve which had soon followed Isabella's marriage on their being left to each other, was yet a dearer, tenderer recollection. It had been a friend and companion such as few possessed, intelligent, well-informed, useful, gentle, knowing all the ways of the family, interested in all its concerns, and peculiarly interested in herself, in every pleasure, every scheme of her's; — one to whom she could speak every thought as it arose, and who had such an affection for her as could never find fault.

How was she to bear the change? — It was true that her friend was going only half a mile from them; but Emma was aware that great must be the difference between a Mrs. Weston only half a mile from them, and a Miss Taylor in the house; and with all her advantages, natural and domestic, she was now in great danger of suffering from intellectual solitude. She dearly loved her father, but he was no companion for her. He could not meet her in conversation, rational or playful.

The evil of the actual disparity in their ages (and Mr. Woodhouse had not married early) was much increased by his constitution and habits; for having been a valetudinarian[1] all his life, without activity of mind or body, he was a much older man in ways than in years; and though everywhere beloved for the friendliness of his heart and his amiable temper, his talents could not have recommended him at any time.

Her sister, though comparatively but little removed by matrimony, being settled in London, only sixteen miles off, was much beyond her daily reach; and many a long October and November evening must be struggled through at Hartfield, before Christmas brought the next visit from Isabella and her husband and their little children to fill the house and give her pleasant society again.

Highbury,[2] the large and populous village almost amounting to a town, to which Hartfield, in spite of its separate lawn and shrubberies and name, did really belong, afforded her no equals. The Woodhouses were first in consequence there. All looked up to them. She had many acquaintance in the place, for her father was universally civil, but not one among them who could be accepted in lieu of Miss Taylor for even half a day. It was a melancholy change; and Emma could not but sigh over it and wish for impossible things, till her father awoke, and made it necessary to be cheerful. His spirits required support. He was a nervous man, easily depressed; fond of every body that he was used to, and hating to part with them; hating change of every kind. Matrimony, as the origin of change, was always disagreeable; and he was by no means yet reconciled to his own daughter's marrying, nor could ever speak of her but with compassion, though it had been entirely a match of affection, when he was now obliged to part with Miss Taylor too; and from his habits of gentle selfishness and of being never able to suppose that other people could feel differently from himself, he was very much disposed to think Miss Taylor had done as sad a thing for herself as for them, and would have been a great deal happier if she had spent all the rest of her life at Hartfield. Emma smiled and chatted as cheerfully as she could, to keep him from such thoughts; but when tea came, it was impossible for him not to say exactly as he had said at dinner,

"Poor Miss Taylor! — I wish she were here again. What a pity it is that Mr. Weston ever thought of her!"

"I cannot agree with you, papa; you know I cannot. Mr. Weston is such a good-humoured, pleasant, excellent man, that he thoroughly deserves a good wife; — and you would not have had Miss Taylor live

---

[1] *valetudinarian:* A person in poor health, especially one excessively concerned with his or her ailments.

[2] *Highbury:* Fictional village with some resemblance to such actual Surrey towns as Cobham and Leatherhead.

with us for ever and bear all my odd humours, when she might have a house of her own?"

"A house of her own! — but where is the advantage of a house of her own? This is three times as large. — And you have never any odd humours, my dear."

"How often we shall be going to see them and they coming to see us! — We shall be always meeting! *We* must begin, we must go and pay our wedding-visit very soon."

"My dear, how am I to get so far? Randalls is such a distance. I could not walk half so far."

"No, papa, nobody thought of your walking. We must go in the carriage to be sure."

"The carriage! But James will not like to put the horses to for such a little way; — and where are the poor horses to be while we are paying our visit?"

"They are to be put into Mr. Weston's stable, papa. You know we have settled all that already. We talked it all over with Mr. Weston last night. And as for James, you may be very sure he will always like going to Randalls, because of his daughter's being housemaid there. I only doubt whether he will ever take us anywhere else. That, was your doing, papa. You got Hannah that good place. Nobody thought of Hannah till you mentioned her — James is so obliged to you!"

"I am very glad I did think of her. It was very lucky, for I would not have had poor James think himself slighted upon any account; and I am sure she will make a very good servant; she is a civil, pretty-spoken girl; I have a great opinion of her. Whenever I see her, she always curtseys and asks me how I do, in a very pretty manner; and when you have had her here to do needlework, I observe she always turns the lock of the door the right way and never bangs it. I am sure she will be an excellent servant; and it will be a great comfort to poor Miss Taylor to have somebody about her that she is used to see. Whenever James goes over to see his daughter you know, she will be hearing of us. He will be able to tell her how we all are."

Emma spared no exertions to maintain this happier flow of ideas, and hoped, by the help of backgammon, to get her father tolerably through the evening, and be attacked by no regrets but her own. The backgammon-table was placed; but a visitor immediately afterwards walked in and made it unnecessary.

Mr. Knightley, a sensible man about seven or eight-and-thirty, was not only a very old and intimate friend of the family, but particularly connected with it as the elder brother of Isabella's husband. He lived about a mile from Highbury, was a frequent visitor and always welcome, and at this time more welcome than usual, as coming directly from their mutual connections in London. He had returned to a late dinner after some days absence, and now walked up to Hartfield to say that all were well in Brunswick-square.[3] It was a happy circumstance and animated Mr. Woodhouse for some time. Mr. Knightley had a cheerful manner which always did him good; and his many inquiries after "poor Isabella" and her children were answered most satisfactorily. When this was over, Mr. Woodhouse gratefully observed,

"It is very kind of you, Mr. Knightley, to come out at this late hour to call upon us. I am afraid you must have had a shocking walk."

"Not at all, sir. It is a beautiful, moonlight night; and so mild that I must draw back from your great fire."

"But you must have found it very damp and dirty. I wish you may not catch cold."

"Dirty, sir! Look at my shoes. Not a speck on them."

"Well! that is quite surprizing, for we have had a vast deal of rain here. It rained dreadfully hard for half an hour, while we were at breakfast. I wanted them to put off the wedding."

"By the bye — I have not wished you joy. Being pretty well aware of what sort of joy you must both be feeling, I have been in no hurry with my congratulations. But I hope it all went off tolerably well. How did you all behave? Who cried most?"

"Ah! poor Miss Taylor! 'tis a sad business."

"Poor Mr. and Miss Woodhouse, if you please; but I cannot possibly say 'poor Miss Taylor.' I have a great regard for you and Emma; but when it comes to the question of dependence or independence! — At any rate, it must be better to have only one to please, than two."

"Especially when *one* of those two is such a fanciful, troublesome creature!" said Emma playfully. "That, is what you have in your head, I know — and what you would certainly say if my father were not by."

"I believe it is very true, my dear, indeed," said Mr. Woodhouse with a sigh. "I am afraid I am sometimes very fanciful and troublesome."

"My dearest papa! You do not think I could mean *you*, or suppose Mr. Knightley to mean *you*. What a horrible idea! Oh, no! I meant only

[3] *Brunswick-square:* Square of Georgian houses in the Bloomsbury district of London.

myself. Mr. Knightley loves to find fault with me you know — in a joke — it is all a joke. We always say what we like to one another."

Mr. Knightley, in fact, was one of the few people who could see faults in Emma Woodhouse, and the only one who ever told her of them: and though this was not particularly agreeable to Emma herself, she knew it would be so much less so to her father, that she would not have him really suspect such a circumstance as her not being thought perfect by every body.

"Emma knows I never flatter her," said Mr. Knightley; "but I meant no reflection on any body. Miss Taylor has been used to have two persons to please; she will now have but one. The chances are that she must be a gainer."

"Well," said Emma, willing to let it pass — "you want to hear about the wedding, and I shall be happy to tell you, for we all behaved charmingly. Every body was punctual, every body in their best looks. Not a tear, and hardly a long face to be seen. Oh! no, we all felt that we were going to be only half a mile apart, and were sure of meeting every day."

"Dear Emma bears every thing so well," said her father. "But, Mr. Knightley, she is really very sorry to lose poor Miss Taylor, and I am sure she *will* miss her more than she thinks for."

Emma turned away her head, divided between tears and smiles.

"It is impossible that Emma should not miss such a companion," said Mr. Knightley. "We should not like her so well as we do, sir, if we could suppose it. But she knows how much the marriage is to Miss Taylor's advantage; she knows how very acceptable it must be at Miss Taylor's time of life to be settled in a home of her own, and how important to her to be secure of a comfortable provision, and therefore cannot allow herself to feel so much pain as pleasure. Every friend of Miss Taylor must be glad to have her so happily married."

"And you have forgotten one matter of joy to me," said Emma, "and a very considerable one — that I made the match myself. I made the match, you know, four years ago; and to have it take place, and be proved in the right, when so many people said Mr. Weston would never marry again, may comfort me for any thing."

Mr. Knightley shook his head at her. Her father fondly relied, "Ah! my dear, I wish you would not make matches and foretel things, for whatever you say always comes to pass. Pray do not make any more matches."

"I promise you to make none for myself, papa; but I must, indeed, for other people. It is the greatest amusement in the world! And after such success you know! — Every body said that Mr. Weston would never marry again. Oh dear, no! Mr. Weston, who had been a widower so long, and who seemed so perfectly comfortable without a wife, so constantly occupied either in his business in town or among his friends here, always acceptable wherever he went, always cheerful — Mr. Weston need not spend a single evening in the year alone if he did not like it. Oh, no! Mr. Weston certainly would never marry again. Some people even talked of a promise to his wife on her death-bed, and others of the son and the uncle not letting him. All manner of solemn nonsense was talked on the subject, but I believed none of it. Ever since the day (about four years ago) that Miss Taylor and I met with him in Broadway-lane, when, because it began to mizzle, he darted away with so much gallantry, and borrowed two umbrellas for us from Farmer Mitchell's, I made up my mind on the subject. I planned the match from that hour; and when such success has blessed me in this instance, dear papa, you cannot think that I shall leave off match-making."

"I do not understand what you mean by 'success;'" said Mr. Knightley. "Success supposes endeavour. Your time has been properly and delicately spent, if you have been endeavouring for the last four years to bring about this marriage. A worthy employment for a young lady's mind! But if, which I rather imagine, your making the match, as you call it, means only your planning it, your saying to yourself one idle day, 'I think it would be a very good thing for Miss Taylor if Mr. Weston were to marry her,' and saying it again to yourself every now and then afterwards, — why do you talk of success? where is your merit? — what are you proud of? — you made a lucky guess; and *that* is all that can be said."

"And have you never known the pleasure and triumph of a lucky guess? — I pity you. — I thought you cleverer — for depend upon it, a lucky guess is never merely luck. There is always some talent in it. And as to my poor word 'success,' which you quarrel with, I do not know that I am so entirely without any claim to it. You have drawn two pretty pictures — but I think there may be a third — a something between the do-nothing and the do-all. If I had not promoted Mr. Weston's visits here, and given many little encouragements, and smoothed many little matters, it might not have come to any thing after all. I think you must know Hartfield enough to comprehend that."

"A straight-forward, open-hearted man, like Weston, and a rational unaffected woman, like Miss Taylor, may be safely left to manage their own concerns. You are more likely to have done harm to yourself, than good to them, by interference."

"Emma never thinks of herself, if she can do good to others;"

rejoined Mr. Woodhouse, understanding but in part. "But, my dear, pray do not make any more matches, they are silly things, and break up one's family circle grievously."

"Only one more, papa; only for Mr. Elton. Poor Mr. Elton! You like Mr. Elton, papa, — I must look about for a wife for him. There is nobody in Highbury who deserves him — and he has been here a whole year, and has fitted up his house so comfortably that it would be a shame to have him single any longer — and I thought when he was joining their hands to-day, he looked so very much as if he would like to have the same kind office done for him! I think very well of Mr. Elton, and this is the only way I have of doing him a service."

"Mr. Elton is a very pretty young man to be sure, and a very good young man, and I have a great regard for him. But if you want to shew him any attention, my dear, ask him to come and dine with us some day. That will be a much better thing. I dare say Mr. Knightley will be so kind as to meet him."

"With a great deal of pleasure, sir, at any time," said Mr. Knightley laughing; "and I agree with you entirely that it will be a much better thing. Invite him to dinner, Emma, and help him to the best of the fish and the chicken, but leave him to chuse his own wife. Depend upon it, a man of six or seven-and-twenty can take care of himself."

CHAPTER II.

MR. WESTON was a native of Highbury, and born of a respectable family, which for the last two or three generations had been rising into gentility and property. He had received a good education, but on succeeding early in life to a small independence, had become indisposed for any of the more homely pursuits in which his brothers were engaged; and had satisfied an active cheerful mind and social temper by entering into the militia[4] of his county, then embodied.

Captain Weston was a general favourite; and when the chances of his military life had introduced him to Miss Churchill, of a great York-

---

[4]*militia:* An auxiliary body of citizen (as opposed to professional) soldiers, raised by the Lord Lieutenant of a county and subject to regular military drills; militias could be "embodied" for service within the kingdom, but not sent abroad except as volunteers. Like Austen's brother Henry, Captain Weston may have been embodied during the invasion scare of the 1790s, when the military defense of England was in the hands of the county militia regiments, numbering some thirty thousand men. See Clive Caplan, "Jane Austen's Soldier Brother: The Military Career of Captain Henry Thomas Austen of the Oxfordshire Regiment of Militia, 1793–1801," *Persuasions* 18 (1996): 122–43, esp. 22.

shire family, and Miss Churchill fell in love with him, nobody was surprized except her brother and his wife, who had never seen him, and
who were full of pride and importance, which the connection would
offend.

Miss Churchill, however, being of age, and with the full command
of her fortune — though her fortune bore no proportion to the family-
estate — was not to be dissuaded from the marriage, and it took place
to the infinite mortification of Mr. and Mrs. Churchill, who threw her
off with due decorum. It was an unsuitable connection, and did not
produce much happiness. Mrs. Weston ought to have found more in it,
for she had a husband whose warm heart and sweet temper made him
think every thing due to her in return for the great goodness of being in
love with him; but though she had one sort of spirit, she had not the
best. She had resolution enough to pursue her own will in spite of her
brother, but not enough to refrain from unreasonable regrets at that
brother's unreasonable anger, nor from missing the luxuries of her former home. They lived beyond their income, but still it was nothing
in comparison of Enscombe: she did not cease to love her husband,
but she wanted at once to be the wife of Captain Weston, and Miss
Churchill of Enscombe.

Captain Weston, who had been considered, especially by the Churchills, as making such an amazing match, was proved to have much the
worst of the bargain; for when his wife died after a three years' marriage, he was rather a poorer man than at first, and with a child to maintain. From the expense of the child, however, he was soon relieved. The
boy had, with the additional softening claim of a lingering illness of his
mother's, been the means of a sort of reconciliation; and Mr. and Mrs.
Churchill, having no children of their own, nor any other young creature of equal kindred to care for, offered to take the whole charge of the
little Frank soon after her decease. Some scruples and some reluctance
the widower-father may be supposed to have felt; but as they were overcome by other considerations, the child was given up to the care and
the wealth of the Churchills, and he had only his own comfort to seek
and his own situation to improve as he could.

A complete change of life became desirable. He quitted the militia
and engaged in trade, having brothers already established in a good way
in London, which afforded him a favourable opening. It was a concern
which brought just employment enough. He had still a small house in
Highbury, where most of his leisure days were spent; and between useful occupation and the pleasures of society, the next eighteen or twenty
years of his life passed cheerfully away. He had, by that time, realized an

easy competence — enough to secure the purchase of a little estate adjoining Highbury, which he had always longed for — enough to marry a woman as portionless even as Miss Taylor, and to live according to the wishes of his own friendly and social disposition.

It was now some time since Miss Taylor had begun to influence his schemes; but as it was not the tyrannic influence of youth on youth, it had not shaken his determination of never settling till he could purchase Randalls, and the sale of Randalls was long looked forward to: but he had gone steadily on, with these objects in view, till they were accomplished. He had made his fortune, bought his house, and obtained his wife; and was beginning a new period of existence with every probability of greater happiness than in any yet passed through. He had never been an unhappy man; his own temper had secured him from that, even in his first marriage; but his second must shew him how delightful a well-judging and truly amiable woman could be, and must give him the pleasantest proof of its being a great deal better to chuse than to be chosen, to excite gratitude than to feel it.

He had only himself to please in his choice: his fortune was his own; for as to Frank, it was more than being tacitly brought up as his uncle's heir, it had become so avowed an adoption as to have him assume the name of Churchill on coming of age. It was most unlikely, therefore, that he should ever want his father's assistance. His father had no apprehension of it. The aunt was a capricious woman, and governed her husband entirely; but it was not in Mr. Weston's nature to imagine that any caprice could be strong enough to affect one so dear, and, as he believed, so deservedly dear. He saw his son every year in London, and was proud of him; and his fond report of him as a very fine young man had made Highbury feel a sort of pride in him too. He was looked on as sufficiently belonging to the place to make his merits and prospects a kind of common concern.

Mr. Frank Churchill was one of the boasts of Highbury, and a lively curiosity to see him prevailed, though the compliment was so little returned that he had never been there in his life. His coming to visit his father had been often talked of but never achieved.

Now, upon his father's marriage, it was very generally proposed, as a most proper attention, that the visit should take place. There was not a dissentient voice on the subject, either when Mrs. Perry drank tea with Mrs. and Miss Bates, or when Mrs. and Miss Bates returned the visit. Now was the time for Mr. Frank Churchill to come among them; and the hope strengthened when it was understood that he had written to his new mother on the occasion. For a few days every morning visit in Highbury included some mention of the handsome letter Mrs. Weston had received. "I suppose you have heard of the handsome letter Mr. Frank Churchill had written to Mrs. Weston? I understand it was a very handsome letter, indeed. Mr. Woodhouse told me of it. Mr. Woodhouse saw the letter, and he says he never saw such a handsome letter in his life."

It was, indeed, a highly-prized letter. Mrs. Weston had, of course, formed a very favourable idea of the young man; and such a pleasing attention was an irresistible proof of his great good sense, and a most welcome addition to every source and every expression of congratulation which her marriage had already secured. She felt herself a most fortunate woman; and she had lived long enough to know how fortunate she might well be thought, where the only regret was for a partial separation from friends, whose friendship for her had never cooled, and who could ill bear to part with her!

She knew that at times she must be missed; and could not think, without pain, of Emma's losing a single pleasure, or suffering an hour's ennui, from the want of her companionableness: but dear Emma was of no feeble character; she was more equal to her situation than most girls would have been, and had sense and energy and spirits that might be hoped would bear her well and happily through its little difficulties and privations. And then there was such comfort in the very easy distance of Randalls from Hartfield, so convenient for even solitary female walking, and in Mr. Weston's disposition and circumstances, which would make the approaching season no hindrance to their spending half the evenings in the week together.

Her situation was altogether the subject of hours of gratitude to Mrs. Weston, and of moments only of regret; and her satisfaction — her more than satisfaction — her cheerful enjoyment was so just and so apparent, that Emma, well as she knew her father, was sometimes taken by surprize at his being still able to pity "poor Miss Taylor," when they left her at Randalls in the centre of every domestic comfort, or saw her go away in the evening attended by her pleasant husband to a carriage of her own. But never did she go without Mr. Woodhouse's giving a gentle sigh, and saying:

"Ah! poor Miss Taylor. She would be very glad to stay."

There was no recovering Miss Taylor — nor much likelihood of ceasing to pity her: but a few weeks brought some alleviation to Mr. Woodhouse. The compliments of his neighbours were over; he was no longer teased by being wished joy of so sorrowful an event; and the wedding-cake, which had been a great distress to him, was all eat up.

His own stomach could bear nothing rich, and he could never believe other people to be different from himself. What was unwholesome to him, he regarded as unfit for any body; and he had, therefore, earnestly tried to dissuade them from having any wedding-cake at all, and when that proved vain, as earnestly tried to prevent any body's eating it. He had been at the pains of consulting Mr. Perry, the apothecary,[5] on the subject. Mr. Perry was an intelligent, gentlemanlike man, whose frequent visits were one of the comforts of Mr. Woodhouse's life; and, upon being applied to, he could not but acknowledge, (though it seemed rather against the bias of inclination,) that wedding-cake might certainly disagree with many — perhaps with most people, unless taken moderately. With such an opinion, in confirmation of his own, Mr. Woodhouse hoped to influence every visitor of the new-married pair; but still the cake was eaten; and there was no rest for his benevolent nerves till it was all gone.

There was a strange rumour in Highbury of all the little Perrys being seen with a slice of Mrs. Weston's wedding-cake in their hands: but Mr. Woodhouse would never believe it.

CHAPTER III.

MR. WOODHOUSE was fond of society in his own way. He liked very much to have his friends come and see him; and from various united causes, from his long residence at Hartfield, and his good nature, from his fortune, his house, and his daughter, he could command the visits of his own little circle, in a great measure as he liked. He had not much intercourse with any families beyond that circle; his horror of late hours and large dinner-parties made him unfit for any acquaintance, but such as would visit him on his own terms. Fortunately for him, Highbury, including Randalls in the same parish, and Donwell Abbey in the parish adjoining, the seat of Mr. Knightley, comprehended many such. Not unfrequently, through Emma's persuasion, he had some of the chosen and the best to dine with him, but evening-parties were what he preferred, and, unless he fancied himself at any time unequal to company,

[5]*apothecary:* The medical role and social status of apothecaries were the subject of contentious debate in the years leading up to the passing of the Apothecaries' Act in July 1815. Though inferior in the medical hierarchy to physicians and surgeons, apothecaries had in many areas effectively become medical practitioners, and not merely dispensers of drugs, a role provided by often untrained druggists. For a discussion of the debates in Parliament and elsewhere over the status of apothecaries, see Roger Sales, *Jane Austen and Representations of Regency England* (New York: Routledge, 1994) 147–55.

there was scarcely an evening in the week in which Emma could not make up a card-table for him.

Real, long-standing regard brought the Westons and Mr. Knightley; and by Mr. Elton, a young man living alone without liking it, the privilege of exchanging any vacant evening of his own blank solitude for the elegancies and society of Mr. Woodhouse's drawing-room and the smiles of his lovely daughter, was in no danger of being thrown away.

After these came a second set; among the most come-at-able of whom were Mrs. and Miss Bates and Mrs. Goddard, three ladies almost always at the service of an invitation from Hartfield, and who were fetched and carried home so often that Mr. Woodhouse thought it no hardship for either James or the horses. Had it taken place only once a year, it would have been a grievance.

Mrs. Bates, the widow of a former vicar of Highbury, was a very old lady, almost past every thing but tea and quadrille.[6] She lived with her single daughter in a very small way, and was considered with all the regard and respect which a harmless old lady, under such untoward circumstances, can excite. Her daughter enjoyed a most uncommon degree of popularity for a woman neither young, handsome, rich, nor married. Miss Bates stood in the very worst predicament in the world for having much of the public favour; and she had no intellectual superiority to make atonement to herself, or frighten those who might hate her, into outward respect. She had never boasted either beauty or cleverness. Her youth had passed without distinction, and her middle of life was devoted to the care of a failing mother, and the endeavour to make a small income go as far as possible. And yet she was a happy woman, and a woman whom no one named without good-will. It was her own universal good-will and contended temper which worked such wonders. She loved every body, was interested in every body's happiness, quick-sighted to every body's merits; thought herself a most fortunate creature, and surrounded with blessings in such an excellent mother and so many good neighbours and friends, and a home that wanted for nothing. The simplicity and cheerfulness of her nature, her contended and grateful spirit, were a recommendation to every body and a mine of felicity to herself. She was a great talker upon little matters, which exactly suited Mr. Woodhouse, full of trivial communications and harmless gossip.

---

[6]*quadrille:* Card game played by four people with a reduced deck; somewhat old-fashioned at the time, having been widely superseded by whist.

Mrs. Goddard was the mistress of a School — not of a seminary, or an establishment, or any thing which professed, in long sentences of refined nonsense, to combine liberal acquirements with elegant moral ity upon new principles and new systems — and where young ladies for enormous pay might be screwed out of health and into vanity — but a real, honest, old-fashioned Boarding-school,[7] where a reasonable quantity of accomplishments were sold at a reasonable price, and where girls might be sent to be out of the way and scramble themselves into a little education, without any danger of coming back prodigies. Mrs. Goddard's school was in high repute — and very deservedly; for Highbury was reckoned a particularly healthy spot: she had an ample house and garden, gave the children plenty of wholesome food, let them run about a great deal in the summer, and in winter dressed their chilblains[8] with her own hands. It was no wonder that a train of twenty young couple now walked after her to church. She was a plain, motherly kind of woman, who had worked hard in her youth, and now thought herself entitled to the occasional holiday of a tea-visit;[9] and having formerly owed much to Mr. Woodhouse's kindness, felt his particular claim on her to leave her neat parlour hung round with fancy-work whenever she could, and win or lose a few sixpences by his fireside.

These were the ladies whom Emma found herself very frequently able to collect; and happy was she, for her father's sake, in the power; though, as far as she was herself concerned, it was no remedy for the absence of Mrs. Weston. She was delighted to see her father look comfortable, and very much pleased with herself for contriving things so well; but the quiet prosings of three such women made her feel that every evening so spent, was indeed one of the long evenings she had fearfully anticipated.

As she sat one morning, looking forward to exactly such a close of the present day, a note was brought from Mrs. Goddard, requesting, in most respectful terms, to be allowed to bring Miss Smith with her; a

---

[7]*a real, honest, old-fashioned Boarding-school:* Similar, perhaps, to the Reading Ladies Boarding School that Jane Austen attended with her sister Cassandra between 1785 and 1786. See T. A. B. Corley, "Jane Austen's 'real, honest, old-fashioned Boarding-School': Miss La Tournelle and Mrs Goddard," *Women's Writing* 5 (1998): 113–30.

[8]*chilblains:* Inflammatory swellings produced by exposure to the cold, affecting the hands and feet, accompanied with heat and itching, and in severe cases leading to ulceration. (*OED*).

[9]*tea-visit:* Tea was generally served in the drawing room after dinner in the evening. At Hartfield, however, as R. W. Chapman points out in his appendix on "The Manners of the Age" in the Oxford edition of *Emma*, tea is untypically ranked as a meal and served at table.

most welcome request: for Miss Smith was a girl of seventeen whom Emma knew very well by sight and had long felt an interest in, on account of her beauty. A very gracious invitation was returned, and the evening no longer dreaded by the fair mistress of the mansion.

Harriet Smith was the natural daughter[10] of somebody. Somebody had placed her, several years back, at Mrs. Goddard's school, and somebody had lately raised her from the condition of scholar to that of parlour-boarder.[11] This was all that was generally known of her history. She had no visible friends but what had been acquired at Highbury, and was now just returned from a long visit in the country to some young ladies who had been at school there with her.

She was a very pretty girl, and her beauty happened to be of a sort which Emma particularly admired. She was short, plump and fair, with a fine bloom, blue eyes, light hair, regular features, and a look of great sweetness; and before the end of the evening, Emma was as much pleased with her manners as her person, and quite determined to continue the acquaintance.

She was not struck by any thing remarkably clever in Miss Smith's conversation, but she found her altogether very engaging — not inconveniently shy, not unwilling to talk — and yet so far from pushing, shewing so proper and becoming a deference, seeming so pleasantly grateful for being admitted to Hartfield, and so artlessly impressed by the appearance of every thing in so superior a style to what she had been used to, that she must have good sense and deserve encouragement. Encouragement should be given. Those soft blue eyes and all those natural graces should not be wasted on the inferior society of Highbury and its connections. The acquaintance she had already formed were unworthy of her. The friends from whom she had just parted, though very good sort of people, must be doing her harm. They were a family of the name of Martin, whom Emma well knew by character, as renting a large farm of Mr. Knightley, and residing in the parish of Donwell — very creditably she believed — she knew Mr. Knightley thought highly of them — but they must be coarse and unpolished, and very unfit to be the intimates of a girl who wanted only a little more knowledge and elegance to be quite perfect. *She* would notice her; she would improve her; she would detach her from her bad acquaintance, and introduce her into good society; she would form her opinions and her manners. It

---

[10] *natural daughter:* Illegitimate.
[11] *parlour-boarder:* Boarding-school pupil with special privileges, such as eating and sleeping in the household of the principal.

would be an interesting, and certainly a very kind undertaking; highly becoming her own situation in life, her leisure, and powers.

She was so busy in admiring those soft blue eyes, in talking and listening, and forming all these schemes in the in-betweens, that the evening flew away at a very unusual rate; and the supper-table, which always closed such parties, and for which she had been used to sit and watch the due time, was all set out and ready, and moved forwards to the fire, before she was aware. With an alacrity beyond the common impulse of a spirit which yet was never indifferent to the credit of doing every thing well and attentively, with the real good-will of a mind delighted with its own ideas, did she then do all the honours of the meal, and help and recommend the minced chicken and scalloped oysters with an urgency which she knew would be acceptable to the early hours and civil scruples of their guests.

Upon such occasions poor Mr. Woodhouse's feelings were in sad warfare. He loved to have the cloth laid, because it had been the fashion of his youth; but his conviction of suppers being very unwholesome made him rather sorry to see any thing put on it; and while his hospitality would have welcomed his visitors to every thing, his care for their health made him grieve that they would eat.

Such another small basin of thin gruel as his own, was all that he could, with thorough self-approbation, recommend, though he might constrain himself, while the ladies were comfortably clearing the nicer things, to say:

"Mrs. Bates, let me propose your venturing on one of these eggs. An egg boiled very soft is not unwholesome. Serle understands boiling an egg better than any body. I would not recommend an egg boiled by any body else — but you need not be afraid — they are very small, you see — one of our small eggs will not hurt you. Miss Bates, let Emma help you to a *little* bit of tart — a *very* little bit. Ours are all apple tarts. You need not be afraid of unwholesome preserves here. I do not advise the custard. Mrs. Goddard, what say you to *half* a glass of wine? A *small* half glass — put into a tumbler of water? I do not think it could disagree with you."

Emma allowed her father to talk — but supplied her visitors in a much more satisfactory style; and on the present evening had particular pleasure in sending them away happy. The happiness of Miss Smith was quite equal to her intentions. Miss Woodhouse was so great a personage in Highbury, that the prospect of the introduction had given as much panic as pleasure — but the humble, grateful, little girl went off with highly gratified feelings, delighted with the affability with which

Miss Woodhouse had treated her all the evening, and actually shaken hands with her at last!

CHAPTER IV.

HARRIET SMITH'S intimacy at Hartfield was soon a settled thing. Quick and decided in her ways, Emma lost no time in inviting, encouraging, and telling her to come very often; and as their acquaintance increased, so did their satisfaction in each other. As a walking companion, Emma had very early foreseen how useful she might find her. In that respect Mrs. Weston's loss had been important. Her father never went beyond the shrubbery, where two divisions of the grounds sufficed him for his long walk, or his short, as the year varied; and since Mrs. Weston's marriage her exercise had been too much confined. She had ventured once alone to Randalls, but it was not pleasant; and a Harriet Smith, therefore, one whom she could summon at any time to a walk, would be a valuable addition to her privileges. But in every respect as she saw more of her, she approved her, and was confirmed in all her kind designs.

Harriet certainly was not clever, but she had a sweet, docile, grateful disposition; was totally free from conceit; and only desiring to be guided by any one she looked up to. Her early attachment to herself was very amiable; and her inclination for good company, and power of appreciating what was elegant and clever, shewed that there was no want of taste, though strength of understanding must not be expected. Altogether she was quite convinced of Harriet Smith's being exactly the young friend she wanted — exactly the something which her home required. Such a friend as Mrs. Weston was out of the question. Two such could never be granted. Two such she did not want. It was quite a different sort of thing — a sentiment distinct and independent. Mrs. Weston was the object of a regard, which had its basis in gratitude and esteem. Harriet would be loved as one to whom she could be useful. For Mrs. Weston there was nothing to be done; for Harriet every thing.

Her first attempts at usefulness were in an endeavour to find out who were the parents; but Harriet could not tell. She was ready to tell every thing in her power, but on this subject questions were vain. Emma was obliged to fancy what she liked — but she could never believe that in the same situation *she* should not have discovered the truth. Harriet had no penetration. She had been satisfied to hear and believe just what Mrs. Goddard chose to tell her; and looked no farther.

Mrs. Goddard, and the teachers, and the girls, and the affairs of the school in general, formed naturally a great part of her conversation — and but for her acquaintance with the Martins of Abbey-Mill-Farm, it must have been the whole. But the Martins occupied her thoughts a good deal; she had spent two very happy months with them, and now loved to talk of the pleasures of her visit, and describe the many comforts and wonders of the place. Emma encouraged her talkativeness — amused by such a picture of another set of beings, and enjoying the youthful simplicity which could speak with so much exultation of Mrs. Martin's having "*two* parlours, two very good parlours indeed; one of them quite as large as Mrs. Goddard's drawing-room; and of her having an upper maid who had lived five-and-twenty years with her; and of their having eight cows, two of them Alderneys, and one a little Welch cow,[12] a very pretty little Welch cow, indeed; and of Mrs. Martin's saying, as she was so fond of it, it should be called *her* cow; and of their having a very handsome summer-house in their garden, where some day next year they were all to drink tea: — a very handsome summer-house, large enough to hold a dozen people."

For some time she was amused, without thinking beyond the immediate cause; but as she came to understand the family better, other feelings arose. She had taken up a wrong idea, fancying it was a mother and daughter, a son and son's wife, who all lived together; but when it appeared that the Mr. Martin, who bore a part in the narrative, and was always mentioned with approbation for his great good-nature in doing something or other, was a single man; that there was no young Mrs. Martin, no wife in the case; she did suspect danger to her poor little friend from all this hospitality and kindness — and that if she were not taken care of, she might be required to sink herself for ever.

With this inspiriting notion, her questions increased in number and meaning; and she particularly led Harriet to talk more of Mr. Martin, — and there was evidently no dislike to it. Harriet was very ready to speak of the share he had had in their moonlight walks and merry evening games; and dwelt a good deal upon his being so very good-humoured and obliging. "He had gone three miles round one day, in order to bring her some walnuts, because she had said how fond she was of them — and in every thing else he was so very obliging! He had his shepherd's son into the parlour one night on purpose to sing to

---

[12] *Alderneys . . . Welch cow:* Respectively, milk cattle named after one of the Channel Islands, their original home, and a small breed of cow indigenous to Wales. The Austens' farm at Steventon in Jane Austen's childhood had a dairy, supervised by her mother, and five Alderney cows.

her. She was very fond of singing. He could sing a little himself. She believed he was very clever, and understood every thing. He had a very fine flock; and while she was with them, he had been bid more for his wool than any body in the country. She believed every body spoke well of him. His mother and sisters were very fond of him. Mrs. Martin had told her one day, (and there was a blush as she said it,) that it was impossible for any body to be a better son; and therefore she was sure whenever he married he would make a good husband. Not that she *wanted* him to marry. She was in no hurry at all."

"Well done, Mrs. Martin!" thought Emma. "You know what you are about."

"And when she had come away, Mrs. Martin was so very kind as to send Mrs. Goddard a beautiful goose: the finest goose Mrs. Goddard had ever seen. Mrs. Goddard had dressed it on a Sunday, and asked all the three teachers, Miss Nash, and Miss Prince, and Miss Richardson, to sup with her."

"Mr. Martin, I suppose, is not a man of information beyond the line of his own business. He does not read?"

"Oh, yes! — that is, no — I do not know — but I believe he has read a good deal — but not what you would think any thing of. He reads the Agricultural Reports[13] and some other books, that lay in one of the window seats — but he reads all *them* to himself. But sometimes of an evening, before we went to cards, he would read something aloud out of the Elegant Extracts[14] — very entertaining. And I know he has read the Vicar of Wakefield.[15] He never read the Romance of the Forest, nor the Children of the Abbey.[16] He had never heard of such books before I mentioned them, but he is determined to get them now as soon as ever he can."

The next question was.

"What sort of looking man is Mr. Martin?"

---

[13] *Agricultural Reports:* Reports submitted to the Board of Agriculture in two series of General Views. The first appeared in 1794 and was printed with wide margins so that farmers could contribute information. A revised and enlarged *General Views* appeared between 1805 and 1817. Reports on matters of interest to farmers were also sent, many of them by tenant farmers, to *The Annals of Agriculture*, a periodical edited by Arthur Young (46 vols., 1784–1815). See John Barrell, *The Idea of Landscape and the Sense of Place* (Cambridge: Cambridge UP, 1972), ch. 2.

[14] *Elegant Extracts:* Anthology of choice pieces of prose and poetry edited by Vicesimus Knox in 1789 and often reprinted.

[15] *The Vicar of Wakefield:* Oliver Goldsmith's novel (1766).

[16] *Romance of the Forest . . . Children of the Abbey:* Gothic novels by Ann Radcliffe (1791) and Regina Maria Roche (1798).

"Oh! not handsome — not at all handsome. I thought him very plain at first, but I do not think him so plain now. One does not, you know, after a time. But, did you never see him? He is in Highbury every now and then, and he is sure to ride through every week in his way to Kingston.[17] He has passed you very often."

"That may be — and I may have seen him fifty times, but without having any idea of his name. A young farmer, whether on horseback or on foot, is the very last sort of person to raise my curiosity. The yeomanry[18] are precisely the order of people with whom I feel I can have nothing to do. A degree or two lower, and a creditable appearance might interest me; I might hope to be useful to their families in some way or other. But a farmer can need none of my help, and is therefore in one sense as much above my notice as in every other he is below it."

"To be sure. Oh! yes, it is not likely you should ever have observed him — but he knows you very well indeed — I mean by sight."

"I have no doubt of his being a very respectable young man. I know indeed that he is so; and as such wish him well. What do you imagine his age to be?"

"He was four-and-twenty the 8th of last June, and my birth-day is the 23d — just a fortnight and a day's difference! which is very odd!"

"Only four-and-twenty. That is too young to settle. His mother is perfectly right not to be in a hurry. They seem very comfortable as they are, and if she were to take any pains to marry him, she would probably repent it. Six years hence, if he could meet with a good sort of young woman in the same rank as his own, with a little money, it might be very desirable."

"Six years hence! dear Miss Woodhouse, he would be thirty years old!"

"Well, and that is as early as most men can afford to marry, who are not born to an independence. Mr. Martin, I imagine, has his fortune entirely to make — cannot be at all beforehand with the world. Whatever money he might come into when his father died, whatever his share of the family property, it is, I dare say, all afloat, all employed in his stock, and so forth; and though, with diligence and good luck, he

---

[17] *Kingston:* Town west of London, where Mr. Martin doubtless went to the farmer's market.

[18] *yeomanry:* Well-respected order of farmers below the rank of the gentry; either small landed proprietors or (like the Martins) tenants working rented land with their own capital.

may be rich in time, it is next to impossible that he should have realised any thing yet."

"To be sure, so it is. But they live very comfortably. They have no in-doors man — else they do not want for any thing; and Mrs. Martin talks of taking a boy another year."

"I wish you may not get into a scrape, Harriet, whenever he does marry; — I mean, as to being acquainted with his wife — for though his sisters, from a superior education, are not to be altogether objected to, it does not follow that he might marry any body at all fit for you to notice. The misfortune of your birth ought to make you particularly careful as to your associates. There can be no doubt of your being a gentleman's daughter, and you must support your claim to that station by every thing within your own power, or there will be plenty of people who would take pleasure in degrading you."

"Yes, to be sure — I suppose there are. But while I visit at Hartfield, and you are so kind to me, Miss Woodhouse, I am not afraid of what any body can do."

"You understand the force of influence pretty well, Harriet; but I would have you so firmly established in good society, as to be independent even of Hartfield and Miss Woodhouse. I want to see you permanently well connected — and to that end it will be advisable to have as few odd acquaintance as may be; and, therefore, I say that if you should still be in this country when Mr. Martin marries, I wish you may not be drawn in, by your intimacy with the sisters, to be acquainted with the wife, who will probably be some mere farmer's daughter, without education."

"To be sure. Yes. Not that I think Mr. Martin would ever marry any body but what had had some education — and been very well brought up. However, I do not mean to set up my opinion against your's — and I am sure I shall not wish for the acquaintance of his wife. I shall always have a great regard for the Miss Martins, especially Elizabeth, and should be very sorry to give them up, for they are quite as well educated as me. But if he marries a very ignorant, vulgar woman, certainly I had better not visit her, if I can help it."

Emma watched her through the fluctuations of this speech, and saw no alarming symptoms of love. The young man had been the first admirer, but she trusted there was no other hold, and that there would be no serious difficulty on Harriet's side to oppose any friendly arrangement of her own.

They met Mr. Martin the very next day, as they were walking on the

Donwell road. He was on foot, and after looking very respectfully at her, looked with most unfeigned satisfaction at her companion. Emma was not sorry to have such an opportunity of survey; and walking a few yards forward, while they talked together, soon made her quick eye sufficiently acquainted with Mr. Robert Martin. His appearance was very neat, and he looked like a sensible young man, but his person had no other advantage; and when he came to be contrasted with gentlemen, she thought he must lose all the ground he had gained in Harriet's inclination. Harriet was not insensible of manner; she had voluntarily noticed her father's gentleness with admiration as well as wonder. Mr. Martin looked as if he did not know what manner was.

They remained but a few minutes together, as Miss Woodhouse must not be kept waiting; and Harriet then came running to her with a smiling face, and in a flutter of spirits, which Miss Woodhouse hoped very soon to compose.

"Only think of our happening to meet him! — How very odd! It was quite a chance, he said, that he had not gone round by Randalls. He did not think we ever walked this road. He thought we walked towards Randalls most days. He has not been able to get the Romance of the Forest yet. He was so busy the last time he was at Kingston that he quite forgot it, but he goes again to-morrow. So very odd we should happen to meet! Well, Miss Woodhouse, is he like what you expected? What do you think of him? Do you think him so very plain?"

"He is very plain, undoubtedly — remarkably plain: — but that is nothing, compared with his entire want of gentility. I had no right to expect much, and I did not expect much; but I had no idea that he could be so very clownish, so totally without air. I had imagined him, I confess, a degree or two nearer gentility."

"To be sure," said Harriet, in a mortified voice, "he is not so genteel as real gentlemen."

"I think, Harriet, since your acquaintance with us, you have been repeatedly in the company of some, such very real gentlemen, that you must yourself be struck with the difference in Mr. Martin. At Hartfield you have had very good specimens of well educated, well bred men. I should be surprized if, after seeing them, you could be in company with Mr. Martin again without perceiving him to be a very inferior creature — and rather wondering at yourself for having ever thought him at all agreeable before. Do not you begin to feel that now? Were not you struck? I am sure you must have been struck by his awkward look and abrupt manner — and the uncouthness of a voice, which I heard to be wholly unmodulated as I stood here."

"Certainly, he is not like Mr. Knightley. He has not such a fine air and way of walking as Mr. Knightley. I see the difference plain enough. But Mr. Knightley is so very fine a man!"

"Mr. Knightley's air is so remarkably good, that it is not fair to compare Mr. Martin with *him*. You might not see one in a hundred, with *gentleman* so plainly written as in Mr. Knightley. But he is not the only gentleman you have been lately used to. What say you to Mr. Weston and Mr. Elton? Compare Mr. Martin with either of *them*. Compare their manner of carrying themselves; of walking; of speaking; of being silent. You must see the difference."

"Oh, yes! — there is a great difference. But Mr. Weston is almost an old man. Mr. Weston must be between forty and fifty."

"Which makes his good manners the more valuable. The older a person grows, Harriet, the more important it is that their manners should not be bad — the more glaring and disgusting any loudness, or coarseness, or awkwardness becomes. What is passable in youth, is detestable in later age. Mr. Martin is now awkward and abrupt; what will he be at Mr. Weston's time of life?"

"There is no saying, indeed!" replied Harriet, rather solemnly.

"But there may be pretty good guessing. He will be a completely gross, vulgar farmer — totally inattentive to appearances, and thinking of nothing but profit and loss."

"Will he, indeed, that will be very bad "

"How much his business engrosses him already, is very plain from the circumstance of his forgetting to inquire for the book you recommended. He was a great deal too full of the market to think of any thing else — which is just as it should be, for a thriving man. What has he to do with books? And I have no doubt that he *will* thrive and be a very rich man in time — and his being illiterate and coarse need not disturb *us*."

"I wonder he did not remember the book" — was all Harriet's answer, and spoken with a degree of grave displeasure which Emma thought might be safely left to itself. She, therefore, said no more for some time. Her next beginning was,

"In one respect, perhaps, Mr. Elton's manners are superior to Mr. Knightley's or Mr. Weston's. They have more gentleness. They might be more safely held up as a pattern. There is an openness, a quickness, almost a bluntness in Mr. Weston, which every body likes in *him* because there is so much good humour with it — but that would not do to be copied. Neither would Mr. Knightley's downright, decided, commanding sort of manner — though it suits *him* very well; his figure and look, and situation in life seem to allow it; but if any young man were to set about copying him, he would not be sufferable. On the contrary, I think a young man might be very safely recommended to take Mr. Elton as a model. Mr. Elton is good humoured, cheerful, obliging, and gentle. He seems to me, to be grown particularly gentle of late. I do not know whether he has any design of ingratiating himself with either of us, Harriet, by additional softness, but it strikes me that his manners are softer than they used to be. If he means anything, it must be to please you. Did not I tell you what he said of you the other day?"

She then repeated some warm personal praise which she had drawn from Mr. Elton, and now did full justice to; and Harriet blushed and smiled, and said she had always thought Mr. Elton very agreeable.

Mr. Elton was the very person fixed on by Emma for driving the young farmer out of Harriet's head. She thought it would be an excellent match; and only too palpably desirable, natural, and probable, for her to have much merit in planning it. She feared it was what every body else must think of and predict. It was not likely, however, that any body should have equalled her in the date of the plan, as it had entered her brain during the very first evening of Harriet's coming to Hartfield. The longer she considered it, the greater was her sense of its expediency. Mr. Elton's situation was most suitable, quite the gentleman himself, and without low connections; at the same time not of any family that could fairly object to the doubtful birth of Harriet. He had a comfortable home for her, and Emma imagined a very sufficient income; for though the vicarage of Highbury was not large, he was known to have some independent property; and she thought very highly of him as a good-humoured, well-meaning, respectable young man, without any deficiency of useful understanding or knowledge of the world.

She had already satisfied herself that he thought Harriet a beautiful girl, which she trusted, with such frequent meetings at Hartfield, was foundation enough on his side; and on Harriet's, there could be little doubt that the idea of being preferred by him would have all the usual weight and efficacy. And he was really a very pleasing young man, a young man whom any woman not fastidious might like. He was reckoned very handsome; his person much admired in general, though not by her, there being a want of elegance of feature which she could not dispense with: — but the girl who could be gratified by a Robert Martin's riding about the country to get walnuts for her, might very well be conquered by Mr. Elton's admiration.

CHAPTER V.

"I DO not know what your opinion may be, Mrs. Weston," said Mr. Knightley, "of this great intimacy between Emma and Harriet Smith, but I think it a bad thing."

"A bad thing! Do you really think it a bad thing? — why so?"

"I think they will neither of them do the other any good."

"You surprize me! Emma must do Harriet good: and by supplying her with a new object of interest, Harriet may be said to do Emma good. I have been seeing their intimacy with the greatest pleasure. How very differently we feel! — Not think they will do each other any good! This will certainly be the beginning of one of our quarrels about Emma, Mr. Knightley."

"Perhaps you think I am come on purpose to quarrel with you, knowing Weston to be out, and that you must still fight your own battle."

"Mr. Weston would undoubtedly support me, if he were here, for he thinks exactly as I do on the subject. We were speaking of it only yesterday, and agreeing how fortunate it was for Emma, that there should be such a girl in Highbury for her to associate with. Mr. Knightley, I shall not allow you to be a fair judge in this case. You are so much used to live alone, that you do not know the value of a companion; and perhaps no man can be a good judge of the comfort a woman feels in the society of one of her own sex, after being used to it all her life. I can imagine your objection to Harriet Smith. She is not the superior young woman which Emma's friend ought to be. But on the other hand, as Emma wants to see her better informed, it will be an inducement to her to read more herself. They will read together. She means it, I know."

"Emma has been meaning to read more ever since she was twelve years old. I have seen a great many lists of her drawing up at various times of books that she meant to read regularly through — and very good lists they were — very well chosen, and very neatly arranged — sometimes alphabetically, and sometimes by some other rule. The list she drew up when only fourteen — I remember thinking it did her judgment so much credit, that I preserved it some time; and I dare say she may have made out a very good list now. But I have done with expecting any course of steady reading from Emma. She will never submit to any thing requiring industry and patience, and a subjection of the fancy to the understanding. Where Miss Taylor failed to stimulate, I may safely affirm that Harriet Smith will do nothing. — You never could persuade her to read half so much as you wished. — You know you could not."

"I dare say," replied Mrs. Weston, smiling, "that I thought so *then;* — but since we have parted, I can never remember Emma's omitting to do any thing I wished."

"There is hardly any desiring to refresh such a memory as *that*" — said Mr. Knightley, feelingly; and for a moment or two he had done. "But I," he soon added, "who have had no such charm thrown over my senses, must still see, hear, and remember. Emma is spoiled by being the cleverest of her family. At ten years old, she had the misfortune of being able to answer questions which puzzled her sister at seventeen. She was always quick and assured: Isabella slow and diffident. And ever since she was twelve, Emma has been mistress of the house and of you all. In her mother she lost the only person able to cope with her. She inherits her mother's talents, and must have been under subjection to her."

"I should have been sorry, Mr. Knightley, to be dependent on *your* recommendation, had I quitted Mr. Woodhouse's family and wanted another situation; I do not think you would have spoken a good word for me to any body. I am sure you always thought me unfit for the office I held."

"Yes," said he, smiling. "You are better placed *here;* very fit for a wife, but not at all for a governess. But you were preparing yourself to be an excellent wife all the time you were at Hartfield. You might not give Emma such a complete education as your powers would seem to promise; but you were receiving a very good education from *her,* on the very material matrimonial point of submitting your own will, and doing as you were bid; and if Weston had asked me to recommend him a wife, I should certainly have named Miss Taylor."

"Thank you. There will be very little merit in making a good wife to such a man as Mr. Weston."

"Why, to own the truth, I am afraid you are rather thrown away, and that with every disposition to bear, there will be nothing to be borne. We will not despair, however. Weston may grow cross from the wantonness of comfort, or his son may plague him."

"I hope not *that.* — It is not likely. No, Mr. Knightley, do not foretel vexation from that quarter."

"Not I, indeed. I only name possibilities. I do not pretend to Emma's genius for foretelling and guessing. I hope, with all my heart, the young man may be a Weston in merit, and a Churchill in fortune. — But Harriet Smith — I have not half done about Harriet Smith. I think her the very worst sort of companion that Emma could possibly have. She knows nothing herself, and looks upon Emma as knowing every thing. She is a flatterer in all her ways, and so much the worse, because undesigned. Her ignorance is hourly flattery. How can Emma imagine she has any thing to learn herself, while Harriet is presenting such a delightful inferiority? And as for Harriet, I will venture to say that *she* cannot gain by the acquaintance. Hartfield will only put her out of conceit with all the other places she belongs to. She will grow just refined enough to be uncomfortable with those among whom birth and circumstances have placed her home. I am much mistaken if Emma's doctrines give any strength of mind, or tend at all to make a girl adapt herself rationally to the varieties of her situation in life. — They only give a little polish."

"I either depend more upon Emma's good sense than you do, or am more anxious for her present comfort; for I cannot lament the acquaintance. How well she looked last night!"

"Oh! you would rather talk of her person than her mind, would you? Very well; I shall not attempt to deny Emma's being pretty."

"Pretty! say beautiful rather. Can you imagine any thing nearer perfect beauty than Emma altogether — face and figure?"

"I do not know what I could imagine, but I confess that I have seldom seen a face or figure more pleasing to me than her's. But I am a partial old friend."

"Such an eye! — the true hazle eye — and so brilliant! regular features, open countenance, with a complexion! oh! what a bloom of full health, and such a pretty height and size; such a firm and upright figure. There is health, not merely in her bloom, but in her air, her head, her glance. One hears sometimes of a child being 'the picture of health;' now Emma always gives me the idea of being the complete picture of grown-up health. She is loveliness itself. Mr. Knightley, is not she?"

"I have not a fault to find with her person," he replied. "I think her all you describe. I love to look at her; and I will add this praise, that I do not think her personally vain. Considering how very handsome she is, she appears to be little occupied with it; her vanity lies another way. Mrs. Weston, I am not to be talked out of my dislike of her intimacy with Harriet Smith, or my dread of its doing them both harm."

"And I, Mr. Knightley, am equally stout in my confidence of its not doing them any harm. With all dear Emma's little faults, she is an excellent creature. Where shall we see a better daughter, or a kinder sister, or a truer friend? No, no; she has qualities which may be trusted; she will never lead any one really wrong; she will make no lasting blunder; where Emma errs once, she is in the right a hundred times."

"Very well; I will not plague you any more. Emma shall be an angel, and I will keep my spleen[19] to myself till Christmas brings John and Isabella. John loves Emma with a reasonable and therefore not a blind affection, and Isabella always thinks as he does; except when he is not quite frightened enough about the children. I am sure of having their opinions with me."

"I know that you all love her really too well to be unjust or unkind; but excuse me, Mr. Knightley, if I take the liberty (I consider myself, you know, as having somewhat of the privilege of speech that Emma's mother might have had) the liberty of hinting that I do not think any possible good can arise from Harriet Smith's intimacy being made a matter of much discussion among you. Pray excuse me; but supposing any little inconvenience may be apprehended from the intimacy, it cannot be expected that Emma, accountable to nobody but her father, who perfectly approves the acquaintance, should put an end to it, so long as it is a source of pleasure to herself. It has been so many years my province to give advice, that you cannot be surprized, Mr. Knightley, at this little remains of office."

"Not at all," cried he; "I am much obliged to you for it. It is very good advice, and it shall have a better fate than your advice has often found; for it shall be attended to."

"Mrs. John Knightley is easily alarmed, and might be made unhappy about her sister."

"Be satisfied," said he, "I will not raise any outcry. I will keep my ill-humour to myself. I have a very sincere interest in Emma. Isabella does not seem more my sister; has never excited a greater interest; perhaps hardly so great. There is an anxiety, a curiosity in what one feels for Emma. I wonder what will become of her!"

"So do I," said Mrs. Weston gently; "very much."

"She always declares she will never marry, which, of course, means just nothing at all. But I have no idea that she has yet ever seen a man she cared for. It would not be a bad thing for her to be very much in love with a proper object. I should like to see Emma in love, and in some doubt of a return; it would do her good. But there is nobody hereabouts to attach her; and she goes so seldom from home."

"There does, indeed, seem as little to tempt her to break her resolution, at present," said Mrs. Weston, "as can well be; and while she is so

[19]*spleen:* Ill-humor (often considered the English disease).

happy at Hartfield, I cannot wish her to be forming any attachment which would be creating such difficulties, on poor Mr. Woodhouse's account. I do not recommend matrimony at present to Emma, though I mean no slight to the state I assure you."

Part of her meaning was to conceal some favourite thoughts of her own and Mr. Weston's on the subject, as much as possible. There were wishes at Randalls respecting Emma's destiny, but it was not desirable to have them suspected; and the quiet transition which Mr. Knightley soon afterwards made to "What does Weston think of the weather; shall we have rain?" convinced her that he had nothing more to say or surmise about Hartfield.

CHAPTER VI.

EMMA could not feel a doubt of having given Harriet's fancy a proper direction and raised the gratitude of her young vanity to a very good purpose, for she found her decidedly more sensible than before of Mr. Elton's being a remarkably handsome man, with most agreeable manners; and as she had no hesitation in following up the assurance of his admiration, by agreeable hints, she was soon pretty confident of creating as much liking on Harriet's side, as there could be any occasion for. She was quite convinced of Mr. Elton's being in the fairest way of falling in love, if not in love already. She had no scruple with regard to him. He talked of Harriet, and praised her so warmly, that she could not suppose any thing wanting which a little time would not add. His perception of the striking improvement of Harriet's manner, since her introduction at Hartfield, was not one of the least agreeable proofs of his growing attachment.

"You have given Miss Smith all that she required," said he; "you have made her graceful and easy. She was a beautiful creature when she came to you, but, in my opinion, the attractions you have added are infinitely superior to what she received from nature."

"I am glad you think I have been useful to her; but Harriet only wanted drawing out, and receiving a few, very few hints. She had all the natural grace of sweetness of temper and artlessness in herself. I have done very little."

"If it were admissible to contradict a lady," said the gallant Mr. Elton —

"I have perhaps given her a little more decision of character, have taught her to think on points which had not fallen in her way before."

"Exactly so; that is what principally strikes me. So much superadded decision of character! Skilful has been the hand."

"Great has been the pleasure, I am sure. I never met with a disposition more truly amiable."

"I have no doubt of it." And it was spoken with a sort of sighing animation, which had a vast deal of the lover. She was not less pleased another day with the manner in which he seconded a sudden wish of her's, to have Harriet's picture.

"Did you ever have your likeness taken, Harriet?" said she: "Did you ever sit for your picture?"

Harriet was on the point of leaving the room, and only stopt to say, with a very interesting naïveté,

"Oh! dear, no, never."

No sooner was she out of sight, than Emma exclaimed,

"What an exquisite possession a good picture of her would be! I would give any money for it. I almost long to attempt her likeness myself. You do not know it I dare say, but two or three years ago I had a great passion for taking likenesses, and attempted several of my friends, and was thought to have a tolerable eye in general. But from one cause or another, I gave it up in disgust. But really, I could almost venture, if Harriet would sit to me. It would be such a delight to have her picture!"

"Let me entreat you," cried Mr. Elton; "it would indeed be a delight! Let me entreat you, Miss Woodhouse, to exercise so charming a talent in favour of your friend. I know what your drawings are. How could you suppose me ignorant? Is not this room rich in specimens of your landscapes and flowers; and has not Mrs. Weston some inimitable figure-pieces in her drawing-room, at Randalls?"

Yes, good man! — thought Emma — but what has all that to do with taking likenesses? You know nothing of drawing. Don't pretend to be in raptures about mine. Keep your raptures for Harriet's face. "Well, if you give me such kind encouragement, Mr. Elton, I believe I shall try what I can do. Harriet's features are very delicate, which makes a likeness difficult; and yet there is a peculiarity in the shape of the eye and the lines about the mouth which one ought to catch."

"Exactly so — The shape of the eye and the lines about the mouth — I have not a doubt of your success. Pray, pray attempt it. As you will do it, it will indeed, to use your own words, be an exquisite possession."

"But I am afraid, Mr. Elton, Harriet will not like to sit. She thinks so little of her own beauty. Did not you observe her manner of answering me? How completely it meant, 'why should my picture be drawn?'"

"Oh! yes, I observed it, I assure you. It was not lost on me. But still I cannot imagine she would not be persuaded."

Harriet was soon back again, and the proposal almost immediately made; and she had no scruples which could stand many minutes against the earnest pressing of both the others. Emma wished to go to work directly, and therefore produced the portfolio containing her various attempts at portraits, for not one of them had ever been finished, that they might decide together on the best size for Harriet. Her many beginnings were displayed. Miniatures, half-lengths, whole-lengths, pencil, crayon, and water-colours had been all tried in turn. She had always wanted to do everything, and had made more progress both in drawing and music than many might have done with so little labour as she would ever submit to. She played and sang; — and drew in almost every style; but steadiness had always been wanting; and in nothing had she approached the degree of excellence which she would have been glad to command, and ought not to have failed of. She was not much deceived as to her own skill either as an artist or a musician, but she was not unwilling to have others deceived, or sorry to know her reputation for accomplishment often higher than it deserved.

There was merit in every drawing — in the least finished, perhaps the most; her style was spirited; but had there been much less, or had there been ten times more, the delight and admiration of her two companions would have been the same. They were both in extasies. A likeness pleases every body; and Miss Woodhouse's performances must be capital.

"No great variety of faces for you," said Emma. "I had only my own family to study from. There is my father — another of my father — but the idea of sitting for his picture made him so nervous, that I could only take him by stealth; neither of them very like therefore. Mrs. Weston again, and again, and again, you see. Dear Mrs. Weston! always my kindest friend on every occasion. She would sit whenever I asked her. There is my sister; and really quite her own little elegant figure! — and the face not unlike. I should have made a good likeness of her, if she would have sat longer, but she was in such a hurry to have me draw her four children that she would not be quiet. Then, here come all my attempts at three of those four children; — there they are, Henry and John and Bella, from one end of the sheet to the other, and any one of them might do for any one of the rest. She was so eager to have them drawn that I could not refuse; but there is no making children of three or four years old stand still you know; nor can it be very easy to take any likeness of them, beyond the air and complexion, unless they are coarser featured than any mama's children ever were. Here is my sketch of the fourth, who was a baby. I took him, as he was sleeping on the sofa, and it is as strong a likeness of his cockade[20] as you would wish to see. He had nestled down his head most conveniently. That's very like. I am rather proud of little George. The corner of the sofa is very good. Then here is my last" — unclosing a pretty sketch of a gentleman in small size, whole-length — "my last and my best — my brother,[21] Mr. John Knightley. — This did not want much of being finished, when I put it away in a pet,[22] and vowed I would never take another likeness. I could not help being provoked; for after all my pains, and when I had really made a very good likeness of it — (Mrs. Weston and I were quite agreed in thinking it *very* like) — only too handsome — too flattering — but that was a fault on the right side — after all this, came poor dear Isabella's cold approbation of — "Yes, it was a little like — but to be sure it did not do him justice." We had had a great deal of trouble in persuading him to sit at all. It was made a great favour of; and altogether it was more than I could bear; and so I never would finish it, to have it apologized over as an unfavourable likeness, to every morning visitor in Brunswick-square; — and, as I said, I did then forswear ever drawing anybody again. But for Harriet's sake, or rather for my own, and as there are no husbands and wives in the case at present, I will break my resolution now."

Mr. Elton seemed very properly struck and delighted by the idea, and was repeating, "No husbands and wives in the case *at present* indeed, as you observe. Exactly so. No husbands and wives," with so interesting a consciousness, that Emma began to consider whether she had not better leave them together at once. But as she wanted to be drawing, the declaration must wait a little longer.

She had soon fixed on the size and sort of portrait. It was to be a whole-length in water-colours, like Mr. John Knightley's, and was destined, if she could please herself, to hold a very honourable station over the mantlepiece.

The sitting began; and Harriet, smiling and blushing, and afraid of not keeping her attitude and countenance, presented a very sweet mixture of youthful expression to the steady eyes of the artist. But there

[20]*cockade:* Ribboned ornament on a baby's cap.
[21]*brother:* Brother-in-law.
[22]*in a pet:* In a fit of annoyance.

was no doing anything, with Mr. Elton fidgetting behind her and watching every touch. She gave him credit for stationing himself where he might gaze and gaze again without offence; but was really obliged to put an end to it, and request him to place himself elsewhere. It then occurred to her to employ him in reading.

"If he would be so good as to read to them, it would be a kindness indeed! It would amuse away the difficulties of her part, and lessen the irksomeness of Miss Smith's."

Mr. Elton was only too happy. Harriet listened, and Emma drew in peace. She must allow him to be still frequently coming to look; anything less would certainly have been too little in a lover; and he was ready at the smallest intermission of the pencil, to jump up and see the progress, and be charmed. — There was no being displeased with such an encourager, for his admiration made him discern a likeness almost before it was possible. She could not respect his eye, but his love and his complaisance were unexceptionable.

The sitting was altogether very satisfactory; she was quite enough pleased with the first day's sketch to wish to go on. There was no want of likeness, she had been fortunate in the attitude, and as she meant to throw in a little improvement to the figure, to give a little more height, and considerably more elegance, she had great confidence of its being in every way a pretty drawing at last, and of its filling its destined place with credit to them both — a standing memorial of the beauty of one, the skill of the other, and the friendship of both; with as many other agreeable associations as Mr. Elton's very promising attachment was likely to add.

Harriet was to sit again the next day; and Mr. Elton, just as he ought, entreated for the permission of attending and reading to them again.

"By all means. We shall be most happy to consider you as one of the party."

The same civilities and courtesies, the same success and satisfaction, took place on the morrow, and accompanied the whole progress of the picture, which was rapid and happy. Every body who saw it was pleased, but Mr. Elton was in continual raptures, and defended it through every criticism.

"Miss Woodhouse has given her friend the only beauty she wanted," — observed Mrs. Weston to him — not in the least suspecting that she was addressing a lover. — "The expression of the eye is most correct, but Miss Smith has not those eye-brows and eye-lashes. It is the fault of her face that she has them not."

"Do you think so?" replied he. "I cannot agree with you. It appears to me a most perfect resemblance in every feature. I never saw such a likeness in my life. We must allow for the effect of shade, you know."

"You have made her too tall, Emma," said Mr. Knightley.

Emma knew that she had, but would not own it, and Mr. Elton warmly added,

"Oh, no! certainly not too tall; not in the least too tall. Consider, she is sitting down — which naturally presents a different — which in short gives exactly the idea — and the proportions must be preserved, you know. Proportions, fore-shortening. — Oh, no! it gives one exactly the idea of such a height as Miss Smith's. Exactly so indeed!"

"It is very pretty," said Mr. Woodhouse. "So prettily done! Just as your drawings always are, my dear. I do not know any body who draws so well as you do. The only thing I do not thoroughly like is, that she seems to be sitting out of doors, with only a little shawl over her shoulders — and it makes one think she must catch cold."

"But, my dear papa, it is supposed to be summer; a warm day in summer. Look at the tree."

"But it is never safe to sit out of doors, my dear."

"You, sir, may say anything," cried Mr. Elton; "but I must confess that I regard it as a most happy thought, the placing of Miss Smith out of doors; and the tree is touched with such inimitable spirit! Any other situation would have been much less in character. The naïveté of Miss Smith's manners — and altogether — Oh, it is most admirable! I cannot keep my eyes from it. I never saw such a likeness."

The next thing wanted was to get the picture framed; and here were a few difficulties. It must be done directly; it must be done in London; the order must go through the hands of some intelligent person whose taste could be depended on; and Isabella, the usual doer of all commissions, must not be applied to, because it was December, and Mr. Woodhouse could not bear the idea of her stirring out of her house in the fogs of December. But no sooner was the distress known to Mr. Elton, than it was removed. His gallantry was always on the alert. "Might he be trusted with the commission, what infinite pleasure should he have in executing it! he could ride to London at any time. It was impossible to say how much he should be gratified by being employed on such an errand."

"He was too good! — she could not endure the thought! — she would not give him such a troublesome office for the world" — brought on the desired repetition of entreaties and assurances, — and a very few minutes settled the business.

Mr. Elton was to take the drawing to London, chuse the frame, and give the directions; and Emma thought she could so pack it as to ensure its safety without much incommoding him, while he seemed mostly fearful of not being incommoded enough

"What a precious deposit!" said he with a tender sigh, as he received it.

"This man is almost too gallant to be in love," thought Emma. "I should say so, but that I suppose there may be a hundred different ways of being in love. He is an excellent young man, and will suit Harriet exactly; it will be an 'Exactly so,' as he says himself; but he does sigh and languish, and study for compliments rather more than I could endure as a principal. I come in for a pretty good share as a second. But it is his gratitude on Harriet's account."

CHAPTER VII.

THE very day of Mr. Elton's going to London produced a fresh occasion for Emma's services towards her friend. Harriet had been at Hartfield, as usual, soon after breakfast; and after a time, had gone home to return again to dinner; she returned, and sooner than had been talked of, and with an agitated, hurried look, announcing something extraordinary to have happened which she was longing to tell. Half a minute brought it all out. She had heard, as soon as she got back to Mrs. Goddard's, that Mr. Martin had been there an hour before, and finding she was not at home, nor particularly expected, had left a little parcel for her from one of his sisters, and gone away; and on opening this parcel, she had actually found, besides the two songs which she had lent Elizabeth to copy, a letter to herself; and this letter was from him, from Mr. Martin, and contained a direct proposal of marriage. "Who could have thought it! She was so surprized she did not know what to do. Yes, quite a proposal of marriage; and a very good letter, at least she thought so. And he wrote as if he really loved her very much — but she did not know — and so, she was come as fast as she could to ask Miss Woodhouse what she should do." — Emma was half ashamed of her friend for seeming so pleased and so doubtful.

"Upon my word," she cried, "the young man is determined not to lose any thing for want of asking. He will connect himself well if he can."

"Will you read the letter?" cried Harriet. "Pray do. I'd rather you would."

Emma was not sorry to be pressed. She read, and was surprized. The style of the letter was much above her expectation. There were not merely no grammatical errors, but as a composition it would not have disgraccd a gentleman; the language, though plain, was strong and unaffected, and the sentiments it conveyed very much to the credit of the writer. It was short, but expressed good sense, warm attachment, liberality, propriety, even delicacy of feeling. She paused over it, while Harriet stood anxiously watching for her opinion, with a "Well, well," and was at last forced to add, "Is it a good letter? or is it too short?"

"Yes, indeed, a very good letter," replied Emma rather slowly — "so good a letter, Harriet, that every thing considered, I think one of his sisters must have helped him. I can hardly imagine the young man whom I saw talking with you the other day could express himself so well, if left quite to his own powers, and yet it is not the style of a woman; no, certainly, it is too strong and concise; not diffuse enough for a woman. No doubt he is a sensible man, and I suppose may have a natural talent for — thinks strongly and clearly — and when he takes a pen in hand, his thoughts naturally find proper words. It is so with some men. Yes, I understand the sort of mind. Vigorous, decided, with sentiments to a certain point, not coarse. A better written letter, Harriet, (returning it,) than I had expected."

"Well," said the still waiting Harriet; — "well — and — and what shall I do?"

"What shall you do! In what respect? Do you mean with regard to this letter?"

"Yes."

"But what are you in doubt of? You must answer it of course — and speedily."

"Yes. But what shall I say? Dear Miss Woodhouse, do advise me."

"Oh, no, no! the letter had much better be all your own. You will express yourself very properly, I am sure. There is no danger of your not being intelligible, which is the first thing. Your meaning must be unequivocal; no doubts or demurs: and such expressions of gratitude and concern for the pain you are inflicting as propriety requires, will present themselves unbidden to *your* mind, I am persuaded. *You* need not be prompted to write with the appearance of sorrow for his disappointment."

"You think I ought to refuse him then," said Harriet, looking down.

"Ought to refuse him! My dear Harriet, what do you mean? Are you in any doubt as to that? I thought — but I beg your pardon, perhaps I have been under a mistake. I certainly have been misunderstanding you, if you feel in doubt as to the *purport* of your answer. I had imagined you were consulting me only as to the wording of it."

Harriet was silent. With a little reserve of manner, Emma continued: "You mean to return a favourable answer, I collect."

"No, I do not; that is, I do not mean — What shall I do? What would you advise me to do? Pray, dear Miss Woodhouse, tell me what I ought to do?"

"I shall not give you any advice, Harriet. I will have nothing to do with it. This is a point which you must settle with your own feelings."

"I had no notion that he liked me so very much," said Harriet, contemplating the letter. For a little while Emma persevered in her silence; but beginning to apprehend the bewitching flattery of that letter might be too powerful, she thought it best to say,

"I lay it down as a general rule, Harriet, that if a woman *doubts* as to whether she should accept a man or not, she certainly ought to refuse him. If she can hesitate as to 'Yes,' she ought to say 'No' directly. It is not a state to be safely entered into with doubtful feelings, with half a heart. I thought it my duty as a friend, and older than yourself, to say thus much to you. But do not imagine that I want to influence you."

"Oh! no, I am sure you are a great deal too kind to —— but if you would just advise me what I had best do — No, no, I do not mean that — As you say, one's mind ought to be quite made up — One should not be hesitating — It is a very serious thing — It will be safer to say 'No,' perhaps. — Do you think I had better say 'No?'"

"Not for the world," said Emma, smiling graciously, "would I advise you either way. You must be the best judge of your own happiness. If you prefer Mr. Martin to every other person; if you think him the most agreeable man you have ever been in company with, why should you hesitate? You blush, Harriet. — Does any body else occur to you at this moment under such a definition? Harriet, Harriet, do not deceive yourself; do not be run away with by gratitude and compassion. At this moment whom are you thinking of?"

The symptoms were favourable. — Instead of answering, Harriet turned away confused, and stood thoughtfully by the fire; and though the letter was still in her hand, it was now mechanically twisted about without regard. Emma waited the result with impatience, but not without strong hopes. At last, with some hesitation, Harriet said —

"Miss Woodhouse, as you will not give me your opinion, I must do as well as I can by myself; and I have now quite determined, and really almost made up my mind — to refuse Mr. Martin. Do you think I am right?"

"Perfectly, perfectly right, my dearest Harriet; you are doing just what you ought. While you were at all in suspense I kept my feelings to myself, but now that you are so completely decided I have no hesitation in approving. Dear Harriet, I give myself joy of this. It would have grieved me to lose your acquaintance, which must have been the consequence of your marrying Mr. Martin. While you were in the smallest degree wavering, I said nothing about it, because I would not influence; but it would have been the loss of a friend to me. I could not have visited Mrs. Robert Martin, of Abbey-Mill Farm. Now I am secure of you for ever."

Harriet had not surmised her own danger, but the idea of it struck her forcibly.

"You could not have visited me!" she cried, looking aghast. "No, to be sure you could not; but I never thought of that before. That would have been too dreadful! — What an escape! — Dear Miss Woodhouse, I would not give up the pleasure and honour of being intimate with you for any thing in the world."

"Indeed, Harriet, it would have been a severe pang to lose you; but it must have been. You would have thrown yourself out of all good society. I must have given you up."

"Dear me! — How should I ever have borne it! It would have killed me never to come to Hartfield any more!"

"Dear affectionate creature! — *You* banished to Abbey-Mill Farm! — *You* confined to the society of the illiterate and vulgar all your life! I wonder how the young man could have the assurance to ask it. He must have a pretty good opinion of himself."

"I do not think he is conceited either, in general," said Harriet, her conscience opposing such censure; "at least he is very good natured, and I shall always feel much obliged to him, and have a great regard for — but that is quite a different thing from — and you know, though he may like me, it does not follow that I should — and certainly I must confess that since my visiting here I have seen people — and if one comes to compare them, person and manners, there is no comparison at all, *one* is so very handsome and agreeable. However, I do really think Mr. Martin a very amiable young man, and have a great opinion of him; and his being so much attached to me — and his writing such a letter — but as to leaving you, it is what I would not do upon any consideration."

"Thank you, thank you, my own sweet little friend. We will not be parted. A woman is not to marry a man merely because she is asked, or because he is attached to her, and can write a tolerable letter."

"Oh! no; — and it is but a short letter too."

Emma felt the bad taste of her friend, but let it pass with a "very true; and it would be a small consolation to her, for the clownish manner which might be offending her every hour of the day, to know that her husband could write a good letter."

"Oh! yes, very. Nobody cares for a letter; the thing is, to be always happy with pleasant companions. I am quite determined to refuse him. But how shall I do? What shall I say?"

Emma assured her there would be no difficulty in the answer, and advised its being written directly, which was agreed to, in the hope of her assistance; and though Emma continued to protest against any assistance being wanted, it was in fact given in the formation of every sentence. The looking over his letter again, in replying to it, had such a softening tendency, that it was particularly necessary to brace her up with a few decisive expressions; and she was so very much concerned at the idea of making him unhappy, and thought so much of what his mother and sisters would think and say, and was so anxious that they should not fancy her ungrateful, that Emma believed if the young man had come in her way at that moment, he would have been accepted after all.

This letter, however, was written, and sealed, and sent. The business was finished, and Harriet safe. She was rather low all the evening, but Emma could allow for her amiable regrets, and sometimes relieved them by speaking of her own affection, sometimes by bringing forward the idea of Mr. Elton.

"I shall never be invited to Abbey-Mill again," was said in rather a sorrowful tone.

"Nor if you were, could I ever bear to part with you, my Harriet. You are a great deal too necessary at Hartfield, to be spared to Abbey-Mill."

"And I am sure I should never want to go there; for I am never happy but at Hartfield."

Some time afterwards it was, "I think Mrs. Goddard would be very much surprized if she knew what had happened. I am sure Miss Nash would — for Miss Nash thinks her own sister very well married and it is only a linen-draper."

"One should be sorry to see greater pride or refinement in the teacher of a school, Harriet. I dare say Miss Nash would envy you such an opportunity as this of being married. Even this conquest would appear valuable in her eyes. As to anything superior for you, I suppose she is quite in the dark. The attentions of a certain person can hardly be among the tittle-tattle of Highbury yet. Hitherto I fancy you and I are the only people to whom his looks and manners have explained themselves."

Harriet blushed and smiled, and said something about wondering that people should like her so much. The idea of Mr. Elton was certainly cheering; but still, after a time, she was tender-hearted again towards the rejected Mr. Martin.

"Now he has got my letter," said she softly. "I wonder what they are all doing — whether his sisters know — if he is unhappy, they will be unhappy too. I hope he will not mind it so very much."

"Let us think of those among our absent friends who are more cheerfully employed," cried Emma. "At this moment, perhaps, Mr. Elton is shewing your picture to his mother and sisters, telling how much more beautiful is the original, and after being asked for it five or six times, allowing them to hear your name, your own dear name."

"My picture! — But he has left my picture in Bond-street."[23]

"Has he so! — Then I know nothing of Mr. Elton. No, my dear little modest Harriet, depend upon it the picture will not be in Bond-street till just before he mounts his horse to-morrow. It is his companion all this evening, his solace, his delight. It opens his designs to his family, it introduces you among them, it diffuses through the party those pleasantest feelings of our nature, eager curiosity and warm prepossession. How cheerful, how animated, how suspicious, how busy their imaginations all are!"

Harriet smiled again, and her smiles grew stronger.

CHAPTER VIII.

HARRIET slept at Hartfield that night. For some weeks past she had been spending more than half her time there, and gradually getting to have a bed-room appropriated to herself; and Emma judged it best in every respect, safest and kindest, to keep her with them as much as possible just at present. She was obliged to go the next morning for an hour or two to Mrs. Goddard's, but it was then to be settled that she should return to Hartfield, to make a regular visit of some days.

While she was gone, Mr. Knightley called, and sat some time with Mr. Woodhouse and Emma, till Mr. Woodhouse, who had previously made up his mind to walk out, was persuaded by his daughter not to defer it, and was induced by the entreaties of both, though against the

[23] *Bond-street:* Street with expensive shops in the fashionable West End of London.

scruples of his own civility, to leave Mr. Knightley for that purpose. Mr. Knightley, who had nothing of ceremony about him, was offering by his short, decided answers, an amusing contrast to the protracted apologies and civil hesitations of the other.

"Well, I believe, if you will excuse me, Mr. Knightley, if you will not consider me as doing a very rude thing, I shall take Emma's advice and go out for a quarter of an hour. As the sun is out, I believe I had better take my three turns while I can. I treat you without ceremony, Mr. Knightley. We invalids think we are privileged people."

"My dear sir, do not make a stranger of me."

"I leave an excellent substitute in my daughter. Emma will be happy to entertain you. And therefore I think I will beg your excuse and take my three turns — my winter walk."

"You cannot do better, sir."

"I would ask for the pleasure of your company, Mr. Knightley, but I am a very slow walker, and my pace would be tedious to you; and besides, you have another long walk before you, to Donwell Abbey."

"Thank you, sir, thank you; I am going this moment myself; and I think the sooner *you* go the better. I will fetch your great coat and open the garden door for you."

Mr. Woodhouse at last was off; but Mr. Knightley, instead of being immediately off likewise, sat down again, seemingly inclined for more chat. He began speaking of Harriet, and speaking of her with more voluntary praise than Emma had ever heard before.

"I cannot rate her beauty as you do," said he; "but she is a pretty little creature, and I am inclined to think very well of her disposition. Her character depends upon those she is with; but in good hands she will turn out a valuable woman."

"I am glad you think so; and the good hands, I hope, may not be wanting."

"Come," said he, "you are anxious for a compliment, so I will tell you that you have improved her. You have cured her of her school-girl's giggle; she really does you credit."

"Thank you. I should be mortified indeed if I did not believe I had been of some use; but it is not every body who will bestow praise where they may. *You* do not often overpower me with it."

"You are expecting her again, you say, this morning?"

"Almost every moment. She has been gone longer already than she intended."

"Something has happened to delay her; some visitors perhaps."

"Highbury gossips! — Tiresome wretches!"

"Harriet may not consider every body tiresome that you would."

Emma knew this was too true for contradiction, and therefore said nothing. He presently added, with a smile,

"I do not pretend to fix on times or places, but I must tell you that I have good reason to believe your little friend will soon hear of something to her advantage."

"Indeed! how so? of what sort?"

"A very serious sort, I assure you;" still smiling.

"Very serious! I can think of but one thing — Who is in love with her? Who makes you their confidant?"

Emma was more than half in hopes of Mr. Elton's having dropt a hint. Mr. Knightley was a sort of general friend and adviser, and she knew Mr. Elton looked up to him.

"I have reason to think," he replied, "that Harriet Smith will soon have an offer of marriage, and from a most unexceptionable quarter: — Robert Martin is the man. Her visit to Abbey-Mill, this summer, seems to have done his business. He is desperately in love and means to marry her."

"He is very obliging," said Emma; "but is he sure that Harriet means to marry him?"

"Well, well, means to make her an offer then. Will that do? He came to the Abbey two evenings ago, on purpose to consult me about it. He knows I have a thorough regard for him and all his family, and, I believe, considers me as one of his best friends. He came to ask me whether I thought it would be imprudent in him to settle so early; whether I thought her too young: in short, whether I approved his choice altogether; having some apprehension perhaps of her being considered (especially since *your* making so much of her) as in a line of society above him. I was very much pleased with all that he said. I never hear better sense from any one than Robert Martin. He always speaks to the purpose; open, straight forward, and very well judging. He told me every thing; his circumstances and plans, and what they all proposed doing in the event of his marriage. He is an excellent young man, both as son and brother. I had no hesitation in advising him to marry. He proved to me that he could afford it; and that being the case, I was convinced he could not do better. I praised the fair lady too, and altogether sent him away very happy. If he had never esteemed my opinion before, he would have thought highly of me then; and, I dare say, left the house thinking me the best friend and counsellor man ever had. This happened the night before last. Now, as we may fairly suppose, he would not allow much time to pass before he spoke to the lady, and as he does not appear to have spoken yesterday, it is not unlikely that he should be at Mrs. Goddard's to day; and she may be detained by a visitor, without thinking him at all a tiresome wretch."

"Pray, Mr. Knightley," said Emma, who had been smiling to herself through a great part of this speech, "how do you know that Mr. Martin did not speak yesterday?"

"Certainly," replied he, surprized, "I do not absolutely know it; but it may be inferred. Was not she the whole day with you?"

"Come," said she, "I will tell you something, in return for what you have told me. He did speak yesterday — that is, he wrote, and was refused."

This was obliged to be repeated before it could be believed; and Mr. Knightley actually looked red with surprize and displeasure, as he stood up, in tall indignation, and said,

"Then she is a greater simpleton than I ever believed her. What is the foolish girl about?"

"Oh! to be sure," cried Emma, "it is always incomprehensible to a man that a woman should ever refuse an offer of marriage. A man always imagines a woman to be ready for anybody who asks her."

"Nonsense! a man does not imagine any such thing. But what is the meaning of this? Harriet Smith refuse Robert Martin? madness, if it is so; but I hope you are mistaken."

"I saw her answer, nothing could be clearer."

"You saw her answer! you wrote her answer too. Emma, this is your doing. You persuaded her to refuse him."

"And if I did, (which, however, I am far from allowing,) I should not feel that I had done wrong. Mr. Martin is a very respectable young man, but I cannot admit him to be Harriet's equal; and am rather surprized indeed that he should have ventured to address her. By your account, he does seem to have had some scruples. It is a pity that they were ever got over."

"Not Harriet's equal!" exclaimed Mr. Knightley loudly and warmly; and with calmer asperity, added, a few moments afterwards, "No, he is not her equal indeed, for he is as much her superior in sense as in situation. Emma, your infatuation about that girl blinds you. What are Harriet Smith's claims, either of birth, nature or education, to any connection higher than Robert Martin? She is the natural daughter of nobody knows whom, with probably no settled provision at all, and certainly no respectable relations. She is known only as parlour-boarder at a common school. She is not a sensible girl, nor a girl of any information. She has been taught nothing useful, and is too young and too simple to have acquired any thing herself. At her age she can have no experience, and with her little wit, is not very likely ever to have any that can avail her. She is pretty, and she is good tempered, and that is all. My only scruple in advising the match was on his account, as being beneath his deserts, and a bad connexion for him. I felt, that as to fortune, in all probability he might do much better; and that as to a rational companion or useful helpmate, he could not do worse. But I could not reason so to a man in love, and was willing to trust to there being no harm in her, to her having that sort of disposition, which, in good hands, like his, might be easily led aright and turn out very well. The advantage of the match I felt to be all on her side; and had not the smallest doubt (nor have I now) that there would be a general cry-out upon her extreme good luck. Even *your* satisfaction I made sure of. It crossed my mind immediately that you would not regret your friend's leaving Highbury, for the sake of her being settled so well. I remember saying to myself, 'Even Emma, with all her partiality for Harriet, will think this a good match.' "[24]

"I cannot help wondering at your knowing so little of Emma as to say any such thing. What! think a farmer, (and with all his sense and all his merit Mr. Martin is nothing more,) a good match for my intimate friend! Not regret her leaving Highbury for the sake of marrying a man whom I could never admit as an acquaintance of my own! I wonder you should think it possible for me to have such feelings. I assure you mine are very different. I must think your statement by no means fair. You are not just to Harriet's claims. They would be estimated very differently by others as well as myself; Mr. Martin may be the richest of the two, but he is undoubtedly her inferior as to rank in society. — The sphere in which she moves is much above his. — It would be a degradation."

"A degradation to illegitimacy and ignorance, to be married to a respectable, intelligent gentleman-farmer!"

"As to the circumstances of her birth, though in a legal sense she may be called Nobody, it will not hold in common sense. She is not to pay for the offence of others, by being held below the level of those with whom she is brought up. — There can scarcely be a doubt that her father is a gentleman — and a gentleman of fortune. — Her allowance is very liberal; nothing has ever been grudged for her improvement or comfort. — That she is a gentleman's daughter, is indubitable to me;

---

[24]*a good match.' "*: An emendation of the first edition, which omits the closing single quotation mark.

that she associates with gentlemen's daughters, no one, I apprehend, will deny. — She is superior to Mr. Robert Martin."

"Whoever might be her parents," said Mr. Knightley, "whoever may have had the charge of her, it does not appear to have been any part of their plan to introduce her into what you would call good society. After receiving a very indifferent education she is left in Mrs. Goddard's hands to shift as she can; — to move, in short, in Mrs. Goddard's line, to have Mrs. Goddard's acquaintance. Her friends evidently thought this good enough for her; and it *was* good enough. She desired nothing better herself. Till you chose to turn her into a friend, her mind had no distaste for her own set, nor any ambition beyond it. She was as happy as possible with the Martins in the summer. She had no sense of superiority then. If she has it now, you have given it. You have been no friend to Harriet Smith, Emma. Robert Martin would never have proceeded so far, if he had not felt persuaded of her not being disinclined to him. I know him well. He has too much real feeling to address any woman on the hap-hazard of selfish passion. And as to conceit, he is the farthest from it of any man I know. Depend upon it he had encouragement."

It was most convenient to Emma not to make a direct reply to this assertion; she chose rather to take up her own line of the subject again.

"You are a very warm friend to Mr. Martin; but, as I said before, are unjust to Harriet. Harriet's claims to marry well are not so contemptible as you represent them. She is not a clever girl, but she has better sense than you are aware of, and does not deserve to have her understanding spoken of so slightingly. Waving that point, however, and supposing her to be, as you describe her, only pretty and good-natured, let me tell you, that in the degree she possesses them, they are not trivial recommendations to the world in general, for she is, in fact, a beautiful girl, and must be thought so by ninety-nine people out of an hundred; and till it appears that men are much more philosophic on the subject of beauty than they are generally supposed; till they do fall in love with well-informed minds instead of handsome faces, a girl, with such loveliness as Harriet, has a certainty of being admired and sought after, of having the power of choosing from among many, consequently a claim to be nice.[25] Her good-nature, too, is not so very slight a claim, comprehending, as it does, real, thorough sweetness of temper and manner, a very humble opinion of herself, and a great readiness to be pleased with other people. I am very much mistaken if your sex in

[25] *nice:* Discriminating.

general would not think such beauty, and such temper, the highest claims a woman could possess."

"Upon my word, Emma, to hear you abusing the reason you have, is almost enough to make me think so too. Better be without sense, than misapply it as you do."

"To be sure!" cried she playfully. "I know *that* is the feeling of you all. I know that such a girl as Harriet is exactly what every man delights in — what at once bewitches his senses and satisfies his judgment. Oh! Harriet may pick and choose. Were you, yourself, ever to marry, she is the very woman for you. And is she, at seventeen, just entering into life, just beginning to be known, to be wondered at because she does not accept the first offer she receives? No — pray let her have time to look about her."

"I have always thought it a very foolish intimacy," said Mr. Knightley presently, "though I have kept my thoughts to myself; but I now perceive that it will be a very unfortunate one for Harriet. You will puff her up with such ideas of her own beauty, and of what she has a claim to, that, in a little while, nobody within her reach will be good enough for her. Vanity working on a weak head, produces every sort of mischief. Nothing so easy as for a young lady to raise her expectations too high. Miss Harriet Smith may not find offers of marriage flow in so fast, though she is a very pretty girl. Men of sense, whatever you may chuse to say, do not want silly wives. Men of family would not be very fond of connecting themselves with a girl of such obscurity — and most prudent men would be afraid of the inconvenience and disgrace they might be involved in, when the mystery of her parentage came to be revealed. Let her marry Robert Martin, and she is safe, respectable, and happy for ever; but if you encourage her to expect to marry greatly, and teach her to be satisfied with nothing less than a man of consequence and large fortune, she may be a parlour-boarder at Mrs. Goddard's all the rest of her life — or, at least, (for Harriet Smith is a girl who will marry somebody or other,) till she grow desperate, and is glad to catch at the old writing master's[26] son."

"We think so very differently on this point, Mr. Knightley, that there can be no use in canvassing[27] it. We shall only be making each other more angry. But as to my *letting* her marry Robert Martin, it is impossible; she has refused him, and so decidedly, I think, as must prevent any second application. She must abide by the evil of having

---

[26] *writing master:* A teacher of writing, penmanship, or calligraphy.
[27] *canvassing:* Discussing (derived from the idea of shaking papers in a canvas bag).

refused him, whatever it may be; and as to the refusal itself, I will not pretend to say that I might not influence her a little; but I assure you there was very little for me or for anybody to do. His appearance is so much against him, and his manner so bad, that if she ever were disposed to favour him, she is not now. I can imagine, that before she had seen anybody superior, she might tolerate him. He was the brother of her friends, and he took pains to please her; and altogether, having seen nobody better (that must have been his great assistant) she might not, while she was at Abbey-Mill, find him disagreeable. But the case is altered now. She knows now what gentlemen are; and nothing but a gentleman in education and manner has any chance with Harriet."

"Nonsense, errant nonsense, as ever was talked!" cried Mr. Knightley. — "Robert Martin's manners have sense, sincerity, and good-humour to recommend them; and his mind has more true gentility than Harriet Smith could understand."

Emma made no answer, and tried to look cheerfully unconcerned, but was really feeling uncomfortable and wanting him very much to be gone. She did not repent what she had done; she still thought herself a better judge of such a point of female right[28] and refinement than he could be; but yet she had a sort of habitual respect for his judgment in general, which made her dislike having it so loudly against her; and to have him sitting just opposite to her in angry state, was very disagreeable. Some minutes passed in this unpleasant silence, with only one attempt on Emma's side to talk of the weather, but he made no answer. He was thinking. The result of his thoughts appeared at last in these words.

"Robert Martin has no great loss — if he can but think so; and I hope it will not be long before he does. Your views for Harriet are best known to yourself; but as you make no secret of your love of match-making, it is fair to suppose that views, and plans, and projects you have; — and as a friend I shall just hint to you that if Elton is the man, I think it will be all labour in vain."

Emma laughed and disclaimed. He continued,

"Depend upon it, Elton will not do. Elton is a very good sort of man, and a very respectable vicar of Highbury, but not at all likely to make an imprudent match. He knows the value of a good income as well as anybody. Elton may talk sentimentally, but he will act rationally. He is as well acquainted with his own claims, as you can be with

---

[28] *female right:* A possible echo of Mary Wollstonecraft's *A Vindication of the Rights of Woman* (1792).

Harriet's. He knows that he is a very handsome young man, and a great favourite wherever he goes; and from his general way of talking in unreserved moments, when there are only men present, I am convinced that he does not mean to throw himself away. I have heard him speak with great animation of a large family of young ladies that his sisters are intimate with, who have all twenty thousand pounds apiece."

"I am very much obliged to you," said Emma, laughing again. "If I had set my heart on Mr. Elton's marrying Harriet, it would have been very kind to open my eyes; but at present I only want to keep Harriet to myself. I have done with match-making indeed. I could never hope to equal my own doings at Randalls. I shall leave off while I am well."

"Good morning to you," — said he, rising and walking off abruptly. He was very much vexed. He felt the disappointment of the young man, and was mortified to have been the means of promoting it, by the sanction he had given; and the part which he was persuaded Emma had taken in the affair, was provoking him exceedingly.

Emma remained in a state of vexation too; but there was more indistinctness in the causes of her's, than in his. She did not always feel so absolutely satisfied with herself, so entirely convinced that her opinions were right and her adversary's wrong, as Mr. Knightley. He walked off in more complete self-approbation than he left for her. She was not so materially cast down, however, but that a little time and the return of Harriet were very adequate restoratives. Harriet's staying away so long was beginning to make her uneasy. The possibility of the young man's coming to Mrs. Goddard's that morning, and meeting with Harriet and pleading his own cause, gave alarming ideas. The dread of such a failure after all became the prominent uneasiness; and when Harriet appeared, and in very good spirits, and without having any such reason to give for her long absence, she felt a satisfaction which settled her with her own mind, and convinced her, that let Mr. Knightley think or say what he would, she had done nothing which woman's friendship and woman's feelings would not justify.

He had frightened her a little about Mr. Elton; but when she considered that Mr. Knightley could not have observed him as she had done, neither with the interest, nor (she must be allowed to tell herself, in spite of Mr. Knightley's pretensions) with the skill of such an observer on such a question as herself, that he had spoken it hastily and in anger, she was able to believe, that he had rather said what he wished resentfully to be true, than what he knew anything about. He certainly might have heard Mr. Elton speak with more unreserve than she had ever done, and Mr. Elton might not be of an imprudent, inconsiderate disposition as to money-matters; he might naturally be rather attentive than otherwise to them; but then, Mr. Knightley did not make due allowance for the influence of a strong passion at war with all interested motives. Mr. Knightley saw no such passion, and of course thought nothing of its effects; but she saw too much of it, to feel a doubt of its overcoming any hesitations that a reasonable prudence might originally suggest; and more than a reasonable, becoming degree of prudence, she was very sure did not belong to Mr. Elton.

Harriet's cheerful look and manner established her's: she came back, not to think of Mr. Martin, but to talk of Mr. Elton. Miss Nash had been telling her something, which she repeated immediately with great delight. Mr. Perry had been to Mrs. Goddard's to attend a sick child, and Miss Nash had seen him, and he had told Miss Nash, that as he was coming back yesterday from Clayton Park, he had met Mr. Elton, and found to his great surprize that Mr. Elton was actually on his road to London, and not meaning to return till the morrow, though it was the whist-club[29] night, which he had been never known to miss before; and Mr. Perry had remonstrated with him about it, and told him how shabby it was in him, their best player, to absent himself, and tried very much to persuade him to put off his journey only one day; but it would not do; Mr. Elton had been determined to go on, and had said in a *very particular* way indeed, that he was going on business which he would not put off for any inducement in the world; and something about a very enviable commission, and being the bearer of something exceedingly precious. Mr. Perry could not quite understand him, but he was very sure there must be a *lady* in the case,[30] and he told him so; and Mr. Elton only looked very conscious and smiling, and rode off in great spirits. Miss Nash had told her all this, and had talked a great deal more about Mr. Elton; and said, looking so very significantly at her, "that she did not pretend to understand what his business might be, but she only knew that any woman whom Mr. Elton could prefer, she should think the luckiest woman in the world; for, beyond a doubt, Mr. Elton had not his equal for beauty or agreeableness."

---

[29] *whist-club:* Group of people meeting regularly to play at whist, a card game for four players made up of two pairs.

[30] *a* lady *in the case:* As R. W. Chapman notes of a later use of the phrase (p. 358), Mr. Perry is quoting a line spoken by a "stately bull" in one of John Gay's *Fables* (1727) entitled "The Hare and Many Friends." In refusing the hare's request for help in order to escape from pursuing hounds, the bull says: "Love calls me hence; a fav'rite cow / Expects me near yon barley mow: / And when a lady's in the case, / You know, all other things give place."

CHAPTER IX.

MR. KNIGHTLEY might quarrel with her, but Emma could not quarrel with herself. He was so much displeased, that it was longer than usual before he came to Hartfield again; and when they did meet, his grave looks shewed that she was not forgiven. She was sorry, but could not repent. On the contrary, her plans and proceedings were more and more justified, and endeared to her by the general appearances of the next few days.

The Picture, elegantly framed, came safely to hand soon after Mr. Elton's return, and being hung over the mantle-piece of the common sitting-room, he got up to look at it, and sighed out his half sentences of admiration just as he ought; and as for Harriet's feelings, they were visibly forming themselves into as strong and steady an attachment as her youth and sort of mind admitted. Emma was soon perfectly satis-fied of Mr. Martin's being no otherwise remembered, than as he fur-nished a contrast with Mr. Elton, of the utmost advantage to the latter.

Her views of improving her little friend's mind, by a great deal of useful reading and conversation, had never yet led to more than a few first chapters, and the intention of going on to-morrow. It was much easier to chat than to study; much pleasanter to let her imagination range and work at Harriet's fortune, than to be labouring to enlarge her comprehension or exercise it on sober facts; and the only literary pursuit which engaged Harriet at present, the only mental provision she was making for the evening of life, was the collecting and transcribing all the riddles of every sort that she could meet with, into a thin quarto of hot-pressed paper,[31] made up by her friend, and ornamented with cyphers and trophies.[32]

In this age of literature, such collections on a very grand scale are not uncommon.[33] Miss Nash, head-teacher at Mrs. Goddard's, had written out at least three hundred; and Harriet, who had taken the first hint of it from her, hoped, with Miss Woodhouse's help, to get a great many more. Emma assisted with her invention, memory and taste; and as Harriet wrote a very pretty hand, it was likely to be an arrangement of the first order, in form as well as quantity.

---

[31] *hot-pressed paper:* Paper made smooth and glossy by being pressed between glazed boards and hot metal plates.

[32] *cyphers and trophies:* Ornamental initials or monograms and elaborate drawings of treasured objects.

[33] *not uncommon:* The narrator speaks the truth; both private and public collections of charades, riddles, and conundrums were common. For further discussion and the title page of one such collection see "Contextual Documents," pp. 395, 399.

Mr. Woodhouse was almost as much interested in the business as the girls and tried very often to recollect something worth their putting in. "So many clever riddles as there used to be when he was young — he wondered he could not remember them! but he hoped he should in time." And it always ended in "Kitty, a fair but frozen maid."[34]

His good friend Perry too, whom he had spoken to on the subject, did not at present recollect any thing of the riddle kind; but he had desired Perry to be upon the watch, and as he went about so much, something, he thought, might come from that quarter.

It was by no means his daughter's wish that the intellects of Highbury in general should be put under requisition. Mr. Elton was the only one whose assistance she asked. He was invited to contribute any really good enigmas, charades, or conundrums that he might recollect; and she had the pleasure of seeing him most intently at work with his recollections; and at the same time, as she could perceive, most earnestly careful that nothing ungallant, nothing that did not breathe a compliment to the sex should pass his lips. They owed to him their two or three politest puzzles; and the joy and exultation with which at last he recalled, and rather sentimentally recited, that well-known charade,

My first doth affliction denote,
  Which my second is destin'd to feel
And my whole is the best antidote
  That affliction to soften and heal. — [35]

made her quite sorry to acknowledge that they had transcribed it some pages ago already.

"Why will not you write one yourself for us, Mr. Elton?" said she; "that is the only security for its freshness; and nothing could be easier to you."

"Oh, no! he had never written, hardly ever, any thing of the kind in his life. The stupidest fellow! He was afraid not even Miss Woodhouse" — he stopt a moment — "or Miss Smith could inspire him."

The very next day however produced some proof of inspiration. He called for a few moments, just to leave a piece of paper on the table containing, as he said, a charade, which a friend of his had addressed to a

---

[34] *"Kitty, a fair but frozen maid":* A riddle by David Garrick (1717–1779). The answer to the riddle is "chimney-sweep." For further discussion and the full text of one version of the riddle see "Contextual Documents," pp. 382, 385.

[35] *My first doth affliction denote . . . ":* The solution to the riddle is "woman" (i.e., "woe" plus "man").

young lady, the object of his admiration, but which, from his manner, Emma was immediately convinced must be his own.

"I do not offer it for Miss Smith's collection," said he. "Being my friend's, I have no right to expose it in any degree to the public eye, but perhaps you may not dislike looking at it."

The speech was more to Emma than to Harriet, which Emma could understand. There was deep consciousness about him, and he found it easier to meet her eye than her friend's. He was gone the next moment: — after another moment's pause,

"Take it," said Emma, smiling, and pushing the paper towards Harriet — "it is for you. Take your own."

But Harriet was in a tremor, and could not touch it; and Emma, never loth to be first, was obliged to examine it herself.

To Miss ———.
CHARADE.
My first displays the wealth and pomp of kings,
    Lords of the earth! their luxury and ease.
Another view of man, my second brings,
    Behold him there, the monarch of the seas!

But, ah! united, what reverse we have!
    Man's boasted power and freedom, all are flown;
Lord of the earth and sea, he bends a slave,
    And woman, lovely woman, reigns alone.

Thy ready wit the word will soon supply,
    May its approval beam in that soft eye!

She cast her eye over it, pondered, caught the meaning, read it through again to be quite certain, and quite mistress of the lines, and then passing it to Harriet, sat happily smiling, and saying to herself, while Harriet was puzzling over the paper in all the confusion of hope and dulness, "Very well, Mr. Elton, very well, indeed. I have read worse charades. *Courtship* — a very good hint. I give you credit for it. This is feeling your way. This is saying very plainly — 'Pray, Miss Smith, give me leave to pay my addresses to you. Approve my charade and my intentions in the same glance.'

May its approval beam in that soft eye!

Harriet exactly. Soft, is the very word for her eye — of all epithets, the justest that could be given.

Thy ready wit the word will soon supply.

Humph — Harriet's ready wit! All the better. A man must be very much in love indeed, to describe her so. Ah! Mr. Knightley, I wish you had the benefit of this; I think this would convince you. For once in your life you would be obliged to own yourself mistaken. An excellent charade indeed! and very much to the purpose. Things must come to a crisis soon now."

She was obliged to break off from these very pleasant observations, which were otherwise of a sort to run into great length, by the eagerness of Harriet's wondering questions.

"What can it be, Miss Woodhouse? — what can it be? I have not an idea — I cannot guess it in the least. What can it possibly be? Do try to find it out, Miss Woodhouse. Do help me. I never saw any thing so hard. Is it kingdom? I wonder who the friend was — and who could be the young lady! Do you think it is a good one? Can it be woman?

And woman, lovely woman, reigns alone.

Can it be Neptune?

Behold him there, the monarch of the seas!

Or a trident? or a mermaid? or a shark? Oh, no! shark is only one syllable. It must be very clever, or he would not have brought it. Oh! Miss Woodhouse, do you think we shall ever find it out?"

"Mermaids and sharks! Nonsense! My dear Harriet, what are you thinking of? Where would be the use of his bringing us a charade made by a friend upon a mermaid or a shark? Give me the paper and listen.

"For Miss ———, read Miss Smith.

My first displays the wealth and pomp of kings,
    Lords of the earth! their luxury and ease.

That is *court.*

Another view of man, my second brings;
    Behold him there, the monarch of the seas!

That is *ship;* — plain as can be. — Now for the cream.

But ah! united, (*courtship,* you know,) what reverse we have!
    Man's boasted power and freedom, all are flown.
Lord of the earth and sea, he bends a slave,
    And woman, lovely woman, reigns alone.

A very proper compliment! — and then follows the application, which I think, my dear Harriet, you cannot find much difficulty in comprehending. Read it in comfort to yourself. There can be no doubt of its being written for you and to you."

Harriet could not long resist so delightful a persuasion. She read the concluding lines, and was all flutter and happiness. She could not speak. But she was not wanted to speak. It was enough for her to feel. Emma spoke for her.

"There is so pointed, and so particular a meaning in this compliment," said she, "that I cannot have a moment's doubt as to Mr. Elton's intentions. You are his object — and you will soon receive the completest proof of it. I thought it must be so. I thought I could not be so deceived; but now, it is clear; the state of his mind is as clear and decided, as my wishes on the subject have been ever since I knew you. Yes, Harriet, just so long have I been wanting the very circumstance to happen which has happened. I could never tell whether an attachment between you and Mr. Elton were most desirable or most natural. Its probability and its eligibility have really so equalled each other! I am very happy. I congratulate you, my dear Harriet, with all my heart. This is an attachment which a woman may well feel pride in creating. This is a connection which offers nothing but good. It will give you every thing that you want — consideration, independence, a proper home — it will fix you in the centre of all your real friends, close to Hartfield and to me, and confirm our intimacy for ever. This, Harriet, is an alliance which can never raise a blush in either of us."

"Dear Miss Woodhouse" — and "Dear Miss Woodhouse," was all that Harriet, with many tender embraces could articulate at first; but when they did arrive at something more like conversation, it was sufficiently clear to her friend that she saw, felt, anticipated, and remembered just as she ought. Mr. Elton's superiority had very ample acknowledgment.

"Whatever you say is always right," cried Harriet, "and therefore I suppose, and believe, and hope it must be so; but otherwise I could not have imagined it. It is so much beyond any thing I deserve. Mr. Elton, who might marry any body! There cannot be two opinions about *him*. He is so very superior. Only think of those sweet verses — 'To Miss ———.' Dear me, how clever! — Could it really be meant for me?"

"I cannot make a question, or listen to a question about that. It is a certainty. Receive it on my judgment. It is a sort of prologue to the play, a motto to the chapter; and will be soon followed by matter-of-fact prose."

"It is a sort of thing which nobody could have expected. I am sure, a month ago, I had no more idea myself! — The strangest things do take place!"

—— "When Miss Smiths and Mr. Eltons get acquainted — they do indeed — and really it is strange; it is out of the common course that what is so evidently, so palpably desirable — what courts the pre-arrangement of other people, should so immediately shape itself into the proper form. You and Mr. Elton are by situation called together; you belong to one another by every circumstance of your respective homes. Your marrying will be equal to the match at Randalls. There does seem to be a something in the air of Hartfield which gives love exactly the right direction, and sends it into the very channel where it ought to flow.

The course of true love never did run smooth — [36]

A Hartfield edition of Shakespeare would have a long note on that passage."

"That Mr. Elton should really be in love with me, — me, of all people, who did not know him, to speak to him, at Michaelmas![37] And he, the very handsomest man that ever was, and a man that every body looks up to, quite like Mr. Knightley! His company so sought after, that every body says he need not eat a single meal by himself if he does not chuse it; that he has more invitations than there are days in the week. And so excellent in the Church! Miss Nash has put down all the texts he has ever preached from since he came to Highbury. Dear me! When I look back to the first time I saw him! How little did I think! — The two Abbots and I ran into the front room and peeped through the blind when we heard he was going by, and Miss Nash came and scolded us away, and staid to look through herself; however, she called me back presently, and let me look too, which was very good-natured. And how beautiful we thought he looked! He was arm in arm with Mr. Cole."

"This is an alliance which, whoever — whatever your friends may be, must be agreeable to them, provided at least they have common sense; and we are not to be addressing our conduct to fools. If they are

[36] *The course of true love . . . :* Shakespeare, *A Midsummer Night's Dream* (I.i.3).
[37] *Michaelmas:* The feast of St. Michael, September 29; also one of the quarter days and the name of a law term and a term at Oxford and Cambridge.

anxious to see you *happily* married, here is a man whose amiable character gives every assurance of it; — if they wish to have you settled in the same country and circle which they have chosen to place you in, here it will be accomplished; and if their only object is that you should, in the common phrase, be *well* married, here is the comfortable fortune, the respectable establishment, the rise in the world which must satisfy them."

"Yes, very true. How nicely you talk; I love to hear you. You understand every thing. You and Mr. Elton are one as clever as the other. This charade! — If I had studied a twelvemonth, I could never have made any thing like it."

"I thought he meant to try his skill, by his manner of declining it yesterday."

"I do think it is, without exception, the best charade I ever read."

"I never read one more to the purpose, certainly."

"It is as long again as almost all we have had before."

"I do not consider its length as particularly in its favour. Such things in general cannot be too short."

Harriet was too intent on the lines to hear. The most satisfactory comparisons were rising in her mind.

"It is one thing," said she, presently — her cheeks in a glow — "to have very good sense in a common way, like every body else, and if there is any thing to say, to sit down and write a letter, and say just what you must, in a short way; and another, to write verses and charades like this."

Emma could not have desired a more spirited rejection of Mr. Martin's prose.

"Such sweet lines!" continued Harriet — "these two last! — But how shall I ever be able to return the paper, or say I have found it out? — Oh! Miss Woodhouse, what can we do about that?"

"Leave it to me. You do nothing. He will be here this evening, I dare say, and then I will give it him back, and some nonsense or other will pass between us, and you shall not be committed. — Your soft eyes shall chuse their own time for beaming. Trust to me."

"Oh! Miss Woodhouse, what a pity that I must not write this beautiful charade into my book! I am sure I have not got one half so good."

"Leave out the two last lines, and there is no reason why you should not write it into your book."

"Oh! but those two lines are" —— "—— The best of all. Granted; — for private enjoyment; and for private enjoyment keep them. They are not at all the less written you know, because you divide them. The couplet does not cease to be, nor does its meaning change. But take it away, and all *appropriation* ceases, and a very pretty gallant charade remains, fit for any collection. Depend upon it, he would not like to have his charade slighted, much better than his passion. A poet in love must be encouraged in both capacities, or neither. Give me the book, I will write it down, and then there can be no possible reflection on you."

Harriet submitted, though her mind could hardly separate the parts, so as to feel quite sure that her friend were not writing down a declaration of love. It seemed too precious an offering for any degree of publicity.

"I shall never let that book go out of my own hands," said she.

"Very well," replied Emma, "a most natural feeling; and the longer it lasts, the better I shall be pleased. But here is my father coming: you will not object to my reading the charade to him. It will be giving him so much pleasure! He loves any thing of the sort, and especially any thing that pays woman a compliment. He has the tenderest spirit of gallantry towards us all! — You must let me read it to him."

Harriet looked grave.

"My dear Harriet, you must not refine too much upon this charade. — You will betray your feelings improperly, if you are too conscious and too quick, and appear to affix more meaning, or even quite all the meaning which may be affixed to it. Do not be overpowered by such a little tribute of admiration. If he had been anxious for secrecy, he would not have left the paper while I was by; but he rather pushed it towards me than towards you. Do not let us be too solemn on the business. He has encouragement enough to proceed, without our sighing out our souls over this charade."

"Oh! no — I hope I shall not be ridiculous about it. Do as you please."

Mr. Woodhouse came in, and very soon led to the subject again, by the recurrence of his very frequent inquiry of "Well, my dears, how does your book go on? — Have you got any thing fresh?"

"Yes, papa, we have something to read you, something quite fresh. A piece of paper was found on the table this morning — (dropt, we suppose, by a fairy) — containing a very pretty charade, and we have just copied it in."

She read it to him, just as he liked to have any thing read, slowly and distinctly, and two or three times over, with explanations of every part as she proceeded — and he was very much pleased, and, as she had foreseen, especially struck with the complimentary conclusion.

"Aye, that's very just, indeed, that's very properly said. Very true. 'Woman, lovely woman.' It is such a pretty charade, my dear, that I can easily guess what fairy brought it. — Nobody could have written so prettily, but you, Emma."

Emma only nodded, and smiled. — After a little thinking, and a very tender sigh, he added,

"Ah! it is no difficulty to see who you take after! Your dear mother was so clever at all those things! If I had but her memory! But I can remember nothing; — not even that particular riddle which you have heard me mention; I can only recollect the first stanza; and there are several.

> Kitty, a fair but frozen maid,
>   Kindled a flame I yet deplore,
> The hood-wink'd boy I called to aid,
> Though of his near approach afraid,
>   So fatal to my suit before.

And that is all that I can recollect of it — but it is very clever all the way through. But I think, my dear, you said you had got it."

"Yes, papa, it is written out in our second page. We copied it from the Elegant Extracts. It was Garrick's,[38] you know."

"Aye, very true. — I wish I could recollect more of it.

> Kitty, a fair but frozen maid.

The name makes me think of poor Isabella; for she was very near being christened Catherine after her grandmama. I hope we shall have her here next week. Have you thought, my dear, where you shall put her — and what room there will be for the children?"

"Oh! yes — she will have her own room, of course; the room she always has; — and there is the nursery for the children, — just as usual, you know. — Why should there be any change?"

"I do not know, my dear — but it is so long since she was here! — not since last Easter, and then only for a few days. — Mr. John Knightley's being a lawyer is very inconvenient. — Poor Isabella! — she is sadly taken away from us all! — and how sorry she will be when she comes, not to see Miss Taylor here!"

"She will not be surprised, papa, at least."

---

[38] *Elegant Extracts.... Garrick's:* Although often reprinted, Garrick's riddle, as Chapman points out, does not seem to appear in *Elegant Extracts.*

"I do not know, my dear. I am sure I was very much surprized when I first heard she was going to be married."

"We must ask Mr. and Mrs. Weston to dine with us, while Isabella is here."

"Yes, my dear, if there is time. — But — (in a very depressed tone) — she is coming for only one week. There will not be time for any thing."

"It is unfortunate that they cannot stay longer — but it seems a case of necessity. Mr. John Knightley must be in town again on the 28th, and we ought to be thankful, papa, that we are to have the whole of the time they can give to the country, that two or three days are not to be taken out for the Abbey. Mr. Knightley promises to give up his claim this Christmas — though you know it is longer since they were with him, than with us."

"It would be very hard indeed, my dear, if poor Isabella were to be anywhere but at Hartfield."

Mr. Woodhouse could never allow for Mr. Knightley's claims on his brother, or any body's claims on Isabella, except his own. He sat musing a little while, and then said,

"But I do not see why poor Isabella should be obliged to go back so soon, though he does. I think, Emma, I shall try and persuade her to stay longer with us. She and the children might stay very well."

"Ah! papa — that is what you never have been able to accomplish, and I do not think you ever will. Isabella cannot bear to stay behind her husband."

This was too true for contradiction. Unwelcome as it was, Mr. Woodhouse could only give a submissive sigh; and as Emma saw his spirits affected by the idea of his daughter's attachment to her husband, she immediately led to such a branch of the subject as must raise them.

"Harriet must give us as much of her company as she can while my brother and sister are here. I am sure she will be pleased with the children. We are very proud of the children, are not we, papa? I wonder which she will think the handsomest, Henry or John?"

"Aye, I wonder which she will. Poor little dears, how glad they will be to come. They are very fond of being at Hartfield, Harriet."

"I dare say they are, sir. I am sure I do not know who is not."

"Henry is a fine boy, but John is very like his mamma. Henry is the eldest, he was named after me, not after his father. John, the second, is named after his father. Some people are surprized, I believe, that the eldest was not, but Isabella would have him called Henry, which I thought very pretty of her. And he is a very clever boy, indeed. They are

all remarkably clever; and they have so many pretty ways. They will
come and stand by my chair, and say, 'Grandpapa, can you give me a bit
of string?' and once Henry asked me for a knife, but I told him knives
were only made for grandpapas. I think their father is too rough with
them very often."

"He appears rough to you," said Emma, "because you are so very
gentle yourself; but if you could compare him with other papas, you
would not think him rough. He wishes his boys to be active and hardy;
and if they misbehave, can give them a sharp word now and then; but
he is an affectionate father — certainly Mr. John Knightley is an affectionate father. The children are all fond of him."

"And then their uncle comes in, and tosses them up to the ceiling in
a very frightful way!"

"But they like it, papa; there is nothing they like so much. It is such
enjoyment to them, that if their uncle did not lay down the rule of their
taking turns, which ever began would never give way to the other."

"Well, I cannot understand it."

"That is the case with us all, papa. One half of the world cannot
understand the pleasures of the other."

Later in the morning, and just as the girls were going to separate in
preparation for the regular four o'clock dinner, the hero of this inimitable charade walked in again. Harriet turned away; but Emma could
receive him with the usual smile, and her quick eye soon discerned in
his the consciousness of having made a push — of having thrown a die;
and she imagined he was come to see how it might turn up. His ostensible reason, however, was to ask whether Mr. Woodhouse's party could
be made up in the evening without him, or whether he should be in
the smallest degree necessary at Hartfield. If he were, every thing else
must give way; but otherwise his friend Cole had been saying so much
about his dining with him — had made such a point of it, that he had
promised him conditionally to come.

Emma thanked him, but could not allow of his disappointing his
friend on their account; her father was sure of his rubber.[39] He re-
urged — she re-declined; and he seemed then about to make his bow,
when taking the paper from the table, she returned it —

"Oh! here's the charade you were so obliging as to leave with us;
thank you for the sight of it. We admired it so much, that I have ventured
to write it into Miss Smith's collection. Your friend will not take it amiss I
hope. Of course I have not transcribed beyond the eight first lines."

[39] *rubber:* A set of card games in which the player (or pair) taking two out of three (or
three out of five) games is the winner.

Mr. Elton certainly did not very well know what to say. He looked rather doubtingly — rather confused; said something about "honour;" — glanced at Emma and at Harriet, and then seeing the book open on the table, took it up, and examined it very attentively. With the view of passing off an awkward moment, Emma smilingly said,

"You must make my apologies to your friend; but so good a charade must not be confined to one or two. He may be sure of every woman's approbation while he writes with such gallantry."

"I have no hesitation in saying," replied Mr. Elton, though hesitating a good deal while he spoke, "I have no hesitation in saying — at least if my friend feels at all as *I* do — I have not the smallest doubt that, could he see his little effusion honoured as *I* see it, (looking at the book again, and replacing it on the table,) he would consider it as the proudest moment of his life."

After this speech he was gone as soon as possible. Emma could not think it too soon; for with all his good and agreeable qualities, there was a sort of parade in his speeches which was very apt to incline her to laugh. She ran away to indulge the inclination, leaving the tender and the sublime of pleasure to Harriet's share.

CHAPTER X.

THOUGH now the middle of December, there had yet been no weather to prevent the young ladies from tolerably regular exercise; and on the morrow, Emma had a charitable visit to pay to a poor sick family, who lived a little way out of Highbury.

Their road to this detached cottage was down Vicarage-lane, a lane leading at right-angles from the broad, though irregular, main street of the place; and, as may be inferred, containing the blessed abode of Mr. Elton. A few inferior dwellings were first to be passed, and then, about a quarter of a mile down the lane rose the Vicarage; an old and not very good house, almost as close to the road as it could be. It had no advantage of situation; but had been very much smartened up by the present proprietor; and, such as it was, there could be no possibility of the two friends passing it without a slackened pace and observing eyes. — Emma's remark was —

"There it is. There go you and your riddle-book one of these days." — Harriet's was —

"Oh! what a sweet house! — How very beautiful! — There are the yellow curtains that Miss Nash admires so much."

"I do not often walk this way *now*," said Emma, as they proceeded, "but *then* there will be an inducement, and I shall gradually get intimately acquainted with all the hedges, gates, pools, and pollards[40] of this part of Highbury."

Harriet, she found, had never in her life been within side the Vicarage, and her curiosity to see it was so extreme, that, considering exteriors and probabilities, Emma could only class it, as a proof of love, with Mr. Elton's seeing ready wit in her.

"I wish we could contrive it," said she; "but I cannot think of any tolerable pretence for going in; — no servant that I want to inquire about of his housekeeper — no message from my father."

She pondered, but could think of nothing. After a mutual silence of some minutes, Harriet thus began again —

"I do so wonder, Miss Woodhouse, that you should not be married, or going to be married! so charming as you are!" —

Emma laughed, and replied,

"My being charming, Harriet, is not quite enough to induce me to marry; I must find other people charming — one other person at least. And I am not only, not going to be married, at present, but have very little intention of ever marrying at all."

"Ah! so you say; but I cannot believe it."

"I must see somebody very superior to any one I have seen yet, to be tempted; Mr. Elton, you know, (recollecting herself,) is out of the question: and I do *not* wish to see any such person. I would rather not be tempted. I cannot really change for the better. If I were to marry, I must expect to repent it."

"Dear me! — it is so odd to hear a woman talk so!" —

"I have none of the usual inducements of women to marry. Were I to fall in love, indeed, it would be a different thing! but I never have been in love; it is not my way, or my nature; and I do not think I ever shall. And, without love, I am sure I should be a fool to change such a situation as mine. Fortune I do not want; employment I do not want; consequence I do not want: I believe few married women are half as much mistress of their husband's house, as I am of Hartfield; and never, never could I expect to be so truly beloved and important; so always first and always right in any man's eyes as I am in my father's."

"But then, to be an old maid at last, like Miss Bates!"

"That is as formidable an image as you could present, Harriet; and

---

[40]*pollards:* Trees that are cut back (or polled) at the top so as to produce a thick growth of young branches each year.

if I thought I should ever be like Miss Bates! so silly — so satisfied — so smiling — so prosing — so undistinguishing and unfastidious — and so apt to tell every thing relative to every body about me, I would marry to-morrow. But between *us,* I am convinced there never can be any likeness, except in being unmarried."

"But still, you will be an old maid! and that's so dreadful!"

"Never mind, Harriet, I shall not be a poor old maid; and it is poverty only which makes celibacy contemptible to a generous public! A single woman, with a very narrow income, must be a ridiculous, disagreeable, old maid! the proper sport of boys and girls; but a single woman, of good fortune, is always respectable, and may be as sensible and pleasant as anybody else. And the distinction is not quite so much against the candour and common sense of the world as appears at first; for a very narrow income has a tendency to contract the mind, and sour the temper. Those who can barely live, and who live perforce in a very small, and generally very inferior, society, may well be illiberal and cross. This does not apply, however, to Miss Bates; she is only too good natured and too silly to suit me; but, in general, she is very much to the taste of everybody, though single and though poor. Poverty certainly has not contracted her mind: I really believe, if she had only a shilling in the world, she would be very likely to give away sixpence of it; and nobody is afraid of her: that is a great charm."

"Dear me! but what shall you do? how shall you employ yourself when you grow old?"

"If I know myself, Harriet, mine is an active, busy mind, with a great many independent resources; and I do not perceive why I should be more in want of employment at forty or fifty than one-and-twenty. Woman's usual occupations of eye and hand and mind will be as open to me then, as they are now; or with no important variation. If I draw less, I shall read more; if I give up music, I shall take to carpet-work. And as for objects of interest, objects for the affections, which is in truth the great point of inferiority, the want of which is really the great evil to be avoided in *not* marrying, I shall be very well off, with all the children of a sister I love so much, to care about. There will be enough of them, in all probability, to supply every sort of sensation that declining life can need. There will be enough for every hope and every fear; and though my attachment to none can equal that of a parent, it suits my ideas of comfort better than what is warmer and blinder. My nephews and nieces! — I shall often have a niece with me."

"Do you know Miss Bates's niece? That is, I know you must have seen her a hundred times — but are you acquainted?"

"Oh! yes; we are always forced to be acquainted whenever she comes to Highbury. By the bye, *that* is almost enough to put one out of conceit with a niece. Heaven forbid! at least, that I should ever bore people half so much about all the Knightleys together, as she does about Jane Fairfax. One is sick of the very name of Jane Fairfax. Every letter from her is read forty times over; her compliments to all friends go round and round again; and if she does but send her aunt the pattern of a stomacher,[41] or knit a pair of garters for her grandmother, one hears of nothing else for a month. I wish Jane Fairfax very well; but she tires me to death."

They were now approaching the cottage, and all idle topics were superseded. Emma was very compassionate; and the distresses of the poor were as sure of relief from her personal attention and kindness, her counsel and her patience, as from her purse. She understood their ways, could allow for their ignorance and their temptations, had no romantic expectations of extraordinary virtue from those, for whom education had done so little; entered into their troubles with ready sympathy, and always gave her assistance with as much intelligence as good-will. In the present instance, it was sickness and poverty together which she came to visit; and after remaining there as long as she could give comfort or advice, she quitted the cottage with such an impression of the scene as made her say to Harriet, as they walked away,

"These are the sights, Harriet, to do one good. How trifling they make every thing else appear! — I feel now as if I could think of nothing but these poor creatures all the rest of the day; and yet, who can say how soon it may all vanish from my mind?"

"Very true," said Harriet. "Poor creatures! one can think of nothing else."

"And really, I do not think the impression will soon be over," said Emma, as she crossed the low hedge, and tottering footstep which ended the narrow, slippery path through the cottage garden, and brought them into the lane again. "I do not think it will," stopping to look once more at all the outward wretchedness of the place, and recal the still greater within.

"Oh! dear, no," said her companion.

They walked on. The lane made a slight bend; and when that bend was passed, Mr. Elton was immediately in sight; and so near as to give Emma time only to say farther,

---

[41]*stomacher:* Ornamental covering for the chest worn by women under the lacing of the bodice.

"Ah! Harriet, here comes a very sudden trial of our stability in good thoughts. Well, (smiling,) I hope it may be allowed that if compassion has produced exertion and relief to the sufferers, it has done all that is truly important. If we feel for the wretched, enough to do all we can for them, the rest is empty sympathy, only distressing to ourselves."

Harriet could just answer, "Oh! dear, yes," before the gentleman joined them. The wants and sufferings of the poor family, however, were the first subject on meeting. He had been going to call on them. His visit he would now defer; but they had a very interesting parley[42] about what could be done and should be done. Mr. Elton then turned back to accompany them.

"To fall in with each other on such an errand as this," thought Emma; "to meet in a charitable scheme; this will bring a great increase of love on each side. I should not wonder if it were to bring on the declaration. It must, if I were not here. I wish I were anywhere else."

Anxious to separate herself from them as far as she could, she soon afterwards took possession of a narrow footpath, a little raised on one side of the lane, leaving them together in the main road. But she had not been there two minutes when she found that Harriet's habits of dependence and imitation were bringing her up too, and that, in short, they would both be soon after her. This would not do; she immediately stopped, under pretence of having some alteration to make in the lacing of her half-boot, and stooping down in complete occupation of the footpath, begged them to have the goodness to walk on, and she would follow in half a minute. They did as they were desired; and by the time she judged it reasonable to have done with her boot, she had the comfort of further delay in her power, being overtaken by a child from the cottage, setting out, according to orders, with her pitcher, to fetch broth from Hartfield. To walk by the side of this child, and talk to and question her, was the most natural thing in the world, or would have been the most natural, had she been acting just then without design; and by this means the others were still able to keep ahead, without any obligation of waiting for her. She gained on them, however, involuntarily; the child's pace was quick, and theirs rather slow; and she was the more concerned at it, from their being evidently in a conversation which interested them. Mr. Elton was speaking with animation, Harriet listening with a very pleased attention; and Emma having sent the child on, was beginning to think how she might draw back a little more, when they both looked around, and she was obliged to join them.

---

[42] *parley:* Conversation back and forth.

Mr. Elton was still talking, still engaged in some interesting detail; and Emma experienced some disappointment when she found that he was only giving his fair companion an account of the yesterday's party at his friend Cole's, and that she was come in herself for the Stilton cheese, the north Wiltshire,[43] the butter, the cellery, the beet-root and all the dessert.

"This would soon have led to something better of course," was her consoling reflection; "any thing interests between those who love; and any thing will serve as introduction to what is near the heart. If I could but have kept longer away!"

They now walked on together quietly, till within view of the vicarage pales, when a sudden resolution, of at least getting Harriet into the house, made her again find something very much amiss about her boot, and fall behind to arrange it once more. She then broke the lace off short, and dexterously throwing it into a ditch, was presently obliged to entreat them to stop, and acknowledge her inability to put herself to rights so as to be able to walk home in tolerable comfort.

"Part of my lace is gone," said she, "and I do not know how I am to contrive. I really am a most troublesome companion to you both, but I hope I am not often so ill-equipped. Mr. Elton, I must beg leave to stop at your house, and ask your housekeeper for a bit of ribband or string, or any thing just to keep my boot on."

Mr. Elton looked all happiness at this proposition; and nothing could exceed his alertness and attention in conducting them into his house and endeavouring to make every thing appear to advantage. The room they were taken into was the one he chiefly occupied, and looking forwards; behind it was another with which it immediately communicated; the door between them was open, and Emma passed into it with the housekeeper to receive her assistance in the most comfortable manner. She was obliged to leave the door ajar as she found it; but she fully intended that Mr. Elton should close it. It was not closed however, it still remained ajar; but by engaging the housekeeper in incessant conversation, she hoped to make it practicable for him to chuse his own subject in the adjoining room. For ten minutes she could hear nothing but herself. It could be protracted no longer. She was then obliged to be finished and make her appearance.

The lovers were standing together at one of the windows. It had a most favourable aspect; and, for half a minute, Emma felt the glory of having schemed successfully. But it would not do; he had not come to

[43] *the north Wiltshire:* Like Stilton, a regional cheese.

the point. He had been most agreeable, most delightful; he had told Harriet that he had seen them go by, and had purposely followed them; other little gallantries and allusions had been dropt, but nothing serious.

"Cautious, very cautious," thought Emma; "he advances inch by inch, and will hazard nothing till he believes himself secure."

Still, however, though every thing had not been accomplished by her ingenious device, she could not but flatter herself that it had been the occasion of much present enjoyment to both, and must be leading them forward to the great event.

CHAPTER XI.

MR. ELTON must now be left to himself. It was no longer in Emma's power to superintend his happiness or quicken his measures. The coming of her sister's family was so very near at hand, that first in anticipation and then in reality, it became henceforth her prime object of interest; and during the ten days of their stay at Hartfield it was not to be expected — she did not herself expect — that any thing beyond occasional, fortuitous assistance could be afford by her to the lovers. They might advance rapidly if they would, however; they must advance somehow or other whether they would or no. She hardly wished to have more leisure for them. There are people, who the more you do for them, the less they will do for themselves.

Mr. and Mrs. John Knightley, from having been longer than usual absent from Surry, were exciting of course rather more than the usual interest. Till this year, every long vacation since their marriage had been divided between Hartfield and Donwell Abbey; but all the holidays of this autumn had been given to sea-bathing for the children, and it was therefore many months since they had been seen in a regular way by their Surry connections, or seen at all by Mr. Woodhouse, who could not be induced to get so far as London, even for poor Isabella's sake; and who consequently was now most nervously and apprehensively happy in forestalling this too short visit.

He thought much of the evils of the journey for her, and not a little of the fatigues of his own horses and coachman who were to bring some of the party the last half of the way; but his alarms were needless; the sixteen miles being happily accomplished, and Mr. and Mrs. John Knightley, their five children, and a competent number of nursery-maids, all reaching Hartfield in safety. The bustle and joy of such an arrival, the many to be talked to, welcomed, encouraged, and variously dispersed and disposed of, produced a noise and confusion which his nerves could not have born under any other cause, nor have endured much longer even for this; but the ways of Hartfield and the feelings of her father were so respected by Mrs. John Knightley, that in spite of maternal solicitude for the immediate enjoyment of her little ones, and for their having instantly all the liberty and attendance, all the eating and drinking, and sleeping and playing, which they could possibly wish for, without the smallest delay, the children were never allowed to be long a disturbance to him, either in themselves or in any restless attendance on them.

Mrs. John Knightley was a pretty, elegant little woman, of gentle, quiet manners, and a disposition remarkably amiable and affectionate; wrapt up in her family; a devoted wife, a doating mother, and so tenderly attached to her father and sister that, but for these higher ties, a warmer love might have seemed impossible. She could never see a fault in any of them. She was not a woman of strong understanding or any quickness; and with this resemblance of her father, she inherited also much of his constitution; was delicate in her own health, over-careful of that of her children, had many fears and many nerves, and was as fond of her own Mr. Wingfield in town as her father could be of Mr. Perry. They were alike too, in a general benevolence of temper, and a strong habit of regard for every old acquaintance.

Mr. John Knightley was a tall, gentleman-like, and very clever man; rising in his profession, domestic, and respectable in his private character; but with reserved manners which prevented his being generally pleasing; and capable of being sometimes out of humour. He was not an ill-tempered man, not so often unreasonably cross as to deserve such a reproach; but his temper was not his great perfection; and, indeed, with such a worshipping wife, it was hardly possible that any natural defects in it should not be increased. The extreme sweetness of her temper must hurt his. He had all the clearness and quickness of mind which she wanted, and he could sometimes act an ungracious, or say a severe thing. He was not a great favourite with his fair sister-in-law. Nothing wrong in him escaped her. She was quick in feeling the little injuries to Isabella, which Isabella never felt herself. Perhaps she might have passed over more had his manners been flattering to Isabella's sister, but they were only those of a calmly kind brother and friend, without praise and without blindness; but hardly any degree of personal compliment could have made her regardless of that greatest fault of all in her eyes which he sometimes fell into, the want of respectful forbearance towards her father. There he had not always the patience that could have been wished. Mr. Woodhouse's peculiarities and fidgettiness were sometimes provoking him to a rational remonstrance or sharp retort equally ill bestowed. It did not often happen; for Mr. John Knightley had really a great regard for his father-in-law, and generally a strong sense of what was due to him; but it was too often for Emma's charity, especially as there was all the pain of apprehension frequently to be endured, though the offence came not. The beginning, however, of every visit displayed none but the properest feelings, and this being of necessity so short might be hoped to pass away in unsullied cordiality. They had not been long seated and composed when Mr. Woodhouse, with a melancholy shake of the head and a sigh, called his daughter's attention to the sad change at Hartfield since she had been there last.

"Ah! my dear," said he, "poor Miss Taylor — It is a grievous business!"

"Oh! yes, sir," cried she with ready sympathy, "how you must miss her! And dear Emma too! — what a dreadful loss to you both! — I have been so grieved for you. — I could not imagine how you could possibly do without her. — It is a sad change indeed. — But I hope she is pretty well, sir."

"Pretty well, my dear — I hope — pretty well. — I do not know but that the place agrees with her tolerably."

Mr. John Knightley here asked Emma quietly whether there were any doubts of the air of Randalls.

"Oh! no — none in the least. I never saw Mrs. Weston better in my life — never looking so well. Papa is only speaking his own regret."

"Very much to the honour of both," was the handsome reply.

"And do you see her, sir, tolerably often?" asked Isabella in the plaintive tone which just suited her father.

Mr. Woodhouse hesitated. — "Not near so often, my dear, as I could wish."

"Oh! papa, we have missed seeing them but one entire day since they married. Either in the morning or evening of every day, excepting one, have we seen either Mr. Weston or Mrs. Weston, and generally both, either at Randalls or here — and as you may suppose, Isabella, most frequently here. They are very, very kind in their visits. Mr. Weston is really as kind as herself. Papa, if you speak in that melancholy way, you will be giving Isabella a false idea of us all. Every body must be aware that Miss Taylor must be missed, but every body ought also to be assured that Mr. and Mrs. Weston do really prevent our missing her by any means to the extent we ourselves anticipated — which is the exact truth."

"Just as it should be," said Mr. John Knightley, "and just as I hoped it was from your letters. Her wish of shewing you attention could not be doubted, and his being a disengaged and social man makes it all easy. I have been always telling you, my love, that I had no idea of the change being so very material to Hartfield as you apprehended; and now you have Emma's account, I hope you will be satisfied."

"Why to be sure," said Mr. Woodhouse — "yes, certainly — I cannot deny that Mrs. Weston, poor Mrs. Weston, does come and see us pretty often — but then — she is always obliged to go away again."

"It would be very hard upon Mr. Weston if she did not, papa. — You quite forget poor Mr. Weston."

"I think, indeed," said John Knightley pleasantly, "that Mr. Weston has some little claim. You and I, Emma, will venture to take the part of the poor husband. I, being a husband, and you not being a wife, the claims of the man may very likely strike us with equal force. As for Isabella, she has been married long enough to see the convenience of putting all the Mr. Westons aside as much as she can."

"Me, my love," cried his wife, hearing and understanding only in part. — "Are you talking about me? — I am sure nobody ought to be, or can be, a greater advocate for matrimony than I am; and if it had not been for the misery of her leaving Hartfield, I should never have thought of Miss Taylor but as the most fortunate woman in the world; and as to slighting Mr. Weston, that excellent Mr. Weston, I think there is nothing he does not deserve. I believe he is one of the very best tempered men that ever existed. Excepting yourself and your brother, I do not know his equal for temper. I shall never forget his flying Henry's kite for him that very windy day last Easter — and ever since his particular kindness last September twelvemonth in writing that note, at twelve o'clock at night, on purpose to assure me that there was no scarlet fever at Cobham,[44] I have been convinced there could not be a more feeling heart nor a better man in existence. — If any body can deserve him, it must be Miss Taylor."

"Where is the young man?" said John Knightley. "Has he been here on this occasion — or has he not?"

"He has not been here yet," replied Emma. "There was a strong

---

[44]*Cobham:* Small town in Surrey, sometimes considered the model for Highbury.

expectation of his coming soon after the marriage, but it ended in nothing; and I have not heard him mentioned lately."

"But you should tell them of the letter, my dear," said her father. "He wrote a letter to poor Mrs. Weston, to congratulate her, and a very proper, handsome letter it was. She shewed it to me. I thought it very well done of him indeed. Whether it was his own idea you know, one cannot tell. He is but young, and his uncle perhaps ——"

"My dear papa, he is three-and-twenty. — You forget how time passes."

"Three-and-twenty! — is he indeed? — Well, I could not have thought it — and he was but two years old when he lost his poor mother! Well, time does fly indeed! — and my memory is very bad. However, it was an exceeding good, pretty letter, and gave Mr. and Mrs. Weston a great deal of pleasure. I remember it was written from Weymouth, and dated Sept. 28th — and began, 'My dear Madam,' but I forget how it went on; and it was signed 'F. C. Weston Churchill.' — I remember that perfectly."

"How very pleasing and proper of him!" cried the good-hearted Mrs. John Knightley. "I have no doubt of his being a most amiable young man. But how sad it is that he should not live at home with his father! There is something so shocking in a child's being taken away from his parents and natural home! I never can comprehend how Mr. Weston could part with him. To give up one's child! I really never could think well of any body who proposed such a thing to any body else."

"Nobody ever did think well of the Churchills, I fancy," observed Mr. John Knightley coolly. "But you need not imagine Mr. Weston to have felt what you would feel in giving up Henry or John. Mr. Weston is rather an easy, cheerful tempered man, than a man of strong feelings; he takes things as he finds them, and makes enjoyment of them somehow or other, depending, I suspect, much more upon what is called *society* for his comforts, that is, upon the power of eating and drinking, and playing whist with his neighbours five times a-week, than upon family affection, or any thing that home affords."

Emma could not like what bordered on a reflection on Mr. Weston, and had half a mind to take it up; but she struggled, and let it pass. She would keep the peace if possible; and there was something honourable and valuable in the strong domestic habits, the all-sufficiency of home to himself, whence resulted her brother's disposition to look down on the common rate of social intercourse, and those to whom it was important. — It had a high claim to forbearance.

CHAPTER XII.

MR. KNIGHTLEY was to dine with them — rather against the inclination of Mr. Woodhouse, who did not like that any one should share with him in Isabella's first day. Emma's sense of right however had decided it; and besides the consideration of what was due to each brother, she had particular pleasure, from the circumstance of the late disagreement between Mr. Knightley and herself, in procuring him the proper invitation.

She hoped they might now become friends again. She thought it was time to make up. Making-up indeed would not do. *She* certainly had not been in the wrong, and *he* would never own that he had. Concession must be out of the question; but it was time to appear to forget that they had ever quarrelled; and she hoped it might rather assist the restoration of friendship, that when he came into the room she had one of the children with her — the youngest, a nice little girl about eight months old, who was now making her first visit to Hartfield, and very happy to be danced about in her aunt's arms. It did assist; for though he began with grave looks and short questions, he was soon led on to talk of them all in the usual way, and to take the child out of her arms with all the unceremoniousness of perfect amity. Emma felt they were friends again; and the conviction giving her at first great satisfaction, and then a little sauciness, she could not help saying, as he was admiring the baby,

"What a comfort it is, that we think alike about our nephews and nieces. As to men and women, our opinions are sometimes very different; but with regard to these children, I observe we never disagree."

"If you were as much guided by nature in your estimate of men and women, and as little under the power of fancy and whim in your dealings with them, as you are where these children are concerned, we might always think alike."

"To be sure — our discordancies must always arise from my being in the wrong."

"Yes," said he, smiling — "and reason good. I was sixteen years old when you were born."

"A material difference then," she replied — "and no doubt you were much my superior in judgment at that period of our lives; but does not the lapse of one-and-twenty years bring our understandings a good deal nearer?"

"Yes — a good deal *nearer.*"

"But still, not near enough to give me a chance of being right, if we think differently."

"I have still the advantage of you by sixteen years' experience, and by not being a pretty young woman and a spoiled child. Come, my dear Emma, let us be friends and say no more about it. Tell your aunt, little Emma, that she ought to set you a better example than to be renewing old grievances, and that if she were not wrong before, she is now."

"That's true," she cried — "very true. Little Emma, grow up a better woman than your aunt. Be infinitely cleverer and not half so conceited. Now, Mr. Knightley, a word or two more, and I have done. As far as good intentions went, we were *both* right, and I must say that no effects on my side of the argument have yet proved wrong. I only want to know that Mr. Martin is not very, very bitterly disappointed."

"A man cannot be more so," was his short, full answer.

"Ah! — Indeed I am very sorry. — Come, shake hands with me."

This had just taken place and with great cordiality, when John Knightley made his appearance, and "How d'ye do, George?" and "John, how are you?" succeeded in the true English style, burying under a calmness that seemed all but indifference, the real attachment which would have led either of them, if requisite, to do every thing for the good of the other.

The evening was quiet and conversible, as Mr. Woodhouse declined cards entirely for the sake of comfortable talk with his dear Isabella, and the little party made two natural divisions; on one side he and his daughter; on the other the two Mr. Knightleys; their subjects totally distinct, or very rarely mixing — and Emma only occasionally joining in one or the other.

The brothers talked of their own concerns and pursuits, but principally of those of the elder, whose temper was by much the most communicative, and who was always the greater talker. As a magistrate, he had generally some point of law to consult John about, or, at least, some curious anecdote to give; and as a farmer, as keeping in hand the home-farm at Donwell, he had to tell what every field was to bear next year, and to give all such local information as could not fail of being interesting to a brother whose home it had equally been the longest part of his life, and whose attachments were strong. The plan of a drain, the change of a fence, the felling of a tree, and the destination of every acre for wheat, turnips, or spring corn,[45] was entered into with as much equality of interest by John, as his cooler manners rendered possible;

[45] *wheat, turnips, or spring corn:* An indication that Mr. Knightley, like Robert Martin, reads the Agricultural Reports (see note 13 on p. 41), especially those advocating the inclusion of turnips in the crop rotation; turnips provided winter feed for livestock and "rested" fields between crops of wheat or corn.

and if his willing brother ever left him any thing to inquire about, his inquiries even approached a tone of eagerness.

While they were thus comfortably occupied, Mr. Woodhouse was enjoying a full flow of happy regrets and fearful affection with his daughter.

"My poor dear Isabella," said he, fondly taking her hand, and interrupting, for a few moments, her busy labours for some one of her five children — "How long it is, how terribly long since you were here! And how tired you must be after your journey! You must go to bed early, my dear — and I recommend a little gruel to you before you go. — You and I will have a nice basin of gruel together. My dear Emma, suppose we all have a little gruel."

Emma could not suppose any such thing, knowing, as she did, that both the Mr. Knightleys were as unpersuadable on that article as herself; — and two basins only were ordered. After a little more discourse in praise of gruel, with some wondering at its not being taken every evening by every body, he proceeded to say, with an air of grave reflection,

"It was an awkward business, my dear, your spending the autumn at South End[46] instead of coming here. I never had much opinion of the sea air."

"Mr. Wingfield most strenuously recommended it, sir — or we should not have gone. He recommended it for all the children, but particularly for the weakness in little Bella's throat, — both sea air and bathing."

"Ah! my dear, but Perry had many doubts about the sea doing her any good; and as to myself, I have been long perfectly convinced, though perhaps I never told you so before, that the sea is very rarely of use to any body. I am sure it almost killed me once."

"Come, come," cried Emma, feeling this to be an unsafe subject, "I must beg you not to talk of the sea. It makes me envious and miserable; — I who have never seen it! South End is prohibited, if you please. My dear Isabella, I have not heard you make one inquiry after Mr. Perry yet; and he never forgets you."

"Oh! good Mr. Perry — how is he, sir?"

"Why, pretty well; but not quite well. Poor Perry is bilious, and he

---

[46]*South End:* Now Southend-on-Sea, watering place in Essex on the north shore of the Thames estuary. The salubrity of sea air and the medical benefit of swimming in the sea (even in November!) were much touted at this period. Sales suggests that South End's reputation may have suffered from its proximity to London (136–37) (cited in note 5, p. 34)

has not time to take care of himself — he tells me he has not time to take care of himself — which is very sad — but he is always wanted all round the country. I suppose there is not a man in such practice any where. But then, there is not so clever a man any where."

"And Mrs. Perry and the children, how are they? do the children grow? — I have a great regard for Mr. Perry. I hope he will be calling soon. He will be so pleased to see my little ones."

"I hope he will be here to-morrow, for I have a question or two to ask him about myself of some consequence. And, my dear, whenever he comes, you had better let him look at little Bella's throat."

"Oh! my dear sir, her throat is so much better that I have hardly any uneasiness about it. Either bathing has been of the greatest service to her, or else it is to be attributed to an excellent embrocation[47] of Mr. Wingfield's, which we have been applying at times ever since August."

"It is not very likely, my dear, that bathing should have been of use to her — and if I had known you were wanting an embrocation, I would have spoken to ——"

"You seem to me to have forgotten Mrs. and Miss Bates," said Emma, "I have not heard one inquiry after them."

"Oh! the good Bateses — I am quite ashamed of myself — but you mention them in most of your letters. I hope they are quite well. Good old Mrs. Bates — I will call upon her to-morrow, and take my children. — They are always so pleased to see my children. — And that excellent Miss Bates! — such thorough worthy people! — How are they, sir?"

"Why, pretty well, my dear, upon the whole. But poor Mrs. Bates had a bad cold about a month ago."

"How sorry I am! But colds were never so prevalent as they have been this autumn. Mr. Wingfield told me that he had never known them more general or heavy — except when it has been quite an influenza."

"That has been a good deal the case, my dear; but not to the degree you mention. Perry says that colds have been very general, but not so heavy as he has very often known them in November. Perry does not call it altogether a sickly season."

"No, I do not know that Mr. Wingfield considers it *very* sickly except —"

"Ah! my poor dear child, the truth is, that in London it is always a sickly season. Nobody is healthy in London, nobody can be. It is a

---

[47] *embrocation:* A liquid, such as warm oil, used to treat a diseased part.

dreadful thing to have you forced to live there! — so far off! — and the air so bad!"

"No, indeed — *we* are not at all in a bad air. Our part of London is so very superior to most others! — You must not confound us with London in general, my dear sir. The neighbourhood of Brunswick Square is very different from almost all the rest. We are so very airy! I should be unwilling, I own, to live in any other part of the town; — there is hardly any other that I could be satisfied to have my children in: — but *we* are so remarkably airy! — Mr. Wingfield thinks the vicinity of Brunswick Square decidedly the most favourable as to air."

"Ah! my dear, it is not like Hartfield. You make the best of it — but after you have been a week at Hartfield, you are all of you different creatures; you do not look like the same. Now I cannot say, that I think you are any of you looking well at present."

"I am sorry to hear you say so, sir; but I assure you, excepting those little nervous head-aches and palpitations which I am never entirely free from any where, I am quite well myself; and if the children were rather pale before they went to bed, it was only because they were a little more tired than usual, from their journey and the happiness of coming. I hope you will think better of their looks to-morrow; for I assure you Mr. Wingfield told me, that he did not believe he had ever sent us off altogether, in such good case. I trust, at least, that you do not think Mr. Knightley looking ill," — turning her eyes with affectionate anxiety towards her husband.

"Middling, my dear; I cannot compliment you. I think Mr. John Knightley very far from looking well."

"What is the matter, sir? — Did you speak to me?" cried Mr. John Knightley, hearing his own name.

"I am sorry to find, my love, that my father does not think you looking well — but I hope it is only from being a little fatigued. I could have wished, however, as you know, that you had seen Mr. Wingfield before you left home."

"My dear Isabella," — exclaimed he hastily — "pray do not concern yourself about my looks. Be satisfied with doctoring and coddling yourself and the children, and let me look as I chuse."

"I did not thoroughly understand what you were telling your brother," cried Emma, "about your friend Mr. Graham's intending to have a bailiff from Scotland, to look after his new estate. But will it answer? Will not the old prejudice be too strong?"

And she talked in this way so long and successfully that, when forced to give her attention again to her father and sister, she had nothing worse to hear than Isabella's kind inquiry after Jane Fairfax; — and Jane Fairfax, though no great favourite with her in general, she was at that moment very happy to assist in praising.

"That sweet, amiable Jane Fairfax!" said Mrs. John Knightley — "It is so long since I have seen her, except now and then for a moment accidentally in town! What happiness it must be to her good old grandmother and excellent aunt, when she comes to visit them! I always regret excessively on dear Emma's account that she cannot be more at Highbury; but now their daughter is married, I suppose Colonel and Mrs. Campbell will not be able to part with her at all. She would be such a delightful companion for Emma."

Mr. Woodhouse agreed to it all, but added,

"Our little friend Harriet Smith, however, is just such another pretty kind of young person. You will like Harriet. Emma could not have a better companion than Harriet."

"I am most happy to hear it — but only Jane Fairfax one knows to be so very accomplished and superior! — and exactly Emma's age."

This topic was discussed very happily, and others succeeded of similar moment, and passed away with similar harmony; but the evening did not close without a little return of agitation. The gruel came and supplied a great deal to be said — much praise and many comments — undoubting decision of its wholesomeness for every constitution, and pretty severe Philippics[48] upon the many houses where it was never met with tolerable; — but, unfortunately, among the failures which the daughter had to instance, the most recent, and therefore most prominent, was in her own cook at South End, a young woman hired for the time, who never had been able to understand what she meant by a basin of nice smooth gruel, thin, but not too thin. Often as she had wished for and ordered it, she had never been able to get any thing tolerable. Here was a dangerous opening.

"Ah!" said Mr. Woodhouse, shaking his head and fixing his eyes on her with tender concern. — The ejaculation in Emma's ear expressed, "Ah! there is no end of the sad consequences of your going to South End. It does not bear talking of." And for a little while she hoped he would not talk of it, and that a silent rumination might suffice to restore him to the relish of his own smooth gruel. After an interval of some minutes, however, he began with,

---

[48] *Philippics:* Bitter denunciations (taking their name from the orations of Demosthenes against Philip of Macedon in defense of Athenian liberty).

"I shall always be very sorry that you went to the sea this autumn, instead of coming here."

"But why should you be sorry, sir? — I assure you, it did the children a great deal of good."

"And, moreover, if you must go to the sea, it had better not have been to South End. South End is an unhealthy place. Perry was surprized to hear you had fixed upon South End."

"I know there is such an idea with many people, but indeed it is quite a mistake, sir. — We all had our health perfectly well there, never found the least inconvenience from the mud; and Mr. Wingfield says it is entirely a mistake to suppose the place unhealthy; and I am sure he may be depended on, for he thoroughly understands the nature of the air, and his own brother and family have been there repeatedly."

"You should have gone to Cromer,[49] my dear, if you went any where. — Perry was a week at Cromer once, and he holds it to be the best of all the sea-bathing places. A fine open sea, he says, and very pure air. And, by what I understand, you might have had lodgings there quite away from the sea — a quarter of a mile off — very comfortable. You should have consulted Perry."

"But, my dear sir, the difference of the journey; — only consider how great it would have been. — A hundred miles, perhaps, instead of forty."

"Ah! my dear, as Perry says, where health is at stake,[50] nothing else should be considered; and if one is to travel, there is not much to chuse between forty miles and an hundred. — Better not move at all, better stay in London altogether than travel forty miles to get into a worse air. This is just what Perry said. It seemed to him a very ill-judged measure."

Emma's attempts to stop her father had been vain; and when he had reached such a point as this, she could not wonder at her brother-in-law's breaking out.

"Mr. Perry," said he, in a voice of very strong displeasure, "would do as well to keep his opinion till it is asked for. Why does he make it any business of his, to wonder at what I do? — at my taking my family

<hr/>

[49] **Cromer:** Small town and resort on the North Sea in Norfolk. Mr. Woodhouse has perhaps been reading Edmund Bartell's *Cromer, Considered as a Watering Place: With Observations on the Picturesque Scenery in its Neighbourhood* (London 1806). See Sales (204) (cited in note 5, p. 34).

[50] **Ah! my dear, as Perry says, where health is at stake:** Emendation of first edition, which has closing double quotes after "dear," and opening double quotes before "where health is at stake."

to one part of the coast or another? — I may be allowed, I hope, the use of my judgment as well as Mr. Perry. — I want his directions no more than his drugs." He paused — and growing cooler in a moment, added, with only sarcastic dryness, "If Mr. Perry can tell me how to convey a wife and five children a distance of an hundred and thirty miles with no greater expense or inconvenience than a distance of forty, I should be as willing to prefer Cromer to South End as he could himself."

"True, true," cried Mr. Knightley, with most ready interposition — "very true. That's a consideration indeed. — But John, as to what I was telling you of my idea of moving the path to Langham, of turning it more to the right that it may not cut through the home meadows, I cannot conceive any difficulty. I should not attempt it, if it were to be the means of inconvenience to the Highbury people, but if you call to mind exactly the present line of the path. . . . . . . The only way of proving it, however, will be to turn to our maps. I shall see you at the Abbey to-morrow morning I hope, and then we will look them over, and you shall give me your opinion."

Mr. Woodhouse was rather agitated by such harsh reflections on his friend Perry, to whom he had, in fact, though unconsciously, been attributing many of his own feelings and expressions; — but the soothing attentions of his daughters gradually removed the present evil, and the immediate alertness of one brother, and better recollections of the other, prevented any renewal of it.

CHAPTER XIII.

THERE could hardly be an happier creature in the world, than Mrs. John Knightley, in this short visit to Hartfield, going about every morning among her old acquaintance with her five children, and talking over what she had done every evening with her father and sister. She had nothing to wish otherwise, but that the days did not pass so swiftly. It was a delightful visit; — perfect, in being much too short.

In general their evenings were less engaged with friends than their mornings: but one complete dinner engagement, and out of the house too, there was no avoiding, though at Christmas. Mr. Weston would take no denial; they must all dine at Randalls one day; — even Mr. Woodhouse was persuaded to think it a possible thing in preference to a division of the party.

How they were all to be conveyed, he would have made a difficulty if he could, but as his son and daughter's carriage and horses were actually at Hartfield, he was not able to make more than a simple question on that head; it hardly amounted to a doubt; nor did it occupy Emma long to convince him that they might in one of the carriages find room for Harriet also.

Harriet, Mr. Elton, and Mr. Knightley, their own especial set, were the only persons invited to meet them; — the hours were to be early, as well as the numbers few; Mr. Woodhouse's habits and inclination being consulted in every thing.

The evening before this great event (for it was a very great event that Mr. Woodhouse should dine out, on the 24th of December) had been spent by Harriet at Hartfield, and she had gone home so much indisposed with a cold, that, but for her own earnest wish of being nursed by Mrs. Goddard, Emma could not have allowed her to leave the house. Emma called on her the next day, and found her doom already signed with regard to Randalls. She was very feverish and had a bad sore-throat: Mrs. Goddard was full of care and affection, Mr. Perry was talked of, and Harriet herself was too ill and low to resist the authority which excluded her from this delightful engagement, though she could not speak of her loss without many tears.

Emma sat with her as long as she could, to attend her in Mrs. Goddard's unavoidable absences, and raise her spirits by representing how much Mr. Elton's would be depressed when he knew her state; and left her at last tolerably comfortable, in the sweet dependence of his having a most comfortless visit, and of their all missing her very much. She had not advanced many yards from Mrs. Goddard's door, when she was met by Mr. Elton himself, evidently coming towards it, and as they walked on slowly together in conversation about the invalid — of whom he, on the rumour of considerable illness, had been going to inquire, that he might carry some report of her to Hartfield — they were overtaken by Mr. John Knightley returning from the daily visit to Donwell, with his two eldest boys, whose healthy, glowing faces shewed all the benefit of a country run, and seemed to ensure a quick dispatch of the roast mutton and rice pudding they were hastening home for. They joined company and proceeded together. Emma was just describing the nature of her friend's complaint; — "a throat very much inflamed, with a great deal of heat about her, a quick low pulse, &c. and she was sorry to find from Mrs. Goddard that Harriet was liable to very bad sore-throats, and had often alarmed her with them." — Mr. Elton looked all alarm on the occasion, as he exclaimed,

"A sore-throat! — I hope not infectious. I hope not of a putrid infectious sort. Has Perry seen her? Indeed you should take care of yourself as well as of your friend. Let me entreat you to run no risks. Why does not Perry see her?"

Emma, who was not really at all frightened herself, tranquillized this excess of apprehension by assurances of Mrs. Goddard's experience and care; but as there must still remain a degree of uneasiness which she could not wish to reason away, which she would rather feed and assist than not, she added soon afterwards — as if quite another subject,

"It is so cold, so very cold — and looks and feels so very much like snow, that if it were to any other place or with any other party, I should really try not to go out to-day — and dissuade my father from venturing; but as he has made up his mind, and does not seem to feel the cold himself, I do not like to interfere, as I know it would be so great a disappointment to Mr. and Mrs. Weston. But, upon my word, Mr. Elton, in your case, I should certainly excuse myself. You appear to me a little hoarse already, and when you consider what demand of voice and what fatigues to-morrow will bring, I think it would be no more than common prudence to stay at home and take care of yourself to-night."

Mr. Elton looked as if he did not very well know what answer to make; which was exactly the case; for though very much gratified by the kind care of such a fair lady, and not liking to resist any advice of her's, he had not really the least inclination to give up the visit; — but Emma, too eager and busy in her own previous conceptions and views to hear him impartially, or see him with clear vision, was very well satisfied with his muttering acknowledgement of its being "very cold, certainly very cold," and walked on, rejoicing in having extricated him from Randalls, and secured him the power of sending to inquire after Harriet every hour of the evening.

"You do quite right," said she; — "We will make your apologies to Mr. and Mrs. Weston."

But hardly had she so spoken, when she found her brother was civilly offering a seat in his carriage, if the weather were Mr. Elton's only objection, and Mr. Elton actually accepting the offer with much prompt satisfaction. It was a done thing; Mr. Elton was to go, and never had his broad handsome face expressed more pleasure than at this moment; never had his smile been stronger, nor his eyes more exulting than when he next looked at her.

"Well," said she to herself, "this is most strange! — After I had got him off so well, to chuse to go into company, and leave Harriet ill behind! — Most strange indeed! — But there is, I believe, in many men, especially single men, such an inclination — such a passion for dining out — a dinner engagement is so high in the class of their pleasures, their employments, their dignities, almost their duties, that any thing gives way to it — and this must be the case with Mr. Elton; a most valuable, amiable, pleasing young man undoubtedly, and very much in love with Harriet; but still, he cannot refuse an invitation, he must dine out wherever he is asked. What a strange thing love is! he can see ready wit in Harriet, but will not dine alone for her."

Soon afterwards Mr. Elton quitted them, and she could not but do him the justice of feeling that there was a great deal of sentiment in his manner of naming Harriet at parting; in the tone of his voice while assuring her that he should call at Mrs. Goddard's for news of her fair friend, the last thing before he prepared for the happiness of meeting her again, when he hoped to be able to give a better report; and he sighed and smiled himself off in a way that left the balance of approbation much in his favour.

After a few minutes of entire silence between them, John Knightley began with —

"I never in my life saw a man more intent on being agreeable than Mr. Elton. It is downright labour to him where ladies are concerned. With men he can be rational and unaffected, but when he has ladies to please every feature works."

"Mr. Elton's manners are not perfect," replied Emma; "but where there is a wish to please, one ought to overlook, and one does overlook a great deal. Where a man does his best with only moderate powers, he will have the advantage over negligent superiority. There is such perfect good temper and good will in Mr. Elton as one cannot but value."

"Yes," said Mr. John Knightley presently, with some slyness, "he seems to have a great deal of good-will towards *you*."

"Me!" she replied with a smile of astonishment, "are you imagining me to be Mr. Elton's object?"

"Such an imagination has crossed me, I own, Emma; and if it never occurred to you before, you may as well take it into consideration now."

"Mr. Elton in love with me! — What an idea!"

"I do not say it is so; but you will do well to consider whether it is so or not, and to regulate your behaviour accordingly. I think your manners to him encouraging. I speak as a friend, Emma. You had better look about you, and ascertain what you do, and what you mean to do."

"I thank you; but I assure you you are quite mistaken. Mr. Elton and I are good friends, and nothing more;" and she walked on, amusing herself in the consideration of the blunders which often arise from a partial knowledge of circumstances, of the mistakes which people of high pretensions to judgment are for ever falling into; and not very well pleased with her brother for imagining her blind and ignorant, and in want of counsel. He said no more.

Mr. Woodhouse had so completely made up his mind to the visit, that in spite of the increasing coldness, he seemed to have no idea of shrinking from it, and set forward at last most punctually with his eldest daughter in his own carriage, with less apparent consciousness of the weather than either of the others; too full of the wonder of his own going, and the pleasure it was to afford at Randalls to see that it was cold, and too well wrapt up to feel it. The cold, however, was severe; and by the time the second carriage was in motion, a few flakes of snow were finding their way down, and the sky had the appearance of being so overcharged as to want only a milder air to produce a very white world in a very short time.

Emma soon saw that her companion was not in the happiest humour. The preparing and the going abroad in such weather, with the sacrifice of his children after dinner, were evils, were disagreeables at least, which Mr. John Knightley did not by any means like; he anticipated nothing in the visit that could be at all worth the purchase; and the whole of their drive to the Vicarage was spent by him in expressing his discontent.

"A man," said he, "must have a very good opinion of himself when he asks people to leave their own fireside, and encounter such a day as this, for the sake of coming to see him. He must think himself a most agreeable fellow; I could not do such a thing. It is the greatest absurdity — Actually snowing at this moment! — The folly of not allowing people to be comfortable at home — and the folly of people's not staying comfortably at home when they can! If we were obliged to go out such an evening as this, by any call of duty or business, what a hardship we should deem it; — and here are we, probably with rather thinner clothing than usual, setting forward voluntarily, without excuse, in defiance of the voice of nature, which tells man, in every thing given to his view or his feelings, to stay at home himself, and keep all under shelter that he can; — here are we setting forward to spend five dull hours in another man's house, with nothing to say or to hear that was not said and heard yesterday, and may not be said and heard again to-morrow. Going in dismal weather, to return probably in worse; — four horses and four servants taken out for nothing but to convey five idle, shivering creatures into colder rooms and worse company than they might have had at home."

Emma did not find herself equal to give the pleased assent, which no doubt he was in the habit of receiving, to emulate the "Very true, my love," which must have been usually administered by his travelling companion; but she had resolution enough to refrain from making any answer at all. She could not be complying, she dreaded being quarrelsome; her heroism reached only to silence. She allowed him to talk, and arranged the glasses,[51] and wrapped herself up, without opening her lips.

They arrived, the carriage turned, the step was let down, and Mr. Elton, spruce, black, and smiling, was with them instantly. Emma thought with pleasure of some change of subject. Mr. Elton was all obligation and cheerfulness; he was so very cheerful in his civilities indeed, that she began to think he must have received a different account of Harriet from what had reached her. She had sent while dressing, and the answer had been, "Much the same — not better."

"*My* report from Mrs. Goddard's," said she presently, "was not so pleasant as I had hoped — 'Not better,' was *my* answer."

His face lengthened immediately; and his voice was the voice of sentiment as he answered.

"Oh! no — I am grieved to find — I was on the point of telling you that when I called at Mrs. Goddard's door, which I did the very last thing before I returned to dress, I was told that Miss Smith was not better, by no means better, rather worse. Very much grieved and concerned — I had flattered myself that she must be better after such a cordial as I knew had been given in the morning."

Emma smiled and answered — "My visit was of use to the nervous part of her complaint, I hope; but not even I can charm away a sore throat; it is a most severe cold indeed. Mr. Perry has been with her, as you probably heard."

"Yes — I imagined — that is — I did not" —

"He has been used to her in these complaints, and I hope to-morrow morning will bring us both a more comfortable report. But it is impossible not to feel uneasiness. Such a sad loss to our party to-day!"

"Dreadful! — Exactly so, indeed. — She will be missed every moment."

This was very proper; the sigh which accompanied it was really es-

---

[51] *arranged the glasses:* Adjusted the windows.

timable; but it should have lasted longer. Emma was rather in dismay when only half a minute afterwards he began to speak of other things, and in a voice of the greatest alacrity and enjoyment.

"What an excellent device," said he, "the use of a sheep skin for carriages. How very comfortable they make it; — impossible to feel cold with such precautions. The contrivances of modern days indeed have rendered a gentleman's carriage perfectly complete. One is so fenced and guarded from the weather, that not a breath of air can find its way unpermitted. Weather becomes absolutely of no consequence. It is a very cold afternoon — but in this carriage we know nothing of the matter. — Ha! snows a little I see."

"Yes," said John Knightley, "and I think we shall have a good deal of it."

"Christmas weather," observed Mr. Elton. "Quite seasonable; and extremely fortunate we may think ourselves that it did not begin yesterday, and prevent this day's party, which it might very possibly have done, for Mr. Woodhouse would hardly have ventured had there been much snow on the ground; but now it is of no consequence. This is quite the season indeed for friendly meetings. At Christmas every body invites their friends about them, and people think little of even the worst weather. I was snowed up at a friend's house once for a week. Nothing could be pleasanter. I went for only one night, and could not get away till that very day se'nnight."[52]

Mr. John Knightley looked as if he did not comprehend the pleasure, but said only, coolly,

"I cannot wish to be snowed up a week at Randalls."

At another time Emma might have been amused, but she was too much astonished now at Mr. Elton's spirits for other feelings. Harriet seemed quite forgotten in the expectation of a pleasant party.

"We are sure of excellent fires," continued he, "and every thing in the greatest comfort. Charming people, Mr. and Mrs. Weston; — Mrs. Weston indeed is much beyond praise, and he is exactly what one values, so hospitable, and so fond of society; — it will be a small party, but where small parties are select, they are perhaps the most agreeable of any. Mr. Weston's dining-room does not accommodate more than ten comfortably; and for my part, I would rather, under such circumstances, fall short by two than exceed by two. I think you will agree with me, (turning with a soft air to Emma,) I think I shall certainly have

---

[52] *se'nnight.*: Archaic word for a period of seven nights, i.e., a week, from the present date.

your approbation, though Mr. Knightley perhaps, from being used to the large parties of London, may not quite enter into our feelings."

"I know nothing of the large parties of London, sir — I never dine with any body."

"Indeed! (in a tone of wonder and pity,) I had no idea that the law had been so great a slavery. Well, sir, the time must come when you will be paid for all this, when you will have little labour and great enjoyment."

"My first enjoyment," replied John Knightley, as they passed through the sweep-gate,[53] "will be to find myself safe at Hartfield again."

CHAPTER XIV.

SOME change of countenance was necessary for each gentleman as they walked into Mrs. Weston's drawing-room; — Mr. Elton must compose his joyous looks, and Mr. John Knightley disperse his ill-humour. Mr. Elton must smile less, and Mr. John Knightley more, to fit them for the place. — Emma only might be as nature prompted, and shew herself just as happy as she was. To her, it was real enjoyment to be with the Westons. Mr. Weston was a great favourite, and there was not a creature in the world to whom she spoke with such unreserve, as to his wife; not any one, to whom she related with such conviction of being listened to and understood, of being always interesting and always intelligible, the little affairs, arrangements, perplexities and pleasures of her father and herself. She could tell nothing of Hartfield, in which Mrs. Weston had not a lively concern; and half an hour's uninterrupted communication of all those little matters on which the daily happiness of private life depends, was one of the first gratifications of each.

This was a pleasure which perhaps the whole day's visit might not afford, which certainly did not belong to the present half hour; but the very sight of Mrs. Weston, her smile, her touch, her voice was grateful to Emma, and she determined to think as little as possible of Mr. Elton's oddities, or of any thing else unpleasant, and enjoy all that was enjoyable to the utmost.

The misfortune of Harriet's cold had been pretty well gone through before her arrival. Mr. Woodhouse had been safely seated long enough to give the history of it, besides all the history of his own and

---

[53]*sweep-gate:* Gate to a curved driveway leading to the main entrance of the house. A sweep was a fashionable feature. In *Sense and Sensibility* the newly married Edward Ferrars and Elinor Dashwood "project shrubberies, and invent a sweep" (374).

Isabella's coming, and of Emma's being to follow, and had indeed just got to the end of his satisfaction that James should come and see his daughter, when the others appeared, and Mrs. Weston, who had been almost wholly engrossed by her attentions to him, was able to turn away and welcome her dear Emma.

Emma's project of forgetting Mr. Elton for a while, made her rather sorry to find, when they had all taken their places, that he was close to her. The difficulty was great of driving his strange insensibility towards Harriet, from her mind, while he not only sat at her elbow, but was continually obtruding his happy countenance on her notice, and solicitously addressing her upon every occasion. Instead of forgetting him, his behaviour was such that she could not avoid the internal suggestion of "Can it really be as my brother imagined? can it be possible for this man to be beginning to transfer his affections from Harriet to me? — Absurd and insufferable!" — Yet he would be so anxious for her being perfectly warm, would be so interested about her father, and so delighted with Mrs. Weston; and at last would begin admiring her drawings with so much zeal and so little knowledge as seemed terribly like a would-be lover, and made it some effort with her to preserve her good manners. For her own sake she could not be rude; and for Harriet's, in the hope that all would yet turn out right, she was even positively civil; but it was an effort; especially as something was going on amongst the others, in the most overpowering period of Mr. Elton's nonsense, which she particularly wished to listen to. She heard enough to know that Mr. Weston was giving some information about his son; she heard the words "my son," and "Frank," and "my son," repeated several times over; and from a few other half-syllables very much suspected that he was announcing an early visit from his son; but before she could quiet Mr. Elton, the subject was so completely past that any reviving question from her would have been awkward.

Now, it so happened that in spite of Emma's resolution of never marrying, there was something in the name, in the idea of Mr. Frank Churchill, which always interested her. She had frequently thought — especially since his father's marriage with Miss Taylor — that if she _were_ to marry, he was the very person to suit her in age, character and condition. He seemed by this connection between the families, quite to belong to her. She could not but suppose it to be a match that every body who knew them must think of. That Mr. and Mrs. Weston did think of it, she was very strongly persuaded; and though not meaning to be induced by him, or by any body else, to give up a situation which she believed more replete with good than any she could change it for,

she had a great curiosity to see him, a decided intention of finding him
pleasant, of being liked by him to a certain degree, and a sort of pleasure in the idea of their being coupled in their friends' imaginations.

With such sensations, Mr. Elton's civilities were dreadfully ill-
timed; but she had the comfort of appearing very polite, while feeling
very cross — and of thinking that the rest of the visit could not possibly
pass without bringing forward the same information again, or the substance of it, from the open-hearted Mr. Weston. — So it proved; — for
when happily released from Mr. Elton, and seated by Mr. Weston, at
dinner, he made use of the very first interval in the cares of hospitality,
the very first leisure from the saddle of mutton, to say to her,

"We want only two more to be just the right number. I should like
to see two more here, — your pretty little friend, Miss Smith, and my
son — and then I should say we were quite complete. I believe you did
not hear me telling the others in the drawing-room that we are expecting Frank? I had a letter from him this morning, and he will be with us
within a fortnight."

Emma spoke with a very proper degree of pleasure; and fully
assented to his proposition of Mr. Frank Churchill and Miss Smith making their party quite complete.

"He has been wanting to come to us," continued Mr. Weston,
"ever since September: every letter has been full of it; but he cannot
command his own time. He has those to please who must be pleased,
and who (between ourselves) are sometimes to be pleased only by a
good many sacrifices. But now I have no doubt of seeing him here
about the second week in January."

"What a very great pleasure it will be to you! and Mrs. Weston is so
anxious to be acquainted with him, that she must be almost as happy as
yourself."

"Yes, she would be, but that she thinks there will be another put-
off. She does not depend upon his coming so much as I do: but she
does not know the parties so well as I do. The case, you see, is — (but
this is quite between ourselves: I did not mention a syllable of it in the
other room. There are secrets in all families, you know) — The case is,
that a party of friends are invited to pay a visit at Enscombe in January;
and that Frank's coming depends upon their being put off. If they are
not put off, he cannot stir. But I know they will, because it is a family
that a certain lady, of some consequence, at Enscombe, has a particular
dislike to: and though it is thought necessary to invite them once in two
or three years, they always are put off when it comes to the point. I have
not the smallest doubt of the issue. I am as confident of seeing Frank

here before the middle of January, as I am of being here myself: but your good friend there (nodding towards the upper end of the table) has so few vagaries herself, and has been so little used to them at Hartfield, that she cannot calculate on their effects, as I have been long in the practice of doing."

"I am sorry there should be any thing like doubt in the case," replied Emma; "but am disposed to side with you, Mr. Weston. If you think he will come, I shall think so too; for you know Enscombe."

"Yes — I have some right to that knowledge; though I have never been at the place in my life. — She is an odd woman! — But I never allow myself to speak ill of her, on Frank's account; for I do believe her to be very fond of him. I used to think she was not capable of being fond of any body, except herself: but she has always been kind to him (in her way — allowing for little whims and caprices, and expecting every thing to be as she likes). And it is no small credit, in my opinion, to him, that he should excite such an affection; for, though I would not say it to any body else, she has no more heart than a stone to people in general; and the devil of a temper."

Emma liked the subject so well, that she began upon it, to Mrs. Weston, very soon after their moving into the drawing-room: wishing her joy — yet observing, that she knew the first meeting must be rather alarming. — Mrs. Weston agreed to it; but added, that she should be very glad to be secure of undergoing the anxiety of a first meeting at the time talked of: "for I cannot depend upon his coming. I cannot be so sanguine as Mr. Weston. I am very much afraid that it will all end in nothing. Mr. Weston, I dare say, has been telling you exactly how the matter stands."

"Yes — it seems to depend upon nothing but the ill-humour of Mrs. Churchill, which I imagine to be the most certain thing in the world."

"My Emma!" replied Mrs. Weston, smiling, "what is the certainty of caprice?" Then turning to Isabella, who had not been attending before — "You must know, my dear Mrs. Knightley, that we are by no means so sure of seeing Mr. Frank Churchill, in my opinion, as his father thinks. It depends entirely upon his aunt's spirits and pleasure; in short, upon her temper. To you — to my two daughters, I may venture on the truth. Mrs. Churchill rules at Enscombe, and is a very odd-tempered woman; and his coming now, depends upon her being willing to spare him."

"Oh, Mrs. Churchill; every body knows Mrs. Churchill," replied Isabella: "and I am sure I never think of that poor young man without the greatest compassion. To be constantly living with an ill-tempered person, must be dreadful. It is what we happily have never known any thing of; but it must be a life of misery. What a blessing, that she never had any children! Poor little creatures, how unhappy she would have made them!"

Emma wished she had been alone with Mrs. Weston. She should then have heard more: Mrs. Weston would speak to her, with a degree of unreserve which she would not hazard with Isabella; and, she really believed, would scarcely try to conceal any thing relative to the Churchills from her, excepting those views on the young man, of which her own imagination had already given her such instinctive knowledge. But at present there was nothing more to be said. Mr. Woodhouse very soon followed them into the drawing-room. To be sitting long after dinner, was a confinement that he could not endure. Neither wine nor conversation was any thing to him; and gladly did he move to those with whom he was always comfortable.

While he talked to Isabella, however, Emma found an opportunity of saying,

"And so you do not consider this visit from your son as by any means certain. I am sorry for it. The introduction must be unpleasant, whenever it takes place; and the sooner it could be over, the better."

"Yes; and every delay makes one more apprehensive of other delays. Even if this family, the Braithwaites, are put off, I am still afraid that some excuse may be found for disappointing us. I cannot bear to imagine any reluctance on his side; but I am sure there is a great wish on the Churchills' to keep him to themselves. There is jealousy. They are jealous even of his regard for his father. In short, I can feel no dependence on his coming, and I wish Mr. Weston were less sanguine."

"He ought to come," said Emma. "If he could stay only a couple of days, he ought to come; and one can hardly conceive a young man's not having it in his power to do as much as that. A young *woman*, if she fall into bad hands, may be teazed, and kept at a distance from those she wants to be with; but one cannot comprehend a young *man*'s being under such restraint, as not to be able to spend a week with his father, if he likes it.'

"One ought to be at Enscombe, and know the ways of the family, before one decides upon what he can do," replied Mrs. Weston. "One ought to use the same caution, perhaps, in judging of the conduct of any one individual of any one family; but Enscombe, I believe, certainly must not be judged by general rules: *she* is so very unreasonable; and every thing gives way to her."

"But she is so fond of the nephew: he is so very great a favourite. Now, according to my idea of Mrs. Churchill, it would be most natural, that while she makes no sacrifice for the comfort of the husband, to whom she owes every thing, while she exercises incessant caprice towards *him*, she should frequently be governed by the nephew, to whom she owes nothing at all."

"My dearest Emma, do not pretend, with your sweet temper, to understand a bad one, or to lay down rules for it: you must let it go its own way. I have no doubt of his having, at times, considerable influence; but it may be perfectly impossible for him to know beforehand *when* it will be."

Emma listened, and then coolly said, "I shall not be satisfied, unless he comes."

"He may have a great deal of influence on some points," continued Mrs. Weston, "and on others, very little: and among those, on which she is beyond his reach, it is but too likely, may be this very circumstance of his coming away from them to visit us."

CHAPTER XV.

MR. WOODHOUSE was soon ready for his tea; and when he had drank his tea he was quite ready to go home, and it was as much as his three companions could do, to entertain away his notice of the lateness of the hour, before the other gentlemen appeared. Mr. Weston was chatty and convivial, and no friend to early separations of any sort; but at last the drawing-room party did receive an augmentation. Mr. Elton, in very good spirits, was one of the first to walk in. Mrs. Weston and Emma were sitting together on a sopha. He joined them immediately, and with scarcely an invitation, seated himself between them.

Emma, in good spirits too, from the amusement afforded her mind by the expectation of Mr. Frank Churchill, was willing to forget his late improprieties, and be as well satisfied with him as before, and on his making Harriet his very first subject, was ready to listen with most friendly smiles.

He professed himself extremely anxious about her fair friend — her fair, lovely, amiable friend. "Did she know? — had she heard any thing about her, since their being at Randalls? — he felt much anxiety — he must confess that the nature of her complaint alarmed him considerably." And in this style he talked on for some time very properly, not much attending to any answer, but altogether sufficiently awake to the terror of a bad sore throat; and Emma was quite in charity with him.

But at last there seemed a perverse turn; it seemed all at once as if he were more afraid of its being a bad sore throat on her account, than on Harriet's — more anxious that she should escape the infection, than that there should be no infection in the complaint. He began with great earnestness to entreat her to refrain from visiting the sick chamber again, for the present — to entreat her to *promise him* not to venture into such hazard till he had seen Mr. Perry and learnt his opinion; and though she tried to laugh it off and bring the subject back into its proper course, there was no putting an end to his extreme solicitude about her. She was vexed. It did appear — there was no concealing it — exactly like the pretence of being in love with her, instead of Harriet; an inconstancy, if real, the most contemptible and abominable! and she had difficulty in behaving with temper. He turned to Mrs. Weston to implore her assistance, "Would not she give him her support? — would not she add her persuasions to his, to induce Miss Woodhouse not to go to Mrs. Goddard's, till it were certain that Miss Smith's disorder had no infection? He could not be satisfied without a promise — would not she give him her influence in procuring it?"

"So scrupulous for others," he continued, "and yet so careless for herself! She wanted me to nurse my cold by staying at home to-day, and yet will not promise to avoid the danger of catching an ulcerated sore throat herself! Is this fair, Mrs. Weston? — Judge between us. Have not I some right to complain? I am sure of your kind support and aid."

Emma saw Mrs. Weston's surprize, and felt that it must be great, at an address which, in words and manner, was assuming to himself the right of first interest in her; and as for herself, she was too much provoked and offended to have the power of directly saying any thing to the purpose. She could only give him a look; but it was such a look as she thought must restore him to his senses; and then left the sopha, removing to a seat by her sister, and giving her all her attention.

She had not time to know how Mr. Elton took the reproof, so rapidly did another subject succeed; for Mr. John Knightley now came into the room from examining the weather, and opened on them all with the information of the ground being covered with snow, and of its still snowing fast, with a strong drifting wind; concluding with these words to Mr. Woodhouse:

"This will prove a spirited beginning of your winter engagements, sir. Something new for your coachman and horses to be making their way through a storm of snow."

Poor Mr. Woodhouse was silent from consternation; but every body else had something to say; every body was either surprized or not surprized, and had some question to ask, or some comfort to offer. Mrs. Weston and Emma tried earnestly to cheer him and turn his attention from his son-in-law, who was pursuing his triumph rather unfeelingly.

"I admired your resolution very much, sir," said he, "in venturing out in such weather, for of course you saw there would be snow very soon. Every body must have seen the snow coming on. I admired your spirit; and I dare say we shall get home very well. Another hour or two's snow can hardly make the road impassable; and we are two carriages; if *one* is blown over in the bleak part of the common field there will be the other at hand. I dare say we shall be all safe at Hartfield before midnight."

Mr. Weston, with triumph of a different sort, was confessing that he had known it to be snowing some time, but had not said a word, lest it should make Mr. Woodhouse uncomfortable, and be an excuse for his hurrying away. As to there being any quantity of snow fallen or likely to fall to impede their return, that was a mere joke; he was afraid they would find no difficulty. He wished the road might be impassable, that he might be able to keep them all at Randalls; and with the utmost good-will was sure that accommodation might be found for every body, calling on his wife to agree with him, that, with a little contrivance, every body might be lodged, which she hardly knew how to do, from the consciousness of there being but two spare rooms in the house.

"What is to be done, my dear Emma? — what is to be done?" was Mr. Woodhouse's first exclamation, and all that he could say for some time. To her he looked for comfort, and her assurances of safety, her representation of the excellence of the horses, and of James, and of their having so many friends about them, revived him a little.

His eldest daughter's alarm was equal to his own. The horror of being blocked up at Randalls, while her children were at Hartfield, was full in her imagination; and fancying the road to be now just passable for adventurous people, but in a state that admitted no delay, she was eager to have it settled, that her father and Emma should remain at Randalls, while she and her husband set forward instantly through all the possible accumulations of drifted snow that might impede them.

"You had better order the carriage directly, my love," said she; "I dare say we shall be able to get along, if we set off directly; and if we do come to any thing very bad, I can get out and walk. I am not at all afraid. I should not mind walking half the way. I could change my shoes, you know, the moment I got home; and it is not the sort of thing that gives me cold."

"Indeed!" replied he. "Then, my dear Isabella, it is the most extraordinary sort of thing in the world, for in general every thing does give you cold. Walk home! — you are prettily shod for walking home, I dare say. It will be bad enough for the horses."

Isabella turned to Mrs. Weston for her approbation of the plan. Mrs. Weston could only approve. Isabella then went to Emma; but Emma could not so entirely give up the hope of their being all able to get away; and they were still discussing the point, when Mr. Knightley, who had left the room immediately after his brother's first report of the snow, came back again, and told them that he had been out of doors to examine, and could answer for there not being the smallest difficulty in their getting home, whenever they liked it, either now or an hour hence. He had gone beyond the sweep — some way along the Highbury road — the snow was no where above half an inch deep — in many places hardly enough to whiten the ground; a very few flakes were falling at present, but the clouds were parting, and there was every appearance of its being soon over. He had seen the coachmen, and they both agreed with him in there being nothing to apprehend.

To Isabella, the relief of such tidings was very great, and they were scarcely less acceptable to Emma on her father's account, who was immediately set as much at ease on the subject as his nervous constitution allowed; but the alarm that had been raised could not be appeased so as to admit of any comfort for him while he continued at Randalls. He was satisfied of there being no present danger in returning home, but no assurances could convince him that it was safe to stay; and while the others were variously urging and recommending, Mr. Knightley and Emma settled it in a few brief sentences: thus —

"Your father will not be easy; why do not you go?"

"I am ready, if the others are."

"Shall I ring the bell?"

"Yes, do."

And the bell was rung, and the carriages spoken for. A few minutes more, and Emma hoped to see one troublesome companion deposited in his own house, to get sober and cool, and the other recover his temper and happiness when this visit of hardship were over.

The carriages came: and Mr. Woodhouse, always the first object on such occasions, was carefully attended to his own by Mr. Knightley and Mr. Weston; but not all that either could say could prevent some renewal of alarm at the sight of the snow which had actually fallen, and the discovery of a much darker night than he had been prepared for. "He was afraid they should have a very bad drive. He was afraid poor Isabella, would not like it. And there would be poor Emma in the carriage behind. He did not know what they had best do. They must keep as much together as they could;" and James was talked to, and given a charge to go very slow and wait for the other carriage.

Isabella stept in after her father; John Knightley, forgetting that he did not belong to their party, stept in after his wife very naturally; so that Emma found, on being escorted and followed into the second carriage by Mr. Elton, that the door was to be lawfully shut on them, and that they were to have a tête-à-tête drive. It would not have been the awkwardness of a moment, it would have been rather a pleasure, previous to the suspicions of this very day; she could have talked to him of Harriet, and the three-quarters of a mile would have seemed but one. But now, she would rather it had not happened. She believed he had been drinking too much of Mr. Weston's good wine, and felt sure that he would want to be talking nonsense.

To restrain him as much as might be, by her own manners, she was immediately preparing to speak with exquisite calmness and gravity of the weather and the night; but scarcely had she begun, scarcely had they passed the sweep-gate and joined the other carriage, than she found her subject cut up — her hand seized — her attention demanded, and Mr. Elton actually making violent love to her: availing himself of the precious opportunity, declaring sentiments which must be already well known, hoping — fearing — adoring — ready to die if she refused him; but flattering himself that his ardent attachment and unequalled love and unexampled passion could not fail of having some effect, and in short, very much resolved on being seriously accepted as soon as possible. It really was so. Without scruple — without apology — without much apparent diffidence, Mr. Elton, the lover of Harriet, was professing himself *her* lover. She tried to stop him; but vainly; he would go on, and say it all. Angry as she was, the thought of the moment made her resolve to restrain herself when she did speak. She felt that half this folly must be drunkenness, and therefore could hope that it might belong only to the passing hour. Accordingly, with a mixture of the serious and the playful, which she hoped would best suit his half and half state, she replied,

"I am very much astonished, Mr. Elton. This to *me!* you forget yourself — you take me for my friend — any message to Miss Smith I shall be happy to deliver; but no more of this to *me,* if you please."

"Miss Smith! — Message to Miss Smith! — What could she possibly mean!" — And he repeated her words with such assurance of accent, such boastful pretence of amazement, that she could not help replying with quickness,

"Mr. Elton, this is the most extraordinary conduct! and I can account for it only in one way; you are not yourself, or you could not speak either to me, or of Harriet, in such a manner. Command yourself enough to say no more, and I will endeavour to forget it."

But Mr. Elton had only drunk wine enough to elevate his spirits, not at all to confuse his intellects. He perfectly knew his own meaning; and having warmly protested against her suspicion as most injurious, and slightly touched upon his respect for Miss Smith as her friend, — but acknowledging his wonder that Miss Smith should be mentioned at all, — he resumed the subject of his own passion, and was very urgent for a favourable answer.

As she thought less of his inebriety, she thought more of his inconstancy and presumption; and with fewer struggles for politeness, replied,

"It is impossible for me to doubt any longer. You have made yourself too clear. Mr. Elton, my astonishment is much beyond any thing I can express. After such behaviour, as I have witnessed during the last month, to Miss Smith — such attentions as I have been in the daily habit of observing — to be addressing me in this manner — this is an unsteadiness of character, indeed, which I had not supposed possible! Believe me, sir, I am far, very far, from gratified in being the object of such professions."

"Good heaven!" cried Mr. Elton, "what can be the meaning of this? — Miss Smith! — I never thought of Miss Smith in the whole course of my existence — never paid her any attentions, but as your friend: never cared whether she were dead or alive, but as your friend. If she has fancied otherwise, her own wishes have misled her, and I am very sorry — extremely sorry — But, Miss Smith, indeed! — Oh! Miss Woodhouse! who can think of Miss Smith, when Miss Woodhouse is near! No, upon my honour, there is no unsteadiness of character. I have thought only of you. I protest against having paid the smallest attention to any one else. Every thing that I have said or done, for many weeks past, has been with the sole view of marking my adoration of yourself. You cannot really, seriously, doubt it. No! — (in an accent meant to be insinuating) — I am sure you have seen and understood me."

It would be impossible to say what Emma felt, on hearing this — which of all her unpleasant sensations was uppermost. She was too completely overpowered to be immediately able to reply: and two moments of silence being ample encouragement for Mr. Elton's sanguine state of mind, he tried to take her hand again, as he joyously exclaimed —

"Charming Miss Woodhouse! allow me to interpret this interesting silence. It confesses that you have long understood me."

"No, sir," cried Emma, "it confesses no such thing. So far from having long understood you, I have been in a most complete error with respect to your views, till this moment. As to myself, I am very sorry that you should have been giving way to any feelings —— Nothing could be farther from my wishes — your attachment to my friend Harriet — your pursuit of her, (pursuit, it appeared,) gave me great pleasure, and I have been very earnestly wishing you success: but had I supposed that she were not your attraction to Hartfield, I should certainly have thought you judged ill in making your visits so frequent. Am I to believe that you have never sought to recommend yourself particularly to Miss Smith? — that you have never thought seriously of her?"

"Never, madam," cried he, affronted, in his turn: "never, I assure you. I think seriously of Miss Smith! — Miss Smith is a very good sort of girl; and I should be happy to see her respectably settled. I wish her extremely well: and, no doubt, there are men who might not object to —— Every body has their level: but as for myself, I am not, I think, quite so much at a loss. I need not so totally despair of an equal alliance, as to be addressing myself to Miss Smith! — No, madam, my visits to Hartfield have been for yourself only; and the encouragement I received" ——

"Encouragement! — I give you encouragement! — sir, you have been entirely mistaken in supposing it. I have seen you only as the admirer of my friend. In no other light could you have been more to me than a common acquaintance. I am exceedingly sorry: but it is well that the mistake ends where it does. Had the same behaviour continued, Miss Smith might have been led into a misconception of your views; not being aware, probably, any more than myself, of the very great inequality which you are so sensible of. But, as it is, the disappointment is single, and, I trust, will not be lasting. I have no thoughts of matrimony at present."

He was too angry to say another word; her manner too decided to invite supplication; and in this state of swelling resentment, and mutually deep mortification, they had to continue together a few minutes longer, for the fears of Mr. Woodhouse had confined them to a foot pace. If there had not been so much anger, there would have been desperate awkwardness; but their straight-forward emotions left no room for the little zigzags of embarrassment. Without knowing when the carriage turned into Vicarage-lane, or when it stopped, they found themselves, all at once, at the door of his house; and he was out before another syllable passed. — Emma then felt it indispensable to wish him a good night. The compliment was just returned, coldly and proudly; and, under indescribable irritation of spirits, she was then conveyed to Hartfield.

There she was welcomed, with the utmost delight, by her father, who had been trembling for the dangers of a solitary drive from Vicarage-lane — turning a corner which he could never bear to think of — and in strange hands — a mere common coachman — no James; and there it seemed as if her return only were wanted to make every thing go well: for Mr. John Knightley, ashamed of his ill-humour, was now all kindness and attention; and so particularly solicitous for the comfort of her father, as to seem — if not quite ready to join him in a basin of gruel — perfectly sensible of its being exceedingly wholesome; and the day was concluding in peace and comfort to all their little party, except herself. — But her mind had never been in such perturbation, and it needed a very strong effort to appear attentive and cheerful till the usual hour of separating allowed her the relief of quiet reflection.

CHAPTER XVI.

THE hair was curled, and the maid sent away, and Emma sat down to think and be miserable. — It was a wretched business, indeed! — Such an overthrow of every thing she had been wishing for! — Such a development of every thing most unwelcome! — Such a blow for Harriet! — That was the worst of all. Every part of it brought pain and humiliation, of some sort or other; but, compared with the evil to Harriet, all was light; and she would gladly have submitted to feel yet more mistaken — more in error — more disgraced by mis-judgment, than she actually was, could the effects of her blunders have been confined to herself.

"If I had not persuaded Harriet into liking the man, I could have born any thing. He might have doubled his presumption to me — But poor Harriet!"

How she could have been so deceived! — He protested that he had never thought seriously of Harriet — never! She looked back as well as she could; but it was all confusion. She had taken up the idea, she supposed, and made every thing bend to it. His manners, however, must have been unmarked, wavering, dubious, or she could not have been so misled

The picture! — How eager he had been about the picture! — and the charade! — and an hundred other circumstances; — how clearly they had seemed to point to Harriet. To be sure, the charade, with its "ready wit" — but then, the "soft eyes" — in fact it suited neither; it was a jumble without taste or truth. Who could have seen through such thick-headed nonsense?

Certainly she had often, especially of late, thought his manners to herself unnecessarily gallant; but it had passed as his way, as a mere error of judgment, of knowledge, of taste, as one proof among others that he had not always lived in the best society, that with all the gentleness of his address, true elegance was sometimes wanting; but, till this very day, she had never, for an instant, suspected it to mean any thing but grateful respect to her as Harriet's friend.

To Mr. John Knightley was she indebted for her first idea on the subject, for the first start of its possibility. There was no denying that those brothers had penetration. She remembered what Mr. Knightley had once said to her about Mr. Elton, the caution he had given, the conviction he had professed that Mr. Elton would never marry indiscreetly; and blushed to think how much truer a knowledge of his character had been there shewn than any she had reached herself. It was dreadfully mortifying; but Mr. Elton was proving himself, in many respects, the very reverse of what she had meant and believed him; proud, assuming, conceited; very full of his own claims, and little concerned about the feelings of others.

Contrary to the usual course of things, Mr. Elton's wanting to pay his addresses to her had sunk him in her opinion. His professions and his proposals did him no service. She thought nothing of his attachment, and was insulted by his hopes. He wanted to marry well, and having the arrogance to raise his eyes to her, pretended to be in love; but she was perfectly easy as to his not suffering any disappointment that need be cared for. There had been no real affection either in his language or manners. Sighs and fine words had been given in abundance; but she could hardly devise any set of expressions, or fancy any tone of voice, less allied with real love. She need not trouble herself to pity him. He only wanted to aggrandize and enrich himself; and if Miss Woodhouse of Hartfield, the heiress of thirty thousand pounds, were not quite so easily obtained as he had fancied, he would soon try for Miss Somebody else with twenty, or with ten.

But — that he should talk of encouragement, should consider her as aware of his views, accepting his attentions, meaning (in short), to marry him! — should suppose himself her equal in connection or mind! — look down upon her friend, so well understanding the gradations of rank below him, and be so blind to what rose above, as to fancy himself shewing no presumption in addressing her! — It was most provoking.

Perhaps it was not fair to expect him to feel how very much he was her inferior in talent, and all the elegancies of mind. The very want of such equality might prevent his perception of it; but he must know that in fortune and consequence she was greatly his superior. He must know that the Woodhouses had been settled for several generations at Hartfield, the younger branch of a very ancient family — and that the Eltons were nobody. The landed property of Hartfield certainly was inconsiderable, being but a sort of notch in the Donwell Abbey estate, to which all the rest of Highbury belonged; but their fortune, from other sources, was such as to make them scarcely secondary to Donwell Abbey itself, in every other kind of consequence; and the Woodhouses had long held a high place in the consideration of the neighbourhood which Mr. Elton had first entered not two years ago, to make his way as he could, without any alliances but in trade, or any thing to recommend him to notice but his situation and his civility. — But he had fancied her in love with him; that evidently must have been his dependence; and after raving a little about the seeming incongruity of gentle manners and a conceited head, Emma was obliged in common honesty to stop and admit that her own behaviour to him had been so complaisant and obliging, so full of courtesy and attention, as (supposing her real motive unperceived) might warrant a man of ordinary observation and delicacy, like Mr. Elton, in fancying himself a very decided favourite. If *she* had so misinterpreted his feelings, she had little right to wonder that *he*, with self-interest to blind him, should have mistaken her's.

The first error and the worst lay at her door. It was foolish, it was wrong, to take so active a part in bringing any two people together. It was adventuring too far, assuming too much, making light of what ought to be serious, a trick of what ought to be simple. She was quite concerned and ashamed, and resolved to do such things no more.

"Here have I," said she, "actually talked poor Harriet into being very much attached to this man. She might never have thought of him but for me; and certainly never would have thought of him with hope, if I had not assured her of his attachment, for she is as modest and humble as I used to think him. Oh! that I had been satisfied with persuading her not to accept young Martin. There I was quite right. That was well done of me; but there I should have stopped, and left the rest to time and chance. I was introducing her into good company, and giving her the opportunity of pleasing some one worth having; I ought not to have attempted more. But now, poor girl, her peace is cut up for some time. I have been but half a friend to her; and if she were *not* to feel this disappointment so very much, I am sure I have not an idea of any body else who would be at all desirable for her; — William Cox — Oh! no, I could not endure William Cox — a pert young lawyer."

She stopt to blush and laugh at her own relapse, and then resumed a more serious, more dispiriting cogitation upon what had been, and might be, and must be. The distressing explanation she had to make to Harriet, and all that poor Harriet would be suffering, with the awkwardness of future meetings, the difficulties of continuing or discontinuing the acquaintance, of subduing feelings, concealing resentment, and avoiding eclat, were enough to occupy her in most unmirthful reflections some time longer, and she went to bed at last with nothing settled but the conviction of her having blundered most dreadfully.

To youth and natural cheerfulness like Emma's, though under temporary gloom at night, the return of day will hardly fail to bring return of spirits. The youth and cheerfulness of morning are in happy analogy, and of powerful operation; and if the distress be not poignant enough to keep the eyes unclosed, they will be sure to open to sensations of softened pain and brighter hope.

Emma got up on the morrow more disposed for comfort than she had gone to bed, more ready to see alleviations of the evil before her, and to depend on getting tolerably out of it.

It was a great consolation that Mr. Elton should not be really in love with her, or so particularly amiable as to make it shocking to disappoint him — that Harriet's nature should not be of that superior sort in which the feelings are most acute and retentive — and that there could be no necessity for any body's knowing what had passed except the three principals, and especially for her father's being given a moment's uneasiness about it.

These were very cheering thoughts; and the sight of a great deal of snow on the ground did her further service, for any thing was welcome that might justify their all three being quite asunder at present.

The weather was most favourable for her; though Christmas-day, she could not go to church. Mr. Woodhouse would have been miserable had his daughter attempted it, and she was therefore safe from either exciting or receiving unpleasant and most unsuitable ideas. The ground covered with snow, and the atmosphere in that unsettled state between frost and thaw, which is of all others the most unfriendly for exercise, every morning beginning in rain or snow, and every evening setting in to freeze, she was for many days a most honourable prisoner. No intercourse with Harriet possible but by note; no church for her on Sunday any more than on Christmas-day; and no need to find excuses for Mr. Elton's absenting himself.

It was weather which might fairly confine every body at home; and though she hoped and believed him to be really taking comfort in some society or other, it was very pleasant to have her father so well satisfied with his being all alone in his own house, too wise to stir out; and to hear him say to Mr. Knightley, whom no weather could keep entirely from them, —

"Ah! Mr. Knightley, why do not you stay at home like poor Mr. Elton?"

These days of confinement would have been, but for her private perplexities, remarkably comfortable, as such seclusion exactly suited her brother, whose feelings must always be of great importance to his companions; and he had, besides, so thoroughly cleared off his ill-humour at Randalls, that his amiableness never failed him during the rest of his stay at Hartfield. He was always agreeable and obliging, and speaking pleasantly of every body. But with all the hopes of cheerfulness, and all the present comfort of delay, there was still such an evil hanging over her in the hour of explanation with Harriet, as made it impossible for Emma to be ever perfectly at ease.

CHAPTER XVII.

Mr. and Mrs. John Knightley were not detained long at Hartfield. The weather soon improved enough for those to move who must move; and Mr. Woodhouse having, as usual, tried to persuade his daughter to stay behind with all her children, was obliged to see the whole party set off, and return to his lamentations over the destiny of poor Isabella; — which poor Isabella, passing her life with those she doated on, full of their merits, blind to their faults, and always innocently busy, might have been a model of right feminine happiness.

The evening of the very day on which they went, brought a note from Mr. Elton to Mr. Woodhouse, a long, civil, ceremonious note, to say, with Mr. Elton's best compliments, "that he was proposing to leave

Highbury the following morning in his way to Bath,[54] where, in compliance with the pressing entreaties of some friends, he had engaged to spend a few weeks, and very much regretted the impossibility he was under, from various circumstances of weather and business, of taking a personal leave of Mr. Woodhouse, of whose friendly civilities he should ever retain a grateful sense — and had Mr. Woodhouse any commands, should be happy to attend to them."

Emma was most agreeably surprized. — Mr. Elton's absence just at this time was the very thing to be desired. She admired him for contriving it, though not able to give him much credit for the manner in which it was announced. Resentment could not have been more plainly spoken than in a civility to her father, from which she was so pointedly excluded. She had not even a share in his opening compliments. — Her name was not mentioned; — and there was so striking a change in all this, and such an ill-judged solemnity of leave-taking in his grateful acknowledgments, as she thought, at first, could not escape her father's suspicion.

It did however. — Her father was quite taken up with the surprize of so sudden a journey, and his fears that Mr. Elton might never get safely to the end of it, and saw nothing extraordinary in his language. It was a very useful note, for it supplied them with fresh matter for thought and conversation during the rest of their lonely evening. Mr. Woodhouse talked over his alarms, and Emma was in spirits to persuade them away with all her usual promptitude.

She now resolved to keep Harriet no longer in the dark. She had reason to believe her nearly recovered from her cold, and it was desirable that she should have as much time as possible for getting the better of her other complaint before the gentleman's return. She went to Mrs. Goddard's accordingly the very next day, to undergo the necessary penance of communication; and a severe one it was. — She had to destroy all the hopes which she had been so industriously feeding — to appear in the ungracious character of the one preferred — and acknowledge herself grossly mistaken and mis-judging in all her ideas on one subject, all her observations, all her convictions, all her prophesies for the last six weeks.

The confession completely renewed her first shame — and the sight of Harriet's tears made her think that she should never be in charity with herself again.

---

[54] **Bath:** The most famous spa in Britain, known for its Roman baths and medicinal waters; its preeminence as a fashionable resort was being challenged by Brighton and other seaside towns at this time.

Harriet bore the intelligence very well — blaming nobody — and in every thing testifying such an ingenuousness of disposition and lowly opinion of herself, as must appear with particular advantage at that moment to her friend.

Emma was in the humour to value simplicity and modesty to the utmost; and all that was amiable, all that ought to be attaching, seemed on Harriet's side, not her own. Harriet did not consider herself as having any thing to complain of. The affection of such a man as Mr. Elton would have been too great a distinction. — She never could have deserved him — and nobody but so partial and kind a friend as Miss Woodhouse would have thought it possible.

Her tears fell abundantly — but her grief was so truly artless, that no dignity could have made it more respectable in Emma's eyes — and she listened to her and tried to console her with all her heart and understanding — really for the time convinced that Harriet was the superior creature of the two — and that to resemble her would be more for her own welfare and happiness than all that genius or intelligence could do.

It was rather too late in the day to set about being simple-minded and ignorant; but she left her with every previous resolution confirmed of being humble and discreet, and repressing imagination all the rest of her life. Her second duty now, inferior only to her father's claims, was to promote Harriet's comfort, and endeavour to prove her own affection in some better method than by match-making. She got her to Hartfield, and shewed her the most unvarying kindness, striving to occupy and amuse her, and by books and conversation, to drive Mr. Elton from her thoughts.

Time, she knew, must be allowed for this being thoroughly done; and she could suppose herself but an indifferent judge of such matters in general, and very inadequate to sympathize in an attachment to Mr. Elton in particular; but it seemed to her reasonable that at Harriet's age, and with the entire extinction of all hope, such a progress might be made towards a state of composure by the time of Mr. Elton's return, as to allow them all to meet again in the common routine of acquaintance, without any danger of betraying sentiments or increasing them.

Harriet did think him all perfection, and maintain the non-existence of any body equal to him in person or goodness — and did, in truth, prove herself more resolutely in love than Emma had foreseen; but yet it appeared to her so natural, so inevitable to strive against an inclination of that sort *unrequited,* that she could not comprehend its continuing very long in equal force.

If Mr. Elton, on his return, made his own indifference as evident and indubitable as she could not doubt he would anxiously do, she could not imagine Harriet's persisting to place her happiness in the sight or the recollection of him.

Their being fixed, so absolutely fixed, in the same place, was bad for each, for all three. Not one of them had the power of removal, or of effecting any material change of society. They must encounter each other, and make the best of it.

Harriet was further unfortunate in the tone of her companions at Mrs. Goddard's; Mr. Elton being the adoration of all the teachers and great girls in the school; and it must be at Hartfield only that she could have any chance of hearing him spoken of with cooling moderation or repellant truth. Where the wound had been given, there must the cure be found if anywhere; and Emma felt that, till she saw her in the way of cure, there could be no true peace for herself.

CHAPTER XVIII.

Mr. Frank Churchill did not come. When the time proposed drew near, Mrs. Weston's fears were justified in the arrival of a letter of excuse. For the present, he could not be spared, to his "very great mortification and regret; but still he looked forward with the hope of coming to Randalls at no distant period."

Mrs. Weston was exceedingly disappointed — much more disappointed, in fact, than her husband, though her dependence on seeing the young man had been so much more sober: but a sanguine temper, though for ever expecting more good than occurs, does not always pay for its hopes by any proportionate depression. It soon flies over the present failure, and begins to hope again. For half an hour Mr. Weston was surprized and sorry; but then he began to perceive that Frank's coming two or three months later would be a much better plan; better time of year; better weather; and that he would be able, without any doubt, to stay considerably longer with them than if he had come sooner.

These feelings rapidly restored his comfort, while Mrs. Weston, of a more apprehensive disposition, foresaw nothing but a repetition of excuses and delays; and after all her concern for what her husband was to suffer, suffered a great deal more herself.

Emma was not at this time in a state of spirits to care really about Mr. Frank Churchill's not coming, except as a disappointment at Randalls.

The acquaintance at present had no charm for her. She wanted, rather, to be quiet, and out of temptation; but still, as it was desirable that she should appear, in general, like her usual self, she took care to express as much interest in the circumstance, and enter as warmly into Mr. and Mrs. Weston's disappointment, as might naturally belong to their friendship.

She was the first to announce it to Mr. Knightley; and exclaimed quite as much as was necessary, (or, being acting a part, perhaps rather more,) at the conduct of the Churchills, in keeping him away. She then proceeded to say a good deal more than she felt, of the advantage of such an addition to their confined society in Surry; the pleasure of look-ing at some body new; the gala-day to Highbury entire, which the sight of him would have made; and ending with reflections on the Churchills again, found herself directly involved in a disagreement with Mr. Knightley; and, to her great amusement, perceived that she was taking the other side of the question from her real opinion, and making use of Mrs. Weston's arguments against herself.

"The Churchills are very likely in fault," said Mr. Knightley, coolly; "but I dare say he might come if he would."

"I do not know why you should say so. He wishes exceedingly to come; but his uncle and aunt will not spare him."

"I cannot believe that he has not the power of coming, if he made a point of it. It is too unlikely, for me to believe it without proof."

"How odd you are! What has Mr. Frank Churchill done, to make you suppose him such an unnatural creature?"

"I am not supposing him at all an unnatural creature, in suspecting that he may have learnt to be above his connections, and to care very little for any thing but his own pleasure, from living with those who have always set him the example of it. It is a great deal more natural than one could wish, that a young man, brought up by those who are proud, luxurious, and selfish, should be proud, luxurious, and selfish too. If Frank Churchill had wanted to see his father, he would have contrived it between September and January. A man at his age — what is he? — three or four-and-twenty — cannot be without the means of doing as much as that. It is impossible."

"That's easily said, and easily felt by you, who have always been your own master. You are the worst judge in the world, Mr. Knightley, of the difficulties of dependence. You do not know what it is to have tempers to manage."

"It is not to be conceived that a man of three or four-and-twenty should not have liberty of mind or limb to that amount. He cannot want money — he cannot want leisure. We know, on the contrary, that he has so much of both, that he is glad to get rid of them at the idlest haunts in the kingdom. We hear of him for ever at some watering-place or other. A little while ago, he was at Weymouth.[55] This proves that he can leave the Churchills."

"Yes, sometimes he can."

"And those times are, whenever he thinks it worth his while; whenever there is any temptation of pleasure."

"It is very unfair to judge of any body's conduct, without an intimate knowledge of their situation. Nobody, who has not been in the interior of a family, can say what the difficulties of any individual of that family may be. We ought to be acquainted with Enscombe, and with Mrs. Churchill's temper, before we pretend to decide upon what her nephew can do. He may, at times, be able to do a great deal more than he can at others."

"There is one thing, Emma, which a man can always do, if he chuses, and that is, his duty; not by manœuvring and finessing,[56] but by vigour and resolution. It is Frank Churchill's duty to pay this attention to his father. He knows it to be so, by his promises and messages; but if he wished to do it, it might be done. A man who felt rightly would say at once, simply and resolutely, to Mrs. Churchill — 'Every sacrifice of mere pleasure you will always find me ready to make to your convenience; but I must go and see my father immediately. I know he would be hurt by my failing in such a mark of respect to him on the present occasion. I shall, therefore, set off to-morrow.' — If he would say so to her at once, in the tone of decision becoming a man, there would be no opposition made to his going."

"No," said Emma, laughing; "but perhaps there might be some made to his coming back again. Such language for a young man entirely dependent, to use! — Nobody but you, Mr. Knightley, would imagine it possible. But you have not an idea of what is requisite in situations directly opposite to your own. Mr. Frank Churchill to be making such a speech as that to the uncle and aunt, who have brought him up, and are to provide for him! — Standing up in the middle of the room, I suppose, and speaking as loud as he could! — How can you imagine such conduct practicable?"

"Depend upon it, Emma, a sensible man would find no difficulty in it. He would feel himself in the right; and the declaration — made, of

---

[55] *Weymouth:* Seaside town in Dorset made fashionable by George III.

[56] *finessing:* Subterfuge like that whereby a card player wins a trick with a card that is not the highest in his hand.

course, as a man of sense would make it, in a proper manner — would do him more good, raise him higher, fix his interest stronger with the people he depended on, than all that a line of shifts and expedients can ever do. Respect would be added to affection. They would feel that they could trust him; that the nephew, who had done rightly by his father, would do rightly by them; for they know, as well as he does, as well as all the world must know, that he ought to pay this visit to his father; and while meanly exerting their power to delay it, are in their hearts not thinking the better of him for submitting to their whims. Respect for right conduct is felt by every body. If he would act in this sort of manner, on principle, consistently, regularly, their little minds would bend to his."

"I rather doubt that. You are very fond of bending little minds; but where little minds belong to rich people in authority, I think they have a knack of swelling out, till they are quite as unmanageable as great ones. I can imagine, that if you, as you are, Mr. Knightley, were to be transported and placed all at once in Mr. Frank Churchill's situation, you would be able to say and do just what you have been recommending for him; and it might have a very good effect. The Churchills might not have a word to say in return; but then, you would have no habits of early obedience and long observance to break through. To him who has, it might not be so easy to burst forth at once into perfect independence, and set all their claims on his gratitude and regard at nought. He may have as strong a sense of what would be right, as you can have, without being so equal under particular circumstances to act up to it."

"Then, it would not be so strong a sense. If it failed to produce equal exertion, it could not be an equal conviction."

"Oh! the difference of situation and habit! I wish you would try to understand what an amiable young man may be likely to feel in directly opposing those, whom as child and boy he has been looking up to all his life."

"Your amiable young man is a very weak young man, if this be the first occasion of his carrying through a resolution to do right against the will of others. It ought to have been an habit with him by this time, of following his duty, instead of consulting expediency. I can allow for the fears of the child, but not of the man. As he became rational, he ought to have roused himself and shaken off all that was unworthy in their authority. He ought to have opposed the first attempt on their side to make him slight his father. Had he begun as he ought, there would have been no difficulty now."

"We shall never agree about him," cried Emma; "but that is nothing extraordinary. I have not the least idea of his being a weak young man: I feel sure that he is not. Mr. Weston would not be blind to folly, though in his own son; but he is very likely to have a more yielding, complying, mild disposition than would suit your notions of man's perfection. I dare say he has; and though it may cut him off from some advantages, it will secure him many others."

"Yes; all the advantages of sitting still when he ought to move, and of leading a life of mere idle pleasure, and fancying himself extremely expert in finding excuses for it. He can sit down and write a fine flourishing letter, full of professions and falsehoods, and persuade himself that he has hit upon the very best method in the world of preserving peace at home and preventing his father's having any right to complain. His letters disgust me."

"Your feelings are singular. They seem to satisfy every body else."

"I suspect they do not satisfy Mrs. Weston. They hardly can satisfy a woman of her good sense and quick feelings: standing in a mother's place, but without a mother's affection to blind her. It is on her account that attention to Randalls is doubly due, and she must doubly feel the omission. Had she been a person of consequence herself, he would have come I dare say; and it would not have signified whether he did or no. Can you think your friend behind-hand in these sort of considerations? Do you suppose she does not often say all this to herself? No, Emma, your amiable young man can be amiable only in French, not in English. He may be very 'aimable,' have very good manners, and be very agreeable; but he can have no English delicacy towards the feelings of other people: nothing really amiable[57] about him."

"You seem determined to think ill of him."

"Me! — not at all," replied Mr. Knightley, rather displeased; "I do not want to think ill of him. I should be as ready to acknowledge his merits as any other man; but I hear of none, except what are merely personal; that he is well grown and good-looking, with smooth, plausible manners."

"Well, if he have nothing else to recommend him, he will be a treasure of Highbury. We do not often look upon fine young men, well-bred and agreeable. We must not be nice and ask for all the virtues into the bargain. Cannot you imagine, Mr. Knightley, what a *sensation* his

[57] *'aimable'... amiable:* The contrast between French and English spellings here (like the contrast between Churchill and Knightley) points to the novel's participation in a long tradition of English distrust of French manners. For further discussion, and for Lord Chesterfield's letter to his son that urges "aimable" behavior, see "Contextual Documents," pp. 383, 389.

coming will produce? There will be but one subject throughout the parishes of Donwell and Highbury; but one interest — one object of curiosity; it will be all Mr. Frank Churchill; we shall think and speak of nobody else."

"You will excuse my being so much overpowered. If I find him conversible, I shall be glad of his acquaintance; but if he is only a chattering coxcomb, he will not occupy much of my time or thoughts."

"My idea of him is, that he can adapt his conversation to the taste of every body, and has the power as well as the wish to being universally agreeable. To you, he will talk of farming; to me, of drawing or music; and so on to every body, having that general information on all subjects which will enable him to follow the lead, or take the lead, just as propriety may require, and to speak extremely well on each; that is my idea of him."

"And mine," said Mr. Knightley warmly, "is, that if he turn out any thing like it, he will be the most insufferable fellow breathing! What! at three-and-twenty to be the king of his company — the great man — the practised politician, who is to read every body's character, and make every body's talents conduce to the display of his own superiority; to be dispensing his flatteries around, that he may make all appear like fools compared with himself! My dear Emma, your own good sense could not endure such a puppy when it came to the point."

"I will say no more about him," cried Emma, "you turn every thing to evil. We are both prejudiced; you against, I for him; and we have no chance of agreeing till he is really here."

"Prejudiced! I am not prejudiced."

"But I am very much, and without being at all ashamed of it. My love for Mr. and Mrs. Weston gives me a decided prejudice in his favour."

"He is a person I never think of from one month's end to another," said Mr. Knightley, with a degree of vexation, which made Emma immediately talk of something else, though she could not comprehend why he should be angry.

To take a dislike to a young man, only because he appeared to be of a different disposition from himself, was unworthy the real liberality of mind which she was always used to acknowledge in him; for with all the high opinion of himself, which she had often laid to his charge, she had never before for a moment supposed it could make him unjust to the merit of another.

Volume II

CHAPTER I.

EMMA and Harriet had been walking together one morning, and, in Emma's opinion, been talking enough of Mr. Elton for that day. She could not think that Harriet's solace or her own sins required more; and she was therefore industriously getting rid of the subject as they returned; — but it burst out again when she thought she had succeeded, and after speaking some time of what the poor must suffer in winter, and receiving no other answer than a very plaintive — "Mr. Elton is so good to the poor!" she found something else must be done.

They were just approaching the house where lived Mrs. and Miss Bates. She determined to call upon them and seek safety in numbers. There was always sufficient reason for such an attention; Mrs. and Miss Bates loved to be called on, and she knew she was considered by the very few who presumed ever to see imperfection in her, as rather negligent in that respect, and as not contributing what she ought to the stock of their scanty comforts.

She had had many a hint from Mr. Knightley and some from her own heart, as to her deficiency — but none were equal to counteract the persuasion of its being very disagreeable, — a waste of time — tiresome women — and all the horror of being in danger of falling in with the second rate and third rate of Highbury, who were calling on them for ever, and therefore she seldom went near them. But now she made the sudden resolution of not passing their door without going in — observing, as she proposed it to Harriet, that, as well as she could calculate, they were just now quite safe from any letter from Jane Fairfax.

The house belonged to people in business. Mrs. and Miss Bates occupied the drawing-room floor; and there, in the very moderate sized apartment, which was every thing to them, the visitors were most cordially and even gratefully welcomed; the quiet neat old lady, who with her knitting was seated in the warmest corner, wanting even to give up her place to Miss Woodhouse, and her more active, talking daughter, almost ready to overpower them with care and kindness, thanks for their visit, solicitude for their shoes, anxious inquiries after Mr. Woodhouse's health, cheerful communications about her mother's, and sweet-cake from the beaufet[58] — "Mrs. Cole had just been there, just called in for ten minutes, and had been so good as to sit an hour with them, and *she* had taken a piece of cake and been so kind as to say she liked it very much; and therefore she hoped Miss Woodhouse and Miss Smith would do them the favour to eat a piece too."

The mention of the Coles was sure to be followed by that of Mr. Elton. There was intimacy between them, and Mr. Cole had heard from Mr. Elton since his going away. Emma knew what was coming; they must have the letter over again, and settle how long he had been gone, and how much he was engaged in company, and what a favourite he was wherever he went, and how full the Master of the Ceremonies' ball had been; and she went through it very well, with all the interest and all the commendation that could be requisite, and always putting forward to prevent Harriet's being obliged to say a word.

This she had been prepared for when she entered the house; but meant, having once talked him handsomely over, to be no farther incommoded by any troublesome topic, and to wander at large amongst all the Mistresses and Misses of Highbury and their card-parties. She had not been prepared to have Jane Fairfax succeed Mr. Elton; but he was actually hurried off by Miss Bates, she jumped away from him at last abruptly to the Coles, to usher in a letter from her niece.

"Oh! yes — Mr. Elton, I understood — certainly as to dancing — Mrs. Cole was telling me that dancing at the rooms at Bath was —— Mrs. Cole was so kind as to sit some time with us, talking of Jane; for as

[58] *beaufet:* Sideboard.

soon as she came in, she began inquiring after her, Jane is so very great a favourite there. Whenever she is with us, Mrs. Cole does not know how to shew her kindness enough; and I must say that Jane deserves it as much as anybody can. And so she began inquiring after her directly, saying, 'I know you cannot have heard from Jane lately, because it is not her time for writing;' and when I immediately said, 'But indeed we have, we had a letter this very morning,' I do not know that I ever saw anybody more surprized. 'Have you, upon your honour!' said she; 'well, that is quite unexpected. Do let me hear what she says.'"

Emma's politeness was at hand directly, to say, with smiling interest —

"Have you heard from Miss Fairfax so lately? I am extremely happy. I hope she is well?"

"Thank you. You are so kind!" replied the happily deceived aunt, while eagerly hunting for the letter. — "Oh! here it is. I was sure it could not be far off; but I had put my huswife[59] upon it, you see, without being aware, and so it was quite hid, but I had it in my hand so very lately that I was almost sure it must be on the table. I was reading it to Mrs. Cole, and since she went away, I was reading it again to my mother, for it is such a pleasure to her — a letter from Jane — that she can never hear it often enough; so I knew it could not be far off, and here it is, only just under my huswife — and since you are so kind as to wish to hear what she says; — but, first of all, I really must, in justice to Jane, apologise for her writing so short a letter — only two pages you see — hardly two — and in general she fills the whole paper and crosses half.[60] My mother often wonders that I can make it out so well. She often says, when the letter is first opened, 'Well, Hetty, now I think you will be put to it to make out all that chequer-work'[61] — don't you, ma'am? — And then I tell her, I am sure she would contrive to make it out herself, if she had nobody to do it for her — every word of it — I am sure she would pore over it till she had made out every word. And, indeed, though my mother's eyes are not so good as they were, she can see amazingly well still, thank God! with the help of spectacles. It is such a blessing! My mother's are really very good indeed. Jane often

---

[59]*huswife:* Container (usually cloth) for needles, pins, scissors, and thread.

[60]*fills the whole paper and crosses half:* To save on paper, letter writers would often turn the completed page ninety degrees and "cross" (i.e., write across) their handwriting. See "Contextual Documents," p. 398, for an example of a crossed letter by Jane Austen to her sister Cassandra.

[61]*chequer-work:* Pattern suggestive of the squares on a chessboard.

says, when she is here, 'I am sure, grandmama, you must have had very
strong eyes to see as you do — and so much fine work as you have done
too! — I only wish my eyes may last me as well.'"

All this spoken extremely fast obliged Miss Bates to stop for breath;
and Emma said something very civil about the excellence of Miss Fairfax's handwriting.

"You are extremely kind," replied Miss Bates highly gratified; "you
who are such a judge, and write so beautifully yourself. I am sure there
is nobody's praise that could give us so much pleasure as Miss Woodhouse's. My mother does not hear; she is a little deaf you know.
Ma'am," addressing her, "do you hear what Miss Woodhouse is so
obliging to say about Jane's handwriting?"

And Emma had the advantage of hearing her own silly compliment
repeated twice over before the good old lady could comprehend it. She
was pondering, in the mean while, upon the possibility, without seeming very rude, of making her escape from Jane Fairfax's letter, and had
almost resolved on hurrying away directly under some slight excuse,
when Miss Bates turned to her again and seized her attention.

"My mother's deafness is very trifling you see — just nothing at all.
By only raising my voice, and saying anything two or three times over,
she is sure to hear; but then she is used to my voice. But it is very
remarkable that she should always hear Jane better than she does me.
Jane speaks so distinct! However, she will not find her grandmama at all
deafer than she was two years ago; which is saying a great deal at my
mother's time of life — and it really is full two years, you know, since
she was here. We never were so long without seeing her before, and as
I was telling Mrs. Cole, we shall hardly know how to make enough of
her now."

"Are you expecting Miss Fairfax here soon?"

"Oh, yes; next week."

"Indeed! — That must be a very great pleasure."

"Thank you. You are very kind. Yes, next week. Every body is so
surprized; and every body says the same obliging things. I am sure she
will be as happy to see her friends at Highbury, as they can be to see her.
Yes, Friday or Saturday; she cannot say which, because Colonel Campbell will be wanting the carriage himself one of those days. So very
good of them to send her the whole way! But they always do, you
know. Oh, yes, Friday or Saturday next. That is what she writes about.
That is the reason of her writing out of rule, as we call it; for, in the
common course, we should not have heard from her before next Tuesday or Wednesday."

"Yes, so I imagined. I was afraid there could be little chance of my hearing any thing of Miss Fairfax to-day."

"So obliging of you! No, we should not have heard, if it had not been for this particular circumstance, of her being to come here so soon. My mother is so delighted! — for she is to be three months with us at least. Three months, she says so, positively, as I am going to have the pleasure of reading to you. The case is, you see, that the Campbells are going to Ireland. Mrs. Dixon has persuaded her father and mother to come over and see her directly. They had not intended to go over till the summer, but she is so impatient to see them again — for till she married, last October, she was never away from them so much as a week, which must make it very strange to be in different kingdoms, I was going to say, but however different countries,[62] and so she wrote a very urgent letter to her mother — or her father, I declare I do not know which it was, but we shall see presently in Jane's letter — wrote in Mr. Dixon's name as well as her own, to press their coming over directly, and they would give them the meeting in Dublin, and take them back to their country-seat, Baly-craig, a beautiful place, I fancy. Jane has heard a great deal of its beauty; from Mr. Dixon I mean — I do not know that she ever heard about it from any body else; but it was very natural, you know, that he should like to speak of his own place while he was paying his addresses — and as Jane used to be very often walking out with them — for Colonel and Mrs. Campbell were very particular about their daughter's not walking out often with only Mr. Dixon, for which I do not at all blame them; of course she heard every-thing he might be telling Miss Campbell about his own home in Ire-land. And I think she wrote us word that he had shewn them some drawings of the place, views that he had taken himself. He is a most amiable, charming young man, I believe. Jane was quite longing to go to Ireland, from his account of things."

At this moment, an ingenious and animating suspicion entering Emma's brain with regard to Jane Fairfax, this charming Mr. Dixon, and the not going to Ireland, she said, with the insidious design of fur-ther discovery,

"You must feel it very fortunate that Miss Fairfax should be allowed to come to you at such a time. Considering the very particular friend-ship between her and Mrs. Dixon, you could hardly have expected her to be excused from accompanying Colonel and Mrs. Campbell."

[62] *different kingdoms, I was going to say, but however different countries:* By the Act of Union (1800), Great Britain and Ireland were joined under a common King, parlia-ment, and flag.

"Very true, very true, indeed. The very thing that we have always been rather afraid of; for we should not have liked to have her at such a distance from us, for months together — not able to come if any thing was to happen. But you see, every thing turns out for the best. They want her (Mr. and Mrs. Dixon) excessively to come over with Colonel and Mrs. Campbell; quite depend upon it; nothing can be more kind or pressing than their *joint* invitation, Jane says, as you will hear presently; Mr. Dixon does not seem in the least backward in any attention. He is a most charming young man. Ever since the service he rendered Jane at Weymouth, when they were out in that party on the water, and she, by the sudden whirling round of something or other among the sails, would have been dashed into the sea at once, and actually was all but gone, if he had not, with the greatest presence of mind, caught hold of her habit — (I can never think of it without trembling!) — But ever since we had the history of that day, I have been so fond of Mr. Dixon!"

"But, in spite of all her friend's urgency, and her own wish of seeing Ireland, Miss Fairfax prefers devoting the time to you and Mrs. Bates?"

"Yes — entirely her own doing, entirely her own choice; and Colonel and Mrs. Campbell think she does quite right, just what they should recommend; and indeed they particularly *wish* her to try her native air, as she has not been quite so well as usual lately."

"I am concerned to hear of it. I think they judge wisely. But Mrs. Dixon must be very much disappointed. Mrs. Dixon, I understand, has no remarkable degree of personal beauty; is not, by any means, to be compared with Miss Fairfax."

"Oh! no. You are very obliging to say such things — but certainly not. There is no comparison between them. Miss Campbell always was absolutely plain — but extremely elegant and amiable."

"Yes, that of course."

"Jane caught a bad cold, poor thing! so long ago as the 7th of November, (as I am going to read to you,) and has never been well since. A long time, is not it, for a cold to hang upon her? She never mentioned it before, because she would not alarm us. Just like her! so considerate! — But however, she is so far from well, that her kind friends the Campbells think she had better come home, and try an air that always agrees with her; and they have no doubt that three or four months at Highbury will entirely cure her — and it is certainly a great deal better that she should come here, than go to Ireland, if she is unwell. Nobody could nurse her, as we should do."

"It appears to me the most desirable arrangement in the world."

"And so she is to come to us next Friday or Saturday, and the Campbells leave town in their way to Holyhead[63] the Monday following — as you will find from Jane's letter. So sudden! — You may guess, dear Miss Woodhouse, what a flurry it has thrown me in! If it was not for the drawback of her illness — but I am afraid we must expect to see her grown thin, and looking very poorly. I must tell you what an unlucky thing happened to me, as to that. I always make a point of reading Jane's letters through to myself first, before I read them aloud to my mother, you know, for fear of there being any thing in them to distress her. Jane desired me to do it, so I always do: and so I began to-day with my usual caution; but no sooner did I come to the mention of her being unwell, than I burst out quite frightened with, 'Bless me! poor Jane is ill!' — which my mother, being on the watch, heard distinctly, and was sadly alarmed at. However, when I read on, I found it was not near so bad as I fancied at first; and I make so light of it now to her, that she does not think much about it. But I cannot imagine how I could be so off my guard! If Jane does not get well soon, we will call in Mr. Perry. The expense shall not be thought of; and though he is so liberal, and so fond of Jane that I dare say he would not mean to charge anything for attendance, we could not suffer it to be so, you know. He has a wife and family to maintain, and is not to be giving away his time. Well, now I have just given you a hint of what Jane writes about, we will turn to her letter, and I am sure she tells her own story a great deal better than I can tell it for her."

"I am afraid we must be running away," said Emma, glancing at Harriet, and beginning to rise — "My father will be expecting us. I had no intention, I thought I had no power of staying more than five minutes, when I first entered the house. I merely called, because I would not pass the door without inquiring after Mrs. Bates; but I have been so pleasantly detained! Now, however, we must wish you and Mrs. Bates good morning."

And not all that could be urged to detain her succeeded. She regained the street — happy in this, that though much had been forced on her against her will, though she had in fact heard the whole substance of Jane Fairfax's letter, she had been able to escape the letter itself.

---

[63] *Holyhead:* Port in north Wales used by travelers to and from Ireland.

CHAPTER II.

JANE FAIRFAX was an orphan, the only child of Mrs. Bates's youngest daughter.

The marriage of Lieut. Fairfax, of the —— regiment of infantry,[64] and Miss Jane Bates, had had its day of fame and pleasure, hope and interest; but nothing now remained of it, save the melancholy remembrance of him dying in action abroad — of his widow sinking under consumption and grief soon afterwards — and this girl.

By birth she belonged to Highbury: and when at three years old, on losing her mother, she became the property, the charge, the consolation, the fondling of her grandmother and aunt, there had seemed every probability of her being permanently fixed there; of her being taught only what very limited means could command, and growing up with no advantages of connection or improvement to be engrafted on what nature had given her in a pleasing person, good understanding, and warm-hearted, well meaning relations.

But the compassionate feelings of a friend of her father gave a change to her destiny. This was Colonel Campbell, who had very highly regarded Fairfax, as an excellent officer and most deserving young man; and farther, had been indebted to him for such attentions, during a severe camp-fever, as he believed had saved his life. These were claims which he did not learn to overlook, though some years passed away from the death of poor Fairfax, before his own return to England put any thing in his power. When he did return, he sought out the child and took notice of her. He was a married man, with only one living child, a girl, about Jane's age: and Jane became their guest, paying them long visits and growing a favourite with all; and, before she was nine years old, his daughter's great fondness for her, and his own wish of being a real friend, united to produce an offer from Colonel Campbell of undertaking the whole charge of her education. It was accepted; and from that period Jane had belonged to Colonel Campbell's family, and had lived with them entirely, only visiting her grandmother from time to time.

The plan was that she should be brought up for educating others; the very few hundred pounds which she inherited from her father making independence impossible. To provide for her otherwise was out of Colonel Campbell's power; for though his income, by pay and appoint-

---

[64]*the* —— *regiment of infantry:* The blank here is a convention inherited from eighteenth-century fiction, the effect of which is to imply a real name withheld out of tact or discretion.

ments, was handsome, his fortune was moderate and must be all his daughter's; but, by giving her an education, he hoped to be supplying the means of respectable subsistance hereafter.

Such was Jane Fairfax's history. She had fallen into good hands, known nothing but kindness from the Campbells, and been given an excellent education. Living constantly with right-minded and well-informed people, her heart and understanding had received every advantage of discipline and culture; and Col. Campbell's residence being in London, every lighter talent had been done full justice to, by the attendance of first-rate masters. Her disposition and abilities were equally worthy of all that friendship could do; and at eighteen or nineteen she was, as far as such an early age can be qualified for the care of children, fully competent to the office of instruction herself; but she was too much beloved to be parted with. Neither father nor mother could promote, and the daughter could not endure it. The evil day was put off. It was easy to decide that she was still too young; and Jane remained with them, sharing, as another daughter, in all the rational pleasures of an elegant society, and a judicious mixture of home and amusement, with only the drawback of the future, the sobering suggestions of her own good understanding to remind her that all this might soon be over.

The affection of the whole family, the warm attachment of Miss Campbell in particular, was the more honourable to each party from the circumstance of Jane's decided superiority both in beauty and acquirements. That nature had given it in feature could not be unseen by the young woman, nor could her higher powers of mind be unfelt by the parents. They continued together with unabated regard however, till the marriage of Miss Campbell, who by that chance, that luck which so often defies anticipation in matrimonial affairs, giving attraction to what is moderate rather than to what is superior, engaged the affections of Mr. Dixon, a young man, rich and agreeable, almost as soon as they were acquainted; and was eligibly and happily settled, while Jane Fairfax had yet her bread to earn.

This event had very lately taken place; too lately for any thing to be yet attempted by her less fortunate friend towards entering on her path of duty; though she had now reached the age which her own judgment had fixed on for beginning. She had long resolved that one-and-twenty should be the period. With the fortitude of a devoted noviciate, she had resolved at one-and-twenty to complete the sacrifice, and retire from all the pleasures of life, of rational intercourse, equal society, peace and hope, to penance and mortification for ever.

The good sense of Colonel and Mrs. Campbell could not oppose such a resolution, though their feelings did. As long as they lived, no exertions would be necessary, their home might be her's for ever; and for their own comfort they would have retained her wholly; but this would be selfishness: — what must be at last, had better be soon. Perhaps they began to feel it might have been kinder and wiser to have resisted the temptation of any delay, and spared her from a taste of such enjoyments of ease and leisure as must now be relinquished. Still, however, affection was glad to catch at any reasonable excuse for not hurrying on the wretched moment. She had never been quite well since the time of their daughter's marriage; and till she should have completely recovered her usual strength, they must forbid her engaging in duties, which, so far from being compatible with a weakened frame and varying spirits, seemed, under the most favourable circumstances, to require something more than human perfection of body and mind to be discharged with tolerable comfort.

With regard to her not accompanying them to Ireland, her account to her aunt contained nothing but truth, though there might be some truths not told. It was her own choice to give the time of their absence to Highbury; to spend, perhaps, her last months of perfect liberty with those kind relations to whom she was so very dear: and the Campbells, whatever might be their motive or motives, whether single, or double, or treble, gave the arrangement their ready sanction, and said, that they depended more on a few months spent in her native air, for the recovery of her health, than on any thing else. Certain it was that she was to come; and that Highbury, instead of welcoming that perfect novelty which had been so long promised it — Mr. Frank Churchill — must put up for the present with Jane Fairfax, who could bring only the freshness of a two years absence.

Emma was sorry; — to have to pay civilities to a person she did not like through three long months! — to be always doing more than she wished, and less than she ought! Why she did not like Jane Fairfax might be a difficult question to answer; Mr. Knightley had once told her it was because she saw in her the really accomplished young woman, which she wanted to be thought herself; and though the accusation had been eagerly refuted at the time, there were moments of self-examination in which her conscience could not quite acquit her. But "she could never get acquainted with her: she did not know how it was, but there was such coldness and reserve — such apparent indifference whether she pleased or not — and then, her aunt was such an eternal talker! — and she was made such a fuss with by every body! — and it had been always imagined that they were to be so intimate — because their ages were the same, every body had supposed they must be so fond of each other." There were her reasons — she had no better.

It was a dislike so little just — every imputed fault was so magnified by fancy, that she never saw Jane Fairfax the first time after any considerable absence, without feeling that she had injured her; and now, when the due visit was paid, on her arrival, after a two years' interval, she was particularly struck with the very appearance and manners, which for those two whole years she had been depreciating. Jane Fairfax was very elegant, remarkably elegant; and she had herself the highest value for elegance. Her height was pretty, just such as almost everybody would think tall, and nobody could think very tall; her figure particularly graceful; her size a most becoming medium, between fat and thin, though a slight appearance of ill-health seemed to point out the likeliest evil of the two. Emma could not but feel all this; and then, her face — her features — there was more beauty in them all together than she had remembered; it was not regular, but it was very pleasing beauty. Her eyes, a deep grey, with dark eye-lashes and eye-brows, had never been denied their praise; but the skin, which she had been used to cavil at, as wanting colour, had a clearness and delicacy which really needed no fuller bloom. It was a style of beauty, of which elegance was the reigning character, and as such, she must, in honour, by all her principles, admire it: — elegance, which, whether of person or of mind, she saw so little in Highbury. There, not to be vulgar, was distinction, and merit.

In short, she sat, during the first visit, looking at Jane Fairfax with two-fold complacency; the sense of pleasure and the sense of rendering justice, and was determining that she would dislike her no longer. When she took in her history, indeed, her situation, as well as her beauty; when she considered what all this elegance was destined to, what she was going to sink from, how she as going to live, it seemed impossible to feel any thing but compassion and respect; especially, if to every well-known particular entitling her to interest, were added the highly probable circumstance of an attachment to Mr. Dixon, which she had so naturally started to herself. In that case, nothing could be more pitiable or more honourable than the sacrifices she had resolved on. Emma was very willing now to acquit her of having seduced Mr. Dixon's affections from his wife, or of any thing mischievous which her imagination had suggested at first. If it were love, it might be simple, single, successless love on her side alone. She might have been unconsciously sucking in the sad poison, while a sharer of his conversation with her friend; and from the best, the purest of motives, might now be denying herself this visit to Ireland, and resolving to divide herself effectually from him and his connections by soon beginning her career of laborious duty.

Upon the whole, Emma left her with such softened, charitable feelings, as made her look around in walking home, and lament that Highbury afforded no young man worthy of giving her independence; nobody that she could wish to scheme about for her.

These were charming feelings — but not lasting. Before she had committed herself by any public profession of eternal friendship for Jane Fairfax, or done more towards a recantation of past prejudices and errors, than saying to Mr. Knightley, "She certainly is handsome; she is better than handsome!" Jane had spent an evening at Hartfield with her grandmother and aunt, and every thing was relapsing much into its usual state. Former provocations re-appeared. The aunt was as tiresome as ever; more tiresome, because anxiety for her health was now added to admiration of her powers; and they had to listen to the description of exactly how little bread and butter she ate for breakfast, and how small a slice of mutton for dinner, as well as to see exhibitions of new caps and new work-bags for her mother and herself; and Jane's offences rose again. They had music; Emma was obliged to play; and the thanks and praise which necessarily followed appeared to her an affectation of candour, an air of greatness, meaning only to shew off in higher style her own very superior performance. She was, besides, which was the worst of all, so cold, so cautious! There was no getting at her real opinion. Wrapt up in a cloak of politeness, she seemed determined to hazard nothing. She was disgustingly, was suspiciously reserved.

If any thing could be more, where all was most, she was more reserved on the subject of Weymouth and the Dixons than any thing. She seemed bent on giving no real insight into Mr. Dixon's character, or her own value for his company, or opinion of the suitableness of the match. It was all general approbation and smoothness; nothing delineated or distinguished. It did her no service however. Her caution was thrown away. Emma saw its artifice, and returned to her first surmises. There probably *was* something more to conceal than her own preference; Mr. Dixon, perhaps, had been very near changing one friend for the other, or been fixed only to Miss Campbell, for the sake of the future twelve thousand pounds.

The like reserve prevailed on other topics. She and Mr. Frank Churchill had been at Weymouth at the same time. It was known that they were a little acquainted; but not a syllable of real information could Emma procure as to what he truly was. "Was he handsome?" —

"She believed he was reckoned a very fine young man." "Was he agreeable?" — "He was generally thought so." "Did he appear a sensible young man; a young man of information?" — "At a watering-place, or in a common London acquaintance, it was difficult to decide on such points. Manners were all that could be safely judged of, under a much longer knowledge than they had yet had of Mr. Churchill. She believed every body found his manners pleasing." Emma could not forgive her.

CHAPTER III.

EMMA could not forgive her; — but as neither provocation nor resentment were discerned by Mr. Knightley, who had been of the party, and had seen only proper attention and pleasing behaviour on each side, he was expressing the next morning, being at Hartfield again on business with Mr. Woodhouse, his approbation of the whole; not so openly as he might have done had her father been out of the room, but speaking plain enough to be very intelligible to Emma. He had been used to think her unjust to Jane, and had now great pleasure in marking an improvement.

"A very pleasant evening," he began, as soon as Mr. Woodhouse had been talked into what was necessary, told that he understood, and the papers swept away; — "particularly pleasant. You and Miss Fairfax gave us some very good music. I do not know a more luxurious state, sir, than sitting at one's ease to be entertained a whole evening by two such young women; sometimes with music and sometimes with conversation. I am sure Miss Fairfax must have found the evening pleasant, Emma. You left nothing undone. I was glad you made her play so much, for having no instrument at her grandmother's, it must have been a real indulgence."

"I am happy you approved," said Emma, smiling; "but I hope I am not often deficient in what is due to guests at Hartfield."

"No, my dear," said her father instantly; "*that* I am sure you are not. There is nobody half so attentive and civil as you are. If any thing, you are too attentive. The muffin[65] last night — if it had been handed round once, I think it would have been enough."

"No," said Mr. Knightley, nearly at the same time; "you are not often deficient; not often deficient either in manner or comprehension. I think you understand me, therefore."

[65] *muffin:* Light, flat, circular, spongy cake, eaten toasted and buttered at breakfast or tea (*OED*).

An arch look expressed — "I understand you well enough;" but she said only, "Miss Fairfax is reserved."

"I always told you she was — a little; but you will soon overcome all that part of her reserve which ought to be overcome, all that has its foundation in diffidence. What arises from discretion must be honoured."

"You think her diffident. I do not see it."

"My dear Emma," said, he, moving from his chair into one close by her, "you are not going to tell me, I hope, that you had not a pleasant evening."

"Oh! no; I was pleased with my own perseverance in asking questions, and amused to think how little information I obtained."

"I am disappointed," was his only answer.

"I hope every body had a pleasant evening," said Mr. Woodhouse, in his quiet way. "I had. Once, I felt the fire rather too much; but then I moved back my chair a little, a very little, and it did not disturb me. Miss Bates was very chatty and good-humoured, as she always is, though she speaks rather too quick. However, she is very agreeable, and Mrs. Bates too, in a different way. I like old friends; and Miss Jane Fairfax is a very pretty sort of young lady, a very pretty and a very well-behaved young lady indeed. She must have found the evening agreeable, Mr. Knightley, because she had Emma."

"True, sir; and Emma, because she had Miss Fairfax."

Emma saw his anxiety, and wishing to appease it, at least for the present, said, and with a sincerity which no one could question —

"She is a sort of elegant creature that one cannot keep one's eyes from. I am always watching her to admire; and I do pity her from my heart."

Mr. Knightley looked as if he were more gratified than he cared to express; and before he could make any reply, Mr. Woodhouse, whose thoughts were on the Bates's, said —

"It is a great pity that their circumstances should be so confined! a great pity indeed! and I have often wished — but it is so little one can venture to do — small, trifling presents, of any thing uncommon — Now we have killed a porker, and Emma thinks of sending them a loin or a leg; it is very small and delicate — Hartfield pork is not like any other pork — but still it is pork — and, my dear Emma, unless one could be sure of their making it into steaks, nicely fried, as our's are fried, without the smallest grease, and not roast it, for no stomach can bear roast pork — I think we had better send the leg — do not you think so, my dear?"

"My dear papa, I sent the whole hind-quarter. I knew you would wish it. There will be the leg to be salted, you know, which is so very nice, and the loin to be dressed directly in any manner they like."

"That's right, my dear, very right. I had not thought of it before, but that was the best way. They must not over-salt the leg; and then, if it is not over-salted, and if it is very thoroughly boiled, just as Serle boils our's, and eaten very moderately of, with a boiled turnip, and a little carrot or parsnip, I do not consider it unwholesome."

"Emma," said Mr. Knightley presently, "I have a piece of news for you. You like news — and I heard an article in my way hither that I think will interest you."

"News! Oh! yes, I always like news. What is it? — why do you smile so? — where did you hear it? — at Randalls?"

He had time only to say,

"No, not at Randalls; I have not been near Randalls,"

When the door was thrown open, and Miss Bates and Miss Fairfax walked into the room. Full of thanks, and full of news, Miss Bates knew not which to give quickest. Mr. Knightley soon saw that he had lost his moment, and that not another syllable of communication could rest with him.

"Oh! my dear sir, how are you this morning? My dear Miss Woodhouse — I come quite overpowered. Such a beautiful hind-quarter of pork! You are too bountiful! Have you heard the news? Mr. Elton is going to be married."

Emma had not had time even to think of Mr. Elton, and she was so completely surprised that she could not avoid a little start, and a little blush, at the sound.

"There is my news — I thought it would interest you," said Mr. Knightley, with a smile which implied a conviction of some part of what had passed between them.

"But where could you hear it?" cried Miss Bates. "Where could you possibly hear it, Mr. Knightley? For it is not five minutes since I received Mrs. Cole's note — no, it cannot be more than five — or at least ten — for I had got my bonnet and spencer[66] on, just ready to come out — I was only gone down to speak to Patty again about the pork — Jane was standing in the passage — were not you, Jane? — for my mother was so afraid that we had not any salting-pan large enough. So I said I would go down and see, and Jane said, 'Shall I go down instead? for I think you have a little cold, and Patty has been washing the kitchen.'

[66]*spencer:* Short, close-fitting coat (named after George John, second earl Spencer).

Oh! my dear, said I[67] — well, and just then came the note. A Miss Hawkins — that's all I know. A Miss Hawkins of Bath. But, Mr. Knightley, how could you possibly have heard it? for the very moment Mr. Cole told Mrs. Cole of it, she sat down and wrote to me. A Miss Hawkins" —

"I was with Mr. Cole on business an hour and half ago. He had just read Elton's letter as I was shewn in, and handed it to me directly."

"Well! that is quite —— I suppose there never was a piece of news more generally interesting. My dear sir, you really are too bountiful. My mother desires her very best compliments and regards, and a thousand thanks, and says you really quite oppress her."

"We consider our Hartfield pork," replied Mr. Woodhouse — "indeed it certainly is, so very superior to all other pork, that Emma and I cannot have a greater pleasure than" —

"Oh! my dear sir, as my mother says, our friends are only too good to us. If ever there were people who, without having great wealth themselves, had every thing they could wish for, I am sure it is us. We may well say that 'our lot is cast in a goodly heritage.'[68] Well, Mr. Knightley, and so you actually saw the letter; well" —

"It was short, merely to announce — but cheerful, exulting, of course." — Here was a sly glance at Emma. "He had been so fortunate as to — I forget the precise words — one has no business to remember them. The information was, as you state, that he was going to be married to a Miss Hawkins. By his style, I should imagine it just settled."

"Mr. Elton going to be married!" said Emma, as soon as she could speak. "He will have everybody's wishes for his happiness."

"He is very young to settle," was Mr. Woodhouse's observation. "He had better not be in a hurry. He seemed to me very well off as he was. We were always glad to see him at Hartfield."

"A new neighbour for us all, Miss Woodhouse!" said Miss Bates, joyfully; "my mother is so pleased! — she says she cannot bear to have the poor old Vicarage without a mistress. This is great news, indeed. Jane, you have never seen Mr. Elton! — no wonder that you have such a curiosity to see him."

Jane's curiosity did not appear of that absorbing nature as wholly to occupy her.

[67] *Oh! My dear, said I:* Emendation of the first edition, which has double opening quotes before "Oh!"

[68] *'our lot is cast in a goodly heritage':* Recalls the language of Psalm 16.7 in the *Book of Common Prayer.*

"No — I have never seen Mr. Elton," she replied, starting on this appeal; "is he — is he a tall man?"

"Who shall answer that question?" cried Emma. "My father would say 'yes,' Mr. Knightley, 'no;' and Miss Bates and I that he is just the happy medium. When you have been here a little longer, Miss Fairfax, you will understand that Mr. Elton is the standard of perfection in Highbury, both in person and mind."

"Very true, Miss Woodhouse, so she will. He is the very best young man — But, my dear Jane, if you remember, I told you yesterday he was precisely the height of Mr. Perry. Miss Hawkins, — I dare say, an excellent young woman. His extreme attention to my mother — wanting her to sit in the vicarage-pew, that she might hear the better, for my mother is a little deaf, you know — it is not much, but she does not hear quite quick. Jane says that Colonel Campbell is a little deaf. He fancied bathing might be good for it — the warm bath — but she says it did him no lasting benefit. Colonel Campbell, you know, is quite our angel. And Mr. Dixon seems a very charming young man, quite worthy of him. It is such a happiness when good people get together — and they always do. Now, here will be Mr. Elton and Miss Hawkins; and there are the Coles, such very good people; and the Perrys — I suppose there never was a happier or a better couple than Mr. and Mrs. Perry. I say, sir," turning to Mr. Woodhouse, "I think there are few places with such society as Highbury. I always say, we are quite blessed in our neighbours. — My dear sir, if there is one thing my mother loves better than another, it is pork — a roast loin of pork" —

"As to who, or what Miss Hawkins is, or how long he has been acquainted with her," said Emma, "nothing I suppose can be known. One feels that it cannot be a very long acquaintance. He has been gone only four weeks."

Nobody had any information to give; and, after a few more wonderings, Emma said,

"You are silent, Miss Fairfax — but I hope you mean to take an interest in this news. You, who have been hearing and seeing so much of late on these subjects, who must have been so deep in the business on Miss Campbell's account — we shall not excuse your being indifferent about Mr. Elton and Miss Hawkins."

"When I have seen Mr. Elton," replied Jane, "I dare say I shall be interested — but I believe it requires *that* with me. And as it is some months since Miss Campbell married, the impression may be a little worn off."

"Yes, he has been gone just four weeks, as you observe, Miss Woodhouse," said Miss Bates, "four weeks yesterday. — A Miss Hawkins. —
Well, I had always rather fancied it would be some young lady hereabouts; not that I ever —— Mrs. Cole once whispered to me — but
I immediately said, 'No, Mr. Elton is a most worthy young man —
but' —— In short, I do not think I am particularly quick at those sort
of discoveries. I do not pretend to it. What is before me, I see. At the
same time, nobody could wonder if Mr. Elton should have aspired ——
Miss Woodhouse lets me chatter on, so good-humouredly. She knows I
would not offend for the world. How does Miss Smith do? She seems
quite recovered now. Have you heard from Mrs. John Knightley lately?
Oh! those dear little children. Jane, do you know I always fancy Mr.
Dixon like Mr. John Knightley? I mean in person — tall, and with that
sort of look — and not very talkative."

"Quite wrong, my dear aunt; there is no likeness at all."

"Very odd! but one never does form a just idea of any body beforehand. One takes up a notion, and runs away with it. Mr. Dixon, you say,
is not, strictly speaking, handsome."

"Handsome! Oh! no — far from it — certainly plain. I told you he
was plain."

"My dear, you said that Miss Campbell would not allow him to be
plain, and that you yourself —"

"Oh! as for me, my judgment is worth nothing. Where I have a
regard, I always think a person well-looking. But I gave what I believed
the general opinion, when I called him plain."

"Well, my dear Jane, I believe we must be running away. The
weather does not look well, and grandmamma will be uneasy. You are
too obliging, my dear Miss Woodhouse; but we really must take leave.
This has been a most agreeable piece of news indeed. I shall just go
round by Mrs. Cole's; but I shall not stop three minutes: and, Jane,
you had better go home directly — I would not have you out in a
shower! — We think she is the better for Highbury already. Thank you,
we do indeed. I shall not attempt calling on Mrs. Goddard, for I really
do not think she cares for any thing but *boiled* pork: when we dress the
leg it will be another thing. Good morning to you, my dear sir. Oh! Mr.
Knightley is coming too. Well, that is so very! — I am sure if Jane is
tired, you will be so kind as to give her your arm. — Mr. Elton, and
Miss Hawkins. — Good morning to you."

Emma, alone with her father, had half her attention wanted by him,
while he lamented that young people would be in such a hurry to
marry — and to marry strangers too — and the other half she could

give to her own view of the subject. It was to herself an amusing and a very welcome piece of news, as proving that Mr. Elton could not have suffered long; but she was sorry for Harriet: Harriet must feel it — and all that she could hope was, by giving the first information herself, to save her from hearing it abruptly from others. It was now about the time that she was likely to call. If she were to meet Miss Bates in her way! — and upon its beginning to rain, Emma was obliged to expect that the weather would be detaining her at Mrs. Goddard's, and that the intelligence would undoubtedly rush upon her without preparation.

The shower was heavy, but short; and it had not been over five minutes, when in came Harriet, with just the heated, agitated look which hurrying thither with a full heart was likely to give; and the "Oh! Miss Woodhouse, what do you think has happened!" which instantly burst forth, had all the evidence of corresponding perturbation. As the blow was given, Emma felt that she could not now shew greater kindness than in listening; and Harriet, unchecked, ran eagerly through what she had to tell. "She had set out from Mrs. Goddard's half an hour ago — she had been afraid it would rain — she had been afraid it would pour down every moment — but she thought she might get to Hartfield first — she had hurried on as fast as possible; but then, as she was passing by the house where a young woman was making up a gown for her, she thought she would just step in and see how it went on; and though she did not seem to stay half a moment there, soon after she came out it began to rain, and she did not know what to do; so she ran on directly, as fast as she could, and took shelter at Ford's." — Ford's was the principal woollen-draper, linen-draper, and haberdasher's shop[69] united; the shop first in size and fashion in the place. — "And so, there she had set,[70] without an idea of any thing in the world, full ten minutes, perhaps — where, all of a sudden, who should come in — to be sure it was so very odd! — but they always dealt at Ford's — who should come in, but Elizabeth Martin and her brother! — Dear Miss Woodhouse! only think. I thought I should have fainted. I did not know what to do. I was sitting near the door — Elizabeth saw me directly; but he did not; he was busy with the umbrella. I am sure she saw me, but she looked away directly, and took no notice; and they both went to quite the farther end of the shop; and I kept sitting near the door! — Oh! dear; I was so miserable! I am sure I must have been as white as my gown. I could not

---

[69] *woollen-draper, linen-draper, and haberdasher's shop:* Shop combining retail dealing in, respectively, cloth, linen, and articles pertaining to dress, such as thread, tape, and ribbons.

[70] *there she had set:* An instance of Harriet's imperfect grammar.

go away you know, because of the rain; but I did so wish myself any where in the world but there. — Oh! dear, Miss Woodhouse — well, at last, I fancy, he looked round and saw me; for instead of going on with their buyings, they began whispering to one another. I am sure they were talking of me; and I could not help thinking that he was persuading her to speak to me — (do you think he was, Miss Woodhouse?) — for presently she came forward — came quite up to me, and asked me how I did, and seemed ready to shake hands, if I would. She did not do any of it in the same way that she used; I could see she was altered; but, however, she seemed to *try* to be very friendly, and we shook hands, and stood talking some time; but I know no more what I said — I was in such a tremble! — I remember she said she was sorry we never met now; which I thought almost too kind! Dear, Miss Woodhouse, I was absolutely miserable! By that time, it was beginning to hold up, and I was determined that nothing should stop me from getting away — and then — only think! — I found he was coming up towards me too — slowly you know, and as if he did not quite know what to do; and so he came and spoke, and I answered — and I stood for a minute, feeling dreadfully, you know, one can't tell how; and then I took courage, and said it did not rain, and I must go: and so off I set; and I had not got three yards from the door, when he came after me, only to say, if I was going to Hartfield, he thought I had much better go round by Mr. Cole's stables, for I should find the near way quite floated by this rain. Oh! dear, I thought it would have been the death of me! So I said, I was very much obliged to him: you know I could not do less; and then he went back to Elizabeth, and I came round by the stables — I believe I did — but I hardly knew where I was, or any thing about it. Oh! Miss Woodhouse, I would rather done any thing[71] than have had it happen: and yet, you know, there was a sort of satisfaction in seeing him behave so pleasantly and so kindly. And Elizabeth, too. Oh! Miss Woodhouse, do talk to me and make me comfortable again."

Very sincerely did Emma wish to do so; but it was not immediately in her power. She was obliged to stop and think. She was not thoroughly comfortable herself. The young man's conduct, and his sister's, seemed the result of real feeling, and she could not but pity them. As Harriet described it, there had been an interesting mixture of wounded affection and genuine delicacy in their behaviour. But she had believed them to be well meaning, worthy people before; and what difference did this make in the evils of the connection? It was folly to be disturbed

---

[71] *I would rather done any thing:* Another instance of imperfect grammar.

by it. Of course, he must be sorry to lose her — they must be all sorry. Ambition, as well as love, had probably been mortified. They might all have hoped to rise by Harriet's acquaintance: and besides, what was the value of Harriet's description? — so easily pleased — so little discerning; — what signified her praise?

She exerted herself; and did try to make her comfortable, by considering all that had passed as a mere trifle, and quite unworthy of being dwelt on.

"It might be distressing, for the moment," said she; "but you seem to have behaved extremely well; and it is over — and may never — can never, as a first meeting, occur again, and therefore you need not think about it."

Harriet said, "very true;" and she "would not think about it;" but still she talked of it — still she could talk of nothing else; and Emma, at last, in order to put the Martins out of her head, was obliged to hurry on the news, which she had meant to give with so much tender caution; hardly knowing herself whether to rejoice or be angry, ashamed or only amused, at such a state of mind in poor Harriet — such a conclusion of Mr. Elton's importance with her!

Mr. Elton's rights, however, gradually revived. Though she did not feel the first intelligence as she might have done the day before, or an hour before, its interest soon increased; and before their first conversation was over, she had talked herself into all the sensations of curiosity, wonder and regret, pain and pleasure, as to this fortunate Miss Hawkins, which could conduce to place the Martins under proper subordination in her fancy.

Emma learned to be rather glad that there had been such a meeting. It had been serviceable in deadening the first shock, without retaining any influence to alarm. As Harriet now lived, the Martins could not get at her, without seeking her, where hitherto they had wanted either the courage or the condescension to seek her; for since her refusal of the brother, the sisters had never been at Mrs. Goddard's; and a twelvemonth might pass without their being thrown together again, with any necessity, or even any power of speech.

CHAPTER IV.

HUMAN nature is so well disposed towards those who are in interesting situations, that a young person, who either marries or dies, is sure of being kindly spoken of.

A week had not passed since Miss Hawkins's name was first mentioned in Highbury, before she was, by some means or other, discovered to have every recommendation of person and mind; to be handsome, elegant, highly accomplished, and perfectly amiable: and when Mr. Elton himself arrived to triumph in his happy prospects, and circulate the fame of her merits, there was very little more for him to do, than to tell her Christian name, and say whose music she principally played.

Mr. Elton returned, a very happy man. He had gone away rejected and mortified — disappointed in a very sanguine hope, after a series of what had appeared to him strong encouragement; and not only losing the right lady, but finding himself debased to the level of a very wrong one. He had gone away deeply offended — he came back engaged to another — and to another as superior, of course, to the first, as under such circumstances what is gained always is to what is lost. He came back gay and self-satisfied, eager and busy, caring nothing for Miss Woodhouse, and defying Miss Smith.

The charming Augusta Hawkins, in addition to all the usual advantages of perfect beauty and merit, was in possession of an independent fortune, of so many thousands as would always be called ten; a point of some dignity, as well as some convenience: the story told well; he had not thrown himself away — he had gained a woman of 10,000*l.* or thereabouts; and he had gained her with such delightful rapidity — the first hour of introduction had been so very soon followed by distinguishing notice; the history which he had to give Mrs. Cole of the rise and progress of the affair was so glorious — the steps so quick, from the accidental rencontre, to the dinner at Mr. Green's, and the party at Mrs. Brown's — smiles and blushes rising in importance — with consciousness and agitation richly scattered — the lady had been so easily impressed — so sweetly disposed — had in short, to use a most intelligible phrase, been so very ready to have him, that vanity and prudence were equally contented.

He had caught both substance and shadow — both fortune and affection, and was just the happy man he ought to be; talking only of himself and his own concerns — expecting to be congratulated — ready to be laughed at — and, with cordial, fearless smiles, now addressing all the young ladies of the place, to whom, a few weeks ago, he would have been more cautiously gallant.

The wedding was no distant event, as the parties had only themselves to please, and nothing but the necessary preparations to wait for; and when he set out for Bath again, there was a general expectation, which a certain glance of Mrs. Cole's did not seem to contradict, that when he next entered Highbury he would bring his bride.

During his present short stay, Emma had barely seen him; but just enough to feel that the first meeting was over, and to give her the impression of his not being improved by the mixture of pique and pretension, now spread over his air. She was, in fact, beginning very much to wonder that she had ever thought him pleasing at all; and his sight was so inseparably connected with some very disagreeable feelings, that except in a moral light, as a penance, a lesson, a source of profitable humiliation to her own mind, she would have been thankful to be assured of never seeing him again. She wished him very well; but he gave her pain, and his welfare twenty miles off would administer most satisfaction.

The pain of his continued residence in Highbury, however, must certainly be lessened by his marriage. Many vain solicitudes would be prevented — many awkwardnesses smoothed by it. A *Mrs. Elton* would be an excuse for any change of intercourse; former intimacy might sink without remark. It would be almost beginning their life of civility again.

Of the lady, individually, Emma thought very little. She was good enough for Mr. Elton, no doubt; accomplished enough for Highbury — handsome enough — to look plain, probably, by Harriet's side. As to connection, there Emma was perfectly easy; persuaded, that after all his own vaunted claims and disdain of Harriet, he had done nothing. On that article, truth seemed attainable. *What* she was, must be uncertain; but *who* she was, might be found out; and setting aside the 10,000*l.* it did not appear that she was at all Harriet's superior. She brought no name, no blood, no alliance. Miss Hawkins was the youngest of the two daughters of a Bristol[72] — merchant, of course, he must be called; but, as the whole of the profits of his mercantile life appeared so very moderate, it was not unfair to guess the dignity of his line of trade had been very moderate also. Part of every winter she had been used to spend in Bath; but Bristol was her home, the very heart of Bristol; for though the father and mother had died some years ago, an uncle remained — in the law line — nothing more distinctly honourable was hazarded of him, than that he was in the law line; and with him the daughter had lived. Emma guessed him to be the drudge of some attorney, and too stupid to rise. And all the grandeur of the connection

---

[72] *Bristol:* Prosperous port city in the west of England; active in trade, including (up to 1807) the slave trade.

seemed dependent on the elder sister, who was *very well married*, to a gentleman in a *great way*, near Bristol, who kept two carriages! That was the wind-up of the history; that was the glory of Miss Hawkins.

Could she but have given Harriet her feelings about it all! She had talked her into love; but alas! she was not so easily to be talked out of it. The charm of an object to occupy the many vacancies of Harriet's mind was not to be talked away. He might be superseded by another; he certainly would indeed; nothing could be clearer; even a Robert Martin would have been sufficient; but nothing else, she feared, would cure her. Harriet was one of those, who, having once begun, would be always in love. And now, poor girl! she was considerably worse from this re-appearance of Mr. Elton. She was always having a glimpse of him somewhere or other. Emma saw him only once; but two or three times every day Harriet was sure *just* to meet with him, or *just* to miss him, *just* to hear his voice, or see his shoulder, *just* to have something occur to preserve him in her fancy, in all the favouring warmth of surprize and conjecture. She was, moreover, perpetually hearing about him; for, excepting when at Hartfield, she was always among those who saw no fault in Mr. Elton, and found nothing so interesting as the discussion of his concerns; and every report, therefore, every guess — all that had already occurred, all that might occur in the arrangement of his affairs, comprehending income, servants, and furniture, was continually in agitation around her. Her regard was receiving strength by invariable praise of him, and her regrets kept alive, and feelings irritated by ceaseless repetitions of Miss Hawkins's happiness, and continual observation of, how much he seemed attached! — his air as he walked by the house — the very sitting of his hat, being all in proof of how much he was in love!

Had it been allowable entertainment, had there been no pain to her friend, or reproach to herself, in the waverings of Harriet's mind, Emma would have been amused by its variations. Sometimes Mr. Elton predominated, sometimes the Martins; and each was occasionally useful as a check to the other. Mr. Elton's engagement had been the cure of the agitation of meeting Mr. Martin. The unhappiness produced by the knowledge of that engagement had been a little put aside by Elizabeth Martin's calling at Mrs. Goddard's a few days afterwards. Harriet had not been at home; but a note had been prepared and left for her, written in the very style to touch; a small mixture of reproach, with a great deal of kindness; and till Mr. Elton himself appeared, she had been much occupied by it, continually pondering over what could be done in return, and wishing to do more than she dared to confess. But Mr.

Elton, in person, had driven away all such cares. While he staid, the Martins were forgotten; and on the very morning of his setting off for Bath again, Emma, to dissipate some of the distress it occasioned, judged it best for her to return Elizabeth Martin's visit.

How that visit was to be acknowledged — what would be necessary — and what might be safest, had been a point of some doubtful consideration. Absolute neglect of the mother and sisters, when invited to come, would be ingratitude. It must not be: and yet the danger of a renewal of the acquaintance! —

After much thinking, she could determine on nothing better, than Harriet's returning the visit; but in a way that, if they had understanding, should convince them that it was to be only a formal acquaintance. She meant to take her in the carriage, leave her at the Abbey Mill, while she drove a little farther, and call for her again so soon, as to allow no time for insidious applications or dangerous recurrences to the past, and give the most decided proof of what degree of intimacy was chosen for the future.

She could think of nothing better: and though there was something in it which her own heart could not approve — something of ingratitude, merely glossed over — it must be done, or what would become of Harriet?

CHAPTER V.

SMALL heart had Harriet for visiting. Only half an hour before her friend called for her at Mrs. Goddard's, her evil stars had led her to the very spot where, at that moment, a trunk, directed to *The Rev. Philip Elton, White-Hart, Bath,* was to be seen under the operation of being lifted into the butcher's cart, which was to convey it to where the coaches past; and every thing in this world, excepting that trunk and the direction, was consequently a blank.

She went, however; and when they reached the farm, and she was to be put down, at the end of the broad, neat gravel-walk, which led between espalier apple-trees[73] to the front door, the sight of every thing which had given her so much pleasure the autumn before, was beginning to revive a little local agitation; and when they parted, Emma observed her to be looking around with a sort of fearful curiosity, which determined her not to allow the visit to exceed the proposed quarter of

---

[73]*espalier apple-trees:* Trees trained on wooden lattices or stakes.

an hour. She went on herself, to give that portion of time to an old servant who was married, and settled in Donwell.

The quarter of an hour brought her punctually to the white gate again; and Miss Smith receiving her summons, was with her without delay, and unattended by any alarming young man. She came solitarily down the gravel walk — a Miss Martin just appearing at the door, and parting with her seemingly with ceremonious civility.

Harriet could not very soon give an intelligible account. She was feeling too much; but at last Emma collected from her enough to understand the sort of meeting, and the sort of pain it was creating. She had seen only Mrs. Martin and the two girls. They had received her doubtingly, if not coolly; and nothing beyond the merest commonplace had been talked almost all the time — till just at last, when Mrs. Martin's saying, all of a sudden, that she thought Miss Smith was grown, had brought on a more interesting subject, and a warmer manner. In that very room she had been measured last September, with her two friends. There were the pencilled marks and memorandums on the wainscot by the window. *He* had done it. They all seemed to remember the day, the hour, the party, the occasion — to feel the same consciousness, the same regrets — to be ready to return to the same good understanding; and they were just growing again like themselves, (Harriet, as Emma must suspect, as ready as the best of them to be cordial and happy,) when the carriage re-appeared, and all was over. The style of the visit, and the shortness of it, were then felt to be decisive. Fourteen minutes to be given to those with whom she had thankfully passed six weeks not six months ago! — Emma could not but picture it all, and feel how justly they might resent, how naturally Harriet must suffer. It was a bad business. She would have given a great deal, or endured a great deal, to have had the Martins in a higher rank of life. They were so deserving, that a *little* higher should have been enough: but as it was, how could she have done otherwise? — Impossible! — She could not repent. They must be separated; but there was a great deal of pain in the process — so much to herself at this time, that she soon felt the necessity of a little consolation, and resolved on going home by way of Randalls to procure it. Her mind was quite sick of Mr. Elton and the Martins. The refreshment of Randalls was absolutely necessary.

It was a good scheme; but on driving to the door they heard that neither "master nor mistress was at home;" they had both been out some time; the man believed they were gone to Hartfield.

"This is too bad," cried Emma, as they turned away. "And now we shall just miss them; too provoking! — I do not know when I have been so disappointed." And she leaned back in the corner, to indulge her murmurs, or to reason them away; probably a little of both — such being the commonest process of a not ill-disposed mind. Presently the carriage stopt; she looked up; it was stopt by Mr. and Mrs. Weston, who were standing to speak to her. There was instant pleasure in the sight of them, and still greater pleasure was conveyed in sound — for Mr. Weston immediately accosted her with,

"How d'ye do? — how d'ye do? — We have been sitting with your father — glad to see him so well. Frank comes to-morrow — I had a letter this morning — we see him to-morrow by dinner time to a cer-tainty — he is at Oxford to-day, and he comes for a whole fortnight; I knew it would be so. If he had come at Christmas he could not have staid three days; I was always glad he did not come at Christmas; now we are going to have just the right weather for him, fine, dry, settled weather. We shall enjoy him completely; every thing has turned out exactly as we could wish."

There was no resisting such news, no possibility of avoiding the influence of such a happy face as Mr. Weston's, confirmed as it all was by the words and the countenance of his wife, fewer and quieter, but not less to the purpose. To know that *she* thought his coming certain was enough to make Emma consider it so, and sincerely did she rejoice in their joy. It was a most delightful re-animation of exhausted spirits. The worn-out past was sunk in the freshness of what was coming; and in the rapidity of half a moment's thought, she hoped Mr. Elton would now be talked of no more.

Mr. Weston gave her the history of the engagements at Enscombe, which allowed his son to answer for having an entire fortnight at his command, as well as the route and the method of his journey; and she listened, and smiled, and congratulated.

"I shall soon bring him over to Hartfield," said he, at the conclusion. Emma could imagine she saw a touch of the arm at this speech, from his wife.

"We had better move on, Mr. Weston," said she, "we are detaining the girls."

"Well, well, I am ready;" — and turning again to Emma, "but you must not be expecting such a *very* fine young man; you have only had *my* account you know; I dare say he is really nothing extraordinary:" — though his own sparkling eyes at the moment were speaking a very dif-ferent conviction.

Emma could look perfectly unconscious and innocent, and answer in a manner that appropriated nothing.

"Think of me to-morrow, my dear Emma, about four o'clock," was Mrs. Weston's parting injunction; spoken with some anxiety, and meant only for her.

"Four o'clock! — depend upon it he will be here by three," was Mr. Weston's quick amendment; and so ended a most satisfactory meeting. Emma's spirits were mounted quite up to happiness; every thing wore a different air; James and his horses seemed not half so sluggish as before. When she looked at the hedges, she thought the elder at least must soon be coming out; and when she turned round to Harriet, she saw something like a look of spring, a tender smile even there.

"Will Mr. Frank Churchill pass through Bath as well as Oxford?" — was a question, however, which did not augur much.

But neither geography nor tranquillity could come all at once, and Emma was now in a humour to resolve that they should both come in time.

The morning of the interesting day arrived, and Mrs. Weston's faithful pupil did not forget either at ten, or eleven, or twelve o'clock, that she was to think of her at four.

"My dear, dear, anxious friend," — said she, in mental soliloquy, while walking down stairs from her own room, "always over-careful for every body's comfort but your own; I see you now in all your little fidgets, going again and again into his room, to be sure that all is right." The clock struck twelve as she passed through the hall. " 'Tis twelve, I shall not forget to think of you four hours hence; and by this time to-morrow, perhaps, or a little later, I may be thinking of the possibility of their all calling here. I am sure they will bring him soon."

She opened the parlour door, and saw two gentlemen sitting with her father — Mr. Weston and his son. They had been arrived only a few minutes, and Mr. Weston had scarcely finished his explanation of Frank's being a day before his time, and her father was yet in the midst of his very civil welcome and congratulations, when she appeared, to have her share of surprize, introduction, and pleasure.

The Frank Churchill so long talked of, so high in interest, was actually before her — he was presented to her, and she did not think too much had been said in his praise; he was a *very* good looking young man; height, air, address, all were unexceptionable, and his countenance had a great deal of the spirit and liveliness of his father's; he looked quick and sensible. She felt immediately that she should like him; and there was a well-bred ease of manner, and a readiness to talk, which convinced her that he came intending to be acquainted with her, and that acquainted they soon must be.

He had reached Randalls the evening before. She was pleased with the eagerness to arrive which had made him alter his plan, and travel earlier, later, and quicker, that he might gain half a day.

"I told you yesterday," cried Mr. Weston with exultation, "I told you all that he would be here before the time named. I remembered what I used to do myself. One cannot creep upon a journey; one cannot help getting on faster than one has planned; and the pleasure of coming in upon one's friends before the look-out begins, is worth a great deal more than any little exertion it needs."

"It is a great pleasure where one can indulge in it," said the young man, "though there are not many houses that I should presume on so far; but in coming *home* I felt I might do any thing."

The word *home* made his father look on him with fresh complacency. Emma was directly sure that he knew how to make himself agreeable; the conviction was strengthened by what followed. He was very much pleased with Randalls, thought it a most admirably arranged house, would hardly allow it even to be very small, admired the situation, the walk to Highbury, Highbury itself, Hartfield still more, and professed himself to have always felt the sort of interest in the country which none but one's *own* country gives, and the greatest curiosity to visit it. That he should never have been able to indulge so amiable a feeling before, passed suspiciously through Emma's brain; but still if it were a falsehood, it was a pleasant one, and pleasantly handled. His manner had no air of study or exaggeration. He did really look and speak as if in a state of no common enjoyment.

Their subjects in general were such as belong to an opening acquaintance. On his side were the inquiries, — "Was she a horsewoman? — Pleasant rides? — Pleasant walks? — Had they a large neighbourhood? — Highbury, perhaps, afforded society enough? — There were several very pretty houses in and about it. — Balls — had they balls? — Was it a musical society?"

But when satisfied on all these points, and their acquaintance proportionably advanced, he contrived to find an opportunity, while their two fathers were engaged with each other, of introducing his mother-in-law,[74] and speaking of her with so much handsome praise, so much warm admiration, so much gratitude for the happiness she secured to his father, and her very kind reception of himself, as was an additional proof of his knowing how to please — and of his certainly thinking it worth while to try to please her. He did not advance a word of praise

[74] *mother-in-law:* Stepmother.

beyond what she knew to be thoroughly deserved by Mrs. Weston; but undoubtedly he could know very little of the matter. He understood what would be welcome; he could be sure of little else. "His father's marriage," he said, "had been the wisest measure, every friend must rejoice in it; and the family from whom he had received such a blessing must be ever considered as having conferred the highest obligation on him."

He got as near as he could to thanking her for Miss Taylor's merits, without seeming quite to forget that in the common course of things it was to be rather supposed that Miss Taylor had formed Miss Woodhouse's character, than Miss Woodhouse Miss Taylor's. And at last, as if resolved to qualify his opinion completely for travelling round to its object, he wound it all up with astonishment at the youth and beauty of her person.

"Elegant, agreeable manners, I was prepared for," said he; "but I confess that, considering every thing, I had not expected more than a very tolerably well-looking woman of a certain age; I did not know that I was to find a pretty young woman in Mrs. Weston."

"You cannot see too much perfection in Mrs. Weston for my feelings," said Emma; "were you to guess her to be *eighteen*, I should listen with pleasure; but *she* would be ready to quarrel with you for using such words. Don't let her imagine that you have spoken of her as a pretty young woman."

"I hope I should know better," he replied; "no, depend upon it, (with a gallant bow,) that in addressing Mrs. Weston I should understand whom I might praise without any danger of being thought extravagant in my terms."

Emma wondered whether the same suspicion of what might be expected from their knowing each other, which had taken strong possession of her mind, had ever crossed his; and whether his compliments were to be considered as marks of acquiescence, or proofs of defiance. She must see more of him to understand his ways; at present she only felt they were agreeable.

She had no doubt of what Mr. Weston was often thinking about. His quick eye she detected again and again glancing towards them with a happy expression; and even, when he might have determined not to look, she was confident that he was often listening.

Her own father's perfect exemption from any thought of the kind, the entire deficiency in him of all such sort of penetration or suspicion, was a most comfortable circumstance. Happily he was not farther from approving matrimony than from foreseeing it. — Though always objecting to every marriage that was arranged, he never suffered beforehand from the apprehension of any; it seemed as if he could not think so ill of any two persons' understanding as to suppose they meant to marry till it were proved against them. She blessed the favouring blindness. He could now, without the drawback of a single unpleasant surmise, without a glance forward at any possible treachery in his guest, give way to all his natural kind-hearted civility in solicitous inquiries after Mr. Frank Churchill's accommodation on his journey, through the sad evils of sleeping two nights on the road, and express very genuine unmixed anxiety to know that he had certainly escaped catching cold — which, however, he could not allow him to feel quite assured of himself till after another night.

A reasonable visit paid, Mr. Weston began to move. — "He must be going. He had business at the Crown about his hay, and a great many errands for Mrs. Weston at Ford's; but he need not hurry any body else." His son, too well bred to hear the hint, rose immediately also, saying,

"As you are going farther on business, sir, I will take the opportunity of paying a visit, which must be paid some day or other, and therefore may as well be paid now. I have the honour of being acquainted with a neighbour of yours, (turning to Emma,) a lady residing in or near Highbury; a family of the name of Fairfax. I shall have no difficulty, I suppose, in finding the house; though Fairfax, I believe, is not the proper name — I should rather say Barnes, or Bates. Do you know any family of that name?"

"To be sure we do," cried his father; "Mrs. Bates — we passed her house — I saw Miss Bates at the window. True, true, you are acquainted with Miss Fairfax; I remember you knew her at Weymouth, and a fine girl she is. Call upon her, by all means."

"There is no necessity for my calling this morning," said the young man; "another day would do as well; but there was that degree of acquaintance at Weymouth which" —

"Oh! go to-day, go to-day. Do not defer it. What is right to be done cannot be done too soon. And, besides, I must give you a hint, Frank; any want of attention to her *here* should be carefully avoided. You saw her with the Campbells when she was the equal of every body she mixed with, but here she is with a poor old grandmother, who has barely enough to live on. If you do not call early it will be a slight."

The son looked convinced.

"I have heard her speak of the acquaintance," said Emma, "she is a very elegant young woman."

He agreed to it, but with so quiet a "Yes," as inclined her almost to doubt his real concurrence; and yet there must be a very distinct sort of elegance for the fashionable world, if Jane Fairfax could be thought only ordinarily gifted with it.

"If you were never particularly struck by her manners before," said she, "I think you will to-day. You will see her to advantage; see her and hear her — no, I am afraid you will not hear her at all, for she has an aunt who never holds her tongue."

"You are acquainted with Miss Jane Fairfax, sir, are you?" said Mr. Woodhouse, always the last to make his way in conversation; "then give me leave to assure you that you will find her a very agreeable young lady. She is staying here on a visit to her grandmamma and aunt, very worthy people; I have known them all my life. They will be extremely glad to see you, I am sure, and one of my servants shall go with you to shew you the way."

"My dear sir, upon no account in the world; my father can direct me."

"But your father is not going so far; he is only going to the Crown, quite on the other side of the street, and there are a great many houses; you might be very much at a loss, and it is a very dirty walk, unless you keep on the foot-path; but my coachman can tell you where you had best cross the street."

Mr. Frank Churchill still declined it, looking as serious as he could, and his father gave his hearty support by calling out, "My good friend, this is quite unnecessary; Frank knows a puddle of water when he sees it, and as to Mrs. Bates's, he may get there from the Crown in a hop, step, and jump."

They were permitted to go alone; and with a cordial nod from one, and a graceful bow from the other, the two gentlemen took leave. Emma remained very well pleased with this beginning of the acquaintance, and could now engage to think of them all at Randalls any hour of the day, with full confidence in their comfort.

CHAPTER VI.

THE next morning brought Mr. Frank Churchill again. He came with Mrs. Weston, to whom and to Highbury he seemed to take very cordially. He had been sitting with her, it appeared, most companionably at home, till her usual hour of exercise; and on being desired to chuse their walk, immediately fixed on Highbury. — "He did not doubt there being very pleasant walks in every direction, but if left to him, he should always chuse the same. Highbury, that airy, cheerful, happy-looking Highbury, would be his constant attraction." — Highbury, with Mrs. Weston, stood for Hartfield; and she trusted to its bearing the same construction with him. They walked thither directly.

Emma had hardly expected them: for Mr. Weston, who had called in for half a minute, in order to hear that his son was very handsome, knew nothing of their plans; and it was an agreeable surprize to her, therefore, to perceive them walking up to the house together, arm in arm. She was wanting to see him again, and especially to see him in company with Mrs. Weston, upon his behaviour to whom her opinion of him was to depend. If he were deficient there, nothing should make amends for it. But on seeing them together, she became perfectly satisfied. It was not merely in fine words or hyperbolical compliment that he paid his duty; nothing could be more proper or pleasing than his whole manner to her — nothing could more agreeably denote his wish of considering her as a friend and securing her affection. And there was time enough for Emma to form a reasonable judgment, as their visit included all the rest of the morning. They were all three walking about together for an hour or two — first round the shrubberies of Hartfield, and afterwards in Highbury. He was delighted with every thing; admired Hartfield sufficiently for Mr. Woodhouse's ear; and when their going farther was resolved on, confessed his wish to be made acquainted with the whole village, and found matter of commendation and interest much oftener than Emma could have supposed.

Some of the objects of his curiosity spoke very amiable feelings. He begged to be shewn the house which his father had lived in so long, and which had been the home of his father's father; and on recollecting that an old woman who had nursed him was still living, walked in quest of her cottage from one end of the street to the other; and though in some points of pursuit or observation there was no positive merit, they shewed, altogether, a good-will towards Highbury in general, which must be very like a merit to those he was with.

Emma watched and decided, that with such feelings as were now shewn, it could not be fairly supposed that he had been ever voluntarily absenting himself; that he had not been acting a part, or making a parade of insincere professions; and that Mr. Knightley certainly had not done him justice.

Their first pause was at the Crown Inn, an inconsiderable house, though the principal one of the sort, where a couple of pair of post-horses were kept, more for the convenience of the neighbourhood than from any run on the road; and his companions had not expected to be detained by any interest excited there; but in passing it they gave the history of the large room visibly added; it had been built many years ago for a ball-room, and while the neighbourhood had been in a particularly populous, dancing state, had been occasionally used as such; — but such brilliant days had long passed away, and now the highest purpose for which it was ever wanted was to accommodate a whist club established among the gentlemen and half-gentlemen of the place. He was immediately interested. Its character as a ball-room caught him; and instead of passing on, he stopt for several minutes at the two superior sashed windows which were open, to look in and contemplate its capabilities, and lament that its original purpose should have ceased. He saw no fault in the room, he would acknowledge none which they suggested. No, it was long enough, broad enough, handsome enough. It would hold the very number for comfort. They ought to have balls there at least every fortnight through the winter. Why had not Miss Woodhouse revived the former good old days of the room? — She who could do any thing in Highbury! The want of proper families in the place, and the conviction that none beyond the place and its immediate environs could be tempted to attend, were mentioned; but he was not satisfied. He could not be persuaded that so many good-looking houses as he saw around him, could not furnish numbers enough for such a meeting; and even when particulars were given and families described, he was still unwilling to admit that the inconvenience of such a mixture would be any thing, or that there would be the smallest difficulty in every body's returning into their proper place the next morning. He argued like a young man very much bent on dancing; and Emma was rather surprized to see the constitution of the Weston prevail so decidedly against the habits of the Churchills. He seemed to have all the life and spirit, cheerful feelings, and social inclinations of his father, and nothing of the pride or reserve of Enscombe. Of pride, indeed, there was, perhaps, scarcely enough; his indifference to a confusion of rank, bordered too much on inelegance of mind. He could be no judge, however, of the evil he was holding cheap. It was but an effusion of lively spirits.

At last he was persuaded to move on from the front of the Crown; and being now almost facing the house where the Bateses lodged, Emma recollected his intended visit the day before, and asked him if he had paid it.

"Yes, oh! yes — he replied; I was just going to mention it. A very successful visit: — I saw all the three ladies; and felt very much obliged to you for your preparatory hint. If the talking aunt had taken me quite by surprize, it must have been the death of me. As it was, I was only betrayed into paying a most unreasonable visit. Ten minutes would have been all that was necessary, perhaps all that was proper; and I had told my father I should certainly be at home before him — but there was no getting away, no pause; and, to my utter astonishment, I found, when he (finding me no where else) joined me there at last, that I had been actually sitting with them very nearly three quarters of an hour. The good lady had not given me the possibility of escape before."

"And how did you think Miss Fairfax looking?"

"Ill, very ill — that is, if a young lady can ever be allowed to look ill. But the expression is hardly admissible, Mrs. Weston, is it? Ladies can never look ill. And, seriously, Miss Fairfax is naturally so pale, as almost always to give the appearance of ill health. — A most deplorable want of complexion."

Emma would not agree to this, and began a warm defence of Miss Fairfax's complexion. "It was certainly never brilliant, but she would not allow it to have a sickly hue in general; and there was a softness and delicacy in her skin which gave peculiar elegance to the character of her face." He listened with all due deference; acknowledged that he had heard many people say the same — but yet he must confess, that to him nothing could make amends for the want of the fine glow of health. Where features were indifferent, a fine complexion gave beauty to them all; and where they were good, the effect was — fortunately he need not attempt to describe what the effect was.

"Well," said Emma, "there is no disputing about taste. — At least you admire her except her complexion."

He shook his head and laughed. — "I cannot separate Miss Fairfax and her complexion."

"Did you see her often at Weymouth? Were you often in the same society?"

At this moment they were approaching Ford's, and he hastily exclaimed, "Ha! this must be the very shop that every body attends every day of their lives, as my father informs me. He comes to High-bury himself, he says, six days out of the seven, and has always business at Ford's. If it be not inconvenient to you, pray let us go in, that I may prove myself to belong to the place, to be a true citizen of Highbury. I must buy something at Ford's. It will be taking out my freedom. — I dare say they sell gloves."

"Oh! yes, gloves and every thing. I do admire your patriotism. You will be adored in Highbury. You were very popular before you came, because you were Mr. Weston's son — but lay out half-a-guinea at Ford's, and your popularity will stand upon your own virtues."

They went in; and while the sleek, well-tied parcels of "Men's Beavers" and "York Tan" were bringing down and displaying on the counter, he said — "But I beg your pardon, Miss Woodhouse, you were speaking to me, you were saying something at the very moment of this burst of my *amor patriæ*.[75] Do not let me lose it. I assure you the utmost stretch of public fame would not make me amends for the loss of any happiness in private life."

"I merely asked, whether you had known much of Miss Fairfax and her party at Weymouth."

"And now that I understand your question, I must pronounce it to be a very unfair one. It is always the lady's right to decide on the degree of acquaintance. Miss Fairfax must already have given her account. — I shall not commit myself by claiming more than she may chuse to allow."

"Upon my word! you answer as discreetly as she could do herself. But her account of every thing leaves so much to be guessed, she is so very reserved, so very unwilling to give the least information about any body, that I really think you may say what you like of your acquaintance with her."

"May I indeed? — Then I will speak the truth, and nothing suits me so well. I met her frequently at Weymouth. I had known the Campbells a little in town; and at Weymouth we were very much in the same set. Col. Campbell is a very agreeable man, and Mrs. Campbell a friendly, warm-hearted woman. I like them all."

"You know Miss Fairfax's situation in life, I conclude; what she is destined to be."

"Yes — (rather hesitatingly) — I believe I do."

"You get upon delicate subjects, Emma," said Mrs. Weston smiling, "remember that I am here. — Mr. Frank Churchill hardly knows what to say when you speak of Miss Fairfax's situation in life. I will move a little farther off."

"I certainly do forget to think of *her*," said Emma, "as having ever been any thing but my friend and my dearest friend."

He looked as if he fully understood and honoured such a sentiment.

When the gloves were bought and they had quitted the shop again, "Did you ever hear the young lady we were speaking of, play?" said Frank Churchill.

---

[75]**amor patriæ:** Latin for love of one's country.

"Ever hear her!" repeated Emma. "You forget how much she belongs to Highbury. I have heard her every year of our lives since we both began. She plays charmingly."

"You think so, do you? — I wanted the opinion of some one who could really judge. She appeared to me to play well, that is, with considerable taste, but I know nothing of the matter myself. — I am excessively fond of music, but without the smallest skill or right of judging of any body's performance. — I have been used to hear her's admired; and I remember one proof of her being thought to play well: — a man, a very musical man, and in love with another woman — engaged to her — on the point of marriage — would yet never ask that other woman to sit down to the instrument, if the lady in question could sit down instead — never seemed to like to hear one if he could hear the other. That I thought, in a man of known musical talent, was some proof."

"Proof, indeed!" said Emma, highly amused. — "Mr. Dixon is very musical, is he? We shall know more about them all, in half an hour, from you, than Miss Fairfax would have vouchsafed in half a year."

"Yes, Mr. Dixon and Miss Campbell were the persons; and I thought it a very strong proof."

"Certainly — very strong it was; to own the truth, a great deal stronger than, if *I* had been Miss Campbell, would have been at all agreeable to me. I could not excuse a man's having more music than love — more ear than eye — a more acute sensibility to fine sounds than to my feelings. How did Miss Campbell appear to like it?"

"It was her very particular friend, you know."

"Poor comfort!" said Emma, laughing. "One would rather have a stranger preferred than one's very particular friend — with a stranger it might not recur again — but the misery of having a very particular friend always at hand, to do every thing better than one does oneself! — Poor Mrs. Dixon! Well, I am glad she is gone to settle in Ireland."

"You are right. It was not very flattering to Miss Campbell; but she really did not seem to feel it."

"So much the better — or so much the worse: — I do not know which. But, be it sweetness or be it stupidity in her — quickness of friendship, or dulness of feeling — there was one person, I think, who must have felt it: Miss Fairfax herself. *She* must have felt the improper and dangerous distinction."

"As to that — I do not ——"

"Oh! do not imagine that I expect an account of Miss Fairfax's sensations from you, or from any body else. They are known to no human being, I guess, but herself. But if she continued to play whenever she was asked by Mr. Dixon, one may guess what one chuses."

"There appeared such a perfectly good understanding among them all —" he began rather quickly, but checking himself, added, "however, it is impossible for me to say on what terms they really were — how it might all be behind the scenes. I can only say that there was smoothness outwardly. But you, who have known Miss Fairfax from a child, must be a better judge of her character, and of how she is likely to conduct herself in critical situations, than I can be."

"I have known her from a child, undoubtedly; we have been children and women together; and it is natural to suppose that we should be intimate, — that we should have taken to each other whenever she visited her friends. But we never did. I hardly know how it has happened; a little, perhaps, from that wickedness on my side which was prone to take disgust towards a girl so idolized and so cried up as she always was, by her aunt and grandmother, and all their set. And then, her reserve — I never could attach myself to any one so completely reserved."

"It is a most repulsive quality, indeed," said he. "Oftentimes very convenient, no doubt, but never pleasing. There is safety in reserve, but no attraction. One cannot love a reserved person."

"Not till the reserve ceases towards oneself; and then the attraction may be the greater. But I must be more in want of a friend, or an agreeable companion, than I have yet been, to take the trouble of conquering any body's reserve to procure one. Intimacy between Miss Fairfax and me is quite out of the question. I have no reason to think ill of her — not the least — except that such extreme and perpetual cautiousness of word and manner, such a dread of giving a distinct idea about any body, is apt to suggest suspicions of there being something to conceal."

He perfectly agreed with her: and after walking together so long, and thinking so much alike, Emma felt herself so well acquainted with him, that she could hardly believe it to be only their second meeting. He was not exactly what she had expected; less of the man of the world in some of his notions, less of the spoiled child of fortune, therefore better than she had expected. His ideas seemed more moderate — his feelings warmer. She was particularly struck by his manner of considering Mr. Elton's house, which, as well as the church, he would go and look at, and would not join them in finding much fault with. No, he could not believe it a bad house; not such a house as a man was to be pitied for having. If it were to be shared with the woman he loved, he could not think any man to be pitied for having that house. There must be ample room in it for every real comfort. The man must be a block-head who wanted more.

Mrs. Weston laughed, and said he did not know what he was talking about. Used only to a large house himself, and without ever thinking how many advantages and accommodations were attached to its size, he could be no judge of the privations inevitably belonging to a small one. But Emma, in her own mind, determined that he *did* know what he was talking about, and that he shewed a very amiable inclination to settle early in life, and to marry, from worthy motives. He might not be aware of the inroads on domestic peace to be occasioned by no house-keeper's room, or a bad butler's pantry, but no doubt he did perfectly feel that Enscombe could not make him happy, and that whenever he were attached, he would willingly give up much of wealth to be allowed an early establishment.

CHAPTER VII.

EMMA's very good opinion of Frank Churchill was a little shaken the fol-lowing day, by hearing that he was gone off to London, merely to have his hair cut. A sudden freak seemed to have seized him at breakfast, and he had sent for a chaise[76] and set off, intending to return to dinner, but with no more important view that appeared than having his hair cut. There was certainly no harm in his travelling sixteen miles twice over on such an errand; but there was an air of foppery and nonsense in it which she could not approve. It did not accord with the rationality of plan, the moderation in expense, or even the unselfish warmth of heart which she had believed herself to discern in him yesterday. Vanity, extravagance, love of change, restlessness of temper, which must be doing something, good or bad; heedlessness as to the pleasure of his father and Mrs. Weston, indifferent as to how his conduct might appear in general; he became liable to all these charges. His father only called him a cox-comb, and thought it a very good story; but that Mrs. Weston did not like it, was clear enough, by her passing it over as quickly as possible, and making no other comment than that "all young people would have their little whims."

---

[76]*chaise:* Here, a closed carriage hired from the Crown Inn; also known as a post-chaise, the carriage was drawn by two or more horses and driven by a mounted postilion or post-boy. A chaise could also be a regular family carriage, such as that owned by the Sucklings (p. 222).

With the exception of this little blot, Emma found that his visit hitherto had given her friend only good ideas of him. Mrs. Weston was very ready to say how attentive and pleasant a companion he made himself — how much she saw to like in his disposition altogether. He appeared to have a very open temper — certainly a very cheerful and lively one; she could observe nothing wrong in his notions, a great deal decidedly right; he spoke of his uncle with warm regard, was fond of talking of him — said he would be the best man in the world if he were left to himself; and though there was no being attached to the aunt, he acknowledged her kindness with gratitude, and seemed to mean always to speak of her with respect. This was all very promising; and, but for such an unfortunate fancy for having his hair cut, there was nothing to denote him unworthy of the distinguished honour which her imagina tion had given him; the honour, if not of being really in love with her, of being at least very near it, and saved only by her own indifference — (for still her resolution held of never marrying) — the honour, in short, of being marked out for her by all their joint acquaintance.

Mr. Weston, on his side, added a virtue to the account which must have some weight. He gave her to understand that Frank admired her extremely — thought her very beautiful and very charming; and with so much to be said for him altogether, she found she must not judge him harshly. As Mrs. Weston observed, "all young people would have their little whims."

There was one person among his new acquaintance in Surry, not so leniently disposed. In general he was judged, throughout the parishes of Donwell and Highbury, with great candour; liberal allowances were made for the little excesses of such a handsome young man — one who smiled so often and bowed so well; but there was one spirit among them not to be softened, from its power of censure, by bows or smiles — Mr. Knightley. The circumstance was told him at Hartfield; for the moment, he was silent; but Emma heard him almost immediately afterwards say to himself, over a newspaper he held in his hand, "Hum! just the trifling, silly fellow I took him for." She had half a mind to resent; but an instant's observation convinced her that it was really said only to relieve his own feelings, and not meant to provoke; and therefore she let it pass.

Although in one instance the bearers of not good tidings, Mr. and Mrs. Weston's visit this morning was in another respect particularly opportune. Something occurred while they were at Hartfield, to make Emma want their advice; and, which was still more lucky, she wanted exactly the advice they gave.

This was the occurrence: — The Coles had been settled some years in Highbury, and were very good sort of people — friendly, liberal, and unpretending; but, on the other hand, they were of low origin, in trade, and only moderately genteel. On their first coming into the country, they had lived in proportion to their income, quietly, keeping little company, and that little unexpensively; but the last year or two had brought them a considerable increase of means — the house in town[77] had yielded greater profits, and fortune in general had smiled on them. With their wealth, their views increased; their want of a larger house, their inclination for more company. They added to their house, to their number of servants, to their expenses of every sort; and by this time were, in fortune and style of living, second only to the family at Hartfield. Their love of society, and their new dining-room, prepared every body for their keeping dinner-company; and a few parties, chiefly among the single men, had already taken place. The regular and best families Emma could hardly suppose they would presume to invite — neither Donwell, nor Hartfield, nor Randalls. Nothing should tempt *her* to go, if they did; and she regretted that her father's known habits would be giving her refusal less meaning than she could wish. The Coles were very respectable in their way, but they ought to be taught that it was not for them to arrange the terms on which the superior families would visit them. This lesson, she very much feared, they would receive only from herself; she had little hope of Mr. Knightley, none of Mr. Weston.

But she had made up her mind how to meet this presumption so many weeks before it appeared, that when the insult came at last, it found her very differently affected. Donwell and Randalls had received their invitation, and none had come for her father and herself; and Mrs. Weston's accounting for it with "I suppose they will not take the liberty with you; they know you do not dine out," was not quite sufficient. She felt that she should like to have had the power of refusal; and afterwards, as the idea of the party to be assembled there, consisting precisely of those whose society was dearest to her, occurred again and again, she did not know that she might not have been tempted to accept. Harriet was to be there in the evening, and the Bateses. They had been speaking of it as they walked about Highbury the day before, and Frank Churchill had most earnestly lamented her absence. Might not the evening end in a dance? had been a question of his. The bare possibility of it acted as a further irritation on her spirits; and her being

---

[77] *house in town:* The Coles' business in London.

left in solitary grandeur, even supposing the omission to be intended as a compliment, was but poor comfort.

It was the arrival of this very invitation while the Westons were at Hartfield, which made their presence so acceptable; for though her first remark, on reading it, was that "of course it must be declined," she so very soon proceeded to ask them what they advised her to do, that their advice for her going was most prompt and successful.

She owned that, considering every thing, she was not absolutely without inclination for the party. The Coles expressed themselves so properly — there was so much real attention in the manner of it — so much consideration for her father. "They would have solicited the honour earlier, but had been waiting the arrival of a folding-screen from London, which they hoped might keep Mr. Woodhouse from any draught of air, and therefore induce him the more readily to give them the honour of his company." Upon the whole, she was very persuadable; and it being briefly settled among themselves how it might be done without neglecting his comfort — how certainly Mrs. Goddard, if not Mrs. Bates, might be depended on for bearing him company — Mr. Woodhouse was to be talked into an acquiescence of his daughter's going out to dinner on a day now near at hand, and spending the whole evening away from him. As for *his* going, Emma did not wish him to think it possible; the hours would be too late, and the party too numerous. He was soon pretty well resigned.

"I am not fond of dinner-visiting," said he — "I never was. No more is Emma. Late hours do not agree with us. I am sorry Mr. and Mrs. Cole should have done it. I think it would be much better if they would come in one afternoon next summer, and take their tea with us — take us in their afternoon walk; which they might do, as our hours are so reasonable, and yet get home without being out in the damp of the evening. The dews of a summer evening are what I would not expose any body to. However, as they are so very desirous to have dear Emma dine with them, and as you will both be there, and Mr. Knightley too, to take care of her, I cannot wish to prevent it, provided the weather be what it ought, neither damp, nor cold, nor windy." Then turning to Mrs. Weston, with a look of gentle reproach — "Ah! Miss Taylor, if you had not married, you would have staid at home with me."

"Well, sir," cried Mr. Weston, "as I took Miss Taylor away, it is incumbent on me to supply her place, if I can; and I will step to Mrs. Goddard in a moment, if you wish it."

But the idea of any thing to be done in a *moment*, was increasing, not lessening Mr. Woodhouse's agitation. The ladies knew better how to allay it. Mr. Weston must be quiet, and every thing deliberately arranged.

With this treatment, Mr. Woodhouse was soon composed enough for talking as usual. "He should be happy to see Mrs. Goddard. He had a great regard for Mrs. Goddard; and Emma should write a line, and invite her. James could take the note. But first of all, there must be an answer written to Mrs. Cole."

"You will make my excuses, my dear, as civilly as possible. You will say that I am quite an invalid, and go no where, and therefore must decline their obliging invitation; beginning with my *compliments*, of course. But you will do every thing right. I need not tell you what is to be done. We must remember to let James know that the carriage will be wanted on Tuesday. I shall have no fears for you with him. We have never been there above once since the new approach was made; but still I have no doubt that James will take you very safely. And when you get there, you must tell him at what time you would have him come for you again; and you had better name an early hour. You will not like staying late. You will get very tired when tea is over."

"But you would not wish me to come away before I am tired, papa?"

"Oh! no, my love; but you will soon be tired. There will be a great many people talking at once. You will not like the noise."

"But, my dear sir," cried Mr. Weston, "if Emma comes away early, it will be breaking up the party."

"And no great harm if it does," said Mr. Woodhouse. "The sooner every party breaks up, the better."

"But you do not consider how it may appear to the Coles. Emma's going away directly after tea might be giving offence. They are good-natured people, and think little of their own claims; but still they must feel that any body's hurrying away is no great compliment; and Miss Woodhouse's doing it would be more thought of than any other person's in the room. You would not wish to disappoint and mortify the Coles, I am sure, sir; friendly, good sort of people as ever lived, and who have been your neighbours these *ten* years."

"No, upon no account in the world. Mr. Weston, I am much obliged to you for reminding me. I should be extremely sorry to be giving them any pain. I know what worthy people they are. Perry tells me that Mr. Cole never touches malt liquor. You would not think it to look at him, but he is bilious — Mr. Cole is very bilious. No, I would not be the means of giving them any pain. My dear Emma, we must consider this. I am sure, rather than run the risk of hurting Mr. and Mrs. Cole, you would stay a little longer than you might wish. You will not regard being tired. You will be perfectly safe, you know, among your friends."

"Oh, yes, papa. I have no fears at all for myself; and I should have no scruples of staying as late as Mrs. Weston, but on your account. I am only afraid of your sitting up for me. I am not afraid of your not being exceedingly comfortable with Mrs. Goddard. She loves piquet,[78] you know; but when she is gone home, I am afraid you will be sitting up by yourself, instead of going to bed at your usual time — and the idea of that would entirely destroy my comfort. You must promise me not to sit up."

He did, on the condition of some promises on her side: such as that, if she came home cold, she would be sure to warm herself thoroughly; if hungry, that she would take something to eat; that her own maid should sit up for her; and that Serle and the butler should see that every thing were safe in the house, as usual.

CHAPTER VIII.

FRANK CHURCHILL came back again; and if he kept his father's dinner waiting, it was not known at Hartfield; for Mrs. Weston was too anxious for his being a favourite with Mr. Woodhouse, to betray any imperfection which could be concealed.

He came back, had had his hair cut, and laughed at himself with a very good grace, but without seeming really at all ashamed of what he had done. He had no reason to wish his hair longer,[79] to conceal any confusion of face; no reason to wish the money unspent, to improve his spirits. He was quite as undaunted and as lively as ever; and after seeing him, Emma thus moralized to herself: —

"I do not know whether it ought to be so, but certainly silly things do cease to be silly if they are done by sensible people in an impudent way. Wickedness is always wickedness, but folly is not always folly. — It depends upon the character of those who handle it. Mr. Knightley, he is *not* a trifling, silly young man. If he were, he would have done this differently. He would either have gloried in the achievement, or been

---

[78]*piquet:* Card game for two players.

[79]*no reason to wish his hair longer:* That the short hair of young men might provoke is shown by Austen's comment in a letter to Cassandra, January 21–23, 1799: "I thought Edward would not approve of Charles being a crop" (i.e., of his younger brother's wearing his hair short and unpowdered) (*Letters* 38).

ashamed of it. There would have been either the ostentation of a cox-comb, or the evasions of a mind too weak to defend its own vanities. — No, I am perfectly sure that he is not trifling or silly "

With Tuesday came the agreeable prospect of seeing him again, and for a longer time than hitherto; of judging of his general manners, and by inference, of the meaning of his manners towards herself; of guess-ing how soon it might be necessary for her to throw coldness into her air; and of fancying what the observations of all those might be, who were now seeing them together for the first time.

She meant to be very happy, in spite of the scene being laid at Mr. Cole's; and without being able to forget that among the failings of Mr. Elton, even in the days of his favour, none had disturbed her more than his propensity to dine with Mr. Cole.

Her father's comfort was amply secured, Mrs. Bates as well as Mrs. Goddard being able to come; and her last pleasing duty, before she left the house, was to pay her respects to them as they sat together after din-ner; and while her father was fondly noticing the beauty of her dress, to make the two ladies all the amends in her power, by helping them to large slices of cake and full glasses of wine, for whatever unwilling self-denial his care of their constitution might have obliged them to practise during the meal. — She had provided a plentiful dinner for them; she wished she could know that they had been allowed to eat it.

She followed another carriage to Mr. Cole's door; and was pleased to see that it was Mr. Knightley's; for Mr. Knightley keeping no horses, having little spare money and a great deal of health, activity, and inde-pendence, was too apt, in Emma's opinion, to get about as he could, and not use his carriage so often as became the owner of Donwell Abbey. She had an opportunity now of speaking her approbation while warm from her heart, for he stopped to hand her out.

"This is coming as you should do," said she, "like a gentleman. — I am quite glad to see you."

He thanked her, observing, "How lucky that we should arrive at the same moment! for, if we had met first in the drawing-room, I doubt whether you would have discerned me to be more of a gentleman than usual. — You might not have distinguished how I came, by my look or manner."

"Yes I should, I am sure I should. There is always a look of con-sciousness or bustle when people come in a way which they know to be beneath them. You think you carry it off very well, I dare say, but with you it is a sort of bravado, an air of affected unconcern; I always ob-serve it whenever I meet you under those circumstances. *Now* you have nothing to try for. You are not afraid of being supposed ashamed. You are not striving to look taller than any body else. *Now* I shall really be very happy to walk into the same room with you."

"Nonsensical girl!" was his reply, but not at all in anger.

Emma had as much reason to be satisfied with the rest of the party as with Mr. Knightley. She was received with a cordial respect which could not but please, and given all the consequence she could wish for. When the Westons arrived, the kindest looks of love, the strongest of admiration were for her, from both husband and wife; the son approached her with a cheerful eagerness which marked her as his peculiar object, and at dinner she found him seated by her — and, as she firmly believed, not without some dexterity on his side.

The party was rather large, as it included one other family, a proper unobjectionable country family, whom the Coles had the advantage of naming among their acquaintance, and the male part of Mr. Cox's family, the lawyer of Highbury. The less worthy females were to come in the evening, with Miss Bates, Miss Fairfax, and Miss Smith; but already, at dinner, they were too numerous for any subject of conversation to be general; and while politics and Mr. Elton were talked over, Emma could fairly surrender all her attention to the pleasantness of her neighbour. The first remote sound to which she felt herself obliged to attend, was the name of Jane Fairfax. Mrs. Cole seemed to be relating something of her that was expected to be very interesting. She listened, and found it well worth listening to. That very dear part of Emma, her fancy, received an amusing supply. Mrs. Cole was telling that she had been calling on Miss Bates, and as soon as she entered the room had been struck by the sight of a pianofortè — a very elegant looking instrument — not a grand, but a large-sized square pianofortè; and the substance of the story, the end of all the dialogue which ensued of surprize, and inquiry, and congratulations on her side, and explanations on Miss Bates's, was, that this pianofortè had arrived from Broadwood's[80] the day before, to the great astonishment of both aunt and niece — entirely unexpected; that at first, by Miss Bates's account, Jane herself was quite at a loss, quite bewildered to think who could possibly have ordered it — but now, they were both perfectly satisfied that it could be from only one quarter; — of course it must be from Col. Campbell.

"One can suppose nothing else," added Mrs. Cole, "and I was only

---

[80]*Broadwood's:* John Broadwood (1732–1812) began selling pianos in 1773 and his firm soon became the leader in the trade from his premises in Great Poulteney Street in London. For an illustration of a square pianofortè of the period, with a "Broadwood's single action," see "Contextual Documents," p. 400.

surprized that there could ever have been a doubt. But Jane, it seems, had a letter from them very lately, and not a word was said about it. She knows their ways best; but I should not consider their silence as any rea son for their not meaning to make the present. They might chuse to surprize her."

Mrs. Cole had many to agree with her; every body who spoke on the subject was equally convinced that it must come from Col. Campbell, and equally rejoiced that such a present had been made; and there were enough ready to speak to allow Emma to think her own way, and still listen to Mrs. Cole.

"I declare, I do not know when I have heard any thing that has given me more satisfaction! — It always has quite hurt me that Jane Fairfax, who plays so delightfully, should not have an instrument. It seemed quite a shame, especially considering how many houses there are where fine instruments are absolutely thrown away. This is like giving ourselves a slap, to be sure! and it was but yesterday I was telling Mr. Cole, I really was ashamed to look at our new grand pianoforté in the drawing-room, while I do not know one note from another, and our little girls, who are but just beginning, perhaps may never make any thing of it; and there is poor Jane Fairfax, who is mistress of music, has not any thing of the nature of an instrument, not even the pitifullest old spinnet in the world, to amuse herself with. — I was saying this to Mr. Cole but yesterday, and he quite agreed with me; only he is so particularly fond of music that he could not help indulging himself in the purchase, hoping that some of our good neighbours might be so obliging occasionally to put it to a better use than we can; and that really is the reason why the instrument was bought — or else I am sure we ought to be ashamed of it. — We are in great hopes that Miss Woodhouse may be prevailed with to try it this evening."

Miss Woodhouse made the proper acquiescence; and finding that nothing more was to be entrapped from any communication of Mrs. Cole's, turned to Frank Churchill.

"Why do you smile?" said she.

"Nay, why do you?"

"Me! — I suppose I smile for pleasure at Col. Campbell's being so rich and so liberal. — It is a handsome present."

"Very."

"I rather wonder that it was never made before."

"Perhaps Miss Fairfax has never been staying here so long before."

"Or that he did not give her the use of their own instrument — which must now be shut up in London, untouched by any body."

"That is a grand pianoforté, and he might think it too large for Mrs. Bates's house."

"You may *say* what you chuse — but your countenance testifies that your *thoughts* on this subject are very much like mine."

"I do not know. I rather believe you are giving me more credit for acuteness than I deserve. I smile because you smile, and shall probably suspect whatever I find you suspect; but at present I do not see what there is to question. If Col. Campbell is not the person, who can be?"

"What do you say to Mrs. Dixon?"

"Mrs. Dixon! very true indeed. I had not thought of Mrs. Dixon. She must know as well as her father, how acceptable an instrument would be; and perhaps the mode of it, the mystery, the surprize, is more like a young woman's scheme than an elderly man's. It is Mrs. Dixon I dare say. I told you that your suspicions would guide mine."

"If so, you must extend your suspicions and comprehend *Mr.* Dixon in them."

"Mr. Dixon. — Very well. Yes, I immediately perceive that it must be the joint present of Mr. and Mrs. Dixon. We were speaking the other day, you know, of his being so warm an admirer of her performance."

"Yes, and what you told me on that head, confirmed an idea which I had entertained before. — I do not mean to reflect upon the good intentions of either Mr. Dixon or Miss Fairfax, but I cannot help suspecting either that, after making his proposals to her friend, he had the misfortune to fall in love with *her,* or that he became conscious of a little attachment on her side. One might guess twenty things without guessing exactly the right; but I am sure there must be a particular cause for her chusing to come to Highbury instead of going with the Campbells to Ireland. Here, she must be leading a life of privation and penance; there it would have been all enjoyment. As to the pretence of trying her native air, I look upon that as a mere excuse. — In the summer it might have passed; but what can any body's native air do for them in the months of January, February, and March? Good fires and carriages would be much more to the purpose in most cases of delicate health, and I dare say in her's. I do not require you to adopt all my suspicions, though you make so noble a profession of doing it, but I honestly tell you what they are."

"And, upon my word, they have an air of great probability. Mr. Dixon's preference for her music to her friend's, I can answer for being very decided."

"And then, he saved her life. Did you ever hear of that? — A water-party; and by some accident she was falling overboard. He caught her."

"He did. I was there — one of the party."

"Were you really? — Well! — But you observed nothing of course, for it seems to be a new idea to you. — If I had been there, I think I should have made some discoveries."

"I dare say you would; but I, simple I, saw nothing but the fact, that Miss Fairfax was nearly dashed from the vessel and that Mr. Dixon caught her. — It was the work of a moment. And though the consequent shock and alarm was very great and much more durable — indeed I believe it was half an hour before any of us were comfortable again — yet that was too general a sensation for any thing of peculiar anxiety to be observable. I do not mean to say, however, that you might not have made discoveries."

The conversation was here interrupted. They were called on to share in the awkwardness of a rather long interval between the courses, and obliged to be as formal and as orderly as the others; but when the table was again safely covered, when every corner dish was placed exactly right, and occupation and ease were generally restored, Emma said,

"The arrival of this pianoforté is decisive with me. I wanted to know a little more, and this tells me quite enough. Depend upon it. We shall soon hear that it is a present from Mr. and Mrs. Dixon."

"And if the Dixons should absolutely deny all knowledge of it we must conclude it to come from the Campbells."

"No, I am sure it is not from the Campbells. Miss Fairfax knows it is not from the Campbells, or they would have been guessed at first. She would not have been puzzled, had she dared fix on them. I may not have convinced you perhaps, but I am perfectly convinced myself that Mr. Dixon is a principal in the business."

"Indeed you injure me if you suppose me unconvinced. Your reasonings carry my judgment along with them entirely. At first, while I supposed you satisfied that Col. Campbell was the giver, I saw it only as paternal kindness, and thought it the most natural thing in the world. But when you mentioned Mrs. Dixon, I felt how much more probable that it should be the tribute of warm female friendship. And now I can see it in no other light than as an offering of love."

There was no occasion to press the matter father. The conviction seemed real; he looked as if he felt it. She said no more, other subjects took their turn; and the rest of the dinner passed away; the dessert succeeded, the children came in, and were talked to and admired amid the usual rate of conversation; a few clever things said, a few downright silly, but by much the larger proportion neither the one nor the other — nothing worse than every day remarks, dull repetitions, old news, and heavy jokes.

The ladies had not been long in the drawing-room, before the other ladies, in their different divisions, arrived. Emma watched the entrée of her own particular little friend; and if she could not exult in her dignity and grace, she could not only love the blooming sweetness and the artless manner, but could most heartily rejoice in that light, cheerful, unsentimental disposition which allowed her so many alleviations of pleasure, in the midst of the pangs of disappointed affection. There she sat — and who would have guessed how many tears she had been lately shedding? To be in company, nicely dressed herself and seeing others nicely dressed, to sit and smile and look pretty, and say nothing, was enough for the happiness of the present hour. Jane Fairfax did look and move superior; but Emma suspected she might have been glad to change feelings with Harriet, very glad to have purchased the mortification of having loved — yes, of having loved even Mr. Elton in vain — by the surrender of all the dangerous pleasure of knowing herself beloved by the husband of her friend.

In so large a party it was not necessary that Emma should approach her. She did not wish to speak of the pianoforté, she felt too much in the secret herself, to think the appearance of curiosity or interest fair, and therefore purposely kept at a distance; but by the others, the subject was almost immediately introduced, and she saw the blush of consciousness with which congratulations were received, the blush of guilt which accompanied the name of "my excellent friend Col. Campbell."

Mrs. Weston, kind-hearted and musical, was particularly interested by the circumstance, and Emma could not help being amused at her perseverance in dwelling on the subject; and having so much to ask and to say as to tone, touch, and pedal, totally unsuspicious of that wish of saying as little about it as possible, which she plainly read in the fair heroine's countenance.

They were soon joined by some of the gentlemen; and the very first of the early was Frank Churchill. In he walked, the first and the handsomest; and after paying his compliments en passant to Miss Bates and her niece, made his way directly to the opposite side of the circle, where sat Miss Woodhouse; and till he could find a seat by her, would not sit at all. Emma divined what every body present must be thinking. She was his object, and every body must perceive it. She introduced him to her friend, Miss Smith, and, at convenient moments afterwards, heard what each thought of the other. "He had never seen so lovely a face, and was delighted with her naïveté." And she, — "Only to be sure it was paying him too great a compliment, but she did think there were some looks a little like Mr. Elton." Emma restrained her indignation, and only turned from her in silence.

Smiles of intelligence passed between her and the gentleman on first glancing towards Miss Fairfax; but it was most prudent to avoid speech. He told her that he had been impatient to leave the dining-room — hated sitting long — was always the first to move when he could — that his father, Mr. Knightley, Mr. Cox, and Mr. Cole, were left very busy over parish business — that as long as he had staid, however, it had been pleasant enough, as he found them in general a set of gentlemen-like, sensible men; and spoke so handsomely of Highbury altogether — thought it so abundant in agreeable families — that Emma began to feel she had been used to despise the place rather too much. She questioned him as to the society in Yorkshire — the extent of the neighbourhood about Enscombe, and the sort; and could make out from his answers that, as far as Enscombe was concerned, there was very little going on; that their visitings were among a range of great families, none very near; and that even when days were fixed, and invitations accepted, it was an even chance that Mrs. Churchill were not in health or spirits for going; that they made a point of visiting no fresh person; and that, though he had his separate engagements, it was not without difficulty, without considerable address *at times,* that he could get away, or introduce an acquaintance for a night.

She saw that Enscombe could not satisfy, and that Highbury, taken in its best, might reasonably please a young man who had more retirement at home than he liked. His importance at Enscombe was very evident. He did not boast, but it naturally betrayed itself, that he had persuaded his aunt where his uncle could do nothing, and on her laughing and noticing it, he owned that he believed (excepting one or two points) he could *with time* persuade her to any thing. One of those points on which his influence failed, he then mentioned. He had wanted very much to go abroad[81] — had been very eager indeed to be allowed to travel — but she would not hear of it. This had happened the year before. *Now,* he said, he was beginning to have no longer the same wish.

[81]*to go abroad:* That Churchill at twenty-three has not taken the Grand Tour to France, Germany, Italy, and other countries, which was common for rich young gentlemen, may be explained not only by his aunt's reluctance but by the enmity between England and France during most of the period of the Revolutionary and Napoleonic wars. Austen's elder brother Edward, adopted in his teens by a rich landed family, took his Grand Tour in 1786–88 on the eve of the French Revolution.

The unpersuadable point, which he did not mention, Emma guessed to be good behaviour to his father.

"I have made a most wretched discovery," said, he, after a short pause. — "I have been here a week to-morrow — half my time. I never knew days fly so fast. A week to-morrow! — And I have hardly begun to enjoy myself. But just got acquainted with Mrs. Weston, and others! — I hate the recollection."

"Perhaps you may now begin to regret that you spent one whole day, out of so few, in having your hair cut."

"No," said he, smiling, "that is no subject of regret at all. I have no pleasure in seeing my friends, unless I can believe myself fit to be seen."

The rest of the gentlemen being now in the room, Emma found herself obliged to turn from him for a few minutes, and listen to Mr. Cole. When Mr. Cole had moved away, and her attention could be restored as before, she saw Frank Churchill looking intently across the room at Miss Fairfax, who was sitting exactly opposite.

"What is the matter?" said she.

He started. "Thank you for rousing me," he replied. "I believe I have been very rude; but really Miss Fairfax has done her hair in so odd a way — so very odd a way — that I cannot keep my eyes from her. I never saw any thing so outrée! — Those curls! — This must be a fancy of her own. I see nobody else looking like her! — I must go and ask her whether it is an Irish fashion. Shall I? — Yes, I will — I declare I will — and you shall see how she takes it; — whether she colours."

He was gone immediately; and Emma soon saw him standing before Miss Fairfax, and talking to her; but as to its effect on the young lady, as he had improvidently placed himself exactly between them, exactly in front of Miss Fairfax, she could absolutely distinguish nothing.

Before he could return to his chair, it was taken by Mrs. Weston.

"This is the luxury of a large party," said she: — "one can get near every body, and say every thing. My dear Emma, I am longing to talk to you. I have been making discoveries and forming plans, just like your-self, and I must tell them while the idea is fresh. Do you know how Miss Bates and her niece came here?"

"How! — They were invited, were not they?"

"Oh! yes — but how they were conveyed hither? — the manner of their coming?"

"They walked, I conclude. How else could they come?"

"Very true. — Well, a little while ago it occurred to me how very sad it would be to have Jane Fairfax walking home again, late at night, and cold as the nights are now. And as I looked at her, though I never saw her appear to more advantage, it struck me that she was heated, and would therefore be particularly liable to take cold. Poor girl! I could not bear the idea of it; so, as soon as Mr. Weston came into the room, and I could get at him, I spoke to him about the carriage. You may guess how readily he came into my wishes; and having his approbation, I made my way directly to Miss Bates, to assure her that the carriage would be at her service before it took us home; for I thought it would be making her comfortable at once. Good soul! she was as grateful as possible, you may be sure. 'Nobody was ever so fortunate as herself!' — but with many, many thanks, — 'there was no occasion to trouble us, for Mr. Knightley's carriage had brought, and was to take them home again.' I was quite surprized; — very glad, I am sure; but really quite surprized. Such a very kind attention — and so thoughtful an atten tion! — the sort of thing that so few men would think of. And, in short, from knowing his usual ways, I am very much inclined to think that it was for their accommodation the carriage was used at all. I do suspect he would not have had a pair of horses for himself, and that it was only as an excuse for assisting them."

"Very likely," said Emma — "nothing more likely. I know no man more likely than Mr. Knightley to do the sort of thing — to do any thing really good-natured, useful, considerate, or benevolent. He is not a gallant man, but he is a very humane one; and this, considering Jane Fairfax's ill health, would appear a case of humanity to him; — and for an act of un-ostentatious kindness, there is nobody whom I would fix on more than on Mr. Knightley. I know he had horses to-day — for we arrived together; and I laughed at him about it, but he said not a word that could betray."

"Well," said Mrs. Weston, smiling, "you give him credit for more simple, disinterested benevolence in this instance than I do; for while Miss Bates was speaking, a suspicion darted into my head, and I have never been able to get it out again. The more I think of it, the more probable it appears. In short, I have made a match between Mr. Knightley and Jane Fairfax. See the consequence of keeping you com-pany! — What do you say to it?"

"Mr. Knightley and Jane Fairfax!" — exclaimed Emma. "Dear Mrs. Weston, how could you think of such a thing? — Mr. Knightley! — Mr. Knightley must not marry! — You would not have little Henry cut out from Donwell? — Oh! no, no, Henry must have Donwell. I cannot at all consent to Mr. Knightley's marrying; and I am sure it is not at all likely. I am amazed that you should think of such a thing."

"My dear Emma, I have told you what led me to think of it. I do not want the match — I do not want to injure dear little Henry — but the idea has been given me by circumstances; and if Mr. Knightley really wished to marry, you would not have him refrain on Henry's account, a boy of six years old, who knows nothing of the matter?"

"Yes, I would. I could not bear to have Henry supplanted. — Mr. Knightley marry! — No, I have never had such an idea, and I cannot adopt it now. And Jane Fairfax, too, of all women!"

"Nay, she has always been a first favourite with him, as you very well know."

"But the imprudence of such a match!"

"I am not speaking of its prudence; merely its probability."

"I see no probability in it, unless you have any better foundation than what you mention. His good-nature, his humanity, as I tell you, would be quite enough to account for the horses. He has a great regard for the Bateses, you know, independent of Jane Fairfax — and is always glad to shew them attention. My dear Mrs. Weston, do not take to match-making. You do it very ill. Jane Fairfax mistress of the Abbey! — Oh! no, no; — every feeling revolts. For his own sake, I would not have him do so mad a thing."

"Imprudent, if you please — but not mad. Excepting inequality of fortune, and perhaps a little disparity of age, I can see nothing unsuitable."

"But Mr. Knightley does not want to marry. I am sure he has not the least idea of it. Do not put it into his head. Why should he marry? — He is as happy as possible by himself; with his farm, and his sheep, and his library, and all the parish to manage; and he is extremely fond of his brother's children. He has no occasion to marry, either to fill up his time or his heart."

"My dear Emma, as long as he thinks so, it is so; but if he really loves Jane Fairfax ———"

"Nonsense! He does not care about Jane Fairfax. In the way of love, I am sure he does not. He would do any good to her, or her family; but ———"

"Well," said Mrs. Weston, laughing, "perhaps the greatest good he could do them, would be to give Jane such a respectable home."

"If it would be good to her, I am sure it would be evil to himself; a very shameful and degrading connection. How would he bear to have Miss Bates belonging to him? — To have her haunting the Abbey, and thanking him all day long for his great kindness in marrying Jane? — 'So very kind and obliging! — But he always had been such a very kind neighbour!' And then fly off, through half a sentence, to her mother's old petticoat. 'Not that it was much a very old petticoat either — for still it would last a great while — and, indeed, she must thankfully say that their petticoats were all very strong.'"

"For shame, Emma! Do not mimic her. You divert me against my conscience. And, upon my word, I do not think Mr. Knightley would be much disturbed by Miss Bates. Little things do not irritate him. She might talk on; and if he wanted to say any thing himself, he would only talk louder, and drown her voice. But the question is not, whether it would be a bad connexion for him, but whether he wishes it; and I think he does. I have heard him speak, and so must you, so very highly of Jane Fairfax! The interest he takes in her — his anxiety about her health — his concern that she should have no happier prospect! I have heard him express himself so warmly on those points! — Such an admirer of her performance on the pianofortè, and of her voice! I have heard him say that he could listen to her for ever. Oh! and I had almost forgotten one idea that occurred to me — this pianofortè that has been sent her by somebody — though we have all been so well satisfied to consider it a present from the Campbells, may it not be from Mr. Knightley? I cannot help suspecting him. I think he is just the person to do it, even without being in love."

"Then it can be no argument to prove that he is in love. But I do not think it is at all a likely thing for him to do. Mr. Knightley does nothing mysteriously."

"I have heard him lamenting her having no instrument repeatedly; oftener than I should suppose such a circumstance would, in the common course of things, occur to him "

"Very well; and if he had intended to give her one, he would have told her so."

"There might be scruples of delicacy, my dear Emma. I have a very strong notion that it comes from him. I am sure he was particularly silent when Mrs. Cole told us of it at dinner."

"You take up an idea, Mrs. Weston, and run away with it; as you have many a time reproached me with doing. I see no sign of attachment — I believe nothing of the pianofortè — and proof only shall convince me that Mr. Knightley has any thought of marrying Jane Fairfax."

They combated the point some time longer in the same way; Emma rather gaining ground over the mind of her friend; for Mrs. Weston was the most used of the two to yield; till a little bustle in the room shewed them that tea was over, and the instrument in preparation; — and at the same moment Mr. Cole approaching to entreat Miss Woodhouse would do them the honour of trying it. Frank Churchill, of whom, in the eagerness of her conversation with Mrs. Weston, she had been seeing nothing, except that he had found a seat by Miss Fairfax, followed Mr. Cole, to add his very pressing entreaties; and as, in every respect, it suited Emma best to lead, she gave a very proper compliance.

She knew the limitations of her own powers too well to attempt more than she could perform with credit; she wanted neither taste nor spirit in the little things which are generally acceptable, and could accompany her own voice well. One accompaniment to her song took her agreeably by surprize — a second, slightly but correctly taken by Frank Churchill. Her pardon was duly begged at the close of the song, and every thing usual followed. He was accused of having a delightful voice, and a perfect knowledge of music; which was properly denied; and that he knew nothing of the matter, and had no voice at all, roundly asserted. They sang together once more; and Emma would then resign her place to Miss Fairfax, whose performance, both vocal and instrumental, she never could attempt to conceal from herself, was infinitely superior to her own.

With mixed feelings, she seated herself at a little distance from the numbers round the instrument, to listen. Frank Churchill sang again. They had sung together once or twice, it appeared, at Weymouth. But the sight of Mr. Knightley among the most attentive, soon drew away half Emma's mind; and she fell into a train of thinking on the subject of Mrs. Weston's suspicions, to which the sweet sounds of the united voices gave only momentary interruptions. Her objections to Mr. Knightley's marrying did not in the least subside. She could see nothing but evil in it. It would be a great disappointment to Mr. John Knightley; consequently to Isabella. A real injury to the children — a most mortifying change, and material loss to them all; — a very great deduction from her father's daily comfort — and, as to herself, she could not at all endure the idea of Jane Fairfax at Donwell Abbey. A Mrs. Knightley for them all to give way to! — No — Mr. Knightley must never marry. Little Henry must remain the heir of Donwell.

Presently Mr. Knightley looked back, and came and sat down by her. They talked at first only of the performance. His admiration was certainly very warm; yet she thought, but for Mrs. Weston, it would not have struck her. As a sort of touchstone, however, she began to speak of his kindness in conveying the aunt and niece; and though his answer was in the spirit of cutting the matter short, she believed it to indicate only his disinclination to dwell on any kindness of his own.

"I often feel concerned," said she, "that I dare not make our carriage more useful on such occasions. It is not that I am without the wish; but you know how impossible my father would deem it that James should put-to for such a purpose."

"Quite out of the question, quite out of the question," he replied; — "but you must often wish it, I am sure." And he smiled with such seeming pleasure at the conviction, that she must proceed another step.

"This present from the Campbells," said she — "This pianoforté is very kindly given."

"Yes," he replied, and without the smallest apparent embarrassment. — "But they would have done better had they given her notice of it. Surprizes are foolish things. The pleasure is not enhanced, and the inconvenience is often considerable. I should have expected better judgment in Colonel Campbell."

From that moment, Emma could have taken her oath that Mr. Knightley had had no concern in giving the instrument. But whether he were entirely free from peculiar attachment — whether there were no actual preference — remained a little longer doubtful. Towards the end of Jane's second song, her voice grew thick.

"That will do," said he, when it was finished, thinking aloud — "You have sung quite enough for one evening — now, be quiet."

Another song, however, was soon begged for. "One more; — they would not fatigue Miss Fairfax on any account, and would only ask for one more." And Frank Churchill was heard to say, "I think you could manage this without effort; the first part is so very trifling. The strength of the song falls on the second."

Mr. Knightley grew angry.

"That fellow," said he, indignantly, "thinks of nothing but shewing off his own voice. This must not be." And touching Miss Bates, who at that moment passed near — "Miss Bates, are you mad, to let your niece sing herself hoarse in this manner? Go, and interfere. They have no mercy on her."

Miss Bates, in her real anxiety for Jane, could hardly stay even to be grateful, before she stept forward and put an end to all further singing. Here ceased the concert part of the evening, for Miss Woodhouse and Miss Fairfax were the only young-lady-performers; but soon (within five minutes) the proposal of dancing — originating nobody exactly knew where — was so effectually promoted by Mr. and Mrs. Cole, that every thing was rapidly clearing away, to give proper space. Mrs. Weston, capital in her country-dances, was seated, and beginning an irresistible waltz;[82] and Frank Churchill, coming up with most becoming gallantry to Emma, had secured her hand, and led her up to the top.

While waiting till the other young people could pair themselves off, Emma found time, in spite of the compliments she was receiving on her voice and her taste, to look about, and see what became of Mr. Knightley. This would be a trial. He was no dancer in general. If he were to be very alert in engaging Jane Fairfax now, it might augur something. There was no immediate appearance. No; he was talking to Mrs. Cole — he was looking on unconcerned; Jane was asked by somebody else, and he was still talking to Mrs. Cole.

Emma had no longer an alarm for Henry; his interest was yet safe; and she led off the dance with genuine spirit and enjoyment. Not more than five couple could be mustered; but the rarity and the suddenness of it made it very delightful, and she found herself well matched in a partner. They were a couple worth looking at.

Two dances, unfortunately, were all that could be allowed. It was growing late, and Miss Bates became anxious to get home, on her mother's account. After some attempts, therefore, to be permitted to begin again, they were obliged to thank Mrs. Weston, look sorrowful, and have done.

"Perhaps it is as well," said Frank Churchill, as he attended Emma to her carriage. "I must have asked Miss Fairfax, and her languid dancing would not have agreed with me, after your's."

CHAPTER IX.

EMMA did not repent her condescension in going to the Coles. The visit afforded her many pleasant recollections the next day; and all that she might be supposed to have lost on the side of dignified seclusion, must be amply repaid in the splendour of popularity. She must have delighted the Coles — worthy people, who deserved to be made happy! — And left a name behind her[83] that would not soon die away.

---

[82] *irresistible waltz:* Not to be confused with the ballroom dance for couples introduced in England in 1812, but not considered acceptable in polite society. Cecil Sharp explains: "Collections of Waltz-airs had been published in England for twenty years or more [before 1812] and used as Country Dance Tunes, furnished with Country Dance figures and called Waltz Country Dances"; quoted in Patrick Piggott, *The Innocent Diversion: Music in the Life and Writings of Jane Austen* (London: Douglas Cleverdon, 1979) 93.

[83] *And left a name behind her:* An echo of Ecclesiasticus xliv.8: "there be of them, that have left a name behind them."

Perfect happiness, even in memory, is not common; and there were two points on which she was not quite easy. She doubted whether she had not transgressed the duty of woman by woman, in betraying her suspicions of Jane Fairfax's feelings to Frank Churchill. It was hardly right; but it had been so strong an idea, that it would escape her, and his submission to all that she told, was a compliment to her penetration which made it difficult for her to be quite certain that she ought to have held her tongue.

The other circumstance of regret related also to Jane Fairfax; and there she had no doubt. She did unfeignedly and unequivocally regret the inferiority of her own playing and singing. She did most heartily grieve over the idleness of her childhood — and sat down and practised vigorously an hour and a half.

She was then interrupted by Harriet's coming in; and if Harriet's praise could have satisfied her, she might soon have been comforted.

"Oh! if I could but play as well as you and Miss Fairfax!"

"Don't class us together, Harriet. My playing is no more like her's, than a lamp is like sunshine."

"Oh! dear — I think you play the best of the two. I think you play quite as well as she does. I am sure I had much rather hear you. Every body last night said how well you played."

"Those who knew any thing about it, must have felt the difference The truth is, Harriet, that my playing is just good enough to be praised, but Jane Fairfax's is much beyond it."

"Well, I always shall think that you play quite as well as she does, or that if there is any difference nobody would ever find it out. Mr. Cole said how much taste you had; and Mr. Frank Churchill talked a great deal about your taste, and that he valued taste much more than execution."

"Ah! but Jane Fairfax has them both, Harriet."

"Are you sure? I saw she had execution, but I did not know she had any taste. Nobody talked about it. And I hate Italian singing. — There is no understanding a word of it. Besides, if she does play so very well, you know, it is no more than she is obliged to do, because she will have to teach. The Coxes were wondering last night whether she would get into any great family. How did you think the Coxes looked?"

"Just as they always do — very vulgar."

"They told me something," said Harriet rather hesitatingly, "but it is nothing of any consequence."

Emma was obliged to ask what they had told her, though fearful of its producing Mr. Elton.

"They told me — that Mr. Martin dined with them last Saturday."

"Oh!"

"He came to their father upon some business, and he asked him to stay dinner."

"Oh!"

"They talked a great deal about him, especially Anne Cox. I do not know what she meant, but she asked me if I thought I should go and stay there again next summer."

"She meant to be impertinently curious, just as such an Anne Cox should be."

"She said he was very agreeable the day he dined there. He sat by her at dinner. Miss Nash thinks either of the Coxes would be very glad to marry him."

"Very likely. — I think they are, without exception, the most vulgar girls in Highbury."

Harriet had business at Ford's. — Emma thought it most prudent to go with her. Another accidental meeting with the Martins was possible, and, in her present state, would be dangerous.

Harriet, tempted by every thing and swayed by half a word, was always very long at a purchase; and while she was still hanging over muslins and changing her mind, Emma went to the door for amusement. — Much could not be hoped from the traffic of even the busiest part of Highbury; — Mr. Perry walking hastily by, Mr. William Cox letting himself in at the office door, Mr. Cole's carriage horses returning from exercise, or a stray letter-boy on an obstinate mule, were the liveliest objects she could presume to expect; and when her eyes fell only on the butcher with his tray, a tidy old woman travelling homewards from shop with her full basket, two curs quarrelling over a dirty bone, and a string of dawdling children round the baker's little bow-window eyeing the gingerbread, she knew she had no reason to complain, and was amused enough; quite enough still to stand at the door. A mind lively and at ease, can do with seeing nothing, and can see nothing that does not answer.

She looked down the Randalls road. The scene enlarged; two persons appeared; Mrs. Weston and her son-in-law; they were walking into Highbury; — to Hartfield of course. They were stopping, however, in the first place at Mrs. Bates's; whose house was a little nearer Randalls than Ford's; and had all but knocked, when Emma caught their eye. — Immediately they crossed the road and came forward to her; and the agreeableness of yesterday's engagement seemed to give fresh pleasure to the present meeting. Mrs. Weston informed her that she was going to call on the Bateses, in order to hear the new instrument.

"For my companion tells me," said she, "that I absolutely promised Miss Bates last night, that I would come this morning. I was not aware of it myself. I did not know that I had fixed a day, but as he says I did, I am going now."

"And while Mrs. Weston pays her visit, I may be allowed, I hope," said Frank Churchill, "to join your party and wait for her at Hartfield — if you are going home."

Mrs. Weston was disappointed.

"I thought you meant to go with me. They would be very much pleased."

"Me! I should be quite in the way. But, perhaps — I may be equally in the way here. Miss Woodhouse looks as if she did not want me. My aunt always sends me off when she is shopping. She says I fidget her to death; and Miss Woodhouse looks as if she could almost say the same. What am I to do?"

"I am here on no business of my own," said Emma, "I am only waiting for my friend. She will probably have soon done, and then we shall go home. But you had better go with Mrs. Weston and hear the instrument."

"Well — if you advise it. — But (with a smile) if Col. Campbell should have employed a careless friend, and if it should prove to have an indifferent tone — what shall I say? I shall be no support to Mrs. Weston. She might do very well by herself. A disagreeable truth would be palatable through her lips, but I am the wretchedest being in the world at a civil falsehood."

"I do not believe any such thing," replied Emma. — "I am persuaded that you can be as insincere as your neighbours, when it is necessary; but there is no reason to suppose the instrument is indifferent. Quite otherwise indeed, if I understood Miss Fairfax's opinion last night."

"Do come with me," said Mrs. Weston, "if it be not very disagreeable to you. It need not detain us long. We will go to Hartfield afterwards. We will follow them to Hartfield. I really wish you to call with me. It will be felt so great an attention! and I always thought you meant it."

He could say no more; and with the hope of Hartfield to reward him, returned with Mrs. Weston to Mrs. Bates's door. Emma watched them in, and then joined Harriet at the interesting counter, — trying, with all the force of her own mind, to convince her that if she wanted plain muslin it was of no use to look at figured; and that a blue ribbon, be it ever so beautiful, would still never match her yellow pattern. At last it was all settled, even to the destination of the parcel.

"Should I send it to Mrs. Goddard's, ma'am?" asked Mrs. Ford.

"Yes — no — yes, to Mrs. Goddard's. Only my pattern gown is at Hartfield. No, you shall send it to Hartfield, if you please. But then, Mrs. Goddard will want to see it — And I could take the pattern gown home any day. But I shall want the ribbon directly — so it had better go to Hartfield — at least the ribbon. You could make it into two parcels, Mrs. Ford, could you not?"

"It is not worth while, Harriet, to give Mrs. Ford the trouble of two parcels."

"No more it is."

"No trouble in the world, ma'am," said the obliging Mrs. Ford.

"Oh! but indeed I would much rather have it only in one. Then, if you please, you shall send it all to Mrs. Goddard's — I do not know — No, I think, Miss Woodhouse, I may just as well have it sent to Hartfield, and take it home with me at night. What do you advise?"

"That you do not give another half-second to the subject. To Hartfield, if you please, Mrs. Ford."

"Aye, that will be much best," said Harriet, quite satisfied, "I should not at all like to have it sent to Mrs. Goddard's."

Voices approached the shop — or rather one voice and two ladies; Mrs. Weston and Miss Bates met them at the door.

"My dear Miss Woodhouse," said the latter, "I am just run across to entreat the favour of you to come and sit down with us a little while, and give us your opinion of our new instrument; you and Miss Smith. How do you do, Miss Smith? — Very well I thank you. — And I begged Mrs. Weston to come with me, that I might be sure of succeeding."

"I hope Mrs. Bates and Miss Fairfax are" ——

"Very well, I am much obliged to you. My mother is delightfully well; and Jane caught no cold last night. How is Mr. Woodhouse? — I am so glad to hear such a good account. Mrs. Weston told me you were here. — Oh! then, said I, I must run across, I am sure Miss Woodhouse will allow me just to run across and entreat her to come in; my mother will be so very happy to see her — and now we are such a nice party, she cannot refuse. 'Aye, pray do,' said Mr. Frank Churchill, 'Miss Woodhouse's opinion of the instrument will be worth having.' — But, said I, I shall be more sure of succeeding if one of you will go with me. —

'Oh!' said he, 'wait half-a-minute till I have finished my job.' — For, would you believe it, Miss Woodhouse, there he is, in the most obliging manner in the world, fastening in the rivet of my mother's spec tacles. — The rivet came out, you know, this morning. — So very obliging! — For my mother had no use of her spectacles — could not put them on. And, by the bye, every body ought to have two pair of spectacles; they should indeed. Jane said so. I meant to take them over to John Saunders the first thing I did, but something or other hindered me all the morning; first one thing, then another, there is no saying what, you know. At one time Patty came to say she thought the kitchen chimney wanted sweeping. Oh! said I, Patty do not come with your bad news to me. Here is the rivet of your mistress's spectacles out. Then the baked apples[84] came home, Mrs. Wallis sent them by her boy; they are extremely civil and obliging to us, the Wallises, always — I have heard some people say that Mrs. Wallis can be uncivil and give a very rude answer, but we have never known any thing but the greatest attention from them. And it cannot be for the value of our custom now, for what is our consumption of bread, you know? Only three of us — besides dear Jane at present — and she really eats nothing — makes such a shocking breakfast, you would be quite frightened if you saw it. I dare not let my mother know how little she eats — so I say one thing and then I say another, and it passes off. But about the middle of the day she gets hungry, and there is nothing she likes so well as these baked apples, and they are extremely wholesome, for I took the opportunity the other day of asking Mr. Perry; I happened to meet him in the street. Not that I had any doubt before — I have so often heard Mr. Woodhouse recommend a baked apple. I believe it is the only way that Mr. Woodhouse thinks the fruit thoroughly wholesome. We have apple dumplings, however, very often. Patty makes an excellent apple-dumpling. Well, Mrs. Weston, you have prevailed, I hope, and these ladies will oblige us."

Emma would be "very happy to wait on Mrs. Bates, &c." and they did at last move out of the shop, with no further delay from Miss Bates than,

"How do you do, Mrs. Ford? I beg your pardon. I did not see you before. I hear you have a charming collection of new ribbons from town. Jane came back delighted yesterday. Thank ye, the gloves do

---

[84]*baked apples:* Though Frank Churchill admires them as "the finest looking home-baked apples I ever saw" (p. 196), these apples, Mr. Knightley's gift from Donwell, have been baked (twice) at the village bakery of Mrs. Wallis. For a discussion of apples and other food in *Emma,* see Maggie Lane, *Jane Austen and Food* (London: Hambledon P, 1995) 41–68.

very well — only a little too large about the wrist; but Jane is taking
them in."

"What was I talking of?" said she, beginning again when they were
all in the street.

Emma wondered on what, of all the medley, she would fix.

"I declare I cannot recollect what I was talking of. — Oh! my
mother's spectacles. So very obliging of Mr. Frank Churchill! 'Oh!' said
he, 'I do think I can fasten the rivet; I like a job of this kind excessively.' — Which you know shewed him to be so very . . . . . Indeed I
must say that, much as I had heard of him before and much as I had
expected, he very far exceeds any thing . . . . . I do congratulate you,
Mrs. Weston, most warmly. He seems every thing the fondest parent
could . . . . .'Oh!' said he, 'I can fasten the rivet. I like a job of that sort
excessively.' I never shall forget his manner. And when I brought out
the baked apples from the closet, and hoped our friends would be so
very obliging as to take some, 'Oh!' said he directly, 'there is nothing in
the way of fruit half so good, and these are the finest looking home-
baked apples I ever saw in my life.' That, you know, was so very . . . . . .
And I am sure, by his manner, it was no compliment. Indeed they are
very delightful apples, and Mrs. Wallis does them full justice — only we
do not have them baked more than twice, and Mr. Woodhouse made us
promise to have them done three times — but Miss Woodhouse will be
so good as not to mention it. The apples themselves are the very finest
sort for baking, beyond a doubt; all from Donwell — some of Mr.
Knightley's most liberal supply. He sends us a sack every year; and certainly there never was such a keeping apple any where as one of his
trees — I believe there is two of them. My mother says the orchard was
always famous in her younger days. But I was really quite shocked the
other day — for Mr. Knightley called one morning, and Jane was eating
these apples, and we talked about them and said how much she enjoyed
them, and he asked whether we were not got to the end of our stock. 'I
am sure you must be,' said he, 'and I will send you another supply; for I
have a great many more than I can ever use. William Larkins let me
keep a larger quantity than usual this year. I will send you some more,
before they get good for nothing.' So I begged he would not — for
really as to ours being gone, I could not absolutely say that we had a
great many left — it was but half a dozen indeed; but they should be all
kept for Jane; and I could not at all bear that he should be sending us
more, so liberal as he had been already; and Jane said the same. And
when he was gone, she almost quarrelled with me — No, I should not
say quarrelled, for we never had a quarrel in our lives; but she was quite

distressed that I had owned the apples were so nearly gone; she wished
I had made him believe we had a great many left. Oh! said I, my dear, I
did say as much as I could. However, the very same evening William
Larkins came over with a large basket of apples, the same sort of apples,
a bushel at least, and I was very much obliged, and went down and
spoke to William Larkins and said every thing, as you may suppose.
William Larkins is such an old acquaintance! I am always glad to see
him. But, however, I found afterwards from Patty, that William said it
was all the apples of *that* sort his master had; he had brought them
all — and now his master had not one left to bake or boil. William did
not seem to mind it himself, he was so pleased to think his master had
sold so many; for William, you know, thinks more of his master's profit
than any thing; but Mrs. Hodges, he said, was quite displeased at their
being all sent away. She could not bear that her master should not be
able to have another apple-tart this spring. He told Patty this, but bid
her not mind it, and be sure not to say any thing to us about it, for Mrs.
Hodges *would* be cross sometimes, and as long as so many sacks were
sold, it did not signify who ate the remainder. And so Patty told me,
and I was excessively shocked indeed! I would not have Mr. Knightley
know any thing about it for the world! He would be so very I
wanted to keep it from Jane's knowledge; but unluckily, I had mentioned it before I was aware."

Miss Bates had just done as Patty opened the door; and her visitors
walked up stairs without having any regular narration to attend to, pursued only by the sounds of her desultory good-will.

"Pray take care, Mrs. Weston, there is a step at the turning. Pray
take care, Miss Woodhouse, ours is rather a dark staircase — rather
darker and narrower than one could wish. Miss Smith, pray take care.
Miss Woodhouse, I am quite concerned, I am sure you hit your foot.
Miss Smith, the step at the turning."

CHAPTER X.

THE appearance of the little sitting-room as they entered, was tranquillity itself; Mrs. Bates, deprived of her usual employment, slumbering on
one side of the fire, Frank Churchill, at a table near her, most deedily[85]
occupied about her spectacles, and Jane Fairfax, standing with her back
to them, intent on her pianoforté.

---

[85]*deedily:* Actively, busily. Of the three illustrative citations in the *OED*, two (including this one) are from Jane Austen.

Busy as he was, however, the young man was yet able to shew a most happy countenance on seeing Emma again.

"This is a pleasure," said he, in rather a low voice, "coming at least ten minutes earlier than I had calculated. You find me trying to be useful; tell me if you think I shall succeed."

"What!" said Mrs. Weston, "have not you finished it yet? you would not earn a very good livelihood as a working-silversmith at this rate."

"I have not been working uninterruptedly," he replied, "I have been assisting Miss Fairfax in trying to make her instrument stand steadily, it was not quite firm; an unevenness in the floor, I believe. You see we have been wedging one leg with paper. This was very kind of you to be persuaded to come. I was almost afraid you would be hurrying home."

He contrived that she should be seated by him; and was sufficiently employed in looking out the best baked apple for her, and trying to make her help or advise him in his work, till Jane Fairfax was quite ready to sit down to the pianoforté again. That she was not immediately ready, Emma did suspect to arise from the state of her nerves; she had not yet possessed the instrument long enough to touch it without emotion; she must reason herself into the power of performance; and Emma could not but pity such feelings, whatever their origin, and could not but resolve never to expose them to her neighbour again.

At last Jane began, and though the first bars were feebly given, the powers of the instrument were gradually done full justice to. Mrs. Weston had been delighted before, and was delighted again; Emma joined her in all her praise; and the pianoforté, with every proper discrimination, was pronounced to be altogether of the highest promise.

"Whoever Col. Campbell might employ," said Frank Churchill, with a smile at Emma, "the person has not chosen ill. I heard a good deal of Col. Campbell's taste at Weymouth; and the softness of the upper notes I am sure is exactly what he and *all that party* would particularly prize. I dare say, Miss Fairfax, that he either gave his friend very minute directions, or wrote to Broadwood himself. Do not you think so?"

Jane did not look round. She was not obliged to hear. Mrs. Weston had been speaking to her at the same moment.

"It is not fair," said Emma in a whisper, "mine was a random guess. Do not distress her."

He shook his head with a smile, and looked as if he had very little doubt and very little mercy. Soon afterwards he began again,

"How much your friends in Ireland must be enjoying your pleasure on this occasion, Miss Fairfax. I dare say they often think of you, and wonder which will be the day, the precise day of the instrument's coming to hand. Do you imagine Col. Campbell knows the business to be going forward just at this time? — Do you imagine it to be the consequence of an immediate commission from him, or that he may have sent only a general direction, an order indefinite as to time, to depend upon contingencies and conveniencies?"

He paused. She could not but hear; she could not avoid answering, "Till I have a letter from Col. Campbell," said she, in a voice of forced calmness, "I can imagine nothing with any confidence. It must be all conjecture."

"Conjecture — aye, sometimes one conjectures right, and sometimes one conjectures wrong. I wish I could conjecture how soon I shall make this rivet quite firm. What nonsense one talks, Miss Woodhouse, when hard at work, if one talks at all; — your real workmen, I suppose, hold their tongues; but we gentlemen labourers if we get hold of a word — Miss Fairfax said something about conjecturing. There, it is done. I have the pleasure, madam, (to Mrs. Bates,) of restoring your spectacles, healed for the present."

He was very warmly thanked both by mother and daughter; to escape a little from the latter, he went to the pianoforté, and begged Miss Fairfax, who was still sitting at it, to play something more.

"If you are very kind," said he, "it will be one of the waltzes we danced last night; — let me live them over again. You did not enjoy them as I did; you appeared tired the whole time. I believe you were glad we danced no longer; but I would have given worlds — all the worlds one ever has to give — for another half hour."

She played.

"What felicity it is to hear a tune again which *has* made one happy! — If I mistake not that was danced at Weymouth."

She looked up at him for a moment, coloured deeply, and played something else. He took some music from a chair near the pianoforté, and turning to Emma, said,

"Here is something quite new to me. Do you know it? — Cramer. — And here are a new set of Irish melodies.[86] That, from such

---

[86] *Cramer. . . . Irish melodies:* John Baptist Cramer (1771–1858), the only composer mentioned in Austen's works, was a well-known composer, pianist, and pianoforté teacher whose concertos, chamber music, sonatas, variations, and studies sold in vast quantities in London at the time. See Piggott (100) (cited in note 82, p. 190). The *Irish Melodies* are probably those of Thomas Moore, a compilation of traditional Irish airs and songs issued in eight published works (or numbers) between 1808 and 1821.

a quarter, one might expect. This was all sent with the instrument. Very thoughtful of Col. Campbell, was not it? — He knew Miss Fairfax could have no music here. I honour that part of the attention particularly; it shews it to have been so thoroughly from the heart. Nothing hastily done; nothing incomplete. True affection only could have prompted it."

Emma wished he would be less pointed, yet could not help being amused; and when on glancing her eye towards Jane Fairfax she caught the remains of a smile, when she saw that with all the deep blush of consciousness, there had been a smile of secret delight, she had less scruple in the amusement, and much less compunction with respect to her. — This amiable, upright, perfect Jane Fairfax was apparently cherishing very reprehensible feelings.

He brought all the music to her, and they looked it over together. — Emma took the opportunity of whispering,

"You speak too plain. She must understand you."

"I hope she does. I would have her understand me. I am not in the least ashamed of my meaning."

"But really, I am half ashamed, and wish I had never taken up the idea."

"I am very glad you did, and that you communicated it to me. I have now a key to all her odd looks and ways. Leave shame to her. If she does wrong, she ought to feel it."

"She is not entirely without it, I think."

"I do not see much sign of it. She is playing *Robin Adair*[87] at this moment — *his* favourite."

Shortly afterwards Miss Bates, passing near the window, descried Mr. Knightley on horseback not far off.

"Mr. Knightley I declare! — I must speak to him if possible, just to thank him. I will not open the window here; it would give you all cold; but I can go into my mother's room you know. I dare say he will come in when he knows who is here. Quite delightful to have you all meet so! — Our little room so honoured!"

She was in the adjoining chamber while she still spoke, and opening the casement there, immediately called Mr. Knightley's attention, and every syllable of their conversation was as distinctly heard by the others, as if it had passed within the same apartment.

[87]*Robin Adair:* Traditional air (originally called "Eileen Aroon") introduced into Scotland from Ireland in the eighteenth century, commonly sung to piano accompaniment. For a fuller discussion of the song's relevance to the novel, and for one version of the words, see "Contextual Documents," pp. 382–83, 386.

"How d'ye do? — how d'ye do? — Very well, I thank you. So obliged to you for the carriage last night. We were just in time; my mother just ready for us. Pray come in, do come in. You will find some friends here."

So began Miss Bates; and Mr. Knightley seemed determined to be heard in his turn, for most resolutely and commandingly did he say,

"How is your niece, Miss Bates? — I want to inquire after you all, but particularly your niece. How is Miss Fairfax? — I hope she caught no cold last night. How is she to-day? Tell me how Miss Fairfax is."

And Miss Bates was obliged to give a direct answer before he would hear her in any thing else. The listeners were amused; and Mrs. Weston gave Emma a look of particular meaning. But Emma still shook her head in steady scepticism.

"So obliged to you! — so very much obliged to you for the carriage," resumed Miss Bates.

He cut her short with,

"I am going to Kingston. Can I do any thing for you?"

"Oh! dear, Kingston — are you? — Mrs. Cole was saying the other day she wanted something from Kingston."

"Mrs. Cole has servants to send. Can I do any thing for *you?*"

"No, I thank you. But do come in. Who do you think is here? — Miss Woodhouse and Miss Smith; so kind as to call to hear the new pianoforté. Do put up your horse at the Crown, and come in."

"Well," said he in a deliberating manner, "for five minutes, perhaps."

"And here is Mrs. Weston and Mr. Frank Churchill too! — Quite delightful; so many friends!"

"No, not now, I thank you. I could not stay two minutes. I must get on to Kingston as fast as I can."

"Oh! do come in. They will be so very happy to see you."

"No, no, your room is full enough. I will call another day, and hear the pianoforté."

"Well, I am so sorry! — Oh! Mr. Knightley, what a delightful party last night; how extremely pleasant. — Did you ever see such dancing? — Was not it delightful? — Miss Woodhouse and Mr. Frank Churchill; I never saw any thing equal to it."

"Oh! very delightful indeed; I can say nothing less, for I suppose Miss Woodhouse and Mr. Frank Churchill are hearing every thing that passes. And (raising his voice still more) I do not see why Miss Fairfax should not be mentioned too. I think Miss Fairfax dances very well; and Mrs. Weston is the very best country-dance player, without exception, in England. Now, if your friends have any gratitude, they will say something pretty loud about you and me in return; but I cannot stay to hear it."

"Oh! Mr. Knightley, one moment more; something of consequence — so shocked! — Jane and I are both so shocked about the apples!"

"What is the matter now?"

"To think of your sending us all your store apples. You said you had a great many, and now you have not one left. We really are so shocked! Mrs. Hodges may well be angry. William Larkins mentioned it here. You should not have done it, indeed you should not. Ah! he is off. He never can bear to be thanked. But I thought he would have staid now, and it would have been a pity not to have mentioned . . . . . Well, (returning into the room,) I have not been able to succeed. Mr. Knightley cannot stop. He is going to Kingston. He asked me if he could do any thing". . . .

"Yes," said Jane, "we heard his kind offers, we heard every thing."

"Oh! yes, my dear, I dare say you might, because you know the door was open, and the window was open, and Mr. Knightley spoke loud. You must have heard every thing to be sure. 'Can I do any thing for you at Kingston?' said he; so I just mentioned . . . . . Oh! Miss Woodhouse, must you be going? — You seem but just come — so very obliging of you."

Emma found it really time to be at home; the visit had already lasted long; and on examining watches, so much of the morning was perceived to be gone, that Mrs. Weston and her companion taking leave also, could allow themselves only to walk with the two young ladies to Hartfield gates, before they set off for Randalls.

CHAPTER XI.

It may be possible to do without dancing entirely. Instances have been known of young people passing many, many months successively, without being at any ball of any description, and no material injury accrue either to body or mind; — but when a beginning is made — when the felicities of rapid motion have once been, though slightly, felt — it must be a very heavy set that does not ask for more.

Frank Churchill had danced once at Highbury, and longed to dance again; and the last half hour of an evening which Mr. Woodhouse was persuaded to spend with his daughter at Randalls, was passed by the two young people in schemes on the subject. Frank's was the first idea; and his the greatest zeal in pursuing it; for the lady was the best judge of the difficulties, and the most solicitous for accommodation and appearance. But still she had inclination enough for shewing people again how delightfully Mr. Frank Churchill and Miss Woodhouse danced — for doing that in which she need not blush to compare herself with Jane Fairfax — and even for simple dancing itself, without any of the wicked aids of vanity — to assist him first in pacing out the room they were in to see what it could be made to hold — and then in taking the dimensions of the other parlour, in the hope of discovering, in spite of all that Mr. Weston could say of their exactly equal size, that it was a little the largest.

His first proposition and request, that the dance begun at Mr. Cole's should be finished there — that the same party should be collected, and the same musician engaged, met with the readiest acquiescence. Mr. Weston entered into the idea with thorough enjoyment, and Mrs. Weston most willingly undertook to play as long as they could wish to dance; and the interesting employment had followed, of reckoning up exactly who there would be, and portioning out the indispensable division of space to every couple.

"You and Miss Smith, and Miss Fairfax, will be three, and the two Miss Coxes five," had been repeated many times over. "And there will be the two Gilberts, young Cox, my father, and myself, besides Mr. Knightley. Yes, that will be quite enough for pleasure. You and Miss Smith, and Miss Fairfax, will be three, and the two Miss Coxes five; and for five couple there will be plenty of room."

But soon it came to be on one side,

"But will there be good room for five couple? — I really do not think there will."

On another,

"And after all, five couple are not enough to make it worth while to stand up. Five couple are nothing, when one thinks seriously about it. It will not do to *invite* five couple. It can be allowable only as the thought of the moment."

Somebody said that *Miss* Gilbert was expected at her brother's, and must be invited with the rest. Somebody else believed *Mrs.* Gilbert would have danced the other evening, if she had been asked. A word was put in for a second young Cox; and at last, Mr. Weston naming one family of cousins who must be included, and another of very old acquaintance who could not be left out, it became a certainty that the five couple would be at least ten, and a very interesting speculation in what possible manner they could be disposed of.

The doors of the two rooms were just opposite each other. "Might not they use both rooms, and dance across the passage?" It seemed the best scheme; and yet it was not so good but that many of them wanted a better. Emma said it would be awkward; Mrs. Weston was in distress about the supper; and Mr. Woodhouse opposed it earnestly, on the score of health. It made him so very unhappy, indeed, that it could not be persevered in.

"Oh! no," said he; "it would be the extreme of imprudence. I could not bear it for Emma! — Emma is not strong. She would catch a dreadful cold. So would poor little Harriet. So you would all. Mrs. Weston, you would be quite laid up; do not let them talk of such a wild thing. Pray do not let them talk of it. That young man (speaking lower) is very thoughtless. Do not tell his father, but that young man is not quite the thing. He has been opening the doors very often this evening, and keeping them open very inconsiderately. He does not think of the draught. I do not mean to set you against him, but indeed he is not quite the thing!"

Mrs. Weston was sorry for such a charge. She knew the importance of it, and said every thing in her power to do it away. Every door was now closed, the passage plan given up, and the first scheme of dancing only in the room they were in resorted to again; and with such good-will on Frank Churchill's part, that the space which a quarter of an hour before had been deemed barely sufficient for five couple, was now endeavoured to be made out quite enough for ten.

"We were too magnificent," said he. "We allowed unnecessary room. Ten couple may stand here very well."

Emma demurred. "It would be a crowd — a sad crowd; and what could be worse than dancing without space to turn in?"

"Very true," he gravely replied; "it was very bad." But still he went on measuring, and still he ended with,

"I think there will be very tolerable room for ten couple."

"No, no," said she, "you are quite unreasonable. It would be dreadful to be standing so close! Nothing can be farther from pleasure than to be dancing in a crowd — and a crowd in a little room!"

"There is no denying it," he replied. "I agree with you exactly. A crowd in a little room — Miss Woodhouse, you have the art of giving pictures in a few words. Exquisite, quite exquisite! — Still, however, having proceeded so far, one is unwilling to give the matter up. It would be a disappointment to my father — and altogether — I do not know that — I am rather of opinion that ten couple might stand here very well."

Emma perceived that the nature of his gallantry was a little self-willed, and that he would rather oppose than lose the pleasure of dancing with her; but she took the compliment, and forgave the rest. Had she intended ever to *marry* him, it might have been worth while to pause and consider, and try to understand the value of his preference, and the character of his temper; but for all the purposes of their acquaintance, he was quite amiable enough.

Before the middle of the next day, he was at Hartfield; and he entered the room with such an agreeable smile as certified the continuance of the scheme. It soon appeared that he came to announce an improvement.

"Well, Miss Woodhouse," he almost immediately began, "your inclination for dancing has not been quite frightened away, I hope, by the terrors of my father's little rooms. I bring a new proposal on the subject: — a thought of my father's, which waits only your approbation to be acted upon. May I hope for the honour of your hand for the two first dances of this little projected ball, to be given, not at Randalls, but at the Crown Inn?"

"The Crown!"

"Yes; if you and Mr. Woodhouse see no objection, and I trust you cannot, my father hopes his friends will be so kind as to visit him there. Better accommodations, he can promise them, and not a less grateful welcome than at Randalls. It is his own idea. Mrs. Weston sees no objection to it, provided you are satisfied. This is what we all feel. Oh! you were perfectly right! Ten couple, in either of the Randalls rooms, would have been insufferable! — Dreadful! — I felt how right you were the whole time, but was too anxious for securing *any thing* to like to yield. Is not it a good exchange? — You consent — I hope you consent?"

"It appears to me a plan that nobody can object to, if Mr. and Mrs. Weston do not. I think it admirable; and, as far as I can answer for myself, shall be most happy —— It seems the only improvement that could be. Papa, do you not think it an excellent improvement?"

She was obliged to repeat and explain it, before it was fully comprehended; and then, being quite new, further representations were necessary to make it acceptable.

"No; he thought it very far from an improvement — a very bad plan — much worse than the other. A room at an inn was always damp and dangerous; never properly aired, or fit to be inhabited. If they must dance, they had better dance at Randalls. He had never been in the room at the Crown in his life — did not know the people who kept it by sight. — Oh! no — a very bad plan. They would catch worse colds at the Crown than any where."

"I was going to observe, sir," said Frank Churchill, "that one of the great recommendations of this change would be the very little danger of any body's catching cold — so much less danger at the Crown than at Randalls! Mr. Perry might have reason to regret the alteration, but nobody else could."

"Sir," said Mr. Woodhouse, rather warmly, "you are very much mistaken if you suppose Mr. Perry to be that sort of character. Mr. Perry is extremely concerned when any of us are ill. But I do not understand how the room at the Crown can be safer for you than your father's house."

"From the very circumstance of its being larger, sir. We shall have no occasion to open the windows at all — not once the whole evening; and it is that dreadful habit of opening the windows, letting in cold air upon heated bodies, which (as you well know, sir) does the mischief."

"Open the windows! — but surely, Mr. Churchill, nobody would think of opening the windows at Randalls. Nobody could be so imprudent! I never heard of such a thing. Dancing with open windows! — I am sure, neither your father nor Mrs. Weston (poor Miss Taylor that was) would suffer it."

"Ah! sir — but a thoughtless young person will sometimes step behind a window-curtain, and throw up a sash, without its being suspected. I have often known it done myself."

"Have you indeed, sir? — Bless me! I never could have supposed it. But I live out of the world, and am often astonished at what I hear. However, this does make a difference; and, perhaps, when we come to talk it over — but these sort of things require a good deal of consideration. One cannot resolve upon them in a hurry. If Mr. and Mrs. Weston will be so obliging as to call here one morning, we may talk it over, and see what can be done."

"But, unfortunately, sir, my time is so limited —"

"Oh!" interrupted Emma, "there will be plenty of time for talking every thing over. There is no hurry at all. If it can be contrived to be at the Crown, papa, it will be very convenient for the horses. They will be so near their own stable."

"So they will, my dear. That is a great thing. Not that James ever complains; but it is right to spare our horses when we can. If I could be sure of the rooms being thoroughly aired — but is Mrs. Stokes to be trusted? I doubt it. I do not know her, even by sight."

"I can answer for every thing of that nature, sir, because it will be under Mrs. Weston's care. Mrs. Weston undertakes to direct the whole."

"There, papa! — Now you must be satisfied — Our own dear Mrs. Weston, who is carefulness itself. Do not you remember what Mr. Perry said, so many years ago, when I had the measles? 'If *Miss Taylor* undertakes to wrap Miss Emma up, you need not have any fears, sir.' How often have I heard you speak of it as such a compliment to her!"

"Aye, very true. Mr. Perry did say so. I shall never forget it. Poor little Emma! You were very bad with the measles; that is, you would have been very bad, but for Perry's great attention. He came four times a day for a week. He said, from the first, it was a very good sort — which was our great comfort; but the measles are a dreadful complaint. I hope whenever poor Isabella's little ones have the measles, she will send for Perry."

"My father and Mrs. Weston are at the Crown at this moment," said Frank Churchill, "examining the capabilities of the house. I left them there and came on to Hartfield, impatient for your opinion, and hoping you might be persuaded to join them and give your advice on the spot. I was desired to say so from both. It would be the greatest pleasure to them, if you could allow me to attend you there. They can do nothing satisfactorily without you."

Emma was most happy to be called to such a council; and her father, engaging to think it all over while she was gone, the two young people set off together without delay for the Crown. There were Mr. and Mrs. Weston, delighted to see her and receive her approbation, very busy and very happy in their different way; she, in some little distress; and he, finding every thing perfect.

"Emma," said she, "this paper is worse than I expected. Look! in places you see it is dreadfully dirty; and the wainscot is more yellow and forlorn than any thing I could have imagined."

"My dear, you are too particular," said her husband. "What does all that signify? You will see nothing of it by candle-light. It will be as clean as Randalls by candle-light. We never see any thing of it on our club-nights."

The ladies here probably exchanged looks which meant, "Men never know when things are dirty or not;" and the gentlemen perhaps thought each to himself, "Women will have their little nonsenses and needless cares."

One perplexity, however, arose, which the gentlemen did not disdain. It regarded a supper-room. At the time of the ball-room's being built, suppers had not been in question; and a small card-room adjoining, was the only addition. What was to be done? This card-room would be wanted as a card-room now; or, if cards were conveniently voted unnecessary by their four selves, still was not it too small for any comfortable supper? Another room of much better size might be secured for the purpose; but it was at the other end of the house, and a long awkward passage must be gone through to get at it. This made a difficulty. Mrs. Weston was afraid of draughts for the young people in that passage; and neither Emma nor the gentlemen could tolerate the prospect of being miserably crowded at supper.

Mrs. Weston proposed having no regular supper; merely sandwiches, &c. set out in the little room; but that was scouted as a wretched suggestion. A private dance, without sitting down to supper, was pronounced an infamous fraud upon the rights of men and women;[88] and Mrs. Weston must not speak of it again. She then took another line of expediency, and looking into the doubtful room, observed,

"I do not think it *is* so very small. We shall not be many, you know."

And Mr. Weston at the same time, walking briskly with long steps through the passage, was calling out,

"You talk a great deal of the length of this passage, my dear. It is a mere nothing after all; and not the least draught from the stairs."

"I wish," said Mrs. Weston, "one could know which arrangement our guests in general would like best. To do what would be most generally pleasing must be our object — if one could but tell what that would be."

"Yes, very true," cried Frank, "very true. You want your neighbours' opinions. I do not wonder at you. If one could ascertain what the chief of them — the Coles, for instance. They are not far off. Shall I call upon them? Or Miss Bates? She is still nearer. — And I do not know whether Miss Bates is not as likely to understand the inclinations of the rest of the people as any body. I think we do want a larger council. Suppose I go and invite Miss Bates to join us?"

"Well — if you please," said Mrs. Weston rather hesitating, "if you think she will be of any use."

"You will get nothing to the purpose from Miss Bates," said Emma.

[88] *rights of men and women:* An allusion to the works of Mary Wollstonecraft (*A Vindication of the Rights of Men* [1790]; *A Vindication of the Rights of Woman* [1792]) and Tom Paine (*The Rights of Man* [1791]).

"She will be all delight and gratitude, but she will tell you nothing. She will not even listen to your questions. I see no advantage in consulting Miss Bates."

"But she is so amusing, so extremely amusing! I am very fond of hearing Miss Bates talk. And I need not bring the whole family, you know."

Here Mr. Weston joined them, and on hearing what was proposed, gave it his decided approbation.

"Aye, do, Frank. — Go and fetch Miss Bates, and let us end the matter at once. She will enjoy the scheme, I am sure; and I do not know a properer person for shewing us how to do away difficulties. Fetch Miss Bates. We are growing a little too nice. She is a standing lesson of how to be happy. But fetch them both. Invite them both."

"Both sir! Can the old lady?". . .

"The old lady! No, the young lady, to be sure. I shall think you a great blockhead, Frank, if you bring the aunt without the niece."

"Oh! I beg your pardon, sir. I did not immediately recollect. Undoubtedly if you wish it, I will endeavour to persuade them both." And away he ran.

Long before he re-appeared, attending the short, neat, brisk-moving aunt, and her elegant niece, — Mrs. Weston, like a sweet-tempered woman and a good wife, had examined the passage again, and found the evils of it much less than she had supposed before — indeed very trifling; and here ended the difficulties of decision. All the rest, in speculation at least, was perfectly smooth. All the minor arrangements of table and chair, lights and music, tea and supper, made themselves; or were left as mere trifles to be settled at any time between Mrs. Weston and Mrs. Stokes. — Every body invited, was certainly to come; Frank had already written to Enscombe to propose staying a few days beyond his fortnight, which could not possibly be refused. And a delightful dance it was to be.

Most cordially, when Miss Bates arrived, did she agree that it must. As a counsellor she was not wanted; but as an approver, (a much safer character,) she was truly welcome. Her approbation, at once general and minute, warm and incessant, could not but please; and for another half-hour they were all walking to and fro, between the different rooms, some suggesting, some attending, and all in happy enjoyment of the future. The party did not break up without Emma's being positively secured for the two first dances by the hero of the evening, nor without her overhearing Mr. Weston whisper to his wife, "He has asked her, my dear. That's right. I knew he would!"

CHAPTER XII.

ONE thing only was wanting to make the prospect of the ball completely satisfactory to Emma — its being fixed for a day within the
granted term of Frank Churchill's stay in Surry; for, in spite of Mr.
Weston's confidence, she could not think it so very impossible that the
Churchills might not allow their nephew to remain a day beyond his
fortnight. But this was not judged feasible. The preparations must take
their time, nothing could be properly ready till the third week were
entered on, and for a few days they must be planning, proceeding and
hoping in uncertainty — at the risk — in her opinion, the great risk, of
its being all in vain.

Enscombe however was gracious, gracious in fact, if not in word.
His wish of staying longer evidently did not please; but it was not
opposed. All was safe and prosperous; and as the removal of one solicitude generally makes way for another, Emma, being now certain of her
ball, began to adopt as the next vexation Mr. Knightley's provoking
indifference about it. Either because he did not dance himself, or
because the plan had been formed without his being consulted, he
seemed resolved that it should not interest him, determined against its
exciting any present curiosity, or affording him any future amusement.
To her voluntary communications Emma could get no more approving
reply, than,

"Very well. If the Westons think it worth while to be at all this
trouble for a few hours of noisy entertainment, I have nothing to say
against it, but that they shall not choose pleasures for me. — Oh! yes, I
must be there; I could not refuse; and I will keep as much awake as I can;
but I would rather be at home, looking over William Larkins's week's
account; much rather, I confess. — Pleasure in seeing dancing! — not
I, indeed — I never look at it — I do not know who does. — Fine
dancing, I believe, like virtue, must be its own reward. Those who are
standing by are usually thinking of something very different."

This Emma felt was aimed at her; and it made her quite angry. It
was not in compliment to Jane Fairfax however that he was so indifferent, or so indignant; he was not guided by *her* feelings in reprobating
the ball, for *she* enjoyed the thought of it to an extraordinary degree. It
made her animated — open hearted — she voluntarily said; —

"Oh! Miss Woodhouse, I hope nothing may happen to prevent the
ball. What a disappointment it would be! I do look forward to it, I own,
with *very* great pleasure."

It was not to oblige Jane Fairfax therefore that he would have preferred the society of William Larkins. No! — she was more and more convinced that Mrs. Weston was quite mistaken in that surmise. There was a great deal of friendly and of compassionate attachment on his side — but no love.

Alas! there was soon no leisure for quarrelling with Mr. Knightley. Two days of joyful security were immediately followed by the overthrow of every thing. A letter arrived from Mr. Churchill to urge his nephew's instant return. Mrs. Churchill was unwell — far too unwell to do without him; she had been in a very suffering state (so said her husband) when writing to her nephew two days before, though from her usual unwillingness to give pain, and constant habit of never thinking of herself, she had not mentioned it; but now she was too ill to trifle, and must entreat him to set off for Enscombe without delay.

The substance of this letter was forwarded to Emma, in a note from Mrs. Weston, instantly. As to his going, it was inevitable. He must be gone within a few hours, though without feeling any real alarm for his aunt, to lessen his repugnance. He knew her illnesses; they never occurred but for her own convenience.

Mrs. Weston added, "that he could only allow himself time to hurry to Highbury, after breakfast, and take leave of the few friends there whom he could suppose to feel any interest in him; and that he might be expected at Hartfield very soon."

This wretched note was the finalé of Emma's breakfast. When once it had been read, there was no doing any thing, but lament and exclaim. The loss of the ball — the loss of the young man — and all that the young man might be feeling! — It was too wretched! — Such a delightful evening as it would have been! — Every body so happy! and she and her partner the happiest! — "I said it would be so," was the only consolation.

Her father's feelings were quite distinct. He thought principally of Mrs. Churchill's illness, and wanted to know how she was treated; and as for the ball, it was shocking to have dear Emma disappointed; but they would all be safer at home.

Emma was ready for her visitor some time before he appeared; but if this reflected at all upon his impatience, his sorrowful look and total want of spirits when he did come might redeem him. He felt the going away almost too much to speak of it. His dejection was most evident. He sat really lost in thought for the first few minutes; and when rousing himself, it was only to say,

"Of all horrid things, leave-taking is the worst."

"But you will come again," said Emma. "This will not be your only visit to Randalls."

"Ah! — (shaking his head) — the uncertainty of when I may be able to return! — I shall try for it with a zeal! — It will be the object of all my thoughts and cares! — and if my uncle and aunt go to town this spring — but I am afraid — they did not stir last spring — I am afraid it is a custom gone for ever."

"Our poor ball must be quite given up."

"Ah! that ball! — why did we wait for any thing? — why not seize the pleasure at once? — How often is happiness destroyed by preparation, foolish preparation! — You told us it would be so. — Oh! Miss Woodhouse, why are you always so right?"

"Indeed, I am very sorry to be right in this instance. I would much rather have been merry than wise."

"If I can come again, we are still to have our ball. My father depends on it. Do not forget your engagement."

Emma looked graciously.

"Such a fortnight as it has been!" he continued; "every day more precious and more delightful than the day before! — every day making me less fit to bear any other place. Happy those, who can remain at Highbury!"

"As you do us such ample justice now," said Emma, laughing, "I will venture to ask, whether you did not come a little doubtingly at first? Do not we rather surpass your expectations? I am sure we do. I am sure you did not much expect to like us. You would not have been so long in coming, if you had had a pleasant idea of Highbury."

He laughed rather consciously; and though denying the sentiment, Emma was convinced that it had been so.

"And you must be off this very morning?"

"Yes; my father is to join me here: we shall walk back together, and I must be off immediately. I am almost afraid that every moment will bring him."

"Not five minutes to spare even for your friends Miss Fairfax and Miss Bates? How unlucky! Miss Bates's powerful, argumentative mind might have strengthened yours."

"Yes — I *have* called there; passing the door, I thought it better. It was a right thing to do. I went in for three minutes, and was detained by Miss Bates's being absent. She was out; and I felt it impossible not to wait till she came in. She is a woman that one may, that one *must* laugh at; but that one would not wish to slight. It was better to pay my visit, then" —

He hesitated, got up, walked to a window.

"In short," said he, "perhaps, Miss Woodhouse —— I think you can hardly be quite without suspicion" —

He looked at her, as if wanting to read her thoughts. She hardly knew what to say. It seemed like the forerunner of something absolutely serious, which she did not wish. Forcing herself to speak, therefore, in the hope of putting it by, she calmly said,

"You were quite in the right; it was most natural to pay your visit, then" —

He was silent. She believed he was looking at her; probably reflecting on what she had said, and trying to understand the manner. She heard him sigh. It was natural for him to feel that he had *cause* to sigh. He could not believe her to be encouraging him. A few awkward moments passed, and he sat down again; and in a more determined manner said,

"It was something to feel that all the rest of my time might be given to Hartfield. My regard for Hartfield is most warm" —

He stopt again, rose again, and seemed quite embarrassed. — He was more in love with her than Emma had supposed; and who can say how it might have ended, if his father had not made his appearance? Mr. Woodhouse soon followed; and the necessity of exertion made him composed.

A very few minutes more, however, completed the present trial. Mr. Weston, always alert when business was to be done, and as incapable of procrastinating any evil that was inevitable, as of foreseeing any that was doubtful, said, "It was time to go;" and the young man, though he might and did sigh, could not but agree, and rise to take leave.

"I shall hear about you all," said he; "that is my chief consolation. I shall hear of every thing that is going on among you. I have engaged Mrs. Weston to correspond with me. She has been so kind as to promise it. Oh! the blessing of a female correspondent, when one is really interested in the absent! — she will tell me every thing. In her letters I shall be at dear Highbury again."

A very friendly shake of the hand, a very earnest "Good bye," closed the speech, and the door had soon shut out Frank Churchill. Short had been the notice — short their meeting; he was gone; and Emma felt so sorry to part, and foresaw so great a loss to their little society from his absence as to begin to be afraid of being too sorry, and feeling it too much.

It was a sad change. They had been meeting almost every day since his arrival. Certainly his being at Randalls had given great spirit to the last two weeks — indescribable spirit; the idea, the expectation of seeing him which every morning had brought, the assurance of his attentions, his liveliness, his manners! It had been a very happy fortnight, and forlorn must be the sinking from it into the common course of Hartfield days. To complete every other recommendation, he had *almost* told her that he loved her. What strength, or what constancy of affection he might be subject to, was another point; but at present she could not doubt his having a decidedly warm admiration, a conscious preference of herself; and this persuasion, joined to all the rest, made her think that she *must* be a little in love with him, in spite of every previous determination against it.

"I certainly must," said she. "This sensation of listlessness, weariness, stupidity, this disinclination to sit down and employ myself, this feeling of every thing's being dull and insipid about the house! — I must be in love; I should be the oddest creature in the world if I were not — for a few weeks at least. Well! evil to some is always good to others. I shall have many fellow-mourners for the ball, if not for Frank Churchill; but Mr. Knightley will be happy. He may spend the evening with his dear William Larkins now if he likes."

Mr. Knightley, however, shewed no triumphant happiness. He could not say that he was sorry on his own account; his very cheerful look would have contradicted him if he had; but he said, and very steadily, that he was sorry for the disappointment of the others, and with considerable kindness added,

"You, Emma, who have so few opportunities of dancing, you are really out of luck; you are very much out of luck!"

It was some days before she saw Jane Fairfax, to judge of her honest regret in this woeful change; but when they did meet, her composure was odious. She had been particularly unwell, however, suffering from headache to a degree, which made her aunt declare, that had the ball taken place, she did not think Jane could have attended it; and it was charity to impute some of her unbecoming indifference to the languor of ill-health.

CHAPTER XIII.

EMMA continued to entertain no doubt of her being in love. Her ideas only varied as to the how much. At first, she thought it was a good deal; and afterwards, but little. She had great pleasure in hearing Frank Churchill talked of; and, for his sake, greater pleasure than ever in seeing Mr. and Mrs. Weston; she was very often thinking of him, and quite impatient for a letter, that she might know how he was, how were his spirits, how was his aunt, and what was the chance of his coming to Randalls again this spring. But, on the other hand, she could not admit herself to be unhappy, nor, after the first morning, to be less disposed for employment than usual; she was still busy and cheerful; and, pleasing as he was, she could yet imagine him to have faults; and farther, though thinking of him so much, and, as she sat drawing or working, forming a thousand amusing schemes for the progress and close of their attachment, fancying interesting dialogues, and inventing elegant letters; the conclusion of every imaginary declaration on his side was that she *refused him.* Their affection was always to subside into friendship. Every thing tender and charming was to mark their parting; but still they were to part. When she became sensible of this, it struck her that she could not be very much in love; for in spite of her previous and fixed determination never to quit her father, never to marry, a strong attachment certainly must produce more of a struggle than she could foresee in her own feelings.

"I do not find myself making any use of the word *sacrifice*," said she. — "In not one of all my clever replies, my delicate negatives, is there any allusion to making a sacrifice. I do suspect that he is not really necessary to my happiness. So much the better. I certainly will not persuade myself to feel more than I do. I am quite enough in love. I should be sorry to be more."

Upon the whole, she was equally contented with her view of his feelings.

"*He* is undoubtedly very much in love — every thing denotes it — very much in love indeed! — and when he comes again, if his affection continue, I must be on my guard not to encourage it. — It would be most inexcusable to do otherwise, as my own mind is quite made up. Not that I imagine he can think I have been encouraging him hitherto. No, if he had believed me at all to share his feelings, he would not have been so wretched. Could he have thought himself encouraged, his looks and language at parting would have been different. —

Still, however, I must be on my guard. This is in the supposition of his attachment continuing what it now is; but I do not know that I expect it will; I do not look upon him to be quite the sort of man — I do not altogether build upon his steadiness or constancy. — His feelings are warm, but I can imagine them rather changeable. — Every consideration of the subject, in short, makes me thankful that my happiness is not more deeply involved. — I shall do very well again after a little while — and then, it will be a good thing over; for they say every body is in love once in their lives, and I shall have been let off easily."

When his letter to Mrs. Weston arrived, Emma had the perusal of it; and she read it with a degree of pleasure and admiration which made her at first shake her head over her own sensations, and think she had undervalued their strength. It was a long, well-written letter, giving the particulars of his journey and of his feelings, expressing all the affection, gratitude, and respect which was natural and honourable, and describing every thing exterior and local that could be supposed attractive, with spirit and precision. No suspicious flourishes now of apology or concern; it was the language of real feeling towards Mrs. Weston; and the transition from Highbury to Enscombe, the contrast between the places in some of the first blessings of social life was just enough touched on to shew how keenly it was felt, and how much more might have been said but for the restraints of propriety. — The charm of her own name was not wanting. *Miss Woodhouse* appeared more than once, and never without a something of pleasing connection, either a compliment to her taste, or a remembrance of what she had said; and in the very last time of its meeting her eye, unadorned as it was by any such broad wreath of gallantry, she yet could discern the effect of her influence and acknowledge the greatest compliment perhaps of all conveyed. Compressed into the very lowest vacant corner were these words — "I had not a spare moment on Tuesday, as you know, for Miss Woodhouse's beautiful little friend. Pray make my excuses and adieus to her." This, Emma could not doubt, was all for herself. Harriet was remembered only from being *her* friend. His information and prospects as to Enscombe were neither worse nor better than had been anticipated; Mrs. Churchill was recovering, and he dared not yet, even in his own imagination, fix a time for coming to Randalls again.

Gratifying, however, and stimulative as was the letter in the material part, its sentiments, she yet found, when it was folded up and returned to Mrs. Weston, that it had not added any lasting warmth, that she could still do without the writer, and that he must learn to do without her. Her intentions were unchanged. Her resolution of refusal only grew more interesting by the addition of a scheme for his subsequent consolation and happiness. His recollection of Harriet, and the words which clothed it, the "beautiful little friend," suggested to her the idea of Harriet's succeeding her in his affections. Was it impossible? — No. — Harriet undoubtedly was greatly his inferior in understanding; but he had been very much struck with the loveliness of her face and the warm simplicity of her manner; and all the probabilities of circumstance and connection were in her favour. — For Harriet, it would be advantageous and delightful indeed.

"I must not dwell upon it," said she. — "I must not think of it. I know the danger of indulging such speculations. But stranger things have happened; and when we cease to care for each other as we do now, it will be the means of confirming us in that sort of true disinterested friendship which I can already look forward to with pleasure."

It was well to have a comfort in store on Harriet's behalf, though it might be wise to let the fancy touch it seldom; for evil in that quarter was at hand. As Frank Churchill's arrival had succeeded Mr. Elton's engagement in the conversation of Highbury, as the latest interest had entirely born down the first, so now upon Frank Churchill's disappearance, Mr. Elton's concerns were assuming the most irresistible form. — His wedding-day was named. He would soon be among them again; Mr. Elton and his bride. There was hardly time to talk over the first letter from Enscombe before "Mr. Elton and his bride" was in every body's mouth, and Frank Churchill was forgotten. Emma grew sick at the sound. She had had three weeks of happy exemption from Mr. Elton; and Harriet's mind, she had been willing to hope, had been lately gaining strength. With Mr. Weston's ball in view at least, there had been a great deal of insensibility to other things; but it was now too evident that she had not attained such a state of composure as could stand against the actual approach — new carriage, bell ringing and all.

Poor Harriet was in a flutter of spirits which required all the reasonings and soothings and attentions of every kind that Emma could give. Emma felt that she could not do too much for her, that Harriet had a right to all her ingenuity and all her patience; but it was heavy work to be for ever convincing without producing any effect, for ever agreed to, without being able to make their opinions the same. Harriet listened submissively, and said "it was very true — it was just as Miss Woodhouse described — it was not worth while to think about them — and she would not think about them any longer" — but no change of subject could avail, and the next half hour saw her as anxious and restless about the Eltons as before. — At last Emma attacked her on another ground.

"Your allowing yourself to be so occupied and so unhappy about Mr. Elton's marrying, Harriet, is the strongest reproach you can make *me*. You could not give me a greater reproof for the mistake I fell into. It was all my doing, I know. I have not forgotten it, I assure you. — Deceived myself, I did very miserably deceive you — and it will be a painful reflection to me for ever. Do not imagine me in danger of forgetting it."

Harriet felt this too much to utter more than a few words of eager exclamation. Emma continued,

"I have not said, exert yourself Harriet for my sake; think less, talk less of Mr. Elton for my sake; because for your own sake rather, I would wish it to be done, for the sake of what is more important than my comfort, a habit of self-command in you, a consideration of what is your duty, an attention to propriety, an endeavour to avoid the suspicions of others, to save your health and credit, and restore your tranquillity. These are the motives which I have been pressing on you. They are very important — and sorry I am that you cannot feel them sufficiently to act upon them. My being saved from pain is a very secondary consideration. I want you to save yourself from greater pain. Perhaps I may sometimes have felt that Harriet would not forget what was due — or rather what would be kind by me."

This appeal to her affections did more than all the rest. The idea of wanting gratitude and consideration for Miss Woodhouse, whom she really loved extremely, made her wretched for a while, and when the violence of grief was comforted away, still remained powerful enough to prompt to what was right and support her in it very tolerably.

"You, who have been the best friend I ever had in my life — Want gratitude to you! — Nobody is equal to you! — I care for nobody as I do for you! — Oh! Miss Woodhouse, how ungrateful I have been!"

Such expressions, assisted as they were by every thing that look and manner could do, made Emma feel that she had never loved Harriet so well, nor valued her affection so highly before.

"There is no charm equal to tenderness of heart," said she afterwards to herself. "There is nothing to be compared to it. Warmth and tenderness of heart, with an affectionate, open manner, will beat all the clearness of head in the world, for attraction. I am sure it will. It is tenderness of heart which makes my dear father so generally beloved — which gives Isabella all her popularity. — I have it not — but I know how to prize and respect it. — Harriet is my superior in all the charm

and all the felicity it gives. Dear Harriet! — I would not change you for
the clearest-headed, longest-sighted, best-judging female breathing. Oh!
the coldness of a Jane Fairfax! Harriet is worth a hundred such. —
And for a wife — a sensible man's wife — it is invaluable. I mention no
names; but happy the man who changes Emma for Harriet!"

CHAPTER XIV.

MRS. ELTON was first seen at church: but though devotion might be
interrupted, curiosity could not be satisfied by a bride in a pew, and it
must be left for the visits in form which were then to be paid, to settle
whether she were very pretty indeed, or only rather pretty, or not pretty
at all.

Emma had feelings, less of curiosity than of pride or propriety, to
make her resolve on not being the last to pay her respects; and she made
a point of Harriet's going with her, that the worst of the business might
be gone through as soon as possible.

She could not enter the house again, could not be in the same room
to which she had with such vain artifice retreated three months ago, to
lace up her boot, without *recollecting*. A thousand vexatious thoughts
would recur. Compliments, charades, and horrible blunders; and it was
not to be supposed that poor Harriet should not be recollecting too;
but she behaved very well, and was only rather pale and silent. The visit
was of course short; and there was so much embarrassment and occupation of mind to shorten it, that Emma would not allow herself
entirely to form an opinion of the lady, and on no account to give one,
beyond the nothing-meaning terms of being "elegantly dressed, and
very pleasing."

She did not really like her. She would not be in a hurry to find fault,
but she suspected that there was no elegance; — ease, but not elegance. — She was almost sure that for a young woman, a stranger, a
bride, there was too much ease. Her person was rather good; her face
not unpretty; but neither feature, nor air, nor voice, nor manner, were
elegant. Emma thought at least it would turn out so.

As for Mr. Elton, his manners did not appear — but no, she would
not permit a hasty or a witty word from herself about his manners. It
was an awkward ceremony at any time to be receiving wedding-visits,
and a man had need be all grace to acquit himself well through it. The
woman was better off; she might have the assistance of fine clothes, and
the privilege of bashfulness, but the man had only his own good sense

to depend on; and when she considered how peculiarly unlucky poor
Mr. Elton was in being in the same room at once with the woman he
had just married, the woman he had wanted to marry, and the woman
whom he had been expected to marry, she must allow him to have the
right to look as little wise, and to be as much affectedly, and as little
really easy as could be.

"Well, Miss Woodhouse," said Harriet, when they had quitted the
house, and after waiting in vain for her friend to begin; "Well, Miss
Woodhouse, (with a gentle sigh,) what do you think of her? — Is not
she very charming?"

There was a little hesitation in Emma's answer.

"Oh! yes — very — a very pleasing young woman."

"I think her beautiful, quite beautiful."

"Very nicely dressed, indeed; a remarkably elegant gown."

"I am not at all surprized that he should have fallen in love."

"Oh! no — there is nothing to surprize one at all. — A pretty fortune; and she came in his way."

"I dare say," returned Harriet, sighing again, "I dare say she was
very much attached to him."

"Perhaps she might; but it is not every man's fate to marry the
woman who loves him best. Miss Hawkins perhaps wanted a home, and
thought this the best offer she was likely to have."

"Yes," said Harriet earnestly, "and well she might, nobody could
ever have a better. Well, I wish them happy with all my heart. And now,
Miss Woodhouse, I do not think I shall mind seeing them again. He is
just as superior as ever; — but being married, you know, it is quite a different thing. No, indeed, Miss Woodhouse, you need not be afraid; I
can sit and admire him now without any great misery. To know that he
has not thrown himself away, is such a comfort! — She does seem a
charming young woman, just what he deserves. Happy creature! He
called her 'Augusta.' How delightful!"

When the visit was returned, Emma made up her mind. She could
then see more and judge better. From Harriet's happening not to be at
Hartfield, and her father's being present to engage Mr. Elton, she had a
quarter of an hour of the lady's conversation to herself, and could composedly attend to her; and the quarter of an hour quite convinced her
that Mrs. Elton was a vain woman, extremely well satisfied with herself,
and thinking much of her own importance; that she meant to shine and
be very superior, but with manners which had been formed in a bad
school, pert and familiar; that all her notions were drawn from one set

of people, and one style of living; that if not foolish she was ignorant, and that her society would certainly do Mr. Elton no good.

Harriet would have been a better match. If not wise or refined herself, she would have connected him with those who were; but Miss Hawkins, it might be fairly supposed from her easy conceit, had been the best of her own set. The rich brother-in-law near Bristol was the pride of the alliance, and his place and his carriages were the pride of him.

The very first subject after being seated was Maple Grove, "My brother Mr. Suckling's seat" — a comparison of Hartfield to Maple Grove. The grounds of Hartfield were small, but neat and pretty; and the house was modern and well-built. Mrs. Elton seemed most favourably impressed by the size of the room, the entrance, and all that she could see or imagine. "Very like Maple Grove indeed! — She was quite struck by the likeness! — That room was the very shape and size of the morning-room at Maple Grove; her sister's favourite room." — Mr. Elton was appealed to. — "Was not it astonishingly like? — She could really almost fancy herself at Maple Grove."

"And the staircase — You know, as I came in, I observed how very like the staircase was; placed exactly in the same part of the house. I really could not help exclaiming! I assure you, Miss Woodhouse, it is very delightful to me, to be reminded of a place I am so extremely partial to as Maple Grove. I have spent so many happy months there! (with a little sigh of sentiment). A charming place, undoubtedly. Every body who sees it is struck by its beauty; but to me, it has been quite a home. Whenever you are transplanted, like me, Miss Woodhouse, you will understand how very delightful it is to meet with any thing at all like what one has left behind. I always say this is quite one of the evils of matrimony."

Emma made as slight a reply as she could; but it was fully sufficient for Mrs. Elton, who only wanted to be talking herself.

"So extremely like Maple Grove! And it is not merely the house — the grounds, I assure you, as far as I could observe, are strikingly like. The laurels at Maple Grove are in the same profusion as here, and stand very much in the same way — just across the lawn; and I had a glimpse of a fine large tree, with a bench round it, which put me so exactly in mind! My brother and sister will be enchanted with this place. People who have extensive grounds themselves are always pleased with any thing in the same style."

Emma doubted the truth of this sentiment. She had a great idea that people who had extensive grounds themselves cared very little for the extensive grounds of any body else; but it was not worth while to attack an error so double-dyed, and therefore only said in reply,

"When you have seen more of this country, I am afraid you will think you have over-rated Hartfield. Surry is full of beauties."

"Oh! yes, I am quite aware of that. It is the garden of England,[89] you know. Surry is the garden of England."

"Yes; but we must not rest our claims on that distinction. Many counties, I believe, are called the garden of England, as well as Surry."

"No, I fancy not," replied Mrs. Elton, with a most satisfied smile. "I never heard any county but Surry called so."

Emma was silenced.

"My brother and sister have promised us a visit in the spring, or summer at farthest," continued Mrs. Elton; "and that will be our time for exploring. While they are with us, we shall explore a great deal, I dare say. They will have their barouche-landau,[90] of course, which holds four perfectly; and therefore, without saying any thing of *our* carriage, we should be able to explore the different beauties extremely well. They would hardly come in their chaise, I think, at that season of the year. Indeed, when the time draws on, I shall decidedly recommend their bringing the barouche-landau; it will be so very much preferable. When people come into a beautiful country of this sort, you know, Miss Woodhouse, one naturally wishes them to see as much as possible; and Mr. Suckling is extremely fond of exploring. We explored to King's-Weston[91] twice last summer, in that way, most delightfully, just after their first having the barouche-landau. You have many parties of that kind here, I suppose, Miss Woodhouse, every summer?"

"No; not immediately here. We are rather out of distance of the very striking beauties which attract the sort of parties you speak of; and we are a very quiet set of people, I believe; more disposed to stay at home than engage in schemes of pleasure."

"Ah! there is nothing like staying at home, for real comfort. No-

---

[89]*garden of England:* Kent, not Surrey, is usually viewed as the garden of England.

[90]*barouche-landau:* Rare four-wheeled carriage built between 1804 and 1811 by Barker & Co., carriage builders in London. The carriage was basically a landau with two "heads" (hoods) that could be lowered front and back in fine weather (a barouche had only one hood, covering the rear seat when raised). For an illustration and further discussion, see "Contextual Documents," pp. 395–96, 401.

[91]*King's-Weston:* (Kings Weston on p. 283) stately house west of Bristol and about two miles from the river Severn; designed by Sir John Vanbrugh in the early eighteenth century, it was celebrated in Austen's time for its beautiful grounds; from a hill tourists such as Mrs. Elton could admire the prospect of the Bristol Channel and the Welsh countryside beyond, no doubt without even descending from the barouche-landau.

body can be more devoted to home than I am. I was quite a proverb for it at Maple Grove. Many a time has Selina said, when she has been going to Bristol, 'I really cannot get this girl to move from the house. I absolutely must go in by myself, though I hate being stuck up in the barouche-landau without a companion; but Augusta, I believe, with her own good will, would never stir beyond the park paling.' Many a time has she said so; and yet I am no advocate for entire seclusion. I think, on the contrary, when people shut themselves up entirely from society, it is a very bad thing; and that it is much more advisable to mix in the world in a proper degree, without living in it either too much or too little. I perfectly understand your situation, however, Miss Wood-house — (looking towards Mr. Woodhouse) — Your father's state of health must be a great drawback. Why does not he try Bath? — Indeed he should. Let me recommend Bath to you. I assure you I have no doubt of its doing Mr. Woodhouse good."

"My father tried it more than once, formerly; but without receiving any benefit; and Mr. Perry, whose name, I dare say, is not unknown to you, docs not conceive it would be at all more likely to be useful now."

"Ah! that's a great pity; for I assure you, Miss Woodhouse, where the waters do agree, it is quite wonderful the relief they give. In my Bath life, I have seen such instances of it! And it is so cheerful a place, that it could not fail of being of use to Mr. Woodhouse's spirits, which, I understand, are sometimes much depressed. And as to its recommen-dations to *you*, I fancy I need not take much pains to dwell on them. The advantages of Bath to the young are pretty generally under-stood. It would be a charming introduction for you, who have lived so secluded a life; and I could immediately secure you some of the best society in the place. A line from me would bring you a little host of acquaintance; and my particular friend, Mrs. Partridge, the lady I have always resided with when in Bath, would be most happy to shew you any attentions, and would be the very person for you to go into public with."

It was as much as Emma could bear, without being impolite. The idea of her being indebted to Mrs. Elton for what was called an *intro-duction* — of her going into public under the auspices of a friend of Mrs. Elton's, probably some vulgar, dashing widow, who, with the help of a boarder, just made a shift to live! — The dignity of Miss Wood-house, of Hartfield, was sunk indeed!

She restrained herself, however, from any of the reproofs she could have given, and only thanked Mrs. Elton coolly; "but their going to Bath was quite out of the question; and she was not perfectly convinced

that the place might suit her better than her father." And then, to prevent further outrage and indignation, changed the subject directly:

"I do not ask whether you are musical, Mrs. Elton. Upon these
occasions, a lady's character generally precedes her; and Highbury has
long known that you are a superior performer."

"Oh! no, indeed; I must protest against any such idea. A superior
performer! — very far from it, I assure you. Consider from how partial
a quarter your information came. I am doatingly fond of music — passionately fond; — and my friends say I am not entirely devoid of taste;
but as to any thing else, upon my honour my performance is *mediocre*
to the last degree. You, Miss Woodhouse, I well know, play delightfully.
I assure you it has been the greatest satisfaction, comfort, and delight to
me, to hear what a musical society I am got into. I absolutely cannot do
without music. It is a necessary of life to me; and having always been
used to a very musical society, both at Maple Grove and in Bath, it
would have been a most serious sacrifice. I honestly said as much to Mr.
E. when he was speaking of my future home, and expressing his fears
lest the retirement of it should be disagreeable; and the inferiority of
the house too — knowing what I had been accustomed to — of course
he was not wholly without apprehension. When he was speaking of it in
that way, I honestly said that *the world* I could give up — parties, balls,
plays — for I had no fear of retirement. Blessed with so many resources
within myself, the world was not necessary to *me*. I could do very well
without it. To those who had no resources it was a different thing; but
my resources made me quite independent. And as to smaller-sized
rooms than I had been used to, I really could not give it a thought. I
hoped I was perfectly equal to any sacrifice of that description. Certainly I had been accustomed to every luxury at Maple Grove; but I did
assure him that two carriages were not necessary to my happiness, nor
were spacious apartments. 'But,' said I, 'to be quite honest, I do not
think I can live without something of a musical society. I condition for
nothing else; but without music, life would be a blank to me.' "

"We cannot suppose," said Emma, smiling, "that Mr. Elton would
hesitate to assure you of there being a *very* musical society in Highbury;
and I hope you will not find he has outstepped the truth more than may
be pardoned, in consideration of the motive."

"No, indeed, I have no doubts at all on that head. I am delighted to
find myself in such a circle. I hope we shall have many sweet little con-
certs together. I think, Miss Woodhouse, you and I must establish a
musical club, and have regular weekly meetings at your house, or ours.
Will not it be a good plan? If *we* exert ourselves, I think we shall not be

long in want of allies. Something of that nature would be particularly desirable for *me*, as an inducement to keep me in practice; for married women, you know — there is a sad story against them, in general. They are but too apt to give up music."

"But you, who are so extremely fond of it — there can be no danger, surely."

"I should hope not; but really when I look round among my acquaintance, I tremble. Selina has entirely given up music — never touches the instrument — though she played sweetly. And the same may be said of Mrs. Jeffereys — Clara Partridge, that was — and of the two Milmans, now Mrs. Bird and Mrs. James Cooper; and of more than I can enumerate. Upon my word it is enough to put one in a fright. I used to be quite angry with Selina; but really I begin now to comprehend that a married woman has many things to call her attention. I believe I was half an hour this morning shut up with my housekeeper."

"But every thing of that kind," said Emma, "will soon be in so regular a train ——"

"Well," said Mrs. Elton, laughing, "we shall see."

Emma, finding her so determined upon neglecting her music, had nothing more to say; and, after a moment's pause, Mrs. Elton chose another subject.

"We have been calling at Randalls," said she, "and found them both at home; and very pleasant people they seem to be. I like them extremely. Mr. Weston seems an excellent creature — quite a first-rate favourite with me already, I assure you. And *she* appears so truly good — there is something so motherly and kind-hearted about her, that it wins upon one directly. She was your governess, I think?"

Emma was almost too much astonished to answer; but Mrs. Elton hardly waited for the affirmative before she went on.

"Having understood as much, I was rather astonished to find her so very lady-like! But she is really quite the gentlewoman."

"Mrs. Weston's manners," said Emma, "were always particularly good. Their propriety, simplicity, and elegance, would make them the safest model for any young woman."

"And who do you think came in while we were there?"

Emma was quite at a loss. The tone implied some old acquaintance — and how could she possibly guess?

"Knightley!" continued Mrs. Elton; — "Knightley himself! — Was not it lucky? — for, not being within when he called the other day, I had never seen him before; and of course, as so particular a friend of Mr. E.'s, I had a great curiosity. 'My friend Knightley' had been so often mentioned, that I was really impatient to see him; and I must do my cara sposo[92] the justice to say that he need not be ashamed of his friend. Knightley is quite the gentleman. I like him very much. Decidedly, I think, a very gentleman-like man."

Happily it was now time to be gone. They were off; and Emma could breathe.

"Insufferable woman!" was her immediate exclamation. "Worse than I had supposed. Absolutely insufferable! Knightley! — I could not have believed it. Knightley! — never seen him in her life before, and call him Knightley! — and discover that he is a gentleman! A little upstart, vulgar being, with her Mr. E., and her *cara sposo*, and her resources, and all her airs of pert pretension and under-bred finery. Actually to discover that Mr. Knightley is a gentleman! I doubt whether he will return the compliment, and discover her to be a lady. I could not have believed it! And to propose that she and I should unite to form a musical club! One would fancy we were bosom friends! And Mrs. Weston! — Astonished that the person who had brought me up should be a gentlewoman! Worse and worse. I never met with her equal. Much beyond my hopes. Harriet is disgraced by any comparison. Oh! what would Frank Churchill say to her, if he were here? How angry and how diverted he would be! Ah! there I am — thinking of him directly. Always the first person to be thought of! How I catch myself out! Frank Churchill comes as regularly into my mind!" ——

All this ran so glibly through her thoughts, that by the time her father had arranged himself, after the bustle of the Eltons' departure, and was ready to speak, she was very tolerably capable of attending.

"Well, my dear," he deliberately began, "considering we never saw her before, she seems a very pretty sort of young lady; and I dare say she was very much pleased with you. She speaks a little too quick. A little quickness of voice there is which rather hurts the ear. But I believe I am nice; I do not like strange voices; and nobody speaks like you and poor Miss Taylor. However, she seems a very obliging, pretty-behaved young lady, and no doubt will make him a very good wife. Though I think he

---

[92]*cara sposo:* (incorrect) Italian for dear husband. The phrase appears four times in the novel, twice on this page as "cara sposo," once as "cara sposa" (p. 244) and once (correctly) as "caro sposo" (p. 284). Chapman corrects the phrase where it is misspelled, but the emendation is problematic since Jane Austen is more likely to have intended the inconsistency as yet another indication of Mrs. Elton's ignorance. Emma's scornful repetition of the mistake may be assumed to be intentional. The phrase appears in many earlier novels; for an argument that Mrs. Elton's use of it was out of date, see Pat Rogers, " 'Caro Sposo': Mrs. Elton, Burneys, Thrales, and Noels," *RES* 45 (1994): 70–75.

had better not have married. I made the best excuses I could for not having been able to wait on him and Mrs. Elton on this happy occasion; I said that I hoped I should in the course of the summer. But I ought to have gone before. Not to wait upon a bride is very remiss. Ah! it shews what a sad invalid I am! But I do not like the corner into Vicarage-lane."

"I dare say your apologies were accepted, sir. Mr. Elton knows you."

"Yes: but a young lady — a bride — I ought to have paid my respects to her if possible. It was being very deficient."

"But, my dear papa, you are no friend to matrimony; and therefore why should you be so anxious to pay your respects to a *bride*? It ought to be no recommendation to *you*. It is encouraging people to marry if you make so much of them."

"No, my dear, I never encouraged any body to marry, but I would always wish to pay every proper attention to a lady — and a bride, especially, is never to be neglected. More is avowedly due to *her*. A bride, you know, my dear, is always the first in company, let the others be who they may."

"Well, papa, if this is not encouragement to marry, I do not know what is. And I should never have expected you to be lending your sanction to such vanity baits for poor young ladies."

"My dear, you do not understand me. This is a matter of mere common politeness and good-breeding, and has nothing to do with any encouragement to people to marry."

Emma had done. Her father was growing nervous, and could not understand *her*. Her mind returned to Mrs. Elton's offences, and long, very long, did they occupy her.

CHAPTER XV.

EMMA was not required, by any subsequent discovery, to retract her ill opinion of Mrs. Elton. Her observation had been pretty correct. Such as Mrs. Elton appeared to her on this second interview, such she appeared whenever they met again, — self-important, presuming, familiar, ignorant, and ill-bred. She had a little beauty and a little accomplishment, but so little judgment that she thought herself coming with superior knowledge of the world, to enliven and improve a country neighbourhood; and conceived Miss Hawkins to have held such a place in society as Mrs. Elton's consequence only could surpass.

There was no reason to suppose Mr. Elton thought at all differently from his wife. He seemed not merely happy with her, but proud. He had the air of congratulating himself on having brought such a woman to Highbury, as not even Miss Woodhouse could equal; and the greater part of her new acquaintance, disposed to commend, or not in the habit of judging, following the lead of Miss Bates's good-will or taking it for granted that the bride must be as clever and as agreeable as she professed herself, were very well satisfied; so that Mrs. Elton's praise passed from one mouth to another as it ought to do, unimpeded by Miss Woodhouse, who readily continued her first contribution and talked with a good grace of her being "very pleasant and very elegantly dressed."

In one respect Mrs. Elton grew even worse than she had appeared at first. Her feelings altered towards Emma. — Offended, probably, by the little encouragement which her proposals of intimacy met with, she drew back in her turn and gradually became much more cold and distant; and though the effect was agreeable, the ill-will which produced it was necessarily increasing Emma's dislike. Her manners too — and Mr. Elton's, were unpleasant towards Harriet. They were sneering and negligent. Emma hoped it must rapidly work Harriet's cure; but the sensations which could prompt such behaviour sunk them both very much. — It was not to be doubted that poor Harriet's attachment had been an offering to conjugal unreserve, and her own share in the story, under a colouring the least favourable to her and the most soothing to him, had in all likelihood been given also. She was, of course, the object of their joint dislike. — When they had nothing else to say, it must be always easy to begin abusing Miss Woodhouse; and the enmity which they dared not shew in open disrespect to her, found a broader vent in contemptuous treatment of Harriet.

Mrs. Elton took a great fancy to Jane Fairfax; and from the first. Not merely when a state of warfare with one young lady might be supposed to recommend the other, but from the very first; and she was not satisfied with expressing a natural and reasonable admiration — but without solicitation, or plea, or privilege, she must be wanting to assist and befriend her. — Before Emma had forfeited her confidence, and about the third time of their meeting, she heard all Mrs. Elton's knight-errantry on the subject. —

"Jane Fairfax is absolutely charming, Miss Woodhouse. — I quite rave about Jane Fairfax. — A sweet, interesting creature. So mild and lady-like — and with such talents! — I assure you I think she has very extraordinary talents. I do not scruple to say that she plays extremely

well. I know enough of music to speak decidedly on that point. Oh! she
is absolutely charming! You will laugh at my warmth — but upon my
word, I talk of nothing but Jane Fairfax.   And her situation is so calculated to affect one! — Miss Woodhouse, we must exert ourselves and
endeavour to do something for her. We must bring her forward. Such
talents as her's must not be suffered to remain unknown. — I dare say
you have heard those charming lines of the poet,

> 'Full many a flower is born to blush unseen,
>   'And waste its fragrance on the desert air.'[93]

We must not allow them to be verified in sweet Jane Fairfax."

"I cannot think there is any danger of it," was Emma's calm
answer — "and when you are better acquainted with Miss Fairfax's situation and understand what her home has been, with Col. and Mrs.
Campbell, I have no idea that you will suppose her talents can be
unknown."

"Oh! but dear Miss Woodhouse, she is now in such retirement,
such obscurity, so thrown away. — Whatever advantages she may have
enjoyed with the Campbells are so palpably at an end! And I think she
feels it. I am sure she does. She is very timid and silent. One can see that
she feels the want of encouragement. I like her the better for it. I must
confess it is a recommendation to me. I am a great advocate for timidity — and I am sure one does not often meet with it. — But in those
who are at all inferior, it is extremely prepossessing. Oh! I assure you,
Jane Fairfax is a very delightful character, and interests me more than I
can express."

"You appear to feel a great deal — but I am not aware how you or
any of Miss Fairfax's acquaintance here, any of those who have known
her longer than yourself, can shew her any other attention than" ——

"My dear Miss Woodhouse, a vast deal may be done by those who
dare to act. You and I need not be afraid. If *we* set the example, many
will follow it as far as they can; though all have not our situations. *We*
have carriages to fetch and convey her home, and *we* live in a style
which could not make the addition of Jane Fairfax, at any time, the least
inconvenient. — I should be extremely displeased if Wright were to
send us up such a dinner, as could make me regret having asked *more*
than Jane Fairfax to partake of it. I have no idea of that sort of thing. It
is not likely that I *should,* considering what I have been used to. My

---

[93] *Full many a flower...':* A citation (slightly misquoted) from Thomas Gray's
"Elegy Written in a Country Churchyard" (1751), l.55.

greatest danger, perhaps, in housekeeping, may be quite the other way, in doing too much, and being too careless of expense. Maple Grove will probably be my model more than it ought to be — for we do not at all affect to equal my brother, Mr. Suckling, in income. — However, my resolution is taken as to noticing Jane Fairfax. — I shall certainly have her very often at my house, shall introduce her wherever I can, shall have musical parties to draw out her talents, and shall be constantly on the watch for an eligible situation. My acquaintance is so very extensive, that I have little doubt of hearing of something to suit her shortly. — I shall introduce her, of course, very particularly to my brother and sister when they come to us. I am sure they will like her extremely; and when she gets a little acquainted with them, her fears will completely wear off, for there really is nothing in the manners of either but what is highly conciliating. — I shall have her very often indeed while they are with me, and I dare say we shall sometimes find a seat for her in the barouche-landau in some of our exploring parties."

"Poor Jane Fairfax!" — thought Emma. — "You have not deserved this. You may have done wrong with regard to Mr. Dixon, but this is a punishment beyond what you can have merited! — The kindness and protection of Mrs. Elton! — 'Jane Fairfax and Jane Fairfax.' Heavens! Let me not suppose that she dares go about, Emma Woodhouse-ing me! — But upon my honour, there seem no limits to the licentiousness of that woman's tongue!"

Emma had not to listen to such paradings again — to any so exclusively addressed to herself — so disgustingly decorated with a "dear Miss Woodhouse." The change on Mrs. Elton's side soon afterwards appeared, and she was left in peace — neither forced to be the very particular friend of Mrs. Elton, nor, under Mrs. Elton's guidance, the very active patroness of Jane Fairfax, and only sharing with others in a general way, in knowing what was felt, what was meditated, what was done.

She looked on with some amusement. — Miss Bates's gratitude for Mrs. Elton's attentions to Jane was in the first style of guileless simplicity and warmth. She was quite one of her worthies — the most amiable, affable, delightful woman — just as accomplished and condescending as Mrs. Elton meant to be considered. Emma's only surprize was that Jane Fairfax should accept those attentions and tolerate Mrs. Elton as she seemed to do. She heard of her walking with the Eltons, sitting with the Eltons, spending a day with the Eltons! This was astonishing! — She could not have believed it possible that the taste or the pride of Miss Fairfax could endure such society and friendship as the Vicarage had to offer.

VOLUME II, CHAPTER XV   231

"She is a riddle, quite a riddle!" said she. — "To chuse to remain
here month after month, under privations of every sort! And now to
chuse the mortification of Mrs. Elton's notice and the penury of her
conversation, rather than return to the superior companions who have
always loved her with such real, generous affection."

Jane had come to Highbury professedly for three months; the
Campbells were gone to Ireland for three months; but now the Campbells had promised their daughter to stay at least till Midsummer, and
fresh invitations had arrived for her to join them there. According to
Miss Bates — it all came from her — Mrs. Dixon had written most
pressingly. Would Jane but go, means were to be found, servants sent,
friends contrived — no travelling difficulty allowed to exist; but still she
had declined it!

"She must have some motive, more powerful than appears, for
refusing this invitation," was Emma's conclusion. "She must be under
some sort of penance, inflicted either by the Campbells or herself. There
is great fear, great caution, great resolution somewhere. — She is *not* to
be with the *Dixons*. The decree is issued by somebody. But why must
she consent to be with the Eltons? — Here is quite a separate puzzle."

Upon her speaking her wonder aloud on that part of the subject,
before the few who knew her opinion of Mrs. Elton, Mrs. Weston ventured this apology for Jane.

"We cannot suppose that she has any great enjoyment at the Vicarage, my dear Emma — but it is better than being always at home. Her
aunt is a good creature, but, as a constant companion, must be very
tiresome. We must consider what Miss Fairfax quits, before we condemn her taste for what she goes to."

"You are right, Mrs. Weston," said Mr. Knightley warmly, "Miss
Fairfax is as capable as any of us of forming a just opinion of Mrs. Elton.
Could she have chosen with whom to associate, she would not have
chosen her. But (with a reproachful smile at Emma) she receives attentions from Mrs. Elton, which nobody else pays her."

Emma felt that Mrs. Weston was giving her a momentary glance;
and she was herself struck by his warmth. With a faint blush, she
presently replied,

"Such attentions as Mrs. Elton's, I should have imagined, would
rather disgust than gratify Miss Fairfax. Mrs. Elton's invitations I
should have imagined any thing but inviting."

"I should not wonder," said Mrs. Weston, "if Miss Fairfax were to
have been drawn on beyond her own inclination, by her aunt's eagerness in accepting Mrs. Elton's civilities for her. Poor Miss Bates may

very likely have committed her niece and hurried her into a greater appearance of intimacy than her own good sense would have dictated, in spite of the very natural wish of a little change."

Both felt rather anxious to hear him speak again; and after a few minutes silence, he said,

"Another thing must be taken into consideration too — Mrs. Elton does not talk *to* Miss Fairfax as she speaks *of* her. We all know the difference between the pronouns he or she and thou, the plainest-spoken amongst us; we all feel the influence of a something beyond common civility in our personal intercourse with each other — a something more early implanted. We cannot give any body the disagreeable hints that we may have been very full of the hour before. We feel things differently. And besides the operation of this, as a general principle, you may be sure that Miss Fairfax awes Mrs. Elton by her superiority both of mind and manner; and that face to face Mrs. Elton treats her with all the respect which she has a claim to. Such a woman as Jane Fairfax probably never fell in Mrs. Elton's way before — and no degree of vanity can prevent her acknowledging her own comparative littleness in action, if not in consciousness."

"I know how highly you think of Jane Fairfax," said Emma. Little Henry was in her thoughts, and a mixture of alarm and delicacy made her irresolute what else to say.

"Yes," he replied, "any body may know how highly I think of her."

"And yet," said Emma, beginning hastily and with an arch look, but soon stopping — it was better, however, to know the worst at once — she hurried on — "And yet, perhaps, you may hardly be aware yourself how highly it is. The extent of your admiration may take you by surprize some day or other."

Mr. Knightley was hard at work upon the lower buttons of his thick leather gaiters, and either the exertion of getting them together, or some other cause, brought the colour into his face, as he answered,

"Oh! are you there? — But you are miserably behind-hand. Mr. Cole gave me a hint of it six weeks ago."

He stopped. — Emma felt her foot pressed by Mrs. Weston, and did not herself know what to think. In a moment he went on —

"That will never be, however, I can assure you. Miss Fairfax, I dare say, would not have me if I were to ask her — and I am very sure I shall never ask her."

Emma returned her friend's pressure with interest; and was pleased enough to exclaim,

"You are not vain, Mr. Knightley. I will say that for you."

He seemed hardly to hear her; he was thoughtful — and in a manner which shewed him not pleased, soon afterwards said, "So you have been settling that I should marry Jane Fairfax." "No indeed I have not. You have scolded me too much for matchmaking, for me to presume to take such a liberty with you. What I said just now, meant nothing. One says those sort of things, of course, without any idea of a serious meaning. Oh! no, upon my word I have not the smallest wish for your marrying Jane Fairfax or Jane any body. You would not come in and sit with us in this comfortable way, if you were married."

Mr. Knightley was thoughtful again. The result of his reverie was, "No, Emma, I do not think the extent of my admiration for her will ever take me by surprize. — I never had a thought of her in that way, I assure you." And soon afterwards, "Jane Fairfax is a very charming young woman — but not even Jane Fairfax is perfect. She has a fault. She has not the open temper which a man would wish for in a wife."

Emma could not but rejoice to hear that she had a fault. "Well," said she, "and you soon silenced Mr. Cole, I suppose?"

"Yes, very soon. He gave me a quiet hint; I told him he was mistaken; he asked my pardon and said no more. Cole does not want to be wiser or wittier than his neighbours."

"In that respect how unlike dear Mrs. Elton, who wants to be wiser and wittier than all the world! I wonder how she speaks of the Coles — what she calls them! How can she find any appellation for them, deep enough in familiar vulgarity? She calls you, Knightley — what can she do for Mr. Cole? And so I am not to be surprized that Jane Fairfax accepts her civilities and consents to be with her. Mrs. Weston, your argument weighs most with me. I can much more readily enter into the temptation of getting away from Miss Bates, than I can believe in the triumph of Miss Fairfax's mind over Mrs. Elton. I have no faith in Mrs. Elton's acknowledging herself the inferior in thought, word, or deed; or in her being under any restraint beyond her own scanty rule of goodbreeding. I cannot imagine that she will not be continually insulting her visitor with praise, encouragement, and offers of service; that she will not be continually detailing her magnificent intentions, from the procuring her a permanent situation to the including her in those delightful exploring parties which are to take place in the barouche-landau."

"Jane Fairfax has feeling," said Mr. Knightley — "I do not accuse her of want of feeling. Her sensibilities, I suspect, are strong — and her temper excellent in its power of forbearance, patience, self-controul;

but it wants openness. She is reserved, more reserved, I think, than she used to be — And I love an open temper. No — till Cole alluded to my supposed attachment, it had never entered my head. I saw Jane Fairfax and conversed with her, with admiration and pleasure always — but with no thought beyond."

"Well, Mrs. Weston," said Emma triumphantly when he left them, "what do you say now to Mr. Knightley's marrying Jane Fairfax?"

"Why really, dear Emma, I say that he is so very much occupied by the idea of *not* being in love with her, that I should not wonder if it were to end in his being so at last. Do not beat me."

CHAPTER XVI.

EVERY body in and about Highbury who had ever visited Mr. Elton, was disposed to pay him attention on his marriage. Dinner-parties and evening-parties were made for him and his lady; and invitations flowed in so fast that she had soon the pleasure of apprehending they were never to have a disengaged day.

"I see how it is," said she. "I see what a life I am to lead among you. Upon my word we shall be absolutely dissipated. We really seem quite the fashion. If this is living in the country, it is nothing very formidable. From Monday next to Saturday, I assure you we have not a disengaged day! — A woman with fewer resources than I have, need not have been at a loss."

No invitation came amiss to her. Her Bath habits made evening-parties perfectly natural to her, and Maple Grove had given her a taste for dinners. She was a little shocked at the want of two drawing rooms, at the poor attempt at rout-cakes,[94] and there being no ice[95] in the Highbury card parties. Mrs. Bates, Mrs. Perry, Mrs. Goddard and others, were a good deal behind hand in knowledge of the world, but *she* would soon shew them how every thing ought to be arranged. In the course of the spring she must return their civilities by one very superior party — in which her card tables should be set out with their separate candles and unbroken packs in the true style — and more waiters engaged for the evening than their own establishment could furnish, to

---

[94]*rout-cakes:* Rich cakes served at social gatherings; made from a mixture of flour, butter, sugar, eggs, and currants and flavored with wine, brandy, etc. For a recipe from 1806, see Lane (69) (cited in note 84, p. 195).

[95]*no ice:* As Stafford points out, by this period larger houses of consequence had ice houses for storing winter ice for summer use.

carry round the refreshments at exactly the proper hour, and in the proper order.

Emma, in the meanwhile, could not be satisfied without a dinner at Hartfield for the Eltons. They must not do less than others, or she should be exposed to odious suspicions, and imagined capable of pitiful resentment. A dinner there must be. After Emma had talked about it for ten minutes, Mr. Woodhouse felt no unwillingness, and only made the usual stipulation of not sitting at the bottom of the table himself, with the usual regular difficulty of deciding who should do it for him.

The persons to be invited, required little thought. Besides the Eltons, it must be the Westons and Mr. Knightley; so far it was all of course — and it was hardly less inevitable that poor little Harriet must be asked to make the eighth: — but this invitation was not given with equal satisfaction, and on many accounts Emma was particularly pleased by Harriet's begging to be allowed to decline it. "She would rather not be in *his* company more than she could help. She was not yet quite able to see him and his charming happy wife together, without feeling uncomfortable. If Miss Woodhouse would not be displeased, she would rather stay at home." It was precisely what Emma would have wished, had she deemed it possible enough for wishing. She was delighted with the fortitude of her little friend — for fortitude she knew it was in her to give up being in company and stay at home; and she could now invite the very person whom she really wanted to make the eighth, Jane Fairfax. — Since her last conversation with Mrs. Weston and Mr. Knightley, she was more conscience-stricken about Jane Fairfax than she had often been. — Mr. Knightley's words dwelt with her. He had said that Jane Fairfax received attentions from Mrs. Elton which nobody else paid her.

"This is very true," said she, "at least as far as relates to me, which was all that was meant — and it is very shameful. — Of the same age — and always knowing her — I ought to have been more her friend. — She will never like me now. I have neglected her too long. But I will shew her greater attention than I have done."

Every invitation was successful. They were all disengaged and all happy. — The preparatory interest of this dinner, however, was not yet over. A circumstance rather unlucky occurred. The two eldest little Knightleys were engaged to pay their grandpapa and aunt a visit of some weeks in the spring, and their papa now proposed bringing them, and staying one whole day at Hartfield — which one day would be the very day of this party. — His professional engagement did not allow of his being put off, but both father and daughter were disturbed by its happening so. Mr. Woodhouse considered eight persons at dinner together as the utmost that his nerves could bear — and here would be a ninth — and Emma apprehended that it would be a ninth very much out of humour at not being able to come even to Hartfield for forty-eight hours without falling in with a dinner-party.

She comforted her father better than she could comfort herself, by representing that though he certainly would make them nine, yet he always said so little, that the increase of noise would be very immaterial. She thought it in reality a sad exchange for herself, to have him with his grave looks and reluctant conversation opposed to her instead of his brother.

The event was more favourable to Mr. Woodhouse than to Emma. John Knightley came; but Mr. Weston was unexpectedly summoned to town and must be absent on the very day. He might be able to join them in the evening, but certainly not to dinner. Mr. Woodhouse was quite at ease; and the seeing him so, with the arrival of the little boys and the philosophic composure of her brother on hearing his fate, removed the chief of even Emma's vexation.

The day came, the party were punctually assembled, and Mr. John Knightley seemed early to devote himself to the business of being agreeable. Instead of drawing his brother off to a window while they waited for dinner, he was talking to Miss Fairfax. Mrs. Elton, as elegant as lace and pearls could make her, he looked at in silence — wanting only to observe enough for Isabella's information — but Miss Fairfax was an old acquaintance and a quiet girl, and he could talk to her. He had met her before breakfast as he was returning from a walk with his little boys, when it had been just beginning to rain. It was natural to have some civil hopes on the subject, and he said,

"I hope you did not venture far, Miss Fairfax, this morning, or I am sure you must have been wet. — *We* scarcely got home in time. I hope you turned directly."

"I went only to the post-office," said she, "and reached home before the rain was much. It is my daily errand. I always fetch the letters when I am here. It saves trouble, and is a something to get me out. A walk before breakfast does me good."

"Not a walk in the rain, I should imagine."

"No, but it did not absolutely rain when I set out."

Mr. John Knightley smiled, and replied,

"That is to say, you chose to have your walk, for you were not six yards from your own door when I had the pleasure of meeting you; and Henry and John had seen more drops than they could count long before. The post-office has a great charm at one period of our lives. When you have lived to my age, you will begin to think letters are never worth going through the rain for."

There was a little blush, and then this answer.

"I must not hope to be ever situated as you are, in the midst of every dearest connection, and therefore I cannot expect that simply growing older should make me indifferent about letters."

"Indifferent! Oh! no — I never conceived you could become indifferent. Letters are no matter of indifference; they are generally a very positive curse."

"You are speaking of letters of business; mine are letters of friendship."

"I have often thought them the worst of the two," replied he coolly. "Business, you know, may bring money, but friendship hardly ever does."

"Ah! you are not serious now. I know Mr. John Knightley too well — I am very sure he understands the value of friendship as well as any body. I can easily believe that letters are very little to you, much less than to me, but it is not your being ten years older than myself which makes the difference, it is not age, but situation. You have every body dearest to you always at hand, I, probably, never shall again; and therefore till I have outlived all my affections, a post-office, I think, must always have power to draw me out, in worse weather than to-day."

"When I talked of your being altered by time, by the progress of years," said John Knightley, "I meant to imply the change of situation which time usually brings. I consider one as including the other. Time will generally lessen the interest of every attachment not within the daily circle — but that is not the change I had in view for you. As an old friend, you will allow me to hope, Miss Fairfax, that ten years hence you may have as many concentrated objects as I have."

It was kindly said, and very far from giving offence. A pleasant "thank you" seemed meant to laugh it off, but a blush, a quivering lip, a tear in the eye, shewed that it was felt beyond a laugh. Her attention was now claimed by Mr. Woodhouse, who being, according to his custom on such occasions, making the circle of his guests, and paying his particular compliments to the ladies, was ending with her — and with all his mildest urbanity, said,

"I am very sorry to hear, Miss Fairfax, of your being out this morning in the rain. Young ladies should take care of themselves. — Young ladies are delicate plants. They should take care of their health and their complexion. My dear, did you change your stockings?"

"Yes, sir, I did indeed; and I am very much obliged by your kind solicitude about me."

"My dear Miss Fairfax, young ladies are very sure to be cared for. — I hope your good grandmamma and aunt are well. They are some of my very old friends. I wish my health allowed me to be a better neighbour. You do us a great deal of honour to-day, I am sure. My daughter and I are both highly sensible of your goodness, and have the greatest satisfaction in seeing you at Hartfield."

The kind-hearted, polite old man might then sit down and feel that he had done his duty, and made every fair lady welcome and easy.

By this time, the walk in the rain had reached Mrs. Elton, and her remonstrances now opened upon Jane.

"My dear Jane, what is this I hear? — Going to the post-office in the rain! — This must not be, I assure you. — You sad girl, how could you do such a thing? — It is a sign I was not there to take care of you."

Jane very patiently assured her that she had not caught any cold.

"Oh! do not tell *me*. You really are a very sad girl, and do not know how to take care of yourself.   To the post-office indeed! Mrs. Weston, did you ever hear the like? You and I must positively exert our authority."

"My advice," said Mrs. Weston kindly and persuasively, "I certainly do feel tempted to give. Miss Fairfax, you must not run such risks. — Liable as you have been to severe colds, indeed you ought to be particularly careful, especially at this time of year. The spring I always think requires more than common care. Better wait an hour or two, or even half a day for your letters, than run the risk of bringing on your cough again. Now do not you feel that you had? Yes, I am sure you are much too reasonable. You look as if you would not do such a thing again."

"Oh! she *shall not* do such a thing again," eagerly rejoined Mrs. Elton. "We will not allow her to do such a thing again:" — and nodding significantly — "there must be some arrangement made, there must indeed. I shall speak to Mr. E. The man who fetches our letters every morning (one of our men, I forget his name) shall inquire for your's too and bring them to you. That will obviate all difficulties you know; and from *us* I really think, my dear Jane, you can have no scruple to accept such an accommodation."

"You are extremely kind," said Jane; "but I cannot give up my early walk. I am advised to be out of doors as much as I can, I must walk somewhere, and the post-office is an object; and upon my word, I have scarcely ever had a bad morning before."

"My dear Jane, say no more about it. The thing is determined, that is (laughing affectedly) as far as I can presume to determine any thing without the concurrence of my lord and master. You know, Mrs. Weston, you and I must be cautious how we express ourselves. But I do flatter myself, my dear Jane, that my influence is not entirely worn out. If I meet with no insuperable difficulties therefore, consider that point as settled."

"Excuse me," said Jane earnestly, "I cannot by any means consent to such an arrangement, so needlessly troublesome to your servant. If the errand were not a pleasure to me, it could be done, as it always is when I am not here, by my grandmamma's."

"Oh! my dear; but so much as Patty has to do! — And it is a kindness to employ our men."

Jane looked as if she did not mean to be conquered; but instead of answering, she began speaking again to Mr. John Knightley.

"The post-office is a wonderful establishment!" said she. — "The regularity and dispatch of it! If one thinks of all that it has to do, and all that it does so well, it is really astonishing!"

"It is certainly very well regulated."

"So seldom that any negligence or blunder appears! So seldom that a letter, among the thousands that are constantly passing about the kingdom, is even[96] carried wrong — and not one in a million, I suppose, actually lost! And when one considers the variety of hands, and of bad hands too, that are to be deciphered, it increases the wonder!"

"The clerks grow expert from habit. — They must begin with some quickness of sight and hand, and exercise improves them. If you want any further explanation," continued he, smiling, "they are paid for it. That is the key to a great deal of capacity. The public pays and must be served well."

The varieties of hand-writing were farther talked of, and the usual observations made.

"I have heard it asserted," said John Knightley, "that the same sort of hand-writing often prevails in a family; and where the same master teaches, it is natural enough. But for that reason, I should imagine the likeness must be chiefly confined to the females, for boys have very little teaching after an early age, and scramble into any hand they can get. Isabella and Emma, I think, do write very much alike. I have not always known their writing apart."

[96]*even:* Possibly a compositor's misreading of "ever."

"Yes," said his brother hesitatingly, "there is a likeness. I know what you mean — but Emma's hand is the strongest."

"Isabella and Emma both write beautifully," said Mr. Woodhouse; "and always did. And so does poor Mrs. Weston" — with half a sigh and half a smile at her.

"I never saw any gentleman's hand-writing" — Emma began, looking also at Mrs. Weston; but stopped, on perceiving that Mrs. Weston was attending to some one else — and the pause gave her time to reflect, "Now, how am I going to introduce him? — Am I unequal to speaking his name at once before all these people? Is it necessary for me to use any roundabout phrase? — Your Yorkshire friend — your correspondent in Yorkshire; — that would be the way, I suppose, if I were very bad. — No, I can pronounce his name without the smallest distress. I certainly get better and better. — Now for it."

Mrs. Weston was disengaged and Emma began again — "Mr. Frank Churchill writes one of the best gentlemen's hands I ever saw."

"I do not admire it," said Mr. Knightley. "It is too small — wants strength. It is like a woman's writing."

This was not submitted to by either lady. They vindicated him against the base aspersion. "No, it by no means wanted strength — it was not a large hand, but very clear and certainly strong. Had not Mrs. Weston any letter about her to produce?" No, she had heard from him very lately, but having answered the letter, had put it away.

"If we were in the other room," said Emma, "if I had my writing-desk, I am sure I could produce a specimen. I have a note of his. — Do not you remember, Mrs. Weston, employing him to write for you one day?"

"He chose to say he was employed" ——

"Well, well, I have that note; and can shew it after dinner to convince Mr. Knightley."

"Oh! when a gallant young man, like Mr. Frank Churchill," said Mr. Knightley drily, "writes to a fair lady like Miss Woodhouse, he will, of course, put forth his best."

Dinner was on table. — Mrs. Elton, before she could be spoken to, was ready; and before Mr. Woodhouse had reached her with his request to be allowed to hand her into the dining-parlour, was saying —

"Must I go first? I really am ashamed of always leading the way."

Jane's solicitude about fetching her own letters had not escaped Emma. She had heard and seen it all; and felt some curiosity to know whether the wet walk of this morning had produced any. She suspected that it *had;* that it would not have been so resolutely encountered but in full expectation of hearing from some one very dear, and that it had not been in vain. She thought there was an air of greater happiness than usual — a glow both of complexion and spirits.

She could have made an inquiry or two, as to the expedition and the expense of the Irish mails; — it was at her tongue's end — but she abstained. She was quite determined not to utter a word that should hurt Jane Fairfax's feelings; and they followed the other ladies out of the room, arm in arm, with an appearance of good-will highly becoming to the beauty and grace of each.

CHAPTER XVII.

WHEN the ladies returned to the drawing-room after dinner, Emma found it hardly possible to prevent their making two distinct parties; — with so much perseverance in judging and behaving ill did Mrs. Elton engross Jane Fairfax and slight herself. She and Mrs. Weston were obliged to be almost always either talking together or silent together. Mrs. Elton left them no choice. If Jane repressed her for a little time, she soon began again; and though much that passed between them was in a half-whisper, especially on Mrs. Elton's side, there was no avoiding a knowledge of their principal subjects: — The post-office — catching cold — fetching letters — and friendship, were long under discussion; and to them succeeded one, which must be at least equally unpleasant to Jane — inquiries whether she had yet heard of any situation likely to suit her, and professions of Mrs. Elton's meditated activity.

"Here is April come!" said she, "I get quite anxious about you. June will soon be here."

"But I have never fixed on June or any other month — merely looked forward to the summer in general."

"But have you really heard of nothing?"

"I have not even made any inquiry; I do not wish to make any yet."

"Oh! my dear, we cannot begin too early; you are not aware of the difficulty of procuring exactly the desirable thing."

"I not aware!" said Jane, shaking her head; "dear Mrs. Elton, who can have thought of it as I have done?"

"But you have not seen so much of the world as I have. You do not know how many candidates there always are for the *first* situations. I saw a vast deal of that in the neighbourhood round Maple Grove. A cousin of Mr. Suckling, Mrs. Bragge, had such an infinity of applications; every body was anxious to be in her family, for she moves in the first circle. Wax-candles in the school-room! You may imagine how desirable! Of all houses in the kingdom Mrs. Bragge's is the one I would most wish to see you in."

"Col. and Mrs. Campbell are to be in town again by midsummer," said Jane. "I must spend some time with them; I am sure they will want it; — afterwards I may probably be glad to dispose of myself. But I would not wish you to take the trouble of making any inquiries at present."

"Trouble! aye, I know your scruples. You are afraid of giving me trouble; but I assure you, my dear Jane, the Campbells can hardly be more interested about you than I am. I shall write to Mrs. Partridge in a day or two, and shall give her a strict charge to be on the look-out for any thing eligible."

"Thank you, but I would rather you did not mention the subject to her; till the time draws nearer, I do not wish to be giving any body trouble."

"But, my dear child, the time *is* drawing near; here is April, and June, or say even July, is very near, with such business to accomplish before us. Your inexperience really amuses me! A situation such as you deserve, and your friends would require for you, is no every day occurrence, is not obtained at a moment's notice; indeed, indeed, we must begin inquiring directly."

"Excuse me, ma'am, but this is by no means my intention; I make no inquiry myself, and should be sorry to have any made by my friends. When I am quite determined as to the time, I am not at all afraid of being long unemployed. There are places in town, offices, where inquiry would soon produce something — Offices for the sale — not quite of human flesh — but of human intellect."[97]

"Oh! my dear, human flesh! You quite shock me; if you mean a fling at the slave-trade,[98] I assure you Mr. Suckling was always rather a friend to the abolition."

---

[97] *Offices for the sale—not quite of human flesh—but of human intellect.":* Though Jane will shortly insist that she is referring to the governess trade and not the slave trade, her words here find ironical counterpoint in William Cowper's "Negro's Complaint" (1788), in which the speaker, a slave, asserts that "Minds are never to be sold." See Thorell Porter Tsomondo, "Temporal, Spatial, and Linguistic Configurations and the Geopolitics of *Emma*," *Persuasions* 21 (1999): 188–220.

[98] *slave-trade:* Mrs. Elton, as a native of Bristol, a slave port, would have reason to be acquainted with the slave trade and the vigorous parliamentary debates leading up to its abolition, which occurred in 1807–08 when a bill was passed into law in two stages. Austen was an admirer of Thomas Clarkson's *The History . . . of the Abolition of the African Slave-Trade* (1808). And she may have intended Mrs. Elton's maiden name—

"I did not mean, I was not thinking of the slave-trade," replied Jane; "governess-trade, I assure you, was all that I had in view; widely different certainly as to the guilt of those who carry it on, but as to the greater misery of the victims, I do not know where it lies. But I only mean to say that there are advertising offices, and that by applying to them I should have no doubt of very soon meeting with something that would do."

"Something that would do!" repeated Mrs. Elton. "Aye, *that* may suit your humble ideas of yourself; — I know what a modest creature you are; but it will not satisfy your friends to have you taking up with any thing that may offer, any inferior, common-place situation, in a family not moving in a certain circle, or able to command the elegancies of life."

"You are very obliging; but as to all that, I am very indifferent; it would be no object to me to be with the rich; my mortifications, I think, would only be the greater; I should suffer more from comparison. A gentleman's family is all that I should condition for."

"I know you, I know you; you would take up with any thing; but I shall be a little more nice, and I am sure the good Campbells will be quite on my side; with your superior talents, you have a right to move in the first circle. Your musical knowledge alone would entitle you to name your own terms, have as many rooms as you like, and mix in the family as much as you chose; — that is — I do not know — if you knew the harp, you might do all that, I am very sure; but you sing as well as play; — yes, I really believe you might, even with the harp, stipulate for what you chose; — and you must and shall be delightfully, honourably and comfortably settled before the Campbells or I have any rest."

"You may well class the delight, the honour, and the comfort of such a situation together," said Jane, "they are pretty sure to be equal; however, I am very serious in not wishing any thing to be attempted at present for me. I am exceedingly obliged to you, Mrs. Elton, I am obliged to any body who feels for me, but I am quite serious in wishing nothing to be done till the summer. For two or three months longer I shall remain where I am, and as I am."

"And I am quite serious too, I assure you," replied Mrs. Elton gaily,

---

Hawkins—to recall that of the Elizabethan sailor and slave trader, Sir John Hawkins. See Ruth Perry, "Austen and Empire: A Thinking Woman's Guide to British Imperialism," *Persuasions* 16 (1994): 96–106; and for the Austen family's tenuous links with slavery in the West Indies, see Claire Tomalin, *Jane Austen: A Life* (New York: Knopf, 1997), Appendix ii.

"in resolving to be always on the watch, and employing my friends to watch also, that nothing really unexceptionable may pass us."

In this style she ran on; never thoroughly stopped by any thing till Mr. Woodhouse came into the room; her vanity had then a change of object, and Emma heard her saying in the same half-whisper to Jane,

"Here comes this dear old beau of mine, I protest! — Only think of his gallantry in coming away before the other men! — what a dear creature he is; — I assure you I like him excessively. I admire all that quaint, old-fashioned politeness; it is much more to my taste than modern ease; modern ease often disgusts me. But this good old Mr. Woodhouse, I wish you had heard his gallant speeches to me at dinner. Oh! I assure you I began to think my cara sposa[99] would be absolutely jealous. I fancy I am rather a favourite; he took notice of my gown. How do you like it? — Selina's choice — handsome, I think, but I do not know whether it is not over-trimmed; I have the greatest dislike to the idea of being over-trimmed — quite a horror of finery. I must put on a few ornaments *now*, because it is expected of me. A bride, you know, must appear like a bride, but my natural taste is all for simplicity; a simple style of dress is so infinitely preferable to finery. But I am quite in the minority, I believe; few people seem to value simplicity of dress, — shew and finery are every thing. I have some notion of putting such a trimming as this to my white and silver poplin. Do you think it will look well?"

The whole party were but just re-assembled in the drawing-room when Mr. Weston made his appearance among them. He had returned to a late dinner, and walked to Hartfield as soon as it was over. He had been too much expected by the best judges, for surprize — but there was great joy. Mr. Woodhouse was almost as glad to see him now, as he would have been sorry to see him before. John Knightley only was in mute astonishment. — That a man who might have spent his evening quietly at home after a day of business in London, should set off again, and walk half-a-mile to another man's house, for the sake of being in mixed company till bed-time, of finishing his day in the efforts of civility and the noise of numbers, was a circumstance to strike him deeply. A man who had been in motion since eight o'clock in the morning, and might now have been still, who had been long talking, and might have been silent, who had been in more than one crowd, and might have been alone! — Such a man, to quit the tranquillity and independence of his own fire-side, and on the evening of a cold sleety April day rush

---

[99] *cara sposa:* See note 92, p. 226.

out again into the world! — Could he by a touch of his finger have instantly taken back his wife, there would have been a motive; but his coming would probably prolong rather than break up the party. John Knightley looked at him with amazement, then shrugged his shoulders, and said, "I could not have believed it even of *him*."

Mr. Weston meanwhile, perfectly unsuspicious of the indignation he was exciting, happy and cheerful as usual, and with all the right of being principal talker, which a day spent any where from home confers, was making himself agreeable among the rest; and having satisfied the inquiries of his wife as to his dinner, convincing her that none of all her careful directions to the servants had been forgotten, and spread abroad what public news he had heard, was proceeding to a family communication, which, though principally addressed to Mrs. Weston, he had not the smallest doubt of being highly interesting to every body in the room. He gave her a letter, it was from Frank, and to herself; he had met with it in his way, and had taken the liberty of opening it.

"Read it, read it," said he, "it will give you pleasure; only a few lines — will not take you long; read it to Emma."

The two ladies looked over it together; and he sat smiling and talking to them the whole time, in a voice a little subdued, but very audible to every body.

"Well, he is coming, you see; good news, I think. Well, what do you say to it? — I always told you he would be here again soon, did not I? — Anne, my dear, did not I always tell you so, and you would not believe me? — In town next week, you see — at the latest, I dare say; for *she* is as impatient as the black gentleman[100] when any thing is to be done; most likely they will be there to-morrow or Saturday. As to her illness, all nothing of course. But it is an excellent thing to have Frank among us again, so near as town. They will stay a good while when they do come, and he will be half his time with us. This is precisely what I wanted. Well, pretty good news, is not it? Have you finished it? Has Emma read it all? Put it up, put it up; we will have a good talk about it some other time, but it will not do now. I shall only just mention the circumstance to the others in a common way."

Mrs. Weston was most comfortably pleased on the occasion. Her looks and words had nothing to restrain them. She was happy, she knew she was happy, and knew she ought to be happy. Her congratulations were warm and open; but Emma could not speak so fluently. *She* was a little occupied in weighing her own feelings, and trying

---

[100] *the black gentleman:* The devil.

to understand the degree of her agitation, which she rather thought was considerable.

Mr. Weston, however, too eager to be very observant, too communicative to want others to talk, was very well satisfied with what she did say, and soon moved away to make the rest of his friends happy by a partial communication of what the whole room must have overheard already.

It was well that he took every body's joy for granted, or he might not have thought either Mr. Woodhouse or Mr. Knightley particularly delighted. They were the first entitled, after Mrs. Weston and Emma, to be made happy; — from them he would have proceeded to Miss Fairfax, but she was so deep in conversation with John Knightley, that it would have been too positive an interruption; and finding himself close to Mrs. Elton, and her attention disengaged, he necessarily began on the subject with her.

CHAPTER XVIII.

"I hope I shall soon have the pleasure of introducing my son to you," said Mr. Weston.

Mrs. Elton, very willing to suppose a particular compliment intended her by such a hope, smiled most graciously.

"You have heard of a certain Frank Churchill, I presume," he continued — "and know him to be my son, though he does not bear my name."

"Oh! yes, and I shall be very happy in his acquaintance. I am sure Mr. Elton will lose no time in calling on him; and we shall both have great pleasure in seeing him at the Vicarage."

"You are very obliging. — Frank will be extremely happy, I am sure. — He is to be in town next week, if not sooner. We have notice of it in a letter to-day. I met the letters in my way this morning, and seeing my son's hand, presumed to open it — though it was not directed to me — it was to Mrs. Weston. She is his principal correspondent, I assure you. I hardly ever get a letter."

"And so you absolutely opened what was directed to her! oh! Mr. Weston — (laughing affectedly) I must protest against that. — A most dangerous precedent indeed! — I beg you will not let your neighbours follow your example. — Upon my word, if this is what I am to expect, we married women must begin to exert ourselves! — Oh! Mr. Weston, I could not have believed it of you!"

"Aye, we men are sad fellows. You must take care of yourself, Mrs. Elton. — This letter tells us — it is a short letter — written in a hurry, merely to give us notice — it tells us that they are all coming up to town directly, on Mrs. Churchill's account — she has not been well the whole winter, and thinks Enscombe too cold for her — so they are all to move southward without loss of time."

"Indeed! — from Yorkshire, I think. Enscombe is in Yorkshire?"

"Yes, they are about 190 miles from London. A considerable journey."

"Yes, upon my word, very considerable. Sixty-five miles farther than from Maple Grove to London. But what is distance, Mr. Weston, to people of large fortune? — You would be amazed to hear how my brother, Mr. Suckling, sometimes flies about. You will hardly believe me — but twice in one week he and Mr. Bragge went to London and back again with four horses."

"The evil of the distance from Enscombe," said Mr. Weston, "is, that Mrs. Churchill, *as we understand,* has not been able to leave the sopha for a week together. In Frank's last letter she complained, he said, of being too weak to get into her conservatory without having both his arm and his uncle's! This, you know, speaks a great degree of weakness — but now she is so impatient to be in town, that she means to sleep only two nights on the road. — So Frank writes word. Certainly, delicate ladies have very extraordinary constitutions, Mrs. Elton. You must grant me that."

"No, indeed, I shall grant you nothing. I always take the part of my own sex. I do indeed. I give you notice — You will find me a formidable antagonist on that point. I always stand up for women — and I assure you, if you knew how Selina feels with respect to sleeping at an inn, you would not wonder at Mrs. Churchill's making incredible exertions to avoid it. Selina says it is quite horror to her — and I believe I have caught a little of her nicety. She always travels with her own sheets; an excellent precaution. Does Mrs. Churchill do the same?"

"Depend upon it, Mrs. Churchill does every thing that any other fine lady ever did. Mrs. Churchill will not be second to any lady in the land for" —

Mrs. Elton eagerly interposed with,

"Oh! Mr. Weston, do not mistake me. Selina is no fine lady, I assure you. Do not run away with such an idea."

"Is not she? Then she is no rule for Mrs. Churchill, who is as thorough a fine lady as any body ever beheld."

Mrs. Elton began to think she had been wrong in disclaiming so warmly. It was by no means her object to have it believed that her sister was *not* a fine lady; perhaps there was want of spirit in the pretence of it; — and she was considering in what way she had best retract, when Mr. Weston went on.

"Mrs. Churchill is not much in my good graces, as you may suspect — but this is quite between ourselves. She is very fond of Frank, and therefore I would not speak ill of her. Besides, she is out of health now; but *that* indeed, by her own account, she has always been. I would not say so to every body, Mrs. Elton, but I have not much faith in Mrs. Churchill's illness."

"If she is really ill, why not go to Bath, Mr. Weston? — To Bath, or to Clifton?"[101]

"She has taken it into her head that Enscombe is too cold for her. The fact is, I suppose, that she is tired of Enscombe. She has now been a longer time stationary there, than she ever was before, and she begins to want change. It is a retired place. A fine place, but very retired."

"Aye — like Maple Grove, I dare say. Nothing can stand more retired from the road than Maple Grove. Such an immense plantation all around it! You seem shut out from every thing — in the most complete retirement. — And Mrs. Churchill probably has not health or spirits like Selina to enjoy that sort of seclusion. Or, perhaps she may not have resources enough in herself to be qualified for a country life. I always say a woman cannot have too many resources — and I feel very thankful that I have so many myself as to be quite independent of society."

"Frank was here in February for a fortnight."

"So I remember to have heard. He will find an *addition* to the society of Highbury when he comes again; that is, if I may presume to call myself an addition. But perhaps he may never have heard of there being such a creature in the world."

This was too loud a call for a compliment to be passed by, and Mr. Weston, with a very good grace, immediately exclaimed,

"My dear madam! Nobody but yourself could imagine such a thing possible. Not heard of you! — I believe Mrs. Weston's letters lately have been full of very little else than Mrs. Elton."

He had done his duty and could return to his son.

---

[101] *Clifton:* Residential district just outside (in Austen's time) the city boundary of Bristol; known for its graceful Georgian and Regency terraces and villas. Jane Austen stayed there briefly with her mother and sister after they left Bath in 1806 and before they took up residence in Southampton.

"When Frank left us," continued he, "it was quite uncertain when
he might see him again, which makes this day's news doubly welcome.
It has been completely unexpected. That is, *I* always had a strong persuasion he would be here again soon, I was sure something favourable
would turn up — but nobody believed me. He and Mrs. Weston were
both dreadfully desponding. 'How could he contrive to come? and how
could it be supposed that his uncle and aunt would spare him again?'
and so forth — I always felt that something would happen in our
favour; and so it has, you see. I have observed, Mrs. Elton, in the course
of my life, that if things are going untowardly one month, they are sure
to mend the next."

"Very true, Mr. Weston, perfectly true. It is just what I used to say
to a certain gentleman in company in the days of courtship, when,
because things did not go quite right, did not proceed with all the
rapidity which suited his feelings, he was apt to be in despair, and
exclaim that he was sure at this rate it would be *May* before Hymen's
saffron robe[102] would be put on for us! Oh! the pains I have been at
to dispel those gloomy ideas and give him cheerfuller views! The carriage — we had disappointments about the carriage; — one morning, I
remember, he came to me quite in despair."

She was stopped by a slight fit of coughing, and Mr. Weston
instantly seized the opportunity of going on.

"You were mentioning May. May is the very month which Mrs.
Churchill is ordered, or has ordered herself, to spend in some warmer
place than Enscombe — in short, to spend in London; so that we have
the agreeable prospect of frequent visits from Frank the whole
spring — precisely the season of the year which one should have chosen
for it: days almost at the longest; weather genial and pleasant, always
inviting one out, and never too hot for exercise. When he was here
before, we made the best of it; but there was a good deal of wet, damp,
cheerless weather; there always is in February, you know, and we could
not do half that we intended. Now will be the time. This will be complete enjoyment; and I do not know, Mrs. Elton, whether the uncertainty of our meetings, the sort of constant expectation there will be of
his coming in to-day or to-morrow, and at any hour, may not be more
friendly to happiness than having him actually in the house. I think it is

---

[102] *Hymen's saffron robe:* Pseudopoetic reference to the Greek god of marriage. As
Chapman and Stafford point out, the phrase recalls Milton's *L'Allegro:* "There let
Hymen oft appear / In saffron robe."

so. I think it is the state of mind which gives most spirit and delight. I hope you will be pleased with my son; but you must not expect a prodigy. He is generally thought a fine young man, but do not expect a prodigy. Mrs. Weston's partiality for him is very great, and, as you may suppose, most gratifying to me. She thinks nobody equal to him."

"And I assure you, Mr. Weston, I have very little doubt that my opinion will be decidedly in his favour. I have heard so much in praise of Mr. Frank Churchill. — At the same time it is fair to observe, that I am one of those who always judge for themselves, and are by no means implicitly guided by others. I give you notice that as I find your son, so I shall judge of him. — I am no flatterer."

Mr. Weston was musing.

"I hope," said he presently, "I have not been severe upon poor Mrs. Churchill. If she is ill I should be sorry to do her injustice; but there are some traits in her character which make it difficult for me to speak of her with the forbearance I could wish. You cannot be ignorant, Mrs. Elton, of my connection with the family, nor of the treatment I have met with; and, between ourselves, the whole blame of it is to be laid to her. She was the instigator. Frank's mother would never have been slighted as she was but for her. Mr. Churchill has pride; but his pride is nothing to his wife's: his is a quiet, indolent, gentlemanlike sort of pride that would harm nobody, and only make himself a little helpless and tiresome; but her pride is arrogance and insolence! And what inclines one less to bear, she has no fair pretence of family or blood. She was nobody when he married her, barely the daughter of a gentleman; but ever since her being turned into a Churchill she has out-Churchill'd them all in high and mighty claims: but in herself, I assure you, she is an upstart."

"Only think! well, that must be infinitely provoking! I have quite a horror of upstarts. Maple Grove has given me a thorough disgust to people of that sort; for there is a family in that neighbourhood who are such an annoyance to my brother and sister from the airs they give themselves! Your description of Mrs. Churchill made me think of them directly. People of the name of Tupman, very lately settled there, and encumbered with many low connections, but giving themselves immense airs, and expecting to be on a footing with the old established families. A year and a half is the very utmost that they can have lived at West Hall; and how they got their fortune nobody knows. They came from Birmingham,[103] which is not a place to promise much, you know,

---

[103] *Birmingham:* Explosively expanding industrial town in the Midlands.

Mr. Weston. One has not great hopes from Birmingham. I always say there is something direful in the sound: but nothing more is positively known of the Tupmans, though a good many things I assure you are suspected; and yet by their manners they evidently think themselves equal even to my brother, Mr. Suckling, who happens to be one of their nearest neighbours. It is infinitely too bad. Mr. Suckling, who has been eleven years a resident at Maple Grove, and whose father had it before him — I believe, at least — I am almost sure that old Mr. Suckling had completed the purchase before his death."

They were interrupted. Tea was carrying round, and Mr. Weston, having said all that he wanted, soon took the opportunity of walking away.

After tea, Mr. and Mrs. Weston, and Mr. Elton sat down with Mr. Woodhouse to cards. The remaining five were left to their own powers, and Emma doubted their getting on very well; for Mr. Knightley seemed little disposed for conversation; Mrs. Elton was wanting notice, which nobody had inclination to pay, and she was herself in a worry of spirits which would have made her prefer being silent.

Mr. John Knightley proved more talkative than his brother. He was to leave them early the next day; and he soon began with —

"Well, Emma, I do not believe I have any thing more to say about the boys; but you have your sister's letter, and every thing is down at full length there we may be sure. My charge would be much more concise than her's, and probably not much in the same spirit; all that I have to recommend being comprised in, do not spoil them, and do not physic them."

"I rather hope to satisfy you both," said Emma, "for I shall do all in my power to make them happy, which will be enough for Isabella; and happiness must preclude false indulgence and physic."

"And if you find them troublesome, you must send them home again."

"That is very likely. You think so, do not you?"

"I hope I am aware that they may be too noisy for your father — or even may be some incumbrance to you, if your visiting-engagements continue to increase as much as they have done lately."

"Increase!"

"Certainly; you must be sensible that the last half year has made a great difference in your way of life."

"Difference! No indeed I am not."

"There can be no doubt of your being much more engaged with company than you used to be. Witness this very time. Here am I come

down for only one day, and you are engaged with a dinner-party! —
When did it happen before, or any thing like it? Your neighbourhood is
increasing, and you mix more with it. A little while ago, every letter to
Isabella brought an account of fresh gaieties; dinners at Mr. Cole's, or
balls at the Crown. The difference which Randalls, Randalls alone
makes in your goings-on, is very great."

"Yes," said his brother quickly, "it is Randalls that does it all."

"Very well — and as Randalls, I suppose, is not likely to have less
influence than heretofore, it strikes me as a possible thing, Emma, that
Henry and John may be sometimes in the way. And if they are, I only
beg you to send them home."

"No," cried Mr. Knightley, "that need not be the consequence. Let
them be sent to Donwell. I shall certainly be at leisure."

"Upon my word," exclaimed Emma, "you amuse me! I should like
to know how many of all my numerous engagements take place without your being of the party; and why I am to be supposed in danger of
wanting leisure to attend to the little boys. These amazing engagements of mine — what have they been? Dining once with the Coles —
and having a ball talked of, which never took place. I can understand
you — (nodding at Mr. John Knightley) — your good fortune in meeting with so many of your friends at once here, delights you too much to
pass unnoticed. But you, (turning to Mr. Knightley,) who know how
very, very seldom I am ever two hours from Hartfield, why you should
foresee such a series of dissipation for me, I cannot imagine. And as to
my dear little boys, I must say, that if aunt Emma has not time for them,
I do not think they would fare much better with uncle Knightley, who
is absent from home about five hours where she is absent one — and
who, when he is at home, is either reading to himself or settling his
accounts."

Mr. Knightley seemed to be trying not to smile; and succeeded
without difficulty, upon Mrs. Elton's beginning to talk to him.

Volume III

CHAPTER I.

A VERY little quiet reflection was enough to satisfy Emma as to the nature of her agitation on hearing this news of Frank Churchill. She was soon convinced that it was not for herself she was feeling at all apprehensive or embarrassed; it was for him. Her own attachment had really subsided into a mere nothing; it was not worth thinking of; — but if he, who had undoubtedly been always so much the most in love of the two, were to be returning with the same warmth of sentiment which he had taken away, it would be very distressing. If a separation of two months should not have cooled him, there were dangers and evils before her: — caution for him and for herself would be necessary. She did not mean to have her own affections entangled again, and it would be incumbent on her to avoid any encouragement of his.

She wished she might be able to keep him from an absolute declaration. That would be so very painful a conclusion of their present acquaintance! — and yet, she could not help rather anticipating something decisive. She felt as if the spring would not pass without bringing a crisis, an event, a something to alter her present composed and tranquil state.

It was not very long, though rather longer than Mr. Weston had foreseen, before she had the power of forming some opinion of Frank

Churchill's feelings. The Enscombe family were not in town quite so soon as had been imagined, but he was at Highbury very soon afterwards. He rode down for a couple of hours; he could not yet do more; but as he came from Randalls[104] immediately to Hartfield, she could then exercise all her quick observation, and speedily determine how he was influenced, and how she must act. They met with the utmost friendliness. There could be no doubt of his great pleasure in seeing her. But she had an almost instant doubt of his caring for her as he had done, of his feeling the same tenderness in the same degree. She watched him well. It was a clear thing he was less in love than he had been. Absence, with the conviction probably of her indifference, had produced this very natural and very desirable effect.

He was in high spirits; as ready to talk and laugh as ever, and seemed delighted to speak of his former visit, and recur to old stories: and he was not without agitation. It was not in his calmness that she read his comparative indifference. He was not calm; his spirits were evidently fluttered; there was restlessness about him. Lively as he was, it seemed a liveliness that did not satisfy himself: but what decided her belief on the subject, was his staying only a quarter of an hour, and hurrying away to make other calls in Highbury. "He had seen a group of old acquaintance in the street as he passed — he had not stopped, he would not stop for more than a word — but he had the vanity to think they would be disappointed if he did not call, and much as he wished to stay longer at Hartfield, he must hurry off."

She had no doubt as to his being less in love — but neither his agitated spirits, nor his hurrying away, seemed like a perfect cure; and she was rather inclined to think it implied a dread of her returning power, and a discreet resolution of not trusting himself with her long.

This was the only visit from Frank Churchill in the course of ten days. He was often hoping, intending to come — but was always prevented. His aunt could not bear to have him leave her. Such was his own account at Randalls. If he were quite sincere, if he really tried to come, it was to be inferred that Mrs. Churchill's removal to London had been of no service to the wilful or nervous part of her disorder. That she was really ill was very certain; he had declared himself convinced of it, at Randalls. Though much might be fancy, he could not doubt, when he looked back, that she was in a weaker state of health than she had been half a year ago. He did not believe it to proceed from

---

[104] *Randalls:* The spelling of the first two volumes has been retained here and in other instances, though in the third volume of the first edition "Randall's" is the form used.

any thing that care and medicine might not remove, or at least that she might not have many years of existence before her; but he could not be prevailed on by all his father's doubts, to say that her complaints were merely imaginary, or that she was as strong as ever.

It soon appeared that London was not the place for her. She could not endure its noise. Her nerves were under continual irritation and suffering; and by the ten days' end, her nephew's letter to Randalls communicated a change of plan. They were going to remove immediately to Richmond.[105] Mrs. Churchill had been recommended to the medical skill of an eminent person there, and had otherwise a fancy for the place. A ready-furnished house in a favourite spot was engaged, and much benefit expected from the change.

Emma heard that Frank wrote in the highest spirits of this arrangement, and seemed most fully to appreciate the blessing of having two months before him of such near neighbourhood to many dear friends — for the house was taken for May and June. She was told that now he wrote with the greatest confidence of being often with them, almost as often as he could even wish.

Emma saw how Mr. Weston understood these joyous prospects. He was considering her as the source of all the happiness they offered. She hoped it was not so. Two months must bring it to the proof.

Mr. Weston's own happiness was indisputable. He was quite delighted. It was the very circumstance he could have wished for. Now, it would be really having Frank in their neighbourhood. What were nine miles to a young man? — An hour's ride. He would be always coming over. The difference in that respect of Richmond and London was enough to make the whole difference of seeing him always and seeing him never. Sixteen miles — nay, eighteen — it must be full eighteen to Manchester-street — was a serious obstacle. Were he ever able to get away, the day would be spent in coming and returning. There was no comfort in having him in London; he might as well be at Enscombe; but Richmond was the very distance for easy intercourse. Better than nearer!

One good thing was immediately brought to a certainty by this removal, — the ball at the Crown. It had not been forgotten before, but it had been soon acknowledged vain to attempt to fix a day. Now, however, it was absolutely to be; every preparation was resumed, and very soon after the Churchills had removed to Richmond, a few lines

[105] *Richmond:* Fashionable town with royal associations on the Thames west of London.

from Frank, to say that his aunt felt already much better for the change, and that he had no doubt of being able to join them for twenty-four hours at any given time, induced them to name as early a day as possible.

Mr. Weston's ball was to be a real thing. A very few to-morrows stood between the young people of Highbury and happiness.

Mr. Woodhouse was resigned. The time of year lightened the evil to him. May was better for every thing than February. Mrs. Bates was engaged to spend the evening at Hartfield, James had due notice, and he sanguinely hoped that neither dear little Henry nor dear little John would have any thing the matter with them, while dear Emma were gone.

CHAPTER II.

No misfortune occurred, again to prevent the ball. The day approached, the day arrived; and, after a morning of some anxious watching, Frank Churchill, in all the certainty of his own self, reached Randalls before dinner, and every thing was safe.

No second meeting had there yet been between him and Emma. The room at the Crown was to witness it; — but it would be better than a common meeting in a crowd. Mr. Weston had been so very earnest in his entreaties for her early attendance, for her arriving there as soon as possible after themselves, for the purpose of taking her opinion as to the propriety and comfort of the rooms before any other persons came, that she could not refuse him, and must therefore spend some quiet interval in the young man's company. She was to convey Harriet, and they drove to the Crown in good time, the Randalls' party just sufficiently before them.

Frank Churchill seemed to have been on the watch; and though he did not say much, his eyes declared that he meant to have a delightful evening. They all walked about together, to see that every thing was as it should be; and within a few minutes were joined by the contents of another carriage, which Emma could not hear the sound of at first, without great surprise. "So unreasonably early!" she was going to exclaim; but she presently found that it was a family of old friends, who were coming, like herself, by particular desire, to help Mr. Weston's judgement; and they were so very closely followed by another carriage of cousins, who had been entreated to come early with the same distinguishing earnestness, on the same errand, that it seemed as if half the company might soon be collected together for the purpose of preparatory inspection.

Emma perceived that her taste was not the only taste on which Mr. Weston depended, and felt, that to be the favourite and intimate of a man who had so many intimates and confidantes, was not the very first distinction in the scale of vanity. She liked his open manners, but a little less of open-heartedness would have made him a higher character. — General benevolence, but not general friendship, made a man what he ought to be. — She could fancy such a man.

The whole party walked about, and looked, and praised again; and then, having nothing else to do, formed a sort of half circle round the fire, to observe in their various modes, till other subjects were started, that, though *May*, a fire in the evening was still very pleasant.

Emma found that it was not Mr. Weston's fault that the number of privy counsellors was not yet larger. They had stopped at Mrs. Bates's door to offer the use of their carriage, but the aunt and niece were to be brought by the Eltons.

Frank was standing by her, but not steadily; there was a restlessness, which showed a mind not at ease. He was looking about, he was going to the door, he was watching for the sound of other carriages, — impatient to begin, or afraid of being always near her.

Mrs. Elton was spoken of. "I think she must be here soon," said he. "I have a great curiosity to see Mrs. Elton, I have heard so much of her. It cannot be long, I think, before she comes."

A carriage was heard. He was on the move immediately; but coming back, said,

"I am forgetting that I am not acquainted with her. I have never seen either Mr. or Mrs. Elton. I have no business to put myself forward."

Mr. and Mrs. Elton appeared; and all the smiles and the proprieties passed.

"But Miss Bates and Miss Fairfax!" said Mr. Weston, looking about. "We thought you were to bring them."

The mistake had been slight. The carriage was sent for them now. Emma longed to know what Frank's first opinion of Mrs. Elton might be; how he was affected by the studied elegance of her dress, and her smiles of graciousness. He was immediately qualifying himself to form an opinion, by giving her very proper attention, after the introduction had passed.

In a few minutes the carriage returned. — Somebody talked of rain. — "I will see that there are umbrellas, sir," said Frank to his father: "Miss Bates must not be forgotten:" and away he went. Mr. Weston was following; but Mrs. Elton detained him, to gratify him by her opinion of his son; and so briskly did she begin, that the young man himself, though by no means moving slowly, could hardly be out of hearing.

"A very fine young man indeed, Mr. Weston. You know I candidly told you I should form my own opinion; and I am happy to say that I am extremely pleased with him. — You may believe me. I never compliment. I think him a very handsome young man, and his manners are precisely what I like and approve — so truly the gentleman, without the least conceit or puppyism.[106] You must know I have a vast dislike to puppies — quite a horror of them. They were never tolerated at Maple Grove. Neither Mr. Suckling nor me[107] had ever any patience with them; and we used sometimes to say very cutting things! Selina, who is mild almost to a fault, bore with them much better."

While she talked of his son, Mr. Weston's attention was chained; but when she got to Maple Grove, he could recollect that there were ladies just arriving to be attended to, and with happy smiles must hurry away.

Mrs. Elton turned to Mrs. Weston. "I have no doubt of its being our carriage with Miss Bates and Jane. Our coachman and horses are so extremely expeditious! — I believe we drive faster than anybody. — What a pleasure it is to send one's carriage for a friend! — I understand you were so kind as to offer, but another time it will be quite unnecessary. You may be very sure I shall always take care of *them*."

Miss Bates and Miss Fairfax, escorted by the two gentlemen, walked into the room; and Mrs. Elton seemed to think it as much her duty as Mrs. Weston's to receive them. Her gestures and movements might be understood by any one who looked on like Emma, but her words, everybody's words, were soon lost under the incessant flow of Miss Bates, who came in talking, and had not finished her speech under many minutes after her being admitted into the circle at the fire. As the door opened she was heard,

"So very obliging of you! — No rain at all. Nothing to signify. I do not care for myself. Quite thick shoes. And Jane declares — Well! — (as soon as she was within the door) Well! This is brilliant indeed! — This is admirable! — Excellently contrived, upon my word. Nothing wanting. Could not have imagined it. — So well lighted up. — Jane, Jane, look — did you ever see any thing? Oh! Mr. Weston, you must really

---

[106]*puppyism:* The vain and impertinent behavior of a "puppy," that is, a silly young man. Mr. Knightley characterizes Frank Churchill as a "puppy" (p. 132).

[107]*Neither Mr. Suckling nor me:* Mrs. Elton's grammar is as bad as her egoism is unrelenting.

have had Aladdin's lamp. Good Mrs. Stokes would not know her own room again. I saw her as I came in; she was standing in the entrance. 'Oh! Mrs. Stokes,' said I — but I had not time for more." — She was now met by Mrs. Weston. — "Very well, I thank you, ma'am. I hope you are quite well. Very happy to hear it. So afraid you might have a headach! — seeing you pass by so often, and knowing how much trouble you must have. Delighted to hear it indeed. Ah! dear Mrs. Elton, so obliged to you for the carriage! — excellent time. — Jane and I quite ready. Did not keep the horses a moment. Most comfortable carriage. — Oh! and I am sure our thanks are due to you, Mrs. Weston, on that score. — Mrs. Elton had most kindly sent Jane a note, or we should have been. — But two such offers in one day! — Never were such neighbours. I said to my mother, 'Upon my word, ma'am ——— .' Thank you, my mother is remarkably well. Gone to Mr. Woodhouse's. I made her take her shawl — for the evenings are not warm — her large new shawl — Mrs. Dixon's wedding present. — So kind of her to think of my mother! Bought at Weymouth, you know — Mr. Dixon's choice. There were three others, Jane says, which they hesitated about some time. Colonel Campbell rather preferred an olive. My dear Jane, are you sure you did not wet your feet? — It was but a drop or two, but I am so afraid: — but Mr. Frank Churchill was so extremely — and there was a mat to step upon — I shall never forget his extreme politeness. — Oh! Mr. Frank Churchill, I must tell you my mother's spectacles have never been in fault since; the rivet never came out again. My mother often talks of your goodnature. Does not she, Jane? — Do not we often talk of Mr. Frank Churchill? — Ah! here's Miss Woodhouse. — Dear Miss Woodhouse, how do you do? — Very well I thank you, quite well. This is meeting quite in fairy-land! — Such a transformation! — Must not compliment, I know — (eyeing Emma most complacently) — that would be rude[108] — but upon my word, Miss Woodhouse, you do look — how do you like Jane's hair? — You are a judge. — She did it all herself. Quite wonderful how she does her hair! — No hair-dresser from London I think could. — Ah! Dr. Hughes I declare — and Mrs. Hughes. Must go and speak to Dr. and Mrs. Hughes for a moment. — How do you do? How do you do? — Very well, I thank you. This is delightful, is not it? — Where's dear Mr. Richard? — Oh! there he is. Don't disturb him. Much better employed talking to the young ladies. How do you do, Mr. Richard? — I saw you the other day as you rode

[108] *Must not compliment . . . that would be rude:* A sign of the formal manners of the time.

through the town —— Mrs. Otway, I protest! — and good Mr. Otway, and Miss Otway and Miss Caroline. — Such a host of friends! — and Mr. George and Mr. Arthur! — How do you do? How do you all do? — Quite well, I am much obliged to you. Never better. — Don't I hear another carriage? — Who can this be? — very likely the worthy Coles. — Upon my word, this is charming to be standing about among such friends! — And such a noble fire! — I am quite roasted. No coffee, I thank you, for me — never take coffee. — A little tea if you please, sir, by and bye, — no hurry — Oh! here it comes. Every thing so good!"

Frank Churchill returned to his station by Emma; and as soon as Miss Bates was quiet, she found herself necessarily overhearing the discourse of Mrs. Elton and Miss Fairfax, who were standing a little way behind her. — He was thoughtful. Whether he were overhearing too, she could not determine. After a good many compliments to Jane on her dress and look, compliments very quietly and properly taken, Mrs. Elton was evidently wanting to be complimented herself — and it was, "How do you like my gown? — How do you like my trimming? — How has Wright done my hair?" — with many other relative questions, all answered with patient politeness. Mrs. Elton then said,

"Nobody can think less of dress in general than I do — but upon such an occasion as this, when everybody's eyes are so much upon me, and in compliment to the Westons — who I have no doubt are giving this ball chiefly to do me honour — I would not wish to be inferior to others. And I see very few pearls in the room except mine. — So Frank Churchill is a capital dancer, I understand. — We shall see if our styles suit. — A fine young man certainly is Frank Churchill. I like him very well."

At this moment Frank began talking so vigorously, that Emma could not but imagine he had overheard his own praises, and did not want to hear more; — and the voices of the ladies were drowned for awhile, till another suspension brought Mrs. Elton's tones again distinctly forward. — Mr. Elton had just joined them, and his wife was exclaiming,

"Oh! you have found us out at last, have you, in our seclusion? — I was this moment telling Jane, I thought you would begin to be impatient for tidings of us."

"Jane!" — repeated Frank Churchill, with a look of surprise and displeasure. —

"That is easy — but Miss Fairfax does not disapprove it, I suppose."

"How do you like Mrs. Elton?" said Emma in a whisper.

"Not at all."

"You are ungrateful."

"Ungrateful! — What do you mean?" Then changing from a frown to a smile — "No, do not tell me — I do not want to know what you mean. — Where is my father? — When are we to begin dancing?"

Emma could hardly understand him; he seemed in an odd humour. He walked off to find his father, but was quickly back again with both Mr. and Mrs. Weston. He had met with them in a little perplexity, which must be laid before Emma. It had just occurred to Mrs. Weston that Mrs. Elton must be asked to begin the ball; that she would expect it; which interfered with all their wishes of giving Emma that distinction. — Emma heard the sad truth with fortitude.

"And what are we to do for a proper partner for her?" said Mr. Weston. "She will think Frank ought to ask her."

Frank turned instantly to Emma, to claim her former promise; and boasted himself an engaged man, which his father looked his most perfect approbation of — and it then appeared that Mrs. Weston was wanting *him* to dance with Mrs. Elton himself, and that their business was to help to persuade him into it, which was done pretty soon. — Mr. Weston and Mrs. Elton led the way, Mr. Frank Churchill and Miss Woodhouse followed. Emma must submit to stand second to Mrs. Elton, though she had always considered the ball as peculiarly for her. It was almost enough to make her think of marrying.

Mrs. Elton had undoubtedly the advantage, at this time, in vanity completely gratified; for though she had intended to begin with Frank Churchill, she could not lose by the change. Mr. Weston might be his son's superior. — In spite of this little rub, however, Emma was smiling with enjoyment, delighted to see the respectable length of the set as it was forming, and to feel that she had so many hours of unusual festivity before her. — She was more disturbed by Mr. Knightley's not dancing, than by any thing else. — There he was, among the standers-by, where he ought not to be; he ought to be dancing, — not classing himself with the husbands, and fathers, and whist-players, who were pretending to feel an interest in the dance till their rubbers were made up, — so young as he looked! — He could not have appeared to greater advantage perhaps any where, than where he had placed himself. His tall, firm, upright figure, among the bulky forms and stooping shoulders of the elderly men, was such as Emma felt must draw every body's eyes; and, excepting her own partner, there was not one among the whole row of young men who could be compared with him. — He moved a few steps nearer, and those few steps were enough to prove in how gentlemanlike a manner, with what natural grace, he must have danced, would he but take the trouble. — Whenever she caught his eye, she forced him to smile; but in general he was looking grave. She wished he could love a ball-room better, and could like Frank Churchill better. — He seemed often observing her. She must not flatter herself that he thought of her dancing, but if he were criticising her behaviour, she did not feel afraid. There was nothing like flirtation between her and her partner. They seemed more like cheerful, easy friends, than lovers. That Frank Churchill thought less of her than he had done, was indubitable.

The ball proceeded pleasantly. The anxious cares, the incessant attentions of Mrs. Weston, were not thrown away. Every body seemed happy; and the praise of being a delightful ball, which is seldom bestowed till after a ball has ceased to be, was repeatedly given in the very beginning of the existence of this. Of very important, very record-able events, it was not more productive than such meetings usually are. There was one, however, which Emma thought something of. — The two last dances before supper were begun, and Harriet had no partner; — the only young lady sitting down; — and so equal had been hitherto the number of dancers, that how there could be any one disen-gaged was the wonder! — But Emma's wonder lessened soon after-wards, on seeing Mr. Elton sauntering about. He would not ask Harriet to dance if it were possible to be avoided: she was sure he would not — and she was expecting him every moment to escape into the card-room.

Escape, however, was not his plan. He came to the part of the room where the sitters-by were collected, spoke to some, and walked about in front of them, as if to show his liberty, and his resolution of maintaining it. He did not omit being sometimes directly before Miss Smith, or speaking to those who were close to her. — Emma saw it. She was not yet dancing; she was working her way up from the bottom, and had therefore leisure to look around, and by only turning her head a little she saw it all. When she was half way up the set, the whole group were exactly behind her, and she would no longer allow her eyes to watch; but Mr. Elton was so near, that she heard every syllable of a dialogue which just then took place between him and Mrs. Weston; and she per-ceived that his wife, who was standing immediately above her, was not only listening also, but even encouraging him by significant glances. — The kind-hearted, gentle Mrs. Weston had left her seat to join him and say, "Do not you dance, Mr. Elton?" to which his prompt reply was, "Most readily, Mrs. Weston, if you will dance with me."

"Me! — oh! no — I would get you a better partner than myself. I am no dancer."

"If Mrs. Gilbert wishes to dance," said he, "I shall have great pleasure, I am sure — for, though beginning to feel myself rather an old married man, and that my dancing days are over, it would give me very great pleasure at any time to stand up with an old friend like Mrs. Gilbert."

"Mrs. Gilbert does not mean to dance, but there is a young lady disengaged whom I should be very glad to see dancing — Miss Smith."

"Miss Smith! — oh! — I had not observed. — You are extremely obliging — and if I were not an old married man. — But my dancing days are over, Mrs. Weston. You will excuse me. Any thing else I should be most happy to do, at your command — but my dancing days are over."

Mrs. Weston said no more; and Emma could imagine with what surprise and mortification she must be returning to her seat. This was Mr. Elton! the amiable, obliging, gentle Mr. Elton. — She looked round for a moment; he had joined Mr. Knightley at a little distance, and was arranging himself for settled conversation, while smiles of high glee passed between him and his wife.

She would not look again. Her heart was in a glow, and she feared her face might be as hot.

In another moment a happier sight caught her; — Mr. Knightley leading Harriet to the set! — Never had she been more surprised, seldom more delighted, than at that instant. She was all pleasure and gratitude, both for Harriet and herself, and longed to be thanking him; and though too distant for speech, her countenance said much, as soon as she could catch his eye again.

His dancing proved to be just what she had believed it, extremely good; and Harriet would have seemed almost too lucky, if it had not been for the cruel state of things before, and for the very complete enjoyment and very high sense of the distinction which her happy features announced. It was not thrown away on her, she bounded higher than ever, flew farther down the middle, and was in a continual course of smiles.

Mr. Elton had retreated into the card-room, looking (Emma trusted) very foolish. She did not think he was quite so hardened as his wife, though growing very like her; — *she* spoke some of her feelings, by observing audibly to her partner,

"Knightley has taken pity on poor little Miss Smith! — Very good-natured, I declare."

Supper was announced. The move began; and Miss Bates might be heard from that moment, without interruption, till her being seated at table and taking up her spoon.

"Jane, Jane, my dear Jane, where are you? — Here is your tippet.[109] Mrs. Weston begs you to put on your tippet. She says she is afraid there will be draughts in the passage, though every thing has been done — One door nailed up — Quantities of matting — My dear Jane, indeed you must. Mr. Churchill, oh! you are too obliging! — How well you put it on! — so gratified! Excellent dancing indeed! — Yes, my dear, I ran home, as I said I should, to help grandmamma to bed, and got back again, and nobody missed me. — I set off without saying a word, just as I told you. Grandmamma was quite well, had a charming evening with Mr. Woodhouse, a vast deal of chat, and backgammon. — Tea was made down stairs, biscuits and baked apples and wine before she came away: amazing luck in some of her throws: and she inquired a great deal about you, how you were amused, and who were your partners. 'Oh!' said I, 'I shall not forestall Jane; I left her dancing with Mr. George Otway; she will love to tell you all about it herself to-morrow: her first partner was Mr. Elton, I do not know who will ask her next, perhaps Mr. William Cox.' My dear sir, you are too obliging. — Is there nobody you would not rather? — I am not helpless. Sir, you are most kind. Upon my word, Jane on one arm, and me on the other! — Stop, stop, let us stand a little back, Mrs. Elton is going; dear Mrs. Elton, how elegant she looks — Beautiful lace! — Now we all follow in her train. Quite the queen of the evening! — Well, here we are at the passage. Two steps, Jane, take care of the two steps. Oh! no, there is but one. Well, I was persuaded there were two. How very odd! I was convinced there were two, and there is but one. I never saw any thing equal to the comfort and style — Candles every where. — I was telling you of your grandmamma, Jane, — There was a little disappointment. — The baked apples and biscuits, excellent in their way, you know; but there was a delicate fricassee of sweetbread and some asparagus brought in at first, and good Mr. Woodhouse, not thinking the asparagus quite boiled enough, sent it all out again. Now there is nothing grandmamma loves better than sweetbread and asparagus — so she was rather disappointed, but we agreed we would not speak of it to any body, for fear of its getting round to dear Miss Woodhouse, who would be so very much concerned! — Well, this is brilliant! I am all amazement! could not have supposed any thing! — Such elegance and profusion! — I have seen nothing like it since — Well, where shall we sit? where shall we sit? Any where, so that Jane is not in a draught. Where *I* sit is of no consequence. Oh! do you recommend this side? — Well, I

---

[109]*tippet:* Garment worn around the neck and shoulders, often with hanging ends.

am sure, Mr. Churchill — only it seems too good — but just as you please. What you direct in this house cannot be wrong. Dear Jane, how shall we ever recollect half the dishes for grandmamma. Soup too! Bless me! I should not be helped so soon, but it smells most excellent, and I cannot help beginning."

Emma had no opportunity of speaking to Mr. Knightley till after supper; but, when they were all in the ball-room again, her eyes invited him irresistibly to come to her and be thanked. He was warm in his reprobation of Mr. Elton's conduct; it had been unpardonable rudeness; and Mrs. Elton's looks also received the due share of censure.

"They aimed at wounding more than Harriet," said he. "Emma, why is it that they are your enemies?"

He looked with smiling penetration; and, on receiving no answer, added, "*She* ought not to be angry with you, I suspect, whatever he may be. — To that surmise, you say nothing, of course; but confess, Emma, that you did want him to marry Harriet."

"I did," replied Emma, "and they cannot forgive me."

He shook his head; but there was a smile of indulgence with it, and he only said,

"I shall not scold you. I leave you to your own reflections."

"Can you trust me with such flatterers? — Does my vain spirit ever tell me I am wrong?"

"Not your vain spirit, but your serious spirit. — If one leads you wrong, I am sure the other tells you of it."

"I do own myself to have been completely mistaken in Mr. Elton. There is a littleness about him which you discovered, and which I did not: and I was fully convinced of his being in love with Harriet. It was through a series of strange blunders!"

"And, in return for your acknowledging so much, I will do you the justice to say, that you would have chosen for him better than he has chosen for himself. — Harriet Smith has some first-rate qualities, which Mrs. Elton is totally without. An unpretending, single-minded, artless girl — infinitely to be preferred by any man of sense and taste to such a woman as Mrs. Elton. I found Harriet more conversable than I expected."

Emma was extremely gratified. — They were interrupted by the bustle of Mr. Weston calling on every body to begin dancing again.

"Come Miss Woodhouse, Miss Otway, Miss Fairfax, what are you all doing? — Come Emma, set your companions the example. Every body is lazy! Every body is asleep!"

"I am ready," said Emma, "whenever I am wanted."

"Whom are you going to dance with?" asked Mr. Knightley.

She hesitated a moment, and then replied, "With you, if you will ask me."

"Will you?" said he, offering his hand.

"Indeed I will. You have shown that you can dance, and you know we are not really so much brother and sister as to make it at all improper."

"Brother and sister! no, indeed."

CHAPTER III.

THIS little explanation with Mr. Knightley gave Emma considerable pleasure. It was one of the agreeable recollections of the ball, which she walked about the lawn the next morning to enjoy. — She was extremely glad that they had come to so good an understanding respecting the Eltons, and that their opinions of both husband and wife were so much alike; and his praise of Harriet, his concession in her favour, was peculiarly gratifying. The impertinence of the Eltons, which for a few minutes had threatened to ruin the rest of her evening, had been the occasion of some of its highest satisfactions; and she looked forward to another happy result — the cure of Harriet's infatuation. — From Harriet's manner of speaking of the circumstance before they quitted the ball-room, she had strong hopes. It seemed as if her eyes were suddenly opened, and she were enabled to see that Mr. Elton was not the superior creature she had believed him. The fever was over, and Emma could harbour little fear of the pulse being quickened again by injurious courtesy. She depended on the evil feelings of the Eltons for supplying all the discipline of pointed neglect that could be further requisite. — Harriet rational, Frank Churchill not too much in love, and Mr. Knightley not wanting to quarrel with her, how very happy a summer must be before her!

She was not to see Frank Churchill this morning. He had told her that he could not allow himself the pleasure of stopping at Hartfield, as he was to be at home by the middle of the day. She did not regret it.

Having arranged all these matters, looked them through, and put them all to rights, she was just turning to the house with spirits freshened up for the demands of the two little boys, as well as of their grandpapa, when the great iron sweep-gate opened, and two persons entered whom she had never less expected to see together — Frank Churchill, with Harriet leaning on his arm — actually Harriet! — A moment sufficed to convince her that something extraordinary had happened. Harriet looked white and frightened, and he was trying to cheer her. — The iron gates and the front door were not twenty yards asunder; — they were all three soon in the hall, and Harriet immediately sinking into a chair fainted away.

A young lady who faints, must be recovered; questions must be answered, and surprises be explained. Such events are very interesting, but the suspense of them cannot last long. A few minutes made Emma acquainted with the whole.

Miss Smith, and Miss Bickerton, another parlour boarder at Mrs. Goddard's, who had been also at the ball, had walked out together, and taken a road, the Richmond road, which, though apparently public enough for safety, had led them into alarm. — About half a mile beyond Highbury, making a sudden turn, and deeply shaded by elms on each side, it became for a considerable stretch very retired; and when the young ladies had advanced some way into it, they had suddenly perceived at a small distance before them, on a broader patch of greensward by the side, a party of gipsies. A child on the watch, came towards them to beg; and Miss Bickerton, excessively frightened, gave a great scream, and calling on Harriet to follow her, ran up a steep bank, cleared a slight hedge at the top, and made the best of her way by a short cut back to Highbury. But poor Harriet could not follow. She had suffered very much from cramp after dancing, and her first attempt to mount the bank brought on such a return of it as made her absolutely powerless — and in this state, and exceedingly terrified, she had been obliged to remain.

How the trampers might have behaved, had the young ladies been more courageous, must be doubtful; but such an invitation for attack could not be resisted; and Harriet was soon assailed by half a dozen children, headed by a stout woman and a great boy, all clamorous, and impertinent in look, though not absolutely in word. — More and more frightened, she immediately promised them money, and taking out her purse, gave them a shilling, and begged them not to want more, or to use her ill. — She was then able to walk, though but slowly, and was moving away — but her terror and her purse were too tempting, and she was followed, or rather surrounded, by the whole gang, demanding more.

In this state Frank Churchill had found her, she trembling and conditioning, they loud and insolent. By a most fortunate chance his leaving Highbury had been delayed so as to bring him to her assistance at this critical moment. The pleasantness of the morning had induced him to walk forward, and leave his horses to meet him by another road, a mile or two beyond Highbury — and happening to have borrowed a pair of scissars the night before of Miss Bates, and to have forgotten to restore them, he had been obliged to stop at her door, and go in for a few minutes: he was therefore later than he had intended; and being on foot, was unseen by the whole party till almost close to them. The terror which the woman and boy had been creating in Harriet was then their own portion. He had left them completely frightened; and Harriet eagerly clinging to him, and hardly able to speak, had just strength enough to reach Hartfield, before her spirits were quite overcome. It was his idea to bring her to Hartfield: he had thought of no other place.

This was the amount of the whole story, — of his communication and of Harriet's as soon as she had recovered her senses and speech. — He dared not stay longer than to see her well; these several delays left him not another minute to lose; and Emma engaging to give assurance of her safety to Mrs. Goddard, and notice of there being such a set of people in the neighbourhood to Mr. Knightley, he set off, with all the grateful blessings that she could utter for her friend and herself.

Such an adventure as this, — a fine young man and a lovely young woman thrown together in such a way, could hardly fail of suggesting certain ideas to the coldest heart and the steadiest brain. So Emma thought, at least. Could a linguist, could a grammarian, could even a mathematician have seen what she did, have witnessed their appearance together, and heard their history of it, without feeling that circumstances had been at work to make them peculiarly interesting to each other? — How much more must an imaginist,[110] like herself, be on fire with speculation and foresight! — especially with such a ground-work of anticipation as her mind had already made.

It was a very extraordinary thing! Nothing of the sort had ever occurred before to any young ladies in the place, within her memory; no rencontre,[111] no alarm of the kind; — and now it had happened to the very person, and at the very hour, when the other very person was chancing to pass by to rescue her! — It certainly was very extraordinary! — And knowing, as she did, the favourable state of mind of each at this period, it struck her the more. He was wishing to get the better of his attachment to herself, she just recovering from her mania for Mr.

[110]*imaginist:* Apparently a word coined by Jane Austen; a person given to imaginative flights.
[111]*rencontre:* Meeting, usually with connotations of violence or conflict.

Elton. It seemed as if every thing united to promise the most interesting consequences. It was not possible that the occurrence should not be strongly recommending each to the other.

In the few minutes' conversation which she had yet had with him, while Harriet had been partially insensible, he had spoken of her terror, her naïveté, her fervor as she seized and clung to his arm, with a sensibility amused and delighted; and just at last, after Harriet's own account had been given, he had expressed his indignation at the abominable folly of Miss Bickerton in the warmest terms. Every thing was to take its natural course, however, neither impelled nor assisted. She would not stir a step, nor drop a hint. No, she had had enough of interference. There could be no harm in a scheme, a mere passive scheme. It was no more than a wish. Beyond it she would on no account proceed.

Emma's first resolution was to keep her father from the knowledge of what had passed, — aware of the anxiety and alarm it would occasion: but she soon felt that concealment must be impossible. Within half an hour it was known all over Highbury. It was the very event to engage those who talk most, the young and the low; and all the youth and servants in the place were soon in the happiness of frightful news. The last night's ball seemed lost in the gipsies. Poor Mr. Woodhouse trembled as he sat, and, as Emma had foreseen, would scarcely be satisfied without their promising never to go beyond the shrubbery again. It was some comfort to him that many inquiries after himself and Miss Woodhouse (for his neighbours knew that he loved to be inquired after), as well as Miss Smith, were coming in during the rest of the day; and he had the pleasure of returning for answer, that they were all very indifferent — which, though not exactly true, for she was perfectly well, and Harriet not much otherwise, Emma would not interfere with. She had an unhappy state of health in general for the child of such a man, for she hardly knew what indisposition was; and if he did not invent illnesses for her, she could make no figure in a message.

The gipsies did not wait for the operations of justice; they took themselves off in a hurry. The young ladies of Highbury might have walked again in safety before their panic began, and the whole history dwindled soon into a matter of little importance but to Emma and her nephews: — in her imagination it maintained its ground, and Henry and John were still asking every day for the story of Harriet and the gipsies, and still tenaciously setting her right if she varied in the slightest particular from the original recital.

CHAPTER IV.

A VERY few days had passed after this adventure, when Harriet came one morning to Emma with a small parcel in her hand, and after sitting down and hesitating, thus began:

"Miss Woodhouse — if you are at leisure — I have something that I should like to tell you — a sort of confession to make — and then, you know, it will be over."

Emma was a good deal surprised; but begged her to speak. There was a seriousness in Harriet's manner which prepared her, quite as much as her words, for something more than ordinary.

"It is my duty, and I am sure it is my wish," she continued, "to have no reserves with you on this subject. As I am happily quite an altered creature in *one respect,* it is very fit that you should have the satisfaction of knowing it. I do not want to say more than is necessary — I am too much ashamed of having given way as I have done, and I dare say you understand me."

"Yes," said Emma, "I hope I do."

"How I could so long a time be fancying myself! . . . ." cried Harriet, warmly. "It seems like madness! I can see nothing at all extraordinary in him now. — I do not care whether I meet him or not — except that of the two I had rather not see him — and indeed I would go any distance round to avoid him — but I do not envy his wife in the least; I neither admire her nor envy her, as I have done: she is very charming, I dare say, and all that, but I think her very ill-tempered and disagreeable — I shall never forget her look the other night! — However, I assure you, Miss Woodhouse, I wish her no evil. — No, let them be ever so happy together, it will not give me another moment's pang: and to convince you that I have been speaking truth, I am now going to destroy — what I ought to have destroyed long ago — what I ought never to have kept — I know that very well (blushing as she spoke). — However, now I will destroy it all — and it is my particular wish to do it in your presence, that you may see how rational I am grown. Cannot you guess what this parcel holds?" said she, with a conscious look.

"Not the least in the world. — Did he ever give you any thing?"

"No — I cannot call them gifts; but they are things that I have valued very much."

She held the parcel towards her, and Emma read the words *Most precious treasures* on the top. Her curiosity was greatly excited. Harriet unfolded the parcel, and she looked on with impatience. Within abundance of silver paper was a pretty little Tunbridge-ware box,[112] which Harriet opened: it was well lined with the softest cotton; but, excepting the cotton, Emma saw only a small piece of court plaister.[113]

"Now," said Harriet, "you *must* recollect."

"No, indeed I do not."

"Dear me! I should not have thought it possible you could forget what passed in this very room about court plaister, one of the very last times we ever met in it! — It was but a very few days before I had my sore throat — just before Mr. and Mrs. John Knightley came — I think the very evening. — Do not you remember his cutting his finger with your new penknife,[114] and your recommending court plaister? — But as you had none about you, and knew I had, you desired me to supply him; and so I took mine out and cut him a piece; but it was a great deal too large, and he cut it smaller, and kept playing some time with what was left, before he gave it back to me. And so then, in my nonsense, I could not help making a treasure of it — so I put it by never to be used, and looked at it now and then as a great treat."

"My dearest Harriet!" cried Emma, putting her hand before her face, and jumping up, "you make me more ashamed of myself than I can bear. Remember it? Ay, I remember it all now; all, except your saving this relick — I knew nothing of that till this moment — but the cutting the finger, and my recommending court plaister, and saying I had none about me! — Oh! my sins, my sins! — And I had plenty all the while in my pocket! — One of my senseless tricks! — I deserve to be under a continual blush all the rest of my life. — Well — (sitting down again) go on — what else?"

"And had you really some at hand yourself? — I am sure I never suspected it, you did it so naturally."

"And so you actually put this piece of court plaister by for his sake!" said Emma, recovering from her state of shame and feeling,[115] divided between wonder and amusement. And secretly she added to herself, "Lord bless me! when should I ever have thought of putting by in cotton a piece of court plaister that Frank Churchill had been pulling about! — I never was equal to this."

---

[112]*Tunbridge-ware box:* Wooden box of the kind made in or near Tunbridge Wells, Kent; characterized by colored mosaic decoration.

[113]*court plaister:* Sticking plaster made of silk coated with isinglass, used for covering superficial cuts and wounds.

[114]*penknife:* A small pocket knife used for the making and mending of quill pens.

[115]*and feeling,:* Comma placement is possibly misleading here; a comma after "shame" makes better sense.

"Here," resumed Harriet, turning to her box again, "here is something still more valuable, I mean that *has been* more valuable, because this is what did really once belong to him, which the court plaister never did."

Emma was quite eager to see this superior treasure. It was the end of an old pencil, — the part without any lead.

"This was really his," said Harriet. — "Do not you remember one morning? — no, I dare say you do not. But one morning — I forget exactly the day — but perhaps it was the Tuesday or Wednesday before *that evening,* he wanted to make a memorandum in his pocket-book; it was about spruce beer.[116] Mr. Knightley had been telling him something about brewing spruce beer, and he wanted to put it down; but when he took out his pencil, there was so little lead that he soon cut it all away, and it would not do, so you lent him another, and this was left upon the table as good for nothing. But I kept my eye on it; and, as soon as I dared, caught it up, and never parted with it again from that moment."

"I do remember it," cried Emma; "I perfectly remember it. — Talking about spruce beer. — Oh! yes — Mr. Knightley and I both saying we liked it, and Mr. Elton's seeming resolved to learn to like it too. I perfectly remember it. — Stop; Mr. Knightley was standing just here, was not he? — I have an idea he was standing just here."

"Ah! I do not know. I cannot recollect. — It is very odd, but I cannot recollect. — Mr. Elton was sitting here, I remember, much about where I am now." —

"Well, go on."

"Oh! that's all. I have nothing more to show you, or to say — except that I am now going to throw them both behind the fire, and I wish you to see me do it."

"My poor dear Harriet! and have you actually found happiness in treasuring up these things?"

"Yes, simpleton as I was! — but I am quite ashamed of it now, and wish I could forget as easily as I can burn them. It was very wrong of me, you know, to keep any remembrances, after he was married. I knew it was — but had not resolution enough to part with them."

"But, Harriet, is it necessary to burn the court plaister? — I have not a word to say for the bit of old pencil, but the court plaister might be useful."

[116]*spruce beer:* Fermented beverage made with an extract from the leaves and branches of the spruce fir: for a more detailed description, including a recipe, see Lane (72–73) (cited in note 84, p. 195).

"I shall be happier to burn it," replied Harriet. "It has a disagree-able look to me. I must get rid of every thing. — There it goes, and there is an end, thank Heaven! of Mr. Elton."

"And when," thought Emma, "will there be a beginning of Mr. Churchill?"

She had soon afterwards reason to believe that the beginning was already made, and could not but hope that the gipsy, though she had *told* no fortune, might be proved to have made Harriet's. — About a fortnight after the alarm, they came to a sufficient explanation, and quite undesignedly. Emma was not thinking of it at the moment, which made the information she received more valuable. She merely said, in the course of some trivial chat, "Well, Harriet, whenever you marry I would advise you to do so and so" — and thought no more of it, till after a minute's silence she heard Harriet say in a very serious tone, "I shall never marry."

Emma then looked up, and immediately saw how it was; and after a moment's debate, as to whether it should pass unnoticed or not, replied,

"Never marry! — This is a new resolution."

"It is one that I shall never change, however."

After another short hesitation, "I hope it does not proceed from —— I hope it is not in compliment to Mr. Elton?"

"Mr. Elton indeed!" cried Harriet indignantly. — Oh! no" — and Emma could just catch the words, "so superior to Mr. Elton!"

She then took a longer time for consideration. Should she proceed no farther? — should she let it pass, and seem to suspect nothing? — Perhaps Harriet might think her cold or angry if she did; or perhaps if she were totally silent, it might only drive Harriet into asking her to hear too much; and against any thing like such an unreserve as had been, such an open and frequent discussion of hopes and chances, she was perfectly resolved. — She believed it would be wiser for her to say and know at once, all that she meant to say and know. Plain dealing was always best. She had previously determined how far she would proceed, on any application of the sort; and it would be safer for both, to have the judicious law of her own brain laid down with speed. — She was decided, and thus spoke —

"Harriet, I will not affect to be in doubt of your meaning. Your res-olution, or rather your expectation of never marrying, results from an idea that the person whom you might prefer, would be too greatly your superior in situation to think of you. Is not it so?"

"Oh! Miss Woodhouse, believe me I have not the presumption to suppose — Indeed I am not so mad. — But it is a pleasure to me to admire him at a distance — and to think of his infinite superiority to all the rest of the world, with the gratitude, wonder, and veneration, which are so proper, in me especially."

"I am not at all surprised at you, Harriet. The service he rendered you was enough to warm your heart."

"Service! oh! it was such an inexpressible obligation! — The very recollection of it, and all that I felt at the time — when I saw him coming — his noble look — and my wretchedness before. Such a change! In one moment such a change! From perfect misery to perfect happiness."

"It is very natural. It is natural, and it is honourable. — Yes, honourable, I think, to choose so well and so gratefully. — But that it will be a fortunate preference is more than I can promise. I do not advise you to give way to it, Harriet. I do not by any means engage for its being returned. Consider what you are about. Perhaps it will be wisest in you to check your feelings while you can: at any rate do not let them carry you far, unless you are persuaded of his liking you. Be observant of him. Let his behaviour be the guide of your sensations. I give you this caution now, because I shall never speak to you again on the subject. I am determined against all interference. Henceforward I know nothing of the matter. Let no name ever pass our lips. We were very wrong before; we will be cautious now. — He is your superior, no doubt, and there do seem objections and obstacles of a very serious nature; but yet, Harriet, more wonderful things have taken place, there have been matches of greater disparity. But take care of yourself. I would not have you too sanguine; though, however it may end, be assured that your raising your thoughts to *him*, is a mark of good taste which I shall always know how to value."

Harriet kissed her hand in silent and submissive gratitude. Emma was very decided in thinking such an attachment no bad thing for her friend. It's tendency would be to raise and refine her mind — and it must be saving her from the danger of degradation.

CHAPTER V.

In this state of schemes, and hopes, and connivance, June opened upon Hartfield. To Highbury in general it brought no material change. The Eltons were still talking of a visit from the Sucklings, and of the use to be made of their barouche-landau; and Jane Fairfax was still at her grandmother's; and as the return of the Campbells from Ireland was again delayed, and August, instead of Mid-summer, fixed for it, she was likely to remain there full two months longer, provided at least she were able to defeat Mrs. Elton's activity in her service, and save herself from being hurried into a delightful situation against her will.

Mr. Knightley, who, for some reason best known to himself, had certainly taken an early dislike to Frank Churchill, was only growing to dislike him more. He began to suspect him of some double dealing in his pursuit of Emma. That Emma was his object appeared indisputable. Every thing declared it; his own attentions, his father's hints, his mother-in-law's[117] guarded silence; it was all in unison; words, conduct, discretion, and indiscretion, told the same story. But while so many were devoting him to Emma, and Emma herself making him over to Harriet, Mr. Knightley began to suspect him of some inclination to trifle with Jane Fairfax. He could not understand it; but there were symptoms of intelligence between them — he thought so at least — symptoms of admiration on his side, which, having once observed, he could not persuade himself to think entirely void of meaning, however he might wish to escape any of Emma's errors of imagination. *She* was not present when the suspicion first arose. He was dining with the Randalls' family, and Jane, at the Eltons'; and he had seen a look, more than a single look, at Miss Fairfax, which, from the admirer of Miss Woodhouse, seemed somewhat out of place. When he was again in their company, he could not help remembering what he had seen; nor could he avoid observations which, unless it were like Cowper and his fire at twilight,

"Myself creating what I saw,"[118]

brought him yet stronger suspicion of there being a something of private liking, of private understanding even, between Frank Churchill and Jane.

He had walked up one day after dinner, as he very often did, to spend his evening at Hartfield. Emma and Harriet were going to walk; he joined them; and, on returning, they fell in with a larger party, who, like themselves, judged it wisest to take their exercise early, as the weather threatened rain; Mr. and Mrs. Weston and their son, Miss Bates

---

[117] *mother-in-law:* See note 74 on p. 161.
[118] *"Myself creating . . . ":* From William Cowper's *The Task* (1785), bk. IV: "Me oft has fancy, ludicrous and wild, / Sooth'd with a waking dream of houses, tow'rs, / Trees, churches, and strange visages, express'd / In the red cinders, while with poring eye / I gaz'd, myself creating what I saw" (ll. 286–90).

and her niece, who had accidentally met. They all united; and, on reaching Hartfield gates, Emma, who knew it was exactly the sort of visiting that would be welcome to her father, pressed them all to go in and drink tea with him. The Randalls' party agreed to it immediately; and after a pretty long speech from Miss Bates, which few persons listened to, she also found it possible to accept dear Miss Woodhouse's most obliging invitation.

As they were turning into the grounds, Mr. Perry passed by on horseback. The gentlemen spoke of his horse.

"By the bye," said Frank Churchill to Mrs. Weston presently, "what became of Mr. Perry's plan of setting up his carriage?"[119]

Mrs. Weston looked surprised, and said, "I did not know that he ever had any such plan."

"Nay, I had it from you. You wrote me word of it three months ago."

"Me! impossible!"

"Indeed you did. I remember it perfectly. You mentioned it as what was certainly to be very soon. Mrs. Perry had told somebody, and was extremely happy about it. It was owing to *her* persuasion, as she thought his being out in bad weather did him a great deal of harm. You must remember it now?"

"Upon my word I never heard of it till this moment."

"Never! really, never! — Bless me! how could it be? — Then I must have dreamt it — but I was completely persuaded — Miss Smith, you walk as if you were tired. You will not be sorry to find yourself at home."

"What is this? — What is this?" cried Mr. Weston, "about Perry and a carriage? Is Perry going to set up his carriage, Frank? I am glad he can afford it. You had it from himself, had you?"

"No, sir," replied his son, laughing, "I seem to have had it from nobody. — Very odd! — I really was persuaded of Mrs. Weston's having mentioned it in one of her letters to Enscombe, many weeks ago, with all these particulars — but as she declares she never heard a syllable of it before, of course it must have been a dream. I am a great dreamer. I dream of every body at Highbury when I am away — and when I have gone through my particular friends, then I begin dreaming of Mr. and Mrs. Perry."

---

[119]*setting up his carriage:* Mr. Perry's plan (or more accurately, Mrs. Perry's) may be seen in the context of the contemporary campaign by apothecaries to improve their social status. See Sales (note 5, p. 34).

"It is odd though," observed his father, "that you should have had such a regular connected dream about people whom it was not very likely you should be thinking of at Enscombe. Perry's setting up his carriage! and his wife's persuading him to it, out of care for his health — just what will happen, I have no doubt, some time or other; only a little premature. What an air of probability sometimes runs through a dream! And at others, what a heap of absurdities it is! Well, Frank, your dream certainly shows that Highbury is in your thoughts when you are absent. Emma, you are a great dreamer, I think?"

Emma was out of hearing. She had hurried on before her guests to prepare her father for their appearance, and was beyond the reach of Mr. Weston's hint.

"Why, to own the truth," cried Miss Bates, who had been trying in vain to be heard the last two minutes, "if I must speak on this subject, there is no denying that Mr. Frank Churchill might have — I do not mean to say that he did not dream it — I am sure I have sometimes the oddest dreams in the world — but if I am questioned about it, I must acknowledge that there was such an idea last spring; for Mrs. Perry herself mentioned it to my mother, and the Coles knew of it as well as ourselves — but it was quite a secret, known to nobody else, and only thought of about three days. Mrs. Perry was very anxious that he should have a carriage, and came to my mother in great spirits one morning because she thought she had prevailed. Jane, don't you remember grandmamma's telling us of it when we got home? — I forget where we had been walking to — very likely to Randalls; yes, I think it was to Randalls. Mrs. Perry was always particularly fond of my mother — indeed I do not know who is not — and she had mentioned it to her in confidence; she had no objection to her telling us, of course, but it was not to go beyond: and, from that day to this, I never mentioned it to a soul that I know of. At the same time, I will not positively answer for my having never dropt a hint, because I know I do sometimes pop out a thing before I am aware. I am a talker, you know; I am rather a talker; and now and then I have let a thing escape me which I should not. I am not like Jane; I wish I were. I will answer for it *she* never betrayed the least thing in the world. Where is she? — Oh! just behind. Perfectly remember Mrs. Perry's coming. — Extraordinary dream indeed!"

They were entering the hall. Mr. Knightley's eyes had preceded Miss Bates's in a glance at Jane. From Frank Churchill's face, where he thought he saw confusion suppressed or laughed away, he had involuntarily turned to her's; but she indeed behind, and too busy with her shawl. Mr. Weston had walked in. The two other gentlemen waited at the door to let her pass. Mr. Knightley suspected in Frank Churchill the determination of catching her eye — he seemed watching her intently — in vain, however, if it were so — Jane passed between them into the hall, and looked at neither.

There was no time for farther remark or explanation. The dream must be borne with, and Mr. Knightley must take his seat with the rest round the large modern circular table which Emma had introduced at Hartfield, and which none but Emma could have had power to place there and persuade her father to use, instead of the small-sized Pembroke,[120] on which two of his daily meals had, for forty years, been crowded. Tea passed pleasantly, and nobody seemed in a hurry to move.

"Miss Woodhouse," said Frank Churchill, after examining a table behind him, which he could reach as he sat, "have your nephews taken away their alphabets — their box of letters? It used to stand here. Where is it? This is a sort of dull-looking evening, that ought to be treated rather as winter than summer. We had great amusement with those letters one morning. I want to puzzle you again."

Emma was pleased with the thought; and producing the box, the table was quickly scattered over with alphabets, which no one seemed so much disposed to employ as their two selves. They were rapidly forming words for each other, or for any body else who would be puzzled. The quietness of the game made it particularly eligible for Mr. Woodhouse, who had often been distressed by the more animated sort, which Mr. Weston had occasionally introduced, and who now sat happily occupied in lamenting, with tender melancholy, over the departure of the "poor little boys," or in fondly pointing out, as he took up any stray letter near him, how beautifully Emma had written it.

Frank Churchill placed a word before Miss Fairfax. She gave a slight glance round the table, and applied herself to it. Frank was next to Emma, Jane opposite to them — and Mr. Knightley so placed as to see them all; and it was his object to see as much as he could, with as little apparent observation. The word was discovered, and with a faint smile pushed away. If meant to be immediately mixed with the others, and buried from sight, she should have looked on the table instead of looking just across, for it was not mixed; and Harriet, eager after every fresh word, and finding out none, directly took it up, and fell to work. She

---

[120] **Pembroke:** A table supported on four fixed legs, with two hinged flaps that can either be folded down or spread out and rested on moveable legs.

was sitting by Mr. Knightley, and turned to him for help. The word was *blunder;* and as Harriet exultingly proclaimed it, there was a blush on Jane's cheek which gave it a meaning not otherwise ostensible. Mr. Knightley connected it with the dream; but how it could all be, was beyond his comprehension. How the delicacy, the discretion of his favourite could have been so lain asleep! He feared there must be some decided involvement. Disingenuousness and double-dealing seemed to meet him at every turn. These letters were but the vehicle for gallantry and trick. It was a child's play, chosen to conceal a deeper game on Frank Churchill's part.

With great indignation did he continue to observe him; with great alarm and distrust, to observe also his two blinded companions. He saw a short word prepared for Emma, and given to her with a look sly and demure. He saw that Emma had soon made it out, and found it highly entertaining, though it was something which she judged it proper to appear to censure; for she said, "Nonsense! for shame!" He heard Frank Churchill next say, with a glance towards Jane, "I will give it to her — shall I?" — and as clearly heard Emma opposing it with eager laughing warmth. "No, no, you must not; you shall not, indeed."

It was done however. This gallant young man, who seemed to love without feeling, and to recommend himself without complaisance, directly handed over the word to Miss Fairfax, and with a particular degree of sedate civility entreated her to study it. Mr. Knightley's excessive curiosity to know what this word might be, made him seize every possible moment for darting his eye towards it, and it was not long before he saw it to be *Dixon.* Jane Fairfax's perception seemed to accompany his; her comprehension was certainly more equal to the covert meaning, the superior intelligence, of those five letters so arranged. She was evidently displeased; looked up, and seeing herself watched, blushed more deeply than he had ever perceived her, and saying only, "I did not know that proper names were allowed," pushed away the letters with even an angry spirit, and looked resolved to be engaged by no other word that could be offered. Her face was averted from those who had made the attack, and turned towards her aunt.

"Ay, very true, my dear," cried the latter, though Jane had not spoken a word — "I was just going to say the same thing. It is time for us to be going indeed. The evening is closing in, and grandmamma will be looking for us. My dear sir, you are too obliging. We really must wish you good night."

Jane's alertness in moving, proved her as ready as her aunt had preconceived. She was immediately up, and wanting to quit the table; but

so many were also moving, that she could not get away; and Mr.
Knightley thought he saw another collection of letters[121] anxiously
pushed towards her, and resolutely swept away by her unexamined. She
was afterwards looking for her shawl — Frank Churchill was looking
also — it was growing dusk, and the room was in confusion; and how
they parted, Mr. Knightley could not tell.

He remained at Hartfield after all the rest, his thoughts full of what
he had seen; so full, that when the candles came to assist his observations, he must — yes, he certainly must, as a friend — an anxious
friend — give Emma some hint, ask her some question. He could not
see her in a situation of such danger, without trying to preserve her. It
was his duty.

"Pray, Emma," said he, "may I ask in what lay the great amusement, the poignant sting of the last word given to you and Miss Fairfax?
I saw the word, and am curious to know how it could be so very entertaining to the one, and so very distressing to the other."

Emma was extremely confused. She could not endure to give him
the true explanation; for though her suspicions were by no means
removed, she was really ashamed of having ever imparted them.

"Oh!" she cried in evident embarrassment, "it all meant nothing; a
mere joke among ourselves."

"The joke," he replied gravely, "seemed confined to you and Mr.
Churchill."

He had hoped she would speak again, but she did not. She would
rather busy herself about any thing than speak. He sat a little while in
doubt. A variety of evils crossed his mind. Interference — fruitless
interference. Emma's confusion, and the acknowledged intimacy,
seemed to declare her affection engaged. Yet he would speak. He owed
it to her, to risk any thing that might be involved in an unwelcome
interference, rather than her welfare; to encounter any thing, rather
than the remembrance of neglect in such a cause.

"My dear Emma," said he at last, with earnest kindness, "do you
think you perfectly understand the degree of acquaintance between the
gentleman and lady we have been speaking of?"

"Between Mr. Frank Churchill and Miss Jane Fairfax? Oh! yes,
perfectly. — Why do you make a doubt of it?"

"Have you never at any time had reason to think that he admired
her, or that she admired him?"

---

[121] *another collection of letters:* According to family tradition, the scrambled letters
spelled the word *pardon.*

"Never, never!" — she cried with a most open eagerness — "Never, for the twentieth part of a moment, did such an idea occur to me. And how could it possibly come into your head?"

"I have lately imagined that I saw symptoms of attachment between them — certain expressive looks, which I did not believe meant to be public."

"Oh! you amuse me excessively. I am delighted to find that you can vouchsafe to let your imagination wander — but it will not do — very sorry to check you in your first essay — but indeed it will not do. There is no admiration between them, I do assure you; and the appearances which have caught you, have arisen from some peculiar circumstances — feelings rather of a totally different nature: — it is impossible exactly to explain: — there is a good deal of nonsense in it — but the part which is capable of being communicated, which is sense, is, that they are as far from any attachment or admiration for one another, as any two beings in the world can be. That is, I *presume* it to be so on her side, and I can *answer* for its being so on his. I will answer for the gentleman's indifference."

She spoke with a confidence which staggered, with a satisfaction which silenced, Mr. Knightley. She was in gay spirits, and would have prolonged the conversation, wanting to hear the particulars of his suspicions, every look described, and all the wheres and hows of a circumstance which highly entertained her: but his gaiety did not meet her's. He found he could not be useful, and his feelings were too much irritated for talking. That he might not be irritated into an absolute fever, by the fire which Mr. Woodhouse's tender habits required almost every evening throughout the year, he soon afterwards took a hasty leave, and walked home to the coolness and solitude of Donwell Abbey.

CHAPTER VI.

AFTER being long fed with hopes of a speedy visit from Mr. and Mrs. Suckling, the Highbury world were obliged to endure the mortification of hearing that they could not possibly come till the autumn. No such importation of novelties could enrich their intellectual stores at present. In the daily interchange of news, they must be again restricted to the other topics with which for a while the Sucklings' coming had been united, such as the last accounts of Mrs. Churchill, whose health seemed every day to supply a different report, and the situation of Mrs. Weston, whose happiness it was to be hoped might eventually be as much increased by the arrival of a child, as that of all her neighbours was by the approach of it.

Mrs. Elton was very much disappointed. It was the delay of a great deal of pleasure and parade. Her introductions and recommendations must all wait, and every projected party be still only talked of. So she thought at first; — but a little consideration convinced her that every thing need not be put off. Why should not they explore to Box Hill[122] though the Sucklings did not come? They could go there again with them in the autumn. It was settled that they should go to Box Hill. That there was to be such a party had been long generally known: it had even given the idea of another. Emma had never been to Box Hill; she wished to see what every body found so well worth seeing, and she and Mr. Weston had agreed to choose some fine morning and drive thither. Two or three more of the chosen only were to be admitted to join them, and it was to be done in a quiet, unpretending, elegant way, infinitely superior to the bustle and preparation, the regular eating and drinking, and pic-nic parade of the Eltons and the Sucklings.

This was so very well understood between them, that Emma could not but feel some surprise, and a little displeasure, on hearing from Mr. Weston that he had been proposing to Mrs. Elton, as her brother and sister had failed her, that the two parties should unite, and go together; and that as Mrs. Elton had very readily acceded to it, so it was to be, if she had no objection. Now, as her objection was nothing but her very great dislike of Mrs. Elton, of which Mr. Weston must already be per- fectly aware, it was not worth bringing forward again: — it could not be done without a reproof to him, which would be giving pain to his wife; and she found herself therefore obliged to consent to an arrangement which she would have done a great deal to avoid; an arrangement which would probably expose her even to the degradation of being said to be of Mrs. Elton's party! Every feeling was offended; and the forbearance of her outward submission left a heavy arrear due of secret severity in her reflections on the unmanageable good-will of Mr. Weston's temper.

"I am glad you approve of what I have done," said he very comfort- ably. "But I thought you would. Such schemes as these are nothing without numbers. One cannot have too large a party. A large party secures its own amusement. And she is a good-natured woman after all. One could not leave her out."

---

[122] **Box Hill:** Well-known beauty spot (named for the boxwood that grew there) offering prospects of the surrounding Surrey countryside. For illustration and further dis- cussion, see "Contextual Documents," pp. 401, 396.

Emma denied none of it aloud, and agreed to none of it in private.

It was now the middle of June, and the weather fine; and Mrs. Elton was growing impatient to name the day, and settle with Mr. Weston as to pigeon-pies and cold lamb, when a lame carriage-horse threw every thing into sad uncertainty. It might be weeks, it might be only a few days, before the horse were useable, but no preparations could be ventured on, and it was all melancholy stagnation. Mrs. Elton's resources were inadequate to such an attack.

"Is not this most vexatious, Knightley?" she cried. — And such weather for exploring! — These delays and disappointments are quite odious. What are we to do? — The year will wear away at this rate, and nothing done. Before this time last year I assure you we had had a delightful exploring party from Maple Grove to Kings Weston."

"You had better explore to Donwell," replied Mr. Knightley. "That may be done without horses. Come, and eat my strawberries. They are ripening fast."

If Mr. Knightley did not begin seriously, he was obliged to proceed so, for his proposal was caught at with delight; and the "Oh! I should like it of all things," was not plainer in words than manner. Donwell was famous for its strawberry-beds, which seemed a plea for the invitation: but no plea was necessary; cabbage-beds would have been enough to tempt the lady, who only wanted to be going somewhere. She promised him again and again to come — much oftener than he doubted — and was extremely gratified by such a proof of intimacy, such a distinguishing compliment as she chose to consider it.

"You may depend upon me," said she. "I certainly will come. Name your day, and I will come. You will allow me to bring Jane Fairfax?"

"I cannot name a day," said he, "till I have spoken to some others whom I would wish to meet you."

"Oh! leave all that to me. Only give me a carte-blanche. — I am Lady Patroness, you know. It is my party. I will bring friends with me."

"I hope you will bring Elton," said he: — but I will not trouble you to give any other invitations."

"Oh! now you are looking very sly. But consider; — you need not be afraid of delegating power to *me*. I am no young lady on her preferment.[123] Married women, you know, may be safely authorized. It is my party. Leave it all to me. I will invite your guests."

"No," — he calmly replied, — "there is but one married woman in

---

[123]*on her preferment:* That is, seeking social advantage through an appointment or post.

the world whom I can ever allow to invite what guests she pleases to Donwell, and that one is ——"

"— Mrs. Weston, I suppose," interrupted Mrs. Elton, rather mortified.

"No — Mrs. Knightley; — and, till she is in being, I will manage such matters myself."

"Ah! you are an odd creature!" she cried, satisfied to have no one preferred to herself. — "You are a humourist, and may say what you like. Quite a humourist. Well, I shall bring Jane with me — Jane and her aunt. — The rest I leave to you. I have no objections at all to meeting the Hartfield family. Don't scruple. I know you are attached to them."

"You certainly will meet them if I can prevail; and I shall call on Miss Bates in my way home."

"That's quite unnecessary; I see Jane every day: — but as you like. It is to be a morning scheme, you know, Knightley; quite a simple thing. I shall wear a large bonnet, and bring one of my little baskets hanging on my arm. Here, — probably this basket with pink ribbon. Nothing can be more simple, you see. And Jane will have such another. There is to be no form or parade — a sort of gipsy party. — We are to walk about your gardens, and gather the strawberries ourselves, and sit under trees; — and whatever else you may like to provide, it is to be all out of doors — a table spread in the shade, you know. Every thing as natural and simple as possible. Is not that your idea?"

"Not quite. My idea of the simple and the natural will be to have the table spread in the dining-room. The nature and the simplicity of gentlemen and ladies, with their servants and furniture, I think is best observed by meals within doors. When you are tired of eating strawberries in the garden, there shall be cold meat in the house."

"Well — as you please; only don't have a great set out. And, by the bye, can I or my housekeeper be of any use to you with our opinion? — Pray be sincere, Knightley. If you wish me to talk to Mrs. Hodges, or to inspect anything — ."

"I have not the least wish for it, I thank you."

"Well — but if any difficulties should arise, my housekeeper is extremely clever."

"I will answer for it, that mine thinks herself full as clever, and would spurn anybody's assistance."

"I wish we had a donkey. The thing would be for us all to come on donkies, Jane, Miss Bates, and me — and my caro sposo[124] walking by.

---

[124]*caro sposo:* See note 92 on page 226.

I really must talk to him about purchasing a donkey. In a country life I conceive it to be a sort of necessary; for, let a woman have ever so many resources, it is not possible for her to be always shut up at home; and very long walks, you know —— in summer there is dust, and in winter there is dirt."

"You will not find either, between Donwell and Highbury. Donwell-lane is never dusty, and now it is perfectly dry. Come on a donkey, however, if you prefer it. You can borrow Mrs. Cole's. I would wish every thing to be as much to your taste as possible."

"That I am sure you would. Indeed I do you justice, my good friend. Under that peculiar sort of dry, blunt manner, I know you have the warmest heart. As I tell Mr. E., you are a thorough humourist. — Yes, believe me, Knightley, I am fully sensible of your attention to me in the whole of this scheme. You have hit upon the very thing to please me."

Mr. Knightley had another reason for avoiding a table in the shade. He wished to persuade Mr. Woodhouse, as well as Emma, to join the party; and he knew that to have any of them sitting down out of doors to eat would inevitably make him ill. Mr. Woodhouse must not, under the specious pretence of a morning drive, and an hour or two spent at Donwell, be tempted away to his misery.

He was invited on good faith. No lurking horrors were to upbraid him for his easy credulity. He did consent. He had not been at Donwell for two years. "Some very fine morning, he, and Emma, and Harriet, could go very well; and he could sit still with Mrs. Weston, while the dear girls walked about the gardens. He did not suppose they could be damp now, in the middle of the day. He should like to see the old house again exceedingly, and should be very happy to meet Mr. and Mrs. Elton, and any other of his neighbours. — He could not see any objection at all to his, and Emma's, and Harriet's, going there some very fine morning. He thought it very well done of Mr. Knightley to invite them — very kind and sensible — much cleverer than dining out. — He was not fond of dining out."

Mr. Knightley was fortunate in every body's most ready concurrence. The invitation was every where so well received, that it seemed as if, like Mrs. Elton, they were all taking the scheme as a particular compliment to themselves. — Emma and Harriet professed very high expectations of pleasure from it; and Mr. Weston, unasked, promised to get Frank over to join them, if possible; a proof of approbation and gratitude which could have been dispensed with. — Mr. Knightley was then obliged to say that he should be glad to see him; and Mr. Weston engaged to lose no time in writing, and spare no arguments to induce him to come.

In the meanwhile the lame horse recovered so fast, that the party to Box Hill was again under happy consideration; and at last Donwell was settled for one day, and Box Hill for the next, — the weather appearing exactly right.

Under a bright mid-day sun, at almost Midsummer, Mr. Woodhouse was safely conveyed in his carriage, with one window down, to partake of this al-fresco[125] party; and in one of the most comfortable rooms in the abbey, especially prepared for him by a fire all the morning, he was happily placed, quite at his ease, ready to talk with pleasure of what had been atchieved, and advise every body to come and sit down, and not to heat themselves. — Mrs. Weston, who seemed to have walked there on purpose to be tired, and sit all the time with him, remained, when all the others were invited or persuaded out, his patient listener and sympathizer.

It was so long since Emma had been at the Abbey, that as soon as she was satisfied of her father's comfort, she was glad to leave him, and look around her; eager to refresh and correct her memory with more particular observation, more exact understanding of a house and grounds which must ever be so interesting to her and all her family.

She felt all the honest pride and complacency which her alliance with the present and future proprietor could fairly warrant, as she viewed the respectable size and style of the building, its suitable, becoming characteristic situation, low and sheltered — its ample gardens stretching down to meadows washed by a stream, of which the Abbey, with all the old neglect of prospect, had scarcely a sight — and its abundance of timber in rows and avenues, which neither fashion nor extravagance had rooted up.[126] — The house was larger than Hartfield, and totally unlike it, covering a good deal of ground, rambling and irregular, with many comfortable and one or two handsome rooms. — It was just what it ought to be, and it looked what it was — and Emma felt an increasing respect for it, as the residence of a family of such true

---

[125] *al-fresco:* Italian for "in the fresh air."

[126] *neither fashion nor extravagance had rooted up:* Though no enemy of tasteful improvements, such as those at Pemberley in *Pride and Prejudice,* Jane Austen had a fondness for old estates like Donwell Abbey that had missed or rejected the extravagant alterations of Capability Brown and other eighteenth-century improvers. See Alistair M. Duckworth, "Improvements," *The Jane Austen Companion,* ed. J. David Grey et al. (New York: Macmillan, 1986) 223–27.

gentility, untainted in blood and understanding. — Some faults of temper John Knightley had; but Isabella had connected herself unexcep-
tionably. She had given them neither men, nor names, nor places, that
could raise a blush. These were pleasant feelings, and she walked about
and indulged them till it was necessary to do as the others did, and collect round the strawberry beds. — The whole party were assembled,
excepting Frank Churchill, who was expected every moment from
Richmond; and Mrs. Elton, in all her apparatus of happiness, her large
bonnet and her basket, was very ready to lead the way in gathering,
accepting, or talking — strawberries, and only strawberries, could now
be thought or spoken of. — "The best fruit in England — every body's
favourite — always wholesome. — These the finest beds and finest
sorts. — Delightful to gather for one's self — the only way of really
enjoying them. — Morning decidedly the best time — never tired —
every sort good — hautboy infinitely superior — no comparison — the
others hardly eatable — hautboys very scarce — Chili[127] preferred —
white wood finest flavour of all — price of strawberries in London —
abundance about Bristol — Maple Grove — cultivation — beds when
to be renewed — gardeners thinking exactly different — no general
rule — gardeners never to be put out of their way — delicious fruit —
only too rich to be eaten much of — inferior to cherries — currants
more refreshing — only objection to gathering strawberries the stooping — glaring sun — tired to death — could bear it no longer — must
go and sit in the shade."
    Such, for half an hour, was the conversation — interrupted only
once by Mrs. Weston, who came out, in her solicitude after her son-in-
law, to inquire if he were come — and she was a little uneasy. — She
had some fears of his horse.
    Seats tolerably in the shade were found; and now Emma was
obliged to overhear what Mrs. Elton and Jane Fairfax were talking
of. — A situation, a most desirable situation, was in question. Mrs.
Elton had received notice of it that morning, and was in raptures. It was
not with Mrs. Suckling, it was not with Mrs. Bragge, but in felicity and
splendour it fell short only of them: it was with a cousin of Mrs. Bragge,
an acquaintance of Mrs. Suckling, a lady known at Maple Grove.
Delightful, charming, superior, first circles, spheres, lines, ranks, every
thing — and Mrs. Elton was wild to have the offer closed with immediately. — On her side, all was warmth, energy, and triumph — and she

---

[127]**Chili:** Presumably, like hautboys, a kind of strawberry.

positively refused to take her friend's negative, though Miss Fairfax
continued to assure her that she would not at present engage in any
thing, repeating the same motives which she had been heard to urge
before. — Still Mrs. Elton insisted on being authorized to write an
acquiescence by the morrow's post. — How Jane could bear it at all,
was astonishing to Emma. — She did look vexed, she did speak pointedly — and at last, with a decision of action unusual to her, proposed a
removal. — "Should not they walk? — Would not Mr. Knightley show
them the gardens — all the gardens? — She wished to see the whole
extent." — The pertinacity of her friend seemed more than she could
bear.

It was hot; and after walking some time over the gardens in a scattered, dispersed way, scarcely any three together, they insensibly followed one another to the delicious shade of a broad short avenue of
limes, which stretching beyond the garden at an equal distance from
the river, seemed the finish of the pleasure grounds. — It led to nothing; nothing but a view at the end over a low stone wall with high pil-
lars, which seemed intended, in their erection, to give the appearance of
an approach to the house, which never had been there. Disputable,
however, as might be the taste of such a termination, it was in itself a
charming walk, and the view which closed it extremely pretty. — The
considerable slope, at nearly the foot of which the Abbey stood, gradually acquired a steeper form beyond its grounds; and at half a mile distant was a bank of considerable abruptness and grandeur, well clothed
with wood; — and at the bottom of this bank, favourably placed and
sheltered, rose the Abbey-Mill Farm, with meadows in front, and the
river making a close and handsome curve around it.

It was a sweet view — sweet to the eye and the mind. English verdure, English culture,[128] English comfort, seen under a sun bright,
without being oppressive.

In this walk Emma and Mr. Weston found all the others assembled;
and towards this view she immediately perceived Mr. Knightley and
Harriet distinct from the rest, quietly leading the way. Mr. Knightley
and Harriet! — It was an odd tête-à-tête; but she was glad to see it. —
There had been a time when he would have scorned her as a companion, and turned from her with little ceremony. Now they seemed in
pleasant conversation. There had been a time also when Emma would
have been sorry to see Harriet in a spot so favourable for the Abbey-

---

[128] *English culture:* Agriculture is the primary meaning.

Mill Farm; but now she feared it not. It might be safely viewed with all its appendages of prosperity and beauty, its rich pastures, spreading flocks, orchard in blossom,[179] and light column of smoke ascending. — She joined them at the wall, and found them more engaged in talking than in looking around. He was giving Harriet information as to modes of agriculture, &c. and Emma received a smile which seemed to say, "These are my own concerns. I have a right to talk on such subjects, without being suspected of introducing Robert Martin." — She did not suspect him. It was too old a story. — Robert Martin had probably ceased to think of Harriet. — They took a few turns together along the walk. — The shade was most refreshing, and Emma found it the pleasantest part of the day.

The next remove was to the house; they must all go in and eat; — and they were all seated and busy, and still Frank Churchill did not come. Mrs. Weston looked, and looked in vain. His father would not own himself uneasy, and laughed at her fears; but she could not be cured of wishing that he would part with his black mare. He had expressed himself as to coming, with more than common certainty. "His aunt was so much better, that he had not a doubt of getting over to them." — Mrs. Churchill's state, however, as many were ready to remind her, was liable to such sudden variation as might disappoint her nephew in the most reasonable dependence — and Mrs. Weston was at last persuaded to believe, or to say, that it must be by some attack of Mrs. Churchill that he was prevented coming. — Emma looked at Harriet while the point was under consideration; she behaved very well, and betrayed no emotion.

The cold repast was over, and the party were to go out once more to see what had not yet been seen, the old Abbey fish-ponds; perhaps get as far as the clover, which was to be begun cutting on the morrow, or, at any rate, have the pleasure of being hot, and growing cool again. — Mr. Woodhouse, who had already taken his little round in the highest part of the gardens, where no damps from the river were imagined even by him, stirred no more; and his daughter resolved to remain

---

[129]*orchard in blossom:* Famous slip, noticed by her landowner brother Edward: "Jane, I wish you would tell me where you get these apple-trees of yours that come into bloom in July"; quoted in William and Richard Austen-Leigh, *Jane Austen: A Family Record* (1913; revised and enlarged by Deirdre Le Faye [London: British Library, 1989]) 207. For further consideration of the question, see John Sutherland, "Jane Austen, *Emma*: Apple-Blossom in June?" in *Is Heathcliff a Murderer? Great Puzzles in Nineteenth-Century Literature* (New York: Oxford UP, 1996) 14–19.

with him, that Mrs. Weston might be persuaded away by her husband
to the exercise and variety which her spirits seemed to need.

Mr. Knightley had done all in his power for Mr. Woodhouse's
entertainment. Books of engravings, drawers of medals, cameos, corals,
shells, and every other family collection within his cabinets, had been
prepared for his old friend, to while away the morning; and the kindness had perfectly answered. Mr. Woodhouse had been exceedingly well
amused. Mrs. Weston had been showing them all to him, and now he
would show them all to Emma; — fortunate in having no other resemblance to a child, than in a total want of taste for what he saw, for he was
slow, constant, and methodical. — Before this second looking over was
begun, however, Emma walked into the hall for the sake of a few
moments' free observation of the entrance and ground-plot of the
house — and was hardly there, when Jane Fairfax appeared, coming
quickly in from the garden, and with a look of escape. — Little expecting to meet Miss Woodhouse so soon, there was a start at first; but Miss
Woodhouse was the very person she was in quest of.

"Will you be so kind," said she, "when I am missed, as to say that I
am gone home? — I am going this moment. — My aunt is not aware
how late it is, nor how long we have been absent — but I am sure we
shall be wanted, and I am determined to go directly. — I have said
nothing about it to any body. It would only be giving trouble and distress. Some are gone to the ponds, and some to the lime walk. Till they
all come in I shall not be missed; and when they do, will you have the
goodness to say that I am gone?"

"Certainly, if you wish it; — but you are not going to walk to Highbury alone?"

"Yes — what should hurt me? — I walk fast. I shall be at home in
twenty minutes."

"But it is too far, indeed it is, to be walking quite alone. Let my
father's servant go with you. — Let me order the carriage. It can be
round in five minutes."

"Thank you, thank you — but on no account. — I would rather
walk. — And for *me* to be afraid of walking alone! — I, who may so
soon have to guard others!"

She spoke with great agitation; and Emma very feelingly replied,
"That can be no reason for your being exposed to danger now. I must
order the carriage. The heat even would be danger. — You are fatigued
already."

"I am" — she answered — "I am fatigued; but it is not the sort of
fatigue — quick walking will refresh me. — Miss Woodhouse, we all

know at times what it is to be wearied in spirits. Mine, I confess, are
exhausted. The greatest kindness you can show me, will be to let me
have my own way, and only say that I am gone when it is necessary."

Emma had not another word to oppose. She saw it all; and entering
into her feelings, promoted her quitting the house immediately, and
watched her safely off with the zeal of a friend. Her parting look was
grateful — and her parting words, "Oh! Miss Woodhouse, the comfort
of being sometimes alone!" — seemed to burst from an overcharged
heart, and to describe somewhat of the continual endurance to be practised by her, even towards some of those who loved her best.

"Such a home, indeed! such an aunt!" said Emma, as she turned
back into the hall again. "I do pity you. And the more sensibility you
betray of their just horrors, the more I shall like you."

Jane had not been gone a quarter of an hour, and they had only
accomplished some views of St. Mark's Place, Venice, when Frank
Churchill entered the room. Emma had not been thinking of him, she
had forgotten to think of him — but she was very glad to see him. Mrs.
Weston would be at ease. The black mare was blameless; *they* were right
who had named Mrs. Churchill as the cause. He had been detained by a
temporary increase of illness in her; a nervous seizure, which had lasted
some hours — and he had quite given up evry thought of coming, till
very late; — and had he known how hot a ride he should have, and how
late, with all his hurry, he must be, he believed he should not have come
at all. The heat was excessive; he had never suffered any thing like it —
almost wished he had staid at home — nothing killed him like heat —
he could bear any degree of cold, &c. but heat was intolerable — and
he sat down, at the greatest possible distance from the slight remains of
Mr. Woodhouse's fire, looking very deplorable.

"You will soon be cooler, if you sit still," said Emma.

"As soon as I am cooler I shall go back again. I could very ill be
spared — but such a point had been made of my coming! You will all be
going soon I suppose; the whole party breaking up. I met *one* as I
came — Madness in such weather! — absolute madness!"

Emma listened, and looked, and soon perceived that Frank Churchill's state might be best defined by the expressive phrase of being out
of humour. Some people were always cross when they were hot. Such
might be his constitution; and as she knew that eating and drinking
were often the cure of such incidental complaints, she recommended
his taking some refreshment; he would find abundance of every thing in
the dining-room — and she humanely pointed out the door.

"No — he should not eat. He was not hungry; it would only make him hotter." In two minutes, however, he relented in his own favour; and muttering something about spruce beer, walked off. Emma returned all her attention to her father, saying in secret —

"I am glad I have done being in love with him. I should not like a man who is so soon discomposed by a hot morning. Harriet's sweet easy temper will not mind it."

He was gone long enough to have had a very comfortable meal, and came back all the better — grown quite cool — and, with good manners, like himself — able to draw a chair close to them, take an interest in their employment; and regret, in a reasonable way, that he should be so late. He was not in his best spirits, but seemed trying to improve them; and, at last, made himself talk nonsense very agreeably. They were looking over views in Swisserland.[130]

"As soon as my aunt gets well, I shall go abroad," said he. I shall never be easy till I have seen some of these places. You will have my sketches, some time or other, to look at — or my tour to read — or my poem. I shall do something to expose myself."

"That may be — but not by sketches in Swisserland. You will never go to Swisserland. Your uncle and aunt will never allow you to leave England."

"They may be induced to go too. A warm climate may be pre-scribed for her. I have more than half an expectation of our all going abroad. I assure you I have. I feel a strong persuasion, this morning, that I shall soon be abroad. I ought to travel. I am tired of doing noth-ing. I want a change. I am serious, Miss Woodhouse, whatever your penetrating eyes may fancy — I am sick of England — and would leave it to-morrow, if I could."

"You are sick of prosperity and indulgence. Cannot you invent a few hardships for yourself, and be contented to stay?"

"*I* sick of prosperity and indulgence! — You are quite mistaken. I do not look upon myself as either prosperous or indulged. I am thwarted in every thing material. I do not consider myself at all a fortu-nate person."

"You are not quite so miserable, though, as when you first came. Go and eat and drink a little more, and you will do very well. Another slice of cold meat, another draught of Madeira and water,[131] will make you nearly on a par with the rest of us."

---

[130] *Swisserland:* Archaic spelling of Switzerland.
[131] *Madeira and water:* Wine, similar to sherry, produced in the island of Madeira, and here served in diluted form.

"No — I shall not stir. I shall sit by you. You are my best cure."

"We are going to Box Hill to-morrow; — you will join us. It is not Swisserland, but it will be something for a young man so much in want of a change. You will stay, and go with us?"

"No, certainly not; I shall go home in the cool of the evening."

"But you may come again in the cool of to-morrow morning."

"No — It will not be worth while. If I come, I shall be cross."

"Then pray stay at Richmond."

"But if I do, I shall be crosser still. I can never bear to think of you all there without me."

"These are difficulties which you must settle for yourself. Choose your own degree of crossness. I shall press you no more."

The rest of the party were now returning, and all were soon collected. With some there was great joy at the sight of Frank Churchill; others took it very composedly; but there was a very general distress and disturbance on Miss Fairfax's disappearance being explained. That it was time for every body to go, concluded the subject; and with a short final arrangement for the next day's scheme, they parted. Frank Churchill's little inclination to exclude himself increased so much, that his last words to Emma were,

"Well; — if *you* wish me to stay, and join the party, I will."

She smiled her acceptance; and nothing less than a summons from Richmond was to take him back before the following evening.

CHAPTER VII.

THEY had a very fine day for Box Hill; and all the other outward circumstances of arrangement, accommodation, and punctuality, were in favour of a pleasant party. Mr. Weston directed the whole, officiating safely between Hartfield and the vicarage, and every body was in good time. Emma and Harriet went together; Miss Bates and her niece, with the Eltons; the gentlemen on horseback. Mrs. Weston remained with Mr. Woodhouse. Nothing was wanting but to be happy when they got there. Seven miles were travelled in expectation of enjoyment, and every body had a burst of admiration on first arriving; but in the general amount of the day there was deficiency. There was a languor, a want of spirits, a want of union, which could not be got over. They separated too much into parties. The Eltons walked together; Mr. Knightley took charge of Miss Bates and Jane; and Emma and Harriet belonged to Frank Churchill. And Mr. Weston tried, in vain, to make them harmonize better. It seemed at first an accidental division, but it never materially varied. Mr. and Mrs. Elton, indeed, showed no unwillingness to mix, and be as agreeable as they could: but during the two whole hours that were spent on the hill, there seemed a principle of separation, between the other parties, too strong for any fine prospects, or any cold collation,[132] or any cheerful Mr. Weston, to remove.

At first it was downright dulness to Emma. She had never seen Frank Churchill so silent and stupid. He said nothing worth hearing — looked without seeing — admired without intelligence — listened without knowing what she said. While he was so dull, it was no wonder that Harriet should be dull likewise, and they were both insufferable.

When they all sat down it was better; to her taste a great deal better, for Frank Churchill grew talkative and gay, making her his first object. Every distinguishing attention that could be paid, was paid to her. To amuse her, and be agreeable in her eyes, seemed all that he cared for — and Emma, glad to be enlivened, not sorry to be flattered, was gay and easy too, and gave him all the friendly encouragement, the admission to be gallant, which she had ever given in the first and most animating period of their acquaintance; but which now, in her own estimation, meant nothing, though in the judgment of most people looking on it must have had such an appearance as no English word but flirtation could very well describe. "Mr. Frank Churchill and Miss Woodhouse flirted together excessively." They were laying themselves open to that very phrase — and to having it sent off in a letter to Maple Grove by one lady, to Ireland by another. Not that Emma was gay and thoughtless from any real felicity; it was rather because she felt less happy than she had expected. She laughed because she was disappointed; and though she liked him for his attentions, and thought them all, whether in friendship, admiration, or playfulness, extremely judicious, they were not winning back her heart. She still intended him for her friend.

"How much I am obliged to you," said he, "for telling me to come to day! — If it had not been for you, I should certainly have lost all the happiness of this party. I had quite determined to go away again."

"Yes, you were very cross; and I do not know what about, except that you were too late for the best strawberries. I was a kinder friend than you deserved. But you were humble. You begged hard to be commanded to come."

"Don't say I was cross. I was fatigued. The heat overcame me."

---

[132]*cold collation:* A light meal consisting of cold meat, fruit, sweets, and perhaps accompanied by wine.

"It is hotter to-day."

"Not to my feelings. I am perfectly comfortable to-day."

"You are comfortable because you are under command."

"Your command? — Yes."

"Perhaps I intended you to say so, but I meant self-command. You had, somehow or other, broken bounds yesterday, and run away from your own management; but to-day you are got back again — and as I cannot be always with you, it is best to believe your temper under your own command rather than mine."

"It comes to the same thing. I can have no self-command without a motive. You order me, whether you speak or not. And you can be always with me. You are always with me."

"Dating from three o'clock yesterday. My perceptual influence could not begin earlier, or you would not have been so much out of humour before."

"Three o'clock yesterday! That is your date. I thought I had seen you first in February."

"Your gallantry is really unanswerable. But (lowering her voice) — nobody speaks except ourselves, and it is rather too much to be talking nonsense for the entertainment of seven silent people."

"I say nothing of which I am ashamed," replied he, with lively impudence. "I saw you first in February. Let every body on the Hill hear me if they can. Let my accents swell to Mickleham on one side, and Dorking on the other. I saw you first in February." And then whispering — "Our companions are excessively stupid. What shall we do to rouse them? Any nonsense will serve. They *shall* talk. Ladies and gentlemen, I am ordered by Miss Woodhouse (who, wherever she is, presides,) to say, that she desires to know what you are all thinking of."

Some laughed, and answered good-humouredly. Miss Bates said a great deal; Mrs. Elton swelled at the idea of Miss Woodhouse's presiding; Mr. Knightley's answer was the most distinct.

"Is Miss Woodhouse sure that she would like to hear what we are all thinking of?"

"Oh! no, no" — cried Emma, laughing as carelessly as she could — "Upon no account in the world. It is the very last thing I would stand the brunt of just now. Let me hear any thing rather than what you are all thinking of. I will not say quite all. There are one or two, perhaps, (glancing at Mr. Weston and Harriet,) whose thoughts I might not be afraid of knowing."

"It is a sort of thing," cried Mrs. Elton emphatically, "which *I* should not have thought myself privileged to inquire into. Though, perhaps, as the *Chaperon* of the party — *I* never was in any circle — exploring parties — young ladies — married women —"

Her mutterings were chiefly to her husband; and he murmured, in reply,

"Very true, my love, very true. Exactly so, indeed — quite unheard of — but some ladies say any thing. Better pass it off as a joke. Every body knows what is due to *you*."

"It will not do," whispered Frank to Emma, "they are most of them affronted. I will attack them with more address. Ladies and gentlemen — I am ordered by Miss Woodhouse to say, that she waves her right of knowing exactly what you may all be thinking of, and only requires something very entertaining from each of you, in a general way. Here are seven of you, besides myself, (who, she is pleased to say, am very entertaining already,) and she only demands from each of you either one thing very clever, be it prose or verse, original or repeated — or two things moderately clever — or three things very dull indeed, and she engages to laugh heartily at them all."

"Oh! very well," exclaimed Miss Bates, "then I need not be uneasy. 'Three things very dull indeed.' That will just do for me, you know. I shall be sure to say three dull things as soon as ever I open my mouth, shan't I? — (looking round with the most good-humoured dependence on every body's assent) — Do not you all think I shall?"

Emma could not resist.

"Ah! ma'am, but there may be a difficulty. Pardon me — but you will be limited as to number — only three at once."

Miss Bates, deceived by the mock ceremony of her manner, did not immediately catch her meaning; but, when it burst on her, it could not anger, though a slight blush showed that it could pain her.

"Ah! — well — to be sure. Yes, I see what she means, (turning to Mr. Knightley,) and I will try to hold my tongue. I must make myself very disagreeable, or she would not have said such a thing to an old friend."

"I like your plan," cried Mr. Weston. "Agreed, agreed. I will do my best. I am making a conundrum. How will a conundrum reckon?"

"Low, I am afraid, sir, very low," answered his son; — "but we shall be indulgent — especially to any one who leads the way."

"No, no," said Emma, "it will not reckon low. A conundrum of Mr. Weston's shall clear him and his next neighbour. Come, sir, pray let me hear it."

"I doubt it's being very clever myself," said Mr. Weston. "It is too much a matter of fact, but here it is. — What two letters of the alphabet are there, that express perfection?"

"What two letters! — express perfection! I am sure I do not know."
"Ah! you will never guess. You, (to Emma), I am certain, will never guess. — I will tell you. — M. and A.[133] — Em — ma. — Do you understand?"

Understanding and gratification came together. It might be a very indifferent piece of wit; but Emma found a great deal to laugh at and enjoy in it — and so did Frank and Harriet. — It did not seem to touch the rest of the party equally; some looked very stupid about it, and Mr. Knightley gravely said,

"This explains the sort of clever thing that is wanted, and Mr. Weston has done very well for himself; but he must have knocked up every body else. *Perfection* should not have come quite so soon."

"Oh! for myself, I protest I must be excused," said Mrs. Elton; "*I* really cannot attempt — I am not at all fond of the sort of thing. I had an acrostic[134] once sent to me upon my own name, which I was not at all pleased with. I knew who it came from. An abominable puppy! — You know who I mean — (nodding to her husband). These kind of things are very well at Christmas, when one is sitting round the fire; but quite out of place, in my opinion, when one is exploring about the country in summer. Miss Woodhouse must excuse me. I am not one of those who have witty things at every body's service. I do not pretend to be a wit. I have a great deal of vivacity in my own way, but I really must be allowed to judge when to speak and when to hold my tongue. Pass us, if you please, Mr. Churchill. Pass Mr. E., Knightley, Jane, and myself. We have nothing clever to say — not one of us."

"Yes, yes, pray pass *me*," added her husband, with a sort of sneering consciousness; "*I* have nothing to say that can entertain Miss Woodhouse, or any other young lady. An old married man — quite good for nothing. Shall we walk, Augusta?"

"With all my heart. I am really tired of exploring so long on one spot. Come, Jane, take my other arm."

Jane declined it, however, and the husband and wife walked off. "Happy couple!" said Frank Churchill, as soon as they were out of hearing: — "How well they suit one another! — Very lucky — marrying as they did, upon an acquaintance formed only in a public place! — They only knew each other, I think, a few weeks in Bath! Peculiarly

---

[133] *M. and A.*: See Mark Loveridge's "Francis Hutcheson and Mr. Weston's Conundrum in *Emma*," *Notes and Queries* (1983) 30.3: 214–16 for the unlikely philosophical source of Mr. Weston's conundrum in Hutcheson's *Enquiry into the Original of Our Ideas of Beauty and Virtue* (1725).

[134] *acrostic:* Poem in which the first letters of successive lines spell a name.

lucky! — for as to any real knowledge of a person's disposition that Bath, or any public place, can give — it is all nothing; there can be no knowledge. It is only by seeing women in their own homes, among their own set, just as they always are, that you can form any just judgment. Short of that, it is all guess and luck — and will generally be ill-luck. How many a man has committed himself on a short acquaintance, and rued it all the rest of his life!"

Miss Fairfax, who had seldom spoken before, except among her own confederates, spoke now.

"Such things do occur, undoubtedly." — She was stopped by a cough. Frank Churchill turned towards her to listen.

"You were speaking," said he, gravely. She recovered her voice.

"I was only going to observe, that though such unfortunate circumstances do sometimes occur both to men and women, I cannot imagine them to be very frequent. A hasty and imprudent attachment may arise — but there is generally time to recover from it afterwards. I would be understood to mean, that it can be only weak, irresolute characters, (whose happiness must be always at the mercy of chance,) who will suffer an unfortunate acquaintance to be an inconvenience, an oppression for ever."

He made no answer; merely looked, and bowed in submission; and soon afterwards said, in a lively tone,

"Well, I have so little confidence in my own judgement, that whenever I marry, I hope somebody will choose my wife for me. Will you? (turning to Emma.) Will you choose a wife for me? — I am sure I should like any body fixed on by you. You provide for the family, you know, (with a smile at his father). Find somebody for me. I am in no hurry. Adopt her, educate her."

"And make her like myself."

"By all means, if you can."

"Very well. I undertake the commission. You shall have a charming wife."

"She must be very lively, and have hazle eyes. I care for nothing else. I shall go abroad for a couple of years — and when I return, I shall come to you for my wife. Remember."

Emma was in no danger of forgetting. It was a commission to touch every favourite feeling. Would not Harriet be the very creature described? — Hazle eyes excepted, two years more might make her all that he wished. He might even have Harriet in his thoughts at the moment; who could say? Referring the education to her seemed to imply it.

"Now, ma'am," said Jane to her aunt, "shall we join Mrs. Elton?"
"If you please, my dear. With all my heart. I am quite ready. I was
ready to have gone with her, but this will do just as well. We shall soon
overtake her. There she is — no, that's somebody else. That's one of
the ladies in the Irish car party, not at all like her. — Well, I declare —"

They walked off, followed in half a minute by Mr. Knightley. Mr.
Weston, his son, Emma, and Harriet, only remained; and the young
man's spirits now rose to a pitch almost unpleasant. Even Emma grew
tired at last of flattery and merriment, and wished herself rather walking
quietly about with any of the others, or sitting almost alone, and quite
unattended to, in tranquil observation of the beautiful views beneath
her. The appearance of the servants looking out for them to give notice
of the carriages was a joyful sight; and even the bustle of collecting and
preparing to depart, and the solicitude of Mrs. Elton to have *her* carriage first, were gladly endured, in the prospect of the quiet drive home
which was to close the very questionable enjoyments of this day of pleasure. Such another scheme, composed of so many ill-assorted people,
she hoped never to be betrayed into again.

While waiting for the carriage, she found Mr. Knightley by her side.
He looked around, as if to see that no one were near, and then said,

"Emma, I must once more speak to you as I have been used to do: a
privilege rather endured than allowed, perhaps, but I must still use it. I
cannot see you acting wrong, without a remonstrance. How could you
be so unfeeling to Miss Bates? How could you be so insolent in your wit
to a woman of her character, age, and situation? — Emma, I had not
thought it possible."

Emma recollected, blushed, was sorry, but tried to laugh it off.

"Nay, how could I help saying what I did? — Nobody could have
helped it. It was not so very bad. I dare say she did not understand me."

"I assure you she did. She felt your full meaning. She has talked of it
since. I wish you could have heard how she talked of it — with what
candour and generosity. I wish you could have heard her honouring
your forbearance, in being able to pay her such attentions, as she was
for ever receiving from yourself and your father, when her society must
be so irksome."

"Oh!" cried Emma, "I know there is not a better creature in the
world: but you must allow, that what is good and what is ridiculous are
most unfortunately blended in her."

"They are blended," said he, "I acknowledge; and, were she prosperous, I could allow much for the occasional prevalence of the ridiculous over the good. Were she a woman of fortune, I would leave every

harmless absurdity to take its chance, I would not quarrel with you for any liberties of manner. Were she your equal in situation — but, Emma, consider how far this is from being the case. She is poor; she has sunk from the comforts she was born to; and, if she live to old age, must probably sink more. Her situation should secure your compassion. It was badly done, indeed! — You, whom she had known from an infant, whom she had seen grow up from a period when her notice was an honour, to have you now, in thoughtless spirits, and the pride of the moment, laugh at her, humble her — and before her niece, too — and before others, many of whom (certainly *some,*) would be entirely guided by *your* treatment of her. — This is not pleasant to you, Emma — and it is very far from pleasant to me; but I must, I will, — I will tell you truths while I can, satisfied with proving myself your friend by very faithful counsel, and trusting that you will some time or other do me greater justice than you can do now."

While they talked, they were advancing towards the carriage; it was ready; and, before she could speak again, he had handed her in. He had misinterpreted the feelings which had kept her face averted, and her tongue motionless. They were combined only of anger against herself, mortification, and deep concern. She had not been able to speak; and, on entering the carriage, sunk back for a moment overcome — then reproaching herself for having taken no leave, making no acknowledgement, parting in apparent sullenness, she looked out with voice and hand eager to show a difference; but it was just too late. He had turned away, and the horses were in motion. She continued to look back, but in vain; and soon, with what appeared unusual speed, they were half way down the hill, and every thing left far behind. She was vexed beyond what could have been expressed — almost beyond what she could conceal. Never had she felt so agitated, mortified, grieved, at any circumstance in her life. She was most forcibly struck. The truth of his representation there was no denying. She felt it at her heart. How could she have been so brutal, so cruel to Miss Bates! — How could she have exposed herself to such ill opinion in any one she valued! And how suffer him to leave her without saying one word of gratitude, of concurrence, of common kindness!

Time did not compose her. As she reflected more, she seemed but to feel it more. She never had been so depressed. Happily it was not necessary to speak. There was only Harriet, who seemed not in spirits herself, fagged, and very willing to be silent; and Emma felt the tears running down her cheeks almost all the way home, without being at any trouble to check them, extraordinary as they were.

CHAPTER VIII.

THE wretchedness of a scheme to Box Hill was in Emma's thoughts all the evening. How it might be considered by the rest of the party, she could not tell. They, in their different homes, and their different ways, might be looking back on it with pleasure; but in her view it was a morning more completely mispent, more totally bare of rational satisfaction at the time, and more to be abhorred in recollection, than any she had ever passed. A whole evening of back-gammon with her father, was felicity to it. *There*, indeed, lay real pleasure, for there she was giving up the sweetest hours of the twenty-four to his comfort; and feeling that, unmerited as might be the degree of his fond affection and confiding esteem, she could not, in her general conduct, be open to any severe reproach. As a daughter, she hoped she was not without a heart. She hoped no one could have said to her, "How could you be so unfeeling to your father? — I must, I will tell you truths while I can." Miss Bates should never again — no, never! If attention, in future, could do away the past, she might hope to be forgiven. She had been often remiss, her conscience told her so; remiss, perhaps, more in thought than fact; scornful, ungracious. But it should be so no more. In the warmth of true contrition, she would call upon her the very next morning, and it should be the beginning, on her side, of a regular, equal, kindly intercourse.

She was just as determined when the morrow came, and went early, that nothing might prevent her. It was not unlikely, she thought, that she might see Mr. Knightley in her way; or, perhaps, he might come in while she were paying her visit. She had no objection. She would not be ashamed of the appearance of the penitence, so justly and truly hers. Her eyes were towards Donwell as she walked, but she saw him not.

"The ladies were all at home." She had never rejoiced at the sound before, nor ever before entered the passage, nor walked up the stairs, with any wish of giving pleasure, but in conferring obligation, or of deriving it, except in subsequent ridicule.

There was a bustle on her approach; a good deal of moving and talking. She heard Miss Bates's voice, something was to be done in a hurry; the maid looked frightened and awkward; hoped she would be pleased to wait a moment, and then ushered her in too soon. The aunt and niece seemed both escaping into the adjoining room. Jane she had a distinct glimpse of, looking extremely ill; and, before the door had shut them out, she heard Miss Bates saying, "Well, my dear, I shall *say* you are laid down upon the bed, and I am sure you are ill enough."

Poor old Mrs. Bates, civil and humble as usual, looked as if she did not quite understand what was going on.

"I am afraid Jane is not very well," said she, "but I do not know; they *tell* me she is well. I dare say my daughter will be here presently, Miss Woodhouse. I hope you find a chair. I wish Hetty had not gone. I am very little able — Have you a chair, ma'am? Do you sit where you like? I am sure she will be here presently."

Emma seriously hoped she would. She had a moment's fear of Miss Bates keeping away from her. But Miss Bates soon came — "Very happy and obliged" — but Emma's conscience told her that there was not the same cheerful volubility as before — less ease of look and manner. A very friendly inquiry after Miss Fairfax, she hoped, might lead the way to a return of old feelings. The touch seemed immediate.

"Ah! Miss Woodhouse, how kind you are! — I suppose you have heard — and are come to give us joy. This does not seem much like joy, indeed, in me — (twinkling away a tear or two) — but it will be very trying for us to part with her, after having had her so long, and she has a dreadful headach just now, writing all the morning: — such long letters, you know, to be written to Colonel Campbell, and Mrs. Dixon. 'My dear,' said I, 'you will blind yourself' — for tears were in her eyes perpetually. One cannot wonder, one cannot wonder. It is a great change; and though she is amazingly fortunate — such a situation, I suppose, as no young woman before ever met with on first going out — do not think us ungrateful, Miss Woodhouse, for such surprising good fortune — (again dispersing her tears) — but, poor dear soul! if you were to see what a headach she has. When one is in great pain, you know one cannot feel any blessing quite as it may deserve. She is as low as possible. To look at her, nobody would think how delighted and happy she is to have secured such a situation. You will excuse her not coming to you — she is not able — she is gone into her own room — I want her to lie down upon the bed. 'My dear,' said I, 'I shall say you are laid down upon the bed:' but, however, she is not; she is walking about the room. But, now that she has written her letters, she says she shall soon be well. She will be extremely sorry to miss seeing you, Miss Woodhouse, but your kindness will excuse her. You were kept waiting at the door — I was quite ashamed — but somehow there was a little bustle — or it so happened that we had not heard the knock, and till you were on the stairs, we did not know any body was coming. 'It is only Mrs. Cole,' said I, 'depend upon it. Nobody else would come so early.' 'Well,' said she, 'it must be borne some time or other, and it may as well be now.' But then Patty came in, and said it was you. 'Oh!' said

I, 'it is Miss Woodhouse: I am sure you will like to see her.' — 'I can see nobody,' said she; and up she got, and would go away; and that was what made us keep you waiting — and extremely sorry and ashamed we were. 'If you must go, my dear,' said I, 'you must, and I will say you are laid down upon the bed.'"

Emma was most sincerely interested. Her heart had been long growing kinder towards Jane; and this picture of her present sufferings acted as a cure of every former ungenerous suspicion, and left her nothing but pity; and the remembrance of the less just and less gentle sensations of the past, obliged her to admit that Jane might very naturally resolve on seeing Mrs. Cole or any other steady friend, when she might not bear to see herself. She spoke as she felt, with earnest regret and solicitude — sincerely wishing that the circumstances which she collected from Miss Bates to be now actually determined on, might be as much for Miss Fairfax's advantage and comfort as possible. "It must be a severe trial to them all. She had understood it was to be delayed till Colonel Campbell's return."

"So very kind!" replied Miss Bates. "But you are always kind."

There was no bearing such an 'always;' and to break through her dreadful gratitude, Emma made the direct inquiry of —

"Where — may I ask? — is Miss Fairfax going?"

"To a Mrs. Smallridge — charming woman — most superior — to have the charge of her three little girls — delightful children. Impossible that any situation could be more replete with comfort; if we except, perhaps, Mrs. Suckling's own family, and Mrs. Bragge's; but Mrs. Smallridge is intimate with both, and in the very same neighbourhood· — lives only four miles from Maple Grove. Jane will be only four miles from Maple Grove."

"Mrs. Elton, I suppose, has been the person to whom Miss Fairfax owes ——"

"Yes, our good Mrs. Elton. The most indefatigable, true friend. She would not take a denial. She would not let Jane say 'No;' for when Jane first heard of it, (it was the day before yesterday, the very morning we were at Donwell,) when Jane first heard of it, she was quite decided against accepting the offer, and for the reasons you mention; exactly as you say, she had made up her mind to close with nothing till Colonel Campbell's return, and nothing should induce her to enter into any engagement at present — and so she told Mrs. Elton over and over again — and I am sure I had no more idea that she would change her mind! — but that good Mrs. Elton, whose judgement never fails her, saw farther than I did. It is not every body that would have stood out in such a kind way as she did, and refuse to take Jane's answer; but she positively declared she would *not* write any such denial yesterday, as Jane wished her; she would wait — and, sure enough, yesterday evening it was all settled that Jane should go. Quite a surprise to me! I had not the least idea! — Jane took Mrs. Elton aside, and told her at once, that upon thinking over the advantages of Mrs. Suckling's situation, she had come to the resolution of accepting it. — I did not know a word of it till it was all settled."

"You spent the evening with Mrs. Elton?"

"Yes, all of us; Mrs. Elton would have us come. It was settled so, upon the hill, while we were walking about with Mr. Knightley. 'You *must all* spend your evening with us,' said she — 'I positively must have you *all* come.'"

"Mr. Knightley was there too, was he?"

"No, not Mr. Knightley; he declined it from the first; and though I thought he would come, because Mrs. Elton declared she would not let him off, he did not; — but my mother, and Jane, and I, were all there, and a very agreeable evening we had. Such kind friends, you know, Miss Woodhouse, one must always find agreeable, though every body seemed rather fagged after the morning's party. Even pleasure, you know, is fatiguing — and I cannot say that any of them seemed very much to have enjoyed it. However, *I* shall always think it a very pleasant party, and feel extremely obliged to the kind friends who included me in it."

"Miss Fairfax, I suppose, though you were not aware of it, had been making up her mind the whole day."

"I dare say she had."

"Whenever the time may come, it must be unwelcome to her and all her friends — but I hope her engagement will have every alleviation that is possible — I mean, as to the character and manners of the family."

"Thank you, dear Miss Woodhouse. Yes, indeed, there is every thing in the world that can make her happy in it. Except the Sucklings and Bragges, there is not such another nursery establishment, so liberal and elegant, in all Mrs. Elton's acquaintance. Mrs. Smallridge, a most delightful woman! — A style of living almost equal to Maple Grove — and as to the children, except the little Sucklings and little Bragges, there are not such elegant sweet children any where. Jane will be treated with such regard and kindness! — It will be nothing but pleasure, a life of pleasure. — And her salary! — I really cannot venture to name her salary to you, Miss Woodhouse. Even you, used as you are to great sums, would hardly believe that so much could be given to a young person like Jane."

"Ah! madam," cried Emma, "if other children are at all like what I remember to have been myself, I should think five times the amount of what I have ever yet heard named as a salary on such occasions, dearly earned."

"You are so noble in your ideas!"

"And when is Miss Fairfax to leave you?"

"Very soon, very soon indeed; that's the worst of it. Within a fort-night. Mrs. Smallridge is in a great hurry. My poor mother does not know how to bear it. So then, I try to put it out of her thoughts, and say, Come ma'am, do not let us think about it any more."

"Her friends must all be sorry to lose her; and will not Colonel and Mrs. Campbell be sorry to find that she has engaged herself before their return?"

"Yes; Jane says she is sure they will; but yet, this is such a situation as she cannot feel herself justified in declining. I was so astonished when she first told me what she had been saying to Mrs. Elton, and when Mrs. Elton at the same moment came congratulating me upon it! It was before tea — stay — no, it could not be before tea, because we were just going to cards — and yet it was before tea, because I remember think-ing — Oh! no, now I recollect, now I have it; something happened before tea, but not that. Mr. Elton was called out of the room before tea, old John Abdy's son wanted to speak with him. Poor old John, I have a great regard for him; he was clerk to my poor father twenty-seven years; and now, poor old man, he is bed-ridden, and very poorly with the rheumatic gout in his joints — I must go and see him to-day; and so will Jane, I am sure, if she gets out at all. And poor John's son came to talk to Mr. Elton about relief from the parish: he is very well to do himself, you know, being head man at the Crown, ostler,[135] and every thing of that sort, but still he cannot keep his father without some help; and so, when Mr. Elton came back, he told us what John ostler had been telling him, and then it came out about the chaise having been sent to Randalls to take Mr. Frank Churchill to Richmond. That was what happened before tea. It was after tea that Jane spoke to Mrs. Elton."

Miss Bates would hardly give Emma time to say how perfectly new this circumstance was to her; but as without supposing it possible that she could be ignorant of any of the particulars of Mr. Frank Churchill's going, she proceeded to give them all, it was of no consequence.

[135] *ostler:* Groom or stableman who attends to horses at an inn.

What Mr. Elton had learnt from the ostler on the subject, being the accumulation of the ostler's own knowledge, and the knowledge of the servants at Randalls, was, that a messenger had come over from Richmond soon after the return of the party from Box Hill — which messenger, however, had been no more than was expected; and that Mr. Churchill had sent his nephew a few lines, containing, upon the whole, a tolerable account of Mrs. Churchill, and only wishing him not to delay coming back beyond the next morning early; but that Mr. Frank Churchill having resolved to go home directly, without waiting at all, and his horse seeming to have got a cold, Tom had been sent off immediately for the Crown chaise, and the ostler had stood out and seen it pass by, the boy going a good pace, and driving very steady.

There was nothing in all this either to astonish or interest, and it caught Emma's attention only as it united with the subject which already engaged her mind. The contrast between Mrs. Churchill's importance in the world, and Jane Fairfax's, struck her; one was every thing, the other nothing — and she sat musing on the difference of woman's destiny, and quite unconscious on what her eyes were fixed, till roused by Miss Bates's saying,

"Ay, I see what you are thinking of, the piano forté. What is to become of that? — Very true. Poor dear Jane was talking of it just now. — 'You must go,' said she. 'You and I must part. You will have no business here. — Let it stay, however,' said she; 'give it house-room till Colonel Campbell comes back. I shall talk about it to him; he will settle for me; he will help me out of all my difficulties.' — And to this day, I do believe, she knows not whether it was his present or his daughter's."

Now Emma was obliged to think of the piano forté; and the remembrance of all her former fanciful and unfair conjectures was so little pleasing, that she soon allowed herself to believe her visit had been long enough; and, with a repetition of every thing that she could venture to say of the good wishes which she really felt, took leave.

CHAPTER IX.

EMMA'S pensive meditations, as she walked home, were not interrupted; but on entering the parlour, she found those who must rouse her. Mr. Knightley and Harriet had arrived during her absence, and were sitting with her father. — Mr. Knightley immediately got up, and in a manner decidedly graver than usual, said,

"I would not go away without seeing you, but I have no time to spare, and therefore must now be gone directly. I am going to London, to spend a few days with John and Isabella. Have you any thing to send or say, besides the 'love,' which nobody carries?"

"Nothing at all. But is not this a sudden scheme?"

"Yes — rather — I have been thinking of it some little time."

Emma was sure he had not forgiven her; he looked unlike himself. Time, however, she thought, would tell him that they ought to be friends again. While he stood, as if meaning to go, but not going — her father began his inquiries.

"Well, my dear, and did you get there safely? — And how did you find my worthy old friend and her daughter? — I dare say they must have been very much obliged to you for coming. Dear Emma has been to call on Mrs. and Miss Bates, Mr. Knightley, as I told you before. She is always so attentive to them!"

Emma's colour was heightened by this unjust praise; and with a smile, and shake of the head, which spoke much, she looked at Mr. Knightley. — It seemed as if there were an instantaneous impression in her favour, as if his eyes received the truth from her's, and all that had passed of good in her feelings were at once caught and honoured. — He looked at her with a glow of regard. She was warmly gratified — and in another moment still more so, by a little movement of more than common friendliness on his part. — He took her hand; — whether she had not herself made the first motion, she could not say — she might, perhaps, have rather offered it — but he took her hand, pressed it, and certainly was on the point of carrying it to his lips — when, from some fancy or other, he suddenly let it go. — Why he should feel such a scruple, why he should change his mind when it was all but done, she could not perceive. — He would have judged better, she thought, if he had not stopped. — The intention, however, was indubitable; and whether it was that his manners had in general so little gallantry, or however else it happened, but she thought nothing became him more. — It was with him, of so simple, yet so dignified a nature. — She could not but recall the attempt with great satisfaction. It spoke such perfect amity. — He left them immediately afterwards — gone in a moment. He always moved with the alertness of a mind which could neither be undecided nor dilatory, but now he seemed more sudden than usual in his disappearance.

Emma could not regret her having gone to Miss Bates, but she wished she had left her ten minutes earlier; — it would have been a great pleasure to talk over Jane Fairfax's situation with Mr. Knightley. — Neither would she regret that he should be going to Brunswick

Square, for she knew how much his visit would be enjoyed — but it might have happened at a better time — and to have had longer notice of it, would have been pleasanter. — They parted thorough friends, however; she could not be deceived as to the meaning of his countenance, and his unfinished gallantry; — it was all done to assure her that she had fully recovered his good opinion. — He had been sitting with them, half an hour, she found. It was a pity that she had not come back earlier!

In the hope of diverting her father's thoughts from the disagreeableness of Mr. Knightley's going to London; and going so suddenly; and going on horseback, which she knew would be all very bad; Emma communicated her news of Jane Fairfax, and her dependence on the effect was justified; it supplied a very useful check, — interested, without disturbing him. He had long made up his mind to Jane Fairfax's going out as governess, and could talk of it cheerfully, but Mr. Knightley's going to London had been an unexpected blow.

"I am very glad indeed, my dear, to hear she is to be so comfortably settled. Mrs. Elton is very good-natured and agreeable, and I dare say her acquaintance are just what they ought to be. I hope it is a dry situation, and that her health will be taken good care of. It ought to be a first object, as I am sure poor Miss Taylor's always was with me. You know, my dear, she is going to be to this new lady what Miss Taylor was to us. And I hope she will be better off in one respect, and not be induced to go away after it has been her home so long."

The following day brought news from Richmond to throw every thing else into the back-ground. An express arrived at Randalls to announce the death of Mrs. Churchill! Though her nephew had had no particular reason to hasten back on her account, she had not lived above six-and-thirty hours after his return. A sudden seizure of a different nature from any thing foreboded by her general state, had carried her off after a short struggle. The great Mrs. Churchill was no more.

It was felt as such things must be felt. Every body had a degree of gravity and sorrow; tenderness towards the departed, solicitude for the surviving friends; and, in a reasonable time, curiosity to know where she would be buried. Goldsmith[136] tells us, that when lovely woman stoops to folly, she has nothing to do but to die; and when she stoops to be disagreeable, it is equally to be recommended as a clearer of ill-fame.

---

[136] *Goldsmith:* "When lovely woman stoops to folly" is the first line of a plangent song that the seduced and abandoned Olivia Primrose sings on her return to her family in chapter 24 of *The Vicar of Wakefield*.

Mrs. Churchill, after being disliked at least twenty-five years, was now spoken of with compassionate allowances. In one point she was fully justified. She had never been admitted before to be seriously ill. The event acquitted her of all the fancifulness, and all the selfishness of imaginary complaints.

"Poor Mrs. Churchill! no doubt she had been suffering a great deal: more than any body had ever supposed — and continual pain would try the temper. It was a sad event — a great shock — with all her faults, what would Mr. Churchill do without her? Mr. Churchill's loss would be dreadful indeed. Mr. Churchill would never get over it." — Even Mr. Weston shook his head, and looked solemn, and said, "Ah! poor woman, who would have thought it!" and resolved, that his mourning should be as handsome as possible; and his wife sat sighing and moralizing over her broad hems[137] with a commiseration and good sense, true and steady. How it would affect Frank was among the earliest thoughts of both. It was also a very early speculation with Emma. The character of Mrs. Churchill, the grief of her husband — her mind glanced over them both with awe and compassion — and then rested with lightened feelings on how Frank might be affected by the event, how benefited, how freed. She saw in a moment all the possible good. Now, an attachment to Harriet Smith would have nothing to encounter. Mr. Churchill, independent of his wife, was feared by nobody; an easy, guidable man, to be persuaded into any thing by his nephew. All that remained to be wished was, that the nephew should form the attachment, as, with all her good will in the cause, Emma could feel no certainty of its being already formed.

Harriet behaved extremely well on the occasion, with great self-command. Whatever she might feel of brighter hope, she betrayed nothing. Emma was gratified, to observe such a proof in her of strengthened character, and refrained from any allusion that might endanger its maintenance. They spoke, therefore, of Mrs. Churchill's death with mutual forbearance.

Short letters from Frank were received at Randalls, communicating all that was immediately important of their state and plans. Mr. Churchill was better than could be expected; and their first removal, on the departure of the funeral for Yorkshire, was to be to the house of a very old friend in Windsor,[138] to whom Mr. Churchill had been promising a visit the last ten years. At present, there was nothing to be

---

[137] *broad hems:* Presumably a sign of mourning.
[138] *Windsor:* Town on the Thames west of London, famous for its royal castle.

done for Harriet; good wishes for the future were all that could yet be possible on Emma's side.

It was a more pressing concern to show attention to Jane Fairfax, whose prospects were closing, while Harriet's opened, and whose engagements now allowed of no delay in any one at Highbury, who wished to show her kindness — and with Emma it was grown into a first wish. She had scarcely a stronger regret than for her past coldness; and the person, whom she had been so many months neglecting, was now the very one on whom she would have lavished every distinction of regard or sympathy. She wanted to be of use to her; wanted to show a value for her society, and testify respect and consideration. She resolved to prevail on her to spend a day at Hartfield. A note was written to urge it. The invitation was refused, and by a verbal message. "Miss Fairfax was not well enough to write;" and when Mr. Perry called at Hartfield, the same morning, it appeared that she was so much indisposed as to have been visited, though against her own consent, by himself, and that she was suffering under severe headachs, and a nervous fever to a degree, which made him doubt the possibility of her going to Mrs. Smallridge's at the time proposed. Her health seemed for the moment completely deranged — appetite quite gone — and though there were no absolutely alarming symptoms, nothing touching the pulmonary complaint, which was the standing apprehension of the family, Mr. Perry was uneasy about her. He thought she had undertaken more than she was equal to, and that she felt it so herself, though she would not own it. Her spirits seemed overcome. Her present home, he could not but observe, was unfavourable to a nervous disorder: — confined always to one room; — he could have wished it otherwise — and her good aunt, though his very old friend, he must acknowledge to be not the best companion for an invalid of that description. Her care and attention could not be questioned; they were, in fact, only too great. He very much feared that Miss Fairfax derived more evil than good from them. Emma listened with the warmest concern; grieved for her more and more, and looked around eager to discover some way of being useful. To take her — be it only an hour or two — from her aunt, to give her change of air and scene, and quiet rational conversation, even for an hour or two, might do her good; and the following morning she wrote again to say, in the most feeling language she could command, that she would call for her in the carriage at any hour that Jane would name — mentioning that she had Mr. Perry's decided opinion, in favour of such exercise for his patient. The answer was only in this short note:

"Miss Fairfax's compliments and thanks, but is quite unequal to any exercise."

Emma felt that her own note had deserved something better; but it was impossible to quarrel with words, whose tremulous inequality showed indisposition so plainly, and she thought only of how she might best counteract this unwillingness to be seen or assisted. In spite of the answer, therefore, she ordered the carriage, and drove to Mrs. Bates's, in the hope that Jane would be induced to join her — but it would not do; — Miss Bates came to the carriage door, all gratitude, and agreeing with her most earnestly in thinking an airing might be of the greatest service — and every thing that message could do was tried — but all in vain. Miss Bates was obliged to return without success; Jane was quite unpersuadable; the mere proposal of going out seemed to make her worse. — Emma wished she could have seen her, and tried her own powers; but, almost before she could hint the wish, Miss Bates made it appear that she had promised her niece on no account to let Miss Woodhouse in. "Indeed, the truth was, that poor dear Jane could not bear to see anybody — anybody at all — Mrs. Elton, indeed, could not be denied — and Mrs. Cole had made such a point — and Mrs. Perry had said so much — but, except them, Jane would really see nobody."

Emma did not want to be classed with the Mrs. Eltons, the Mrs. Perry's, and the Mrs. Coles, who would force themselves anywhere; neither could she feel any right of preference herself — she submitted, therefore, and only questioned Miss Bates farther as to her niece's appetite and diet, which she longed to be able to assist. On that subject poor Miss Bates was very unhappy, and very communicative; Jane would hardly eat any thing: — Mr Perry recommended nourishing food; but every thing they could command (and never had anybody such good neighbours) was distasteful.

Emma, on reaching home, called the housekeeper directly, to an examination of her stores; and some arrow-root[139] of very superior quality was speedily despatched to Miss Bates with a most friendly note. In half an hour the arrow-root was returned, with a thousand thanks from Miss Bates, but "dear Jane would not be satisfied without its

---

[139] *arrow-root:* Pure nutritious starch prepared from the Maranta plant and used in food prepared for invalids. As Maggie Lane points out (cited in note 84, p. 195), it is not clear whether the arrowroot is the raw ingredient or the made-up dish, which was served as a mould. For the latter, the arrowroot "was dissolved in a small quantity of cold milk; then boiling milk, sweetened and flavored with cinnamon and lemon peel was poured on whilst stirring briskly, since it thickened instantly" (Lane 74).

being sent back; it was a thing she could not take — and, moreover, she insisted on her saying, that she was not at all in want of any thing."

When Emma afterwards heard that Jane Fairfax had been seen wandering about the meadows, at some distance from Highbury, on the afternoon of the very day on which she had, under the plea of being unequal to any exercise, so peremptorily refused to go out with her in the carriage, she could have no doubt — putting every thing together — that Jane was resolved to receive no kindness from *her.* She was sorry, very sorry. Her heart was grieved for a state which seemed but the more pitiable from this sort of irritation of spirits, inconsistency of action, and inequality of powers; and it mortified her that she was given so little credit for proper feeling, or esteemed so little worthy as a friend: but she had the consolation of knowing that her intentions were good, and of being able to say to herself, that could Mr. Knightley have been privy to all her attempts of assisting Jane Fairfax, could he even have seen into her heart, he would not, on this occasion, have found any thing to reprove.

CHAPTER X.

ONE morning, about ten days after Mrs. Churchill's decease, Emma was called down stairs to Mr. Weston, who "could not stay five minutes, and wanted particularly to speak with her." — He met her at the parlour door, and hardly asking her how she did, in the natural key of his voice, sunk it immediately, to say, unheard by her father,

"Can you come to Randalls at any time this morning? — Do, if it be possible. Mrs. Weston wants to see you. She must see you."

"Is she unwell?"

"No, no, not at all — only a little agitated. She would have ordered the carriage, and come to you, but she must see you *alone,* and that you know — (nodding towards her father) — Humph! — Can you come?"

"Certainly. This moment, if you please. It is impossible to refuse what you ask in such a way. But what can be the matter? — Is she really not ill?"

"Depend upon me — but ask no more questions. You will know it all in time. The most unaccountable business! But hush, hush!"

To guess what all this meant, was impossible even for Emma. Something really important seemed announced by his looks; but, as her friend was well, she endeavoured not to be uneasy, and settling it with

her father, that she would take her walk now, she and Mr. Weston were
soon out of the house together, and on their way at a quick pace for
Randalls.

"Now," — said Emma, when they were fairly beyond the sweep
gates, — "now Mr. Weston, do let me know what has happened."

"No, no," — he gravely replied. — "Don't ask me. I promised my
wife to leave it all to her. She will break it to you better than I can. Do
not be impatient, Emma; it will all come out too soon."

"Break it to me," cried Emma, standing still with terror. — "Good
God! — Mr. Weston, tell me at once. — Something has happened in
Brunswick Square. I know it has. Tell me, I charge you tell me this
moment what it is."

"No, indeed you are mistaken." —

"Mr. Weston do not trifle with me. — Consider how many of my
dearest friends are now in Brunswick Square. Which of them is it? — I
charge you by all that is sacred, not to attempt concealment."

"Upon my word, Emma." —

"Your word! — why not your honour! — why not say upon your
honour, that it has nothing to do with any of them? Good Heavens! —
What can be to be *broke* to me, that does not relate to one of that
family?"

"Upon my honour," said he very seriously, "it does not. It is not in
the smallest degree connected with any human being of the name of
Knightley."

Emma's courage returned, and she walked on.

"I was wrong," he continued, "in talking of its being *broke* to you. I
should not have used the expression. In fact, it does not concern you —
it concerns only myself, — that is, we hope. — Humph! — In short,
my dear Emma, there is no occasion to be so uneasy about it. I don't
say that it is not a disagreeable business — but things might be much
worse. — If we walk fast, we shall soon be at Randalls."

Emma found that she must wait; and now it required little effort.
She asked no more questions therefore, merely employed her own
fancy, and that soon pointed out to her the probability of its being some
money concern — something just come to light, of a disagreeable
nature in the circumstances of the family, — something which the late
event at Richmond had brought forward. Her fancy was very active.
Half a dozen natural children, perhaps — and poor Frank cut off! —
This, though very undesirable, would be no matter of agony to her. It
inspired little more than an animating curiosity.

"Who is that gentleman on horseback?" said she, as they proceeded — speaking more to assist Mr. Weston in keeping his secret,
than with any other view.

"I do not know. — One of the Otways. — Not Frank; — it is not
Frank, I assure you. You will not see him. He is half way to Windsor by
this time."

"Has your son been with you, then?"

"Oh! yes — did not you know? — Well, well, never mind."

For a moment he was silent; and then added, in a tone much more
guarded and demure,

"Yes, Frank came over this morning just to ask us how we did."

They hurried on, and were speedily at Randalls. — "Well, my dear,"
said he, as they entered the room — "I have brought her, and now I
hope you will soon be better. I shall leave you together. There is no use
in delay. I shall not be far off, if you want me." — And Emma distinctly
heard him add, in a lower tone, before he quitted the room, — "I have
been as good as my word. She has not the least idea."

Mrs. Weston was looking so ill, and had an air of so much perturbation, that Emma's uneasiness increased; and the moment they were
alone, she eagerly said,

"What is it my dear friend? Something of a very unpleasant nature, I
find, has occurred; — do let me know directly what it is. I have been
walking all this way in complete suspense. We both abhor suspense. Do
not let mine continue longer. It will do you good to speak of your distress, whatever it may be."

"Have you indeed no idea?" said Mrs. Weston in a trembling voice.
"Cannot you, my dear Emma — cannot you form a guess as to what
you are to hear?"

"So far as that it relates to Mr. Frank Churchill, I do guess."

"You are right. It does relate to him, and I will tell you directly;"
(resuming her work, and seeming resolved against looking up.) "He
has been here this very morning, on a most extraordinary errand. It is
impossible to express our surprise. He came to speak to his father on a
subject, — to announce an attachment —"

She stopped to breathe. Emma thought first of herself, and then of
Harriet.

"More than an attachment, indeed," resumed Mrs. Weston; "an
engagement — a positive engagement. — What will you say, Emma —
what will anybody say, when it is known that Frank Churchill and Miss
Fairfax are engaged; — nay, that they have been long engaged!"

Emma even jumped with surprise; — and, horror-struck, exclaimed,

"Jane Fairfax! — Good God! You are not serious? You do not mean it?"

"You may well be amazed," returned Mrs. Weston, still averting hei eyes, and talking on with eagerness, that Emma might have time to recover — "You may well be amazed. But it is even so. There has been a solemn engagement between them ever since October — formed at Weymouth, and kept a secret from everybody. Not a creature knowing it but themselves — neither the Campbells, nor her family, nor his. — It is so wonderful, that though perfectly convinced of the fact, it is yet almost incredible to myself. I can hardly believe it. — I thought I knew him."

Emma scarcely heard what was said. — Her mind was divided between two ideas — her own former conversations with him about Miss Fairfax; and poor Harriet; — and for some time she could only exclaim, and require confirmation, repeated confirmation.

"Well," said she at last, trying to recover herself; "this is a circumstance which I must think of at least half a day, before I can at all comprehend it. What! — engaged to her all the winter — before either of them came to Highbury?"

"Engaged since October, — secretly engaged. — It has hurt me, Emma, very much. It has hurt his father equally. *Some part* of his conduct we cannot excuse."

Emma pondered a moment, and then replied, "I will not pretend *not* to understand you; and to give you all the relief in my power, be assured that no such effect has followed his attentions to me, as you are apprehensive of."

Mrs. Weston looked up, afraid to believe; but Emma's countenance was as steady as her words.

"That you may have less difficulty in believing this boast, of my present perfect indifference," she continued, "I will farther tell you, that there was a period in the early part of our acquaintance, when I did like him, when I was very much disposed to be attached to him — nay, was attached — and how it came to cease, is perhaps the wonder. Fortunately, however, it did cease. I have really for some time past, for at least these three months, cared nothing about him. You may believe me, Mrs. Weston. This is the simple truth."

Mrs. Weston kissed her with tears of joy; and when she could find utterance, assured her, that this protestation had done her more good than any thing else in the world could do.

"Mr. Weston will be almost as much relieved as myself," said she. "On this point we have been wretched. It was our darling wish that you might be attached to each other — and we were persuaded that it was so. — Imagine what we have been feeling on your account."

"I have escaped; and that I should escape, may be a matter of grateful wonder to you and myself. But this does not acquit *him,* Mrs. Weston; and I must say, that I think him greatly to blame. What right had he to come among us with affection and faith engaged, and with manners so *very* disengaged? What right had he to endeavour to please, as he certainly did — to distinguish any one young woman with persevering attention, as he certainly did — while he really belonged to another? — How could he tell what mischief he might be doing? — How could he tell that he might not be making me in love with him? — very wrong, very wrong indeed."

"From something that he said, my dear Emma, I rather imagine —"

"And how could *she* bear such behaviour! Composure with a witness! to look on, while repeated attentions were offering to another woman, before her face, and not resent it. — That is a degree of placidity, which I can neither comprehend nor respect."

"There were misunderstandings between them, Emma; he said so expressly. He had not time to enter into much explanation. He was here only a quarter of an hour, and in a state of agitation which did not allow the full use even of the time he could stay — but that there had been misunderstandings he decidedly said. The present crisis, indeed, seemed to be brought on by them; and those misunderstandings might very possibly arise from the impropriety of his conduct."

"Impropriety! Oh! Mrs. Weston — it is too calm a censure. Much, much beyond impropriety! — It has sunk him, I cannot say how it has sunk him in my opinion. So unlike what a man should be! — None of that upright integrity, that strict adherence to truth and principle, that disdain of trick and littleness, which a man should display in every transaction of his life."

"Nay, dear Emma, now I must take his part; for though he has been wrong in this instance, I have known him long enough to answer for his having many, very many, good qualities; and —"

"Good God!" cried Emma, not attending to her. — "Mrs. Smallridge, too! Jane actually on the point of going as governess! What could he mean by such horrible indelicacy? To suffer her to engage herself — to suffer her even to think of such a measure!"

"He knew nothing about it, Emma. On this article I can fully acquit him. It was a private resolution of her's, not communicated to him — or at least not communicated in a way to carry conviction. — Till yesterday, I know he said he was in the dark as to her plans. They burst on him, I do not know how, but by some letter or message — and it was the discovery of what she was doing, of this very project of her's, which determined him to come forward at once, own it all to his uncle, throw himself on his kindness, and, in short, put an end to the miserable state of concealment that had been carrying on so long."

Emma began to listen better.

"I am to hear from him soon," continued Mrs. Weston. "He told me at parting, that he should soon write; and he spoke in a manner which seemed to promise me many particulars that could not be given now. Let us wait, therefore, for this letter. It may bring many extenuations. It may make many things intelligible and excusable which now are not to be understood. Don't let us be severe, don't let us be in a hurry to condemn him. Let us have patience. I must love him; and now that I am satisfied on one point, the one material point, I am sincerely anxious for its all turning out well, and ready to hope that it may. They must both have suffered a great deal under such a system of secresy and concealment."

"*His* sufferings," replied Emma drily, "do not appear to have done him much harm. Well, and how did Mr. Churchill take it?"

"Most favourably for his nephew — gave his consent with scarcely a difficulty. Conceive what the events of a week have done in that family! While poor Mrs. Churchill lived, I suppose there could not have been a hope, a chance, a possibility; — but scarcely are her remains at rest in the family vault, than her husband is persuaded to act exactly opposite to what she would have required. What a blessing it is, when undue influence does not survive the grave! — He gave his consent with very little persuasion."

"Ah!" thought Emma, "he would have done as much for Harriet."

"This was settled last night, and Frank was off with the light this morning. He stopped at Highbury, at the Bates's, I fancy, some time — and then came on hither; but was in such a hurry to get back to his uncle, to whom he is just now more necessary than ever, that, as I tell you, he could stay with us but a quarter of an hour. — He was very much agitated — very much, indeed — to a degree that made him appear quite a different creature from any thing I had ever seen him before. — In addition to all the rest, there had been the shock of finding her so very unwell, which he had had no previous suspicion of — and there was every appearance of his having been feeling a great deal."

"And do you really believe the affair to have been carrying on with such perfect secresy? — The Campbells, the Dixons, did none of them know of the engagement?"

Emma could not speak the name of Dixon without a little blush.

"None; not one. He positively said that it had been known to no being in the world but their two selves."

"Well," said Emma, "I suppose we shall gradually grow reconciled to the idea, and I wish them very happy. But I shall always think it a very abominable sort of proceeding. What has it been but a system of hypocrisy and deceit, — espionage, and treachery? — To come among us with professions of openness and simplicity; and such a league in secret to judge us all! — Here have we been, the whole winter and spring, completely duped, fancying ourselves all on an equal footing of truth and honour, with two people in the midst of us who may have been carrying round, comparing and sitting in judgment on sentiments and words that were never meant for both to hear. — They must take the consequence, if they have heard each other spoken of in a way not perfectly agreeable!"

"I am quite easy on that head," replied Mrs. Weston. "I am very sure that I never said any thing of either to the other, which both might not have heard."

"You are in luck. — Your only blunder was confined to my ear, when you imagined a certain friend of our's in love with the lady."

"True. But as I have always had a thoroughly good opinion of Miss Fairfax, I never could, under any blunder, have spoken ill of her; and as to speaking ill of him, there I must have been safe."

At this moment Mr. Weston appeared at a little distance from the window, evidently on the watch. His wife gave him a look which invited him in; and, while he was coming round, added, "Now, dearest Emma, let me intreat you to say and look every thing that may set his heart at ease, and incline him to be satisfied with the match. Let us make the best of it — and, indeed, almost every thing may be fairly said in her favour. It is not a connexion to gratify; but if Mr. Churchill does not feel that, why should we? and it may be a very fortunate circumstance for him, for Frank, I mean, that he should have attached himself to a girl of such steadiness of character and good judgment as I have always given her credit for — and still am disposed to give her credit for, in spite of this one great deviation from the strict rule of right. And how much may be said in her situation for even that error!"

"Much, indeed!" cried Emma, feelingly. "If a woman can ever be excused for thinking only of herself, it is in a situation like Jane Fairfax's. — Of such, one may almost say, that 'the world is not their's, nor the world's law' "[140]

She met Mr. Weston on his entrance with a smiling countenance, exclaiming,

"A very pretty trick you have been playing me, upon my word! This was a device, I suppose, to sport with my curiosity, and exercise my talent of guessing. But you really frightened me. I thought you had lost half your property, at least. And here, instead of its being a matter of condolence, it turns out to be one of congratulation. — I congratulate you, Mr. Weston, with all my heart, on the prospect of having one of the most lovely and accomplished young women in England for your daughter."

A glance or two between him and his wife, convinced him that all was as right as this speech proclaimed; and its happy effect on his spirits was immediate. His air and voice recovered their usual briskness: he shook her heartily and gratefully by the hand, and entered on the subject in a manner to prove, that he now only wanted time and persuasion to think the engagement no very bad thing. His companions suggested only what could palliate imprudence, or smooth objections; and by the time they had talked it all over together, and he had talked it all over again with Emma, in their walk back to Hartfield, he was become perfectly reconciled, and not far from thinking it the very best thing that Frank could possibly have done.

CHAPTER XI.

"HARRIET, poor Harriet!" — Those were the words; in them lay the tormenting ideas which Emma could not get rid of, and which constituted the real misery of the business to her. Frank Churchill had behaved very ill by herself — very ill in many ways, — but it was not so much *his* behaviour as her *own*, which made her so angry with him. It was the scrape which he had drawn her into on Harriet's account, that gave the deepest hue to his offence. — Poor Harriet! to be a second time the dupe of her misconceptions and flattery. Mr. Knightley had spoken prophetically, when he once said, "Emma, you have been no friend to

---

[140] *'the world is not their's, nor the world's law'*: Compare *Romeo and Juliet* V.I.72. Mary Lascelles, in a note to the Oxford edition of *Emma*, proposes that Austen has Emma cite (not quite accurately) a line from *Rambler* 107, in which the writer adapts Shakespeare's words to the plight of friendless women: "The world is not their friend, nor the world's law."

Harriet Smith." — She was afraid she had done her nothing but disservice — It was true that she had not to charge herself, in this instance as in the former, with being the sole and original author of the mischief; with having suggested such feelings as might otherwise never have entered Harriet's imagination; for Harriet had acknowledged her admiration and preference of Frank Churchill before she had ever given her a hint on the subject; but she felt completely guilty of having encouraged what she might have repressed. She might have prevented the indulgence and increase of such sentiments. Her influence would have been enough. And now she was very conscious that she ought to have prevented them. — She felt that she had been risking her friend's happiness on most insufficient grounds. Common sense would have directed her to tell Harriet, that she must not allow herself to think of him, and that there were five hundred chances to one against his ever caring for her. — "But, with common sense," she added, "I am afraid I have had little to do."

She was extremely angry with herself. If she could not have been angry with Frank Churchill too, it would have been dreadful. — As for Jane Fairfax, she might at least relieve her feelings from any present solicitude on her account. Harriet would be anxiety enough; she need no longer be unhappy about Jane, whose troubles and whose ill health having, of course, the same origin, must be equally under cure. — Her days of insignificance and evil were over. — She would soon be well, and happy, and prosperous. — Emma could now imagine why her own attentions had been slighted. This discovery laid many smaller matters open. No doubt it had been from jealousy. — In Jane's eyes she had been a rival; and well might any thing she could offer of assistance or regard be repulsed. An airing in the Hartfield carriage would have been the rack, and arrow-root from the Hartfield store-room must have been poison. She understood it all; and as far as her mind could disengage itself from the injustice and selfishness of angry feelings, she acknowledged that Jane Fairfax would have neither elevation nor happiness beyond her desert. But poor Harriet was such an engrossing charge! There was little sympathy to be spared for any body else. Emma was sadly fearful that this second disappointment would be more severe than the first. Considering the very superior claims of the object, it ought; and judging by its apparently stronger effect on Harriet's mind, producing reserve and self-command, it would. — She must communicate the painful truth, however, and as soon as possible. An injunction of secrecy had been among Mr. Weston's parting words. "For the present, the whole affair was to be completely a secret. Mr. Churchill had made a point of it, as a token of respect to the wife he had so very recently lost, and everybody admitted it to be no more than due decorum." — Emma had promised; but still Harriet must be excepted. It was her superior duty.

In spite of her vexation, she could not help feeling it almost ridiculous, that she should have the very same distressing and delicate office to perform by Harriet, which Mrs. Weston had just gone through by herself. The intelligence, which had been so anxiously announced to her, she was now to be anxiously announcing to another. Her heart beat quick on hearing Harriet's footstep and voice; so, she supposed, had poor Mrs. Weston felt when *she* was approaching Randalls. Could the event of the disclosure bear an equal resemblance! — But of that, unfortunately, there could be no chance.

"Well, Miss Woodhouse!" cried Harriet, coming eagerly into the room — "is not this the oddest news that ever was?"

"What news do you mean?" replied Emma, unable to guess, by look or voice, whether Harriet could indeed have received any hint.

"About Jane Fairfax. Did you ever hear any thing so strange? Oh! — you need not be afraid of owning it to me, for Mr. Weston has told me himself. I met him just now. He told me it was to be a great secret; and, therefore, I should not think of mentioning it to any body but you, but he said you knew it."

"What did Mr. Weston tell you?" — said Emma, still perplexed.

"Oh! he told me all about it; that Jane Fairfax and Mr. Frank Churchill are to be married, and that they have been privately engaged to one another this long while. How very odd!"

It was, indeed, so odd; Harriet's behaviour was so extremely odd, that Emma did not know how to understand it. Her character appeared absolutely changed. She seemed to propose showing no agitation, or disappointment, or peculiar concern in the discovery. Emma looked at her, quite unable to speak.

"Had you any idea," cried Harriet, "of his being in love with her? — You, perhaps, might. — You (blushing as she spoke) who can see into everybody's heart; but nobody else ——"

"Upon my word," said Emma, "I begin to doubt my having any such talent. Can you seriously ask me, Harriet, whether I imagined him attached to another woman at the very time that I was — tacitly, if not openly — encouraging you to give way to your own feelings? — I never had the slightest suspicion, till within the last hour, of Mr. Frank Churchill's having the least regard for Jane Fairfax. You may be very sure that if I had, I should have cautioned you accordingly."

"Me!" cried Harriet, colouring, and astonished. "Why should you caution me? — You do not think I care about Mr. Frank Churchill."

"I am delighted to hear you speak so stoutly on the subject," replied Emma, smiling; "but you do not mean to deny that there was a time — and not very distant either — when you gave me reason to understand that you did care about him?"

"Him! — never, never. Dear Miss Woodhouse, how could you so mistake me?" turning away distressed.

"Harriet!" cried Emma, after a moment's pause — "What do you mean? — Good Heaven! what do you mean? — Mistake you! — Am I to suppose then? ——"

She could not speak another word. — Her voice was lost; and she sat down, waiting in great terror till Harriet should answer.

Harriet, who was standing at some distance, and with face turned from her, did not immediately say any thing; and when she did speak, it was in a voice nearly as agitated as Emma's.

"I should not have thought it possible," she began, "that you could have misunderstood me! I know we agreed never to name him — but considering how infinitely superior he is to every body else, I should not have thought it possible that I could be supposed to mean any other person. Mr. Frank Churchill, indeed! I do not know who would ever look at him in the company of the other. I hope I have a better taste than to think of Mr. Frank Churchill, who is like nobody by his side. And that you should have been so mistaken, is amazing! — I am sure, but for believing that you entirely approved and meant to encourage me in my attachment, I should have considered it at first too great a presumption almost, to dare to think of him. At first, if you had not told me that more wonderful things had happened; that there had been matches of greater disparity (those were your very words); — I should not have dared to give way to — I should not have thought it possible — But if *you*, who had been always acquainted with him ——"

"Harriet!" cried Emma, collecting herself resolutely — "Let us understand each other now, without the possibility of farther mistake. Are you speaking of — Mr. Knightley?"

"To be sure I am. I never could have an idea of anybody else — and so I thought you knew. When we talked about him, it was clear as possible."

"Not quite," returned Emma, with forced calmness, "for all that you then said, appeared to me to relate to a different person. I could almost assert that you had *named* Mr. Frank Churchill. I am sure the service Mr. Frank Churchill had rendered you, in protecting you from the gipsies, was spoken of"

"Oh! Miss Woodhouse, how you do forget!"

"My dear Harriet, I perfectly remember the substance of what I said on the occasion. I told you that I did not wonder at your attachment; that considering the service he had rendered you, it was extremely natural: — and you agreed to it, expressing yourself very warmly as to your sense of that service, and mentioning even what your sensations had been in seeing him come forward to your rescue. — The impression of it is strong on my memory."

"Oh, dear," cried Harriet, "now I recollect what you mean; but I was thinking of something very different at the time. It was not the gipsies — it was not Mr. Frank Churchill that I meant. No! (with some elevation) I was thinking of a much more precious circumstance — of Mr. Knightley's coming and asking me to dance, when Mr. Elton would not stand up with me; and when there was no other partner in the room. That was the kind action; that was the noble benevolence and generosity; that was the service which made me begin to feel how superior he was to every other being upon earth."

"Good God!" cried Emma, "this has been a most unfortunate — most deplorable mistake! What is to be done?"

"You would not have encouraged me, then, if you had understood me. At least, however, I cannot be worse off than I should have been, if the other had been the person; and now — it *is* possible ——"

She paused a few moments. Emma could not speak.

"I do not wonder, Miss Woodhouse," she resumed, "that you should feel a great difference between the two, as to me or as to anybody. You must think one five hundred million times more above me than the other. But I hope, Miss Woodhouse, that supposing — that if — strange as it may appear — . But you know they were your own words, that *more* wonderful things had happened, matches of *greater* disparity had taken place than between Mr. Frank Churchill and me; and, therefore, it seems as if such a thing even as this, may have occurred before — and if I should be so fortunate, beyond expression, as to — if Mr. Knightley should really — if *he* does not mind the disparity, I hope, dear Miss Woodhouse, you will not set yourself against it, and try to put difficulties in the way. But you are too good for that, I am sure."

Harriet was standing at one of the windows. Emma turned round to look at her in consternation, and hastily said,

"Have you any idea of Mr. Knightley's returning your affection?"

"Yes," replied Harriet modestly, but not fearfully — "I must say that I have."

Emma's eyes were instantly withdrawn; and she sat silently meditating, in a fixed attitude, for a few minutes. A few minutes were sufficient for making her acquainted with her own heart. A mind like her's, once opening to suspicion, made rapid progress. She touched — she admitted — she acknowledged the whole truth. Why was it so much worse that Harriet should be in love with Mr. Knightley, than with Frank Churchill? Why was the evil so dreadfully increased by Harriet's having some hope of a return? It darted through her, with the speed of an arrow, that Mr. Knightley must marry no one but herself!

Her own conduct, as well as her own heart, was before her in the same few minutes. She saw it all with a clearness which had never blessed her before. How improperly had she been acting by Harriet! How inconsiderate, how indelicate, how irrational, how unfeeling had been her conduct! What blindness, what madness, had led her on! It struck her with dreadful force, and she was ready to give it every bad name in the world. Some portion of respect for herself, however, in spite of all these demerits — some concern for her own appearance, and a strong sense of justice by Harriet — (there would be no need of *compassion* to the girl who believed herself loved by Mr. Knightley — but justice required that she should not be made unhappy by any coldness now,) gave Emma the resolution to sit and endure farther with calmness, with even apparent kindness. — For her own advantage indeed, it was fit that the utmost extent of Harriet's hopes should be enquired into; and Harriet had done nothing to forfeit the regard and interest which had been so voluntarily formed and maintained — or to deserve to be slighted by the person, whose counsels had never led her right. — Rousing from reflection, therefore, and subduing her emotion, she turned to Harriet again, and, in a more inviting accent, renewed the conversation; for as to the subject which had first introduced it, the wonderful story of Jane Fairfax, that was quite sunk and lost. — Neither of them thought but of Mr. Knightley and themselves.

Harriet, who had been standing in no unhappy reverie, was yet very glad to be called from it, by the now encouraging manner of such a judge, and such a friend as Miss Woodhouse, and only wanted invitation, to give the history of her hopes with great, though trembling delight. — Emma's tremblings as she asked, and as she listened, were better concealed than Harriet's, but they were not less. Her voice was not unsteady; but her mind was in all the perturbation that such a development of self, such a burst of threatening evil, such a confusion of sudden and perplexing emotions, must create. — She listened with much inward suffering, but with great outward patience, to Harriet's detail. — Methodical, or well arranged, or very well delivered, it could not be expected to be; but it contained, when separated from all the feebleness and tautology of the narration, a substance to sink her spirit — especially with the corroborating circumstances, which her own memory brought in favour of Mr. Knightley's most improved opinion of Harriet.

Harriet had been conscious of a difference in his behaviour ever since those two decisive dances. — Emma knew that he had, on that occasion, found her much superior to his expectation. From that evening, or at least from the time of Miss Woodhouse's encouraging her to think of him, Harriet had begun to be sensible of his talking to her much more than he had been used to do, and of his having indeed quite a different manner towards her; a manner of kindness and sweetness! — Latterly she had been more and more aware of it. When they had been all walking together, he had so often come and walked by her, and talked so very delightfully! — He seemed to want to be acquainted with her. Emma knew it to have been very much the case. She had often observed the change, to almost the same extent. — Harriet repeated expressions of approbation and praise from him — and Emma felt them to be in the closest agreement with what she had known of his opinion of Harriet. He praised her for being without art or affectation, for having simple, honest, generous, feelings. — She knew that he saw such recommendations in Harriet; he had dwelt on them to her more than once. — Much that lived in Harriet's memory, many little particulars of the notice she had received from him, a look, a speech, a removal from one chair to another, a compliment implied, a preference inferred, had been unnoticed, because unsuspected by Emma. Circumstances that might swell to half an hour's relation, and contained multiplied proofs to her who had seen them, had passed undiscerned by her who now heard them; but the two latest occurrences to be mentioned, the two of strongest promise to Harriet, were not without some degree of witness from Emma herself. — The first, was his walking with her apart from the others, in the lime walk at Donwell, where they had been walking some time before Emma came, and he had taken pains (as she was convinced) to draw her from the rest to himself — and at first, he had talked to her in a more particular way than he had ever done before, in a very particular way indeed! — (Harriet could not recall it without a blush.) He seemed to be almost asking her, whether her affections were engaged. — But as soon as she (Miss Woodhouse) appeared likely to join them, he changed the subject, and began talking about farming: — The second, was his having sat talking with her nearly half an hour before Emma came back from her visit, the very last morning of his being at Hartfield — though, when he first came in, he had said that he could not stay five minutes — and his having told her, during their conversation, that though he must go to London, it was very much against his inclination that he left home at all, which was much more (as Emma felt) than he had acknowledged to *her*. The superior degree of confidence towards Harriet, which this one article marked, gave her severe pain.

On the subject of the first of the two circumstances, she did, after a little reflection, venture the following question. "Might he not? — Is not it possible, that when enquiring, as you thought, into the state of your affections, he might be alluding to Mr. Martin — he might have Mr. Martin's interest in view?" — But Harriet rejected the suspicion with spirit.

"Mr. Martin! No indeed! — There was not a hint of Mr. Martin. I hope I know better now, than to care for Mr. Martin, or to be suspected of it."

When Harriet had closed her evidence, she appealed to her dear Miss Woodhouse, to say whether she had not good ground for hope.

"I never should have presumed to think of it at first," said she, "but for you. You told me to observe him carefully, and let his behaviour be the rule of mine — and so I have. But now I seem to feel that I may deserve him; and that if he does choose me, it will not be any thing so very wonderful."

The bitter feelings occasioned by this speech, the many bitter feelings, made the utmost exertion necessary on Emma's side, to enable her to say on reply,

"Harriet, I will only venture to declare, that Mr. Knightley is the last man in the world, who would intentionally give any woman the idea of his feeling for her more than he really does."

Harriet seemed ready to worship her friend for a sentence so satisfactory; and Emma was only saved from raptures and fondness, which at that moment would have been dreadful penance, by the sound of her father's footsteps. He was coming through the hall. Harriet was too much agitated to encounter him. "She could not compose herself — Mr. Woodhouse would be alarmed — she had better go;" — with most ready encouragement from her friend, therefore, she passed off through another door — and the moment she was gone, this was the spontaneous burst of Emma's feelings: "Oh God! that I had never seen her!"

The rest of the day, the following night, were hardly enough for her thoughts. — She was bewildered amidst the confusion of all that had rushed on her within the last few hours. Every moment had brought a fresh surprise; and every surprise must be matter of humiliation to her. — How to understand it all! How to understand the deceptions she had been thus practising on herself, and living under! — The blunders, the blindness of her own head and heart! — she sat still, she walked about, she tried her own room, she tried the shrubbery — in every place, every posture, she perceived that she had acted most weakly; that she had been imposed on by others in a most mortifying degree; that she had been imposing on herself in a degree yet more mortifying; that she was wretched, and should probably find this day but the beginning of wretchedness.

To understand, thoroughly understand her own heart, was the first endeavour. To that point went every leisure moment which her father's claims on her allowed, and every moment of involuntary absence of mind.

How long had Mr. Knightley been so dear to her, as every feeling declared him now to be? When had his influence, such influence begun? — When had he succeeded to that place in her affection, which Frank Churchill had once, for a short period, occupied? — She looked back; she compared the two — compared them, as they had always stood in her estimation, from the time of the latter's becoming known to her — and as they must at any time have been compared by her, had it — oh! had it, by any blessed felicity, occurred to her, to institute the comparison. — She saw that there never had been a time when she did not consider Mr. Knightley as infinitely the superior, or when his regard for her had not been infinitely the most dear. She saw, that in persuading herself, in fancying, in acting to the contrary, she had been entirely under a delusion, totally ignorant of her own heart — and, in short, that she had never really cared for Frank Churchill at all!

This was the conclusion of the first series of reflection. This was the knowledge of herself, on the first question of inquiry, which she reached; and without being long in reaching it. — She was most sorrowfully indignant; ashamed of every sensation but the one revealed to her — her affection for Mr. Knightley. — Every other part of her mind was disgusting.

With insufferable vanity had she believed herself in the secret of everybody's feelings; with unpardonable arrogance proposed to arrange everybody's destiny. She was proved to have been universally mistaken; and she had not quite done nothing — for she had done mischief. She had brought evil on Harriet, on herself, and she too much feared, on Mr. Knightley. — Were this most unequal of all connexions to take place, on her must rest all the reproach of having given it a beginning; for his attachment, she must believe to be produced only by a consciousness of Harriet's; — and even were this not the case, he would never have known Harriet at all but for her folly.

Mr. Knightley and Harriet Smith! — It was an union to distance every wonder of the kind. — The attachment of Frank Churchill and Jane Fairfax became common-place, threadbare, stale in the comparison, exciting no surprise, presenting no disparity, affording nothing to be said or thought. — Mr. Knightley and Harriet Smith! — Such an elevation on her side! Such a debasement on his! — It was horrible to Emma to think how it must sink him in the general opinion, to foresee the smiles, the sneers, the merriment it would prompt at his expense; the mortification and disdain of his brother, the thousand inconveniences to himself. — Could it be? — No; it was impossible. And yet it was far, very far, from impossible. — Was it a new circumstance for a man of first-rate abilities to be captivated by very inferior powers? Was it new for one, perhaps too busy to seek, to be the prize of a girl who would seek him? — Was it new for any thing in this world to be unequal, inconsistent, incongruous — or for chance and circumstance (as second causes[141]) to direct the human fate?

Oh! had she never brought Harriet forward! Had she left her where she ought, and where he had told her she ought! — Had she not, with a folly which no tongue could express, prevented her marrying the unexceptionable young man who would have made her happy and respectable in the line of life to which she ought to belong — all would have been safe; none of this dreadful sequel would have been.

How Harriet could ever have had the presumption to raise her thoughts to Mr. Knightley! — How she could dare to fancy herself the chosen of such a man till actually assured of it! — But Harriet was less humble, had fewer scruples than formerly. — Her inferiority, whether of mind or situation, seemed little felt. — She had seemed more sensible of Mr. Elton's being to stoop in marrying her, than she now seemed of Mr. Knightley's. — Alas! was not that her own doing too?

[141]*second causes:* As distinguished from the first cause, God, who directs all human events.

Who had been at pains to give Harriet notions of self-consequence but herself? — Who but herself had taught her, that she was to elevate herself if possible, and that her claims were great to a high worldly establishment? — If Harriet, from being humble, were grown vain, it was her doing too.

CHAPTER XII.

TILL now that she was threatened with its loss, Emma had never known how much of her happiness depended on being *first* with Mr. Knightley, first in interest and affection. — Satisfied that it was so, and feeling it her due, she had enjoyed it without reflection; and only in the dread of being supplanted, found how inexpressibly important it had been. — Long, very long, she felt she had been first; for, having no female connexions of his own, there had been only Isabella whose claims could be compared with hers, and she had always known exactly how far he loved and esteemed Isabella. She had herself been first with him for many years past. She had not deserved it; she had often been negligent or perverse, slighting his advice, or even wilfully opposing him, insensible of half his merits, and quarrelling with him because he would not acknowledge her false and insolent estimate of her own — but still, from family attachment and habit, and thorough excellence of mind, he had loved her, and watched over her from a girl, with an endeavour to improve her, and an anxiety for her doing right, which no other creature had at all shared. In spite of all her faults, she knew she was dear to him; might she not say very dear? — When the suggestions of hope, however, which must follow here, presented themselves, she could not presume to indulge them. Harriet Smith might think herself not unworthy of being peculiarly, exclusively, passionately loved by Mr. Knightley. *She* could not. She could not flatter herself with any idea of blindness in his attachment to *her*. She had received a very recent proof of its impartiality. — How shocked had he been by her behaviour to Miss Bates! How directly, how strongly had he expressed himself to her on the subject! — Not too strongly for the offence — but far, far too strongly to issue from any feeling softer than upright justice and clear-sighted good will. — She had no hope, nothing to deserve the name of hope, that he could have that sort of affection for herself which was now in question; but there was a hope (at times a slight one, at times much stronger,) that Harriet might have deceived herself, and be over-rating his regard for *her*. — Wish it she must, for his sake — be the consequence nothing to herself, but his remaining single all his life. Could she be secure of that, indeed, of his never marrying at all, she believed she should be perfectly satisfied. — Let him but continue the same Mr. Knightley to her and her father, the same Mr. Knightley to all the world; let Donwell and Hartfield lose none of their precious intercourse of friendship and confidence, and her peace would be fully secured. — Marriage, in fact, would not do for her. It would be incompatible with what she owed to her father, and with what she felt for him. Nothing should separate her from her father. She would not marry, even if she were asked by Mr. Knightley.

It must be her ardent wish that Harriet might be disappointed; and she hoped, that when able to see them together again, she might at least be able to ascertain what the chances for it were. — She should see them henceforward with the closest observance; and wretchedly as she had hitherto misunderstood even those she was watching, she did not know how to admit that she could be blinded here. — He was expected back every day. The power of observation would be soon given — frightfully soon it appeared when her thoughts were in one course. In the meanwhile, she resolved against seeing Harriet. — It would do neither of them good, it would do the subject no good, to be talking of it farther. — She was resolved not to be convinced, as long as she could doubt, and yet had no authority for opposing Harriet's confidence. To talk would be only to irritate. — She wrote to her, therefore, kindly, but decisively, to beg that she would not, at present, come to Hartfield; acknowledging it to be her conviction, that all farther confidential discussion of *one* topic had better be avoided; and hoping, that if a few days were allowed to pass before they met again, except in the company of others — she objected only to a tête-à-tête — they might be able to act as if they had forgotten the conversation of yesterday. — Harriet submitted, and approved, and was grateful.

This point was just arranged, when a visitor arrived to tear Emma's thoughts a little from the one subject which had engrossed them, sleeping or waking, the last twenty-four hours — Mrs. Weston, who had been calling on her daughter-in-law elect, and took Hartfield in her way home, almost as much in duty to Emma as in pleasure to herself, to relate all the particulars of so interesting an interview.

Mr. Weston had accompanied her to Mrs. Bates's, and gone through his share of this essential attention most handsomely; but she having then induced Miss Fairfax to join her in an airing, was now returned with much more to say, and much more to say with satisfaction, than a quarter of an hour spent in Mrs. Bates's parlour, with all the incumbrance of awkward feelings, could have afforded.

A little curiosity Emma had; and she made the most of it while her friend related. Mrs. Weston had set off to pay the visit in a good deal of agitation herself; and in the first place had wished not to go at all at present, to be allowed merely to write to Miss Fairfax instead, and to defer this ceremonious call till a little time had passed, and Mr. Churchill could be reconciled to the engagement's becoming known; as, considering every thing, she thought such a visit could not be paid without leading to reports: — but Mr. Weston had thought differently; he was extremely anxious to shew his approbation to Miss Fairfax and her family, and did not conceive that any suspicion could be excited by it; or if it were, that it would be of any consequence; for "such things," he observed, "always got about." Emma smiled, and felt that Mr. Weston had very good reason for saying so. They had gone, in short — and very great had been the evident distress and confusion of the lady. She had hardly been able to speak a word, and every look and action had shown how deeply she was suffering from consciousness. The quiet, heartfelt satisfaction of the old lady, and the rapturous delight of her daughter — who proved even too joyous to talk as usual, had been a gratifying, yet almost an affecting, scene. They were both so truly respectable in their happiness, so disinterested in every sensation; thought so much of Jane; so much of everybody, and so little of themselves, that every kindly feeling was at work for them. Miss Fairfax's recent illness had offered a fair plea for Mrs. Weston to invite her to an airing; she had drawn back and declined at first, but on being pressed had yielded; and in the course of their drive, Mrs. Weston had, by gentle encouragement, overcome so much of her embarrassment, as to bring her to converse on the important subject. Apologies for her seemingly ungracious silence in their first reception, and the warmest expressions of the gratitude she was always feeling towards herself and Mr. Weston, must necessarily open the cause; but when these effusions were put by, they had talked a good deal of the present and of the future state of the engagement. Mrs. Weston was convinced that such conversation must be the greatest relief to her companion, pent up within her own mind as every thing had so long been, and was very much pleased with all that she had said on the subject.

"On the misery of what she had suffered, during the concealment of so many months," continued Mrs. Weston, "she was energetic. This was one of her expressions. 'I will not say, that since I entered into the engagement I have not had some happy moments; but I can say, that I have never known the blessing of one tranquil hour:' — and the quivering lip, Emma, which uttered it, was an attestation that I felt at my heart."

"Poor girl!" said Emma. "She thinks herself wrong, then, for having consented to a private engagement?"

"Wrong! — No one, I believe, can blame her more than she is disposed to blame herself. 'The consequence,' said she, 'has been a state of perpetual suffering to me; and so it ought. But after all the punishment that misconduct can bring, it is still not less misconduct. Pain is no expiation. I never can be blameless. I have been acting contrary to all my sense of right; and the fortunate turn that every thing has taken, and the kindness I am now receiving, is what my conscience tells me ought not to be. Do not imagine, madam,' she continued, 'that I was taught wrong. Do not let any reflection fall on the principles or the care of the friends who brought me up. The error has been all my own; and I do assure you that, with all the excuse that present circumstances may appear to give, I shall yet dread making the story known to Colonel Campbell.' "

"Poor girl!" said Emma again. "She loves him then excessively, I suppose. It must have been from attachment only that she could be led to form the engagement. Her affection must have overpowered her judgment."

"Yes, I have no doubt of her being extremely attached to him."

"I am afraid," returned Emma, sighing, "that I must often have contributed to make her unhappy."

"On your side, my love, it was very innocently done. But she probably had something of that in her thoughts, when alluding to the misunderstandings which he had given us hints of before. One natural consequence of the evil she had involved herself in, she said, was[142] that of making her *unreasonable*. The consciousness of having done amiss, had exposed her to a thousand inquietudes, and made her captious and irritable to a degree that must have been — that had been — hard for him to bear. 'I did not make the allowances,' said she, 'which I ought to have done, for his temper and spirits — his delightful spirits, and that gaiety, that playfulness of disposition, which, under any other circumstances, would, I am sure, have been as constantly bewitching to me, as they were at first.' She then began to speak of you, and of the great

---

[142]*One natural consequence of the evil she had involved herself in, she said, was:* Emendation of the first edition, which has double closing quotes after "in" and double opening quotes before "was."

kindness you had shown her during her illness; and with a blush which showed me how it was all connected, desired me, whenever I had an opportunity, to thank you — I could not thank you too much — for every wish and every endeavour to do her good. She was sensible that you had never received any proper acknowledgment from herself."

"If I did not know her to be happy now," said Emma, seriously, "which in spite of every little drawback from her scrupulous conscience, she must be, I could not bear these thanks; — for, oh! Mrs. Weston, if there were an account drawn up of the evil and the good I have done Miss Fairfax! — Well, (checking herself, and trying to be more lively), this is all to be forgotten. You are very kind to bring me these interesting particulars. They show her to the greatest advantage. I am sure she is very good — I hope she will be very happy. It is fit that the fortune should be on his side, for I think the merit will be all on her's."

Such a conclusion could not pass unanswered by Mrs. Weston. She thought well of Frank in almost every respect; and, what was more, she loved him very much, and her defence was, therefore, earnest. She talked with a great deal of reason, and at least equal affection — but she had too much to urge for Emma's attention; it was soon gone to Brunswick Square or to Donwell; she forgot to attempt to listen; and when Mrs. Weston ended with, "We have not yet had the letter we are so anxious for, you know, but I hope it will soon come," she was obliged to pause before she answered, and at last obliged to answer at random, before she could at all recollect what letter it was which they were so anxious for.

"Are you well, my Emma?" was Mrs. Weston's parting question.

"Oh! perfectly. I am always well, you know. Be sure to give me intelligence of the letter as soon as possible."

Mrs. Weston's communications furnished Emma with more food for unpleasant reflection, by increasing her esteem and compassion, and her sense of past injustice towards Miss Fairfax. She bitterly regretted not having sought a closer acquaintance with her, and blushed for the envious feelings which had certainly been, in some measure, the cause. Had she followed Mr. Knightley's known wishes, in paying that attention to Miss Fairfax, which was every way her due; had she tried to know her better; had she done her part towards intimacy; had she endeavoured to find a friend there instead of in Harriet Smith; she must, in all probability, have been spared from every pain which pressed on her now. — Birth, abilities, and education, had been equally marking one as an associate for her, to be received with gratitude; and the other — what was she? — Supposing even that they had never become intimate friends; that she had never been admitted into Miss Fairfax's confidence on this important matter — which was most probable — still, in knowing her as she ought, and as she might, she must have been preserved from the abominable suspicions of an improper attachment to Mr. Dixon, which she had not only so foolishly fashioned and harboured herself, but had so unpardonably imparted; an idea which she greatly feared had been made a subject of material distress to the delicacy of Jane's feelings, by the levity or carelessness of Frank Churchill's. Of all the sources of evil surrounding the former, since her coming to Highbury, she was persuaded that she must herself have been the worst. She must have been a perpetual enemy. They never could have been all three together, without her having stabbed Jane Fairfax's peace in a thousand instances; and on Box Hill, perhaps, it had been the agony of a mind that would bear no more.

The evening of this day was very long, and melancholy, at Hartfield. The weather added what it could of gloom. A cold stormy rain set in, and nothing of July appeared but in the trees and shrubs, which the wind was despoiling, and the length of the day, which only made such cruel sights the longer visible.

The weather affected Mr. Woodhouse, and he could only be kept tolerably comfortable by almost ceaseless attention on his daughter's side, and by exertions which had never cost her half so much before. It reminded her of their first forlorn tête-à-tête, on the evening of Mrs. Weston's wedding-day; but Mr. Knightley had walked in then, soon after tea, and dissipated every melancholy fancy. Alas! such delightful proofs of Hartfield's attraction, as those sort of visits conveyed, might shortly be over. The picture which she had then drawn of the privations of the approaching winter, had proved erroneous; no friends had deserted them, no pleasures had been lost. — But her present forebodings she feared would experience no similar contradiction. The prospect before her now, was threatening to a degree that could not be entirely dispelled — that might not be even partially brightened. If all took place that might take place among the circle of her friends, Hartfield must be comparatively deserted; and she left to cheer her father with the spirits only of ruined happiness.

The child to be born at Randalls must be a tie there even dearer than herself; and Mrs. Weston's heart and time would be occupied by it. They should lose her; and, probably, in great measure, her husband also. — Frank Churchill would return among them no more; and Miss Fairfax, it was reasonable to suppose, would soon cease to belong to Highbury. They would be married, and settled either at or near

Enscombe. All that were good would be withdrawn; and if to these losses, the loss of Donwell were to be added, what would remain of cheerful or of rational society within their reach? Mr. Knightley to be no longer coming there for his evening comfort! — No longer walking in at all hours, as if ever willing to change his own home for their's! — How was it to be endured? And if he were to be lost to them for Harriet's sake; if he were to be thought of hereafter, as finding in Harriet's society all that he wanted; if Harriet were to be the chosen, the first, the dearest, the friend, the wife to whom he looked for all the best blessings of existence; what could be increasing Emma's wretchedness but the reflection never far distant from her mind, that it had been all her own work?

When it came to such a pitch as this, she was not able to refrain from a start, or a heavy sigh, or even from walking about the room for a few seconds — and the only source whence any thing like consolation or composure could be drawn, was in the resolution of her own better conduct, and the hope that, however inferior in spirit and gaiety might be the following and every future winter of her life to the past, it would yet find her more rational, more acquainted with herself, and leave her less to regret when it were gone.

CHAPTER XIII.

THE weather continued much the same all the following morning; and the same loneliness, and the same melancholy, seemed to reign at Hartfield — but in the afternoon it cleared; the wind changed into a softer quarter; the clouds were carried off; the sun appeared; it was summer again. With all the eagerness which such a transition gives, Emma resolved to be out of doors as soon as possible. Never had the exquisite sight, smell, sensation of nature, tranquil, warm, and brilliant after a storm, been more attractive to her. She longed for the serenity they might gradually introduce; and on Mr. Perry's coming in soon after dinner, with a disengaged hour to give her father, she lost no time in hurrying into the shrubbery. — There, with spirits freshened, and thoughts a little relieved, she had taken a few turns, when she saw Mr. Knightley passing through the garden door, and coming towards her. — It was the first intimation of his being returned from London. She had been thinking of him the moment before, as unquestionably sixteen miles distant. — There was time only for the quickest arrangement of mind. She must be collected and calm. In half a minute they were together. The "How d'ye do's," were quiet and constrained on each side. She asked after their mutual friends; they were all well. — When had he left them? — Only that morning. He must have had a wet ride. — Yes. — He meant to walk with her, she found. "He had just looked into the dining-room, and as he was not wanted there, preferred being out of doors." — She thought he neither looked nor spoke cheerfully; and the first possible cause for it, suggested by her fears, was, that he had perhaps been communicating his plans to his brother, and was pained by the manner in which they had been received.

They walked together. He was silent. She thought he was often looking at her, and trying for a fuller view of her face than it suited her to give. And this belief produced another dread. Perhaps he wanted to speak to her, of his attachment to Harriet; he might be watching for encouragement to begin. — She did not, could not, feel equal to lead the way to any such subject. He must do it all himself. Yet she could not bear this silence. With him it was most unnatural. She considered — resolved — and, trying to smile, began —

"You have some news to hear, now you are come back, that will rather surprise you."

"Have I?" said he quietly, and looking at her; "of what nature?"

"Oh! the best nature in the world — a wedding."

After waiting a moment, as if to be sure she intended to say no more, he replied,

"If you mean Miss Fairfax and Frank Churchill, I have heard that already."

"How is it possible?" cried Emma, turning her glowing cheeks towards him; for while she spoke, it occurred to her that he might have called at Mrs. Goddard's in his way.

"I had a few lines on parish business from Mr. Weston this morning, and at the end of them he gave me a brief account of what had happened."

Emma was quite relieved, and could presently say, with a little more composure,

"*You* probably have been less surprised than any of us, for you have had your suspicions. — I have not forgotten that you once tried to give me a caution. — I wish I had attended to it — but — (with a sinking voice and a heavy sigh) I seem to have been doomed to blindness."

For a moment or two nothing was said, and she was unsuspicious of having excited any particular interest, till she found her arm drawn within his, and pressed against his heart, and heard him thus saying, in a tone of great sensibility, speaking low,

"Time, my dearest Emma, time will heal the wound. — Your own excellent sense — your exertions for your father's sake — I know you will not allow yourself — ." Her arm was pressed again, as he added, in a more broken and subdued accent, "The feelings of the warmest friendship — Indignation — Abominable scoundrel!" — And in a louder, steadier tone, he concluded with, "He will soon be gone. They will soon be in Yorkshire. I am sorry for *her*. She deserves a better fate."

Emma understood him; and as soon as she could recover from the flutter of pleasure, excited by such tender consideration, replied,

"You are very kind — but you are mistaken — and I must set you right. — I am not in want of that sort of compassion. My blindness to what was going on, led me to act by them in a way that I must always be ashamed of, and I was very foolishly tempted to say and do many things which may well lay me open to unpleasant conjectures, but I have no other reason to regret that I was not in the secret earlier."

"Emma!" cried he, looking eagerly at her, "are you, indeed?" — but checking himself — "No, no, I understand you — forgive me — I am pleased that you can say even so much. — He is no object of regret, indeed! and it will not be very long, I hope, before that becomes the acknowledgment of more than your reason. — Fortunate that your affections were not farther entangled! — I could never, I confess, from your manners, assure myself as to the degree of what you felt — I could only be certain that there was a preference — and a preference which I never believed him to deserve. — He is a disgrace to the name of man. — And is he to be rewarded with that sweet young woman? — Jane, Jane, you will be a miserable creature."

"Mr Knightley," said Emma, trying to be lively, but really confused — "I am in a very extraordinary situation. I cannot let you continue in your error; and yet, perhaps, since my manners gave such an impression, I have as much reason to be ashamed of confessing that I never have been at all attached to the person we are speaking of, as it might be natural for a woman to feel in confessing exactly the reverse. — But I never have."

He listened in perfect silence. She wished him to speak, but he would not. She supposed she must say more before she were entitled to his clemency; but it was a hard case to be obliged still to lower herself in his opinion. She went on, however.

"I have very little to say for my own conduct. — I was tempted by his attentions, and allowed myself to appear pleased. — An old story, probably — a common case — and no more than has happened to hundreds of my sex before; and yet it may not be the more excusable in one who sets up as I do for Understanding. Many circumstances assisted the temptation. He was the son of Mr. Weston — he was continually here — I always found him very pleasant — and, in short, for (with a sigh) let me swell out the causes ever so ingeniously, they all centre in this at last — my vanity was flattered, and I allowed his attentions. Latterly, however — for some time, indeed — I have had no idea of their meaning any thing. — I thought them a habit, a trick, nothing that called for seriousness on my side. He has imposed on me, but he has not injured me. I have never been attached to him. And now I can tolerably comprehend his behaviour. He never wished to attach me. It was merely a blind to conceal his real situation with another. — It was his object to blind all about him; and no one, I am sure, could be more effectually blinded than myself — except that I was *not* blinded — that it was my good fortune — that, in short, I was somehow or other safe from him."

She had hoped for an answer here — for a few words to say that her conduct was at least intelligible; but he was silent; and, as far as she could judge, deep in thought. At last, and tolerably in his usual tone, he said,

"I have never had a high opinion of Frank Churchill. — I can suppose, however, that I may have under-rated him. My acquaintance with him has been but trifling. — And even if I have not under-rated him hitherto, he may yet turn out well. — With such a woman he has a chance. — I have no motive for wishing him ill — and for her sake, whose happiness will be involved in his good character and conduct, I shall certainly wish him well."

"I have no doubt of their being happy together," said Emma; "I believe them to be very mutually and very sincerely attached."

"He is a most fortunate man!" returned Mr. Knightley, with energy. "So early in life — at three and twenty — a period when, if a man chooses a wife, he generally chooses ill. At three and twenty to have drawn such a prize! — What years of felicity that man, in all human calculation, has before him! — Assured of the love of such a woman — the disinterested love, for Jane Fairfax's character vouches for her disinterestedness; every thing in his favour, — equality of situation — I mean, as far as regards society, and all the habits and manners that are important; equality in every point but one — and that one, since the purity of her heart is not to be doubted, such as must increase his felicity, for it will be his to bestow the only advantages she wants. — A man would always wish to give a woman a better home than the one he takes her from; and he who can do it, where there is no doubt of *her* regard, must, I think, be the happiest of mortals. — Frank Churchill is, indeed, the favourite of fortune. Every thing turns out for his good. — He meets with a young woman at a watering-place, gains her affection, cannot even weary her by negligent treatment — and had he and all his family sought round the world for a perfect wife for him, they could not have found her superior. — His aunt is in the way. — His aunt dies. — He has only to speak. — His friends are eager to promote his happiness. — He has used everybody ill — and they are all delighted to forgive him. — He is a fortunate man indeed!"

"You speak as if you envied him."

"And I do envy him, Emma. In one respect he is the object of my envy."

Emma could say no more. They seemed to be within half a sentence of Harriet, and her immediate feeling was to avert the subject, if possible. She made her plan; she would speak of something totally different — the children in Brunswick Square; and she only waited for breath to begin, when Mr. Knightley startled her, by saying,

"You will not ask me what is the point of envy. — You are determined, I see, to have no curiosity. — You are wise — but I cannot be wise. Emma, I must tell what you will not ask, though I may wish it unsaid the next moment."

"Oh! then, don't speak it, don't speak it," she eagerly cried. "Take a little time, consider, do not commit yourself."

"Thank you," said he, in an accent of deep mortification, and not another syllable followed.

Emma could not bear to give him pain. He was wishing to confide in her — perhaps to consult her; — cost her what it would, she would listen. She might assist his resolution, or reconcile him to it; she might give just praise to Harriet, or, by representing to him his own independence, relieve him from that state of indecision, which must be more intolerable than any alternative to such a mind as his. — They had reached the house.

"You are going in, I suppose," said he.

"No" — replied Emma — quite confirmed by the depressed manner in which he still spoke — "I should like to take another turn. Mr. Perry is not gone." And, after proceeding a few steps, she added — "I stopped you ungraciously, just now, Mr. Knightley, and, I am afraid, gave you pain. — But if you have any wish to speak openly to me as a friend, or to ask my opinion of any thing that you may have in contemplation — as a friend, indeed, you may command me. — I will hear whatever you like. I will tell you exactly what I think."

"As a friend!" — repeated Mr. Knightley. — "Emma, that I fear is a word — No, I have no wish — Stay, yes, why should I hesitate? — I have gone too far already for concealment. — Emma, I accept your offer — Extraordinary as it may seem, I accept it, and refer myself to you as a friend. — Tell me, then, have I no chance of ever succeeding?"

He stopped in his earnestness to look the question, and the expression of his eyes overpowered her.

"My dearest Emma," said he, "for dearest you will always be, whatever the event of this hour's conversation, my dearest, most beloved Emma — tell me at once. Say 'No,' if it is to be said." — She could really say nothing. — "You are silent," he cried, with great animation; "absolutely silent! at present I ask no more."

Emma was almost ready to sink under the agitation of this moment. The dread of being awakened from the happiest dream, was perhaps the most prominent feeling.

"I cannot make speeches, Emma:" — he soon resumed; and in a tone of such sincere, decided, intelligible tenderness as was tolerably convincing. — "If I loved you less, I might be able to talk about it more. But you know what I am. — You hear nothing but truth from me. — I have blamed you, and lectured you, and you have borne it as no other woman in England would have borne it. — Bear with the truths I would tell you now, dearest Emma, as well as you have borne with them. The manner, perhaps, may have as little to recommend them. God knows, I have been a very indifferent lover. — But you understand me. — Yes, you see, you understand my feelings — and will return them if you can. At present, I ask only to hear, once to hear your voice."

While he spoke, Emma's mind was most busy, and, with all the wonderful velocity of thought, had been able — and yet without losing a word — to catch and comprehend the exact truth of the whole; to see that Harriet's hopes had been entirely groundless, a mistake, a delusion, as complete a delusion as any of her own — that Harriet was nothing; that she was every thing herself; that what she had been saying relative to Harriet had been all taken as the language of her own feelings; and that her agitation, her doubts, her reluctance, her discouragement, had been all received as discouragement from herself. — And not only was there time for these convictions, with all their glow of attendant happiness; there was time also to rejoice that Harriet's secret had not escaped her, and to resolve that it need not and should not. — It was all the service she could now render her poor friend; for as to any of that heroism of sentiment which might have prompted her to entreat him to transfer his affection from herself to Harriet, as infinitely the most worthy of the two — or even the more simple sublimity of resolving to refuse him at once and for ever, without vouchsafing any motive, because he could not marry them both, Emma had it not. She felt for Harriet, with pain and with contrition; but no flight of generosity run mad, opposing all that could be probable or reasonable, entered her brain. She had led her friend astray, and it would be a reproach to her for ever; but her judgment was as strong as her feelings, and as strong as it had ever been before, in reprobating any such alliance for him, as most unequal and degrading. Her way was clear, though not quite smooth. — She spoke then, on being so entreated. — What did she say? — Just what she ought, of course. A lady always does. — She said enough to show there need not be despair — and to invite him to say more himself. He *had* despaired at one period; he had received such an injunction to caution and silence, as for the time crushed every hope; — she had begun by refusing to hear him. — The change had perhaps been somewhat sudden; — her proposal of taking another turn, her renewing the conversation which she had just put an end to, might be a little extraordinary! — She felt its inconsistency; but Mr. Knightley was so obliging as to put up with it, and seek no farther explanation.

Seldom, very seldom, does complete truth belong to any human disclosure; seldom can it happen that something is not a little disguised, or a little mistaken; but where, as in this case, though the conduct is mistaken, the feelings are not, it may not be very material. — Mr. Knightley could not impute to Emma a more relenting heart than she possessed, or a heart more disposed to accept of his.

He had, in fact, been wholly unsuspicious of his own influence. He had followed her into the shrubbery with no idea of trying it. He had come, in his anxiety to see how she bore Frank Churchill's engagement, with no selfish view, no view at all, but of endeavouring, if she allowed him an opening, to soothe or to counsel her. — The rest had been the work of the moment, the immediate effect of what he heard, on his feelings. The delightful assurance of her total indifference towards Frank Churchill, of her having a heart completely disengaged from him, had given birth to the hope, that, in time, he might gain her affection himself; — but it had been no present hope — he had only, in the momentary conquest of eagerness over judgment, aspired to be told that she did not forbid his attempt to attach her. — The superior hopes which gradually opened were so much the more enchanting. — The affection, which he had been asking to be allowed to create if he could, was already his! — Within half an hour, he had passed from a thoroughly distressed state of mind, to something so like perfect happiness, that it could bear no other name.

Her change was equal. — This one half hour had given to each the same precious certainty of being beloved, had cleared from each the same degree of ignorance, jealousy, or distrust. — On his side, there had been a long-standing jealousy, old as the arrival, or even the expectation, of Frank Churchill. — He had been in love with Emma, and jealous of Frank Churchill, from about the same period, one sentiment having probably enlightened him as to the other. It was his jealousy of Frank Churchill that had taken him from the country. — The Box-Hill party had decided him on going away. He would save himself from witnessing again such permitted, encouraged attentions. — He had gone to learn to be indifferent. — But he had gone to a wrong place. There was too much domestic happiness in his brother's house; woman wore too amiable a form in it; Isabella was too much like Emma — differing only in those striking inferiorities, which always brought the other in brilliancy before him, for much to have been done, even had his time been longer. — He had staid on, however, vigorously, day after day — till this very morning's post had conveyed the history of Jane Fairfax. — Then, with the gladness which must be felt, nay, which he did not scruple to feel, having never believed Frank Churchill to be at all deserving Emma, was there so much fond solicitude, so much keen anxiety for her, that he could stay no longer. He had ridden home through the rain; and had walked up directly after dinner, to see how this sweetest and best of all creatures, faultless in spite of all her faults,[143] bore the discovery.

He had found her agitated and low. — Frank Churchill was a villain. — He heard her declare that she had never loved him. Frank Churchill's character was not desperate. — She was his own Emma, by hand and word, when they returned into the house; and if he could have thought of Frank Churchill then, he might have deemed him a very good sort of fellow.

---

[143]*faultless in spite of all her faults:* As several scholars have recognized, this is an echo of Mirabel's tribute to Millamant in William Congreve's *The Way of the World* (1700), I.iii: "I like her with all her faults; nay, I like her for all her faults."

CHAPTER XIV.

WHAT totally different feelings did Emma take back into the house from what she had brought out! — she had then been only daring to hope for a little respite of suffering; — she was now in an exquisite flutter of happiness, and such happiness moreover as she believed must still be greater when the flutter should have passed away.

They sat down to tea — the same party round the same table — how often it had been collected! — and how often had her eyes fallen on the same shrubs in the lawn, and observed the same beautiful effect of the western sun! - But never in such a state of spirits, never in anything like it; and it was with difficulty that she could summon enough of her usual self to be the attentive lady of the house, or even the attentive daughter.

Poor Mr. Woodhouse little suspected what was plotting against him in the breast of that man whom he was so cordially welcoming, and so anxiously hoping might not have taken cold from his ride. — Could he have seen the heart, he would have cared very little for the lungs; but without the most distant imagination of the impending evil, without the slightest perception of anything extraordinary in the looks or ways of either, he repeated to them very comfortably all the articles of news he had received from Mr. Perry, and talked on with much self-contentment, totally unsuspicious of what they could have told him in return.

As long as Mr. Knightley remained with them, Emma's fever continued; but when he was gone, she began to be a little tranquillized and subdued — and in the course of the sleepless night, which was the tax for such an evening, she found one or two such very serious points to consider, as made her feel, that even her happiness must have some alloy. Her father — and Harriet. She could not be alone without feeling the full weight of their separate claims; and how to guard the comfort of both to the utmost, was the question. With respect to her father, it was a question soon answered. She hardly knew yet what Mr. Knightley would ask; but a very short parley with her own heart produced the most solemn resolution of never quitting her father. — She even wept over the idea of it, as a sin of thought. While he lived, it must be only an engagement; but she flattered herself, that if divested of the danger of drawing her away, it might become an increase of comfort to him. — How to do her best by Harriet, was of more difficult decision; — how to spare her from any unnecessary pain; how to make her any possible atonement; how to appear least her enemy? — On these subjects, her perplexity and distress were very great — and her mind had to pass again and again through every bitter reproach and sorrowful regret that had ever surrounded it. — She could only resolve at last, that she would still avoid a meeting with her, and communicate all that need be told by letter; that it would be inexpressibly desirable to have her removed just now for a time from Highbury, and — indulging in one scheme more — nearly resolve, that it might be practicable to get an invitation for her to Brunswick Square. — Isabella had been pleased with Harriet; and a few weeks spent in London must give her some amusement. — She did not think it in Harriet's nature to escape being benefited by novelty and variety, by the streets, the shops, and the children. — At any rate, it would be a proof of attention and kindness in herself, from whom every thing was due; a separation for the present; an averting of the evil day, when they must all be together again.

She rose early, and wrote her letter to Harriet; an employment which left her so very serious, so nearly sad, that Mr. Knightley, in walking up to Hartfield to breakfast, did not arrive at all too soon; and half an hour stolen afterwards to go over the same ground again with him, literally and figuratively, was quite necessary to reinstate her in a proper share of the happiness of the evening before.

He had not left her long, by no means long enough for her to have the slightest inclination for thinking of anybody else, when a letter was brought her from Randalls — a very thick letter; — she guessed what it must contain, and deprecated the necessity of reading it. — She was now in perfect charity with Frank Churchill; she wanted no explanations, she wanted only to have her thoughts to herself — and as for understanding any thing he wrote, she was sure she was incapable of it. — It must be waded through, however. She opened the packet; it was too surely so; — a note from Mrs. Weston to herself, ushered in the letter from Frank to Mrs. Weston.

"I have the greatest pleasure, my dear Emma, in forwarding to you the enclosed. I know what thorough justice you will do it, and have scarcely a doubt of its happy effect. — I think we shall never materially disagree about the writer again; but I will not delay you by a long preface. — We are quite well. — This letter has been the cure of all the little nervousness I have been feeling lately. — I did not quite like your looks on Tuesday, but it was an ungenial morning; and though you will never own being affected by weather, I think every body feels a north-east wind. — I felt for your dear father very much in the storm of Tues-

day afternoon and yesterday morning, but had the comfort of hearing
last night, by Mr Perry, that it had not made him ill.

"Your's ever,

"A. W."

[*To Mrs. Weston.*]

MY DEAR MADAM,   Windsor — July.
"IF I made myself intelligible yesterday, this letter will be expected;
but expected or not, I know it will be read with candour and indulgence. — You are all goodness, and I believe there will be need of even
all your goodness to allow for some parts of my past conduct. — But I
have been forgiven by one who had still more to resent. My courage
rises while I write. It is very difficult for the prosperous to be humble. I
have already met with such success in two applications for pardon, that
I may be in danger of thinking myself too sure of your's, and of those
among your friends who have had any ground of offence. — You must
all endeavour to comprehend the exact nature of my situation when I
first arrived at Randalls; you must consider me as having a secret which
was to be kept at all hazards. This was the fact. My right to place myself
in a situation requiring such concealment, is another question. I shall
not discuss it here. For my temptation to *think* it a right, I refer every
caviller[144] to a brick house, sashed windows below, and casements
above, in Highbury. I dared not address her openly; my difficulties in
the then state of Enscombe must be too well known to require definition; and I was fortunate enough to prevail, before we parted at Weymouth, and to induce the most upright female mind in the creation to
stoop in charity to a secret engagement. — Had she refused, I should
have gone mad. — But you will be ready to say, what was your hope in
doing this? — What did you look forward to? — To any thing, every
thing — to time, chance, circumstance, slow effects, sudden bursts,
perseverance and weariness, health and sickness. Every possibility of
good was before me, and the first of blessings secured, in obtaining
her promises of faith and correspondence. If you need farther explanation, I have the honour, my dear madam, of being your husband's
son, and the advantage of inheriting a disposition to hope for good,
which no inheritance of houses or lands can ever equal the value of. —
See me, then, under these circumstances, arriving on my first visit to

---

[144]*caviller:* One who makes frivolous objections.

Randalls; — and here I am conscious of wrong, for that visit might have been sooner paid. You will look back and see that I did not come till Miss Fairfax was in Highbury; and as *you* were the person slighted, you will forgive me instantly; but I must work on my father's compassion, by reminding him, that so long as I absented myself from his house, so long I lost the blessing of knowing you. My behaviour, during the very happy fortnight which I spent with you, did not, I hope, lay me open to reprehension, excepting on one point. And now I come to the principal, the only important part of my conduct while belonging to you, which excites my own anxiety, or requires very solicitous explanation. With the greatest respect, and the warmest friendship, do I mention Miss Woodhouse; my father perhaps will think I ought to add, with the deepest humiliation. — A few words which dropped from him yesterday spoke his opinion, and some censure I acknowledge myself liable to. — My behaviour to Miss Woodhouse indicated, I believe, more than it ought. — In order to assist a concealment so essential to me, I was led on to make more than an allowable use of the sort of intimacy into which we were immediately thrown. — I cannot deny that Miss Woodhouse was my ostensible object — but I am sure you will believe the declaration, that had I not been convinced of her indifference, I would not have been induced by any selfish views to go on. — Amiable and delightful as Miss Woodhouse is, she never gave me the idea of a young woman likely to be attached; and that she was perfectly free from any tendency to being attached to me, was as much my conviction as my wish. — She received my attentions with an easy, friendly, good-humoured playfulness, which exactly suited me. We seemed to understand each other. From our relative situation, those attentions were her due, and were felt to be so. — Whether Miss Woodhouse began really to understand me before the expiration of that fortnight, I cannot say; — when I called to take leave of her, I remember that I was within a moment of confessing the truth, and I then fancied she was not without suspicion; but I have no doubt of her having since detected me, at least in some degree. — She may not have surmised the whole, but her quickness must have penetrated a part. I cannot doubt it. You will find, whenever the subject becomes freed from its present restraints, that it did not take her wholly by surprise. She frequently gave me hints of it. I remember her telling me at the ball, that I owed Mrs. Elton gratitude for her attentions to Miss Fairfax. — I hope this history of my conduct towards her will be admitted by you and my father as great extenuation of what you saw amiss. While you considered me as having sinned against Emma Woodhouse, I could deserve nothing from either. Acquit me here, and procure for me, when it is allowable, the acquittal and good wishes of that said Emma Woodhouse, whom I regard with so much brotherly affection, as to long to have her as deeply and as happily in love as myself. — Whatever strange things I said or did during that fortnight, you have now a key to. My heart was in Highbury, and my business was to get my body thither as often as might be, and with the least suspicion. If you remember any queernesses, set them all to the right account. — Of the pianoforté so much talked of, I feel it only necessary to say, that its being ordered was absolutely unknown to Miss F——, who would never have allowed me to send it, had any choice been given her. — The delicacy of her mind throughout the whole engagement, my dear madam, is much beyond my power of doing justice to. You will soon, I earnestly hope, know her thoroughly yourself. — No description can describe her. She must tell you herself what she is — yet not by word, for never was there a human creature who would so designedly suppress her own merit. — Since I began this letter, which will be longer than I foresaw, I have heard from her. — She gives a good account of her own health; but as she never complains, I dare not depend. I want to have your opinion of her looks. I know you will soon call on her; she is living in dread of the visit. Perhaps it is paid already. Let me hear from you without delay; I am impatient for a thousand particulars. Remember how few minutes I was at Randalls, and in how bewildered, how mad a state: and I am not much better yet; still insane either from happiness or misery. When I think of the kindness and favour I have met with, of her excellence and patience, and my uncle's generosity, I am mad with joy: but when I recollect all the uneasiness I occasioned her, and how little I deserve to be forgiven, I am mad with anger. If I could but see her again! — But I must not propose it yet. My uncle has been too good for me to encroach. — I must still add to this long letter. You have not heard all that you ought to hear. I could not give any connected detail yesterday; but the suddenness, and, in one light, the unseasonableness, with which the affair burst out, needs explanation; for though the event of the 26th ult.,[145] as you will conclude, immediately opened to me the happiest prospects, I should not have presumed on such early measures, but from the very particular circumstances, which left me not an hour to lose. I should myself have shrunk from any thing so hasty, and she would have felt every scruple of mine with multiplied strength and refinement. — But I had no choice. The hasty engagement she had entered into with that

---

[145]*the 26th ult.:* The 26th of the last month (here June).

woman —— Here, my dear madam, I was obliged to leave off abruptly, to recollect and compose myself. — I have been walking over the country, and am now, I hope, rational enough to make the rest of my letter what it ought to be. — It is, in fact, a most mortifying retrospect for me. I behaved shamefully. And here I can admit, that my manners to Miss W., in being unpleasant to Miss F., were highly blamable. *She* disapproved them, which ought to have been enough. — My plea of concealing the truth she did not think sufficient. — She was displeased; I thought unreasonably so: I thought her, on a thousand occasions, unnecessarily scrupulous and cautious: I thought her even cold. But she was always right. If I had followed her judgment, and subdued my spirits to the level of what she deemed proper, I should have escaped the greatest unhappiness I have ever known. — We quarrelled. — Do you remember the morning spent at Donwell? — *There* every little dissatisfaction that had occurred before came to a crisis. I was late; I met her walking home by herself, and wanted to walk with her, but she would not suffer it. She absolutely refused to allow me, which I then thought most unreasonable. Now, however, I see nothing in it but a very natural and consistent degree of discretion. While I, to blind the world to our engagement, was behaving one hour with objectionable particularity to another woman, was she to be consenting the next to a proposal which might have made every previous caution useless? — Had we been met walking together between Donwell and Highbury, the truth must have been suspected. — I was mad enough, however, to resent. — I doubted her affection. I doubted it more the next day on Box-Hill; when, provoked by such conduct on my side, such shameful, insolent neglect of her, and such apparent devotion to Miss W., as it would have been impossible for any woman of sense to endure, she spoke her resentment in a form of words perfectly intelligible to me. — In short, my dear madam, it was a quarrel blameless on her side, abominable on mine; and I returned the same evening to Richmond, though I might have staid with you till the next morning, merely because I would be as angry with her as possible. Even then, I was not such a fool as not to mean to be reconciled in time; but I was the injured person, injured by her coldness, and I went away determined that she should make the first advances. — I shall always congratulate myself that you were not of the Box-Hill party. Had you witnessed my behaviour there, I can hardly suppose you would ever have thought well of me again. Its effect upon her appears in the immediate resolution it produced: as soon as she found I was really gone from Randalls, she closed with the offer of that officious Mrs. Elton; the whole system of whose treatment of her, by the bye, has ever filled me with indignation and hatred. I must not quarrel with a spirit of forbearance which has been so richly extended towards myself; but, otherwise, I should loudly protest against the share of it which that woman has known. — "Jane," indeed! — You will observe that I have not yet indulged myself in calling her by that name, even to you. Think, then, what I must have endured in hearing it bandied between the Eltons with all the vulgarity of needless repetition, and all the insolence of imaginary superiority. Have patience with me, I shall soon have done. — She closed with this offer, resolving to break with me entirely, and wrote the next day to tell me that we never were to meet again. — *She felt the engagement to be a source of repentance and misery to each: she dissolved it.* — This letter reached me on the very morning of my poor aunt's death. I answered it within an hour; but from the confusion of my mind, and the multiplicity of business falling on me at once, my answer, instead of being sent with all the many other letters of that day, was locked up in my writing-desk; and I, trusting that I had written enough, though but a few lines, to satisfy her, remained without any uneasiness. — I was rather disappointed that I did not hear from her again speedily; but I made excuses for her, and was too busy, and — may I add? — too cheerful in my views to be captious. — We removed to Windsor; and two days afterwards I received a parcel from her, my own letters all returned! — and a few lines at the same time by the post, stating her extreme surprise at not having had the smallest reply to her last; and adding, that as silence on such a point could not be misconstrued, and as it must be equally desirable to both to have every subordinate arrangement concluded as soon as possible, she now sent me, by a safe conveyance, all my letters, and requested, that if I could not directly command her's, so as to send them to Highbury within a week, I would forward them after that period to her at ——— : in short, the full direction to Mr. Smallridge's, near Bristol, stared me in the face. I knew the name, the place, I knew all about it, and instantly saw what she had been doing. It was perfectly accordant with that resolution of character which I knew her to possess; and the secrecy she had maintained, as to any such design in her former letter, was equally descriptive of its anxious delicacy. For the world would not she have seemed to threaten me. — Imagine the shock; imagine how, till I had actually detected my own blunder, I raved at the blunders of the post. — What was to be done? — One thing only. — I must speak to my uncle. Without his sanction I could not hope to be listened to again. — I spoke; circumstances were in my favour; the late event had softened away his pride, and he was, earlier than I could have anticipated, wholly reconciled and complying; and could say at last, poor man! with a deep sigh, that he wished I might find as much happiness in the marriage state as he had done. — I felt that it would be of a different sort. — Are you disposed to pity me for what I must have suffered in opening the cause to him, for my suspense while all was at stake? — No; do not pity me till I reached Highbury, and saw how ill I had made her. Do not pity me till I saw her wan, sick looks. — I reached Highbury at the time of day when, from my knowledge of their late breakfast hour, I was certain of a good chance of finding her alone. — I was not disappointed; and at last I was not disappointed either in the object of my journey. A great deal of very reasonable, very just displeasure I had to persuade away. But it is done; we are reconciled, dearer, much dearer, than ever, and no moment's uneasiness can ever occur between us again. Now, my dear madam, I will release you; but I could not conclude before. A thousand and a thousand thanks for all the kindness you have ever shown me, and ten thousand for the attentions your heart will dictate towards her. — If you think me in a way to be happier than I deserve, I am quite of your opinion. — Miss W. calls me the child of good fortune. I hope she is right. — In one respect, my good fortune is undoubted, that of being able to subscribe myself,

Your obliged and affectionate Son,

F. C. Weston Churchill.

CHAPTER XV.

This letter must make its way to Emma's feelings. She was obliged, in spite of her previous determination to the contrary, to do it all the justice that Mrs. Weston foretold. As soon as she came to her own name, it was irresistible; every line relating to herself was interesting, and almost every line agreeable; and when this charm ceased, the subject could still maintain itself, by the natural return of her former regard for the writer, and the very strong attraction which any picture of love must have for her at that moment. She never stopt till she had gone through the whole; and though it was impossible not to feel that he had been wrong, yet he had been less wrong than she had supposed — and he had suffered, and was very sorry — and he was so grateful to Mrs.

Weston, and so much in love with Miss Fairfax, and she was so happy herself, that there was no being severe; and could he have entered the room, she must have shaken hands with him as heartily as ever.

She thought so well of the letter, that when Mr. Knightley came again, she desired him to read it. She was sure of Mrs. Weston's wishing it to be communicated; especially to one, who, like Mr. Knightley, had seen so much to blame in his conduct.

"I shall be very glad to look it over," said he, "but it seems long. I will take it home with me at night."

But that would not do. Mr. Weston was to call in the evening, and she must return it by him.

"I would rather be talking to you," he replied; "but as it seems a matter of justice, it shall be done."

He began — stopping, however, almost directly to say, "Had I been offered the sight of one of this gentleman's letters to his mother-in-law a few months ago, Emma, it would not have been taken with such indifference."

He proceeded a little farther, reading to himself; and then, with a smile, observed, "Humph! — a fine complimentary opening: — But it is his way. One man's style must not be the rule of another's. We will not be severe."

"It will be natural for me," he added shortly afterwards, "to speak my opinion aloud as I read. By doing it, I shall feel that I am near you. It will not be so great a loss of time: but if you dislike it ——"

"Not at all. I should wish it."

Mr. Knightley returned to his reading with greater alacrity.

"He trifles here," said he, "as to the temptation. He knows he is wrong, and has nothing rational to urge. — Bad. — He ought not to have formed the engagement. — 'His father's disposition:' — he is unjust, however, to his father. Mr. Weston's sanguine temper was a blessing on all his upright and honourable exertions; but Mr. Weston earned every present comfort before he endeavoured to gain it. — Very true; he did not come till Miss Fairfax was here."

"And I have not forgotten," said Emma, "how sure you were that he might have come sooner if he would. You pass it over very handsomely — but you were perfectly right."

"I was not quite impartial in my judgment, Emma: — but yet, I think — had *you* not been in the case — I should still have distrusted him."

When he came to Miss Woodhouse, he was obliged to read the whole of it aloud — all that related to her, with a smile; a look; a shake of the head; a word or two of assent, or disapprobation; or merely of love, as the subject required; concluding, however, seriously, and, after steady reflection, thus —

"Very bad — though it might have been worse. — Playing a most dangerous game. Too much indebted to the event for his acquittal. — No judge of his own manners by you. — Always deceived in fact by his own wishes, and regardless of little besides his own convenience. — Fancying you to have fathomed his secret. Natural enough! — his own mind full of intrigue, that he should suspect it in others. — Mystery; Finesse — how they pervert the understanding! My Emma, does not every thing serve to prove more and more the beauty of truth and sincerity in all our dealings with each other?"

Emma agreed to it, and with a blush of sensibility on Harriet's account, which she could not give any sincere explanation of.

"You had better go on," said she.

He did so, but very soon stopt again to say, "the piano-forte! Ah! That was the act of a very, very young man, one too young to consider whether the inconvenience of it might not very much exceed the pleasure. A boyish scheme, indeed! — I cannot comprehend a man's wishing to give a woman any proof of affection which he knows she would rather dispense with; and he did know that she would have prevented the instrument's coming if she could."

After this, he made some progress without any pause. Frank Churchill's confession of having behaved shamefully was the first thing to call for more than a word in passing.

"I perfectly agree with you, sir," — was then his remark. "You did behave very shamefully. You never wrote a truer line." And having gone through what immediately followed of the basis of their disagreement, and his persisting to act in direct opposition to Jane Fairfax's sense of right, he made a fuller pause to say, "This is very bad. — He had induced her to place herself, for his sake, in a situation of extreme difficulty and uneasiness, and it should have been his first object to prevent her from suffering unnecessarily. — She must have had much more to contend with, in carrying on the correspondence, than he could. He should have respected even unreasonable scruples, had there been such; but her's were all reasonable. We must look to her one fault, and remember that she had done a wrong thing in consenting to the engagement, to bear that she should have been in such a state of punishment."

Emma knew that he was now getting to the Box-Hill party, and grew uncomfortable. Her own behaviour had been so very improper!

She was deeply ashamed, and a little afraid of his next look. It was all read, however, steadily, attentively, and without the smallest remark; and, excepting one momentary glance at her, instantly withdrawn, in the fear of giving pain — no remembrance of Box-Hill seemed to exist.

"There is no saying much for the delicacy of our good friends, the Eltons," was his next observation. — "His feelings are natural. — What! actually resolve to break with him entirely! — She felt the engagement to be a source of repentance and misery to each — she dissolved it. — What a view this gives of her sense of his behaviour! — Well, he must be a most extraordinary ——"

"Nay, nay, read on. — You will find how very much he suffers."

"I hope he does," replied Mr. Knightley coolly, and resuming the letter. — "'Smallridge!' — What does this mean? What is all this?"

"She had engaged to go as governess to Mrs. Smallridge's children — a dear friend of Mrs. Elton's — a neighbour of Maple Grove; and, by the bye, I wonder how Mrs. Elton bears the disappointment."

"Say nothing, my dear Emma, while you oblige me to read — not even of Mrs. Elton. Only one page more. I shall soon have done. What a letter the man writes!"

"I wish you would read it with a kinder spirit towards him."

"Well, there is feeling here. He does seem to have suffered in finding her ill. — Certainly, I can have no doubt of his being fond of her. 'Dearer, much dearer than ever.' I hope he may long continue to feel all the value of such a reconciliation. — He is a very liberal thanker, with his thousands and tens of thousands. — 'Happier than I deserve.' Come, he knows himself there. 'Miss Woodhouse calls me the child of good fortune.' — Those were Miss Woodhouse's words, were they? — And a fine ending — and there is the letter. The child of good fortune! That was your name for him, was it?"

"You do not appear so well satisfied with his letter as I am; but still you must, at least I hope you must, think the better of him for it. I hope it does him some service with you."

"Yes, certainly it does. He has had great faults, faults of inconsideration and thoughtlessness; and I am very much of his opinion in thinking him likely to be happier than he deserves: but still as he is, beyond a doubt, really attached to Miss Fairfax, and will soon, it may be hoped, have the advantage of being constantly with her, I am very ready to believe his character will improve, and acquire from her's the steadiness and delicacy of principle that it wants. And now, let me talk to you of something else. I have another person's interest at present so much at heart, that I cannot think any longer about Frank Churchill. Ever since

I left you this morning, Emma, my mind has been hard at work on one subject."

The subject followed; it was in plain, unaffected, gentleman-like English, such as Mr. Knightley used even to the woman he was in love with, how to be able to ask her to marry him, without attacking the happiness of her father. Emma's answer was ready at the first word. "While her dear father lived, any change of condition must be impossible for her. She could never quit him." Part only of this answer, however, was admitted. The impossibility of her quitting her father, Mr. Knightley felt as strongly as herself; but the inadmissibility of any other change, he could not agree to. He had been thinking it over most deeply, most intently; he had at first hoped to induce Mr. Woodhouse to remove with her to Donwell; he had wanted to believe it feasible, but his knowledge of Mr. Woodhouse would not suffer him to deceive himself long; and now he confessed his persuasion, that such a transplantation would be a risk of her father's comfort, perhaps even of his life, which must not be hazarded. Mr. Woodhouse taken from Hartfield! — No, he felt that it ought not to be attempted. But the plan which had arisen on the sacrifice of this, he trusted his dearest Emma would not find in any respect objectionable; it was, that he should be received at Hartfield; that so long as her father's happiness — in other words his life — required Hartfield to continue her home, it should be his likewise.

Of their all removing to Donwell, Emma had already had her own passing thoughts. Like him, she had tried the scheme and rejected it; but such an alternative as this had not occurred to her. She was sensible of all the affection it evinced. She felt that, in quitting Donwell, he must be sacrificing a great deal of independence of hours and habits; that in living constantly with her father, and in no house of his own, there would be much, very much, to be borne with. She promised to think of it, and advised him to think of it more; but he was fully convinced, that no reflection could alter his wishes or his opinion on the subject. He had given it, he could assure her, very long and calm consideration; he had been walking away from William Larkins the whole morning, to have his thoughts to himself.

"Ah! there is one difficulty unprovided for," cried Emma. "I am sure William Larkins will not like it. You must get his consent before you ask mine."

She promised, however, to think of it; and pretty nearly promised, moreover, to think of it, with the intention of finding it a very good scheme.

It is remarkable, that Emma, in the many, very many, points of view in which she was now beginning to consider Donwell Abbey, was never struck with any sense of injury to her nephew Henry, whose rights as heir expectant had formerly been so tenaciously regarded. Think she must of the possible difference to the poor little boy; and yet she only gave herself a saucy conscious smile about it, and found amusement in detecting the real cause of that violent dislike of Mr. Knightley's marrying Jane Fairfax, or any body else, which at the time she had wholly imputed to the amiable solicitude of the sister and the aunt.

This proposal of his, this plan of marrying and continuing at Hartfield — the more she contemplated it, the more pleasing it became. His evils seemed to lessen, her own advantages to increase, their mutual good to outweigh every drawback. Such a companion for herself in the periods of anxiety and cheerlessness before her! — Such a partner in all those duties and cares to which time must be giving increase of melancholy!

She would have been too happy but for poor Harriet; but every blessing of her own seemed to involve and advance the sufferings of her friend, who must now be even excluded from Hartfield. The delightful family-party which Emma was securing for herself, poor Harriet must, in mere charitable caution, be kept at a distance from. She would be a loser in every way. Emma could not deplore her future absence as any deduction from her own enjoyment. In such a party, Harriet would be rather a dead weight than otherwise; but for the poor girl herself, it seemed a peculiarly cruel necessity that was to be placing her in such a state of unmerited punishment.

In time, of course, Mr. Knightley would be forgotten, that is, supplanted; but this could not be expected to happen very early. Mr. Knightley himself would be doing nothing to assist the cure; — not like Mr. Elton. Mr. Knightley, always so kind, so feeling, so truly considerate for every body, would never deserve to be less worshipped than now; and it really was too much to hope even of Harriet, that she could be in love with more than *three* men in one year.

CHAPTER XVI.

It was a very great relief to Emma to find Harriet as desirous as herself to avoid a meeting. Their intercourse was painful enough by letter. How much worse, had they been obliged to meet!

Harriet expressed herself very much, as might be supposed, without reproaches, or apparent sense of ill usage; and yet Emma fancied there was a something of resentment, a something bordering on it in her style, which increased the desirableness of their being separate. — It might be only her own consciousness; but it seemed as if an angel only could have been quite without resentment under such a stroke.

She had no difficulty in procuring Isabella's invitation; and she was fortunate in having a sufficient reason for asking it, without resorting to invention. — There was a tooth amiss. Harriet really wished, and had wished some time, to consult a dentist. Mrs. John Knightley was delighted to be of use; any thing of ill-health was a recommendation to her — and though not so fond of a dentist as of a Mr. Wingfield, she was quite eager to have Harriet under her care. — When it was thus settled on her sister's side, Emma proposed it to her friend, and found her very persuadable. — Harriet was to go; she was invited for at least a fortnight; she was to be conveyed in Mr. Woodhouse's carriage. — It was all arranged, it was all completed, and Harriet was safe in Brunswick Square.

Now Emma could, indeed, enjoy Mr. Knightley's visits; now she could talk, and she could listen with true happiness, unchecked by that sense of injustice, of guilt, of something most painful, which had haunted her when remembering how disappointed a heart was near her, how much might at that moment, and at a little distance, be enduring by the feelings which she had led astray herself.

The difference of Harriet at Mrs. Goddard's, or in London, made perhaps an unreasonable difference in Emma's sensations; but she could not think of her in London without objects of curiosity and employment, which must be averting the past, and carrying her out of herself.

She would not allow any other anxiety to succeed directly to the place in her mind which Harriet had occupied. There was a communication before her, one which *she* only could be competent to make — the confession of her engagement to her father; but she would have nothing to do with it at present. — She had resolved to defer the disclosure till Mrs. Weston were safe and well. No additional agitation should be thrown at this period among those she loved — and the evil should not act on herself by anticipation before the appointed time. — A fortnight, at least, of leisure and peace of mind, to crown every warmer, but more agitating, delight, should be her's.

She soon resolved, equally as a duty and a pleasure, to employ half an hour of this holiday of spirits in calling on Miss Fairfax. — She ought to go — and she was longing to see her; the resemblance of their present situations increasing every other motive of good will. It would be a *secret* satisfaction; but the consciousness of a similarity of prospect would certainly add to the interest with which she should attend to any thing Jane might communicate.

She went — she had driven once unsuccessfully to the door, but had not been into the house since the morning after Box-Hill, when poor Jane had been in such distress as had filled her with compassion, though all the worst of her sufferings had been unsuspected. — The fear of being still unwelcome, determined her, though assured of their being at home, to wait in the passage, and send up her name. — She heard Patty announcing it; but no such bustle succeeded as poor Miss Bates had before made so happily intelligible. — No; she heard nothing but the instant reply of, "Beg her to walk up;" — and a moment afterwards she was met on the stairs by Jane herself, coming eagerly forward, as if no other reception of her were felt sufficient. — Emma had never seen her look so well, so lovely, so engaging. There was consciousness, animation, and warmth; there was every thing which her countenance or manner could ever have wanted. — She came forward with an offered hand; and said, in a low, but very feeling tone,

"This is most kind, indeed! — Miss Woodhouse, it is impossible for me to express —— I hope you will believe —— Excuse me for being so entirely without words."

Emma was gratified, and would soon have shown no want of words, if the sound of Mrs. Elton's voice from the sitting-room had not checked her, and made it expedient to compress all her friendly and all her congratulatory sensations into a very, very earnest shake of the hand.

Mrs. Bates and Mrs. Elton were together. Miss Bates was out, which accounted for the previous tranquillity. Emma could have wished Mrs. Elton elsewhere; but she was in a humour to have patience with every body; and as Mrs. Elton met her with unusual graciousness, she hoped the rencontre would do them no harm.

She soon believed herself to penetrate Mrs. Elton's thoughts, and understand why she was, like herself, in happy spirits; it was being in Miss Fairfax's confidence, and fancying herself acquainted with what was still a secret to other people. Emma saw symptoms of it immediately in the expression of her face; and while paying her own compliments to Mrs. Bates, and appearing to attend to the good old lady's replies, she saw her with a sort of anxious parade of mystery fold up a letter which she had apparently been reading aloud to Miss Fairfax, and return it into the purple and gold ridicule[146] by her side, saying, with significant nods,

"We can finish this some other time, you know. You and I shall not want opportunities. And, in fact, you have heard all the essential already. I only wanted to prove to you that Mrs. S. admits our apology, and is not offended. You see how delightfully she writes. Oh! she is a sweet creature! You would have doated on her, had you gone. — But not a word more. Let us be discreet — quite on our good behaviour. — Hush! — You remember those lines — I forget the poem at this moment:

"For when a lady's in the case,
"You know all other things give place."[147]

Now I say, my dear, in *our* case, for *lady*, read — mum! a word to the wise. — I am in a fine flow of spirits, an't I? But I want to set your heart at ease as to Mrs. S. — *My* representation, you see, has quite appeased her."

And again, on Emma's merely turning her head to look at Mrs. Bates's knitting, she added, in a half whisper,

"I mentioned no *names*, you will observe. — Oh! no; cautious as a minister of state. I managed it extremely well."

Emma could not doubt. It was a palpable display, repeated on every possible occasion. When they had all talked a little while in harmony of the weather and Mrs. Weston, she found herself abruptly addressed with,

"Do not you think, Miss Woodhouse, our saucy little friend here is charmingly recovered? — Do not you think her cure does Perry the highest credit? — (here was a side-glance of great meaning at Jane.) Upon my word, Perry has restored her in a wonderful short time! — Oh! if you had seen her, as I did, when she was at the worst!" — And when Mrs. Bates was saying something to Emma, whispered farther, "We do not say a word of any *assistance* that Perry might have; not a word of a certain young physician from Windsor. — Oh! no; Perry shall have all the credit."

"I have scarce had the pleasure of seeing you, Miss Woodhouse," she shortly afterwards began, "since the party to Box-Hill. Very pleas-

---

[146] *ridicule:* (Usually reticule), the name for a lady's small handbag made of woven material.
[147] *"For when a lady's in the case . . . ":* See note 30, p. 71.

ant party. But yet I think there was something wanting. Things did not seem — that is, there seemed a little cloud upon the spirits of some. — So it appeared to me at least, but I might be mistaken. However, I think it answered so far as to tempt one to go again. What say you both to our collecting the same party, and exploring to Box-Hill again, while the fine weather lasts? — It must be the same party, you know, quite the same party, not *one* exception."

Soon after this Miss Bates came in, and Emma could not help being diverted by the perplexity of her first answer to herself, resulting, she supposed, from doubt of what might be said, and impatience to say every thing.

"Thank you, dear Miss Woodhouse, you are all kindness. — It is impossible to say — Yes, indeed, I quite understand — dearest Jane's prospects — that is, I do not mean. — But she is charmingly recovered. — How is Mr. Woodhouse? — I am so glad. — Quite out of my power. — Such a happy little circle as you find us here. — Yes, indeed. — Charming young man! — that is — so very friendly; I mean good Mr. Perry! — such attention to Jane!" — And from her great, her more than commonly thankful delight towards Mrs. Elton for being there, Emma guessed that there had been a little show of resentment towards Jane, from the vicarage quarter, which was now graciously overcome. — After a few whispers, indeed, which placed it beyond a guess, Mrs. Elton, speaking louder, said,

"Yes, here I am, my good friend; and here I have been so long, that anywhere else I should think it necessary to apologize: but the truth is, that I am waiting for my lord and master. He promised to join me here, and pay his respects to you."

"What! are we to have the pleasure of a call from Mr. Elton? — That will be a favour indeed! for I know gentlemen do not like morning visits, and Mr. Elton's time is so engaged."

"Upon my word it is, Miss Bates. — He really is engaged from morning to night. — There is no end of people's coming to him, on some pretence or other. — The magistrates, and overseers, and church-wardens, are always wanting his opinion. They seem not able to do any thing without him. — 'Upon my word, Mr. E., I often say, rather you than I. — I do not know what would become of my crayons and my instrument, if I had half so many applicants.' — Bad enough as it is, for I absolutely neglect them both to an unpardonable degree. — I believe I have not played a bar this fortnight. — However, he is coming, I assure you: yes, indeed, on purpose to wait on you all." — And putting up her hand to screen her words from Emma — "A congratulatory visit, you know. — Oh! yes, quite indispensable."

Miss Bates looked about her, so happily! —

"He promised to come to me as soon as he could disengage himself from Knightley; but he and Knightley are shut up together in deep consultation. — Mr. E. is Knightley's right hand."

Emma would not have smiled for the world, and only said, "Is Mr. Elton gone on foot to Donwell? — He will have a hot walk."

"Oh! no, it is a meeting at the Crown, a regular meeting. Weston and Cole will be there too; but one is apt to speak only of those who lead. — I fancy Mr. E. and Knightley have every thing their own way."

"Have not you mistaken the day?" said Emma. I am almost certain that the meeting at the Crown is not till to-morrow. — Mr. Knightley was at Hartfield yesterday, and spoke of it as for Saturday."

"Oh! no; the meeting is certainly to-day," was the abrupt answer, which denoted the impossibility of any blunder on Mrs. Elton's side. — "I do believe," she continued, "this is the most troublesome parish that ever was. We never heard of such things at Maple Grove."

"Your parish there was small," said Jane.

"Upon my word, my dear, I do not know, for I never heard the subject talked of."

"But it is proved by the smallness of the school, which I have heard you speak of, as under the patronage of your sister and Mrs. Bragge; the only school, and not more than five-and-twenty children."

"Ah! you clever creature, that's very true. What a thinking brain you have! I say, Jane, what a perfect character you and I should make, if we could be shaken together. My liveliness and your solidity would produce perfection. — Not that I presume to insinuate, however, that *some* people may not think *you* perfection already. — But hush! — not a word, if you please."

It seemed an unnecessary caution; Jane was wanting to give her words, not to Mrs. Elton, but to Miss Woodhouse, as the latter plainly saw. The wish of distinguishing her, as far as civility permitted, was very evident, though it could not often proceed beyond a look.

Mr. Elton made his appearance. His lady greeted him with some of her sparkling vivacity.

"Very pretty, sir, upon my word; to send me on here, to be an encumbrance to my friends, so long before you vouchsafe to come! — But you knew what a dutiful creature you had to deal with. You knew I should not stir till my lord and master appeared. — Here have I been sitting this hour, giving these young ladies a sample of true conjugal obedience — for who can say, you know, how soon it may be wanted?"

Mr. Elton was so hot and tired, that all this wit seemed thrown away. His civilities to the other ladies must be paid; but his subsequent object was to lament over himself for the heat he was suffering, and the walk he had had for nothing.

"When I got to Donwell," said he, "Knightley could not be found. Very odd! very unaccountable! after the note I sent him this morning, and the message he returned, that he should certainly be at home till one."

"Donwell!" cried his wife — "My dear Mr. E., you have not been to Donwell! — You mean the Crown; you come from the meeting at the Crown."

"No, no, that's to-morrow; and I particularly wanted to see Knightley to-day on that very account. — Such a dreadful broiling morning! — I went over the fields too — (speaking in a tone of great ill usage,) which made it so much the worse. And then not to find him at home! I assure you I am not at all pleased. And no apology left, no message for me. The housekeeper declared she knew nothing of my being expected. — Very extraordinary! — And nobody knew at all which way he was gone. Perhaps to Hartfield, perhaps to the Abbey Mill, perhaps into his woods. — Miss Woodhouse, this is not like our friend Knightley. — Can you explain it?"

Emma amused herself by protesting that it was very extraordinary indeed, and that she had not a syllable to say for him.

"I cannot imagine," cried Mrs. Elton, (feeling the indignity as a wife ought to do,) "I cannot imagine how he could do such a thing by you, of all people in the world! The very last person whom one should expect to be forgotten! — My dear Mr. E., he must have left a message for you, I am sure he must. — Not even Knightley could be so very eccentric; — and his servants forgot it. Depend upon it, that was the case: and very likely to happen with the Donwell servants, who are all, I have often observed, extremely awkward and remiss. — I am sure I would not have such a creature as his Harry stand at our sideboard for any consideration. And as for Mrs. Hodges, Wright holds her very cheap indeed. — She promised Wright a receipt,[148] and never sent it."

---

[148] *receipt:* The usual meaning at this time is recipe, but the more modern meaning of "a written acknowledgment of money or goods" is not entirely implausible, given the hostility between Mrs. Elton and Mrs. Hodges.

"I met William Larkins," continued Mr. Elton, "as I got near the house, and he told me I should not find his master at home, but I did not believe him. — William seemed rather out of humour. He did not know what was come to his master lately, he said, but he could hardly ever get the speech of him. I have nothing to do with William's wants, but it really is of very great importance that I should see Knightley to day; and it becomes a matter, therefore, of very serious inconvenience that I should have had this hot walk to no purpose."

Emma felt that she could not do better than go home directly. In all probability she was at this very time waited for there; and Mr. Knightley might be preserved from sinking deeper in aggression towards Mr. Elton, if not towards William Larkins.

She was pleased, on taking leave, to find Miss Fairfax determined to attend her out of the room, to go with her even down stairs; it gave her an opportunity which she immediately made use of, to say,

"It is as well, perhaps, that I have not had the possibility. Had you not been surrounded by other friends, I might have been tempted to introduce a subject, to ask questions, to speak more openly than might have been strictly correct. — I feel that I should certainly have been impertinent."

"Oh!" cried Jane, with a blush and an hesitation which Emma thought infinitely more becoming to her than all the elegance of all her usual composure — "there would have been no danger. The danger would have been of my wearying you. You could not have gratified me more than by expressing an interest —— . Indeed, Miss Woodhouse, (speaking more collectedly,) with the consciousness which I have of misconduct, very great misconduct, it is particularly consoling to me to know that those of my friends, whose good opinion is most worth pre-serving, are not disgusted to such a degree as to — I have not time for half that I could wish to say. I long to make apologies, excuses, to urge something for myself. I feel it so very due. But, unfortunately — in short, if your compassion does not stand my friend ——"

"Oh! you are too scrupulous, indeed you are," cried Emma, warmly, and taking her hand. "You owe me no apologies; and every body to whom you might be supposed to owe them, is so perfectly sat-isfied, so delighted even —"

"You are very kind, but I know what my manners were to you. — So cold and artificial! — I had always a part to act. — It was a life of deceit! — I know that I must have disgusted you."

"Pray say no more. I feel that all the apologies should be on my side. Let us forgive each other at once. We must do whatever is to be done quickest, and I think our feelings will lose no time there. I hope you have pleasant accounts from Windsor?"

"Very."

"And the next news, I suppose, will be, that we are to lose you — just as I begin to know you."

"Oh! as to all that, of course nothing can be thought of yet. I am here till claimed by Colonel and Mrs. Campbell."

"Nothing can be actually settled yet, perhaps," replied Emma, smiling — "but, excuse me, it must be thought of."

The smile was returned as Jane answered,

"You are very right; it has been thought of. And I will own to you, (I am sure it will be safe), that so far as our living with Mr. Churchill at Enscombe, it is settled. There must be three months, at least, of deep mourning; but when they are over, I imagine there will be nothing more to wait for."

"Thank you, thank you. — This is just what I wanted to be assured of. — Oh! if you knew how much I love every thing that is decided and open! — Good bye, good bye."

CHAPTER XVII.

MRS. WESTON's friends were all made happy by her safety; and if the satisfaction of her well-doing could be increased to Emma, it was by knowing her to be the mother of a little girl. She had been decided in wishing for a Miss Weston. She would not acknowledge that it was with any view of making a match for her, hereafter, with either of Isabella's sons; but she was convinced that a daughter would suit both father and mother best. It would be a great comfort to Mr. Weston as he grew older — and even Mr. Weston might be growing older ten years hence — to have his fireside enlivened by the sports and the nonsense, the freaks and the fancies of a child never banished from home;[149] and Mrs. Weston — no one could doubt that a daughter would be most to her; and it would be quite a pity that any one who so well knew how to teach, should not have their powers in exercise again.

"She has had the advantage, you know, of practising on me," she continued — "like La Baronne d'Almane on La Comtesse d'Ostalis, in

---

[149] *never banished from home:* As Jane Austen may have wished had been the case in her youth. With Cassandra, she was sent to boarding schools in Oxford and Southampton (1783) and in Reading (1785–86).

Madame de Genlis' Adelaide and Theodore,[150] and we shall now see
her own little Adelaide educated on a more perfect plan."

"That is," replied Mr. Knightley, "she will indulge her even more
than she did you, and believe that she does not indulge her at all. It will
be the only difference."

"Poor child!" cried Emma; "at that rate, what will become of her?"

"Nothing very bad. — The fate of thousands. She will be disagreeable in infancy, and correct herself as she grows older. I am losing all my
bitterness against spoilt children, my dearest Emma, I, who am owing
all my happiness to *you*, would not it be horrible ingratitude in me to be
severe on them?"

Emma laughed, and replied: "But I had the assistance of all your
endeavours to counteract the indulgence of other people. I doubt
whether my own sense would have corrected me without it."

"Do you? — I have no doubt. Nature gave you understanding: —
Miss Taylor gave you principles. You must have done well. My interference was quite as likely to do harm as good. It was very natural for you
to say, what right has he to lecture me? — and I am afraid very natural
for you to feel that it was done in a disagreeable manner. I do not
believe I did you any good. The good was all to myself, by making you
an object of the tenderest affection to me. I could not think about you
so much without doating on you, faults and all; and by dint of fancying
so many errors, have been in love with you ever since you were thirteen
at least."

"I am sure you were of use to me," cried Emma. "I was very often
influenced rightly by you — oftener than I would own at the time. I am
very sure you did me good. And if poor little Anna Weston is to be
spoiled, it will be the greatest humanity in you to do as much for her
as you have done for me, except falling in love with her when she is
thirteen."

"How often, when you were a girl, have you said to me, with one of
your saucy looks — 'Mr. Knightley, I am going to do so and so; papa
says I may, or, I have Miss Taylor's leave' — something which, you
knew, I did not approve. In such cases my interference was giving you
two bad feelings instead of one."

---

[150]*Adelaide and Theodore:* 1783 translation of *Adèle et Théodore, ou Lettres sur L'Éd-
ucation* (3 vols., 1782) by Madame de Genlis (Stéphanie Félicité du Crest de Genlis
[1746–1830]). For a discussion of Austen's indebtedness to, and creative rewriting of,
this pedagogical novel, see Susan Allen Ford, "Romance, Pedagogy and Power: Jane
Austen Re-writes Madame de Genlis," *Persuasions* 21 (1999) 172–87.

"What an amiable creature I was! — No wonder you should hold my speeches in such affectionate remembrance."

"'Mr. Knightley.' — You always called me, 'Mr. Knightley;' and, from habit, it has not so very formal a sound. — And yet it is formal. I want you to call me something else, but I do not know what."

"I remember once calling you 'George,' in one of my amiable fits, about ten years ago. I did it because I thought it would offend you; but, as you made no objection, I never did it again."

"And cannot you call me 'George' now?"

"Impossible! — I never can call you any thing but 'Mr. Knightley.' I will not promise even to equal the elegant terseness of Mrs. Elton, by calling you Mr. K. — But I will promise," she added presently, laughing and blushing — "I will promise to call you once by your Christian name. I do not say when, but perhaps you may guess where; — in the building in which N. takes M. for better, for worse."[151]

Emma grieved that she could not be more openly just to one important service which his better sense would have rendered her, to the advice which would have saved her from the worst of all her womanly follies — her wilful intimacy with Harriet Smith; but it was too tender a subject. — She could not enter on it. — Harriet was very seldom mentioned between them. This, on his side, might merely proceed from her not being thought of; but Emma was rather inclined to attribute it to delicacy, and a suspicion, from some appearances, that their friendship were declining. She was aware herself, that, parting under any other circumstances, they certainly should have corresponded more, and that her intelligence would not have rested, as it now almost wholly did, on Isabella's letters. He might observe that it was so. The pain of being obliged to practise concealment towards him, was very little inferior to the pain of having made Harriet unhappy.

Isabella sent quite as good an account of her visitor as could be expected; on her first arrival she had thought her out of spirits, which appeared perfectly natural, as there was a dentist to be consulted; but, since that business had been over, she did not appear to find Harriet different from what she had known her before. — Isabella, to be sure, was no very quick observer; yet if Harriet had not been equal to playing with the children, it would not have escaped her. Emma's comforts and

---

[151] *in which N. takes M. for better, for worse:* Another example of phonetic wordplay, similar to Mr. Weston's conundrum about "M." and "A." (note 133, p. 297) but here affirmed by association with the marriage ceremony in the Anglican *Book of Common Prayer.* For the text of *The Form of Solemnization of Matrimony,* see <www.pemberley.com /janeinfo/compraym.html>.

hopes were most agreeably carried on, by Harriet's being to stay longer; her fortnight was likely to be a month at least. Mr. and Mrs. John Knightley were to come down in August, and she was invited to remain till they could bring her back.

"John does not even mention your friend," said Mr. Knightley. "Here is his answer, if you like to see it."

It was the answer to the communication of his intended marriage. Emma accepted it with a very eager hand, with an impatience all alive to know what he would say about it, and not at all checked by hearing that her friend was unmentioned.

"John enters like a brother into my happiness," continued Mr. Knightley, "but he is no complimenter; and though I well know him to have, likewise, a most brotherly affection for you, he is so far from making flourishes, that any other young woman might think him rather cool in her praise. But I am not afraid of your seeing what he writes."

"He writes like a sensible man," replied Emma, when she had read the letter. "I honour his sincerity. It is very plain that he considers the good fortune of the engagement as all on my side, but that he is not without hope of my growing, in time, as worthy of your affection, as you think me already. Had he said any thing to bear a different construction, I should not have believed him."

"My Emma, he means no such thing. He only means ——"

"He and I should differ very little in our estimation of the two," — interrupted she, with a sort of serious smile — "much less, perhaps, than he is aware of, if we could enter without ceremony or reserve on the subject."

"Emma, my dear Emma ——"

"Oh!" she cried with more thorough gaiety, "if you fancy your brother does not do me justice, only wait till my dear father is in the secret, and hear his opinion. Depend upon it, he will be much farther from doing *you* justice. He will think all the happiness, all the advantage, on your side of the question; all the merit on mine. I wish I may not sink into 'poor Emma' with him at once. — His tender compassion towards oppressed worth can go no farther."

"Ah!" he cried, "I wish your father might be half as easily convinced as John will be, of our having every right that equal worth can give, to be happy together. I am amused by one part of John's letter — did you notice it? — where he says, that my information did not take him wholly by surprise, that he was rather in expectation of hearing something of the kind."

"If I understand your brother, he only means so far as your having some thoughts of marrying. He had no idea of me. He seems perfectly unprepared for that."

"Yes, yes — but I am amused that he should have seen so far into my feelings. What has he been judging by? — I am not conscious of any difference in my spirits or conversation that could prepare him at this time for my marrying any more than at another. — But it was so, I suppose. I dare say there was a difference when I was staying with them the other day. I believe I did not play with the children quite so much as usual. I remember one evening the poor boys saying, 'Uncle seems always tired now.'"

The time was coming when the news must be spread farther, and other persons' reception of it tried. As soon as Mrs. Weston was sufficiently recovered to admit Mr. Woodhouse's visits, Emma having it in view that her gentle reasonings should be employed in the cause, resolved first to announce it at home, and then at Randalls. — But how to break it to her father at last! — She had bound herself to do it, in such an hour of Mr. Knightley's absence, or when it came to the point her heart would have failed her, and she must have put it off; but Mr. Knightley was to come at such a time, and follow up the beginning she was to make. — She was forced to speak, and to speak cheerfully too. She must not make it a more decided subject of misery to him, by a melancholy tone herself. She must not appear to think it a misfortune. — With all the spirits she could command, she prepared him first for something strange, and then, in few words, said, that if his consent and approbation could be obtained — which, she trusted, would be attended with no difficulty, since it was a plan to promote the happiness of all — she and Mr. Knightley meant to marry; by which means Hartfield would receive the constant addition of that person's company whom she knew he loved, next to his daughters and Mrs. Weston, best in the world.

Poor man! — it was at first a considerable shock to him, and he tried earnestly to dissuade her from it. She was reminded, more than once, of her having always said she would never marry, and assured that it would be a great deal better for her to remain single; and told of poor Isabella, and poor Miss Taylor. — But it would not do. Emma hung about him affectionately, and smiled, and said it must be so; and that he must not class her with Isabella and Mrs. Weston, whose marriages taking them from Hartfield, had, indeed, made a melancholy change: but she was not going from Hartfield; she should be always there; she was

introducing no change in their numbers or their comforts but for the
better; and she was very sure that he would be a great deal the happier
for having Mr. Knightley always at hand, when he were once got used
to the idea. — Did not he love Mr. Knightley very much? — He would
not deny that he did, she was sure. — Whom did he ever want to consult on business but Mr. Knightley? — Who was so useful to him, who
so ready to write his letters, who so glad to assist him? — Who so cheerful, so attentive, so attached to him? — Would not he like to have him
always on the spot? — Yes. That was all very true. Mr. Knightley could
not be there too often; he should be glad to see him every day; — but
they did see him every day as it was. — Why could not they go on as
they had done?

Mr. Woodhouse could not be soon reconciled; but the worst was
overcome, the idea was given; time and continual repetition must
do the rest. — To Emma's entreaties and assurances succeeded Mr.
Knightley's, whose fond praise of her gave the subject even a kind of
welcome; and he was soon used to be talked to by each, on every fair
occasion. — They had all the assistance which Isabella could give, by
letters of the strongest approbation; and Mrs. Weston was ready, on the
first meeting, to consider the subject in the most serviceable light —
first, as a settled, and secondly, as a good one — well aware of the nearly
equal importance of the two recommendations to Mr. Woodhouse's
mind. — It was agreed upon, as what was to be; and every body by
whom he was used to be guided assuring him that it would be for his
happiness; and having some feelings himself which almost admitted it,
he began to think that some time or other — in another year or two,
perhaps — it might not be so very bad if the marriage did take place.

Mrs. Weston was acting no part, feigning no feelings in all that she
said to him in favour of the event. — She had been extremely surprised,
never more so, than when Emma first opened the affair to her; but she
saw in it only increase of happiness to all, and had no scruple in urging
him to the utmost. — She had such a regard for Mr. Knightley, as to
think he deserved even her dearest Emma; and it was in every respect so
proper, suitable, and unexceptionable a connexion, and in one respect,
one point of the highest importance, so peculiarly eligible, so singularly
fortunate, that now it seemed as if Emma could not safely have attached
herself to any other creature, and that she had herself been the stupidest
of beings in not having thought of it, and wished it long ago. — How
very few of those men in a rank of life to address Emma would have
renounced their own home for Hartfield! And who but Mr. Knightley
could know and bear with Mr. Woodhouse, so as to make such an

arrangement desirable! — The difficulty of disposing of poor Mr. Woodhouse had been always felt in her husband's plans and her own, for a marriage between Frank and Emma. How to settle the claims of Enscombe and Hartfield had been a continual impediment — less acknowledged by Mr. Weston than by herself — but even he had never been able to finish the subject better than by saying — "Those matters will take care of themselves; the young people will find a way." — But here there was nothing to be shifted off in a wild speculation on the future. It was all right, all open, all equal. No sacrifice on any side worth the name. It was a union of the highest promise of felicity in itself, and without one real, rational difficulty to oppose or delay it.

Mrs. Weston, with her baby on her knee, indulging in such reflections as these, was one of the happiest women in the world. If any thing could increase her delight, it was perceiving that the baby would soon have outgrown its first set of caps.

The news was universally a surprise wherever it spread; and Mr. Weston had his five minutes share of it; but five minutes were enough to familiarize the idea to his quickness of mind. — He saw the advantages of the match, and rejoiced in them with all the constancy of his wife; but the wonder of it was very soon nothing; and by the end of an hour he was not far from believing that he had always foreseen it.

"It is to be a secret, I conclude," said he. "These matters are always a secret, till it is found out that every body knows them. Only let me be told when I may speak out. — I wonder whether Jane has any suspicion."

He went to Highbury the next morning, and satisfied himself on that point. He told her the news. Was not she like a daughter, his eldest daughter? — he must tell her; and Miss Bates being present, It passed, of course, to Mrs. Cole, Mrs. Perry, and Mrs. Elton, immediately afterwards. It was no more than the principals were prepared for; they had calculated from the time of its being known at Randalls, how soon it would be over Highbury; and were thinking of themselves, as the evening wonder in many a family circle, with great sagacity.

In general, it was a very well approved match. Some might think him, and others might think her, the most in luck. One set might recommend their all removing to Donwell, and leaving Hartfield for the John Knightleys; and another might predict disagreements among their servants; but yet, upon the whole, there was no serious objection raised, except in one habitation, the vicarage. — There, the surprise was not softened by any satisfaction. Mr. Elton cared little about it, compared with his wife; he only hoped "the young lady's pride would now

be contented;" and supposed "she had always meant to catch Knightley
if she could;" and, on the point of living at Hartfield, could daringly
exclaim, "Rather he than I!" — But Mrs. Elton was very much discomposed indeed. — "Poor Knightley! poor fellow! — sad business for
him. — She was extremely concerned; for, though very eccentric, he
had a thousand good qualities. — How could he be so taken in? — Did
not think him at all in love — not in the least. — Poor Knightley! —
There would be an end of all pleasant intercourse with him. — How
happy he had been to come and dine with them whenever they asked
him! But that would be all over now. — Poor fellow! — No more
exploring parties to Donwell made for *her*. Oh! no; there would be a
Mrs. Knightley to throw cold water on every thing. — Extremely disagreeable! But she was not at all sorry that she had abused the housekeeper the other day. — Shocking plan, living together. It would never
do. She knew a family near Maple Grove who had tried it, and been
obliged to separate before the end of the first quarter."[152]

CHAPTER XVIII.

TIME passed on. A few more to-morrows, and the party from London
would be arriving. It was an alarming change; and Emma was thinking
of it one morning as what must bring a great deal to agitate and grieve
her, when Mr. Knightley came in, and distressing thoughts were put by.
After the first chat of pleasure he was silent; and then, in a graver tone,
began with,

"I have something to tell you, Emma; some news."

"Good or bad?" said she, quickly, looking up in his face.

"I do not know which it ought to be called."

"Oh! good I am sure. — I see it in your countenance. You are trying not to smile."

"I am afraid," said he, composing his features, "I am very much
afraid, my dear Emma, that you will not smile when you hear it."

"Indeed! but why so? — I can hardly imagine that any thing which
pleases or amuses you, should not please and amuse me too."

"There is one subject," he replied, "I hope but one, on which we
do not think alike." He paused a moment, again smiling, with his eyes
fixed on her face. "Does nothing occur to you? — Do not you recollect? — Harriet Smith."

---

[152]*of the first quarter"*: Emendation of the first edition, which has no closing double
quotes.

Her cheeks flushed at the name, and she felt afraid of something, though she knew not what.

"Have you heard from her yourself this morning?" cried he. "You have, I believe, and know the whole."

"No, I have not; I know nothing; pray tell me."

"You are prepared for the worst, I see — and very bad it is. Harriet Smith marries Robert Martin."

Emma gave a start, which did not seem like being prepared — and her eyes, in eager gaze, said, "No, this is impossible!" but her lips were closed.

"It is so, indeed," continued Mr. Knightley; "I have it from Robert Martin himself. He left me not half an hour ago."

She was still looking at him with the most speaking amazement.

"You like it, my Emma, as little as I feared. — I wish our opinions were the same. But in time they will. Time, you may be very sure, will make one or the other of us think differently; and, in the meanwhile, we need not talk much on the subject."

"You mistake me, you quite mistake me," she replied, exerting herself. "It is not that such a circumstance would now make me unhappy, but I cannot believe it. It seems an impossibility! — You cannot mean to say, that Harriet Smith has accepted Robert Martin. You cannot mean that he has even proposed to her again — yet. You only mean, that he intends it."

"I mean that he has done it," answered Mr. Knightley, with smiling but determined decision, "and been accepted."

"Good God!" she cried. — "Well!" — Then having recourse to her workbasket, in excuse for leaning down her face, and concealing all the exquisite feelings of delight and entertainment which she knew she must be expressing, she added, "Well, now tell me every thing; make this intelligible to me. How, where, when? — Let me know it all. I never was more surprised — but it does not make me unhappy, I assure you. — How — how has it been possible?"

"It is a very simple story. He went to town on business three days ago, and I got him to take charge of some papers which I was wanting to send to John. — He delivered these papers to John, at his chambers, and was asked by him to join their party the same evening to Astley's.[153] They were going to take the two eldest boys to Astley's. The party was to be our brother and sister, Henry, John —— and Miss Smith. My

---

[153] *Astley's:* Royal Amphiteatre founded in 1798 by Philip Astley (1742–1814), an equestrian performer and circus manager.

friend Robert could not resist. They called for him in their way; were all extremely amused; and my brother asked him to dine with them the next day — which he did — and in the course of that visit (as I understand) he found an opportunity of speaking to Harriet; and certainly did not speak in vain. — She made him, by her acceptance, as happy even as he is deserving. He came down by yesterday's coach, and was with me this morning immediately after breakfast, to report his proceedings, first on my affairs, and then on his own. This is all that I can relate of the how, where, and when. Your friend Harriet will make a much longer history when you see her. — She will give you all the minute particulars, which only woman's language can make interesting. — In our communications we deal only in the great. — However, I must say that Robert Martin's heart seemed for *him*, and to *me*, very overflowing; and that he did mention, without its being much to the purpose, that on quitting their box at Astley's, my brother took charge of Mrs. John Knightley and little John, and he followed with Miss Smith and Henry; and that at one time they were in such a crowd, as to make Miss Smith rather uneasy."

He stopped. — Emma dared not attempt any immediate reply. To speak, she was sure would be to betray a most unreasonable degree of happiness. She must wait a moment, or he would think her mad. Her silence disturbed him; and after observing her a little while, he added,

"Emma, my love, you said that this circumstance would not now make you unhappy; but I am afraid it gives you more pain than you expected. His situation is an evil — but you must consider it as what satisfies your friend; and I will answer for your thinking better and better of him as you know him more. His good sense and good principles would delight you. — As far as the man is concerned, you could not wish your friend in better hands. His rank in society I would alter if I could; which is saying a great deal I assure you, Emma. — You laugh at me about William Larkins; but I could quite as ill spare Robert Martin."

He wanted her to look up and smile; and having now brought herself not to smile too broadly — she did — cheerfully answering,

"You need not be at any pains to reconcile me to the match. I think Harriet is doing extremely well. *Her* connexions may be worse than *his*. In respectability of character, there can be no doubt that they are. I have been silent from surprise merely, excessive surprise. You cannot imagine how suddenly it has come on me! how peculiarly unprepared I was! — for I had reason to believe her very lately more determined against him, much more, than she was before."

"You ought to know your friend best," replied Mr. Knightley; "but I should say she was a good-tempered, soft-hearted girl, not likely to be very, very determined against any young man who told her he loved her."

Emma could not help laughing as she answered, "Upon my word, I believe you know her quite as well as I do. — But, Mr. Knightley, are you perfectly sure that she has absolutely and downright *accepted* him. — I could suppose she might in time — but can she already? — Did not you misunderstand him? — You were both talking of other things; of business, shows of cattle, or new drills — and might not you, in the confusion of so many subjects, mistake him? — It was not Harriet's hand that he was certain of — it was the dimensions of some famous ox."[154]

The contrast between the countenance and air of Mr. Knightley and Robert Martin was, at this moment, so strong to Emma's feelings, and so strong was the recollection of all that had so recently passed on Harriet's side, so fresh the sound of those words, spoken with such emphasis, "No, I hope I know better than to think of Robert Martin," that she was really expecting the intelligence to prove, in some measure, premature. It could not be otherwise.

"Do you dare say this?" cried Mr. Knightley. "Do you dare to suppose me so great a blockhead, as not to know what a man is talking of? — What do you deserve?"

"Oh! I always deserve the best treatment, because I never put up with any other; and, therefore, you must give me a plain, direct answer. Are you quite sure that you understand the terms on which Mr. Martin and Harriet now are?"

"I am quite sure," he replied, speaking very distinctly, "that he told me she had accepted him; and that there was no obscurity, nothing doubtful, in the words he used; and I think I can give you a proof that it must be so. He asked my opinion as to what he was now to do. He knew of no one but Mrs. Goddard to whom he could apply for information of her relations or friends. Could I mention any thing more fit to be done, than to go to Mrs. Goddard? I assured him that I could not. Then, he said, he would endeavour to see her in the course of this day."

---

[154] *the dimensions of some famous ox:* Such as "The Lincolnshire Ox," an ox of prodigious size exhibited in London in 1790–91; George Stubbs's painting of the ox was exhibited at the Royal Academy in 1790. For a reproduction of Stubbs's painting, and for further discussion, see "Contextual Documents," pp. 402, 396–97.

"I am perfectly satisfied," replied Emma, with the brightest smiles, "and most sincerely wish them happy."

"You are materially changed since we talked on this subject before."

"I hope so — for at that time I was a fool."

"And I am changed also; for I am now very willing to grant you all Harriet's good qualities. I have taken some pains for your sake, and for Robert Martin's sake, (whom I have always had reason to believe as much in love with her as ever,) to get acquainted with her. I have often talked to her a good deal. You must have seen that I did. Sometimes, indeed, I have thought you were half suspecting me of pleading poor Martin's cause, which was never the case: but, from all my observations, I am convinced of her being an artless, amiable girl, with very good notions, very seriously good principles, and placing her happiness in the affections and utility of domestic life. — Much of this, I have no doubt, she may thank you for."

"Me!" cried Emma, shaking her head. — "Ah! poor Harriet!"

She checked herself, however, and submitted quietly to a little more praise than she deserved.

Their conversation was soon afterwards closed by the entrance of her father. She was not sorry. She wanted to be alone. Her mind was in a state of flutter and wonder, which made it impossible for her to be collected. She was in dancing, singing, exclaiming spirits; and till she had moved about, and talked to herself, and laughed and reflected, she could be fit for nothing rational.

Her father's business was to announce James's being gone out to put the horses to, preparatory to their now daily drive to Randalls; and she had, therefore, an immediate excuse for disappearing.

The joy, the gratitude, the exquisite delight of her sensations may be imagined. The sole grievance and alloy thus removed in the prospect of Harriet's welfare, she was really in danger of becoming too happy for security. — What had she to wish for? Nothing, but to grow more worthy of him, whose intentions and judgment had been ever so superior to her own. Nothing, but that the lessons of her past folly might teach her humility and circumspection in future.

Serious she was, very serious in her thankfulness, and in her resolutions; and yet there was no preventing a laugh, sometimes in the very midst of them. She must laugh at such a close! Such an end of the doleful disappointment of five weeks back! Such a heart — such a Harriet!

Now there would be pleasure in her returning. — Every thing would be a pleasure. It would be a great pleasure to know Robert Martin.

High in the rank of her most serious and heartfelt felicities, was the reflection that all necessity of concealment from Mr. Knightley would soon be over. The disguise, equivocation, mystery, so hateful to her to practise, might soon be over. She could now look forward to giving him that full and perfect confidence which her disposition was most ready to welcome as a duty.

In the gayest and happiest spirits she set forward with her father; not always listening, but always agreeing to what he said; and, whether in speech or silence, conniving at the comfortable persuasion of his being obliged to go to Randalls every day, or poor Mrs. Weston would be disappointed.

They arrived. — Mrs. Weston was alone in the drawing-room: — but hardly had they been told of the baby, and Mr. Woodhouse received the thanks for coming, which he asked for, when a glimpse was caught through the blind, of two figures passing near the window.

"It is Frank and Miss Fairfax," said Mrs. Weston. "I was just going to tell you of our agreeable surprise in seeing him arrive this morning. He stays till to-morrow, and Miss Fairfax has been persuaded to spend the day with us. — They are coming in, I hope."

In half a minute they were in the room. Emma was extremely glad to see him — but there was a degree of confusion — a number of embarrassing recollections on each side. They met readily and smiling, but with a consciousness which at first allowed little to be said; and having all sat down again, there was for some time such a blank in the circle, that Emma began to doubt whether the wish now indulged, which she had long felt, of seeing Frank Churchill once more, and of seeing him with Jane, would yield its proportion of pleasure. When Mr. Weston joined the party, however, and when the baby was fetched, there was no longer a want of subject or animation — or of courage and opportunity for Frank Churchill to draw near her and say,

"I have to thank you, Miss Woodhouse, for a very kind forgiving message in one of Mrs. Weston's letters. I hope time has not made you less willing to pardon. I hope you do not retract what you then said."

"No, indeed," cried Emma, most happy to begin, "not in the least. I am particularly glad to see and shake hands with you — and to give you joy in person."

He thanked her with all his heart, and continued some time to speak with serious feeling of his gratitude and happiness.

"Is not she looking well?" said he, turning his eyes towards Jane. "Better than she ever used to do? — You see how my father and Mrs. Weston doat upon her."

But his spirits were soon rising again, and with laughing eyes, after mentioning the expected return of the Campbells, he named the name of Dixon. — Emma blushed, and forbad its being pronounced in her hearing.

"I can never think of it," she cried, "without extreme shame."

"The shame," he answered, "is all mine, or ought to be. But is it possible that you had no suspicion? — I mean of late. Early, I know you had none."

"I never had the smallest, I assure you."

"That appears quite wonderful. I was once very near — and I wish I had — it would have been better. But though I was always doing wrong things, they were very *bad* wrong things, and such as did me no service. — It would have been a much better transgression had I broken the bond of secrecy and told you every thing."

"It is not now worth a regret," said Emma.

"I have some hope," resumed he, "of my uncle's being persuaded to pay a visit at Randalls; he wants to be introduced to her. When the Campbells are returned, we shall meet them in London, and continue there, I trust, till we may carry her northward. — But now, I am at such a distance from her — is not it hard, Miss Woodhouse? — Till this morning, we have not once met since the day of reconciliation. Do not you pity me?"

Emma spoke her pity so very kindly, that, with a sudden accession of gay thought, he cried,

"Ah! by the bye," — then sinking his voice, and looking demure for the moment — "I hope Mr. Knightley is well?" He paused. — She coloured and laughed. — "I know you saw my letter, and think you may remember my wish in your favour. Let me return your congratulations. — I assure you that I have heard the news with the warmest interest and satisfaction. — He is a man whom I cannot presume to praise."

Emma was delighted, and only wanted him to go on in the same style; but his mind was the next moment in his own concerns and with his own Jane, and his next words were,

"Did you ever see such a skin? — such smoothness! such delicacy! — and yet without being actually fair. — One cannot call her fair. It is a most uncommon complexion, and her dark eye-lashes and hair — a most distinguishing complexion! — So peculiarly the lady in it. — Just colour enough for beauty."

"I have always admired her complexion," replied Emma, archly; "but do not I remember the time when you found fault with her for being so pale? — When we first began to talk of her. — Have you quite forgotten?"

"Oh! no — what an impudent dog I was! — How could I dare —"

But he laughed so heartily at the recollection, that Emma could not help saying,

"I do suspect that in the midst of your perplexities at that time, you had very great amusement in tricking us all. — I am sure you had. — I am sure it was a consolation to you."

"Oh! no, no, no — how can you suspect me of such a thing? — I was the most miserable wretch!"

"Not quite so miserable as to be insensible to mirth. I am sure it was a source of high entertainment to you, to feel that you were taking us all in. — Perhaps I am the readier to suspect, because, to tell you the truth, I think it might have been some amusement to myself in the same situation. I think there is a little likeness between us."

He bowed.

"If not in our dispositions," she presently added, with a look of true sensibility, "there is a likeness in our destiny; the destiny which bids fair to connect us with two characters so much superior to our own."

"True, true," he answered, warmly. "No, not true on your side. You can have no superior, but most true on mine. — She is a complete angel. Look at her. Is not she an angel in every gesture? Observe the turn of her throat. Observe her eyes, as she is looking up at my father. — You will be glad to hear (inclining his head, and whispering seriously) that my uncle means to give her all my aunt's jewels. They are to be new set. I am resolved to have some in an ornament for the head. Will not it be beautiful in her dark hair?"

"Very beautiful, indeed," replied Emma: and she spoke so kindly, that he gratefully burst out,

"How delighted I am to see you again! and to see you in such excellent looks! — I would not have missed this meeting for the world. I should certainly have called at Hartfield, had you failed to come."

The others had been talking of the child, Mrs. Weston giving an account of a little alarm she had been under, the evening before, from the infant's appearing not quite well. She believed she had been foolish, but it had alarmed her, and she had been within half a minute of sending for Mr. Perry. Perhaps she ought to be ashamed, but Mr. Weston had been almost as uneasy as herself. — In ten minutes, however, the child had been perfectly well again. This was her history; and particularly interesting it was to Mr. Woodhouse, who commended her very much for thinking of sending for Perry, and only regretted that she had not done it. "She should always send for Perry, if the child appeared in the slightest degree disordered, were it only for a moment. She could not be too soon alarmed, nor send for Perry too often. It was a pity, perhaps, that he had not come last night; for, though the child seemed well now, very well considering, it would probably have been better if Perry had seen it."

Frank Churchill caught the name.

"Perry!" said he to Emma, and trying, as he spoke, to catch Miss Fairfax's eye. "My friend Mr. Perry! What are they saying about Mr. Perry? — Has he been here this morning? — and how does he travel now? — Has he set up his carriage?"

Emma soon recollected, and understood him; and while she joined in the laugh, it was evident from Jane's countenance that she too was really hearing him, though trying to seem deaf.

"Such an extraordinary dream of mine!" he cried. "I can never think of it without laughing. — She hears us, she hears us, Miss Woodhouse. I see it in her cheek, her smile, her vain attempt to frown. Look at her. Do not you see that, at this instant, the very passage of her own letter, which sent me the report, is passing under her eye — that the whole blunder is spread before her — that she can attend to nothing else, though pretending to listen to the others?"

Jane was forced to smile completely, for a moment; and the smile partly remained as she turned towards him, and said in a conscious, low, yet steady voice,

"How you can bear such recollections, is astonishing to me! — They *will* sometimes obtrude — but how you can *court* them!"

He had a great deal to say in return, and very entertainingly; but Emma's feelings were chiefly with Jane, in the argument; and on leaving Randalls, and falling naturally into a comparison of the two men, she felt, that pleased as she had been to see Frank Churchill, and really regarding him as she did with friendship, she had never been more sensible of Mr. Knightley's high superiority of character. The happiness of this most happy day, received its completion, in the animated contemplation of his worth which this comparison produced.

CHAPTER XIX.

IF Emma had still, at intervals, an anxious feeling for Harriet, a momentary doubt of its being possible for her to be really cured of her attachment to Mr. Knightley, and really able to accept another man from unbiassed inclination, it was not long that she had to suffer from the recurrence of any such uncertainty. A very few days brought the party from London, and she had no sooner an opportunity of being one hour alone with Harriet, than she became perfectly satisfied — unaccountable as it was! — that Robert Martin had thoroughly supplanted Mr. Knightley, and was now forming all her views of happiness.

Harriet was a little distressed — did look a little foolish at first; but having once owned that she had been presumptuous and silly, and self-deceived, before, her pain and confusion seemed to die away with the words, and leave her without a care for the past, and with the fullest exultation in the present and future; for, as to her friend's approbation, Emma had instantly removed every fear of that nature, by meeting her with the most unqualified congratulations. — Harriet was most happy to give every particular of the evening at Astley's, and the dinner the next day; she could dwell on it all with the utmost delight. But what did such particulars explain? — The fact was, as Emma could now acknowledge, that Harriet had always liked Robert Martin; and that his continuing to love her had been irresistible. — Beyond this, it must ever be unintelligible to Emma.

The event, however, was most joyful, and every day was giving her fresh reason for thinking so. — Harriet's parentage became known. She proved to be the daughter of a tradesman, rich enough to afford her the comfortable maintenance which had ever been her's, and decent enough to have always wished for concealment. — Such was the blood of gentility which Emma had formerly been so ready to vouch for! — It was likely to be as untainted, perhaps, as the blood of many a gentleman: but what a connexion had she been preparing for Mr. Knightley — or for the Churchills — or even for Mr. Elton! — The stain of illegitimacy, unbleached by nobility or wealth, would have been a stain indeed.

No objection was raised on the father's side; the young man was treated liberally; it was all as it should be: and as Emma became acquainted with Robert Martin, who was now introduced at Hartfield, she fully acknowledged in him all the appearance of sense and worth which could bid fairest for her little friend. She had no doubt of Harriet's happiness with any good tempered man; but with him, and in the home he offered, there would be the hope of more, of security, stability, and improvement. She would be placed in the midst of those who loved her, and who had better sense than herself; retired enough for safety, and occupied enough for cheerfulness. She would be never led into temptation, nor left for it to find her out. She would be respectable and happy; and Emma admitted her to be the luckiest creature in the world, to have created so steady and persevering an affection in such a man; — or, if not quite the luckiest, to yield only to herself.

Harriet, necessarily drawn away by her engagements with the Martins, was less and less at Hartfield; which was not to be regretted. — The intimacy between her and Emma must sink; their friendship must change into a calmer sort of goodwill; and, fortunately, what ought to be, and must be, seemed already beginning, and in the most gradual, natural manner.

Before the end of September, Emma attended Harriet to church, and saw her hand bestowed on Robert Martin with so complete a satisfaction, as no remembrances, even connected with Mr. Elton as he stood before them, could impair. — Perhaps, indeed, at that time she scarcely saw Mr. Elton, but as the clergyman whose blessing at the altar might next fall on herself. — Robert Martin and Harriet Smith, the latest couple engaged of the three, were the first to be married.

Jane Fairfax had already quitted Highbury, and was restored to the comforts of her beloved home with the Campbells. — The Mr. Churchills were also in town; and they were only waiting for November.

The intermediate month was the one fixed on, as far as they dared, by Emma and Mr. Knightley. — They had determined that their marriage ought to be concluded while John and Isabella were still at Hartfield, to allow them the fortnight's absence in a tour to the sea-side, which was the plan. — John and Isabella, and every other friend, were agreed in approving it. But Mr. Woodhouse — how was Mr. Woodhouse to be induced to consent? — he, who had never yet alluded to their marriage but as a distant event.

When first sounded on the subject, he was so miserable, that they were almost hopeless. — A second allusion, indeed, gave less pain. — He began to think it was to be, and that he could not prevent it — a very promising step of the mind on its way to resignation. Still, however, he was not happy. Nay, he appeared so much otherwise, that his daughter's courage failed. She could not bear to see him suffering, to know him fancying himself neglected; and though her understanding almost acquiesced in the assurance of both the Mr. Knightleys, that when once the event were over, his distress would be soon over too, she hesitated — she could not proceed.

In this state of suspense they were befriended, not by any sudden illumination of Mr. Woodhouse's mind, or any wonderful change of his nervous system, but by the operation of the same system in another way. — Mrs. Weston's poultry-house was robbed one night of all her turkies — evidently by the ingenuity of man. Other poultry-yards in the neighbourhood also suffered. — Pilfering was *housebreaking* to Mr. Woodhouse's fears. — He was very uneasy; and but for the sense of his son-in-law's protection, would have been under wretched alarm every night of his life. The strength, resolution, and presence of mind of the Mr. Knightleys, commanded his fullest dependance. While either of them protected him and his, Hartfield was safe. — But Mr. John Knightley must be in London again by the end of the first week in November.

The result of this distress was, that, with a much more voluntary, cheerful consent than his daughter had ever presumed to hope for at the moment, she was able to fix her wedding-day — and Mr. Elton was called on, within a month from the marriage of Mr. and Mrs. Robert Martin, to join the hands of Mr. Knightley and Miss Woodhouse.

The wedding was very much like other weddings, where the parties have no taste for finery or parade; and Mrs. Elton, from the particulars detailed by her husband, thought it all extremely shabby, and very inferior to her own. — "Very little white satin, very few lace veils; a most pitiful business! — Selina would stare when she heard of it." — But, in spite of these deficiencies, the wishes, the hopes, the confidence, the predictions of the small band of true friends who witnessed the ceremony, were fully answered in the perfect happiness of the union.

Contextual Documents
and Illustrations

EDITOR'S NOTE ON DOCUMENTS

The following documents and illustrations bear on some of the novel's central concerns and are intended to add to readers' appreciation of the novel while also suggesting issues of interpretation and topics for further discussion.

The entry for **"Kitty, a Fair but Frozen Maid,"** p. 385, provides a full-length version of the riddle that Mr. Woodhouse knew in his youth but now has trouble remembering. Composed by the actor and playwright David Garrick, the riddle, first published in 1757 and reprinted later, would probably have been known to many of Austen's readers. Though the answer (chimney-sweep) seems innocuous, the riddle may contain sexually suggestive material and is thus an odd choice for Mr. Woodhouse. For an exploration of its use of double entendre see Alice Chandler, "'A Pair of Fine Eyes': Jane Austen's Treatment of Sex," *Studies in the Novel* 7.1 (1975): 91–92; and Jill Heydt-Stevenson, "'Slipping into the Ha-Ha': Bawdy Humor and Body Politics in Jane Austen's Novels," *Nineteenth-Century Literature* 55.3 (2000): 316–23.

"Robin Adair," p. 386, is an even less gratuitous reference, as Peter F. Alexander has argued in "'Robin Adair' as a Musical Clue in Jane Austen's *Emma*," *Review of English Studies*, 39.153 (1988): 84–86.

The words of the song poignantly express Jane's current situation and foreshadow her possible bleak future. According to *The Oxford Companion to Music*, ed. Percy Scholes (Oxford: Oxford UP, 1976), "Robin Adair" was introduced into Scotland from Ireland in the early eighteenth century, but only acquired the "Scotch snap" in the early nineteenth century. Though it is not specified which musical version Jane played, the words (which many of Austen's readers would have known) are likely to have been those here printed; they are by Lady Caroline Keppel, who in about 1750 thus addressed a young Irish surgeon (also named Robin Adair) with whom she was in love and whom, in 1758, she married.

The extract from Mary Wollstonecraft's *Thoughts on the Education of Daughters*, p. 387, also bears on Jane Fairfax. Discussing the "unfortunate situation of females, fashionably educated, and left without a fortune," Wollstonecraft might almost be anticipating the predicament of Austen's character. Her subsequent description of the humiliations suffered by governesses, together with their tendency to fall in love with men of position and power who seduce and abandon them, provides a bleak picture of the future that Jane fortuitously avoids in *Emma*.

The extract from Lord Chesterfield's *"Letter to His Son,"* p. 389, is notable for its anticipation of Mr. Knightley's use of the word "aimable" to characterize the French manners of Frank Churchill; but whereas Chesterfield saw French manners as a model for conduct, Mr. Knightley deplores them. His country distrust of courtly manners and English distrust of French airs place him as the inheritor of a long tradition of distrust of aristocratic refinement; see Michael Curtin, "A Question of Manners: Status and Gender in Etiquette and Courtesy," *Journal of Modern History* 57 (1985): 395–423.

The extract from Uvedale Price's *Essays on the Picturesque*, p. 390, is part of his attack — first published in 1794 — on Lancelot ("Capability") Brown and his followers, designers who removed houses and gardens in their pursuit of a landscape aesthetic that Price found not only monotonous but politically "despotic." In advocating a "picturesque" alternative, Price invokes the "humanizing" influence of painters. Austen hardly ever refers to painting in her novels, and she can be ironic about the picturesque, but her verbal descriptions of Donwell Abbey (p. 286 in this volume) and the Abbey-Mill farm (p. 288), as seen through Emma's eyes in chapter six of the third volume, accord with Price's criticism of the "general system of improvement" and his advocacy of social "connection." Similarly, the paternalist care that Mr. Knightley extends to the inhabitants of Highbury echoes that of the landlord Price praises in the extract.

Paternalism of a Tory kind characterizes the argument of Robert Southey's 1829 essay *Our Domestic Policy,* p. 391. If Price was responding to the threats posed to the landed order by the French Revolution, Southey was opposing liberal reform measures in the years before the Reform Bill of 1832. Written more than a decade after *Emma,* Southey's essay is an expression of an ideology of mutual rights and responsibilities: social ranks are to be maintained, but those with power and possessions are obligated to protect the poor. Stated thus, the extract corresponds to elements of conservatism in Austen's novel, which in one of its dimensions calls on Emma to recognize the responsibilities her rank entails. But Southey's abstract exposition of "Tory principles" may serve less as a gloss than as an opportunity for observing how *Emma* — like all great novels — complicates rather than defines an ideological position. *Emma* certainly affirms a moral economy of the kind both Price (a Whig) and Southey (a Tory) espouse; but Mr. Knightley is no Tory stick figure. In his relations with Robert Martin he shows himself open to the advancement of merit. Concerning Jane Fairfax, however, he has nothing to offer but sympathy and understanding. For some readers, Jane's predicament measures the limitations of a protective paternalism, though whether she intended such a recognition is doubtful.

The **"Opinions of *Emma,*"** p, 392, collected and transcribed by Jane Austen, probably in 1816, offer an interesting window on the reception of the novel at the time. Fragmentary and often superficial as the opinions are, they were clearly valued by Austen, who evidently wished to learn which of her intentions had succeeded and which had not. They are presented without marginal comment; even the most fatuous opinions are preserved. Which would have pleased her most? Surely the comments of those who praised the natural quality of the novel's style, the consistency of the characterization, and the skill of the plot's resolution. That the Knights should have liked Mr. Knightley would not have surprised her, since the character is an idealized version of her brother Edward Knight, squire of Godmersham. Nor would she have been surprised by the admiration expressed for Mrs. Elton, since unlike some modern readers she could distinguish between skill in characterization and flaw in character. She would not have been displeased by the loyalty of readers to *Pride and Prejudice,* which she considered her "darling child." Perhaps her sister's preference for *Mansfield Park* would have surprised her, though she would probably have attributed this preference to Cassandra's evangelical views, views that are also evident in those opinions that deplore the representation of a clergyman in Mr. Elton. Of special interest to her, perhaps, would have been Miss Sharp's dissatisfaction with Jane Fairfax, for Miss Sharp, whom Austen liked and admired, and to whom she gave a presentation copy of *Emma*, had served as governess at Godmersham.

DAVID GARRICK

A Riddle[1]

Kitty, a fair but frozen maid,
    Kindled a flame I still deplore;
The hood-wink'd boy I call'd in aid,
Much of his near approach afraid,
    So fatal to my suit before.

At length, propitious to my pray'r,
    The little urchin came;
At once he sought the midway air
And soon he clear'd, with dextrous care,
    The bitter relicks of my flame.

To Kitty, Fanny now succeeds,
    She kindles slow, but lasting fires:
With care my appetite she feeds;
Each day some willing victim bleeds,
    To satisfy my strange desires.

Say, by what title, or what name,
    Must I this youth address?[2]
Cupid and he are not the same,
Tho' both can raise, or quench a flame —
    I'll kiss you, if you guess.

---

[1]As Fiona Stafford notes, this riddle by Garrick was first published in a three-stanza version in *The London Chronicle*, May 19–21 (1757), as "Written by a Lady, whose Maid had set her Chimney on Fire." The version printed here is taken from *The Poetical Works of David Garrick*, 2 vols. (1785, rpt. New York: Benjamin Blom, 1968), II, 507.
[2]The answer to the riddle is *chimney-sweep*.

Robin Adair [1]

What's this dull town to me?
    Robin's not near.
What was't I wish'd to see?
    What wish't to hear?
Where's all the joy and mirth
Made this town a heav'n on earth?
Oh! they're all fled with thee,
    Robin Adair.

What made th'assembly shine?
    Robin Adair.
What made the ball so fine?
    Robin was there.
What, when the play was o'er,
What made my heart so sore?
Oh! it was parting with
    Robin Adair.

But now thou'rt cold to me,
    Robin Adair,
But now thou'rt cold to me,
    Robin Adair.
Yet him I lov'd so well
Still in my heart shall dwell;
Oh! I can ne'er forget
    Robin Adair.

[1]P. C. Buck, ed., *The Oxford Song Book*, vol. 1 (London: Oxford UP, 1916), 153.

MARY WOLLSTONECRAFT

From Unfortunate Situation of Females, Fashionably Educated, and Left without a Fortune.[1] (1787)

I have hitherto only spoken of those females, who will have a provision made for them by their parents. But many who have been well, or at least fashionably educated, are left without a fortune, and if they are not entirely devoid of delicacy, they must frequently remain single.

Few are the modes of earning a subsistence, and those very humiliating. Perhaps to be an humble companion to some rich old cousin, or what is still worse, to live with strangers, who are so intolerably tyrannical, that none of their own relations can bear to live with them, though they should even expect a fortune in reversion. It is impossible to enumerate the many hours of anguish such a person must spend. Above the servants, yet considered by them as a spy, and ever reminded of her inferiority when in conversation with the superiors. If she cannot condescend to mean flattery, she has not a chance of being a favourite; and should any of the visitors take notice of her, and she for a moment forget her subordinate state, she is sure to be reminded of it.

Painfully sensible of unkindness, she is alive to every thing, and many sarcasms reach her, which were perhaps directed another way. She is alone, shut out from equality and confidence, and the concealed anxiety impairs her constitution; for she must wear a cheerful face, or be dismissed. The being dependant on the caprice of a fellow-creature, though certainly very necessary in this state of discipline, is yet a very bitter corrective, which we would fain shrink from.

A teacher at a school is only a kind of upper servant, who has more work than the menial ones.

A governess to young ladies is equally disagreeable. It is ten to one if they meet with a reasonable mother; and if she is not so, she will be continually finding fault to prove she is not ignorant, and be displeased if her pupils do not improve, but angry if the proper methods are taken to make them do so. The children treat them with disrespect, and often with insolence. In the mean time life glides away, and the spirits with it; "and when youth and genial years are flown," they have nothing to

---

[1] From *Thoughts on the Education of Daughters, with Reflections on Female Conduct in the More Important Duties of Life* (London, 1787).

subsist on; or, perhaps, on some extraordinary occasion, some small allowance may be made for them, which is thought a great charity.

The few trades which are left, are now gradually falling into the hands of the men, and certainly they are not very respectable.

It is hard for a person who has a relish for polished society, to herd with the vulgar, or to condescend to mix with her former equals when she is considered in a different light. What unwelcome heart-breaking knowledge is then poured in on her! I mean a view of the selfishness and depravity of the world; for every other acquirement is a source of pleasure, though they may occasion temporary inconveniences. How cutting is the contempt she meets with! — A young mind looks round for love and friendship; but love and friendship fly from poverty: expect them not if you are poor! The mind must then sink into meanness, and accommodate itself to its new state, or dare to be unhappy. Yet I think no reflecting person would give up the experience and improvement they have gained, to have avoided the misfortunes; on the contrary, they are thankfully ranked amongst the choicest blessings of life, when we are not under their immediate pressure.

How earnestly does a mind full of sensibility look for disinterested friendship, and long to meet with good unalloyed. When fortune smiles they hug the dear delusion; but dream not that it is one. The painted cloud disappears suddenly, the scene is changed, and what an aching void is left in the heart! a void which only religion can fill up — and how few seek this internal comfort!

A woman, who has beauty without sentiment, is in great danger of being seduced; and if she has any, cannot guard herself from painful mortifications. It is very disagreeable to keep up a continual reserve with men she has been formerly familiar with; yet if she places confidence, it is ten to one but she is deceived. Few men seriously think of marrying an inferior; and if they have honour enough not to take advantage of the artless tenderness of a woman who loves, and thinks not of the difference of rank, they do not undeceive her until she has anticipated happiness, which, contrasted with her dependant situation, appears delightful. The disappointment is severe; and the heart receives a wound which does not easily admit of a compleat cure, as the good that is missed is not valued according to its real worth: for fancy drew the picture, and grief delights to create food to feed on.

If what I have written should be read by parents, who are now going on in thoughtless extravagance, and anxious only that their daughters may be *genteelly educated,* let them consider to what sorrows they may expose them; for I have not over-coloured the picture.

PHILIP STANHOPE, EARL OF CHESTERFIELD

From Letter to His Son[1] (1750)

There should be in the least, as well as in the greatest parts of a gentleman, *les manières nobles*. Sense will teach you some, observation others; attend carefully to the manners, the diction, the motions, of people of the first fashion, and form your own upon them. On the other hand, observe a little those of the vulgar, in order to avoid them; for though the things which they say or do may be the same, the manner is always totally different; and in that, and nothing else, consists the characteristic of the man of fashion. The lowest peasant speaks, moves, dresses, eats, and drinks, as much as a man of the first fashion; but does them all quite differently; so that by doing and saying most things in a manner opposite to that of the vulgar, you have a great chance of doing and saying them right. There are graduations in awkwardness and vulgarism, as there are in everything else. Les *manières de robe*, though not quite right, are still better than *les manières bourgeoises;* and these, though bad, are better than *les manières de campagne*. But the language, the air, the dress, and the manners of the Court, are the only true standard *des manières nobles, et d'un honnête homme. Ex pede Herculem* is an old and true saying, and very applicable to our present subject; for a man of parts, who has been bred at Courts, and used to keep the best company, will distinguish himself, and is to be known from the vulgar, by every word, attitude, gesture, and even look. . . .

Having said all this, I cannot help reflecting what a formal dull fellow, or a cloistered pedant, would say, if they were to read this letter; they would look upon it with the utmost contempt, and say that surely a father might find much better topics for advice to a son. I would admit it, if I had given you, or that you were capable of receiving no better; but if sufficient pains have been taken to form your heart and improve your mind, and, as I hope, not without success, I will tell those solid gentlemen, that all these trifling things, as they think them, collectively form that pleasing *je ne sçais quoi,* that *ensemble,* which they are utter strangers to, both in themselves and others. The word *aimable* is not known in their language, or the thing in their manners. Great usage of the world, great attention, and a great desire of pleasing, can alone give it; and it is no trifle.

[1]From *Lord Chesterfield's Letters to His Son,* intro. R. K. Root (New York: Dutton, 1969) 200–01.

UVEDALE PRICE

From Essays on the Picturesque[1] (1810)

There is, indeed, something despotic in the general system of improvement; all must be laid open; all that obstructs, levelled to the ground; houses, orchards, gardens, all swept away. *Painting*, on the contrary, tends to humanize the mind: where a despot thinks every person an intruder who enters his domain, and wishes to destroy cottages and pathways, and to reign alone, the lover of painting, considers the dwellings, the inhabitants, and the marks of their intercourse, as ornaments to the landscape.

For the honour of humanity there *are* minds, which require no other motive than what passes within. And here I cannot resist paying a tribute to the memory of a beloved uncle, and recording a benevolence towards all the inhabitants around him, that struck me from my earliest remembrance; and it is an impression I wish always to cherish. It seemed as if he had made his extensive walks as much for them as for himself; they used them as freely, and their enjoyment was his. The village bore as strong marks of his and of his brother's attentions (for in that respect they appeared to have but one mind) to the comforts and pleasures of its inhabitants. Such attentive kindnesses are amply repaid by affectionate regard and reverence; and were they general throughout the kingdom, they would do much more towards guarding us against democratical opinions,

"Than twenty thousand soldiers arm'd in proof."

The cheerfulness of the scene I have mentioned, and all the interesting circumstances attending to it, so different from those of solitary grandeur, have convinced me, that he who destroys dwellings, gardens, and inclosures, for the sake of mere extent and parade of property, only extends the bounds of monotony, and of dreary selfish pride; but contracts those of variety, amusement, and humanity.

[1]Uvedale Price, *Essays on the Picturesque*, vol. 1 (London, 1810) 338–40.

ROBERT SOUTHEY

From Our Domestic Policy. No I.[1] (1829)

[W]e have . . . to rejoice in the sympathy of feeling, with which those whose sympathy we more regard, have hailed our exposition of true Tory principles — of principles which, while they maintain the due order and proportion of each separate rank in the state, maintain also that protection and support are the right of all, so long as there are the means, within the state, of affording them. In opposition to those cold and heartless politicians, who, with the words liberty and liberality ever in their mouths, look with scientific composure upon a people's sufferings, we would say, govern the people, and govern them strictly, for their good, but see that they are fed. The sort of liberty which the Liberals afford, is something like that which he would bestow who should turn his steed loose in the desert, with many encomiums upon his own magnaminity, forgetting, or not caring to remember, that while he gave the animal his freedom, he deprived him of his food. As Tories, we maintain that it is the duty of the people to pay obedience to those set in authority over them: but it is also the duty of those in authority to protect the people who are placed below them. They are not to sit in stately grandeur, and see the people perish, nor, indeed, are they ever to forget that they hold their power and their possessions upon the understanding that they administer both more for the good of the people at large, than the people would do, if they had the administration of both themselves.

If this were not Tory doctrine, we should be ashamed of the name in which we glory; but because it is Tory doctrine; because it is the doctrine of genuine practical freedom, deduced from the precepts of our religion, and sanctioned by the principles of humanity; because it is all this, we . . . are filled with disgust and indignation, at the pernicious folly which runs counter to it.

---

[1]From Blackwood's *Edinburgh Magazine* 26, Nov. 1829: 768–69.

Opinions of *Emma*[1] (Ca. 1816)

Captn. Austen. — liked it extremely, observing that though there might be more Wit in P & P — & an higher Morality in M P — yet altogether, on account of it's peculiar air of Nature throughout, he preferred it to either.

Mrs. F. A. — liked & admired it very much indeed, but must still prefer P. & P.

Mrs. J. Bridges — preferred it to all the others.

Miss Sharp — better than M P. — but not so well as P. & P. — pleased with the Heroine for her Originality, delighted with Mr K — & called Mrs Elton beyond praise. — dissatisfied with Jane Fairfax.

Cassandra — better than P. & P. — but not so well as M. P. —

Fanny K. — not so well as either P. & P. or M P. — could not bear *Emma* herself. — Mr Knightley delightful. — Should like J. F. — if she knew more of her. —

Mr and Mrs J. A. — did not like it so well as either of the 3 others. Language different from the others, not so easily read. —

Edward — preferred it to M P. — *only*. — Mr. K. liked by every body.

Miss Bigg — not equal to either P & P. — or M P. — objected to the sameness of the subject (Match-making) all through. — Too much of Mr Elton and H. Smith. Language superior to the others. —

My Mother — thought it more entertaining than M. P. — but not so interesting as P. & P. — No characters in it equal to Ly Catherine & Mr Collins. —

Miss Lloyd — thought it as *clever* as either of the others, but did not receive so much pleasure from it as from P. & P — & M P. —

Mrs and Miss Craven — liked it very much, but not so much as the others. —

Fanny Cage — liked it very much indeed & classed it between P & P. — & M P. —

Mr. Sherer — did not think it equal to either M P — (which he liked the best of all) or P & P. — Displeased with my pictures of Clergymen. —

Miss Bigg — on reading it a second time, liked Miss Bates much better than at first, & expressed herself as liking all the people of High-

[1]From *The Works of Jane Austen. Volume VI. Minor Works*. Ed. R. W. Chapman (Oxford: Oxford UP, 1988), pp. 436–39. The opinions were collected and written out by Jane Austen, probably in 1816.

bury in general, except Harriet Smith — but cd not help still thinking *her* too silly in her Loves.

The family at Upton Gray — all very amused with it. — Miss Bates a great favourite with Mrs Beaufoy.

Mr & Mrs Leigh Perrot — saw many beauties in it, but cd not think it equal to P. & P. — Darcy & Elizth had spoilt them for anything else. — Mr K. however, an excellent Character; Emma better luck than a Matchmaker often has. Pitied Jane Fairfax — thought Frank Churchill better treated than he deserved. —

Countess Craven — admired it very much, but did not think it equal to P & P. — which she ranked as the very first of it's sort. —

Mrs Guiton — thought it too natural to be interesting.

Mrs Digweed — did not like it so well as the others, in fact if she had not known the Author, could hardly have got through it. —

Miss Terry — admired it very much, particularly Mrs Elton.

Henry Sanford — very much pleased with it — delighted with Miss Bates, but thought Mrs Elton the best-drawn Character in the Book. Mansfield Park however, still his favourite.

Mr Haden — *quite* delighted with it. Admired the Character of Emma. —

Miss Isabella Herries — did not like it — objected to my exposing the sex in the character of the Heroine — convinced that I had meant Mrs & Miss Bates for some acquaintance of theirs — People whom I never heard of before. —

Miss Harriet Moore — admired it very much, but M. P. still her favourite of all. —

Countess Morley — delighted with it. —

Mr Cockerelle — liked it so little, that Fanny wd not send me his opinion. —

Mrs Dickson — did not much like it — thought it *very* inferior to P. & P. — Liked it the less, from there being a Mr. & Mrs Dixon in it. —

Mrs Brandreth — thought the 3d vol: superior to anything I had ever written — quite beautiful! —

Mr B. Lefroy — thought that if there had been more Incident, it would be equal to any of the others. — The Characters quite as well drawn & supported as in any, & from being more everyday ones, the more entertaining. — Did not like the Heroine so well as any of the others. Miss Bates excellent, but rather too much of her. Mr & Mrs Elton admirable & John Knightley a sensible Man. —

Mrs B. Lefroy — rank'd *Emma* as a composition with S & S. — not so *Brilliant* as P. & P — nor so *equal* as M P. — Preferred Emma herself to all the heroines. — The Characters like all the others admirably well drawn & supported — perhaps rather less strongly marked than some, but only the more natural for that reason. — Mr Knightley Mrs Elton & Miss Bates her favourites. — Thought one or two of the conversations too long. —

Mrs Lefroy — preferred it to M P — but liked M P. the least of all.

Mr Fowle — read only the first & last Chapters, because he had heard it was not interesting. —

Mrs Lutley Sclater — liked it very much, better than M P — & thought I had "brought it all about very cleverly in the last volume." —

Mrs C. Cage wrote thus to Fanny — "A very great many thanks for the loan of *Emma,* which I am delighted with. I like it better than any. Every character is thoroughly kept up. I must enjoy reading it again with Charles. Miss Bates is incomparable, but I was nearly killed with those precious treasures! They are Unique, & really with more fun than I can express. I am at Highbury all day, & I can't help feeling I have just got into a new set of acquaintance. No one writes such good sense. & so very comfortable.

Mrs Wroughton — did not like so well as P. & P. — Thought the Authoress wrong, in such times as these, to draw such Clergymen as Mr Collins & Mr Elton.

Sir J. Langham — thought it much inferior to the others. —

Mr Jeffery (of the Edinburgh Review) was kept up by it three nights.

Miss Murden — certainly inferior to all the others.

Capt. C. Austen wrote — "Emma arrived in time to a moment. I am delighted with her, more so I think than even with my favourite Pride & Prejudice, & have read it three times in the Passage."

Mrs D. Dundas — thought it very clever, but did not like it so well as either of the others.

EDITOR'S NOTE ON ILLUSTRATIONS

Jane Austen's letter to Cassandra of June 20, 1808 illustrates a **"crossed letter,"** p. 398. "[I]n general," Miss Bates tells Emma, Jane Fairfax "fills the whole paper and crosses half," and her mother adds: "Well, Hetty, now I think you will be put to it to make out all that chequer-work" (p. 135 in this volume). Though crossed letters were written to save the cost of paper and postage, their existence in *Emma* (very much a novel of "cross" purposes) suggests the problems that all of the characters encounter in the decipherment of meanings

Problems in communication recur in the word games that are a recurring feature of the novel. The title page of *The Frolics of the Sphynx*, p. 399, here illustrated, is a reminder of how common collections of charades, riddles, and conundrums were at the time. That the Austen family delighted in word puzzles is shown by the publication of *Charades, etc. written by Jane Austen and her Family* (London: Spottiswoode, 1895); this had twenty-three pieces, of which three are by Jane Austen. And that Austen herself delighted in the word games that she describes disparagingly in *Emma* as "the only mental provision [Harriet] was making for the evening of life" (p. 72) is shown in a letter she wrote to Cassandra on January 29, 1813: "We admire your Charades excessively, but as yet have guessed only the 1st. The others seem very difficult. There is so much beauty in the Versification however, that the finding them out is but a secondary pleasure" (*Letters* 202). *The Frolics of the Sphynx* contains 214 riddles, most of which follow the same format of "My first . . . My second . . . My whole" that characterizes Mr. Elton's courtship charade (p. 74). At the end of the volume the solutions are provided, and on the endpapers of the copy I consulted, handwritten additions of more riddles appear — doubtless a common practice. As with crossed letters, so with word games, Austen in *Emma* transformed a common family practice into theme and motif for her own fictional purposes.

The illustration of the **square pianoforté**, p. 400, relates, of course, to the mysterious gift that Jane Fairfax receives: "a pianoforté — a very elegant looking instrument — not a grand, but a large-sized square pianoforté" (p. 178). Though the pianoforte illustrated was made by Andrew Rochead in Edinburgh, and not by John Broadwood in London, it has a "Broadwood's single action," and is otherwise similar to the one that arrives at the Bates's house from Broadwood's. Patrick Piggot (cited in note on p. 190) describes the elegance and high cost (between 20 and 30 guineas) of a square pianoforte of this kind at the time (p. 86). In a novel much concerned with gifts, this stands out as a token of the regard — and thoughtlessness — of the giver.

The **barouche-landau** from *Le Beau Monde, or Literary and Fashionable Magazine*, p. 401, illustrates the carriage that the parvenu Mrs. Elton boastfully refers to as being in the possession of her sister and brother-in-law, the Sucklings of Maple Grove: "They will have their barouche-landau, of course, which holds four perfectly" (p. 222). As C. J. Nicholson has written (personal letter), the four-wheeled carriage was basically a landau with two heads (or hoods) that could be lowered front and back in fine weather (a barouche had only one hood, covering the rear seat when raised). A barouche-landau (sometimes confusingly named a landau-barouche) provided room for four people on two facing seats, and would thus be suitable in fine weather, with lowered hoods, for the exploring parties Mrs. Elton plans to direct. Mr. Nicholson writes that the barouche-landau was built between 1804 and 1811 by Barker & Co, carriage builders in London. It remained rare, however, and a passage from the *Morning Post* of January 5, 1804 may suggest why, as well as confirming the suspicion that the carriage became associated with nouveau riche families such as the Sucklings: "Mr. Buxton, the celebrated whip, has just launched a new-fangled machine, a kind of *nondescript*. It is described by the inventor to be the due medium between a landau and a barouche, but all who have seen it say it more resembles a fish-cart or a music-caravan" (citation indebted to R. W. Chapman's addendum in his Oxford UP edition of *Mansfield Park* [various dates]).

Box Hill, illustrated here in George Lambert's painting, p. 401, was celebrated in the eighteenth century for its beautiful prospects of the surrounding Surrey countryside. From at least the time of John Macky's *Tour* (1709), however, it also had a more dubious reputation — of being a place where it was easy "for Gentlemen and Ladies insensibly to lose their company in these pretty labyrinths of Box-wood, and divert themselves unperceived" (citation from John E. Rogers Jr., "Emma Woodhouse: Betrayed by Place," *Persusasions* 21 [1999]: 165). Austen provides little in the way of descriptive detail of Box Hill, but something of its reputation for sexual impropriety appears in Emma's own formulation of how her behavior will be judged: "Mr. Frank Churchill and Miss Woodhouse flirted together excessively" (p. 294). That Box Hill was becoming in Austen's time a major tourist site is suggested by one of Miss Bates's comments — the more telling for being immediately denied — as she and Jane set off after Mrs. Elton: "There she is — no, that's somebody else. That's one of the ladies in the Irish car party, not at all like her" (p. 299).

George Stubbs's painting of *The Lincolnshire Ox,* p. 402, illustrates the novel's muted affirmation of the Agrarian Revolution then in progress. Though Emma is both amused and irritated at the time Mr. Knightley spends with his steward, William Larkins, and his tenant farmer, Robert Martin, the novel's representation of agriculture

("English culture" in Emma's view of the Abbey-Mill Farm from Donwell Abbey [p. 288]) is entirely positive. That Robert Martin should read the Agricultural Reports is, Emma's distaste notwithstanding, a mark in his favor; and that Mr. Knightley should share a first name with George III, the farmer king, is also of interest. When told of Robert Martin's proposal to Harriet — a proposal Emma had earlier prevented — Emma responds teasingly:

> "But, Mr. Knightley, are you perfectly sure that she has absolutely and downright *accepted* him. . . . Did not you misunderstand him? — You were both talking of other things; of business, shows of cattle, or new drills — and might not you, in the confusion of so many subjects, mistake him? — It was not Harriet's hand that he was certain of — it was the dimensions of some famous ox." (p. 373)

For the period's interest in the improvement of cattle breeds, and for an argument that Austen in her inconspicuous fictional ways shared Stubbs's promotion of progressive farming, see Alistair M. Duckworth, "Jane Austen and George Stubbs: Two Speculations," *Eighteenth-Century Fiction* 13.1 (2000): 53–66.

On page 398: *Crossed letter from Jane Austen to Cassandra, front and back pages (June 20, 1808).* ". . . [I]n general she fills the whole paper and crosses half." " 'Well, Hetty, now I think you will be put to it to make out all that chequer-work' " (p. 135).

delightfully — more than he can always understand.

The two Middletons are come to dine & spend the day with him. I wd. rather any Hour to say whatever she thinks necessary, but cannot settle — & I hope to see her at Steventon soon after the 1st of the [...] of that time is as convenient to my Brother as any other. I have hardly done justice to what she means on this subject, as her intention is that my Mother shd. come at whatever time she likes best. They will be at home on or [...] I always wd. wish for a morning visit from Bookham, & [...] & Mrs Cooke have just given me my share. He & I talked a vast quantity of Southampton. The [...] Walter [...] Having sent to his bookseller to call, all [...] will write to [...] very soon. Yours very affecly

THE

FROLICS

OF THE

Sphynx;

OR,

AN ENTIRELY-ORIGINAL COLLECTION

OF

CHARADES,

RIDDLES, AND CONUNDRUMS.

Oxford:

PRINTED AND SOLD BY MUNDAY AND SLATTER;
SOLD ALSO BY
MESSRS. LONGMAN, HURST, REES, ORME, AND BROWN,
PATERNOSTER-ROW, LONDON.

1820.

The Frolics of the Sphinx (1820). ". . . [T]he only mental provision [Harriet] was making for the evening of life, was the collecting and transcribing all the riddles of every sort that she could meet with . . ." (p. 72).

Square Pianoforté (Rochead, 1805), with "Broadwood's Single Action."
". . . [A] pianoforté — a very elegant looking instrument — not a grand,
but a large-sized square pianoforté" (p. 178).

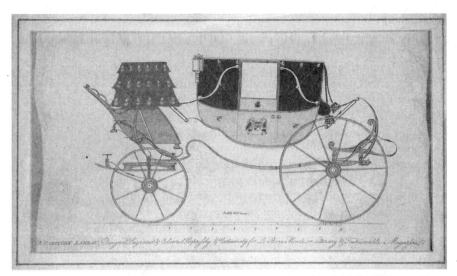

A Barouche Landau, engraving in Le Beau Monde *(1805).* "They will have their barouche-landau, of course, which holds four perfectly" (p. 222).
Reprinted by permission of C. J. Nicholson, Esq.

George Lambert, A View of Box Hill, Surrey *(1733).* "It was settled that they should go to Box Hill" (p. 282).
Copyright © Tate, London 2000.

George Stubbs, The Lincolnshire Ox *(1790).* "It was not Harriet's hand that he was certain of — it was the dimensions of some famous ox" (p. 373).

PART TWO

Emma:
A Case Study in
Contemporary Criticism

A Critical History of
Emma

In 1995, Colin Firth parties were held across England during the showing of the BBC serial *Pride and Prejudice* (Firth, playing Darcy, became a sexual icon), while in the United States viewers were delighted by *Clueless*, Amy Heckerling's brilliantly idiomatic transposition of *Emma* into a teenage Beverly Hills milieu. In the same year Emma Thompson won an Oscar for her screenplay of *Sense and Sensibility*, and Roger Michell directed *Persuasion* in the grittiest of the adaptations. In 1996 two films of *Emma* appeared — Douglas McGrath's for Miramax, in which Gwyneth Paltrow played the heroine, and Diarmud Lawrence's less frothy version jointly sponsored by Meridian (ITV) and A & E. In 1999 Patricia Rozema wrote and directed *Mansfield Park* in a controversial adaptation featuring lesbian subtexts and a critique of colonialism.

What E. M. Forster had been in the previous decade — a novelist profitably recycled for the silver screen — Jane Austen became in the second half of the 1990s. Except that Austenmania exceeds by far the Forster vogue. Her name and face appear on T-shirts and bumper stickers ("I'd rather be reading Jane Austen"), in *Entertainment Weekly* (where Theo Westenberg's "photo" showed a glamorous Jane Austen lounging by a pool in Beverly Hills), in innumerable journals and newspapers, and even on CNN. Sequels to her novels abound. Spin-off books on music, food, dress, houses and landscapes in her novels appear regularly, along with "quiz" books and collections of her sayings. In tribute to the detective aspects of *Emma* Stephanie Barron writes "Jane Austen Mysteries." At annual meetings of JASNA (the Jane Austen Society of North America) members dress in Regency costumes.

The Austen boom is doubtless a function of a rapidly changing technology (Troost and Greenfield 2). Web sites, such as Henry Churchyard's *Republic of Pemberley,* open her works to a larger audience, and e-mail allows for the free circulation of ideas. Her popularity, though resented by some, is a significant social phenomenon. For present purposes, the importance of Austenmania lies in the contrast it offers to the modest reception of her novels during and after her lifetime. In the critical history that follows I trace responses to Austen's fiction (particularly *Emma*) through four phases: (1) from 1816 to 1870 when she was not yet a canonical author; (2) from 1870 to 1939 when, following the memoir published by her nephew, she became a cult figure; (3) from 1939 to about 1970 when her novels were the focus of intense analysis by academic critics, most of whom were male; and (4) from 1970 until the present when her fictional achievement was read politically from a number of theoretical perspectives, many provided by women.

Jane Austen's relative obscurity during her life and for years after may come as a surprise. She had admirers, such as Sir Walter Scott, Archbishop Whately, and Lord Macaulay, but she was far from being a popular author. Her lifetime earnings from her novels came to less than £700, compared with more than £11,000 for her contemporary Maria Edgeworth (Fergus 28). *Emma* was published at the end of 1815 in an edition of 2,000 copies. It found readers outside England, with an imprint in Philadelphia (1816) and a translation in Paris (1816); but four years after publication, only 1,461 copies of the English edition had sold, and the rest were remaindered. Hannah More's *Coelebs in Search of a Wife* (1808), by contrast, earned £2,000 in the first year, and thirty editions of 1,000 copies each sold before her death in 1834 (Jones cited in Looser, p. 584 in this volume).

Emma's failure to equal the success of *Pride and Prejudice,* which was published in January 1813 and went into a second edition in October of the same year, was not the fault of her publisher. John Murray did what he could for the novel by persuading Walter Scott to review it in an issue of the *Quarterly Review* that appeared in March 1816. In his generous review, Scott sees *Emma* as offering in its depiction of "characters and incidents . . . from the current of ordinary life" a new style of novel quite different from gothic and romantic novels of the recent past (Southam, 1968 59). That Scott admired Austen is clear from a later journal entry (March 14, 1826) in which he opposes his "Big Bow-wow strain" to Austen's "exquisite touch which renders ordinary commonplace things and characters interesting from the truth of the description and the sentiment" (106). But in the review his praise is not unmixed. His comparison of her novels to the Flemish school of painting, his description of Mr. Woodhouse and Miss Bates as "prosing," and his landscape analogy (Austen's novels are to cornfield, cottages, and meadows as romantic novels are to sublime mountainous scenery) would set the terms for later depreciation as well as praise. Charlotte Brontë, for example, found in Pride and Prejudice "a carefully fenced, highly cultivated garden, with neat borders and delicate flowers; but . . . no open country, no fresh air, no blue hill, no bonny beck" (Southam, 1968 126); and of Emma she wrote: "there is a Chinese fidelity, a miniature delicacy in the painting: she ruffles her reader by nothing vehement, disturbs him by nothing profound: the Passions are perfectly unknown to her" (128).

In the most important early review, Richard Whately, Archbishop of Dublin, preferred her novels to those of Maria Edgeworth, which he found too didactic. Austen, he proposed, was comparable to Shakespeare in the "dramatic air" she gave to the narrative and in the variety of her characterization (Southam, 1968 97–98). Whately's Aristotelian attention to Austen's integration of plot, character, and narrative style looks forward to mid-twentieth-century humanist criticism, with which it shares the assumption that great literature can transcend partisanship and achieve a nonideological representation of human experience. Yet in granting Austen "the merit of . . . being evidently a Christian writer" (95), Whately was in fact appropriating Austen's novels for his own faith, and even in the nineteenth century his view did not go unchallenged. Before his conversion to Catholicism, John Henry Newman, who liked the character of Emma ("I feel kind to her whenever I think of her"), disliked Austen's representation of religion: "What vile creatures her parsons are! she has not a dream of the high Catholic ethos" (Southam, 1968 117).

For fifty years after her death, however, Austen's novels were hardly sites of conflict over her ideology. Lord Macaulay followed Whately in comparing her to Shakespeare, but most writers saw her (for better or worse) as the mistress of a limited world. Seldom are we surprised by challenging proposals, such as Julia Kavanaugh's, that Austen could not represent happy love (Southam, 1968 194). Of all her critics of this period, G. H. Lewes (in 1859) is the most perceptive. Like Scott, he mixes criticism with praise. While admiring her "economy of art" (in which he finds her comparable to Molière and Sophocles), her perfectly discriminated characters, and her "dramatic ventriloquism," Lewes concedes that her novels lack "breadth, picturesqueness, and passion," and, with his consort George Eliot in mind, he questions her "culture, reach of mind, and depth of emotional sensibility" (153–62). His conclusion is that "her place is among the Immortals; but the pedestal is erected in a quiet niche of the great temple" (166).

Following publication of James Edward Austen-Leigh's *A Memoir of Jane Austen* in 1870, Austen's novels achieved the kind of popularity given to the novels of Scott, Thackeray, Dickens, the Brontës, and Trollope. But her popularity was of a distinctive kind. As Southam (1987) shows, the *Memoir* encouraged a view of Austen as a ladylike amateur whose quiet pictures of rural England provided an antidote to the violence found in the novels of Dickens and Wilkie Collins. At a time when women were seen as angels of the hearth, Austen-Leigh's portrait of "dear Aunt Jane" provided comforting confirmation. George Saintsbury, in 1894, was glad to report that Elizabeth Bennet had "nothing for the 'New Woman' about her" (Southam, 1987 218). Austen was viewed as a delineator of gentry manners; she became, in Southam's words, a kind of "cultural shibboleth" separating those with taste from those lacking it (Southam, 1987 21). By the 1880s "Austenolatry" (174) was in full swing, encouraged by sumptuous editions such as the Steventon edition of 1882. This, the first collected edition of Austen's novels, included the *Memoir, Lady Susan,* a prettified portrait of the author, and woodcuts of Chawton Church and Steventon parsonage — Austen's little world in a "tidy bundle," as Claudia Johnson writes ("Austen Cults and Cultures" 211). By the 1890s publishers were vying for the services of artists, notably Hugh Thomson, whose illustrations, sentimentally conceived and featuring period costumes, evoked the peace of an earlier and simpler time.

The Austen boom was too much for Henry James. In "The Lesson of Balzac" (1905) he applauded the "rectification of estimate" that had made Austen popular at last, but deplored the process whereby "the body of publishers, editors, illustrators, producers of the pleasant twaddle of magazines . . . found their 'dear,' our dear, everybody's dear, Jane so infinitely to their material purpose" (230). The "Janeiteism" he attacked, however, not to mention the commercial opportunism of publishers, persisted well into the twentieth century; it is still to be found in the antiquarian articles that appear in the journals of Jane Austen societies, for example, and in the fervor with which "heretical" proposals (such as Terry Castle's in a *London Review* essay of 1995 claiming homoerotic elements in Austen's relations with her sister Cassandra) are seized on and denounced in correspondence columns. The persistence of the cult is partly explained by the support it received from R. W. Chapman's monumental Clarendon edition of her novels in 1923. This was the first critical edition of any English novelist, and as revised in 1932 and later, it remains the standard scholarly text. Based on a collation of the early editions, it brought to Austen's texts the meticulous scholarship hitherto reserved for classical texts; but in its selective annotations, indexes, notes, and illustrations, it pressed Austen into the service of a postwar "national nostalgia," in which a comforting rather than disturbing Regency past was recalled ("Austen Cults and Cultures" 218–19).

Only seldom in the period between 1870 and 1940 do we encounter criticism of high order. The novelist Margaret Oliphant tried in 1870 to correct the cozy picture painted in the *Memoir* by discovering in the novels a "fine vein of feminine cynicism" (Southam, 1968 216). But as Southam points out, by 1882 in her *Literary History of England*, Oliphant was following the conventional line. Another fine piece largely dropped out of sight until Lionel Trilling called attention to it in 1957. The essay, by Richard Simpson, a Shakespearian scholar, appeared anonymously in the *North British Review* in 1870; in it he sees Austen as saturated with "the Platonic idea that the giving and receiving of knowledge, the active formation of another's character, or the more passive growth under another's guidance, is the truest and strongest foundation of love" (244).

Compared with Simpson's criticism, that of another Shakespearian scholar, A. C. Bradley, given in a lecture in 1911, sounds Janeite tones: "As for Mr. Woodhouse, whose most famous sentences hang like texts in frames on the four walls of our memories, he is, next to Don Quixote, perhaps the most perfect gentleman in fiction" (Southam, 1987 237–38). Not everyone responded with this degree of belletristic enthusiasm. The attacks by Emerson and Mark Twain, evincing an American dislike of insular Englishness, are well-known. In an 1861 journal entry, Emerson found her novels "vulgar in tone, sterile in artistic invention, imprisoned in the wretched conventions of English society, without genius, wit, or knowledge of the world" (qtd. in Southam,

1968 28); and Twain felt "like a barkeeper entering the kingdom of heaven" when he took up one of her novels (232–33). Other Americans, however, notably William Dean Howells and Edith Wharton, read Austen's fiction with anglophile enthusiasm.

Sustained attention to Austen is not to be found in the essays of Henry James, E. M. Forster, and Virginia Woolf. Woolf made the obligatory comparison with Shakespeare (but ambivalently as we will see), and she proposed that, had Austen lived longer and experienced more, she would have been "the forerunner of Henry James and of Proust" (283). She was neither the first nor the last to make the connection with James; James himself, however, though in a letter of 1883 he appreciated "her narrow unconscious perfection of form" (179), eschewed any attempt to analyze her style. Forster, a self-declared "Austenite," reviewed Chapman's edition of the letters, distinguishing between the "Miss Austen" of the letters, who engaged in triviality and rancor, and the "Jane Austen" of the novels who somehow, through the alchemy of form, transcended the limitations of her personality. And in *Aspects of the Novel* (1927) he illustrated the difference between "flat" and "round" characters by discussing Lady Bertram. But in sum his critical contribution seems rather slight, his real tribute to Austen being found in his five novels, which everywhere reveal the influence of her techniques of irony and characterization.

In 1917, on the hundredth anniversary of Austen's death, appeared in the *Quarterly Review* what may be the single most interesting essay ever written on Austen. Reginald Farrer deplored the "fantasies of propriety" attaching to her reputation (248). For Farrer, Austen's novels exhibited "a most perfect mastery of her weapons, a most faultless and precise adjustment of means to end" (250). Developing Simpson's argument, he saw Austen's primary concern to be with "character unfolded through love, not with that love's crudities of appetite and incident" (252). Like Whately, he appreciated her avoidance of the didactic. In his reading of *Mansfield Park*, a novel he saw as "vitiated throughout by a radical dishonesty" (262), Farrer anticipated the "subversive" criticism of Marvin Mudrick. But his praise of *Emma* is unstinted: "Take it all in all, 'Emma' is the very climax of Jane Austen's work; and a real appreciation of 'Emma' is the final test of citizenship in her kingdom" (266).

In the thirty or so years following Mary Lascelles's *Jane Austen and Her Art* (1939) — the first substantial academic study of Austen's novels — Austen became a major figure in literary criticism. Her remarkable rise to eminence in the canon was promoted by her inclusion in two of the most influential books of the period. In F. R. Leavis's *The Great Tradition* (1948), she inaugurates the main tradition of English fiction (to be developed in the work of George Eliot, James, and Conrad); this tradition, Leavis argued, was characterized by technical innovation and "a marked moral intensity" (8–9). In Ian Watt's *The Rise of the Novel* (1957), Austen completes rather than initiates a fictional tradition. For Watt her achievement was to bring the novel to its mature form (especially in *Emma*) through a synthesis of Henry Fielding's objective "realism of assessment" and Samuel Richardson's subjective "realism of presentation" (296–97).

Appearing at the beginning of Leavis's study and at the end of Watt's, Austen had achieved a niche in a patrilineal pantheon more prominent than Lewes could have imagined. Her prestige as artist and moralist was high indeed. As if in illustration of Leavis's claim that Austen, "in her indebtedness to others, provides an exceptionally illuminating study of the nature of originality" (5), several scholars stressed her relation to male predecessors. C. S. Lewis believed we breathe the air of Samuel Johnson's *Rambler* and *Idler* in her novels; his Oxford colleague Gilbert Ryle derived her ethics from the writings of the third earl of Shaftesbury; and later at Harvard, Douglas Bush extended the context to an even wider and more distant (but still male) past comprising nothing less than the Christian humanism of Spenser, Milton, Johnson, and Burke. More commonly, however, critics responded to Leavis's insistence that she did not offer an aesthetic value separable from moral significance (7). In 1962, Malcolm Bradbury wrote that, after reading *Emma*, "we have been persuaded . . . to consider every human action as a crucial, committing act of self-definition" (345–46). Bradbury's humanist reading stemmed not only from Leavis but from Lionel Trilling who in a famous 1957 essay made high claims for *Emma*.

Trilling sees the world of *Emma* as an "idyll" separated from the complexities of the modern world and the modern self; but he also speaks of Austen's conception of a "specifically English way of life" (40–41) that is endangered by the heroine when, in an act of "national import," she snobbishly dismisses Robert Martin, the worthy yeoman farmer (40). The danger is averted, however, and through her representation of Emma's conflicted subjectivity, Austen becomes one of Trilling's liberal humanists, whose novel reveals to us "the possibility of controlling the personal life, of becoming acquainted with ourselves, of creating a community of 'intelligent love'" (55). (Trilling's citation is to Richard Simpson.)

An equally influential, if differently based, affirmation of Austen's humanism appeared in Wayne Booth's chapter on *Emma* in *The Rhetoric of Fiction* (1961). Booth displayed the formidable power of the Chicago school's "neo-Aristotelian" methodology (see Glossary under "Chicago School" and "Formalism" for definition). Focusing on point of view, he proposed that Austen's problem in *Emma* was how to retain the reader's sympathy for Emma, despite her many faults; and he argued that Austen's solution lay in her decision to involve us in the heroine's subjective reflections, while at the same time containing these reflections within a narrative discourse that provides, more subtly than Mr. Knightley's overt criticisms, a measure of Emma's aberrations from sense and responsibility. Guided by the narrator, the reader hopes for her happiness and rejoices when she gains it in her marriage to Mr. Knightley at the end.

Not all criticism was affirmative. Indeed, if we take the period as beginning, not with Lascelles's study, but with D. W. Harding's "Regulated Hatred" essay of 1940, a very different view appears. Anticipating Marvin Mudrick (1952), Harding described a "subversive" author who hid her resentments behind a conventional mask. Irony was Austen's means of "defense and discovery," to cite Mudrick's subtitle. Her books, Harding stated, "are enjoyed by precisely the sort of people whom she disliked: she is a literary classic of the society which attitudes like hers, held widely enough, would undermine" (167). Subversive criticism was not entirely new; Farrer employed it in his attack on *Mansfield Park*. But armed with Freudian insights (Harding was a psychologist as well as a literary critic), these critics found repression and displacement in the novels. In *Sense and Sensibility,* Mudrick claimed, Marianne Dashwood is betrayed, not by her lover Willoughby, but by Austen — who thus represses her own insurgent desires (91–93). Reading *Emma,* Mudrick goes further. Recalling Farrer's warning that "'Emma' is not an easy book to read [and] should never be a beginner's primer," he finds intimations of lesbianism: "Emma is in love with [Harriet]: a love unphysical and inadmissable, even perhaps undefinable in such a society; and therefore safe" (203).

Beginning in the 1970s, the hegemony of the English department, with its commitment to a formalist and humanist pedagogy, and its limited pluralism, was progressively challenged and ultimately overthrown. Jane Austen played no small part in the process. In 1971, my work *The Improvement of the Estate* was considered a new departure by some reviewers. I read Austen as a conservative author, who in a revolutionary time affirmed a Burkean conception of society (or "estate"), while uncovering the threats posed to the transmission of a cultural heritage by irresponsible heirs ("improvers") Mr. Knightley, despite some jealousy of Frank Churchill, seemed to me an exemplary figure; and just as the play in *Mansfield Park* carried subversive cultural implications, so, I argued, the secret games that run through *Emma* threatened the open and public communication on which a stable community relied. The book was perhaps less of a departure than some thought; it remained formalist in its assumption that Austen's novels were aesthetic wholes; and it remained literary-historical in its discovery of eighteenth-century contexts for Austen's deployment of such motifs as landscape and laughter.

Marxists and cultural critics, while often agreeing with my characterization of Austen's political position, objected to the book's idealist methodology and nonevaluative stance. New historicist critics took issue with the book's moral orientation. Deconstructive critics distrusted its reliance on binary oppositions in which one term (Mr. Knightley) was preferred to another (Frank Churchill). And feminists found the book insufficiently attentive to the pernicious role of the marriage plot in the political subordination of women. In the preface to the 1994 reissue I sought to come to terms with such criticisms. Here I look at selected instances of the above approaches, reserving a separate section for feminism, by any measure the most important contribution to Austen criticism in the last generation, and a final section for gender studies and other recent work whose relation to feminism is often anxious.

After Raymond Williams's *The Country and the City* (1973), Marxist criticism of Austen became common. Austen had an important place in Williams's history of England; under the surface of domestic life in country villages, she revealed interactions between landed and trading wealth at a period when the split between "culture" and "society" seriously widened. Typically, he saw her morality as based in class interest, but his stance was not condemnatory. In her novels Williams found a unity of tone that allowed Austen not only to expose the economic basis of society but also to make confident judgments, founded on a belief that moral and social improvement should coexist. In David Aers's "Community and Morality" (1981) a harsher view emerged. Aers found in her fiction an unresolved conflict between market values and a neo-feudal morality. James Thompson in *Between Self and World* (1988) also saw a conflict between exchange and landed values in her novels, but following Pierre Macherey, he argued that a "bourgeois" ideology, entailing an increased privatization of experience, sustains contradictions, particularly as regards courtship and marriage. Austen's heroines "are sent out to do business in a bad market" (143); but rather than focus on marriage as a problem, Austen portrays it as a "refuge from commodification" (156). Thompson's view of romantic love as detrimental to women is, as he acknowledges, close to Mary Poovey's argument in *The Proper Lady and the Woman Writer* (1984), while his critique of Austen's failure to conceive of options besides marriage (such as female friendship) accords with the views of other feminists, notably Ruth Perry.

Two other studies, closer perhaps to cultural criticism than to Marxism, also reveal Austen's fictional responses to economic pressures. In 1983, David Spring described Austen's family as "pseudo-gentry"; by this term, he meant a professional rather than landed family, who were nevertheless well-connected to gentry kinsmen and who strategically adopted gentry standards in a highly aggressive capitalist world. Responding to this milieu in her novels, Austen combined, in Spring's witty phrase, "the gifts of an estate agent, family lawyer, and auctioneer" (61). In *Women Writing about Money* (1995), Edward Copeland placed Austen in a commodity culture, suggesting that, while she seeks to define a moral economics by distinguishing between acceptable and unacceptable consumption, her motives may be less moral than defensive. Like Spring, Copeland sees her as intent on retaining her links with the landed order, and influenced by the sociologist Pierre Bourdieu, he reads manners in her novels as a means of legitimating status.

New historicist criticism of Austen shares some of the de-idealizing tendencies of the above approaches, though the tutor influence is Foucault more than Marx. The exemplar of this approach is Nancy Armstrong. In her influential *Desire and Domestic Criticism* (1987), she places Austen midway in an ambitious history of bourgeois disciplinary practices and of "sexuality," considered as a cultural system of signs. In novels before Austen, and especially in Samuel Richardson's *Pamela* (1740), the domestic woman, in whom value existed "inside" as a gendered subjectivity, opposed her aristocratic counterpart, in whom value was an external function of fortune and status. After Austen, however, the domestic woman performs a containing rather than a liberating function; her middle-class domesticity is set against working-class discontents, and the household she oversees becomes a counterimage of the marketplace, an interior space in which women have circumscribed power. Austen's position in Armstrong's history is pivotal. In *Pride and*

Prejudice, the marriage plot plays a significant role in the inscription of heterosexual monogamy as the social norm (50–51). And in *Emma* an emphasis on the need for "literacy" produces a new domestic form of cultural authority. Representing a fictional community "free of all traces of the regional, religious, social, or factional dialects that marked other kinds of writing" (136), *Emma* provided a norm of polite English, based on the speech of country gentlefolk, which newly empowered social groups could, and did, emulate.

In "What Is an Author?" (1979), Michel Foucault saw interpretative reliance upon the author as the means whereby an institution was able to organize critical discourse so as to protect its vested interests. By positing an author as the origin of a coherent vision, readers could exclude what was surplus, or fortuitous, or uncontrolled in a text. Though Foucault seemed to be calling for the free dissemination of textual meanings, Foucauldian critics tended to make the same claim: that novels in general, and Austen's novels in particular, are prime agents in the construction of bourgeois subjectivity. No wonder, then, that Armstrong's reading should provoke debate from some Marxist and cultural critics, who sought a more historical specification of Austen's politics, and from some feminists, who in their desire to see Austen's novels positively, returned to a notion of human agency. Meanwhile, it was another critical approach, deconstruction, that sought to unravel her texts and discover the delights of the fortuitous and the uncontrolled.

If one were to choose a novel ripe for the deconstructive picking (apart), that novel might well be *Emma.* The novel is not only filled with binary oppositions — Knightley and Churchill, English and French manners, seriousness and play — it is also packed with riddles, charades, puzzles, and conundrums, and it returns again and again to letters: letters written and (mis)read, letters sent and received, letters delivered to and picked up from the post office, letters that fail to reach their destination. What lover of Jacques Derrida's *The Post Card: From Socrates to Freud and Beyond* or Jacques Lacan's "Seminar on 'The Purloined Letter'" could resist a "writerly" engagement with the novel? Joseph Litvak's "Reading Characters: Self, Society, and Text in *Emma*" (1985) was an early attempt to see the novel as staging a battle "between figurative language and figuring out, between ciphers and deciphering, between Emma's deep superficiality and Knightley's superficial depth" (98). Opposing readings in which Emma submits to the objective perspectives of an older man, Litvak celebrates the free play of the reader's imagination enabled by the slipperiness of the novel's language. More recent studies that address games, letters, or

the post office in *Emma* include Mary Favret's "Jane Austen and the
Look of Letters" (1993), Valentine Cunningham's "Games Texts Play"
(1994), Mack Smith's "Fancy and Understanding and the Ekphrastic
Riddles of *Emma*" (1995), and Diane Cousineau's "Letters and the
Post Office: Epistolary Exchange in Jane Austen's *Emma*" (1997).

Derrida is an influence on such studies; for example, his proposal
that the letter is not so much a genre, but all genres, even literature
itself, underlies Cunningham's deconstruction of stable meanings in
Emma (320). Cunningham sees Emma's mentor Mr. Knightley as a fal-
lible figure: "Reading letters is for him like reading Austen's novel is for
us, a matter of engaging with the definition of moral terms"(322). But
such a "hermeneutic" enterprise invites failure. In the alphabet game,
Mr. Knightley deciphers two of the anagrams, but the third eludes him,
just as it eludes us. Family tradition had it that the solution was "pardon," Frank Churchill's secret plea of forgiveness from Jane; but Cunningham will have none of it. The text is silent, rebuking those who
insist on recoverable meanings. Cunningham's reading (or rather writing) is itself a kind of play, witty, fluid, and responsive to Austen's own
dazzling games with words. Compared with a traditional structural
analysis (e.g., that of Edgar Shannon 1956), Cunningham's essay scin-
tillates. But its own interpretative failures raise questions. The author
mistakenly assumes, for example, that Mr. Knightley converses with
Jane Fairfax about the post office, when in fact the speaker is his
brother, Mr. John Knightley (321–22). Is the misreading a consequence of the uncertainty of language, forever sliding from signifier to
signifier in a chain of deferred meanings? Or is it, simply, error? Perhaps
meanings in *Emma* are recoverable. Some critics, including some feminist critics, have thought so.

Feminist criticism came late to Austen's novels. Astute nineteenth-
century writers such as Julia Kavanaugh and Mrs. Oliphant did not find
her politically progressive. Nor did the crusading Millicent Fawcett
when, in essays contributed to *The Mother's Companion* (1877–78), she
recruited Austen for Victorian feminism; what Fawcett stressed were
her womanly "habits, manners, and occupations" (qtd. in Southam,
1987 39). Virginia Woolf praised Austen's artistry and included her in
A Room of One's Own (1929), but neither there nor in any of several
essays and reviews does Woolf see her as an ally in a critique of the patriarchy. Rather the reverse: in a 1913 review Woolf describes Austen's
"conservative spirit," and finds that she had "too little of the rebel in
her composition" (Southam, 1987 241–42). Even her praise of Austen's

Shakespearean impersonality and nonpolemical style was ambivalent; Woolf, Janet Todd concludes, was hostile to Austen's reticence and control ("Who's Afraid of Jane Austen?" 162). Only Rebecca West proves to be a significant early exception. In a preface to an edition of *Northanger Abbey* (1932), she described the feminism of the novel as so "marked" as to cause her publisher to leave the manuscript on the shelf (294–95). But West's review went largely unnoticed at the time.

Feminist voices were, in fact, largely absent from Austen criticism until the late 1970s. Marilyn Butler's landmark *Jane Austen and the War of Ideas* (1975) was not only prefeminist but in some ways anti-feminist. Butler set Austen's novels in the highly politicized decade of the revolutionary 1790s, comparing them to other novels, many by women, that were polemically engaged in a "war of ideas." The trouble for feminists was that Butler saw Austen as belonging to the conservative side of the question, as an unequivocally anti-Jacobin novelist whose works resemble those of reactionary novelists like Jane West and Elizabeth Hamilton rather than those of a progressive author such as Maria Edgeworth or a radical such as Mary Hays. Her conservatism is evident, Butler argued, in her preference for rationality over intuition and in her respect for inherited moral or religious systems over individual choice; it also appears through her plots, which either bring individualistic heroines to a recognition of their social duty (Elizabeth, Emma) or present them as principled from the beginning (Elinor, Fanny).

In 1975 Butler conceded that Austen's morality was so distinct from modern morality that it might prove "antipathetic" to current readers (296). But in a 1987 introduction to the reissue of her book — an introduction that gives an excellent survey of the contributions of such feminist critics as Patricia Spacks, Ellen Moers, Elaine Showalter, Margaret Kirkham, Ruth Perry, Sandra Gilbert, and Susan Gubar (xx–xxxiii) — Butler took a more open view, seeing Austen as a feminist in a tradition of Tory women's writing. Even so, she remained skeptical of critics such as Margaret Kirkham who, in *Jane Austen, Feminism and Fiction* (1983), placed Austen in the camp of Enlightenment feminism and of those, such as Gilbert and Gubar, who viewed gender independently of class, religion, and politics.

If feminism was late in arriving, its effects, when it did arrive, were electric. Gilbert and Gubar's *The Madwoman in the Attic* (1979) provided the strongest shock. Their Austen is far distant from the controlled author whose acquiescence in the patriarchy troubled Woolf. Though her novels camouflage the rebelliousness that is openly expressed in her juvenile works, it is there, Gilbert and Gubar argue, beneath the surface. Austen's heroines may seem to enact the submission required of women in male-dominated societies, but her anger erupts in such female characters as Lady Susan, Lady Catherine de Bourgh, and Mrs. Norris (169–74). Gilbert and Gubar's construction of Austen as a subversive feminist was seen by others besides Butler as ahistorical and essentialist in its assumption that female predicaments and responses were uniform across time (Todd, "Jane Austen, politics and sensibility"). Yet the verve of their analysis inspired many to return to topics treated, if not always first raised, in *The Madwoman in the Attic:* the disciplinary role of the marriage plot; the tyranny of fathers and brothers; the importance accorded, or not accorded, to female friendship.

Persistent disagreements regarding Austen's feminism, or lack thereof, have marked recent criticism. Though some, such as Kirkham and Alison Sulloway, affirmed Austen as a consciously feminist author whose "viewpoint on the moral nature and status of women, female education, marriage, authority and the family, and the representation of women in literature is strikingly similar to that shown by Mary Wollstonecraft in *A Vindication of the Rights of Woman*" (Kirkham xi), others were skeptical. Comparisons with Wollstonecraft are certainly possible (see the extract from Wollstonecraft in "Contextual Documents," p. 387). Like Wollstonecraft, Austen attacked those who valued female "accomplishments" and undervalued female reason and intelligence. But the contrasts seem even greater. Unlike Wollstonecraft, for example, Austen had no programmatic plans for improving woman's lot. Her apparent political quietism, indeed, led some feminist critics to deny or qualify Austen's feminism. For them, she relied too much on the marriage plot, bought into the ideology of romantic love, gave short shrift to female friendship, tamed her independent heroines, and avoided institutional criticism (Duckworth x–xi, xxiv). In a polemical essay, Julia Prewitt Brown countered "the feminist depreciation of Austen," by interpreting marriages in the novels not as "cowardly accommodations" to "the central institution of bourgeois culture" but as unions in which hero and heroine come together in the service of "national purpose" (304–07).

Claudia Johnson's *Jane Austen: Women, Politics, and the Novel* (1988), the book that occasioned Brown's review, has proved to be the most influential book on Austen in recent years. Like Butler, Johnson saw Austen's novels as emerging out of the fiction of the revolutionary 1790s; unlike Butler, she did not see Austen as an anti-Jacobin novelist. In Johnson's view, Austen could have found, even in such conservative predecessors as Frances Burney, Elizabeth Hamilton, and Amelia Opie, various techniques of double plotting, antithetical characterization, and irony allowing her to smuggle social criticism into her fiction. Consequently, she was able to show, "beneath the nominally conventional surfaces of [her] novels, truths about the absence or arbitrariness of fathers, the self-importance of brothers, and the bad faith of mentors which, if not as daring or sweeping, are still as disturbing as any of the indictments made by radical novelists" (26). In Johnson's view, if Austen adopted conservative fictional models, she did so for strategic reasons, and not because, like Edmund Burke, she wished to defend an inherited culture in time of revolutionary danger. In her root and branch extirpation of patrilineal influence, there would seem to be some overcompensation; there can be no doubt, however, that Johnson's book, along with Sulloway's equally affirmative study, has helped persuade recent critics, such as Devoney Looser, that Austen may properly be termed a feminist.

In her recent work, Johnson has moved from feminist criticism to gender criticism. Casting her lot with "the queer Austen" ("Divine Miss Jane" 146), she explores the irony that, just as novel criticism was becoming an academic "discipline," it — and not Austen's fiction — was exerting a disciplinary control over reading practices. From 1940 on, she observes, a middle-class "professorate" championed "bourgeois virtue" over the "Bloomsburian aestheticism" of Lord David Cecil and the "Janeitism" of upper-class amateurs. Such criticism sowed the seeds for the normalizing value accorded to the marriage plot in such different critics as Marvin Mudrick and Wayne Booth. Mudrick, expecting Austen's novels "to narrativize the maturing processes of heterosexual love," could only deplore the heroine's penchant for same-sex love in *Emma* (158), while Booth, blind to what Mudrick and Edmund Wilson (1944) saw, engaged in "a massively definitive normalization," in which the telos of marriage, implied from the first page of *Emma*, corrects the heroine's potential deviance (159).

Like Eve Sedgwick, Johnson is offended by the bottom-spanking "Girl Being Taught a Lesson" mode of criticism that disciplines wayward heroines like Emma. She finds it typical of an academy intent on straightening Austen up. In the very Janeitism excluded by professional scholars, but reappearing in Jane Austen societies in America, Britain, and Australia, she finds an openness to questions foreclosed by most critics — to the "unnerving" possibility, for example, that manners and morals, contrary to the views of Leavis, Booth, Trilling, and many others, are different things in Austen, and that manners, separate from morals, may be both civilizing and productive in ways that are better understood by reference to the works of Oscar Wilde than those of Samuel Johnson.

A similar shift of emphasis is found in Judy Simons's "Classics and Trash: Reading Austen in the 1990s" (1998), in which Austen's current place in popular culture is not deplored but interpreted as a response akin to Austen's own delight in the popular culture of her time. Like the circulating libraries of Austen's period, which displayed her novels on the same tables as the pulp fiction of the Minerva Press (Copeland 114), the Internet today has declassified Austen's fiction. As Simons writes, "other pens" have fun with her, adding to "the catalogue of Jane Austen jokes, the Jane Austen Top Ten Song List and the Jane Austen Punishment list," imagining how her characters would act if alive today ("The Woodhouse Diet Plan"), and sending letters to the advice column ("Can I trust Emma's judgement?") (32–33). How far such fun will extend is hard to predict. That Austen's novels will remain central to the illumination of successive intellectual discourses, however, seems certain. Patricia Rozema's brilliantly tendentious film of *Mansfield Park* (1999) reflects an awareness not only of postcolonial criticism that has implicated the novel in issues of slavery but of gender criticism that has discovered alternative sexual possibilities in her novels. Perhaps it is their responsiveness to multiple ideological demands, rather than their achievement of universal truths transcending culture and period, that makes her novels classic. That so many conflicting thinkers want to claim her as an ally — or alternatively to identify what is pernicious in her influence — offers yet more evidence that she is, indeed, comparable to Shakespeare.

WORKS CITED

Aers, David. "Community and Morality: Towards Reading Jane Austen." *Romanticism and Ideology: Studies in English Writing, 1765–1830.* Ed. David Aers et al. Boston: Routledge, 1981. 118–36.

Armstrong, Nancy. *Desire and Domestic Fiction: A Political History of the Novel.* New York: Oxford UP, 1987.

Austen-Leigh, James Edward. *A Memoir of Jane Austen.* London: Bentley, 1870.

Booth, Wayne C. "Control of Distance in Jane Austen's *Emma*." *The Rhetoric of Fiction*. By Booth. Chicago: U of Chicago P, 1961. 243–66.

Bradbury, Malcolm. "Jane Austen's *Emma*." *Critical Quarterly* 4 (Winter 1962): 335–46.

Brontë, Charlotte. Letter to G. H. Lewes, January 12, 1848. Southam, 1968. 126–27.

———. Letter to W. S. Williams, April 12, 1850. Southam, 1968. 127–28.

Brown, Julia Prewitt. "The Feminist Depreciation of Austen: A Polemical Reading." *Novel* 23 (Spring 1990): 303–13.

Bush, Douglas. *Jane Austen*. New York: Macmillan, 1975.

Butler, Marilyn. *Jane Austen and the War of Ideas*. 1975. Rpt. with new intro. Oxford: Clarendon, 1987.

Castle, Terry. "Sister-sister." *London Review of Books*, 3 August 1995: 3–4.

Churchyard, Henry, ed. *Republic of Pemberley*. <http://www.pemberley.com/>.

Copeland, Edward, and Juliet McMaster, eds. *The Cambridge Companion to Jane Austen*. Cambridge: Cambridge UP, 1997.

Copeland, Edward. *Women Writing about Money: Women's Fiction in England, 1790–1820*. Cambridge: Cambridge UP, 1995.

Cousineau, Diane. "Letters and the Post Office: Epistolary Exchange in Jane Austen's *Emma*." *Letters and Labyrinths: Women Writing/Cultural Codes*. By Cousineau. Newark: U of Delaware P, 1997. 26–51.

Cunningham, Valentine. "Games Texts Play." *In the Reading Gaol: Postmodernity, Texts, and History*. By Cunningham. Oxford: Blackwell, 1994. 259–336.

Derrida, Jacques. *The Post Card: From Socrates to Freud and Beyond*. Trans. Alan Bass. Chicago: U of Chicago P, 1987.

Duckworth, Alistair M. *The Improvement of the Estate: A Study of Jane Austen's Novels*. 1971. Rpt. with new pref. Baltimore: Johns Hopkins UP, 1994.

Farrer, Reginald. "Jane Austen, ob. July 18, 1817." 1917. Southam, 1987. 245–72.

Favret, Mary A. "Jane Austen and the Look of Letters." *Romantic Correspondence: Women, Politics, and the Fiction of Letters*. By Favret. Cambridge: Cambridge UP, 1993.

Fergus, Jan. "The Professional Woman Writer." Copeland and McMaster 12–31.

Forster, E. M. *Aspects of the Novel*. New York: Harcourt, 1927.

Foucault, Michel. "What Is an Author?" *Textual Strategies*. Ed. Josué V. Harari. Ithaca: Cornell UP, 1979. 141–60.

Gilbert, Sandra M., and Susan Gubar, *The Madwoman in the Attic: The Woman Writer and the Nineteenth-Century Literary Imagination*. New Haven: Yale UP, 1979.

Harding, D. W. "Regulated Hatred: An Aspect of the Work of Jane Austen." 1940. Watt, *Jane Austen* 166–79.

James, Henry. "The Lesson of Balzac." 1905. Southam, 1987. 229–31.

Johnson, Claudia J. "Austen cults and cultures." Copeland and McMaster 211–26.

———. "The Divine Miss Jane: Jane Austen, Janeites, and the Discipline of Novel Studies." *Boundary 2: An International Journal of Literature and Culture* 23 (Fall 1996): 143–63.

———. *Jane Austen: Women, Politics, and the Novel*. Chicago: U of Chicago P, 1988.

Kirkham, Margaret. *Jane Austen, Feminism, and Fiction*. 1983. Rpt. with new pref. London: Athlone, 1997.

Lacan, Jacques. "Seminar on 'The Purloined Letter.'" Trans. Jeffrey Mehlman. *The Purloined Poe: Lacan, Derrida, and Psychoanalytic Reading*. Ed. John P. Muller and William J. Richardson. Baltimore: Johns Hopkins UP, 1988. 28–54.

Lascelles, Mary. *Jane Austen and Her Art*. 1939. Oxford UP, 1963.

Leavis, F. R. *The Great Tradition*. London: Chatto, 1948.

Lewes, G. H. "The Novels of Jane Austen." 1859. Southam, 1968. 148–66.

Lewis, C. S. "A Note on Jane Austen." Watt, *Jane Austen* 25–34.

Litvak, Joseph. "Reading Characters: Self, Society, and Text in *Emma*." 1985. Monaghan 89–109.

Looser, Devoney, ed. *Jane Austen and Discourses of Feminism*. New York: St. Martin's, 1995.

Monaghan, David, ed. *"Emma": Jane Austen*. New Casebooks. New York: St. Martin's, 1992.

Mudrick, Marvin. *Jane Austen: Irony as Defense and Discovery*. Princeton: Princeton UP, 1952.

Perry, Ruth. "Interrupted Friendships in Jane Austen's *Emma*." 1986. Monaghan 185–202.

Poovey, Mary. *The Proper Lady and the Woman Writer: Ideology as Style in the Works of Mary Wollstonecraft, Mary Shelley, and Jane Austen*. Chicago: U of Chicago P, 1984.

Ryle, Gilbert. "Jane Austen and the Moralists." *Critical Essays on Jane Austen*. Ed. B.C. Southam. London: Routledge, 1968. 106–22.

Scott, Walter. Unsigned review of *Emma*. 1816. Southam, 1968. 58–69.

Sedgwick, Eve Kosofsky. "Jane Austen and the Masturbating Girl." *Critical Inquiry* 17 (1991): 818–37.

Shannon, Edgar F., Jr. "*Emma*: Character and Construction." *PMLA* 71 (1956): 637–50.

Simons, Judy. "Classics and Trash: Reading Austen in the 1990s." *Women's Writing* 5 (1998): 27–39.

Simpson, Richard. Unsigned review of the *Memoir*. 1870. Southam, 1968. 241–65.

Smith, Mack. "Fancy and Understanding and the Ekphrastic Riddles of *Emma*." *Literary Realism and the Ekphrastic Tradition*. By Smith. University Park: Pennsylvania State UP, 1995. 77–113.

Southam, B. C., ed. *Jane Austen: The Critical Heritage*. New York: Barnes & Noble, 1968.

———, ed. *Jane Austen: The Critical Heritage: Volume 2, 1870–1940*. New York: Routledge, 1987.

Spring, David A. "Interpreters of Jane Austen's Social World: Literary Critics and Historians." *Jane Austen: New Perspectives*. Ed. Janet Todd. New York: Holmes & Meier, 1983. 53–72.

Sulloway, Alison G. *Jane Austen and the Province of Womanhood*. Philadelphia: U of Pennsylvania P, 1989.

Thompson, James. *Between Self and World: The Novels of Jane Austen*. University Park: Pennsylvania State UP, 1988.

Todd, Janet. "Jane Austen, politics and sensibility." *Gender, Art and Death*. By Todd. New York: Continuum, 1993. 136–54.

———. "Who's Afraid of Jane Austen?" *Jane Austen: New Perspectives*. Ed. by Todd. New York: Holmes & Meier, 1983. 107–27.

Trilling, Lionel. "*Emma* and the Legend of Jane Austen." 1957. *Beyond Culture: Essays on Literature and Learning*. By Trilling. New York: Viking, 1965. 31–55

Troost, Linda, and Sayre Greenfield, eds. *Jane Austen in Hollywood*. Lexington: UP of Kentucky, 1998.

Twain, Mark. 1912. Quoted in A. B. Paine, *Mark Twain*. Southam, 1987. 232–33.

Watt, Ian, ed. *Jane Austen: A Collection of Critical Essays*. Englewood Cliffs, NJ: Prentice-Hall, 1963.

———. *The Rise of the Novel: Studies in Defoe, Richardson, and Fielding*. London: Chatto, 1957.

West, Rebecca. "Preface" to *Northanger Abbey*. 1932. Southam, 1987. 293–97.

Whately, Richard. Unsigned review of *Northanger Abbey* and *Persuasion*. 1821. Southam, 1968. 87–105.

Williams, Raymond. *The Country and the City*. Oxford: Oxford UP, 1973.

Wilson, Edmund. 1944. "A Long Talk about Jane Austen." *Classics and Commercials: A Literary Chronicle of the Forties*. By Wilson. New York: Farrar, 1950. 196–203.

Woolf, Virginia. "Jane Austen at Sixty." 1923. Southam, 1987. 281–83.

Gender Criticism
and *Emma*

WHAT IS GENDER CRITICISM?

Feminist criticism was accorded academic legitimacy in American universities "around 1981," Jane Gallop claims in her book *Around 1981: Academic Feminist Literary Theory.* With Gallop's title and amusing approximation in mind, Naomi Schor has since estimated that, "around 1985, feminism began to give way to what has come to be called gender studies" (Schor 275).

In explaining her reason for saying that feminism began to give way to gender studies "around 1985," Schor says that she chose that date "in part because it marks the publication of *Between Men,*" a book whose author, the influential gender critic Eve Kosofsky Sedgwick, "articulates the insights of feminist criticism onto those of gay-male studies, which had up to then pursued often parallel but separate courses (affirming the existence of a homosexual or female imagination, recovering lost traditions, decoding the cryptic discourse of works already in the canon by homosexual or feminist authors)" (Schor 276). Today, gay and lesbian criticism is so much a part of gender criticism that some people equate "sexualities criticism" with the gender approach.

Many would quarrel with the notion that feminist criticism and women's studies have been giving way to gender criticism and gender studies — and with the either/or distinction that such a claim implies.

Some would argue that feminist criticism is by definition gender criticism. (When Simone de Beauvoir declared in 1949 that "one is not born a woman, one becomes one" [301], she was talking about the way in which individuals of the female sex assume the feminine gender — that is, that elaborate set of restrictive, socially prescribed attitudes and behaviors that we associate with femininity.) Others would point out that one critic whose work *everyone* associates with feminism (Julia Kristeva) has problems with the feminist label, while another critic whose name, like Sedgwick's, is continually linked with the gender approach (Teresa de Lauretis) continues to refer to herself and her work as feminist.

Certainly, feminist and gender criticism are not polar opposites but, rather, exist along a continuum of attitudes toward sex and sexism, sexuality and gender, language and the literary canon. There are, however, a few distinctions to be made between those critics whose writings are inevitably identified as being toward one end of the continuum or the other.

One distinction is based on focus: as the word implies, "feminists" have concentrated their efforts on the study of women and women's issues. Gender criticism, by contrast, has not been woman centered. It has tended to view the male and female sexes — and the masculine and feminine genders — in terms of a complicated continuum, much as we are viewing feminist and gender criticism. Critics like Diane K. Lewis have raised the possibility that black women may be more like white men in terms of familial and economic roles, like black men in terms of their relationships with whites, and like white women in terms of their relationships with men. Lesbian gender critics have asked whether lesbian women are really more like straight women than they are like gay (or for that matter straight) men. That we refer to gay and lesbian studies as gender studies has led some to suggest that gender studies is a misnomer; after all, homosexuality is not a gender. This objection may easily be answered once we realize that one purpose of gender criticism is to criticize gender as we commonly conceive of it, to expose its insufficiency and inadequacy as a category.

Another distinction between feminist and gender criticism is based on the terms *gender* and *sex*. As de Lauretis suggests in *Technologies of Gender* (1987), feminists of the 1970s tended to equate gender with sex, gender difference with sexual difference. But that equation doesn't help us explain "the differences among women, . . . the differences *within women*." After positing that "we need a notion of gender that is not so bound up with sexual difference," de Lauretis provides just such a notion by arguing that "gender is not a property of bodies or something originally existent in human beings"; rather, it is "the product of various social technologies, such as cinema" (2). Gender is, in other words, a construct, an effect of language, culture, and its institutions. It is gender, not sex, that causes a weak old man to open a door for an athletic young woman. And it is gender, not sex, that may cause one young woman to expect old men to behave in this way, another to view this kind of behavior as chauvinistic and insulting, and still another to have mixed feelings (hence de Lauretis's phrase "differences *within women*") about "gentlemanly gallantry."

Still another, related distinction between feminist and gender criticism is based on the *essentialist* views of many feminist critics and the *constructionist* views of many gender critics (both those who would call themselves feminists and those who would not). Stated simply and perhaps too reductively, the term *essentialist* refers to the view that women are essentially different from men. *Constructionist,* by contrast, refers to the view that most of those differences are characteristics not of the male and female sex (nature) but, rather, of the masculine and feminine genders (nurture). Because of its essentialist tendencies, "radical feminism," according to Sedgwick, "tends to deny that the meaning of gender or sexuality has ever significantly changed; and more damagingly, it can make future change appear impossible" (*Between Men* 13).

Most obviously essentialist would be those feminists who emphasize the female body, its difference, and the manifold implications of that difference. The equation made by some avant-garde French feminists between the female body and the *maternal* body has proved especially troubling to some gender critics, who worry that it may paradoxically play into the hands of extreme conservatives and fundamentalists seeking to reestablish patriarchal family values. In her book *The Reproduction of Mothering* (1978), Nancy Chodorow, a sociologist of gender, admits that what we call "mothering"— not having or nursing babies but mothering more broadly conceived — is commonly associated not just with the feminine gender but also with the female sex, often considered nurturing by nature. But she critically interrogates the common assumption that it is in women's nature or biological destiny to "mother" in this broader sense, arguing that the separation of home and workplace brought about by the development of capitalism and the ensuing industrial revolution made mothering *appear* to be essentially a woman's job in modern Western society.

If sex turns out to be gender where mothering is concerned, what differences *are* grounded in sex — that is, nature? *Are* there *essential* differences between men and women — other than those that are purely anatomical and anatomically determined (for example, a man can exclusively take on the job of feeding an infant milk, but he may not do so from his own breast)? A growing number of gender critics would answer the question in the negative. Sometimes referred to as "extreme constructionists" and "postfeminists," these critics have adopted the viewpoint of philosopher Judith Butler, who in her book *Gender Trouble* (1990) predicts that "sex, by definition, will be shown to have been gender all along" (8). As Naomi Schor explains their position, "there is nothing outside or before culture, no nature that is not always and already enculturated" (278).

Whereas a number of feminists celebrate women's difference, postfeminist gender critics would agree with Chodorow's statement that men have an "investment in difference that women do not have" (Eisenstein and Jardine 14). They see difference as a symptom of oppression, not a cause for celebration, and would abolish it by dismantling gender categories and, ultimately, destroying gender itself. Because gender categories and distinctions are embedded in and perpetuated through language, gender critics like Monique Wittig have called for the wholesale transformation of language into a nonsexist, and nonheterosexist, medium.

Language has proved the site of important debates between feminist and gender critics, essentialists and constructionists. Gender critics have taken issue with those French feminists who have spoken of a feminine language and writing and who have grounded differences in language and writing in the female body.[1] For much the same reason, they have disagreed with those French-influenced Anglo-American critics who, like Toril Moi and Nancy K. Miller, have posited an essential relationship between sexuality and textuality. (In an essentialist sense, such critics have suggested that when women write, they tend to break the rules of plausibility and verisimilitude that men have created to evaluate fiction.) Gender critics like Peggy Kamuf posit a relationship only between *gender* and textuality, between what most men and women *become* after they are born and the way in which they write. They are

---

[1]Because feminist/gender studies, not unlike sex/gender, should be thought of as existing along a continuum of attitudes and not in terms of simple opposition, attempts to highlight the difference between feminist and gender criticism are inevitably prone to reductive overgeneralization and occasional distortion. Here, for instance, French feminism is made out to be more monolithic than it actually is. Hélène Cixous has said that a few men (such as Jean Genet) have produced "feminine writing," although she suggests that these are exceptional men who have acknowledged their own bisexuality.

therefore less interested in the author's sexual "signature"— in whether the author was a woman writing — than in whether the author was (to borrow from Kamuf) "Writing like a Woman."

Feminists such as Miller have suggested that no man could write the "female anger, desire, and selfhood" that Emily Brontë, for instance, inscribed in her poetry and in *Wuthering Heights* (*Subject* 72). In the view of gender critics, it is and has been possible for a man to write like a woman, a woman to write like a man. Shari Benstock, a noted feminist critic whose investigations into psychoanalytic and poststructuralist theory have led her increasingly to adopt the gender approach, poses the following question to herself in *Textualizing the Feminine* (1991): "Isn't it precisely 'the feminine' in Joyce's writings and Derrida's that carries me along?" (45). In an essay entitled "Unsexing Language: Pronomial Protest in Emily Dickinson's 'Lay This Laurel,'" Anna Shannon Elfenbein has argued that "like Walt Whitman, Emily Dickinson crossed the gender barrier in some remarkable poems," such as "We learned to like the Fire / By playing Glaciers — when a Boy —" (215).

It is also possible, in the view of most gender critics, for women to read as men, men as women. The view that women can, and indeed have been forced to, read as men has been fairly noncontroversial. Everyone agrees that the literary canon is largely "androcentric" and that writings by men have tended to "immasculate" women, forcing them to see the world from a masculine viewpoint. But the question of whether men can read as women has proved to be yet another issue dividing feminist and gender critics. Some feminists suggest that men and women have some essentially different reading strategies and outcomes, while gender critics maintain that such differences arise entirely out of social training and cultural norms. One interesting outcome of recent attention to gender and reading is Elizabeth A. Flynn's argument that women in fact make the best interpreters of imaginative literature. Based on a study of how male and female students read works of fiction, she concludes that women come up with more imaginative, open-ended readings of stories. Quite possibly the imputed hedging and tentativeness of women's speech, often seen by men as disadvantages, are transformed into useful interpretive strategies — receptivity combined with critical assessment of the text — in the act of reading (Flynn and Schweickart 286).

In singling out a catalyst of gender studies, many historians of criticism have pointed to Michel Foucault. In his *History of Sexuality* (1976, trans. 1978), Foucault distinguished sexuality from sex, calling

the former a "technology of sex." De Lauretis, who has deliberately
developed her theory of gender "along the lines of . . . Foucault's theory of sexuality," explains his use of "technology" this way: "sexuality,
commonly thought to be a natural as well as a private matter, is in fact
completely constructed in culture according to the political aims of the
society's dominant class" (*Technologies* 2, 12).

Foucault suggests that homosexuality as we now think of it was to a
great extent an invention of the nineteenth century. In earlier periods
there had been "acts of sodomy" and individuals who committed them,
but the "sodomite" was, according to Foucault, "a temporary aberration," not the "species" he became with the advent of the modern concept of homosexuality (42–43). According to Foucault, in other words,
sodomitic acts did not define people so markedly as the word *homosexual* tags and marks people now. Sodomitic *acts* have been replaced by
homosexual *persons,* and in the process the range of acceptable relationships between individuals of the same gender has been restrictively
altered. As Sedgwick writes, "to specify someone's sexuality [today] is
not to locate her or him on a map teeming with zoophiles, gyneco-
masts, sexoesthetic inverts, and so forth. . . . In the late twentieth century, if I ask you what your sexual orientation or sexual preference is,
you will understand me to be asking precisely one thing: whether you
are homosexual or heterosexual" ("Gender" 282).

By historicizing sexuality, Foucault made it possible for his succes-
sors to consider the possibility that all of the categories and assumptions
that currently come to mind when we think about sex, sexual difference, gender, and sexuality are social artifacts, the products of cultural
discourses. Following Foucault's lead, some gay and lesbian critics have
argued that the heterosexual/homosexual distinction is as much a cultural construct as is the masculine/feminine dichotomy.

Arguing that sexuality is a continuum, not a fixed and static set of
binary oppositions, a number of gay and lesbian critics have critiqued
heterosexuality arguing that it has been an enforced corollary and consequence of what Gayle Rubin has referred to as the "sex/gender system" ("Traffic"). According to this system, persons of the male sex are
assumed to be masculine, masculine men are assumed to be attracted to
women, and therefore it is supposedly natural for men to be attracted
to women and unnatural for them to be attracted to men. Lesbian critics have also taken issue with some feminists on the grounds that they
proceed from fundamentally heterosexual and even heterosexist assumptions. Particularly offensive to lesbians have been those feminists
who, following Doris Lessing, have implied that to affirm a lesbian

identity is to act out feminist hostility against men. According to poet-critic Adrienne Rich:

> The fact is that women in every culture throughout history have undertaken the task of independent, nonheterosexual, women-centered existence, to the extent made possible by their context, often in the belief that they were the "only ones" ever to have done so. They have undertaken it even though few women have been in an economic position to resist marriage altogether; and even though attacks against [them] have ranged from aspersions and mockery to deliberate gynocide. ("Compulsory" 141)

Rich goes on to suggest, in her essay entitled "Compulsory Heterosexuality and Lesbian Existence," that "heterosexuality [is] a beachhead of male dominance," and that, "like motherhood, [it] needs to be recognized and studied as a political institution" (143, 145).

If there is such a thing as reading like a woman and such a thing as reading like a man, how then do lesbians read? Are there gay and lesbian ways of reading? Many would say that there are. Rich, by reading Emily Dickinson's poetry as a lesbian — by not assuming that "heterosexual romance is the key to a woman's life and work"— has introduced us to a poet somewhat different from the one heterosexual critics have made familiar (*Lies* 158). As for gay reading, Wayne Koestenbaum has defined "the (male twentieth-century first world) gay reader" as one who "reads resistantly for inscriptions of his condition, for texts that will confirm a social and private identity founded on a desire for other men. . . . Reading becomes a hunt for histories that deliberately foreknow or unwittingly trace a desire felt not by author but by reader, who is most acute when searching for signs of himself" (176–77).

Lesbian critics have produced a number of compelling reinterpretations, or inscriptions, of works by authors as diverse as Emily Dickinson, Virginia Woolf, and Toni Morrison. As a result of these provocative readings, significant disagreements have arisen between straight and lesbian critics and among lesbian critics as well. Perhaps the most famous and interesting example of this kind of interpretive controversy involves the claim by Barbara Smith and Adrienne Rich that Morrison's novel *Sula* can be read as a lesbian text — and author Toni Morrison's counterclaim that it cannot.

Gay male critics have produced a body of readings no less revisionist and controversial, focusing on writers as staidly classic as Henry James and Wallace Stevens. In Melville's *Billy Budd* and *Moby-Dick*, Robert K. Martin suggests, a triangle of homosexual desire exists. In the latter novel, the hero must choose between a captain who represents "the imposition of the male on the female" and a "Dark Stranger" (Queequeg) who "offers the possibility of an alternate sexuality, one that is less dependent upon performance and conquest" (5).

Masculinity as a complex construct producing and reproducing a constellation of behaviors and goals, many of them destructive (like performance and conquest) and most of them injurious to women, has become the object of an unprecedented number of gender studies. A 1983 issue of *Feminist Review* contained an essay entitled "Anti-Porn: Soft Issue, Hard World," in which B. Ruby Rich suggested that the "legions of feminist men" who examine and deplore the effects of pornography on women might better "undertake the analysis that can tell us why men like porn (not, piously, why this or that exceptional man does *not*)" (Clark 185). The advent of gender criticism makes precisely that kind of analysis possible. Stephen H. Clark, who alludes to Ruby Rich's challenge, reads T. S. Eliot "as a man." Responding to "Eliot's implicit appeal to a specifically masculine audience — 'You! hypocrite lecteur! — mon semblable, — mon *frère!*'"— Clark concludes that poems such as "Sweeney among the Nightingales" and "Gerontion," rather than offering what they are usually said to offer — "a social critique into which a misogynistic language accidentally seeps"— instead articulate a masculine "psychology of sexual fear and desired retaliation" (Clark 173).

Some gender critics focusing on masculinity have analyzed "the anthropology of boyhood," a phrase coined by Mark Seltzer in an article in which he comparatively reads, among other things, Stephen Crane's *Red Badge of Courage,* Jack London's *White Fang,* and the first *Boy Scouts of America* handbook (150). Others have examined the fear men have that artistry is unmasculine, a guilty worry that surfaces perhaps most obviously in "The Custom-House," Hawthorne's lengthy preface to *The Scarlet Letter.* Still others have studied the representation in literature of subtly erotic disciple-patron relationships, relationships like the ones between Nick Carraway and Jay Gatsby, Charlie Marlow and Lord Jim, Doctor Watson and Sherlock Holmes, and any number of characters in Henry James's stories. Not all of these studies have focused on literary texts. Because the movies have played a primary role in gender construction during our lifetimes, gender critics have analyzed the dynamics of masculinity (vis-à-vis femininity and androgyny) in films from *Rebel without a Cause* to *Tootsie* to last year's Best Picture. One of the "social technologies" most influential in (re)constructing gender, film is one of the media in which today's sexual politics is most evident.

Necessary as it is, in an introduction such as this one, to define the difference between feminist and gender criticism, it is equally necessary to conclude by unmaking the distinction, at least partially. The two topics just discussed (film theory and so-called queer theory) give us grounds for undertaking that necessary deconstruction. The alliance I have been creating between gay and lesbian criticism on the one hand and gender criticism on the other is complicated greatly by the fact that not all gay and lesbian critics are constructionists. Indeed, a number of them (Robert K. Martin included) share with many feminists the *essentialist* point of view; that is, they believe homosexuals and heterosexuals to be essentially different, different by nature, just as a number of feminists believe men and women to be different.

In film theory and criticism, feminist and gender critics have so influenced one another that their differences would be difficult to define based on any available criteria, including the ones just outlined. Cinema has been of special interest to contemporary feminists like Trinh T. Minh-ha (herself a filmmaker) and Gayatri Chakravorty Spivak (whose critical eye has focused on movies including *My Beautiful Laundrette* and *Sammie and Rosie Get Laid*). Teresa de Lauretis, whose *Technologies of Gender* (1987) has proved influential in the area of gender studies, continues to publish film criticism consistent with earlier, unambiguously feminist works in which she argued that "the representation of woman as spectacle — body to be looked at, place of sexuality, and object of desire — so pervasive in our culture, finds in narrative cinema its most complex expression and widest circulation" (*Alice* 4).

Feminist film theory has developed alongside a feminist performance theory grounded in Joan Riviere's recently rediscovered essay "Womanliness as a Masquerade" (1929), in which the author argues that there is no femininity that is *not* masquerade. Marjorie Garber, a contemporary cultural critic with an interest in gender, has analyzed the constructed nature of femininity by focusing on men who have apparently achieved it — through the transvestism, transsexualism, and other forms of "cross-dressing" evident in cultural productions from Shakespeare to Elvis, from "Little Red Riding Hood" to *La Cage aux Folles*. The future of feminist and gender criticism, it would seem, is not one of further bifurcation but one involving a refocusing on femininity, masculinity, and related sexualities, not only as represented in poems, novels, and films but also as manifested and developed in video, on television, and along the almost infinite number of waystations rapidly being developed on the information highways running through an exponentially expanding cyberspace.

In the essay that follows, gender critic Claudia L. Johnson states that although Jane Austen is often perceived in terms of her difference from women writers who preceded her (e.g., Fanny Burney, Ann Radcliffe, and Mary Wollstonecraft), she in fact began her career by writing a novel (*Northanger Abbey*) that asserted "solidarity with a distinctively feminine tradition of novelists that developed in the late eighteenth century, a tradition in which Burney and Radcliffe ranked very high." And in *Emma*, a later work, Austen achieved "Wollstonecraft's grand aim better than Wollstonecraft did: diminishing the authority of male sentimentality and reimmasculating" — by which Johnson means "making more masculine again" — "men and women alike with a high sense of national purpose" (p. 441).

Johnson goes on to point out that, for decades, influential critics including Lionel Trilling, Edmund Wilson, and Marvin Mudrick have suggested that Emma Woodhouse is "unsexed" or "manly" or perhaps even a "lesbian." They have questioned her interest in men, accused her of being infatuated with young women, and wondered whether she could ever "give herself" in heterosexual love and marriage. What they have not done, by and large, is attempt to understand these supposed features of Emma's character — these "slippages of sex and gender" (p. 445) — in light of certain social developments taking place in Austen's day — for instance, the eighteenth- and nineteenth-century debates about women's rights and an emerging national, even nationalistic, feeling for English culture and life. By "historicizing the treatment of femininity *and* masculinity in *Emma*," Johnson hopes to "integrate the arguments about female manliness and national feeling that Trilling keeps apart" and "show that Austen engages the work of her predecessors more positively and more intricately than is generally supposed" (p. 442).

Comparing Emma to a number of intentionally unattractive "proto-feminist characters who occupy novels by Austen's contemporaries" — characters designed to "make the [more] proper heroine cringe with horror" — Johnson argues for Emma Woodhouse's difference, maintaining that we are not "invited to consider her infractions against 'femininity' per se to be the cause of her problem"; nor is the novel "interested in subjecting the masculine independence of its heroine to disciplinary correctives" (pp. 445–46). Indeed, "where this novel *is* concerned with gender transgression, it is from the masculine, not the feminine side"; it "persistently asks how a *man* should behave and what he ought to do. Thus, whereas " '[c]lassic' Austenian critics assumed the constancy of feminine norms, and policed Emma's womanhood accordingly," they tended to overlook the possibility that "masculinity could be something the novel contests and constructs" (pp. 447–48).

In fact, however, *Emma* turns out to be very interested in masculinity, as Trilling, Mudrick, and Tony Tanner have noted in their analyses of Emma's father — a man Tanner describes in terms of his "weak emasculate" characteristics. Johnson argues that Mr. Woodhouse is not unmanly but, rather, a historically determined *kind* of man (indeed, the sensitive, tender, benevolent, polite, kind-hearted "man of feeling" found throughout Burney and Radcliffe's novels [p. 449]). Johnson goes on to argue that, by the time *Emma* was written, this "tradition of sentimental masculinity" had become "archaic, . . . somewhat of a joke," much as the "gallant" kind of man represented by Mr. Elton was similarly on the wane (pp. 450–51). "Mr. Woodhouse is dearly beloved and fondly indulged, but his sensitivity is not revered" — any more than the gallantry of Mr. Elton is revered. For "the novel," Johnson argues, "works instead to redefine masculinity" (p. 450).

Although Johnson agrees with other critics who have argued that Mr. Knightley represents that redefined ideal, she resists the common notion that his masculinity is of a traditional sort which Austen would like to see her society reembrace. She also makes the original point that part of Knightley's uniqueness is that "he does not make a big deal out of sexual difference" (p. 451) (he disapproves of gallants like Frank Churchill but also puts down bossy women like Mrs. Elton). Partly because of that fact, his sort of "masculine" virtue is made "accessible to women as well." He is a "humane" and "*fraternal*" figure rather than a gallant or sentimental hero in the "heterosexual" mold, both of which forms of masculinity are, interestingly enough, "feminized" by Austen's novel (p. 452). And the things that define his humanity — "true feelings," "real attachments," honest sympathy, self-effacing effort, and so forth — may be aspired to regardless of gender.

In the later stages of her argument, Johnson states that although Knightley is not traditional, "it is the work of *Emma* to make Mr. Knightley seem traditional," to make his "brisk, energetic, . . . unaffected, reserved, businesslike" qualities seem manly (pp. 452–53). But

Emma, Johnson points out, does other work as well; it makes not only conventionally masculine but also conventionally feminine characters seem downright silly. (Johnson has in mind "Harriet, who is willing to marry any man who asks; Mrs. Elton, with her fulsome little love names for her husband; [and] Isabella, whose wifely devotion verges on sheer stupidity" — women who "give heterosexuality a rather revolting appearance, against which Emma's coolness looks sane and enviable" [p. 453]). Thus, Johnson argues that when Emma seems masculine in the way that Knightley seems masculine — that is (to quote Trilling) "when she has a moral life as a man has a moral life" — she is "rejecting conventional femininity," just as when she acts like a gallant or sentimental man (relying on espionage and small tricks, doting on women with "endearing irrationality") she is guilty not so much of being "unlike what a *woman* should be" (pp. 453–54) but, rather, to quote Emma's rebuke of Frank Churchill, "unlike what a man should be!" (p. 453).

Johnson's essay represents contemporary gender criticism in a number of ways. For one thing, it includes but goes beyond the feminist focus, showing how Austen's *Emma* both uses and transforms features found in contemporary novels by women to address women's issues — of then and now — but also questions about masculinity as well. Johnson's sense that masculinity is not a given but, rather, a social construct or set of constructs (she speaks of various "kinds of masculinity," all of which seem to be historical products or manifestations, and some of which can even be "feminized" by a novel like *Emma*), reflects the attitude of gender critics, that is, the belief that gender and sexuality are social constructs or artifacts, not givens of nature.

Johnson's essay, then, exemplifies gender criticism not only insofar as it argues that a novel attempts to "redefine" gender (in this case to "redefine masculinity") but also insofar as it "doesn't make a big deal of sexual difference." Johnson argues that the manliness Knightley represents is as available to, and represented by, Emma as it is by the man she marries. Finally, Johnson's essay does raise the question of sexuality (that is to say, gay and lesbian sexuality) by dealing sympathetically and creatively with critical assessments that would have it that Emma is, in fact, a lesbian — and by suggesting that terms like *lesbian* and *straight, masculine* and *feminine,* are extremely complex markers that must be understood within the context of changing social and sexual definitions.

Ross C Murfin

GENDER CRITICISM:
A SELECTED BIBLIOGRAPHY

Studies of Gender and Sexuality

Berg, Temma F., ed., and Anna Shannon Elfenbein, Jeanne Larsen, and Elisa K. Sparks, co-eds. *Engendering the Word: Feminist Essays in Psychosexual Poetics.* Urbana: U of Illinois P, 1989.

Boone, Joseph A., and Michael Cadden, eds. *Engendering Men: The Question of Male Feminist Criticism.* New York: Routledge, 1990.

Butler, Judith. *Gender Trouble: Feminism and the Subversion of Identity.* New York: Routledge, 1990.

Chodorow, Nancy. *The Reproduction of Mothering: Psychoanalysis and the Sociology of Gender.* Berkeley: U of California P, 1978.

Claridge, Laura, and Elizabeth Langland, eds. *Out of Bounds: Male Writing and Gender(ed) Criticism.* Amherst: U of Massachusetts P, 1990.

de Lauretis, Teresa. *Technologies of Gender: Essays on Theory, Film, and Fiction.* Bloomington: Indiana UP, 1987.

Doane, Mary Ann. "Masquerade Reconsidered: Further Thoughts on the Female Spectator." *Discourse* 11 (1988 89): 42–54.

Eisenstein, Hester, and Alice Jardine, eds. *The Future of Difference.* Boston: G. K. Hall, 1980.

Flynn, Elizabeth A., and Patrocinio P. Schweickart, eds. *Gender and Reading: Essays on Readers, Texts, and Contexts.* Baltimore: Johns Hopkins UP, 1986.

Foucault, Michel. *The History of Sexuality.* Vol. 1. Trans. Robert Hurley. New York: Random, 1978.

Kamuf, Peggy. "Writing Like a Woman." *Women and Language in Literature and Society.* Ed. Sally McConnell-Ginet et al. New York: Praeger, 1980. 284–99.

Laqueur, Thomas. *Making Sex: Body and Gender from the Greeks to Freud.* Cambridge: Harvard UP, 1990.

Riviere, Joan. "Womanliness as a Masquerade." 1929. Rpt. in *Formations of Fantasy.* Ed. Victor Burgin, James Donald, and Cora Kaplan. London: Methuen, 1986. 35–44.

Rubin, Gayle. "Thinking Sex: Notes for a Radical Theory of the Politics of Sexuality." Abelove et al. 3–44.

———. "The Traffic in Women: Notes on the 'Political Economy' of Sex." *Toward an Anthropology of Women.* Ed. Rayna R. Reiter. New York: Monthly Review, 1975. 157–210.

Schor, Naomi. "Feminist and Gender Studies." *Introduction to Scholarship in Modern Languages and Literatures.* Ed. Joseph Gibaldi. New York: MLA, 1992. 262–87.

Sedgwick, Eve Kosofsky. *Between Men: English Literature and Male Homosocial Desire.* New York: Columbia UP, 1988.

———. "Gender Criticism." *Redrawing the Boundaries: The Transformation of English and American Literary Studies.* Ed. Stephen Greenblatt and Giles Gunn. New York: MLA, 1992. 271–302.

Lesbian and Gay Criticism

Abelove, Henry, Michèle Aina Barale, and David Halperin, eds. *The Lesbian and Gay Studies Reader.* New York: Routledge, 1993.

Butters, Ronald, John M. Clum, and Michael Moon, eds. *Displacing Homophobia: Gay Male Perspectives in Literature and Culture.* Durham: Duke UP, 1989.

Clark, Stephen H. "Testing the Razor: T. S. Eliot's Poems." Berg et al. 167–89.

Craft, Christopher. *Another Kind of Love: Male Homosexual Desire in English Discourse, 1850–1920.* Berkeley: U of California P, 1994.

de Lauretis, Teresa. *The Practice of Love: Lesbian Sexuality and Perverse Desire.* Bloomington: Indiana UP, 1994.

Dollimore, Jonathan. *Sexual Dissidence: Augustine to Wilde, Freud to Foucault.* Oxford: Clarendon, 1991.

Elfenbein, Anna Shannon. "Unsexing Language: Pronomial Protest in Emily Dickenson's 'Lay This Laurel.'" Berg et al. 208–23.

Fuss, Diana, ed. *Inside/Out: Lesbian Theories, Gay Theories.* New York: Routledge, 1991.

Garber, Marjorie. *Vested Interests: Cross-Dressing and Cultural Anxiety.* New York: Routledge, 1992.

Halperin, David M. *One Hundred Years of Homosexuality and Other Essays on Greek Love.* New York: Routledge, 1990.

Koestenbaum, Wayne. "Wilde's Hard Labour and the Birth of Gay Reading." Boone and Cadden 176–89.

The Lesbian Issue. Spec. issue of *Signs* 9 (1984).

Martin, Robert K. *Hero, Captain, and Stranger: Male Friendship, Social Critique, and Literary Form in the Sea Novels of Herman Melville.* Chapel Hill: U of North Carolina P, 1986.

Munt, Sally, ed. *New Lesbian Criticism: Literary and Cultural Readings.* New York: Harvester Wheatsheaf, 1992.

Rich, Adrienne. "Compulsory Heterosexuality and Lesbian
Existence." *The "Signs" Reader: Women, Gender, and Scholarship.*
Ed. Elizabeth Abel and Emily K. Abel. Chicago: U of Chicago P,
1983. 139–68.

Seltzer, Mark. "The Love Master." Boone and Cadden 140–58.

Smith, Barbara. "Toward a Black Feminist Criticism." *The New
Feminist Criticism.* Ed. Elaine Showalter. New York: Pantheon,
1985. 168–85.

Stimpson, Catherine R. "Zero Degree Deviancy: The Lesbian Novel
in English." *Critical Inquiry* 8 (1981): 363–79.

Weeks, Jeffrey. *Sexuality and Its Discontents: Meanings, Myths, and
Modern Sexualities.* London: Routledge, 1985.

Wittig, Monique. "The Mark of Gender." *The Poetics of Gender.* Ed.
Nancy K. Miller. New York: Columbia UP, 1986. 63–73.

———. "One Is Not Born a Woman." *Feminist Issues* 1.2 (1981):
47–54.

———. *The Straight Mind and Other Essays.* Boston: Beacon, 1992.

Queer Theory

Butler, Judith. *Bodies That Matter: On the Discursive Limits of "Sex."*
New York: Routledge, 1993.

Cohen, Ed. *Talk on the Wilde Side: Towards a Genealogy of Discourse
on Male Sexualities.* New York: Routledge, 1993.

de Lauretis, Teresa, ed. Spec. issue on queer theory, *Differences* 3.2
(1991).

Sedgwick, Eve Kosofsky. *Epistemology of the Closet.* Berkeley: U of
California P, 1991.

———. *Tendencies.* Durham: Duke UP, 1993.

Sinfield, Alan. *Cultural Politics — Queer Reading.* Philadelphia: U of
Pennsylvania P, 1994.

———. *The Wilde Century: Effeminacy, Oscar Wilde, and the Queer
Moment.* New York: Columbia UP, 1994.

Other Works Referred to in
"What Is Gender Criticism?"

Benstock, Shari. *Textualizing the Feminine: On the Limits of Genre.*
Norman: U of Oklahoma P, 1991.

de Beauvoir, Simone. *The Second Sex.* 1949. Ed. and trans. H. M.
Parshley. New York: Modern Library, 1952.

de Lauretis, Teresa. *Alice Doesn't: Feminism, Semiotics, Cinema.*
   Bloomington: Indiana UP, 1989.
Gallop, Jane. *Around 1981: Academic Feminist Literary Theory.* New
   York: Routledge, 1992.
Miller, D. A. *The Novel and the Police.* Berkeley: U of California P,
   1988.
Miller, Nancy K. *Subject to Change: Reading Feminist Writing.* New
   York: Columbia UP, 1988.
Rich, Adrienne. *On Lies, Secrets, and Silence: Selected Prose,
   1966–1979.* New York: Norton, 1979.
Tate, Claudia. *Black Women Writers at Work.* New York: Continuum,
   1983.

Gender Criticism Relating to *Emma*

Johnson, Claudia L. "The Divine Miss Jane: Jane Austen, Janeites,
   and the Discipline of Novel Studies." *Boundary 2: An
   International Journal of Literature and Culture* 23 (Fall 1996):
   143–63.
Kestner, Joseph A. "Jane Austen: Revolutionizing Masculinities."
   Persuasions 16 (1994): 147–60.
Korba, Susan M. " 'Improper and Dangerous Distinctions': Female
   Relationships and Erotic Domination in *Emma*." *Studies in the
   Novel* 29.2 (1997): 139–63.
Potter, Tiffany F. " 'A Low But Very Feeling Tone': The Lesbian
   Continuum and Power Relations in Jane Austen's *Emma*."
   English Studies in Canada 20 (June 1994): 187–203.
Roulston, Christine. "Discourse, Gender, and Gossip: Some
   Reflections on Bakhtin and *Emma*." *Ambiguous Discourse:
   Feminist Narratology and British Women Writers.* Ed. Kathy
   Mezei. Chapel Hill: U of North Carolina P, 1996. 40–65.
Sedgwick, Eve Kosofsky. "Jane Austen and the Masturbating Girl."
   Critical Inquiry 17 (1991): 818–37.
Todd, Janet. "Jane Austen, politics and sensibility." *Gender, Art and
   Death.* By Todd. New York: Continuum, 1993. 136–54.

A GENDER STUDIES PERSPECTIVE

CLAUDIA L. JOHNSON
"Not at all what a man should be!":
Remaking English Manhood in *Emma*

For many years, it was universally acknowledged that Jane Austen defined herself negatively vis-à-vis the novelists of her time, shunning the plots of Mary Wollstonecraft's radical feminism, Ann Radcliffe's exaggerated gothicism, and Frances Burney's escalated melodrama, and opting instead to exercise the cameoist's meticulously understated craft. But effects are not intentions. In *Northanger Abbey*, that novel which was to have been her first published work, Austen launches into a spirited defense of her chosen genre over and against those who would decry it as "only a novel." Rather than proceed through negations, she inaugurates her career by asserting solidarity with a distinctively feminine tradition of novelists that developed in the late eighteenth century, a tradition in which Burney and Radcliffe ranked very high. Though Wollstonecraft remained an unmentionable throughout Austen's career, there is ample evidence that she too was a figure Austen reckoned with. Indeed, in many respects *Emma* actually succeeds at Wollstonecraft's grand aim better than Wollstonecraft did: diminishing the authority of male sentimentality, and reimmasculating men and women alike with a high sense of national purpose.

This claim may sound highfalutin'. Given the lingering grip of janeism in Anglophone culture, however, virtually any large claim about Austen tends to sound excessive and desecratory. Besides, no less discriminating a critic than Lionel Trilling himself advanced a similar thesis in 1957, when he declared that *Emma* "is touched — lightly but indubitably — by national feeling." With its tribute to "English verdure, English culture, English comfort," *Emma* tends, as Trilling put it, "to conceive of a specifically English ideal of life" (125). As it so happens, Trilling also regards Emma as what I call an "equivocal being": "The extraordinary thing about Emma," he argues, "is that she has a moral life as a man has a moral life" (124). Beyond alluding to de Tocqueville, however, Trilling is not interested in pondering what these assertions mean historically. By calling *Emma* an "idyll" (130) — a genre he considers definitionally cut off from "real" history — he forecloses the possibility that *Emma* may be enmeshed in the national ideals of its period,

just as he insists that Emma's manliness has no relation to eighteenth-
and nineteenth-century debates about women's rights when he remarks that she possesses it not "as a special instance, as an example of
a new kind of woman, which is the way George Eliot's Dorothea
Brooke has her moral life, but quite as a matter of course, as a given
quality of her nature" (124). For Trilling, these assertions remain at
some distance from each other: there is and can be no connection
between Emma's manly moral life and *Emma*'s "national feeling." By
historicizing the treatment of femininity *and* masculinity in *Emma*, I
will integrate the arguments about female manliness and national feeling which Trilling keeps apart and show that Austen engages the work
of her predecessors more positively and more intricately than is generally supposed.

In part because Austen's canonization — unlike Wollstonecraft's,
Radcliffe's, or Burney's — was so steady and so assured, we have had as
a rule very little historical imagination about her and about our relation
to her. Before considering the subjects of nationality and gender in
Emma it will be instructive to review Austenian commentary on this
subject as well. Eve Kosofsky Sedgwick's Modern Language Association paper "Jane Austen and the Masturbating Girl" was, as Sedgwick
relates, savagely attacked in the press for having violated the monumen-
tally self-evident truth that Austen had the good fortune to predate such
indecorous sexual irregularities as homo- and autoeroticism (818–19).
In her novels, the supposition runs, men are gentlemen; women are
ladies; and the desires of gentlemen and ladies for each other are
unproblematic, inevitable, and mutually fulfilling. As any full-time
Austenian knows, however, a lively and explicit interest in the sexual
irregularities of Emma Woodhouse has been the stuff of "establishment" criticism for almost fifty years now. Indeed, Trilling's assertion
about Emma's manliness was certainly the least original thing about his
essay. For post-World War II critics Emma was as "unsexed" a female as
any of the heroines of Wollstonecraft, Radcliffe, or Burney. The difference between late-eighteenth- and mid-twentieth-century notions of
what it means to be "unsexed" is that discourses of deviance drawn
from psychoanalysis came to occupy this category during our century,
so that far from signifying immodest heterosexuality, it has now meant
being homosexual, manhating, or frigid. The sexual ambiguities of
Radcliffe's and Burney's happily or unhappily equivocal heroines were,
to be sure, spared commentary on their deviance by literary scholars
only because no one paid attention to them at all. Wollstonecraft was
not always so lucky. In *Modern Woman: The Lost Sex* (1947), Ferdinand

Lundberg and Marynia Farnham maintained that modern-day "feminists" too were unsexed, and that they had Wollstonecraft to thank for their debilitatingly "severe case of penis-envy" (143). Postwar discussions of Emma Woodhouse were rarely as clinical as that, but they were fixated on Emma's lack of heterosexual feeling to such a degree that Emma's supposed *coldness* became the central question of the novel: was Emma responsive to men? could she ever really give herself in love, and thus give up trying to control other people's lives? would marriage "cure" her? Ever since Edmund Wilson's review essay "A Long Talk about Jane Austen" (1944), Emma was commonly charged with lesbianism. Wilson does not actually use the *L*-word, but his attention to Emma's lack of "interest . . . in men" and to "her infatuations with women" — along with his allusion to a certain, unspecified "Freudian formula" — makes his point clear (202). Pooh-poohing G. B. Stern's and Sheila Kaye-Smith's book *Speaking of Jane Austen* (1944) for treating characters as "actual people . . . and speculating about their lives beyond the story" (197), Wilson does the same, arguing that Emma's offstage lesbianism is that "something outside the picture which is never made explicit in the story but which has to be recognized by the reader before it is possible for him to appreciate the book" (201). In the following meditation on the conclusion, especially as it relates to Knightley's imprudent decision to move in at Hartfield, Wilson trails off into a fantasy about ménages-à-trois that threaten the domestic and erotic sovereignty to which a husband is entitled:

> Emma, who was relatively indifferent to men, was inclined to infatuations with women; and what reason is there to believe that her marriage with Knightley would prevent her from going on as she had done before: from discovering a new young lady as appealing as Harriet Smith, dominating her personality and situating her in a dream-world of Emma's own in which Emma would be able to confer on her all kinds of imaginary benefits but which would have no connection whatever with her condition or her real possibilities. This would worry and exasperate Knightley and be hard for him to do anything about. He would be lucky if he did not presently find himself saddled, along with the other awkward features of the arrangement, with one of Emma's young protégées as an actual member of the household. (202)

Try as Wilson did to dignify his commentary by differentiating it from the merely gossipy discussions of the women critics he is reviewing, his dilatory sixth-act fantasy about Emma's extramarital infatuations with women and her autonomy from male authority is on a par not only with Miss Stern's effusions but also with Miss Bates's. And like Miss Bates's prattle, I hasten to add, Wilson's here is in its own way exceedingly sensitive to the drama represented or hinted at in the novel.

On the subject of Emma's sexual irregularity, Marvin Mudrick is Wilson's direct descendant. For him, Emma's "attention never falls so warmly upon a man" as on Harriet, whom she observes "with far more warmth than anyone else" (190). Wilson's discussion of Emma's homosexuality, though aligned in sympathy with a husband bewildered to find himself displaced by a woman, nevertheless takes the liberal tone of a man of the world. Mudrick is more censorious: Emma's interest in women is pathological, stemming from the same defensive fear of commitment, the same detachment, and the same need to control that he diagnoses in Austen herself on virtually every page of *Irony as Defense and Discovery:* a woman's emotions ought to be passionately committed to a man, even if this means she might not, then, wish to write brilliant novels. But when Mudrick's scolding ceases, his discussion of Emma is astute: "Emma's interest in Harriet is not merely mistress-and-pupil, but quite emotional and particular: for a time, at least. . . . Emma is in love with her: a love unphysical and inadmissible, even perhaps undefinable in such a society; and therefore safe" (203). Without knowing and certainly without intending it, Mudrick verges here on a theory of the closet: aware that sex and gender are not equivalent, and alert to the relation between sexuality, gender, and social power, he suggests that sexuality is a discursive practice: "inadmissible" forms of sexuality become undiscussable, "undefinable," and therefore under certain circumstances, even "safe."

Wilson's and Mudrick's essays on *Emma* had an incalculable impact on Austen studies from the 1950s through the mid-1970s. Their work is discernible in Mark Schorer's widely reprinted "The Humiliation of Emma Woodhouse" (1959), which accepts the gothically strained love of Jane Fairfax for Frank Churchill as wholesome and normal and treats Emma's chilliness as a pathology deserving of the wondrously salubrious humiliation heralded in his title; and they are the targets of Wayne Booth's indignation in his "Control of Distance in Jane Austen's *Emma*" (1961). This immeasurably influential essay, which links an intensely normative reading of Emma to the genre of fiction itself, attacks Mudrick and Wilson for suggesting that Emma "has not been cured of her inclination to 'infatuations with women'" and thus for doubting that "marriage to an intelligent, amiable, good, and attractive

man is the best thing that can happen to" her (259–60). For Booth —
and a generation of Aristotelian-oriented formalists — the novel's
comic structure and moral lesson are the same. Because heterosexuality
is encoded teleologically onto a rhetoric of fiction, Emma's drama, her
"development" and "growth," are inseparable from her learning to
desire a man. Booth's rebuttal equates the perversity of women who
indulge such "infatuations" with the perversity of novel critics who
refuse to accept a happy ending when they see one.

Clearly, a long time before feminists came along, "classic" Austenian critics considered the sex and gender transgression of Emma their
business. The generation of male academics returning to American culture after the war made Emma go the way of Rosie the Riveter, and
enforced imperatives of masculine dominance and feminine domesticity
without examining the historical contingencies of these imperatives and
their own investment in them. Pained as I am by the cheeriness of their
misogyny, I also think they were basically right about Emma: quite sus-
ceptible to the stirrings of homoerotic pleasure, Emma *is* enchanted by
Harriet's "soft blue eyes" (p. 37, 38 in this volume); displaying all the
captivating enjoyment of "a mind delighted with its own ideas" (p. 38),
Emma *is* highly autonomous and autoerotic; and, finally, displaying
shockingly little reverence for dramas of heterosexual love, Emma's
energies and desires are *not* fully contained within the grid imposed by
the courtship plot. By restoring Austen to a specific social and political
context, we can examine in a more sustained and responsible way the
slippages of sex and gender which post–World War II critics discussed
by fits and starts.

Emma indeed pays conspicuous attention to gender definition. But
whereas mid-twentieth-century critics were mostly preoccupied with
Emma's waywardness as a woman, *Emma* itself evinces amazingly little
anxiety on the subject. This omission itself is highly unusual, and it
demands an explanation. Many late-eighteenth- and early-nineteenth-
century novels responded directly to Mary Wollstonecraft or her "disciple" Mary Hays by introducing into their novels protofeminists who
challenged the ways in which sexual difference had been defined. In the
same year Austen started *Emma* she also read Burney's belated *The
Wanderer* (1814), where Elinor Joddrel torments herself as well as the
women and men around her with her doomed feminist mania. Austen
also knew and admired Edgeworth's *Belinda* (1801), featuring the
mannish Harriot Freke, who erupts into feminist diatribes. It is also
likely that Austen read Charlotte Smith's *Montalbert* (1795), which

includes an "Amazonian" who is (like Emma) destitute of vanity about her personal appearance and who exhibits other "symptoms of a masculine spirit" that make the proper heroine cringe with horror (118); Elizabeth Hamilton's *Memoirs of Modern Philosophers* (1800), whose Bridgetina Botherim is a malicious spoof on Mary Hays; and Amelia Opie's more sympathetic *Adeline Mowbray* (1805), whose heroine strives not only for emancipation from specific sexual mores, particularly as these relate to the institution of marriage, but also for the autonomous, self-responsible "moral life" Trilling detects in *Emma*.

Considered in the context of these heroines, Austen's prediction that no one but herself would like Emma makes enormous sense. Although precedents for doing so were abundantly at hand, Austen never faults Emma's "masculine spirit." Postwar critics groove on what they are pleased to call Emma's *humiliation,* her *chastisement,* her *submission.* But *Emma* is not interested in subjecting the masculine independence of its heroine to disciplinary correctives.[1] To be sure, Emma has flawed and unattractive ideas about the class structure of her world and unlike her feminist prototypes, she is ridiculed for being too little rather than too much of a democrat — but we are never invited to consider her infractions against "femininity" per se to be the cause of her problem as a snob. On the contrary, the narrator trots out Emma's sister, Isabella Knightley, as a "model of right feminine happiness" (p. 124), an indulgent mother and adoring spouse, as blissfully oblivious to the faults of her husband's temper as she is to the vapidity of her own conversation. Rather than pathologize Emma's deviations from "right feminine happiness," the novel introduces Isabella for the sole purpose of making Emma look better by comparison. The narrator says that Isabella's "striking inferiorities" (p. 342) throw Emma's strengths into higher relief in Knightley's own mind. And when the novel explicitly describes Emma's behavior in ways that bend gender, it does so without the slightest hint of horror. As Mr. Knightley puts it, for example, taking care of Emma at Hartfield proves a sort of conjugal training camp for Miss Taylor: "[Y]ou were preparing yourself to be an excellent wife all the time you were at Hartfield. . . . on the very material matrimonial point of submitting your own will, and doing as you were bid"

---

[1]The "humiliation" school of *Emma* criticism is almost too populous to give an accounting for. Along with discussions by Booth and Schorer, other notable celebrations of Emma's humiliation appear in C. S. Lewis, Bernard J. Paris, and Jane Nardin. Eve Sedgwick's critique of the "Girl Being Taught a Lesson" mode of Austenian criticism ought, in my view, to be required reading for everyone interested in writing and reading about Austen (Sedgwick 833–34).

(p. 48). While the strong-willed Emma here is a surrogate husband, claiming submission as marital privilege, elsewhere she comes near to usurping what Henry Tilney in *Northanger Abbey* called the exclusively male "prerogative of choice":

> "Whom are you going to dance with?" asked Mr. Knightley. [Emma] hesitated a moment, and then replied, "With you, if you will ask me." (p. 266)

It is not necessary to overstate this point. Austen's Emma Woodhouse is not like Mary Hays's Emma Courtnay in *The Memoirs of Emma Courtnay* (1796), who proposes marriage outright. Unlike the latter and other protofeminist characters who occupy novels by Austen's contemporaries, Emma Woodhouse stops short of transgressing at least one very important gender rule: by the end of the novel, she finds herself in the certifiably orthodox position of having passively to wait to be proposed to. But the ending does not entirely cancel out what has come before, however it may delimit it. The novel basically accepts as attractive and as legitimate Emma's forcefulness. As Knightley says when comparing Emma's handwriting to that of others, "Emma's hand is the strongest" (p. 240), and this observation is tinged with fondness rather than censure.

Where this novel *is* concerned with gender transgression, it is from the masculine, not the feminine side. What "true" masculinity is like — what a "man" is, how a man speaks and behaves, what a man really wants — is the subject of continual debate, even when characters appear to be discussing women. The following sampling is typical of the novel's tendentiousness on the ever-recurrent subject *man:*

"A man of six or seven-and-twenty can take care of himself." (p. 30)

"A man always imagines a woman to be ready for anybody who asks her."

"Nonsense! a man does not imagine any such thing." (p. 65)

"There is one thing, Emma, which a man can always do, if he chuses, and that is, his duty." (p. 129)

"I can allow for the fears of the child, but not of the man." (p. 130)

"She has not the open temper which a man would wish for in a wife." (p. 233)

"General benevolence, but not general friendship, made a man what he ought to be." (p. 257)

"He is a disgrace to the name of man." (p. 337)

"A man would always wish to give a woman a better home than the one he takes her from." (p. 338)

Emma attaches no opprobrium to the manly Emma, nor does it — unlike a novel such as *Mansfield Park* — dwell on the (contradictory) qualities typifying a truly feminine woman. But it persistently asks how a *man* should behave and what he ought to do. Committing itself to the discussion of true manhood and disparaging men who do not measure up, *Emma* demonstrates that manhood is *not*, as Trilling supposed, a given quality of a man's nature, any more than manhood can ever be a matter of course of a woman's nature. This is my point. "Classic" Austenian critics assumed the constancy of feminine norms, and policed Emma's womanhood accordingly, but they sometimes cast an eye toward errant males too, even if they once again did not imagine that masculinity could be something the novel contests and constructs. Edmund Wilson appears to have been the first to call Mr. Woodhouse a "silly old woman" (201), and this epithet has proved horribly durable. Mudrick once again follows suit when he declares that Mr. Woodhouse possesses no "masculine trait," that he is "really an old woman" (192–93). Refraining from the grossness of name-calling, others beheld Mr. Woodhouse's anility with fascination or alarm. For Joseph Duffy, Mr. Woodhouse is "otiose and androgynous" (42), much like Lady Bertram, a judgment echoed by Trilling years later (130). For Tony Tanner, on the other hand, Mr. Woodhouse is a gender-derelict of dangerous proportions, a "moribund patriarch," the "type of male who would indeed bring his society — any society — to a stop," the "weak emasculate voice of definitive negations and terminations" (180). Mr. Woodhouse's transgressions — his "weak emasculate" qualities — would spell doom for all of society, if it weren't for the counterexample of Knightley, whom Tanner calls the "responsible active male" (180).

The assumption behind these readings is that there is one, continuous mode of manliness against which Mr. Woodhouse is to be judged and found lacking, though the assumption is at odds with their perception that manliness is already multiple and problematic. When Trilling attempted (and chivalrously so) to defend Mr. Woodhouse from Mudrick's attacks by insisting that in the novel he is a "kind-hearted, polite old gentleman" (134), he was right in more ways than one: Mr. Woodhouse is both a kindly old gentleman and an old kind of gentleman. We see his old-fashionedness first in his resistance to change — his desire to keep the family circle unbroken, his wish to retain the hospitable customs of his youth, his "strong habit of regard for every old acquaintance" (p. 90); and second in his attitude towards women — as Emma puts it, Mr Woodhouse loves "any thing that pays woman a compliment. He has the tenderest spirit of gallantry towards us all" (p. 79). Historically considered, far from being an unusual, deviant, emasculated, or otherwise deficient figure, Mr. Woodhouse represents the ideal of sentimental masculinity described throughout this book. The qualities that typify him — sensitivity, tenderness, "benevolent nerves," allegiance to the good old ways, courtesies to the fair sex, endearing irrationality, and even slowness, frailty, and ineptitude itself — also typify the venerated paternal figures crowding the pages of Burney and Radcliffe, to say nothing of those of Edmund Burke.

During the 1790s, a man's "benevolent nerves" carried a national agenda: they were formed by and guaranteed the continuation of the charm, the beauty, the hospitality, and the goodness of Old England itself, which liked its gallant old ways even if they did not make sense, and which won our love, veneration, and loyalty. In a world where the age of chivalry was ebbing, where the courtesies of the old regime were being displaced by the cold economic calculations of the new one, a Woodhousian man of feeling held out for civility; his attachment to the old ways preserved continuity and order, while qualities such as energy, penetration, forcefulness, brusqueness, bluntness, and decision were deemed dangerous, volatile, and cold. The heroically sentimental "man of feeling" presided over his neighborhood and family by virtue of the love he inspired in others, not by virtue of the power he wielded over them; his sensitivity legitimized his authority, enabling him to rule by weakness rather than force. In Burney's *Camilla* (1796), Sir Hugh Tyrold never holds more sway in the minds and hearts of his extended family than when he weeps and takes to his bed — which happens rather often. In Radcliffe's *The Mysteries of Udolpho* (1790), St. Aubert flinches when Quesnel plans to hew down "that noble chestnut, which has flourished for centuries, the glory of the estate!" (13); his tears make his injunctions sacred to his daughter, just as his faintness and infirmity consolidate as well as conceal his authority, making him a fitter object of "gallantry" than a woman like Emily. And in Edmund Burke's *Reflections*, Englishmen like Mr. Woodhouse are proud members of a "dull sluggish race" (106), and are celebrated for their instinctive aversion to change, their frankly irrational attachment to prejudices because they are prejudices, and their fond love for their "little platoon," their attachment "to the subdivision" (97), to diminutive, pathos-driven units of national identity.

Emma is written after the crisis that launched the reemergence of male sentimentality had abated. In it, this tradition of sentimental masculinity is archaic, and it has become somewhat of a joke. Mr. Woodhouse is dearly beloved and fondly indulged, but his sensitivity is not revered. The novel works instead to redefine masculinity. We will miss what is distinctive about Austen's achievement if we assume that masculine self-definitions were givens rather than qualities under reconstruction. Critics commonly agree that Mr. Knightley represents an ideal, but what has *not* been adequately appreciated, I think, is the novelty of that ideal, for by representing a "humane" rather than "gallant" hero, Austen desentimentalizes and deheterosexualizes virtue, and in the process makes it accessible to women as well. Twentieth-century critics assailed Mr. Woodhouse for "effeminacy," and as unpleasant as this charge is in its blend of misogyny and homophobia, there is a good deal in *Emma* that corroborates it, although the novel is careful to spare Mr. Woodhouse the full brunt of such opprobrium and to deflect it onto Mr. Elton and Frank Churchill instead.

Knightley frequently faults men for crossing the masculine/feminine divide. It is Mr. Woodhouse who first refers to Mr. Elton as a "very pretty young man," (p. 30) and coming from Mr. Woodhouse, this is a compliment to Elton's dapperness. From Knightley's viewpoint, however — the viewpoint generally endorsed by the narrator — male prettiness is small, weak, and self-preening. Mr. Knightley finds the company of fellow farmers such as Robert Martin and William Larkins just as absorbing, if not more so, than the society of women; but Mr. Elton disgraces himself in his studied attentions to women. In *Emma,* gallantry — that generous loyalty to rank and sex — rather than representing the acme of manliness, is figured as an effeminating proximity with and submission to women, and as patently absurd. Unlike *Northanger Abbey* and *Mansfield Park, Emma* is permeated with petticoat government, and heroes here show their mettle not by standing up to men with power and authority, but rather by resisting tyrannical female rule. True: Mr. Knightley impresses Emma by his heroic rescue of Harriet-in-distress; but he also proves himself to be a man by bringing bossy women — like Mrs. Elton — up short. Indeed, when "the great Mrs. Churchill" not only henpecks her husband but also bullies Frank Churchill, Mr. Knightley complains that Frank lacks the gumption to stand up to her like a man and to do what is right by that man, his father: "If he would say so to her at once, in the tone of decision becoming a man, there would be no opposition made to his going" (p. 129). As Emma says, Knightley is "not a gallant man, but he is a very humane one" (p. 185), and this means not only that he resists the encroachments of female authority, but also that he does not make a big deal out of sexual difference and the benevolizing sentiments that emerge from it in sentimental culture. Implying a counterdiscourse of "true feeling," *Emma* suggests in a most unBurkean way that "humanity" and gallantry are two different things. The "gallant Mr. Elton" by contrast damns himself when he avows that it is impossible "to contradict a lady" (p. 51); when he takes care "that nothing ungallant, nothing that did not breathe a compliment to the sex should pass his lips" (p. 73), and when he "sigh[s] and languish[es] and stud[ies] for compliments" (p. 57). As presented here, gallantry is intrinsically nonsensical: artificial and disingenuous, taking on the very femininity it courts. No man, as the logic of this novel would have it, talks or believes such rubbish. When Mr. Elton is alone among men, as Mr. Knightley informs us, he makes it clear that he wants to marry into money and that his attentions to the fair sex are only a means to this end, that he is not really a man of feeling at all.

Knightley waxes even more magisterially censorious on the subject of Frank Churchill, rebuking his derelictions from true manliness in highly loaded terms. Before Knightley even meets Frank, he predicts that he will be a "chattering coxcomb" (p. 132). Manifestly, the word "coxcomb" — like "puppy," "foppish," and "trifling," which come up later — connotes the shameful insufficiency already lambasted in Mr. Elton. But the epithet "chattering" interests me more here, *chatter* being a word reserved for feminine speech (like Miss Bates's) — excessive, undisciplined, diffuse, frivolous — and applied to a man, it is an insult. I dwell on this because *Emma* pays a lot of attention to the language of true manliness. Privileging gender over class, Austen grants to Robert Martin what Frank Churchill lacks: a manly style of writing, where manly is defined (by Emma herself) as "concise," "vigorous," "decided," and "strong" (p. 58) — *strong*, of course, also being the term Knightley uses to describe the manly Emma's hand. Knightley delivers an emasculating blow to Frank Churchill when he declares of his handwriting, "I do not admire it. It is too small — wants strength. It is like a woman's writing" (p. 240). But Mr. Knightley casts what his company terms "base aspersions" on more than the mere size of Frank Churchill's handwriting. The related style of Frank's letter also degrades him as being somehow "like a woman." Having already remarked, and more than once, on the prolixity of Frank's final letter, Knightley goes on to censure its hyperbole: "He is a very liberal thanker, with his thousands and tens of thousands" (p. 353). The real man, it is implied here, is a man of few words. Whereas an earlier generation of sentimental men had made a spectacle of their affect — of honorable feelings so powerful as to exceed all possibility of control, thus saturating handkerchiefs and liberally bedewing eloquent pages — the manful Mr. Knightley retreats from display, cultivating containment rather than excess, and "burying under a calmness that seemed all but indifference" (p. 95) the "real attachment" he feels toward his brother and toward Emma as well. And this new, plain style of manliness is a matter of national import, constituting the *amiable*, "the true English style," as opposed of course, to the *aimable*, the artificial, the courtly, the dissembling, the servile, and (as the tradition goes) the feminized French.[2]

It is the work of *Emma* to make Mr. Knightley seem traditional. Combining as it does the patron saint of England with the knight of chivalry, his name itself conduces to his traditional-seeming status. But as I hope I have indicated, he is not a traditional and certainly not a chivalric figure, and far from embodying fixed or at the very least commonly shared notions of masculinity, there is nothing in Scott, Burney, More, Burke, Radcliffe, or Edgeworth remotely like him. On one hand, Knightley is impeccably landed, a magistrate, a gentleman of "untainted" blood and judicious temper, and as such emphatically not the impetuous, combustible masculine type Burke so feared, the mere man of talent who is dangerous precisely because he has nothing to lose. But on the other hand, Knightley avows himself a farmer and a man of business, absorbed in the figures and computations Emma considers so vulgar, a man of energy, vigor, and decision, and as such emphatically not an embodiment of the stasis unto sluggishness Burke commended in country squires. The exemplary love of this "humane" as opposed to "gallant" man is *fraternal* rather than heterosexual. If Emma has difficulty realizing that Knightley is in love with her, it is not because she is impercipient, but rather because he is highly unusual in loving a woman in the same manner he loves his brother rather than the other way around: in the ambient light of sentimental hyperbole, such love seems "indifferent." But while Knightley is in some respects a new man, Austen also harkens back to some older ideals in creating him, looking not to the chivalric pseudotraditionalism celebrated by Burke, but instead bypassing the trauma of 1790s sentimentality altogether to

---

[2]For an excellent discussion of the opposition of the "impure, dishonest, dissembling, imitative, servile" French to the "moral sobriety, individual independence, and collective fellowship" of the English, see Newman 230, 231ff.

recover a native tradition of gentry liberty, which valued its manly independence from tyrannical rule, where that rule is figured as courtly,
feminine, and feminizing (as with the absolute monarchy of Louis XIV,
for example) — a tradition which the French Revolution made dangerous by fulfilling.

Emma puts pressure not on deviance from femininity, then, but on
deviance from masculinity, and it is engaged in the enterprise of purg-
ing masculine gender codes from the ostensible "excesses" of sentimental gallantry and "feminized" display, redefining English manhood
instead as brisk, energetic, downright, "natural," unaffected, reserved,
businesslike, plain-speaking; gentlemanly, to be sure, but not courtly.
What does this reconfiguration mean for Emma? For one, it demotes
the moral importance of heterosexual feeling for women. The more
conventionally feminine women in the novel — one thinks of Harriet,
who is willing to marry any man who asks; of Mrs. Elton, with her fulsome little love-names for her husband; or of Isabella, whose wifely
devotion verges on sheer stupidity — give heterosexuality a rather
revolting appearance, against which Emma's coolness looks sane and
enviable. *Emma*'s patience with Emma's gender transgressions and its
impatience with Mr. Elton's and Frank Churchill's are related. *Emma*
disdains not only the effeminacy of men, but also the femininity of
women. There appears to me as little doubt on Austen's part as there
is on Mr. Knightley's that Emma's masculine strength is better than
Isabella's "proper," "feminine" weakness, weaknesses that link her to
her father. Here, conventional femininity is a degradation to which
Emma does not submit. But it is not merely femininity that Emma's
portion designedly lacks. It is effeminacy as well, as Emma's rebuke of
Frank Churchill's double-dealing and trickery makes clear: "Impropriety! Oh! Mrs. Weston — it is too calm a censure. Much, much beyond
impropriety! — It has sunk him, I cannot say how much it has sunk him
in my opinion. So unlike what a man should be! — None of that
upright integrity, that strict adherence to truth and principle, that disdain of trick and littleness, which a man should display in every transaction of his life!" (p. 316).

To the extent that Emma's condemnation here reprises Mr. Knightley's — and even Emma's own — initial gender-based censure of Frank,
it indicates that Emma has come back to her basically sound senses at
last. But of course, the full import of Emma's censure falls not so much
on Frank Churchill at this point as on Emma herself. Every bit as guilty
of espionage, trick, littleness, and slack waywardness from truth and
principle, Emma is convicting herself not for being unlike what a

woman should be, but rather for being "unlike what a man should be!" And as is generally the case under the sentimental dispensation, its claims to love and protect notwithstanding, sentimental effeminacy harms other women. An effeminate man herself, the gallant Emma is gratified by Harriet Smith's infantine sweetness and malleability, just as she is even less generously invested in and fascinated by Jane Fairfax's gothicized debility, by the stalwart yet visibly wavering fortitude she tries to sustain in the face of her "female difficulty." Having magnified rather than alleviated the "wrongs of woman," Emma reproaches herself for transgressing the duty of woman to woman; this momentous duty is better honored when women too are like "what a man should be."[3]

When *Emma* was published in 1816, Mary Wollstonecraft had been dead for some twenty years; Ann Radcliffe was still alive but had not published since 1797; and Frances Burney had just published the long-awaited *The Wanderer; or, Female Difficulties* (1814), which assumed that the concerns of the 1790s were still pressing, only to fall with a thud. Their careers did not survive the decade that inspired them to such magnificence. In light of this silencing, Austen's achievement in *Emma* impresses me as an act of homage; in the second decade of the nineteenth century, she is still thinking about them, still working through the problems their fiction represented, albeit in a necessarily different social context. Chivalric sentimentality was an incitement to the forces of reaction and reconsolidation, and once its success was assured, sentimentality was refeminized, and the dignity more readily accorded to women's affectivity would go on to authorize their activity in charity work, education, nursing, reform societies, and the like. But *Emma* does not look forward to Victorian visions of feminine puissance; it harkens backwards still to the norms of manly independence which Burke's paean to Marie-Antoinette interrupted.

WORKS CITED

Booth, Wayne. "Control of Distance in Jane Austen's *Emma*." *A Rhetoric of Fiction*. By Booth. Chicago: U of Chicago P, 1961. 243–66.

---

[3]For a compelling study of Emma's reproduction with Harriet of the same heterosexual protocols Wollstonecraft lambastes in *Rights of Woman*, see Sulloway; for a reading of *Emma* as a plea for the enlargement of female friendship, see Perry.

Burke, Edmund. *Reflections on the Revolution in France.* 1790. *The French Revolution 1790–94.* Ed. L. G. Mitchell. Oxford: Clarendon, 1989. Vol. 8 of *The Writings and Speeches of Edmund Burke.*

Duffy, Joseph M. "*Emma*: The Awakening from Innocence." *ELH* 21 (1954): 39–53.

Lewis, C. S. "A Note on Jane Austen." 1954. Watt 25–34.

Lundberg, Ferdinand, and Marynia Farnham. *Modern Woman: The Lost Sex.* New York: Harper, 1947.

Mudrick, Marvin. *Jane Austen: Irony as Defense and Discovery.* Princeton: Princeton UP, 1952.

Nardin, Jane. *Those Elegant Decorums: The Concept of Propriety in Jane Austen's Novels.* Albany: State U of New York P, 1973.

Newman, Gerald. *The Rise of English Nationalism: A Cultural History 1740–1830.* New York: St. Martin's, 1987.

Paris, Bernard J. *Character and Conflict in Jane Austen's Novels: A Psychological Approach.* Detroit: Wayne State UP, 1978.

Perry, Ruth. "Interrupted Friendships in Jane Austen's *Emma.*" *Tulsa Studies in Women's Literature* 5 (1986): 185–202.

Radcliffe, Ann. *The Mysteries of Udolpho.* 1790. Ed. Bonamy Dobrée. Oxford: Oxford UP, 1966.

Schorer, Mark. "The Humiliation of Emma Woodhouse." 1959. Watt 25–34.

Sedgwick, Eve Kosofsky. "Jane Austen and the Masturbating Girl." *Critical Inquiry* 17 (1991): 818–37.

Smith, Charlotte. *Montalbert.* London, 1795.

Sulloway, Alison. "Emma Woodhouse and *A Vindication of the Rights of Woman.*" *Wordsworth Circle* 7 (1976): 320–32.

Tanner, Tony. *Jane Austen.* Cambridge: Harvard UP, 1986.

Trilling, Lionel. "*Emma* and the Legend of Jane Austen." 1957. *Jane Austen's "Emma": A Casebook.* Ed. David Lodge. London: Macmillan, 1991. 118–37.

Watt, Ian, ed. *Jane Austen: A Collection of Critical Essays.* Englewood Cliffs, NJ: Prentice-Hall, 1963.

Wilson, Edmund. "A Long Talk about Jane Austen." 1944. *Classics and Commercials: A Literary Chronicle of the Forties.* By Wilson. New York: Farrar, 1950. 190–203.

Marxist Criticism and
Emma

WHAT IS MARXIST CRITICISM?

To the question "What is Marxist criticism?" it may be tempting to respond with another question: "What does it matter?" In light of the rapid and largely unanticipated demise of Soviet-style communism in the former USSR and throughout Eastern Europe, it is understandable to suppose that Marxist literary analysis would disappear too, quickly becoming an anachronism in a world enamored with full-market capitalism.

In fact, however, there is no reason why Marxist criticism should weaken, let alone disappear. It is, after all, a phenomenon distinct from Soviet and Eastern European communism, having had its beginnings nearly eighty years before the Bolshevik revolution and having thrived since the 1940s, mainly in the West — not as a form of communist propaganda but rather as a form of critique, a discourse for interrogating *all* societies and their texts in terms of certain specific issues. Those issues — including race, class, and the attitudes shared within a given culture — are as much with us as ever, not only in contemporary Russia but also in the United States.

The argument could even be made that Marxist criticism has been strengthened by the collapse of Soviet-style communism. There was a time, after all, when few self-respecting Anglo-American journals would use Marxist terms or models, however illuminating, to analyze Western issues or problems. It smacked of sleeping with the enemy. With the collapse of the Kremlin, however, old taboos began to give way. Even the staid *Wall Street Journal* now seems comfortable using phrases like "worker alienation" to discuss the problems plaguing the American business world.

The assumption that Marxist criticism will die on the vine of a moribund political system rests in part on another mistaken assumption, namely, that Marxist literary analysis is practiced only by people who would like to see society transformed into a Marxist-communist state, one created through land reform, the redistribution of wealth, a tightly and centrally managed economy, the abolition of institutionalized religion, and so on. In fact, it has never been necessary to be a communist political revolutionary to be classified as a Marxist literary critic. (Many of the critics discussed in this introduction actually *fled* communist societies to live in the West.) Nor is it necessary to like only those literary works with a radical social vision or to dislike books that represent or even reinforce a middle-class, capitalist worldview. It is necessary, however, to adopt what most students of literature would consider a radical definition of the purpose and function of literary criticism.

More traditional forms of criticism, according to the Marxist critic Pierre Macherey, "set . . . out to deliver the text from its own silences by coaxing it into giving up its true, latent, or hidden meaning." Inevitably, however, non-Marxist criticism "intrude[s] its own discourse between the reader and the text" (qtd. in Bennett 107). Marxist critics, by contrast, do not attempt to discover hidden meanings in texts. Or if they do, they do so only after seeing the text, first and foremost, as a material product to be understood in broadly historical terms. That is to say, a literary work is first viewed as a product *of* work (and hence of the realm of production and consumption we call economics). Second, it may be looked upon as a work that *does* identifiable work of its own. At one level, that work is usually to enforce and reinforce the prevailing ideology, that is, the network of conventions, values, and opinions to which the majority of people uncritically subscribe.

This does not mean that Marxist critics merely describe the obvious. Quite the contrary: the relationship that the Marxist critic Terry Eagleton outlines in *Criticism and Ideology* (1978) among the soaring cost of books in the nineteenth century, the growth of lending libraries, the practice of publishing "three-decker" novels (so that three borrowers could be reading the same book at the same time), and the changing *content* of those novels is highly complex in its own way. But the complexity Eagleton finds is not that of the deeply buried meaning of the text. Rather, it is that of the complex web of social and economic relationships that were prerequisite to the work's production. Marxist criticism does not seek to be, in Eagleton's words, "a passage from text to reader." Indeed, "its task is to show the text as it cannot know itself, to manifest those conditions of its making (inscribed in its very letter) about which it is necessarily silent" (43).

As everyone knows, Marxism began with Karl Marx, the nineteenth-century German philosopher best known for writing *Das Kapital*, the seminal work of the communist movement. What everyone doesn't know is that Marx was also the first Marxist literary critic (much as Sigmund Freud, who psychoanalyzed E. T. A. Hoffmann's supernatural tale "The Sandman," was the first Freudian literary critic). During the 1830s Marx wrote critical essays on writers such as Goethe and Shakespeare (whose tragic vision of Elizabethan disintegration he praised).

The fact that Marxist literary criticism began with Marx himself is hardly surprising, given Marx's education and early interests. Trained in the classics at the University of Bonn, Marx wrote literary imitations, his own poetry, a failed novel, and a fragment of a tragic drama *(Oulanem)* before turning to contemplative and political philosophy. Even after he met Friedrich Engels in 1843 and began collaborating on works such as *The German Ideology* and *The Communist Manifesto,* Marx maintained a keen interest in literary writers and their works. He and Engels argued about the poetry of Heinrich Heine, admired Hermann Freiligrath (a poet critical of the German aristocracy), and faulted the playwright Ferdinand Lassalle for writing about a reactionary knight in the Peasants' War rather than about more progressive aspects of German history.

As these examples suggest, Marx and Engels would not — indeed, could not — think of aesthetic matters as being distinct and independent from such things as politics, economics, and history. Not surprisingly, they viewed the alienation of the worker in industrialized, capitalist societies as having grave consequences for the arts. How can people mechanically stamping out things that bear no mark of their producer's individuality (people thereby "reified," turned into things themselves) be expected to recognize, produce, or even consume things of beauty? And if there is no one to consume something, there will soon be no one to produce it, especially in an age in which production (even of something like literature) has come to mean *mass* (and therefore profitable) production.

In *The German Ideology* (1846), Marx and Engels expressed their sense of the relationship between the arts, politics, and basic economic reality in terms of a general social theory. Economics, they argued, provides the "base" or "infrastructure" of society, but from that base emerges a "superstructure" consisting of law, politics, philosophy, religion, and art.

Marx later admitted that the relationship between base and superstructure may be indirect and fluid: every change in economics may not be reflected by an immediate change in ethics or literature. In *The Eighteenth Brumaire of Louis Bonaparte* (1852), he came up with the word *homology* to describe the sometimes unbalanced, often delayed, and almost always loose correspondence between base and superstructure. And later in that same decade, while working on an introduction to his *Political Economy,* Marx further relaxed the base–superstructure relationship. Writing on the excellence of ancient Greek art (versus the primitive nature of ancient Greek economics), he conceded that a gap sometimes opens up between base and superstructure — between economic forms and those produced by the creative mind.

Nonetheless, *at* base the old formula was maintained. Economics remained basic and the connection between economics and superstructural elements of society was reaffirmed. Central to Marxism and Marxist literary criticism was and is the following "materialist" insight: consciousness, without which such things as art cannot be produced, is not the source of social forms and economic conditions. It is, rather, their most important product.

Marx and Engels, drawing upon the philosopher G. W. F. Hegel's theories about the dialectical synthesis of ideas out of theses and antitheses, believed that a revolutionary class war (pitting the capitalist class against a proletarian, antithetical class) would lead eventually to the synthesis of a new social and economic order. Placing their faith not in the idealist Hegelian dialectic but, rather, in what they called "dialectical materialism," they looked for a secular and material salvation of humanity — one in, not beyond, history — via revolution and not via divine intervention. And they believed that the communist society eventually established would be one capable of producing new forms of consciousness and belief and therefore, ultimately, great art.

The revolution anticipated by Marx and Engels did not occur in their century, let alone lifetime. When it finally did take place, it didn't happen in places where Marx and Engels had thought it might be successful: the United States, Great Britain, and Germany. It happened, rather, in 1917 Russia, a country long ruled by despotic czars but also enlightened by the works of powerful novelists and playwrights, including Chekhov, Pushkin, Tolstoy, and Dostoyevsky.

Perhaps because of its significant literary tradition, Russia produced revolutionaries like V. I. Lenin, who shared not only Marx's interest in literature but also his belief in literature's ultimate importance. But it was not without some hesitation that Lenin endorsed the significance of texts written during the reign of the czars. Well before 1917 he had questioned what the relationship should be between a society undergoing a revolution and the great old literature of its bourgeois past.

Lenin attempted to answer that question in a series of essays on Tolstoy that he wrote between 1908 and 1911. Tolstoy — the author of *War and Peace* and *Anna Karenina* — was an important nineteenth-century Russian writer whose views did not accord with all of those of young Marxist revolutionaries. Continuing interest in a writer like Tolstoy may be justified, Lenin reasoned, given the primitive and unenlightened economic order of the society that produced him. Since superstructure usually lags behind base (and is therefore usually *more* primitive), the attitudes of a Tolstoy were relatively progressive when viewed in light of the monarchical and precapitalist society out of which they arose.

Moreover, Lenin also reasoned, the writings of the great Russian realists would *have* to suffice, at least in the short run. Lenin looked forward, in essays like "Party Organization and Party Literature," to the day in which new artistic forms would be produced by progressive writers with revolutionary political views and agendas. But he also knew that a great proletarian literature was unlikely to evolve until a thoroughly literate proletariat had been produced by the educational system.

Lenin was hardly the only revolutionary leader involved in setting up the new Soviet state who took a strong interest in literary matters. In 1924 Leon Trotsky published a book called *Literature and Revolution*, which is still acknowledged as a classic of Marxist literary criticism.

Trotsky worried about the direction in which Marxist aesthetic theory seemed to be going. He responded skeptically to groups like Proletkult, which opposed tolerance toward pre- and nonrevolutionary writers, and which called for the establishment of a new, proletarian culture. Trotsky warned of the danger of cultural sterility and risked unpopularity by pointing out that there is no necessary connection between the quality of a literary work and the quality of its author's politics.

In 1927 Trotsky lost a power struggle with Josef Stalin, a man who believed, among other things, that writers should be "engineers" of "human souls." After Trotsky's expulsion from the Soviet Union, views held by groups like Proletkult and the Left Front of Art (LEF), and by theorists such as Nikolai Bukharin and A. A. Zhdanov, became more prevalent. Speaking at the First Congress of the Union of Soviet Writers in 1934, the Soviet author Maxim Gorky called for writing that would "make labor the principal hero of our books." It was at the same writers' congress that "socialist realism," an art form glorifying workers and the revolutionary State, was made Communist party policy and the official literary form of the USSR.

Of the writers active in the USSR after the expulsion of Trotsky and the unfortunate triumph of Stalin, two critics stand out. One, Mikhail Bakhtin, was a Russian, later a Soviet, critic who spent much of his life in a kind of internal exile. Many of his essays were written in the 1930s and not published in the West or translated until the late 1960s. His work comes out of an engagement with the Marxist intellectual tradition as well as out of an indirect, even hidden, resistance to the Soviet government. It has been important to Marxist critics writing in the West because his theories provide a means to decode submerged social critique, especially in early modern texts. He viewed language — especially literary texts — in terms of discourses and dialogues. Within a novel written in a society in flux, for instance, the narrative may include an official, legitimate discourse, plus another infiltrated by challenging comments and even retorts. In a 1929 book on Dostoyevsky and a 1940 study titled *Rabelais and His World*, Bakhtin examined what he calls "polyphonic" novels, each characterized by a multiplicity of voices or discourses. In Dostoyevsky the independent status of a given character is marked by the difference of his or her language from that of the narrator. (The narrator's voice, too, can in fact be a dialogue.) In works by Rabelais, Bakhtin finds that the (profane) language of the carnival and of other popular festivals plays against and parodies the more official discourses, that is, of the king, church, or even socially powerful intellectuals. Bakhtin influenced modern cultural criticism by showing, in a sense, that the conflict between "high" and "low" culture takes place not only between classic and popular texts but also between the "dialogic" voices that exist within many books — whether "high" or "low."

The other subtle Marxist critic who managed to survive Stalin's dictatorship and his repressive policies was Georg Lukács. A Hungarian who had begun his career as an "idealist" critic, Lukács had converted to Marxism in 1919; renounced his earlier, Hegelian work shortly thereafter; visited Moscow in 1930–31; and finally emigrated to the USSR in 1933, just one year before the First Congress of the Union of Soviet Writers met. Lukács was far less narrow in his views than the most strident Stalinist Soviet critics of the 1930s and 1940s. He disliked much socialist realism and appreciated prerevolutionary, realistic novels that broadly reflected cultural "totalities"— and were populated with characters representing human "types" of the author's place and time. (Lukács was particularly fond of the historical canvasses painted by the early nineteenth-century novelist Sir Walter Scott.) But like his more rigid and censorious contemporaries, he drew the line at accepting nonrevolutionary, modernist works like James Joyce's *Ulysses*. He condemned movements like expressionism and symbolism, preferring works with "content" over more decadent, experimental works characterized mainly by "form."

With Lukács its most liberal and tolerant critic from the early 1930s until well into the 1960s, the Soviet literary scene degenerated to the point that the works of great writers like Franz Kafka were no longer read, either because they were viewed as decadent, formal experiments or because they "engineered souls" in "nonprogressive" directions. Officially sanctioned works were generally ones in which artistry lagged far behind the politics (no matter how bad the politics were).

Fortunately for the Marxist critical movement, politically radical critics *outside* the Soviet Union were free of its narrow, constricting policies and, consequently, able fruitfully to develop the thinking of Marx, Engels, and Trotsky. It was these non-Soviet Marxists who kept Marxist critical theory alive and useful in discussing all *kinds* of literature, written across the entire historical spectrum.

Perhaps because Lukács was the best of the Soviet communists writing Marxist criticism in the 1930s and 1940s, non-Soviet Marxists tended to develop their ideas by publicly opposing those of Lukács. German dramatist and critic Bertolt Brecht countered Lukács by arguing that art ought to be viewed as a field of production, not as a container of "content." Brecht also criticized Lukács for his attempt to enshrine realism at the expense not only of other "isms" but also of poetry and drama, both of which had been largely ignored by Lukács.

Even more outspoken was Brecht's critical champion Walter Benjamin, a German Marxist who, in the 1930s, attacked those conventional and traditional literary forms conveying a stultifying "aura" of culture. Benjamin praised dadaism and, more important, new forms of art ushered in by the age of mechanical reproduction. Those forms — including radio and film — offered hope, he felt, for liberation from capitalist culture, for they were too new to be part of its stultifyingly ritualistic traditions.

But of all the anti-Lukácsians outside the USSR who made a contribution to the development of Marxist literary criticism, the most important was probably Theodor Adorno. Leader since the early 1950s of the Frankfurt school of Marxist criticism, Adorno attacked Lukács for his dogmatic rejection of nonrealist modern literature and for his belief in the primacy of content over form. Art does not equal science, Adorno insisted. He went on to argue for art's autonomy from empirical forms of knowledge and to suggest that the interior monologues of modernist works (by Beckett and Proust) reflect the fact of modern alienation in a way that Marxist criticism ought to find compelling.

In addition to turning against Lukács and his overly constrictive canon, Marxists outside the Soviet Union were able to take advantage of insights generated by non-Marxist critical theories being developed in post–World War II Europe. One of the movements that came to be of interest to non-Soviet Marxists was structuralism, a scientific approach to the study of humankind whose proponents believed that all elements of culture, including literature, could be understood as parts of a system of signs. Using modern linguistics as a model, structuralists like Claude Lévi-Strauss broke down the myths of various cultures into "mythemes" in an attempt to show that there are structural correspondences, or homologies, between the mythical elements produced by various human communities across time.

Of the European structuralist Marxists, one of the most influential was Lucien Goldmann, a Rumanian critic living in Paris. Goldmann combined structuralist principles with Marx's base–superstructure model in order to show how economics determines the mental structures of social groups, which are reflected in literary texts. Goldmann rejected the idea of individual human genius, choosing to see works, instead, as the "collective" products of "trans-individual" mental structures. In early studies, such as *The Hidden God* (1955), he related seventeenth-century French texts (such as Racine's *Phèdre*) to the ideology of Jansenism. In later works, he applied Marx's base–superstructure model even more strictly, describing a relationship between economic conditions and texts unmediated by an intervening, collective consciousness.

In spite of his rigidity and perhaps because of his affinities with structuralism, Goldmann came to be seen in the 1960s as the proponent of a kind of watered-down, "humanist" Marxism. He was certainly viewed that way by the French Marxist Louis Althusser, a disciple not of Lévi-Strauss and structuralism but rather of the psychoanalytic theorist Jacques Lacan and of the Italian communist Antonio Gramsci, famous for his writings about ideology and "hegemony." (Gramsci used the latter word to refer to the pervasive, weblike system of assumptions and values that shapes the way things look, what they mean, and therefore what reality *is* for the majority of people within a culture.)

Like Gramsci, Althusser viewed literary works primarily in terms of their relationship to ideology, the function of which, he argued, is to (re)produce the existing relations of production in a given society. Dave Laing, in *The Marxist Theory of Art* (1978), has attempted to explain this particular insight of Althusser by saying that ideologies, through the "ensemble of habits, moralities, and opinions" that can be found in any literary text, "ensure that the work-force (and those responsible for re-producing them in the family, school, etc.) are maintained in their position of subordination to the dominant class" (91). This is not to say that Althusser thought of the masses as a brainless multitude following only the dictates of the prevailing ideology: Althusser followed Gramsci in suggesting that even working-class people have some freedom to struggle against ideology and to change history. Nor is it to say that Althusser saw ideology as being a coherent, consistent force. In fact, he saw it as being riven with contradictions that works of literature sometimes expose and even widen. Thus Althusser followed Marx and Gramsci in believing that although literature must be seen in *relation* to ideology, it — like all social forms — has some degree of autonomy.

Althusser's followers included Pierre Macherey, who in *A Theory of Literary Production* (1978) developed Althusser's concept of the relationship between literature and ideology. A realistic novelist, he argued, attempts to produce a unified, coherent text, but instead ends up producing a work containing lapses, omissions, gaps. This happens because within ideology there are subjects that cannot be covered, things that cannot be said, contradictory views that aren't recognized as contradictory. (The critic's challenge, in this case, is to supply what the text cannot say, thereby making sense of gaps and contradictions.)

But there is another reason why gaps open up and contradictions become evident in texts. Works don't just reflect ideology (which Goldmann had referred to as "myth" and which Macherey refers to as a system of "illusory social beliefs"); they are also "fictions," works of art, *products* of ideology that have what Goldmann would call a "world-view" to offer. What kind of product, Macherey implicitly asks, is identical to the thing that produced it? It is hardly surprising, then, that Balzac's fiction shows French peasants in two different lights, only one of which is critical and judgmental, only one of which is baldly ideological. Writing approvingly on Macherey and Macherey's mentor Althusser in *Marxism and Literary Criticism* (1976), Terry Eagleton says: "It is by giving ideology a determinate form, fixing it within certain fictional limits, that art is able to distance itself from [ideology], thus revealing . . . [its] limits" (19).

A follower of Althusser, Macherey is sometimes referred to as a "post-Althusserian Marxist." Eagleton, too, is often described that way, as is his American contemporary Fredric Jameson. Jameson and Eagleton, as well as being post-Althusserians, are also among the few Anglo-American critics who have closely followed and significantly developed Marxist thought.

Before them, Marxist interpretation in English was limited to the work of a handful of critics: Christopher Caudwell, Christopher Hill, Arnold Kettle, E. P. Thompson, and Raymond Williams. Of these, Williams was perhaps least Marxist in orientation: he felt that Marxist critics, ironically, tended too much to isolate economics from culture; that they overlooked the individualism of people, opting instead to see them as "masses"; and that even more ironically, they had become an elitist group. But if the least Marxist of the British Marxists, Williams was also by far the most influential. Preferring to talk about "culture" instead of ideology, Williams argued in works such as *Culture and Society 1780–1950* (1958) that culture is "lived experience" and, as such, an interconnected set of social properties, each and all grounded in and influencing history.

Terry Eagleton's *Criticism and Ideology* is in many ways a response to the work of Williams. Responding to Williams's statement in *Culture and Society* that "there are in fact no masses; there are only ways of seeing people as masses" (289), Eagleton writes:

That men and women really are now unique individuals was Williams's (unexceptionable) insistence; but it was a proposition bought at the expense of perceiving the fact that they must mass and fight to achieve their full individual humanity. One has only to adapt Williams's statement to "There are in fact no classes; there are only ways of seeing people as classes" to expose its theoretical paucity. (*Criticism* 29)

Eagleton goes on, in *Criticism and Ideology*, to propose an elaborate theory about how history — in the form of "general," "authorial," and "aesthetic" ideology — enters texts, which in turn may revivify, open up, or critique those same ideologies, thereby setting in motion a process that may alter history. He shows how texts by Jane Austen, Matthew Arnold, Charles Dickens, George Eliot, Joseph Conrad, and T. S. Eliot deal with and transmute conflicts at the heart of the general and authorial ideologies behind them: conflicts between morality and individualism, and between individualism and social organicism and utilitarianism.

As all this emphasis on ideology and conflict suggests, a modern British Marxist like Eagleton, even while acknowledging the work of a British Marxist predecessor like Williams, is more nearly developing the ideas of Continental Marxists like Althusser and Macherey. That holds, as well, for modern American Marxists like Fredric Jameson. For although he makes occasional, sympathetic references to the works of Williams, Thompson, and Hill, Jameson makes far more *use* of Lukács, Adorno, and Althusser as well as non-Marxist structuralist, psychoanalytic, and poststructuralist critics.

In the first of several influential works, *Marxism and Form* (1971), Jameson takes up the question of form and content, arguing that the former is "but the working out" of the latter "in the realm of superstructure" (329). (In making such a statement Jameson opposes not only the tenets of Russian formalists, for whom content had merely been the fleshing out of form, but also those of so-called vulgar Marxists, who tended to define form as mere ornamentation or window dressing.) In his later work *The Political Unconscious* (1981), Jameson uses what in *Marxism and Form* he had called "dialectical criticism" to synthesize out of structuralism and poststructuralism, Freud and Lacan, Althusser and Adorno, a set of complex arguments that can only be summarized reductively.

The fractured state of societies and the isolated condition of individuals, he argues, may be seen as indications that there originally existed an unfallen state of something that may be called "primitive communism." History — which records the subsequent divisions and alienations — limits awareness of its own contradictions and of that lost, Better State, via ideologies and their manifestation in texts whose strategies essentially contain and repress desire, especially revolutionary desire, into the collective unconscious. (In Conrad's *Lord Jim*, Jameson shows, the knowledge that governing classes don't *deserve* their power is contained and repressed by an ending that metaphysically blames Nature for the tragedy and that melodramatically blames wicked Gentleman Brown.)

As demonstrated by Jameson in analyses like the one mentioned above, textual strategies of containment and concealment may be discovered by the critic, but only by the critic practicing dialectical criticism, that is to say, a criticism aware, among other things, of its *own* status as ideology. All thought, Jameson concludes, is ideological; only through ideological thought that knows itself as such can ideologies be seen through and eventually transcended.

In the essay that follows, Beth Fowkes Tobin focuses on the Box Hill picnic scene in *Emma*, arguing that although it has often been read as one describing the prototypical transformation of a "narcissistic adolescent" into a "thoughtful and responsible adult," the scene may be more properly understood in terms of certain "political, social, and economic problems specific to early-nineteenth-century Britain" (pp. 473–74). More specifically, Tobin reads the scene as "Austen's attempt to deal with the threatened erosion of the old social order and the conflicting claims and ideologies of the emergent middle classes" (p. 474).

Tobin begins her analysis by focusing on the novel's "impoverished gentlewomen," particularly Miss Bates, "the middle-aged daughter of the late vicar of Highbury . . . [who] is 'neither young, handsome, rich, nor married'" (p. 475). Austen, Tobin argues, explored the plight of such women because, as a well-born spinster herself, she was "acutely aware of how economically vulnerable and socially powerless [such] women were in this society" (p. 475). (That powerlessness, Tobin argues, was to a great extent due to the powerful ideology of "different spheres," the emerging notion that "to men belonged the world of work and to women the hearth and home" [p. 476]).

"Placed against this background of impoverished, powerless gentlewomen is Emma," who happens to be independent as well as beautiful and rich. She not only has "social prestige and economic privilege that give her power over . . . Highbury, but she also has complete control over her father, the only man to whom she is legally accountable" (p. 478). But she does not know how to use her prestige and power, Tobin argues; in her failures to be a successful "patron" or "benefactor" (p. 479), she shows that she does not — and how could she, being a young woman? — fully understand that her society depends on a pater-nalistic system of protection and support.

"As a powerful and wealthy woman," Tobin argues, "Emma has a special responsibility to assist and protect women who are economically vulnerable and socially disadvantaged" (p. 479). She does get involved with economically vulnerable women, "adopt[ing] Harriet [Smith] as if she were a pet," (p. 479), but, as Tobin points out, Mr. Knightley criti-cizes her matchmaking endeavor on Harriet's behalf, suggesting that it amounts to inappropriate behavior for a lady and, indeed, an abuse of her social and economic powers. (For a different view of Emma's patronage of poor, less powerful women see Devoney Looser's " 'The Duty of Woman by Woman': Reforming Feminism in *Emma*" [p. 577 in this volume].)

Emma also, Tobin maintains, "abuses her power in her neglect of Jane Fairfax," a "well-educated and accomplished woman" who, instead of Harriet, "should be the object of Emma's interest and atten-tion" (p. 480). Neglect turns to outright meanness during the Box Hill expedition, where Emma "proceeds to make Jane Fairfax miserable" as well as impugning Mrs. Elton's status. But "[i]nsulting Mrs. Elton and being insensitive to Jane Fairfax," Tobin goes on to point out, "are rel-atively minor abuses of social and economic privilege when compared to Emma's cruel remark to Miss Bates, who as a poor, unmarried, and aging gentlewoman deserves not Emma's contempt and ridicule but her charity and protection" (p. 481).

All these "insults and slights," these abuses by Emma of her power, turn out to have "enormous political significance" (p. 481) in Tobin's reading of the novel, for they are actions that ultimately threaten the social structure of Emma's — and Austen's — hierarchical world. For instance, "[b]y adopting Harriet Smith and trying to marry her off to Mr. Elton and then to Frank Churchill," Emma "undermines her soci-ety's elaborate discriminations of social standing" (p. 482). Even more threatening to the delicate social structure is Emma's "insensitive han-dling of her neighbors" such as Robert Martin and his family. By abus-ing the power of her rank, Emma threatens to sever "the chain of connection" that binds the emerging middle class to the gentry and to disabuse them of the belief that they and their social betters "share a common cause" (pp. 481–82).

According to Tobin, "Austen clearly supports the old order and enlists her reader's sympathies in support of [its] institutions and ide-ologies" (p. 482). She "idealizes the gentry, offering Mr. Knightley" as "an exemplary member" (p. 482). Thus, it is important that the still-powerful old order not be threatened by individuals, such as Emma, who abuse its power. This is why Austen has Emma fall in love with Knightley, why Knightley's scolding of her after the Box Hill episode is so emphatic, and why she modifies her behavior as a result. "Mr. Knightley's reprimand echoes in Emma's head as she rides home from Box Hill in tears" (p. 483), Tobin writes. Repentant, she "acknowledges the justness of his remarks and turns a critical eye on her own behavior, especially as it affects the Bateses and Jane Fairfax." From then on "she tries to emulate [Knightley's] style of benevolence" (p. 483).

Although Tobin says she runs "the risk of seeming to allegorize *Emma*," she concludes her essay by drawing a parallel between "Emma's abuse of power" and what the Victorian essayist Thomas Carlyle referred to as an "abdication on the part of the governors" (p. 483), particularly with respect to the gentry's support of Corn Laws that artificially supported the high price of English grain by banning imports. Stating that it is "hard to imagine readers in 1816 reading *Emma* without thinking of the Corn Laws or similarly divisive political and economic issues," Tobin suggests that "Emma's punishment and reform may have had the effect of reassuring nineteenth century readers anxious about the upper classes' abuse of power and neglect of duty, encouraging them to believe that the abuses of the system were isolated individual acts that could be corrected" (p. 484).

Tobin's essay typifies Marxist criticism in its attention to the role class played in Emma's — and Austen's — society. More important, it represents Marxist criticism insofar as it is interested in the *way* Austen represents, in her fiction, political and economic issues based in class differences. That representation, Tobin argues, is ideologically grounded; Austen is "ultimately an apologist for the landed classes" (p. 485) and, therefore, has written a novel that defends their status, in part by acknowledging and correcting their deficiencies and even abuses. She does acknowledge the plight of impoverished gentlewomen, but by translating their problem into Emma's personal problem, she shifts the reader's focus from economic inequities in her society to the moral failings of individuals. Thus, "*Emma* has the effect of brushing away most of the concerns that might arise in the reader's mind regarding the way women are treated in this society," for it "focus[es] on the individual's power to change and control" that treatment (p. 485). This focus, Tobin argues, has led most scholars to focus on the character of Emma and to "read the novel as a Bildungsroman," as a story of individual "moral and psychological development" rather than as a narrative growing out of political and economic conditions, as a text that performs "ideological work" (p. 486).

Ross C Murfin

MARXIST CRITICISM:
A SELECTED BIBLIOGRAPHY

Marx, Engels, Lenin, and Trotsky

Engels, Friedrich. *The Condition of the Working Class in England.* Ed. and trans. W. O. Henderson and W. H. Chaloner. Stanford: Stanford UP, 1968.

Lenin, V. I. *On Literature and Art.* Moscow: Progress, 1967.

Marx, Karl. *Selected Writings.* Ed. David McLellan. Oxford: Oxford UP, 1977.

Trotsky, Leon. *Literature and Revolution.* 1924. New York: Russell, 1967.

General Introductions to and
Reflections on Marxist Criticism

Bennett, Tony. *Formalism and Marxism.* London: Methuen, 1979.

Demetz, Peter. *Marx, Engels, and the Poets.* Chicago: U of Chicago P, 1967.

Eagleton, Terry. *Literary Theory: An Introduction.* Minneapolis: U of Minnesota P, 1983.

———. *Marxism and Literary Criticism.* Berkeley: U of California P, 1976.

Elster, Jon. *An Introduction to Karl Marx.* Cambridge: Cambridge UP, 1985.

———. *Nuts and Bolts for the Social Sciences.* Cambridge: Cambridge UP, 1989.

Fokkema, D. W., and Elrud Kunne-Ibsch. *Theories of Literature in the Twentieth Century: Structuralism, Marxism, Aesthetics of Reception, Semiotics.* New York: St. Martin's, 1977. See ch. 4, "Marxist Theories of Literature."

Frow, John. *Marxism and Literary History.* Cambridge: Harvard UP, 1986.

Jefferson, Ann, and David Robey. *Modern Literary Theory: A Critical Introduction.* Totowa, NJ. Barnes, 1982. See the essay "Marxist Literary Theories," by David Forgacs.

Laing, Dave. *The Marxist Theory of Art.* Brighton: Harvester, 1978.

Selden, Raman, Peter Widdowson, and Peter Brooker. *A Readers' Guide to Contemporary Literary Theory.* 4th ed. Lexington: U of Kentucky P, 1997. See ch. 5, "Marxist Theories."

Slaughter, Cliff. *Marxism, Ideology, and Literature.* Atlantic Highlands: Humanities, 1980.

Some Classic Marxist Studies and Statements

Adorno, Théodor. *Prisms: Cultural Criticism and Society.* Trans. Samuel Weber and Sherry Weber. Cambridge: MIT P, 1982.

Althusser, Louis. *For Marx.* Trans. Ben Brewster. New York: Pantheon, 1969.

Althusser, Louis, and Étienne Balibar. *Reading Capital.* Trans. Ben Brewster. New York: Pantheon, 1971.

Bakhtin, Mikhail. *The Dialogic Imagination: Four Essays.* Ed. Michael Holquist. Trans. Caryl Emerson. Austin: U of Texas P, 1981.

―――. *Rabelais and His World.* Trans. Hélène Iswolsky. Cambridge: MIT P, 1968.

Benjamin, Walter. *Illuminations.* Ed. with introd. by Hannah Arendt. Trans. H. Zohn. New York: Harcourt, 1968.

Brecht, Bertolt. *Brecht on Theatre: The Development of an Aesthetic.* Ed. and trans. John Willett. New York: Hill, 1964.

―――. *William Morris: Romantic to Revolutionary.* New York: Pantheon, 1977.

Caudwell, Christopher. *Illusion and Reality.* 1935. New York: Russell, 1955.

―――. *Studies in a Dying Culture.* London: Lawrence, 1938.

Goldmann, Lucien. *The Hidden God.* New York: Humanities, 1964.

―――. *Towards a Sociology of the Novel.* London: Tavistock, 1975.

Gramsci, Antonio. *Selections from the Prison Notebooks.* Ed. Quintin Hoare and Geoffrey Nowell Smith. New York: International UP, 1971.

Kettle, Arnold. *An Introduction to the English Novel.* New York: Harper, 1960.

Lukács, Georg. *The Historical Novel.* Trans. H. Mitchell and S. Mitchell. Boston: Beacon, 1963.

―――. *Studies in European Realism.* New York: Grosset, 1964.

————. *The Theory of the Novel.* Cambridge: MIT P, 1971.

Marcuse, Herbert. *One-Dimensional Man.* Boston: Beacon, 1964.

Thompson, E. P. *The Making of the English Working Class.* New York: Pantheon, 1964.

Williams, Raymond. *Culture and Society 1780–1950.* New York: Harper, 1958.

————. *The Long Revolution.* New York: Columbia UP, 1961.

————. *Marxism and Literature.* Oxford: Oxford UP, 1977.

Wilson, Edmund. *To the Finland Station.* Garden City: Doubleday, 1953.

Studies by and of Post-Althusserian Marxists

Dowling, William C. *Jameson, Althusser, Marx: An Introduction to "The Political Unconscious."* Ithaca: Cornell UP, 1984.

Eagleton, Terry. *Criticism and Ideology: A Study in Marxist Literary Theory.* London: Verso, 1978.

————. *Exiles and Émigrés.* New York: Schocken, 1970.

Goux, Jean-Joseph. *Symbolic Economies after Marx and Freud.* Trans. Jennifer Gage. Ithaca: Cornell UP, 1990.

Jameson, Fredric. *Marxism and Form: Twentieth-Century Dialectical Theories of Literature.* Princeton: Princeton UP, 1971.

————. *The Political Unconscious: Narrative as a Socially Symbolic Act.* Ithaca: Cornell UP, 1981.

Macherey, Pierre. *A Theory of Literary Production.* Trans. G. Wall. London: Routledge, 1978.

Marxist Criticism Relating to *Emma*

Aers, David. "Community and Morality: Towards Reading Jane Austen." *Romanticism and Ideology: Studies in English Writing, 1765–1830.* Ed. David Aers et al. London: Routledge, 1981. 118–36.

Evans, Mary. *Jane Austen and the State.* London: Tavistock, 1987.

Grossman, Jonathan H. "The Labor of the Leisured in *Emma:* Class, Manners, and Austen." *Nineteenth-Century Literature* 54.2 (1999): 143–64.

Lovell, Terry. "Jane Austen and Gentry Society." *Literature, Society and the Sociology of Literature.* Ed. Francis Barker. [Colchester]: U of Essex, 1977. 118–32.

Parker, Mark. "The End of *Emma:* Drawing the Boundaries of Class in Austen." *JEGP* 91 (1992): 344–59.

Thompson, James. "Austen and the Novel." *Models of Value: Eighteenth-Century Political Economy and the Novel.* Durham: Duke UP, 1996. 185–98.

Watts, Cedric. "'Self-Interest to Blind': Jane Austen, *Emma,* and Myopia." *Literature and Money: Financial Myth and Literary Truth.* New York: Harvester Wheatsheaf, 1990. 122–43.

Williams, Raymond. *The Country and the City.* Oxford: Oxford UP, 1973. 112–19.

A MARXIST PERSPECTIVE

BETH FOWKES TOBIN

Aiding Impoverished Gentlewomen: Power and Class in *Emma*

While picnicking on Box Hill, Emma commits several serious improprieties: she offends the Eltons; she hurts Jane Fairfax by ostentatiously flirting with Frank Churchill; and she devastates Miss Bates by wittily implying that she is a garrulous bore. As the party prepares to leave Box Hill, the scene of Emma's distasteful display of wit and power, Mr. Knightley chastises Emma for her cruelty, saying, "How could you be so unfeeling to Miss Bates? How could you be so insolent in your wit to a woman of her character, age, and situation?" (p. 299 in this volume); and for the first time in the novel Emma experiences the discomfort and vexation that the narrator implies are necessary to secure her happiness.

The Box Hill scene has been read by many critics as a crucial moment in Emma's moral development from a selfish and narcissistic adolescent who suffers from "the power of having rather too much her own way, and a disposition to think a little too well of herself" (p. 24) to a thoughtful and responsible adult aware of her own needs and those of others around her. Such critics, assuming that human nature is transhistorical, have interpreted Emma's thoughts and actions as a variation of the growing pains endemic to a universal young adulthood (Hughes, Schorer, Shannon). I will argue that Austen encourages this humanist reading of moral development and in the process mystifies the economic and social relations she has so precisely depicted in her novel.

Despite the ease with which *Emma* lends itself to humanist interpretation, I would like to follow the lead of such critics as Nancy Armstrong and Judith Newton and such historians as David Spring and
R. S. Neale to argue that *Emma* addresses political, social, and economic problems specific to early-nineteenth-century Britain. *Emma*
can, in fact, be read as Austen's attempt to deal with the threatened erosion of the old social order and the conflicting claims and ideologies of
the emergent middle classes.[1] The novel asks to be analyzed from an
economic and political perspective because the power relations that surface during the Box Hill expedition result, at least in part, from the
material conditions that determine Emma's power, Miss Bates's powerlessness, and Mr. Knightley's role as the arbitrator of Highbury's social
relations.[2]

THE IMPOVERISHED GENTLEWOMAN:
"SHE CANNOT WORK — SHE CANNOT BEG"

In *Emma*, Austen portrays the economic and social conditions of a
surprisingly large number of female characters, describing in the first
eight chapters the lives of fourteen women mostly of the "middling
ranks" of society. For instance, the first chapter tells us of Miss Taylor's
marriage to Mr. Weston, a man from a "respectable family, which for
the last two or three generations had been rising into gentility and
property" (p. 30). Miss Taylor thus moves from being Emma's governess, a position that despite Emma's affection and friendship still suffers from the stigma of service, to a position of "independence" as
mistress of her own home. This marriage is very advantageous, espe-

---

[1]For convenience I use *middle class,* a term that was not used with any consistency
until after 1815. Before that date people were more apt to refer to the "middling" ranks,
which included lawyers, physicians, officers in the army and navy, manufacturers, merchants, and tradesmen and their wives. See *The Female Aegis; or The Duties of Woman*
(120–40). Within this very fluid middle class, and between the gentry and the middle
class, there was much movement. As Lovell and Spring have shown, Austen's novels
describe the rise into gentility and property of families that were once in trade (e.g, Bing-
ley in *Pride and Prejudice,* Mr. Weston in *Emma*), as well as the pursuit of professional
careers by younger sons (e.g., John Knightley). Since those in the middling ranks identified with the interests and values of the gentry, despite their lack of landed property, some
historians have described them as "pseudo-gentry"; David Spring has been influential in
using this term to describe both members of Austen's family and characters in her fiction.
[2]For other historically informed readings of Austen's novels, see Lovell for a sociological reading of the novels, Armstrong for a Foucauldian analysis of *Emma,* Evans and
Neale for Marxist perspectives. For materialist feminist approaches, see Newton and
Poovey. For more traditionally oriented historical analyses, see Butler and Duckworth.

cially "at Miss Taylor's time of life" as Mr. Knightley comments, for it gives Miss Taylor a chance "to be settled in a home of her own, and to be secure of a comfortable provision" (p. 28). Also portrayed are the other members of the Bateses' set: Mrs. Goddard, who had "worked hard in her youth" (p. 36) as the mistress of a plain "old-fashioned Boarding-school" where girls might "scramble themselves into a little education" for a "reasonable price" (p. 36), and Miss Nash, a teacher at Mrs. Goddard's school, who thinks "her own sister very well married and it is only a linen-draper" (p. 61). Later we hear the economic details of Jane Fairfax's life: Jane was orphaned as a child and informally adopted by Colonel Campbell, a man whose "moderate" means (p. 141) were enough to give her an education that would prepare her to be a governess but not enough to give her financial independence.

Of the many impoverished gentlewomen in this book, Miss Bates is most important; as the middle-aged daughter of the late vicar of Highbury, she is "neither young, handsome, rich, nor married" (p. 35). Miss Bates's life is "devoted to the care of a failing mother, and the endeavour to make a small income go as far as possible" (p. 35). They live "in a very small way" (p. 35) in cramped quarters, renting the second floor drawing room — "ours is rather a dark staircase — rather darker and narrower than one could wish" (p. 197) — in a house that "belonged to people in business" (p. 134). The Bateses' economic vulnerability is underscored by their receipt of frequent gifts of hams (from Hartfield) and apples (from Donwell) to supplement their scanty stores. They rely on charity because, as Mr. Knightley says of Miss Bates, "She is poor; she has sunk from the comforts she was born to; and, if she live to old age, must probably sink more" (p. 300).

Austen explores in *Emma* the plight of impoverished gentlewomen, not just their scrimping and saving and constant worry about financial security, but also their depression over their loss of social status and shame at all the small indignities accompanying their social exclusion. Herself a spinster, who like Miss Bates was the daughter of a clergyman and who also lived with her widowed mother in a "small way," Austen was acutely aware of how economically vulnerable and socially powerless women were in this society. Miss Bates, Mrs. Bates, Jane Fairfax, Mrs. Goddard, Miss Nash, and Miss Taylor had real life counterparts, representing a large segment of nineteenth-century British society — women of the middle and upper middle classes who either lived in genteel poverty or worked as governesses or teachers. Girls of genteel families in Austen's time did not receive an education that would prepare them for entrance into the professional, mercantile, or manufacturing worlds of industrialized capitalism. Instead they learned to speak a smattering of French, to do intricate needlepoint, to play a keyboard instrument, to sing and dance prettily, and to sketch and paint but not well enough to be mistaken for a professional. "A lady," wrote Margretta Greg in her diary, "must be a mere lady, and nothing else. She must not work for profit, or engage in any occupation that money can command, lest she invade the rights of the working classes" (qtd. in Pinchbeck 315).[3] A life of enforced, genteel idleness was a necessary sign of class rank.

One reason why such women did not receive an education like their brothers, an education that would enable them to earn their livelihood or even, perhaps, to make their fortune, was the powerful notion that men and women inhabited different spheres of influence and action. To men belonged the world of work and to women the hearth and home. Social, cultural, and economic historians have traced this splitting of work and home life, this division of labor by gender, and the consequent estrangement of men and women, to the beginning of the industrial revolution, when work was taken out of the home or living area and put into the factory (Chodorow, Zaretsky). Before the advent of the factory, work such as brewing, baking, carding, spinning, weaving, and sewing was all done in the home by women (and children) as well as men. Up until the seventeenth century middle-class women were producers, not just consumers, their only role in the late-eighteenth and nineteenth century. Ruth Perry argues that the capitalization of the hand industries — "the arranging of industry by middlemen who hired labor and sold the product" — created the need for larger work places and a more consolidated work force, both of which contributed to pushing women out of the work force and into a life of leisure (38). Perry also argues that as women lost their role as producers in the economy, they also lost important legal rights, such as the right to inherit land and the belongings of a husband, father, or brother, the right as married women to engage in legal transactions without the consent of their husbands, and the right to manage their own property, since this became the husband's on marriage (30–33).

Losing access to skilled trades and professions left eighteenth-century women entirely dependent on men for their livelihood, and thus marriage, despite its consequent loss of legal rights, became for most women with no independent fortune the only way to support them-

---

[3]The literature on women's changing roles in the British economy is huge; for a representative sampling, see Perry, Richards, and Tickner.

selves. Preparation for marriage through the acquisition of accomplishments that would please men became a preoccupation (Tickner 67).
But even marriage might prove only a temporary solution; for example,
a woman married to a military man or clergyman whose salary was just
sufficient for a modestly genteel life faced penury if widowed. When a
father or a husband died, or a brother could no longer support her,
what could an unmarried gentlewoman with little money do? Caring
for and educating children were the only respectable money-earning
occupations open to women, other than writing (and that authorship
itself might not be lady-like is suggested by Austen's own choice of
anonymity). Not fit by training or inclination for any work other than
teaching or governessing, a gentlewomen without a source of support
was in a potentially desperate situation. As Mary Wollstonecraft points
out in *A Vindication of The Rights of Woman* (1792), poor middle-class
women, because their upbringing instilled in them the desire to remain
a "lady" at all costs, were "unable to work, and ashamed to beg" (111).
Another woman borrowed this line in her 1801 letter to the *Times* urging the formation of a charity for impoverished gentlewomen, because
"she cannot work — she cannot beg" (qtd. in Prochaska 5).

Not trained to work and their education limited to dilettantish
endeavors, unmarried gentlewomen without a personal fortune were
forced to rely on the benevolence of male relatives. This dependency
often produced resentment, as the situation of a character in Maria
Edgeworth's *Belinda* reveals: "She finds herself at five or six-and-thirty
a burden to her friends, destitute of the means of rendering herself
independent . . . yet obliged to hang upon all her acquaintance, who
wish her in heaven" (2). In *Rights of Woman* Wollstonecraft eloquently
describes what happens to young unmarried women who have been
"cruelly left by their parents without any provision" and have to
depend on the "bounty of their brothers." Some of these sisters eat
"the bitter bread of dependence" as they perform the role of mistress of
their unmarried brothers' homes. In this "equivocal humiliating situation, a docile female may remain some time, with a tolerable degree of
comfort." But when the brothers marry and bring home their wives,
unmarried sisters are viewed as "an unnecessary burden on the benevolence of the master of the house, and his new partner," and these
"unfortunate beings" suffer greatly when displaced from their brothers'
homes" (110–11).

Protesting women's lack of education and lamenting her own
inability to provide for herself, Mary Hays' heroine Emma Courtney
exclaims: "Why was not I educated for commerce, for a profession, for

labour? Why have I been rendered feeble and delicate by bodily constraint and fastidious by artificial refinement?" (1:55). In *The Female
Advocate* Mary Anne Radcliffe urges that the "great number of unfortunate women" who are displaced and impoverished should receive an
education that would prepare them for work in the skilled trades, professions, and business world so that they may have some means of support other than the rare benevolence of a "tender father, or an
affectionate and kind husband; or . . . a friend, or brother" (441). She
describes the plight of these "poor helpless females" who for a variety of
reasons are now the "most miserable of beings." Radcliffe gives the
example of widows, who having once lived a life of affluence in "ease
and comfort," are "now wandering about through this vale of tears, in
the abject and forlorn condition just described; possibly driven from
their homes by keen adversity, naked and destitute, in the most
inclement season of the year, without a prospect, or means of any sort,
for providing the common necessaries of life . . . till, at length, quite
weary with fatigue and pining with hunger, the dreaded period arrives,
'when, like a hunted bird, she becomes quite exhausted with fatigue,'
and weariness obliges her to fall to the ground" (449).

   Austen, of course, was acutely aware of the predicament of the impoverished gentlewoman. As one herself, she knew the need for careful
economy and the frustration of waiting to be remembered by wealthier
friends and family. In *Emma* Austen creates this world of impoverished
gentlewomen by showing us glimpses of the lives of minor characters
like the pathetic Miss Nash, by detailing the Bateses' life of dependence
and gratitude, and by letting us see Jane Fairfax's suffering as she braces
herself for the distasteful fate of becoming a governess.

"THE POWER OF HAVING RATHER
TOO MUCH HER OWN WAY"

   Placed against this background of impoverished, powerless gentlewomen is Emma Woodhouse, "handsome, clever, and rich" (p. 23). No
other Austen heroine is as beautiful, as rich, or as independent as
Emma. Not only does she have social prestige and economic privilege
that give her power over her small community of Highbury, but she
also has complete control over her father, the only man to whom she is
legally accountable. Emma realizes that if she were to marry she would
have to relinquish much of her power to a husband, a man she could
not possibly hope to manage as easily as she manages her father. Emma

tells Harriet that she will never marry: "Fortune I do not want; employment I do not want; consequence I do not want: I believe few married
women are half as much mistress of their husband's house, as I am of
Hartfield; and never, never could I expect to be so truly beloved and
important; so always first and always right in any man's eyes as I am in
my father's" (p. 84).

Without a mother and with a father who has absented himself from
all concerns beyond his own comfort and diet, Emma, only twenty-
one, is an indulged, socially naive young woman, guided principally by
her vanity. She focuses on what is due to her, on being first and right.
Desperately in need of a guide, someone to teach her how to use her
privileged social and economic position and how to conduct herself in
her small but socially and politically complex world of Highbury,
Emma rarely thinks of what she owes others unless nudged by Mr.
Knightley. Though she does voluntarily visit the home of a sick cot-
tager, her motives are not unclouded: Emma seems to enjoy the image
of herself as a dispenser of charity and is too little touched by the family's distresses to be sincere in her attentions.[4]

Emma's neglect of her role as patron and benefactor clearly demonstrates that she does not understand that her society depends on a system of "paternal protection and responsibility" (Perkin 182). Emma
does not understand that to be first in Highbury society involves much
more than accepting praise and flattery; it requires exertion and the
performance of not particularly pleasant duties such as being kind to
people like the Bateses, inviting them to tea, visiting them in their own
home, and providing them with the necessities they lack. As a powerful
and wealthy woman, Emma has a special responsibility to assist and
protect women who are economically vulnerable and socially disadvantaged. This novel abounds with distressed gentlewomen who by the
rights of the old paternal society deserve Emma's protection and
benevolence. But failing to grasp her proper role in relationship to
these women who are less privileged than she, Emma chooses inappropriate ways to relate to Harriet Smith, Jane Fairfax, and Miss Bates.
Eager to form some kind of relationship with Harriet, and claiming she
wants to be "useful" and of service (p. 39), Emma adopts Harriet as if
she were a pet, and Harriet's grateful and fawning manner encourages

[4]Except for these cottagers, the real poor are noticeably absent from this novel. I
explain this phenomenon in part by arguing that *Emma* is about the relationship of the
gentry to the new middle class rather than the gentry's relationship to the poor. Although
Austen avoids dealing with the gentry's relationship to the poor, Maria Edgeworth con-
fronts the topic directly in *The Absentee* (1812).

Emma's sense of her own superiority. Emma plays with Harriet as if Harriet were a doll, using her to experience vicariously the flirtation and flattery of courtship activities.

When Emma gets involved in match-making schemes for Harriet, Mr. Knightley criticizes her endeavors as not being the proper occupation for a lady, arguing, in effect, that it is an abuse of her powers, that is to say, her abilities. But her match-making activity is also an abuse of her social and economic powers. By assuming the role of match-maker, Emma assumes the right to tinker with the very delicate social and economic adjustments involved in arranging a marriage in her highly structured world. Emma also abuses her power in her neglect of Jane Fairfax who, as the only other well-educated and accomplished woman of her own age in Highbury society, should be the object of Emma's interest and attention. Alone in her community, Emma has the power to relieve Jane Fairfax from what must be a tedious confinement with her talkative aunt and deaf grandmother. Emma can provide Jane a retreat from her cramped and confining home and offer her the opportunity to indulge her taste for the genteel style of life she was accustomed to in the Campbell home. Mr. Knightley urges Emma to invite Jane to Hartfield so that she may have a chance to play Emma's little-used pianoforte. And yet, Emma will not extend to Jane Fairfax any friendly gesture beyond what civility demands. She is threatened by Jane's talents, recognizing that without her inherited status and wealth, she would fall short in a comparison with Miss Fairfax. Envious of Jane's real accomplishments, Emma cannot tolerate equality with a woman who, without property and position, lays claims to elegance and gentility. Preferring the nonthreatening and clearly inferior Harriet, who is without property, position, gentility or accomplishments, Emma rejects Miss Bates's niece as too cold and reserved for her taste, thus preserving her sense of superiority.

The most serious single instance of Emma's abuse of power takes place during the Box Hill expedition. Emma makes it clear that she is in charge of the picnic and demands that everyone acknowledge her as the queen of the proceedings, effectively putting Mrs. Elton in her place. As the daughter of a Bristol merchant of "moderate" mercantile profits (p. 155), Mrs. Elton is a social upstart, in Emma's eyes, a member of the vulgar rising middle classes who naively presumes to equality with the landed gentry. Emma then proceeds to make Jane Fairfax miserable by soliciting Frank Churchill's flattering attentions, something she can do because of her rank and position in this microworld of Highbury. In this scene Jane Fairfax's vulnerability is underscored by our recognition that if she possessed wealth and social position, she could be courted openly by Frank Churchill; instead, she has to suffer the humiliation of their secret engagement and the pain of having to watch Frank Churchill flirt with another woman, callous behavior that is only partly motivated by his wish to avoid arousing suspicions. Jane is confined to silence and circumspection; she must remain passive, her will unvoiced, while Emma, the heiress, is active, even aggressive in her domination of the discourse.

Insulting Mrs. Elton and being insensitive to Jane Fairfax are relatively minor abuses of social and economic privilege when compared to Emma's cruel remark to Miss Bates, who as a poor, unmarried, and aging gentlewoman deserves not Emma's contempt and ridicule but her charity and protection. As Mr. Knightley says, "She is poor. . . . Her situation should secure your compassion" (p. 300). Emma's insult is deeply hurtful to Miss Bates — "I must make myself very disagreeable, or she would not have said such a thing to an old friend" (p. 296) — and, despite their wit and truth, her words are a shocking violation of the "good manners" which, in a traditional society, are designed to lessen the sting of inequality. During the picnic Emma had been pushing against the boundaries of socially accepted behavior with her attack on Mrs. Elton and her obvious neglect of Jane Fairfax, but with her cruel jest she goes too far. By dropping the veil of chivalrous manners, she reveals the true nature of social relations, which are based on property and privilege, on wealth and rank.

BOX HILL:
"THERE WAS A . . . WANT OF UNION,
WHICH COULD NOT BE GOT OVER"

Emma's insults and slights on Box Hill have enormous political significance. In neglecting her duty as a member of the gentry to care for those members of her society who are less fortunate than she, Emma has clearly violated the rules of an intricate and delicately balanced system of duty and obligation, of benevolence and gratitude. Neglecting her charitable duties, she has severed the "chain of connection" that William Cobbett found in the old hierarchical social order (qtd. in Briggs, "Language" 45) and broken "the bond of attachment" that, for Robert Southey, characterized the pre-industrial society of England.

Without "the generous bounty" of the gentry, Southey believed, there could be no "grateful and honest dependence" (224–25).

Many of Emma's actions threaten her society's structure. By adopting Harriet Smith and trying to marry her off to Mr. Elton and then to Frank Churchill, she undermines her society's elaborate discriminations of social standing. Most destructive is her insensitive handling of her neighbors: her highhanded treatment of Robert Martin and his family who, as reliable and productive farmers, are solid members of the yeomanry, traditionally one of the most respected of social ranks; her snobbish dismissal of the Coles, a rising merchant family; her pointed neglect of Jane Fairfax who, though poor, is the most accomplished and genteel young woman in Highbury; and her cruelty to Miss Bates, who, as a harmless impoverished gentlewoman, deserves Emma's pity and protection. Abusing her power, Emma threatens to alienate members of her community from the interests of the gentry. Snobbery like Emma's, which threatens to destroy the illusion that the gentry and the middle class share a common cause, endangers the landed order's ability to maintain its political and economic hegemony. As one conservative member of Parliament cautioned his anti-reform colleagues in the politically turbulent years after the Napoleonic War, to offend the middle class by restricting franchise to the upper classes was to drive the "middle and respectable ranks of society" into "a union, founded on dissatisfaction[,] with the lower orders." Recognizing the potential power of a politically and ideologically consolidated middle class, he warned the landed interests that they could not maintain their power without the support of the middle classes and it was, therefore, "of the utmost importance to associate the middle with the higher orders of society in the love and support of the institutions and government of the country" (qtd. in Briggs, "Middle-Class" 70).

Austen clearly supports the old order and enlists her readers' sympathies in support of the institutions and ideologies of the landed classes. She idealizes the gentry, offering Mr. Knightley with his true gentlemanly manners, his "English delicacy toward the feelings of other people" (p. 131), and his clear sense of "right conduct" (p. 130) as a solution to the social ills of emergent capitalism. It is Mr. Knightley who chastises Emma, reminds her of her duty as a member of the gentry, teaches her how to curb her willful nature, and encourages her to follow his example of neighborly benevolence. Mr. Knightley, as his name suggests, is an exemplary member of the gentry. He is a "true Englishman" in his taste and style of interaction and a model landowner, for he is both a knowledgeable farmer and an excellent landlord, as concerned about improving the quality of his land as he is attentive to his tenants' desires and needs. Above all he is a responsible member of his community, a good friend to his neighbors, and a kind benefactor to those in need of his assistance. Emma comments on Mr. Knightley's kindness in putting his carriage at the service of Miss Bates: "I know no man more likely than Mr. Knightley to do the sort of thing — to do any thing really good-natured, useful, considerate, or benevolent. He is not a gallant man, but he is a very humane one . . ." (p. 185). He is everything Emma admires, and when she realizes she loves him and needs his approval, she moves much closer to aligning herself with his values.

Mr. Knightley's reprimand echoes in Emma's head as she rides home from Box Hill in tears, experiencing a great deal of pain at the loss of his esteem. She acknowledges the justness of his remarks and turns a critical eye on her own behavior, especially as it affects the Bateses and Jane Fairfax; she heartily repents of her insensitivity to the Bateses' needs, recognizing for the first time how much Mr. Knightley does for them in an inconspicuous manner. Repentant, she tries to emulate his style of benevolence by visiting Jane Fairfax and inquiring after her welfare. She offers Jane her carriage for airings, medicine for her sickness, and books to beguile into tranquillity a tense and anxious mind. Emma learns rather belatedly what her role should be in relationship to impoverished gentlewomen made vulnerable by a new capitalist economy; she learns to offer them assistance, sympathy, respect, and a sense of place and purpose in their community. Emma learns not just the proper feminine role of benefactress and sympathetic friend but also how to be a responsible member of the gentry who, in this novel at least, hold the social fabric of this little community together with compassion and patronage, with a blend of Christian and chivalric values that prescribe charitable acts as a remedy not only for the ills of the poor and dispossessed but for the ennui of the privileged.

At the risk of seeming to allegorize *Emma*, I believe that there is a parallel between Emma's abuse of power, her betrayal of Miss Bates and her neglect of Jane Fairfax, and what the English middle classes, somewhat later in the century, felt was an "abdication on the part of governors" (Carlyle 156). When Parliament, which was dominated by the aristocracy and the gentry, passed the Corn Law of 1815, an act that aimed to keep up the high wartime prices of grain by prohibiting the import of foreign grain until the home price reached 80s. a quarter, the landed interests were trying, according to Francis Place, "to keep up the rent of land" (qtd. in Perkin 192). According to Briggs, the Corn Law "affronted . . . some of the most powerful commercial and industrial interests in the country. Manchester millowners protested that the bill would raise the price of labour and handicap manufacturers in their conquest of foreign markets" (*Age* 202). The passage of the Corn Law angered the middle classes; they felt that as soon as their loyalty and cooperation were no longer needed to conduct the Napoleonic wars, the upper classes, acting out of unrestrained self-interest and ignoring the special needs of the mercantile and manufacturing classes, betrayed the trust placed in them as caretakers of the country's and especially of the middle classes' well-being. Cobbett with his usual force of conviction declared that "the landlords deserve ruin. They abandoned the public cause the moment they thought that they saw a prospect of getting rents" (132). More reasonable in his criticisms of the landed interests was James Mill in his *Essay on Government* (1820); Mill argued that "if powers are put into the hands of a comparatively small number, called an Aristocracy, powers which make them stronger than the rest of the community, they will take from the rest of the community as much as they please of the objects of desire" (qtd. in Perkin 277). Alienated by the Corn Laws, the middle classes in retaliation demanded that the landed interests, who in the name of the nation had shaped policy for nearly two hundred years, forfeit their role as political leaders. They pushed for parliamentary reform which would expand enfranchisement and representation for the middle classes.

Though the Corn Laws may seem an unlikely intertextual association for modern readers of *Emma*, it is hard to imagine readers in 1816 reading *Emma* without thinking of the Corn Laws or similarly divisive political and economic issues. Emma's punishment and reform may have had the effect of reassuring nineteenth-century readers anxious about the upper classes' abuse of power and neglect of duty, encouraging them to believe that the abuses of the system were isolated individual acts that could be corrected and eradicated from within and were not endemic to the system. For more patrician English readers, *Emma*'s example would have been prescriptive, suggesting not just a wealthy young woman's duties to the less fortunate middle classes but also the broader responsibilities of the landed classes to the merchants, manufacturers, farmers, and artisans who should be their political allies. Reading *Emma* with its idyllic representation of the gentry may have caused readers to repress their criticism of the old system of patronage and dependence. The novel certainly portrayed, if it did not contribute to, what Perkin calls the "remarkable revival of the aristocratic ideal" in the 1820s (227).

Ultimately an apologist for the landed classes, Austen explores the plight of impoverished gentlewomen as an unfortunate feature of this particular economic and political system only to conclude that the benefits of a patriarchal society governed by the landed interests far outweigh the costs. Despite Austen's detailed and sympathetic portrayal of the plight of impoverished gentlewomen, *Emma* has the effect of brushing away most of the concerns that might arise in the reader's mind concerning the way women are treated in this society. While managing to convey women's lack of power and legal authority, Austen subverts the seriousness of their situation by providing solutions to their problems, solutions that deny the seriousness of the problem. Austen depicts the plight of impoverished gentlewomen through her portrayal of the Bateses' "confined" circumstances (p. 146) and "scanty comforts" (p. 133) and Jane Fairfax's ordeal as she readies herself for life humiliatingly close to that of an upper servant. And yet when Jane Fairfax is married and Emma learns from Mr. Knightley how to carry out her charitable duties as a member of the gentry, the recognition of the seriousness of the plight of the impoverished gentlewoman dissolves in the pleasure readers feel in seeing Jane Fairfax happy and Emma reproved, reformed, and united to Mr. Knightley.

One of the ways Austen mitigates the harshness of her picture of a middle-class woman's economic and social helplessness is by focusing on the individual's power to change and to control her life. Set against this background which shows women as victims of forces beyond their control is Austen's most independent heroine, Emma, whose economic and social power is enormous. Another way that Austen assuages the painful recognition that impoverished middle-class women are victims of a capitalist system that has no use for them because they fail as consumers — the only role available to them — is by translating the plight of the impoverished gentlewoman into Emma's personal problem, into her failure to recognize her proper role as benefactress and custodian of those who are less fortunate than she. Austen takes large economic problems caused by uncontrollable forces and reduces their threatening aspect by transplanting them into the realm of the personal, over which one can have the illusion of some control. Austen introduces only those economic and social problems that Emma's reformation will cure or a marriage will sweep away.

Though Austen depicts harsh political and economic conditions in this novel, she denies their importance in shaping individuals' lives; she mystifies the very material conditions she describes by belying their power to determine the conditions of happiness and by giving to other forces such as romantic love, Christian morality, and chivalry the power to shape her characters' fate. Given this novel's tendency to translate the political and economic into the personal and moral, it is not surprising that many critics, despite recent criticism historicizing Austen's fiction, still read the novel as a Bildungsroman, as a variation on the story of moral and psychological development of an individual, ignoring the social, economic, and political content of the novel, not consciously aware of the ideological work the narrative performs.

WORKS CITED

Armstrong, Nancy. *Desire and Domestic Fiction: A Political History of the Novel.* New York: Oxford UP, 1987. Esp. 134–60.

Briggs, Asa. *The Age of Improvement.* London: Longman, 1959.

———. "The Language of 'Class' in Early Nineteenth-Century England." *Essays in Labour History.* Ed. Asa Briggs and John Saville. London: Macmillan, 1960.

———. "Middle-Class Consciousness in English Politics, 1780–1846." *Past and Present* 9 (1956): 65–94.

Butler, Marilyn. *Jane Austen and the War of Ideas.* Oxford: Clarendon, 1975.

Carlyle, Thomas. "Chartism." 1839. *The Works of Thomas Carlyle.* 1899. Vol. 29. rpt. New York: AMS P, 1974.

Chodorow, Nancy. *The Reproduction of Mothering: Psychoanalysis and the Sociology of Gender.* Berkeley: U of California P, 1978.

Cobbett, William. *Rural Rides.* 1830. London: Penguin, 1967.

Duckworth, Alistair M. *The Improvement of the Estate.* Baltimore: Johns Hopkins UP, 1971.

Edgeworth, Maria. *Belinda.* 1801. London: Pandora, 1986.

Evans, Mary. *Jane Austen and the State.* London: Tavistock, 1987.

The Female Aegis; or The Duties of Women. London, 1798.

Hays, Mary. *The Memoirs of Emma Courtney.* Ed. Gina Luria. 1796. New York: Garland, 1974.

Hughes, R. E. "The Education of Emma Woodhouse." Lodge 188–94.

Lodge, David, ed. *Jane Austen: Emma, A Casebook.* London: Aurora Publishers, 1970.

Lovell, Terry. "Jane Austen and Gentry Society." *Literature, Society and the Sociology of Literature.* Ed. Francis Barker. [Colchester]: U of Essex, 1977. 118–32.

Neale, R.S. "Zapp Zapped: Property and Alienation in *Mansfield Park.*" *Writing Marxist History: British Society, Economy, and Culture since 1700.* Oxford: Blackwell, 1985. 87–108.

Newton, Judith Lowder. *Women, Power, and Subversion: Social Strategies in British Fiction, 1770–1860.* New York: Methuen, 1985. 55–85.

Perkin, Harold. *Origins of Modern English Society.* London: Routledge, 1985.

Perry, Ruth. *Women, Letters, and the Novel.* New York: AMS P, 1980.

Pinchbeck, Ivy. *Women Workers and the Industrial Revolution: 1750–1850.* 1930. London: Cass, 1969.

Poovey, Mary. *The Proper Lady and the Woman Writer: Ideology as Style in the Works of Mary Wollstonecraft, Mary Shelley, and Jane Austen.* Chicago: U of Chicago P, 1984.

Prochaska, F. K. *Women and Philanthropy in Nineteenth-Century England.* Oxford: Clarendon, 1980.

Radcliffe, Mary Anne. *The Female Advocate.* 1799. Rpt. in *First Feminists: British Women Writers, 1578–1799.* Ed. Moira Ferguson. Bloomington: Indiana UP, 1985. 437–55.

Richards, Eric. "Women in the British Economy since about 1700: An Interpretation." *History* 59 (1974): 337–57.

Schorer, Mark. "The Humiliation of Emma Woodhouse." *Lodge* 170–87.

Shannon, Edgar F., Jr. "*Emma:* Character and Construction." *Lodge* 130–47.

Southey, Robert. *Sir Thomas More: or, Colloquies on the Progress and Prospects of Society.* Vol. 2. London, 1829.

Spring, David A. "Interpreters of Jane Austen's Social World." *Jane Austen: New Perspectives.* Ed. Janet Todd. New York: Holmes & Meier, 1983. 53–72.

Tickner, F. W. *Women in English Economic History.* 1923. Westport, CT: Hyperion, 1981.

Wollstonecraft, Mary. *A Vindication of the Rights of Woman.* 1792. New York: Norton, 1967.

Zaretsky, Eli. *Capitalism, the Family, and Personal Life.* New York: Harper, 1976.

Cultural Criticism
and
Emma

WHAT IS CULTURAL CRITICISM?

What do you think of when you think of culture? The opera or ballet? A performance of a Mozart symphony at Lincoln Center or a Rembrandt show at the De Young Museum in San Francisco? Does the phrase "cultural event" conjure up images of young people in jeans and T-shirts — or of people in their sixties dressed formally? Most people hear "culture" and think "high culture." Consequently, when they first hear of cultural criticism, most people assume it is more formal than, well, say, formalism. They suspect it is "highbrow," in both subject and style.

Nothing could be further from the truth. Cultural critics oppose the view that culture refers exclusively to high culture, Culture with a capital *C*. Cultural critics want to make the term refer to popular, folk, urban, and mass (mass-produced, -disseminated, -mediated, and -consumed) culture, as well as to that culture we associate with the so-called classics. Raymond Williams, an early British cultural critic whose ideas will later be described at greater length, suggested that "art and culture are ordinary"; he did so not to "pull art down" but rather to point out that there is "creativity in all our living. . . . We create our human world as we have thought of art being created" (*Revolution* 37).

Cultural critics have consequently placed a great deal of emphasis on what Michel de Certeau has called "the practice of everyday life." Rather than approaching literature in the elitist way that academic literary critics have traditionally approached it, cultural critics view it more as an anthropologist would. They ask how it emerges from and competes with other forms of discourse within a given culture (science, for instance, or television). They seek to understand the social contexts in which a given text was written, and under what conditions it was — and is — produced, disseminated, read, and used.

Contemporary cultural critics are as willing to write about *Star Trek* as they are to analyze James Joyce's *Ulysses*, a modern literary classic full of allusions to Homer's *Odyssey*. And when they write about *Ulysses*, they are likely to view it as a collage reflecting and representing cultural forms common to Joyce's Dublin, such as advertising, journalism, film, and pub life. Cultural critics typically show how the boundary we tend to envision between high and low forms of culture — forms thought of as important on one hand and relatively trivial on the other — is transgressed in all sorts of exciting ways within works on both sides of the putative cultural divide.

A cultural critic writing about a revered classic might contrast it with a movie, or even a comic-strip version produced during a later period. Alternatively, the literary classic might be seen in a variety of other ways: in light of some more common form of reading material (a novel by Jane Austen might be viewed in light of Gothic romances or ladies' conduct manuals); as the reflection of some common cultural myths or concerns (*Adventures of Huckleberry Finn* might be shown to reflect and shape American myths about race and concerns about juvenile delinquency); or as an example of how texts move back and forth across the alleged boundary between "low" and "high" culture. For instance, one group of cultural critics has pointed out that although Shakespeare's history plays probably started off as popular works enjoyed by working people, they were later considered "highbrow" plays that only the privileged and educated could appreciate. That view of them changed, however, due to film productions geared toward a national audience. A film version of *Henry V* produced during World War II, for example, made a powerful, popular, patriotic statement about England's greatness during wartime (Humm, Stigant, and Widdowson 6–7). More recently, cultural critics have analyzed the "cultural work" accomplished cooperatively by Shakespeare and Kenneth Branagh in the latter's 1992 film production of *Henry V*.

In combating old definitions of what constitutes culture, of course, cultural critics sometimes end up contesting old definitions of what constitutes the literary canon, that is, the once-agreed-upon honor roll of Great Books. They tend to do so, however, neither by adding books (and movies and television sitcoms) *to* the old list of texts that every "culturally literate" person should supposedly know nor by substituting some kind of counterculture canon. Instead, they tend to critique the very *idea* of canon.

Cultural critics want to get us away from thinking about certain works as the "best" ones produced by a given culture. They seek to be more descriptive and less evaluative, more interested in relating than in rating cultural products and events. They also aim to discover the (often political) reasons *why* a certain kind of aesthetic or cultural product is more valued than others. This is particularly true when the product in question is one produced since 1945, for most cultural critics follow Jean Baudrillard (*Simulations,* 1981) and Andreas Huyssen (*The Great Divide,* 1986) in thinking that any distinctions that may once have existed between high, popular, and mass culture collapsed after the end of World War II. Their discoveries have led them beyond the literary canon, prompting them to interrogate many other value hierarchies. For instance, Pierre Bourdieu in *Distinction: A Social Critique of the Judgment of Taste* (1984) and Dick Hebdige in *Hiding the Light: On Images and Things* (1988) have argued that definitions of "good taste"— which are instrumental in fostering and reinforcing cultural discrimination — tell us at least as much about prevailing social, economic, and political conditions as they do about artistic quality and value.

In an article entitled "The Need for Cultural Studies," four groundbreaking cultural critics have written that "Cultural Studies should . . . abandon the goal of giving students access to that which represents a culture." A literary work, they go on to suggest, should be seen in relation to other works, to economic conditions, or to broad social discourses (about childbirth, women's education, rural decay, and so on) within whose contexts it makes sense. Perhaps most important, critics practicing cultural studies should counter the prevalent notion of culture as some preformed whole. Rather than being static or monolithic, culture is really a set of interactive *cultures,* alive and changing, and cultural critics should be present- and even future-oriented. They should be "resisting intellectuals," and cultural studies should be "an emancipatory project" (Giroux et al. 478–80).

The paragraphs above are peppered with words like *oppose, counter, deny, resist, combat, abandon,* and *emancipatory.* What such words quite accurately suggest is that a number of cultural critics view themselves in political, even oppositional, terms. Not only are they likely to take on the literary canon, they are also likely to oppose the institution of the university, for that is where the old definitions of culture as high culture (and as something formed, finished, and canonized) have been most vigorously preserved, defended, and reinforced.

Cultural critics have been especially critical of the departmental structure of universities, which, perhaps more than anything else, has kept the study of the "arts" relatively distinct from the study of history, not to mention from the study of such things as television, film, advertising, journalism, popular photography, folklore, current affairs, shoptalk, and gossip. By maintaining artificial boundaries, universities have tended to reassert the high/low culture distinction, implying that all the latter subjects are best left to historians, sociologists, anthropologists, and communication theorists. Cultural critics have taken issue with this implication, arguing that the way of thinking reinforced by the departmentalized structure of universities keeps us from seeing the aesthetics of an advertisement as well as the propagandistic elements of a work of literature. Cultural critics have consequently mixed and matched the analytical procedures developed in a variety of disciplines. They have formed — and encouraged other scholars to form — networks and centers, often outside of those enforced departmentally.

Some initially loose interdisciplinary networks have, over time, solidified to become cultural studies programs and majors. As this has happened, a significant if subtle danger has arisen. Richard Johnson, who along with Hebdige, Stuart Hall, and Richard Hoggart was instrumental in developing the Center for Contemporary Cultural Studies at Birmingham University in England, has warned that cultural studies must not be allowed to turn into yet another traditional academic discipline — one in which students encounter a canon replete with soap operas and cartoons, one in which belief in the importance of such popular forms has become an "orthodoxy" (39). The only principles that critics doing cultural studies can doctrinally espouse, Johnson suggests, are the two that have thus far been introduced: the principle that "culture" has been an "inegalitarian" concept, a "tool" of "condescension," and the belief that a new, "interdisciplinary (and even anti-disciplinary)" approach to *true* culture (that is, to the forms in which culture currently lives) is required now that history, art, and the communications media are so complex and interrelated (42).

The object of cultural study should not be a body of works assumed to comprise or reflect a given culture. Rather, it should be human consciousness, and the goal of that critical analysis should be to understand and show how that consciousness is itself forged and formed, to a great extent, by cultural forces. "Subjectivities," as Johnson has put it, are "produced, not given, and are . . . objects of inquiry" inevitably related to "social practices," whether those involve factory rules, supermarket behavior patterns, reading habits, advertisements, myths, or languages and other signs to which people are exposed (44–45).

Although the United States has probably contributed more than any other nation to the *media* through which culture is currently expressed, and although many if not most contemporary practitioners of cultural criticism are North American, the evolution of cultural criticism and, more broadly, cultural studies has to a great extent been influenced by theories developed in Great Britain and on the European continent.

Among the Continental thinkers whose work allowed for the development of cultural studies are those whose writings we associate with structuralism and poststructuralism. Using the linguistic theory of Ferdinand de Saussure, structuralists suggested that the structures of language lie behind all human organization. They attempted to create a *semiology* — a science of signs — that would give humankind at once a scientific and holistic way of studying the world and its human inhabitants. Roland Barthes, a structuralist who later shifted toward poststructuralism, attempted to recover literary language from the isolation in which it had been studied and to show that the laws that govern it govern all signs, from road signs to articles of clothing. Claude Lévi-Strauss, an anthropologist who studied the structures of everything from cuisine to villages to myths, looked for and found recurring, common elements that transcended the differences within and between cultures.

Of the structuralist and poststructuralist thinkers who have had an impact on the evolution of cultural studies, Jacques Lacan is one of three whose work has been particularly influential. A structuralist psychoanalytic theorist, Lacan posited that the human unconscious is structured like a language and treated dreams not as revealing symptoms of repression but, rather, as forms of discourse. Lacan also argued that the ego, subject, or self that we think of as being natural (our individual human nature) is in fact a product of the social order and its symbolic systems (especially, but not exclusively, language). Lacan's thought has served as the theoretical underpinning for cultural critics seeking to show the way in which subjectivities are produced by social discourses and practices.

Jacques Derrida, a French philosopher whose name has become synonymous with poststructuralism, has had an influence on cultural criticism at least as great as that of Lacan. The linguistic focus of structuralist thought has by no means been abandoned by poststructuralists, despite their opposition to structuralism's tendency to find universal patterns instead of textual and cultural contradictions. Indeed, Derrida has provocatively asserted that *"there is nothing outside the text"* (158), by which he means something like the following: we come to know the world through language, and even our most worldly actions and practices (the Gulf War, the wearing of condoms) are dependent upon discourses (even if they deliberately contravene those discourses). Derrida's "deconstruction" of the world/text distinction, like his deconstruction of so many of the hierarchical oppositions we habitually use to interpret and evaluate reality, has allowed cultural critics to erase the boundaries between high and low culture, classic and popular literary texts, and literature and other cultural discourses that, following Derrida, may be seen as manifestations of the same textuality.

Michel Foucault is the third Continental thinker associated with structuralism and/or poststructuralism who has had a particularly powerful impact on the evolution of cultural studies — and perhaps *the* strongest influence on American cultural criticism and the so-called new historicism, an interdisciplinary form of cultural criticism whose evolution has often paralleled that of cultural criticism. Although Foucault broke with Marxism after the French student uprisings of 1968, he was influenced enough by Marxist thought to study cultures in terms of power relationships. Unlike Marxists, however, Foucault refused to see power as something exercised by a dominant class over a subservient class. Indeed, he emphasized that power is not just repressive power, that is, a tool of conspiracy by one individual or institution against another. Power, rather, is a whole complex of forces; it is that which produces what happens.

Thus even a tyrannical aristocrat does not simply wield power but is empowered by "discourses"— accepted ways of thinking, writing, and speaking — and practices that embody, exercise, and amount to power. Foucault tried to view all things, from punishment to sexuality, in terms of the widest possible variety of discourses. As a result, he traced what he called the "genealogy" of topics he studied through texts that more traditional historians and literary critics would have overlooked, examining (in Lynn Hunt's words) "memoirs of deviants, diaries, political treatises, architectural blueprints, court records, doctors' reports — appl[ying] consistent principles of analysis in search of moments of reversal in discourse, in search of events as loci of the conflict where social practices were transformed" (39). Foucault tended not only to build interdisciplinary bridges but also, in the process, to bring into the study of culture the "histories of women, homosexuals, and minorities"— groups seldom studied by those interested in Culture with a capital *C* (Hunt 45).

Of the British influences on cultural studies and criticism, two stand out prominently. One, the Marxist historian E. P. Thompson, revolutionized the study of the industrial revolution by writing about its impact on human attitudes, even consciousness. He showed how a shared cultural view, specifically that of what constitutes a fair or just price, influenced crowd behavior and caused such things as the "food riots" of the eighteenth and nineteenth centuries (during which the women of Nottingham repriced breads in the shops of local bakers, paid for the goods they needed, and carried them away). The other, even more important early British influence on contemporary cultural criticism and cultural studies was Raymond Williams, who coined the phrase "culture is ordinary." In works like *Culture and Society: 1780– 1950* (1958) and *The Long Revolution* (1961) Williams demonstrated that culture is not fixed and finished but, rather, living and evolving. One of the changes he called for was the development of a common socialist culture.

Although Williams dissociated himself from Marxism during the period 1945–58, he always followed the Marxist practice of viewing culture in relation to ideologies, which he defined as the "residual," "dominant," or "emerging" ways of viewing the world held by classes or individual holding power in a given social group. He avoided dwelling on class conflict and class oppression, however, tending instead to focus on people as people, on how they experience the conditions in which they find themselves and creatively respond to those conditions through their social practices. A believer in the resiliency of the individual, Williams produced a body of criticism notable for what Stuart Hall has called its "humanism" (63).

As is clearly suggested in several of the preceding paragraphs, Marxism is the background to the background of cultural criticism. What isn't as clear is that some contemporary cultural critics consider themselves Marxist critics as well. It is important, therefore, to have some familiarity with certain Marxist concepts — those that would have been familiar to Foucault, Thompson, and Williams, plus those espoused by contemporary cultural critics who self-identify with Marxism. That familiarity can be gained from an introduction to the works of four important Marxist thinkers: Mikhail Bakhtin, Walter Benjamin, Antonio Gramsci, and Louis Althusser.

Bakhtin was a Russian, later a Soviet, critic so original in his thinking and wide-ranging in his influence that some would say he was never a Marxist at all. He viewed literary works in terms of discourses and dialogues *between* discourses. The narrative of a novel written in a society in flux, for instance, may include an official, legitimate discourse, plus others that challenge its viewpoint and even its authority. In a 1929 book on Dostoyevsky and the 1940 study *Rabelais and His World,* Bakhtin examined what he calls "polyphonic" novels, each characterized by a multiplicity of voices or discourses. In Dostoyevsky the independent status of a given character is marked by the difference of his or her language from that of the narrator. (The narrator's language may itself involve a dialogue between opposed points of view.) In works by Rabelais, Bakhtin finds that the (profane) languages of Carnival and of other popular festivities play against and parody the more official discourses of the magistrates and the church. Bakhtin's relevance to cultural criticism lies in his suggestion that the dialogue involving high and low culture takes place not only between classic and popular texts but also between the "dialogic" voices that exist within all great books.

Walter Benjamin was a German Marxist who, during roughly the same period, attacked fascism and questioned the superior value placed on certain traditional literary forms that he felt conveyed a stultifying "aura" of culture. He took this position in part because so many previous Marxist critics (and, in his own day, Georg Lukács) had seemed to prefer nineteenth-century realistic novels to the modernist works of their own time. Benjamin not only praised modernist movements, such as dadaism, but also saw as promising the development of new art forms utilizing mechanical production and reproduction. These forms, including photography, radio, and film, promised that the arts would become a more democratic, less exclusive, domain. Anticipating by decades the work of those cultural critics interested in mass-produced, mass-mediated, and mass-consumed culture, Benjamin analyzed the meanings and (defensive) motivations behind words like *unique* and *authentic* when used in conjunction with mechanically reproduced art.

Antonio Gramsci, an Italian Marxist best known for his *Prison Notebooks* (first published in 1947), critiqued the very concept of literature and, beyond that, of culture in the old sense, stressing the importance of culture more broadly defined and the need for nurturing and developing proletarian, or working-class, culture. He argued that all intellectual or cultural work is fundamentally political and expressed the need for what he called "radical organic" intellectuals. Today's cultural critics urging colleagues to "legitimate the notion of writing reviews and books for the general public," to "become involved in the political reading of popular culture," and more generally to "repoliticize" scholarship have viewed Gramsci as an early precursor (Giroux et al. 482).

Gramsci related literature to the ideologies — the prevailing ideas, beliefs, values, and prejudices — of the culture in which it was produced. He developed the concept of "hegemony," which refers at once to the process of consensus formation and to the authority of the ideologies so formed, that is to say, their power to shape the way things look, what they would seem to mean, and, therefore, what reality *is* for the majority of people. But Gramsci did not see people, even poor people, as the helpless victims of hegemony, as ideology's pathetic robots. Rather, he believed that people have the freedom and power to struggle against and shape ideology, to alter hegemony, to break out of the weblike system of prevailing assumptions and to form a new consensus. As Patrick Brantlinger has suggested in *Crusoe's Footprints: Cultural Studies in Britain and America* (1990), Gramsci rejected the "intellectual arrogance that views the vast majority of people as deluded zombies, the victims or creatures of ideology" (100).

Of those Marxists who, after Gramsci, explored the complex relationship between literature and ideology, the French Marxist Louis Althusser had a significant impact on cultural criticism. Unlike Gramsci, Althusser tended to portray ideology as being in control of people, and not vice versa. He argued that the main function of ideology is to reproduce the society's existing relations of production, and that that function is even carried out in literary texts. In many ways, though, Althusser is as good an example of how Marxism and cultural criticism part company as he is of how cultural criticism is indebted to Marxists and their ideas. For although Althusser did argue that literature is relatively autonomous — more independent of ideology than, say, church, press, or state — he meant literature in the high cultural sense, certainly not the variety of works that present-day cultural critics routinely examine alongside those of Tolstoy and Joyce, Eliot and Brecht. Popular fictions, Althusser assumed, were mere packhorses designed (however unconsciously) to carry the baggage of a culture's ideology, or mere brood mares destined to reproduce it.

Thus, while a number of cultural critics would agree both with Althusser's notion that works of literature reflect certain ideological formations and with his notion that, at the same time, literary works may be relatively distant from or even resistant to ideology, they have rejected the narrow limits within which Althusser and some other Marxists (such as Georg Lukács) have defined literature. In "Marxism and Popular Fiction" (1986), Tony Bennett uses *Monty Python's Flying Circus* and another British television show, *Not the 9 O'clock News*, to argue that the Althusserian notion that all forms of culture belong "among [all those] many material forms which ideology takes . . . under capitalism" is "simply not true." The "entire field" of "popular fiction"— which Bennett takes to include films and television shows as well as books — is said to be "replete with instances" of works that do what Bennett calls the "work" of "distancing." That is, they have the effect of separating the audience from, not rebinding the audience to, prevailing ideologies (249).

Although Marxist cultural critics exist (Bennett himself is one, carrying on through his writings what may be described as a lovers' quarrel with Marxism), most cultural critics are not Marxists in any strict sense. Anne Beezer, in writing about such things as advertisements and women's magazines, contests the "Althusserian view of ideology as the construction of the subject" (qtd. in Punter 103). That is, she gives both the media she is concerned with and their audiences more credit than Althusserian Marxists presumably would. Whereas they might argue that such media make people what they are, she points out that the same magazines that, admittedly, tell women how to please their men may, at the same time, offer liberating advice to women about how to preserve their independence by not getting too serious romantically. And, she suggests, many advertisements advertise their status as ads, just as many people who view or read them see advertising as advertising and interpret it accordingly.

The complex sort of analysis that Beezer has brought to bear on women's magazines and advertisements has been focused on paperback romance novels by Tania Modleski and Janice A. Radway in *Loving with a Vengeance* (1982) and *Reading the Romance* (1984), respectively. Radway, a feminist cultural critic who uses but ultimately goes beyond Marxism, points out that many women who read romances do so in order to carve out a time and space that is wholly their own, not to be intruded upon by husbands or children. Although many such novels end in marriage, the marriage is usually between a feisty and independent heroine and a powerful man she has "tamed," that is, made sensitive and caring. And why do so many of these stories involve such heroines and end as they do? Because, as Radway demonstrates through painstaking research into publishing houses, bookstores, and reading communities, their consumers *want* them to. They don't buy — or, if they buy they don't recommend — romances in which, for example, a heroine is raped: thus, in time, fewer and fewer such plots find their way onto the racks by the supermarket checkout.

Radway's reading is typical of feminist cultural criticism in that it is *political,* but not exclusively about oppression. The subjectivities of women may be "produced" by romances — the thinking of romance readers may be governed by what is read — but the same women also govern, to a great extent, what gets written or produced, thus performing "cultural work" of their own. Rather than seeing all forms of popular culture as manifestations of ideology, soon to be remanifested in the minds of victimized audiences, cultural critics tend to see a sometimes disheartening but always dynamic synergy between cultural forms and the culture's consumers. Their observations have increasingly led to an analysis of consumerism, from a feminist but also from a more general point of view. This analysis owes a great deal to the work of de Certeau, Hall, and, especially, Hebdige, whose 1979 book *Subculture: The Meaning of Style* paved the way for critics like John Fiske (*Television Culture,* 1987), Greil Marcus (*Dead Elvis,* 1991), and Rachel Bowlby (*Shopping with Freud,* 1993). These latter critics have analyzed everything from the resistance tactics employed by television audiences to the influence of consumers on rock music styles to the psychology of consumer choice.

The overlap between feminist and cultural criticism is hardly surprising, especially given the recent evolution of feminism into various femin*isms,* some of which remain focused on "majority" women of European descent, others of which have focused instead on the lives and writings of minority women in Western culture and of women living in Third World (now preferably called postcolonial) societies. The culturalist analysis of value hierarchies within and between cultures has inevitably focused on categories that include class, race, national origin, gender, and sexualities; the terms of its critique have proved useful to contemporary feminists, many of whom differ from their predecessors insofar as they see *woman* not as a universal category but, rather, as one of several that play a role in identity- or subject-formation. The influence of cultural criticism (and, in some cases, Marxist class analysis) can be seen in the work of contemporary feminist critics such as Gayatri Spivak, Trinh T. Minh-ha, and Gloria Anzaldúa, each of whom has stressed that while all women are female, they are something else as well (such as working-class, lesbian, Native American, Muslim, Pakistani) and that that something else must be taken into account when their writings are read and studied.

The expansion of feminism and feminist literary criticism to include multicultural analysis, of course, parallels a transformation of education in general. On college campuses across North America, the field of African-American studies has grown and flourished. African-American critics have been influenced by and have contributed to the cultural approach by pointing out that the white cultural elite of North America has tended to view the oral-musical traditions of African Americans (traditions that include jazz, the blues, sermons, and folktales) as entertaining, but nonetheless inferior. Black writers, in order not to be similarly marginalized, have produced texts that, as Henry Louis Gates has pointed out, fuse the language and traditions of the white Western canon with a black vernacular and traditions derived from African and Caribbean cultures. The resulting "hybridity" (to use Homi K. Bhabha's word), although deplored by a handful of black separatist critics, has proved both rich and complex — fertile ground for many cultural critics practicing African-American criticism.

Interest in race and ethnicity at home has gone hand in hand with a new, interdisciplinary focus on colonial and postcolonial societies abroad, in which issues of race, class, and ethnicity also loom large. Edward Said's book *Orientalism* (1978) is generally said to have inaugurated postcolonial studies, which in Bhabha's words "bears witness to the unequal and uneven forces of cultural representation involved in the contest for political and social authority within the modern world order" ("Postcolonial Criticism" 437). *Orientalism* showed how Eastern and Middle Eastern peoples have for centuries been systematically stereotyped by the West, and how that stereotyping facilitated the colonization of vast areas of the East and Middle East by Westerners. Said's more recent books, along with postcolonial studies by Bhabha and Patrick Brantlinger, are among the most widely read and discussed works of literary scholarship. Brantlinger focuses on British literature of the Victorian period, examining representations of the colonies in

works written during an era of imperialist expansion. Bhabha complements Brantlinger by suggesting that modern Western culture is best
understood from the postcolonial perspective.

Thanks to the work of scholars like Brantlinger, Bhabha, Said,
Gates, Anzaldúa, and Spivak, education in general and literary study in
particular is becoming more democratic, decentered (less patriarchal
and Eurocentric), and multicultural. The future of literary criticism will
owe a great deal indeed to those early cultural critics who demonstrated
that the boundaries between high and low culture are at once repressive
and permeable, that culture is common and therefore includes all forms
of popular culture, that cultural definitions are inevitably political, and
that the world we see is seen through society's ideology. In a very real
sense, the future of education *is* cultural studies.

In the essay that follows, Paul Delany attempts to clarify the debate
about whether Jane Austen was a "conservative" or a "subversive" by
making a distinction between "class" and "status" (p. 508). Class, as
defined by Delany, could be "precisely quantified, and Austen is notoriously fond of such quantifications: Darcy [a character in *Pride and
Prejudice*] has £10,000 a year; Emma . . . will inherit £30,000; Captain
Wentworth (a character in *Persuasion*) has £25,000 in prize money"
(p. 508) and so forth. Status, by contrast, was much more difficult to
quantify, for it implied a certain "*style of life*," in the words of social historian Max Weber (qtd. in Delany, p. 509).

Style could survive economic misfortune, for it involved far more
than money; it implied "honor" and social associations with other persons of status. (Indeed, status carried with it certain behavioral expectations and restrictions, particularly regarding social interactions and
marriage. A person with status was unlikely to marry a person without
it, no matter how wealthy they were.) Generally speaking, status was
earned slowly, across several generations. Although land ownership,
especially if recent, might only signify wealth (and therefore class,
rather than status), most people with status did, in fact, own land.
Austen, Delany points out, uses words like *blood, name, rank, connection, family,* or *consequence* to signify status, whereas class is indicated
by words like *wealth* and *fortune*. In *Emma*, for example, Mr. Knightley
warns Emma that Harriet Smith cannot expect to marry "a man of consequence and large fortune" (p. 510).

As his argument unfolds, Delany argues that Austen critiques these
distinctions even as she uses them. Some characters who have status

(e.g., Mr. Elton) prove to be mercenary lovers, attracted to wealth far more than to the "honor" associated with status. Conversely, although Emma expects Robert Martin "to marry for economic advantage, as would be suitable for someone of his class" (p. 511) — in Emma's words, he is "a great deal too full of the market to think of any thing else" (p. 45) — Martin exhibits "truly romantic feelings for Harriet" (p. 511) that show his love for her to be disinterested.

To say that Austen critiqued the class, status, and the supposed differences between them is not to imply that she didn't understand the importance of these concepts and distinctions. Whereas Karl Marx later dismissed status as a feudal anachronism (choosing to view old, landowning families as mere capitalists interested in profit), Austen knew that people's behavior can be governed by their view of their own — or another person's — status. Indeed, in Delany's words, "[m]uch in *Emma* hinges on Mr. Knightley's being Emma's equal in class, but her superior in status" (p. 512). (Knightley's family has owned land longer than Emma's, which in previous generations probably made its money in business and now draws income from investments.) Many of the novel's events and situations are driven by the status that the society of Highbury assigns to people — and that they believe themselves to have.

Emma's constant attempt to regulate her "social world" (e.g., her attempt to move Harriet Smith up — and the Coles down — in it) is, in Delany's view, a "*symptom* [emphasis added] of the kind of . . . status insecurity described by Pierre Bourdieu," who argued that "the fiercest and most fundamental [social] conflicts" involve "groups occupying a neighboring [status] position," for members of the status group just below one's own "most directly threaten" the "identity" and "*distinction*" of those in the group above (pp. 515–16). Mr. Knightley's conduct, by contrast, is determined by "the solid prestige he enjoys in his position at the top of the status hierarchy" (p. 517). He "regulates the distribution of status" by insisting "that due deference be paid to the gentility of the Bateses, regardless of their present poverty"; that limits be set on "Emma's aspirations for Harriet"; and that the Coles and Robert Martin be admitted "into the lower ranks of the genteel" (p. 518).

Like many cultural critics, Delany writes at the edge of Marxist, feminist, and gender criticism while differentiating his approach from all three. He implicitly distinguishes his approach from that of Marxist criticism insofar as he privileges issues of status over those of class. He

more explicitly delineates his difference from feminist and gender critics
(he refers, in particular, to the work of Claudia Johnson, whose essay
" 'Not at all what a man should be!': Remaking English Manhood in
Emma," represents gender criticism in this volume [p. 441]). Delany is
less interested in the subordination of women to men at the same social
level than he is in the fact that "solidarity between [women] can be
motivated by commonality of status as well as of gender" (p. 518) and
that "the power of their status rather than their gender" shapes "their
relations with subaltern [i.e., lower-status] groups" (p. 519).

   Continuing his disagreement with Johnson, Delany points out that
"Emma's eventual willingness to subordinate herself to the moral
authority of Mr. Knightley is a notorious crux for feminist criticism of
Austen," adding that Knightley is, in the view of Johnson (and many
other feminists), " 'a fantastically wishful creation of benign authority' "
and remarking that "feminists lament the romance imperative that spirited heroines like Emma . . . should accept the diminished status of a
wife" (p. 520). Delany resists such readings, stating that "many of
Austen's protagonists welcome the increase of status relative to other
women that marriage promises them" (p. 520). Responding to the
question, "Does Emma's moral reform entail her becoming a complacent and submissive country gentleman's wife?" (p. 520), Delany concludes that "[m]arriage into the gentry will provide Emma with a
legitimate outlet for her energies, in the care of her estate and its
people. It would be both anachronistic and futile to blame Austen for
failure to envision other kinds of opportunities for women" (p. 521).

   In addition to differentiating his approach from Marxist, feminist, and gender criticism, Delany defines his approach as more broadly
cultural by emphasizing what Pierre Bourdieu calls "the field of cultural production." The "status insecurity" represented in Austen's
novels, along with the search for social "distinction," argues against
readings that would define her fiction as patriarchal or antipatriarchal,
capitalist or anticapitalist, "conservative" or "subversive." Emma, who
for so long sought to regulate the boundaries of her world, comes to
realize that, "in the long run, her best self-assertion can be achieved
only as the wife of Mr. Knightley and the mistress of Donwell Abbey.
That is the place where, for her, the contending claims of status, class,
and gender can be most fully and reciprocally satisfied" (p. 521).

                                                      Ross C Murfin

CULTURAL CRITICISM:
A SELECTED BIBLIOGRAPHY

General Introductions to
Cultural Criticism, Cultural Studies

Bathrick, David. "Cultural Studies." *Introduction to Scholarship in Modern Languages and Literatures*. Ed. Joseph Gibaldi. New York: MLA, 1992. 320–40.

Brantlinger, Patrick. *Crusoe's Footprints: Cultural Studies in Britain and America*. New York: Routledge, 1990.

———. "Cultural Studies vs. the New Historicism." *English Studies/Cultural Studies: Institutionalizing Dissent*. Ed. Isaiah Smithson and Nancy Ruff. Urbana: U of Illinois P, 1994. 43–58.

Brantlinger, Patrick, and James Naremore, eds. *Modernity and Mass Culture*. Bloomington: Indiana UP, 1991.

Brummett, Barry. *Rhetoric in Popular Culture*. New York: St. Martin's, 1994.

Desan, Philippe, Priscilla Parkhurst Ferguson, and Wendy Griswold. "Editors' Introduction: Mirrors, Frames, and Demons: Reflections on the Sociology of Literature." *Literature and Social Practice*. Ed. Desan, Ferguson, and Griswold. Chicago: U of Chicago P, 1989. 1–10.

During, Simon, ed. *The Cultural Studies Reader*. New York: Routledge, 1993.

Eagleton, Terry. "Two Approaches in the Sociology of Literature." *Critical Inquiry* 14 (1988): 469–76.

Easthope, Antony. *Literary into Cultural Studies*. New York: Routledge, 1991.

Fisher, Philip. "American Literary and Cultural Studies since the Civil War." *Redrawing the Boundaries: The Transformation of English and American Literary Studies*. Ed. Stephen Greenblatt and Giles Gunn. New York: MLA, 1992. 232–50.

Giroux, Henry, David Shumway, Paul Smith, and James Sosnoski. "The Need for Cultural Studies: Resisting Intellectuals and Oppositional Public Spheres." *Dalhousie Review* 64.2 (1984): 472–86.

Graff, Gerald, and Bruce Robbins. "Cultural Criticism." *Redrawing the Boundaries: The Transformation of English and American Literary Studies*. Ed. Stephen Greenblatt and Giles Gunn. New York: MLA, 1992. 419–36.

Grossberg, Lawrence, Cary Nelson, and Paula A. Treichler, eds. *Cultural Studies.* New York: Routledge, 1992.

Gunn, Giles. *The Culture of Criticism and the Criticism of Culture.* New York: Oxford UP, 1987.

Hall, Stuart. "Cultural Studies: Two Paradigms." *Media, Culture and Society* 2 (1980): 57–72.

Humm, Peter, Paul Stigant, and Peter Widdowson, eds. *Popular Fictions: Essays in Literature and History.* New York: Methuen, 1986.

Hunt, Lynn, ed. *The New Cultural History: Essays.* Berkeley: U of California P, 1989.

Johnson, Richard. "What Is Cultural Studies Anyway?" *Social Text* 16 (1986–87): 38–80.

Pfister, Joel. "The Americanization of Cultural Studies." *Yale Journal of Criticism* 4 (1991): 199–229.

Punter, David, ed. *Introduction to Contemporary Critical Studies.* New York: Longman, 1986. See especially Punter's "Introduction: Culture and Change" 1–18, Tony Dunn's "The Evolution of Cultural Studies" 71–91, and the essay "Methods for Cultural Studies Students" by Anne Beezer, Jean Grimshaw, and Martin Barker 95–118.

Storey, John. *An Introductory Guide to Cultural Theory and Popular Culture.* Athens: U of Georgia P, 1993.

Turner, Graeme. *British Cultural Studies: An Introduction.* Boston: Unwin Hyman, 1990.

Cultural Studies:
Some Early British Examples

Hoggart, Richard. *Speaking to Each Other.* 2 vols. London: Chatto, 1970.

———. *The Uses of Literacy: Changing Patterns in English Mass Culture.* Boston: Beacon, 1961.

Thompson, E. P. *The Making of the English Working Class.* New York: Harper, 1958.

———. *William Morris: Romantic to Revolutionary.* New York: Pantheon, 1977.

Williams, Raymond. *Culture and Society, 1780–1950.* New York: Harper, 1966.

———. *The Long Revolution.* New York: Columbia UP, 1961.

Cultural Studies:
Continental and Marxist Influences

Althusser, Louis. *For Marx*. Trans. Ben Brewster. New York: Pantheon, 1969.

————. "Ideology and Ideological State Apparatuses." *Lenin and Philosophy*. Trans. Ben Brewster. New York: Monthly Review P, 1971. 127–86.

Althusser, Louis, and Étienne Balibar. *Reading Capital*. Trans. Ben Brewster. New York: Pantheon, 1971.

Bakhtin, Mikhail. *The Dialogic Imagination: Four Essays*. Ed. Michael Holquist. Trans. Caryl Emerson. Austin: U of Texas P, 1981.

————. *Rabelais and His World*. Trans. Hélène Iswolsky. Cambridge: MIT P, 1968.

Baudrillard, Jean. *Simulations*. Trans. Paul Foss, Paul Patton, and Philip Beitchnan. 1981. New York: Semiotext(e), 1983.

Benjamin, Walter. *Illuminations*. Ed. with intro. by Hannah Arendt. Trans. H. Zohn. New York: Harcourt, 1968.

Bennett, Tony. "Marxism and Popular Fiction." Humm, Stigant, and Widdowson 237–65.

Bourdieu, Pierre. *Distinction: A Social Critique of the Judgment of Taste*. Trans. Richard Nice. Cambridge: Harvard UP, 1984.

de Certeau, Michel. *The Practice of Everyday Life*. Trans. Steven F. Rendall. Berkeley: U of California P, 1984.

Derrida, Jacques. *Of Grammatology*. 1969. Trans. Gayatri C. Spivak. Baltimore: Johns Hopkins UP, 1976.

Foucault, Michel. *Discipline and Punish: The Birth of the Prison*. Trans. Alan Sheridan. New York: Pantheon, 1978.

————. *The History of Sexuality*. Trans. Robert Hurley. Vol. 1. New York: Pantheon, 1978.

Gramsci, Antonio. *Selections from the Prison Notebooks*. Ed. Quintin Hoare and Geoffrey Nowell Smith. New York: International, 1971.

Modern Cultural Studies:
Selected British and American Examples

Bagdikian, Ben H. *The Media Monopoly*. Boston: Beacon, 1983.

Bowlby, Rachel. *Shopping with Freud*. New York: Routledge, 1993.

Chambers, Iain. *Popular Culture: The Metropolitan Experience*. New York: Methuen, 1986.

Colls, Robert, and Philip Dodd, eds. *Englishness: Politics and Culture, 1880–1920.* London: Croom Helm, 1986.

Denning, Michael. *Mechanic Accents: Dime Novels and Working-Class Culture in America.* New York: Verso, 1987.

Fiske, John. "British Cultural Studies and Television." *Channels of Discourse: Television and Contemporary Criticism.* Ed. Robert C. Allen. Chapel Hill: U of North Carolina P, 1987.

———. *Television Culture.* New York: Methuen, 1987.

Hebdige, Dick. *Hiding the Light: On Images and Things.* New York: Routledge, 1988.

———. *Subculture: The Meaning of Style.* London: Methuen, 1979.

Huyssen, Andreas. *After the Great Divide: Modernism, Mass Culture, Postmodernism.* Bloomington: Indiana UP, 1986.

Marcus, Greil. *Dead Elvis: A Chronicle of a Cultural Obsession.* New York: Doubleday, 1991.

———. *Lipstick Traces: A Secret History of the Twentieth Century.* Cambridge: Harvard UP, 1989.

Modleski, Tania. *Loving with a Vengeance: Mass-Produced Fantasies for Women.* Hamden: Archon, 1982.

Poovey, Mary. *Uneven Developments: The Ideological Work of Gender in Mid-Victorian England.* Chicago: U of Chicago P, 1988.

Radway, Janice A. *Reading the Romance: Women, Patriarchy, and Popular Literature.* Chapel Hill: U of North Carolina P, 1984.

Reed, T. V. *Fifteen Jugglers, Five Believers: Literary Politics and the Poetics of American Social Movements.* Berkeley: U of California P, 1992.

Ethnic and Minority Criticism, Postcolonial Studies

Anzaldúa, Gloria. *Borderlands: La Frontera = The New Mestiza.* San Francisco: Spinsters/Aunt Lute, 1987.

Baker, Houston. *Blues, Ideology, and Afro-American Literature: A Vernacular Theory.* Chicago: U of Chicago P, 1984.

———. *The Journey Back: Issues in Black Literature and Criticism.* Chicago: U of Chicago P, 1980.

Bhabha, Homi K. *The Location of Culture.* New York: Routledge, 1994.

———, ed. *Nation and Narration.* New York: Routledge, 1990.

———. "Postcolonial Criticism." *Redrawing the Boundaries: The Transformation of English and American Literary Studies.* Ed.

Stephen Greenblatt and Giles Gunn. New York: MLA, 1992. 437–65.

Brantlinger, Patrick. *Rule of Darkness: British Literature and Imperialism, 1830–1914.* Ithaca: Cornell UP, 1988.

Gates, Henry Louis, Jr. *Black Literature and Literary Theory.* New York: Methuen, 1984.

———, ed. *"Race," Writing, and Difference.* Chicago: U of Chicago P, 1986.

Gayle, Addison. *The Black Aesthetic.* Garden City: Doubleday, 1971.

———. *The Way of the New World: The Black Novel in America.* Garden City: Doubleday, 1975.

JanMohamed, Abdul. *Manichean Aesthetics: The Politics of Literature in Colonial Africa.* Amherst: U of Massachusetts P, 1983.

JanMohamed, Abdul, and David Lloyd, eds. *The Nature and Context of Minority Discourse.* New York: Oxford UP, 1991.

Kaplan, Amy, and Donald E. Pease, eds. *Cultures of United States Imperialism.* Durham: Duke UP, 1983.

Neocolonialism. Spec. issue of *Oxford Literary Review* 13 (1991).

Said, Edward. *After the Last Sky: Palestinian Lives.* New York: Pantheon, 1986.

———. *Culture and Imperialism.* New York: Knopf, 1993.

———. *Orientalism.* New York: Pantheon, 1978.

———. *The World, the Text, and the Critic.* Cambridge: Harvard UP, 1983.

Spivak, Gayatri Chakravorty. *In Other Worlds: Essays in Cultural Politics.* New York: Methuen, 1987.

Stepto, Robert B. *From Behind the Veil: A Study of Afro-American Narrative.* Urbana: U of Illinois P, 1979.

Young, Robert. *White Mythologies: Writing, History, and the West.* London: Routledge, 1990.

Cultural Criticism Relating to *Emma*

Copeland, Edward. "Money." *The Cambridge Companion to Jane Austen.* Ed. Edward Copeland and Juliet McMaster. Cambridge: Cambridge UP, 1997. 131–48.

Lynch, Deidre. "At Home with Jane Austen." *Cultural Institutions of the Novel.* Ed. Deidre Lynch and William B. Warner. Durham: Duke UP, 1996. 159–92.

———, ed. *Janeites: Austen's Disciples and Devotees.* Princeton: Princeton UP, 2000.

Macdonagh, Oliver. "Highbury and Chawton: Social Convergence in *Emma.*" *Historical Studies* 18 (1978): 37–51.

Thompson, James. "Jane Austen's Clothing: Things, Property, and Materialism in Her Novels." *Studies in Eighteenth-Century Culture.* Ed. O M Brack, Jr. Vol. 13. Madison: U of Wisconsin P, 1984. 217–31.

Wiltshire, John. *Jane Austen and the Body: "The Picture of Health."* New York: Cambridge UP, 1992.

A CULTURAL PERSPECTIVE

PAUL DELANY

"A Sort of Notch in the Donwell Estate": Intersections of Status and Class in *Emma*

I

Many critics have addressed the question of Jane Austen's exact class position and loyalties. Marilyn Butler (1975) argued influentially that Austen was a conservative who should be placed within the anti-Jacobin reaction; more recently, Claudia L. Johnson (1988) and James Thompson (1988), among others, have read her fiction as implicitly subversive of patriarchal and even capitalist values. I will argue that disagreements about Austen's specific position on the political spectrum can be clarified if we recognize that, for her, there are two distinct social hierarchies, one of "class" and one of "status." Class is the more modern concept: a stratification by capital, income and economic productivity. It is the outcome of competition, driven by man's natural "propensity to truck, barter and exchange one thing for another," as Adam Smith put it (1:17). Class can be precisely quantified, and Austen is notoriously fond of such quantifications: Darcy has £10,000 a year; Emma will inherit £30,000; Captain Wentworth has £25,000 in prize money; and so on. A large number in Austen is sure to have a pound sign attached to it.

But in Austen's England, wealth is only one axis of rank (if it were the only one, Emma could have no objection to Harriet Smith's marrying a man who is much better off than she is, Robert Martin). The other axis measures what Max Weber calls status:

In contrast to the purely economically determined "class situation" we wish to designate as "status situation" every typical component of the life fate of men that is determined by a specific, positive or negative, social estimation of *honor*. . . .

In content, status honor is normally expressed by the fact that above all else a specific *style of life* can be expected from all those who wish to belong to the circle. Linked with this expectation are restrictions on "social" intercourse (that is, intercourse which is not subservient to economic . . . purposes). These restrictions may confine normal marriages to within the status circle and may lead to complete endogamous closure. (187–88)

Status groups form cultures of stability, exclusion, and distinction, and place great value on sheer length of tenure. An important determinant of Mr. Knightley's status, for example, is that his family have been landowners in Highbury since at least 1540; Emma's family have been there for perhaps a hundred years; the Coles have had a house in the village for about ten years; Mr. Elton has recently arrived. Status groups tend to fear the levelling potential of "market forces"; though, as Weber observes, it is impossible for them to ignore wealth altogether:

[C]lass distinctions are linked in the most varied ways with status distinctions. Property as such is not always recognized as a status qualification, but in the long run it is, and with extraordinary regularity. . . .

Both propertied and propertyless people can belong to the same status group, and frequently they do with very tangible consequences. This "equality" of social esteem may, however, in the long run become quite precarious. (187)

In her novels, Austen refers to status in terms like "blood" or "name," which signify some connection with a landed estate. The aristocracy and gentry comprised only about 13,000 landed families in 1800 (when the population of England was about nine million), but they owned more than three quarters of all land, held a virtual monopoly of political power and presided over an extensive system of familial and social influence (Mingay). David Spring makes a useful distinction in identifying the gentry as a "reference group" for a much larger group of "pseudo-gentry" — in which he includes Austen's family — who deferred to the social prestige of landowners and mimicked their style of life (60). Like most subordinate groups, the pseudo-gentry were eager also to distinguish themselves from the group next below them in status, the commercial middle class who engaged in "trade."

Some of Austen's other status-terms are "rank," "connection," "family," or "consequence." A word-search of her novels shows that she regularly makes the distinction between "wealth" or "fortune" (which defines a person's class) and "consequence" (which defines his or her status).[1] Wickham, in *Pride and Prejudice*, for example, complains that "The world is blinded by [Darcy's] fortune and consequence" (78), and Mr. Knightley warns Emma that Harriet Smith cannot expect to marry "a man of consequence and large fortune" (p. 68 in this volume). When J. A. Froude observes that "No form of property gives its owners so much consequence as land," he means that landed wealth confers a supplement of prestige, unlike newer money based on trade.[2] William Elliot, in *Persuasion*, first sets his sights on money, then comes to appreciate the status that only land can bring. As Mrs. Smith recognizes: "Having long had as much money as he could spend, nothing to wish for on the side of avarice or indulgence, he has been gradually learning to pin his happiness upon the consequence he is heir to" (206–07). Persons of consequence can exact deference from others by virtue of their status — a more direct form of power than the ability to purchase goods and services in the market.

Status and class are also qualitatively different modes of classification (Poovey). Status belongs to nature and is ascribed: each person is born with a certain quality of "blood" that gives them a fixed social rank. Class belongs to culture and is achieved: people make themselves through productive enterprise. Such industriousness arouses suspicion among status holders, since it enables people to pass themselves off, through purchased goods and learned manners, as having better blood than they were born with. Status cannot be diminished by economic misfortune (this is Mr. Knightley's lesson to Emma, over her treatment of Miss Bates at Box Hill); class depends on the constant revaluations of the market, where human worth is relativized and rendered unstable.

From status and class a further series of metonymic oppositions arise: between "prestige culture" and "material culture," land and trade, gentry and merchants, old money and new money, gentility and wealth, the romance and the novel, the passions and the interests. Albert Hirschman has shown the importance of this last pair of terms for early modern understanding of social psychology. While matchmaking for Harriet, Emma attributes to Mr. Elton "a strong passion at war with all

---

[1]The text of Austen's fiction may be searched at www.pemberley.com/janeinfo/novlsrch.html

[2]*OED*, see under "Consequence."

interested motives" (p. 71): she expects someone who belongs to her own social circle to be magnanimous in affairs of the heart, and not be deterred in his suit by Harriet's lack of money. Robert Martin, on the other hand, she expects to marry for economic advantage, as would be suitable for someone of his class: "Six years hence, if he could meet with a good sort of young woman in the same rank as his own, with a little money, it might be very desirable" (p. 42). Emma's assumption about Martin is that he is "a great deal too full of the market to think of any thing else" — specifically, of the romantic novel that Harriet wanted him to get for her but he forgot (p. 45).

Austen's ironic viewpoint on this is expressed by Mr. Knightley, who has discerned that, when it comes to love, Mr. Elton is interested rather than passionate. He is attracted to Emma's thirty thousand pounds at least as much as to her social position or her personal charms; when he is rejected by her his passions are jealousy and spite rather than amorous disappointment. Mr. Knightley's view of him is soon confirmed when he settles for a merchant's daughter with something less than ten thousand pounds (p. 154). The genteel Mr. Elton is in fact a mercenary lover, whereas Robert Martin, whom Emma dismissed as coarse and materialistic, has truly romantic feelings for Harriet (and can write a good love letter, too [p 58]). Mr. Knightley himself, of course, is motivated by an unacknowledged passion: jealousy, which leads him to ascribe base motives to Elton's pursuit of Emma (one can be jealous and right, however). In accordance with the conventions of romance, Emma and Mr. Knightley are free at the end to be passionate about each other, because their fortunes are both large and roughly equal, thus canceling out any motive of "interest." Everywhere else in the novel, though, Austen takes it for granted that pure "disinterestedness" — lack of concern for financial gain — can only be a self-serving myth of status culture, and therefore a legitimate target for her irony. Ambition, whether for money or rank, is universal; those who, like Emma, have all the money they want, still want to improve or defend their social position.

Austen's world is one of continuous "status struggle." Marx, with his focus on an ultimately economic "class struggle," wrote off the Weberian status order as a "feudal remnant" in nineteenth-century England. For him, large landowners were really capitalists whose imperatives were efficiency and profit. But the status struggle in *Emma* should not be reduced to a mere reflection of a determining class struggle at the base. It is not just that class issues remain occluded in the novel (how did the Woodhouse family make its money? how much

does Robert Martin pay his agricultural laborers?), but also that the status struggle has its own arena, defined by separation from the market
and the silencing of any direct economic concerns. This separation may
be spatial: a rising bourgeois family like the Coles pursues its economic
interests in town, its status interests in the country (p. 173). Or it may
be gendered: genteel women are excluded from economic production,
but they take the lead in defining and exchanging tokens of status. This
is the business that fills their days and determines their social capital.

II

Much in *Emma* hinges on Mr. Knightley's being Emma's equal in
class, but her superior in status. Although the Woodhouses are indeed
"first in consequence" in Highbury, Mr. Knightley is not a resident of
the town (though he owns the land on which it is built). The Woodhouses rank below him because the source of their fortune cannot be
named (pp. 34, 122), and because of their lack of land: "The landed
property of Hartfield certainly was inconsiderable, being but a sort of
notch in the Donwell Abbey estate, to which all the rest of Highbury
belonged; but their fortune, from other sources, was such as to make
them scarcely secondary to Donwell Abbey itself, in every other kind of
consequence" (p. 122). The Woodhouses are roughly even with Mr.
Knightley in wealth, but they are rentiers who live off their capital,
probably in government bonds ("the funds"). Mr. Knightley's wealth is
in a landed estate that has been in his family since the dissolution of the
monasteries in the 1540s, and part of which he farms himself. Given its
closeness to London, an estate like Donwell Abbey might well have
been acquired in the Reformation by an office holder or rich merchant,
rather than by an aristocratic family (Stone). The name "Knightley,"
however, asserts a direct link with the days of chivalry. The Woodhouse
residence, Hartfield, is subordinated to the estate that encompasses it
on three sides (though it is also, in anticipation of the ending, something desirable to round out its greater neighbor).[3]

The Woodhouses trace their descent from a younger son of the aristocracy who, under primogeniture, would not have inherited any land.
In some generation before Emma's father one of them must have either
married the daughter of a rich merchant, or gone into trade himself.

---

[3]It can also be thought of as the "Heart Field" needed to make Mr. Knightley
complete emotionally. John McAleer links the name "Woodhouse" to the aristocratic
Wentworth-Woodhouse family, to which the Austens were related.

For "several generations" (p. 122) now they have lived at Hartfield, though the house may have been built originally as a weekend retreat from a London business. Emma's father certainly has spent his entire existence there, as a rentier who has taken no part in the active life of pursuing economic gain (the few pigs that they keep are useful for bestowing legs of pork on their dependents; but this is no more than a gesture towards the gentry ideal, and pigs, unlike cattle or sheep, can be raised without land).

The stigma of family connections with "trade" is a common motif in Austen's plots; it generates an interplay between status and class that provides opportunities for her double-sided irony — directed both against those who violate social barriers, and those who defend them too zealously. The status hierarchy of Highbury is determined by the quality of one's "blood." Connections with trade create a taint that gradually may be diluted by withdrawal from active business and the adoption of genteel manners. When Emma praises Mr. Knightley's "true gentility, untainted in blood and understanding" (pp. 286–87), "tainted" covers different kinds of stigma — connections with trade are comparable to illegitimacy or madness.[4] Membership in the highest status-group requires possession of a family landed estate of several hundred acres, held for at least a century; members of the family should have married only within their own caste for successive generations. Darcy, in *Pride and Prejudice*, at first rules out Elizabeth Bennet as a potential wife because of the inferiority of her "connections": her maternal uncle is a London merchant and, in Elizabeth's view, "Mr. Darcy may perhaps have *heard* of such a place as Gracechurch Street [where her uncle has his business], but he would hardly think a month's ablution enough to cleanse him from his impurities, were he once to enter it" (127). His squeamishness may appear extreme, given that the British system of primogeniture created the paradox that younger sons would have to seek their fortune away from the estate in each genera-tion, raising the danger of "defilement" by involvement in, or intermar-riage with, trade. The four genteel professions — the Church, the Law, the Army, and Medicine — provided acceptable livings for cadet mem-bers of the gentry (younger sons and their descendants); Jane Austen's father belonged to this category. In practice, the status system of the gentry was far from watertight, allowing for a circulation of elites between land and trade that was peculiarly English; but the supremacy

---

[4]Compare the assessment of Harriet's "blood" (p. 379), and Tony Tanner's com-mentary on it (184–85).

of gentry values and styles was maintained until at least the later nineteenth century (Stone and Stone; Mingay; Mason).

Aligned with the gentry are an upper-middle class who are subordinated by some combination of insufficient wealth (the Bateses), recent connections with trade (Mrs. Elton), or lack of land (the Woodhouses). Mr. Weston's successive incarnations are instructive: having an independent income, he dissociates himself from the "trade" of his family and enters the militia; he marries the sister of a landed gentleman, but is not accepted by the family because of his origins; he returns to trade in London for twenty years, keeping a small weekend house in Highbury; when he has enough money he abandons trade and buys a small landed estate, Randalls. His second wife is Emma's poor but genteel governess, Miss Taylor (p. 32). When, like Mr. Weston, tenant farmers (Robert Martin) or tradespeople (the Coles) become sufficiently prosperous and mannered, they can win social acceptance from the gentry. Harriet Smith's illegitimacy makes her classification uncertain: Emma assumes that her father was of the gentry; Mr. Elton considers her suspect but accepts her in order to ingratiate himself with Emma; Mr. Knightley decries her "illegitimacy and ignorance" (p. 66) but, characteristically, comes to her aid when she is snubbed by the Eltons at the ball.

In social intercourse, status is confirmed by *recognition* of the other — as distinct from merely seeing them:

> They met Mr. Martin the very next day, as they were walking on the Donwell road. He was on foot, and after looking very respectfully at her, looked with most unfeigned satisfaction at her companion. Emma was not sorry to have such an opportunity of survey; and walking a few yards forward, while they talked together, soon made her quick eye sufficiently acquainted with Mr. Robert Martin. (pp. 43–44)

The social significance of these "few yards forward" is made explicit in a parallel scene from *Persuasion:*

> It did not surprise, but it grieved Anne to observe that Elizabeth would not know [Captain Wentworth]. She saw that he saw Elizabeth, that Elizabeth saw him, that there was complete internal recognition on each side; she was convinced that he was ready to be acknowledged as an acquaintance, expecting it, and she had the pain of seeing her sister turn away with unalterable coldness. (176)

In these encounters, two women of high status (Emma Woodhouse and Elizabeth Elliot) treat someone as if he were "not there." Emma's "sufficient acquaintance" with Robert Martin is to scrutinize him like a domestic animal; Elizabeth won't even look. One of the things Emma notices about Martin is that he is "very neat," just as Captain Wentworth would have been when he encountered Elizabeth. Emma's criticisms belong entirely to "air" and "manner"; her point is that clothes alone do not make a gentleman or a lady (p. 44). In the dual system that still prevails in Austen's world, it is not enough to look right; one must *be* right. What counts most are breeding, "connection" and "consequence," which are not sold in shops.

Historians who have established the idea of an eighteenth-century "consumer revolution" see it as the beginning of a fully economized modern society, in which status is a direct function of purchasing power (Brewer and Porter; McKendrick, Brewer, and Plumb). Edward Copeland has emphasized the role of female consumption in claiming status in Austen's novels: "There is no over-estimating the significance of material possessions in pseudo-gentry life" (91). But consumption, insofar as it is available to anyone with money, remains closer to class than to status. In a sentence that both sparkles and cuts, Austen shows us the difference between appraising consumption and according recognition: "Mrs. Elton, as elegant as lace and pearls could make her, [John Knightley] looked at in silence — wanting only to observe enough for Isabella's information — but Miss Fairfax was an old acquaintance and a quiet girl, and he could talk to her" (p. 236)

The novel pays little attention to Emma's clothing or other purchases, and Mrs. Elton's sister's barouche-landau or the Coles' grand piano stigmatize rather than distinguish their owners. Emma's main occupation is not shopping, but rather regulating boundary disputes at the borders between status groups. She wants to keep the "unworthy" in their place, to raise Harriet Smith (though only as a dependent on herself), and to move the Bateses down towards the very margin of gentility. In her own eyes, these are her duties as the leader of Highbury society and the arbiter of its tables of precedence. But for Austen, for Mr. Knightley, and for the initiated reader, Emma's regulation of her social world appears as a symptom of the kind of restless status insecurity described by Pierre Bourdieu:

> We should pay particular attention to the strategies employed in relation to groups occupying a neighbouring position in the field. The law of the search for distinction explains the apparent paradox which has it that the fiercest and most fundamental conflicts oppose each group to its immediate neighbours, for it is these

who most directly threaten its identity, hence its *distinction* and even its specifically cultural existence. (293)

Mr. Knightley is never more the true gentleman than when he strolls into some social gathering in his "thick leather gaiters," having walked rather than taken his carriage; and Emma betrays her want of true gentility when she judges him to have "little spare money" and wishes that he would be more formal (pp. 232, 177). Securely ensconced at the center of his status group, Mr. Knightley need have no anxiety about conditions at the border, and can actually gain prestige by affecting a rumpled manner.

In theory, Emma recognizes this relaxed gentry ideal: "[she] did not want to be classed with the Mrs. Eltons, the Mrs. Perrys, and the Mrs. Coles, who would force themselves anywhere" (p. 311). All are social climbers, she judges, who betray themselves by their over-eagerness. But Emma's "active, busy mind" (p. 85) also craves occupation in the struggle going on around her for status, acceptance and precedence — a struggle she enters vicariously on behalf of Harriet Smith:

> "There can be no doubt of your being a gentleman's daughter, and you must support your claim to that station by every thing within your own power, or there will be plenty of people who would take pleasure in degrading you."
>
> "Yes, to be sure — I suppose there are. But while I visit at Hartfield, and you are so kind to me, Miss Woodhouse, I am not afraid of what any body can do."
>
> "You understand the force of influence pretty well, Harriet; but I would have you so firmly established in good society, as to be independent even of Hartfield and Miss Woodhouse. I want to see you permanently well connected." (p. 43)

Harriet's only way of achieving such "permanence" is by a marriage into the gentry. But the argument with Mr. Knightley about Harriet's marriageability (pp. 64–70) reveals Emma's naiveté about the interaction between status and class. She argues that most men judge women superficially, so that prettiness and a veneer of good manners will easily make them forget their status expectations; Knightley says that they will only do this if a dowry of several thousand pounds is thrown into the scale.[5] Frank Churchill will marry Jane Fairfax without a dowry, but Jane is *already* genteel, as well as being more beautiful, more accom-

---

[5] This is the point of one of Austen's sly jokes: Mr. Knightley comments on Emma's picture of Harriet "You have made her too tall." The reader should add a second meaning: "You think her status is higher than it actually is."

plished and better educated than Harriet. If he had loved her, Knightley too could have chosen Jane without loss of status.

James Thompson attacks Mr. Knightley's motives by placing him among the "financially ailing rural squirearchy," and therefore someone in need of the "infusion of capital" that Emma's £30,000 could bring (40–41). But although Mr. Knightley chooses to live modestly, Austen shows him to be a diligent, "improving" landlord at a time of general agricultural prosperity. Rents in Surrey rose by a hundred and fifteen percent in the twenty-one years to 1815: the war increased the demand for home-grown food, and agriculture became more efficient in response (Halévy 229). Abbey-Mill Farm is described by Emma as "large" (p. 37), which to the contemporary Board of Agriculture meant more than five hundred acres. This suggests that Mr. Knightley (or one of his recent predecessors) has been an "engrosser" of several small tenant farms into the one large one now held by Robert Martin. If Martin held five hundred acres, he would pay a rent of about £750 to Mr. Knightley and have a similar profit for himself. This would make his income already larger than Mrs. Elton's; and Emma, with her usual shrewdness about money, observes that "with diligence and good luck, he may be rich in time" (pp. 42–43). If Mr. Knightley personally farmed the same amount of land as Martin, his gross agricultural income would be about £2,250 a year and the capitalized value of his estate about £22,500. Ground rents from Highbury village, which is built on his land, would be in addition. Emma's £30,000 (actually what she expects to inherit from her father) would yield £1500 a year at five percent (Halévy 230 34).

Mr. Knightley is no backwoods Squire Western, but a sophisticated agricultural capitalist, keeping one eye on the land and the other on nearby London. This may help to explain why he is much less suspicious of "trade" than Emma is, certainly when it appears in the modest and deferential guise of the Coles. But the main determinant of his social conduct is the solid prestige he enjoys in his position at the top of the status hierarchy; as Ronald Blythe puts it, "The total acceptability of his status hasn't shifted a fraction since Jane Austen invented him" (16).[6] Mr. Knightley can afford an Olympian perspective on the struggle for gentility because no one below has any chance of elbowing him out of his own position — as Mrs. Elton, for example, strives to displace Emma. He will allow people to rise, but will also protect the

---

[6]Duckworth (155–56) and Tobin (229) also make the case for Mr. Knightley as an exemplary landowner.

Bates women from falling; in all cases, he makes it clear that money alone will not determine his judgment.

Emma's plans for revising the status order of Highbury are inconsistent: she wants to see less of the Bateses, in part because of their poverty, but with Harriet she argues that lack of money doesn't matter. The Eltons want to humiliate the shabby-genteel (Mrs. and Miss Bates, Jane Fairfax) and the would-be genteel (Harriet). Only Mr. Knightley, with his inherited gentry virtues, regulates the distribution of status with the right mixture of principle and flexibility. He insists that due deference be paid to the gentility of the Bateses, regardless of their present poverty; he sets limits to Emma's aspirations for Harriet; and he facilitates the admission of the Coles and Robert Martin into the lower ranks of the genteel. His only acts of social aggression are against Frank Churchill, for his failure to observe the rules of his own caste, and against the Eltons, for their attempts to usurp his authority in Highbury.

III

Is there a "gender struggle" in *Emma* corresponding to the struggles over status and class? Attention to status issues tends to complicate feminist readings that are oriented to the disabilities suffered by Emma and other female characters. Claudia Johnson proposes that Austen's "fiction represents the construction and enforcement of sexual difference as politically motivated elements of gentry life, and it protests against the costs these exact from women" (118). A problem with such a reading is that, most of the time, female self-assertion finds expression within the status order — which means both that competition between women is one of Austen's constant moral concerns, and that solidarity between them can be motivated by commonality of status as well as of gender. When a repentant Emma decides to be nicer to Miss Bates and Jane Fairfax, for example, it is partly because of the gentility that they, unlike the upstart Mrs. Elton, share with Emma, even in their poverty.

In the status struggle, female aggressors inflict harm on female victims, and are implicitly condemned for it by the narrator's judgment. Both Mrs. Elton and the friend with whom she wants Jane Fairfax to find employment, would enjoy humiliating Jane *because* she is more genteel than they are. "I am a great advocate for timidity," Mrs. Elton says of Jane, "in those who are at all inferior, it is extremely prepossessing" (p. 229); but it is Mrs. Elton who is inferior to Jane in status. Conversely, Emma's eventual discovery of her sympathy for Jane is a crucial index of her improvement after Mr. Knightley's rebuke at Box Hill. Austen's presumed identification with Miss Bates — because she shares her condition of being "neither young, handsome, rich, nor married" (p. 35) — is a critical truism; but what also needs to be acknowledged is that it is the genteel *women* of Highbury who hold the threat of ostracism and persecution over the Bateses' heads. Miss Bates is attacked by Emma and Mrs. Elton, Harriet by Mrs. Elton, Jane Fairfax by Mrs. Elton and indirectly by Mrs. Churchill. None of the victims has any power to hit back. Austen motivates the aggressions of Mrs. Elton and Mrs. Churchill by revealing that their own origins are suspect: they take advantage of the status they have gained through marriage to become self-appointed guardians of the boundaries they themselves have crossed. They have gained power from their association with men, then use it to oppress women. When Mrs. Elton proclaims herself a feminist ("I always stand up for women" [p. 247]), Austen is not discrediting feminism as such, but exposing Mrs. Elton's hypocrisy. She deals similarly with Mrs. Elton's claim to be an enemy of slavery (p. 242).

Austen shows that, in the status struggle, female power is often misused. The gender system prevailing among the gentry subordinates women to men, and unmarried to married women, at the same social level; but it gives women the power of their status rather than their gender in relations with subaltern groups. Emma can therefore humiliate Robert Martin, and Mrs. Churchill do the same to Mr. Weston, without fear of reprisal. Yet Claudia Johnson argues that any discomfort with Emma, as we first come to know her, is tinged with sexism:

> In endowing attractive female characters like Emma Woodhouse and Elizabeth Bennet with rich and unapologetic senses of self-consequence, Austen defies every dictum about female propriety and deference. . . . Unlike us, Austen is not embarrassed by power . . . [Emma] is a woman who possesses and enjoys power, without bothering to demur about it. . . . Emma's power is generally presented as the problem she must overcome. (xxiii, 125)

People only criticize Emma's treatment of Robert Martin because she is a woman, the argument goes; nobody minds when Darcy behaves with comparable arrogance. But Emma's tears in the carriage home from Box Hill, after she has been rebuked by Mr. Knightley, make no sense unless Austen means them as Emma's becoming a different and better person. Emma recognizes that she was egged on by Frank Churchill to attack a defenseless woman, and feels guilt for her betrayal of "the duty of woman by woman" (p. 191). To offer a feminist vindication of Emma's early behavior is to remove the possibility of her moral development later on. In *Pride and Prejudice,* similarly, Darcy's capacity for change has to be the point. He is cured of the worst of his arrogance by Elizabeth's rebuke when she rejects his first proposal, just as Emma is cured by Mr. Knightley's rebuke over Miss Bates.

Emma's eventual willingness to subordinate herself to the moral authority of Mr. Knightley is a notorious crux for feminist criticism of Austen. Claudia Johnson calls him "a fantastically wishful creation of benign authority" (141), and other feminists lament the romance imperative that spirited heroines like Emma or Elizabeth Bennet should accept the diminished status of a wife. Karen Newman seeks to evade this choice by reading Austen's endings as *parodies* which "measure the distance between novelistic conventions with their culturally coded sentiments and the social realities of patriarchal power" (708). I am not convinced that Austen felt coerced into a conventional ending to *Emma,* and therefore wrote it with tongue in cheek. Such a reading requires the late Emma to be as much a target of authorial irony as the early one. But one does not have to join the conservative camp of critics, who read Emma's marriage as "the overcoming of egoism and the mark of psychic development" (Newman 693–94), to recognize that many of Austen's protagonists welcome the increase of status relative to other women that marriage promises them.

The difficulty for feminist criticism is that Emma, in discarding that part of her nature that had been abusing her power, seems also to embrace a set of gentry values closely associated with paternalism and male dominance. Does Emma's moral reform entail her becoming a complacent and submissive country gentleman's wife? The resolution of *Emma* is in the tradition of the romance: a providential harmonization between status and class. Those who are deservedly wealthy (Robert Martin and the Coles) acquire prestige, while those who are deservedly genteel (Jane Fairfax) acquire wealth — not through capitalist accumulation, but through a fortunate marriage. It is Mrs. Churchill's timely death that removes the barrier between Frank and Jane; a stroke of poetic justice in that her snobbery was that of the parvenu, one whose own blood is less than pure (p. 250). Most important of all, Emma's own early inclination to parvenu snobbery, in the style of Mrs. Churchill or Mrs. Elton, will dissolve as she assumes the gentry values of her husband. Any gap between her status and his will be definitively erased once she has given birth to a son and heir for the Donwell Abbey estate.[7]

Austen's resolution subordinates both gender and class to a status ideal of benevolence. Like Fielding's Allworthy, Mr. Knightley's social authority depends largely on his dissociation from masculine sexual energy (which, in the case of Frank Churchill, is shown to be subversive of community values). Mr. Knightley's willingness to cater to Mr. Woodhouse's timidity and inertia suggests that he will not be too insistent about his other marital prerogatives. The marriage of Emma and Knightley will be one in which *both* partners will renounce much of their former energy and independence: Mr. Knightley is not the romance figure of the predatory male who practices marriage-by-capture, but someone willing to submit to the inanition of Hartfield. On Emma's side, her early restlessness and lack of judgment do not have to be attributed to a lack of male supervision; rather, as Tony Tanner has noted, it is a problem of too much money and too little worthwhile occupation. Marriage into the gentry will provide Emma with a *legitimate* outlet for her energies, in the care of her estate and its people. It would be both anachronistic and futile to blame Austen for failure to envision other kinds of opportunities for women in the public sphere: in spite of her earlier praise of celibate independence (p. 85), Emma comes to see that, in the long run, her best self-assertion can be achieved only as the wife of Mr. Knightley and the mistress of Donwell Abbey. That is the place where, for her, the contending claims of status, class, and gender can be most fully and reciprocally satisfied.

WORKS CITED

Austen, Jane. *Persuasion*. Ed. R. W. Chapman. London: Oxford UP, 1933.

———. *Pride and Prejudice*. Ed. R. W. Chapman. Oxford: Oxford UP, 1983.

———. *Emma*. Ed. Ronald Blythe. Harmondsworth: Penguin, 1985.

Bourdieu, Pierre. *The Field of Cultural Production: Essays on Art and Literature*. Ed. Randal Johnson. Cambridge: Polity, 1993.

[7]The heir expectant has been Mr. Knightley's nephew Henry. Emma showed concern for his loss of expectation when there was talk of Mr. Knightley marrying Jane Fairfax (pp. 185–86), but Austen wryly notes the disappearance of these scruples when Emma herself becomes the instrument of Henry's dispossession (p. 355).

Brewer, John, and Roy Porter, eds. *Consumption and the World of Goods*. London and New York: Routledge, 1993.

Butler, Marilyn. *Jane Austen and the War of Ideas*. Oxford: Clarendon, 1975.

Copeland, Edward. *Women Writing about Money: Women's Fiction in England, 1790–1820*. Cambridge: Cambridge UP, 1995.

Duckworth, Alistair M. *The Improvement of the Estate: A Study of Jane Austen's Novels*. 1971. Baltimore: Johns Hopkins UP, 1994.

Halévy, Elie. *England in 1815*. London: Ernest Benn, 1961.

Hirschman, Albert. *The Passions and the Interests: Political Arguments for Capitalism Before Its Triumph*. Princeton: Princeton UP, 1997.

Johnson, Claudia L. *Jane Austen: Women, Politics, and the Novel*. Chicago: U of Chicago P, 1988.

Marx, Karl. "Economic and Philosophical Manuscripts (1844)." *Karl Marx: Early Writings*. Ed. Lucio Colletti. Harmondsworth: Penguin, 1975. 309–22.

Mason, Philip. *The English Gentleman: The Rise and Fall of an Ideal*. London: André Deutsch, 1982.

McAleer, John. "What a Biographer Can Learn About Jane Austen from *Emma*." *Persuasions* 13 (1991): 69–81.

McKendrick, Neil, John Brewer, and J. H. Plumb. *The Birth of a Consumer Society: The Commercialization of Eighteenth-Century England*. London: Europa, 1982.

Mingay, G. E. *Land and Society in England 1750–1980*. London: Longman, 1994.

Newman, Karen. "Can This Marriage Be Saved: Jane Austen Makes Sense of an Ending." *ELH* 50.4 (Winter 1983): 693–710.

The Oxford English Dictionary. 2nd ed. Oxford: Clarendon, 1989.

Poovey, Mary. "The Social Constitution of 'Class': Toward a History of Classificatory Thinking." *Rethinking Class: Literary Studies and Social Formations*. Ed. Wai Chee Dimock and Michael Gilmore. New York: Columbia UP, 1994. 15–56.

Smith, Adam. *An Inquiry into the Nature and Causes of the Wealth of Nations*. Ed. E. Cannan. 2 vols. Chicago: U of Chicago P, 1976.

Spring, David. "Interpreters of Jane Austen's Social World: Literary Critics and Historians." *Jane Austen: New Perspectives*. Ed. Janet Todd. New York: Holmes & Meier, 1983. 53–72.

Stone, Lawrence, and Jeanne Fawtier Stone. *An Open Elite? England 1540–1800*. Oxford: Clarendon, 1984.

Tanner, Tony. *Jane Austen*. Houndmills: Macmillan, 1986.

Thompson, James. *Between Self and World: The Novels of Jane Austen.* University Park: Pennsylvania State UP, 1988.

Tobin, Beth Fowkes. "The Moral and Political Economy of Property in Austen's *Emma.*" *Eighteenth Century Fiction* 2.3 (April 1990): 229–54.

Weber, Max. *From Max Weber: Essays in Sociology.* Trans. H. H. Gerth and C. Wright Mills. New York: Oxford UP, 1958. 187–88.

The New Historicism
and
Emma

WHAT IS THE NEW HISTORICISM?

The title of Brook Thomas's *The New Historicism and Other Old-Fashioned Topics* (1991) is telling. Whenever an emergent theory, movement, method, approach, or group gets labeled with the adjective "new," trouble is bound to ensue, for what is new today is either established, old, or forgotten tomorrow. Few of you will have heard of the band called The New Kids on the Block. New Age bookshops and jewelry may seem "old hat" by the time this introduction is published. The New Criticism, or formalism, is just about the oldest approach to literature and literary study currently being practiced. The new historicism, by contrast, is *not* as old-fashioned as formalism, but it is hardly new, either. The term *new* eventually and inevitably requires some explanation. In the case of the new historicism, the best explanation is historical.

Although a number of influential critics working between 1920 and 1950 wrote about literature from a psychoanalytic perspective, the majority took what might generally be referred to as the historical approach. With the advent of the New Criticism, however, historically oriented critics almost seemed to disappear from the face of the earth. The dominant New Critics, or formalists, tended to treat literary works as if they were self-contained, self-referential objects. Rather than basing their interpretations on parallels between the text and historical contexts (such as the author's life or stated intentions in writing the work), these critics concentrated on the relationships *within* the text that give it its form and meaning. During the heyday of the New Criticism, concern about the interplay between literature and history virtually disappeared from literary discourse. In its place was a concern about intratextual repetition, particularly of images or symbols but also of rhythms and sound effect.

About 1970 the New Criticism came under attack by reader-response critics (who believe that the meaning of a work is not inherent in its internal form but rather is cooperatively produced by the reader and the text) and poststructuralists (who, following the philosophy of Jacques Derrida, argue that texts are inevitably self-contradictory and that we can find form in them only by ignoring or suppressing conflicting details or elements). In retrospect it is clear that, their outspoken opposition to the New Criticism notwithstanding, the reader-response critics and poststructuralists of the 1970s were very much *like* their formalist predecessors in two important respects: for the most part, they ignored the world beyond the text and its reader, and, for the most part, they ignored the historical contexts within which literary works are written and read.

Jerome McGann first articulated this retrospective insight in 1985, writing that "a text-only approach has been so vigorously promoted during the last thirty-five years that most historical critics have been driven from the field, and have raised the flag of their surrender by yielding the title 'critic,' and accepting the title 'scholar' for themselves" (*Inflections* 17). Most, but not all. The American Marxist Fredric Jameson had begun his 1981 book *The Political Unconscious* with the following two-word challenge: "Always historicize!" (9). Beginning about 1980, a form of historical criticism practiced by Louis Montrose and Stephen Greenblatt had transformed the field of Renaissance studies and begun to influence the study of American and English Romantic literature as well. And by the mid-1980s, Brook Thomas was working on an essay in which he suggests that classroom discussions of Keats's "Ode on a Grecian Urn" might begin with questions such as the following: Where would Keats have seen such an urn? How did a Grecian urn end up in a museum in England? Some very important historical and political realities, Thomas suggests, lie behind and inform Keats's definitions of art, truth, beauty, the past, and timelessness.

When McGann lamented the surrender of "most historical critics," he no doubt realized what is now clear to everyone involved in the study of literature. Those who have *not* yet surrendered — had not yet "yield[ed] the title 'critic' " to the formalist, reader-response, and post-structuralist "victors" — were armed with powerful new arguments and intent on winning back long-lost ground. Indeed, at about the same time that McGann was deploring the near-complete dominance of critics advocating the text-only approach, Herbert Lindenberger was sounding a more hopeful note: "It comes as something of a surprise," he wrote in 1984, "to find that history is making a powerful comeback" ("New History" 16).

We now know that history was indeed making a powerful comeback in the 1980s, although the word is misleading if it causes us to imagine that the historical criticism being practiced in the 1980s by Greenblatt and Montrose, McGann and Thomas, was the same as the historical criticism that had been practiced in the 1930s and 1940s. Indeed, if the word *new* still serves any useful purpose in defining the historical criticism of today, it is in distinguishing it from the old historicism. The new historicism is informed by the poststructuralist and reader-response theory of the 1970s, plus the thinking of feminist, cultural, and Marxist critics whose work was also "new" in the 1980s. New historicist critics are less fact- and event-oriented than historical critics used to be, perhaps because they have come to wonder whether the truth about what really happened can ever be purely and objectively known. They are less likely to see history as linear and progressive, as something developing toward the present or the future ("teleological"), and they are also less likely to think of it in terms of specific eras, each with a definite, persistent, and consistent Zeitgeist ("spirit of the times"). Consequently, they are unlikely to suggest that a literary text has a single or easily identifiable historical context.

New historicist critics also tend to define the discipline of history more broadly than it was defined before the advent of formalism. They view history as a social science and the social sciences as being properly historical. In *Historical Studies and Literary Criticism* (1985), McGann speaks of the need to make "sociohistorical" subjects and methods central to literary studies; in *The Beauty of Inflections: Literary Investigations in Historical Method and Theory* (1985), he links sociology and the future of historical criticism. "A sociological poetics," he writes, "must be recognized not only as relevant to the analysis of poetry, but in fact as central to the analysis" (62). Lindenberger cites anthropology as particularly useful in the new historical analysis of literature, especially anthropology as practiced by Victor Turner and Clifford Geertz. Geertz, who has related theatrical traditions in nineteenth-century Bali to forms of political organization that developed during the same period, has influenced some of the most important critics writing the new kind of historical criticism. Due in large part to Geertz's anthropological influence, new historicists such as Greenblatt have asserted that literature is not a sphere apart or distinct from the history that is relevant to it. That is what the old criticism tended to do: present the background information you needed to know before you could fully appreciate the separate world of art. The new historicists have used what Geertz would call "thick description" to blur distinctions, not only between history and the other social sciences but also between background and foreground, historical and literary materials, political and poetical events. They have erased the old boundary line dividing historical and literary materials, showing that the production of one of Shakespeare's historical plays was a political act and historical event, while at the same time showing that the coronation of Elizabeth I was carried out with the same care for staging and symbol lavished on works of dramatic art.

In addition to breaking down barriers that separate literature and history, history and the social sciences, new historicists have reminded us that it is treacherously difficult to reconstruct the past as it really was, rather than as we have been conditioned by our own place and time to believe that it was. And they know that the job is utterly impossible for those who are unaware of that difficulty and insensitive to the bent or bias of their own historical vantage point. Historical criticism must be "conscious of its status as interpretation," Greenblatt has written (*Renaissance* 4). McGann obviously concurs, writing that "historical criticism can no longer make any part of [its] sweeping picture unselfconsciously, or treat any of its details in an untheorized way" (*Studies* 11).

Unselfconsciously and *untheorized* are the key words in McGann's statement. When new historicist critics of literature describe a historical change, they are highly conscious of, and even likely to discuss, the *theory* of historical change that informs their account. They know that the changes they happen to see and describe are the ones that their theory of change allows or helps them to see and describe. And they know, too, that their theory of change is historically determined. They seek to minimize the distortion inherent in their perceptions and representations by admitting that they see through preconceived notions; in other words, they learn to reveal the color of the lenses in the glasses that they wear.

Nearly everyone who wrote on the new historicism during the 1980s cited the importance of the late Michel Foucault. A French philosophical historian who liked to think of himself as an archaeologist of human knowledge, Foucault brought together incidents and phenomena from areas of inquiry and orders of life that we normally regard as being unconnected. As much as anyone, he encouraged the new historicist critic of literature to redefine the boundaries of historical inquiry.

Foucault's views of history were influenced by the philosopher Friedrich Nietzsche's concept, *wirkliche* ("real" or "true") history that is neither melioristic (that is, "getting better all the time") nor metaphysical. Like Nietzsche, Foucault didn't see history in terms of a continuous development toward the present. Neither did he view it as an abstraction, idea, or ideal, as something that began "In the beginning" and that will come to THE END, a moment of definite closure, a Day of Judgment. In his own words, Foucault "abandoned [the old history's] attempts to understand events in terms of . . . some great evolutionary process" (*Discipline and Punish* 129). He warned a new generation of historians to be aware of the fact that investigators are themselves "situated." It is difficult, he reminded them, to see present cultural practices critically from within them, and because of the same cultural practices, it is extremely difficult to enter bygone ages. In *Discipline and Punish: The Birth of the Prison* (1975), Foucault admitted that his own interest in the past was fueled by a passion to write the history of the present.

Like Marx, Foucault saw history in terms of power, but his view of power probably owed more to Nietzsche than to Marx. Foucault seldom viewed power as a repressive force. He certainly did not view it as a tool of conspiracy used by one specific individual or institution against another. Rather, power represents a whole web or complex of forces; it is that which produces what happens. Not even a tyrannical aristocrat simply wields power, for the aristocrat is himself formed and empowered by a network of discourses and practices that constitute power. Viewed by Foucault, power is "positive and productive," not "repressive" and "prohibitive" (Smart 63). Furthermore, no historical event, according to Foucault, has a single cause; rather, it is intricately connected with a vast web of economic, social, and political factors.

A brief sketch of one of Foucault's major works may help clarify some of his ideas. *Discipline and Punish* begins with a shocking but accurate description of the public drawing and quartering of a Frenchman who had botched his attempt to assassinate King Louis XV in 1757. Foucault proceeds by describing rules governing the daily life of modern Parisian felons. What happened to torture, to punishment as public spectacle? he asks. What complex network of forces made it disappear? In working toward a picture of this "power," Foucault turns up many interesting puzzle pieces, such as the fact that in the early years of the nineteenth century, crowds would sometimes identify with the prisoner and treat the executioner as if *he* were the guilty party. But Foucault sets forth a related reason for keeping prisoners alive, moving punishment indoors, and changing discipline from physical torture into mental rehabilitation: colonization. In this historical period, people were needed to establish colonies and trade, and prisoners could be used for that purpose. Also, because these were politically unsettled times, governments needed infiltrators and informers. Who better to fill those roles than prisoners pardoned or released early for showing a willingness to be rehabilitated? As for rehabilitation itself, Foucault compares it to the old form of punishment, which began with a torturer extracting a confession. In more modern, "reasonable" times, psychologists probe the minds of prisoners with a scientific rigor that Foucault sees as a different kind of torture, a kind that our modern perspective does not allow us to see as such.

Thus, a change took place, but perhaps not as great a change as we generally assume. It may have been for the better or for the worse; the point is that agents of power didn't make the change because mankind is evolving and, therefore, more prone to perform good-hearted deeds. Rather, different objectives arose, including those of a new class of doctors and scientists bent on studying aberrant examples of the human mind. And where do we stand vis-à-vis the history Foucault tells? We are implicated by it, for the evolution of discipline as punishment into the study of the human mind includes the evolution of the "disciplines" as we now understand that word, including the discipline of history, the discipline of literary study, and now a discipline that is neither and both, a form of historical criticism that from the vantage point of the 1980s looked "new."

Foucault's type of analysis has been practiced by a number of literary critics at the vanguard of the back-to-history movement. One of them is Greenblatt, who along with Montrose was to a great extent responsible for transforming Renaissance studies in the early 1980s and revitalizing historical criticism in the process. Greenblatt follows Foucault's lead in interpreting literary devices as if they were continuous with all other representational devices in a culture; he therefore turns to scholars in other fields in order to better understand the workings of literature. "We wall off literary symbolism from the symbolic structures operative elsewhere," he writes, "as if art alone were a human creation, as if humans themselves were not, in Clifford Geertz's phrase, cultural artifacts" (*Renaissance* 4).

Greenblatt's name, more than anyone else's, is synonymous with the new historicism; his essay entitled "Invisible Bullets" (1981) has been said by Patrick Brantlinger to be "perhaps the most frequently cited example of New Historicist work" (45). An English professor at the University of California, Berkeley — the early academic home of the new historicism — Greenblatt was a founding editor of *Representations,* a journal published by the University of California Press that is still considered today to be *the* mouthpiece of the new historicism.

In *Learning to Curse* (1990), Greenblatt cites as central to his own intellectual development his decision to interrupt his literary education at Yale University by accepting a Fulbright fellowship to study in England at Cambridge University. There he came under the influence of the great Marxist cultural critic Raymond Williams, who made Greenblatt realize how much — and what — was missing from his Yale education. "In Williams' lectures," Greenblatt writes, "all that had been carefully excluded from the literary criticism in which I had been trained — who controlled access to the printing press, who owned the land and the factories, whose voices were being repressed as well as represented in literary texts, what social strategies were being served by the aesthetic values we constructed — came pressing back in upon the act of interpretation" (2).

Greenblatt returned to the United States determined not to exclude such matters from his own literary investigations. Blending what he had learned from Williams with poststructuralist thought about the indeterminacy or "undecidability" of meaning, he eventually developed a critical method that he now calls "cultural poetics." More tentative and less overtly political than cultural criticism, it involves what Thomas calls "the technique of montage. Starting with the analysis of a particular historical event, it cuts to the analysis of a particular literary text. The point is not to show that the literary text reflects the historical event but to create a field of energy between the two so that we come to see the event as a social text and the literary text as a social event" ("New Literary Historicism" 490). Alluding to deconstructor Jacques Derrida's assertion that "there is nothing outside the text," Montrose explains that the goal of this new historicist criticism is to show the "historicity of texts and the textuality of history" (Veeser 20).

The relationship between the cultural poetics practiced by a number of new historicists and the cultural criticism associated with Marxism is important, not only because of the proximity of the two approaches but also because one must recognize the difference between the two to understand the new historicism. Still very much a part of the contemporary critical scene, cultural criticism (sometimes called "cultural studies" or "cultural critique") nonetheless involves several tendencies more compatible with the old historicism than with the thinking of new historicists such as Greenblatt. These include the tendency to believe that history is driven by economics; that it is determinable even as it determines the lives of individuals; and that it is progressive, its dialectic one that will bring about justice and equality.

Greenblatt does not privilege economics in his analyses and views individuals as agents possessing considerable productive power. (He says that "the work of art is the product of a negotiation between a creator or class of creators . . . and the institutions and practices of a society" [*Learning* 158]: he also acknowledges that artistic productions are "intensely marked by the private obsessions of individuals," however much they may result from "collective negotiation and exchange" [*Negotiations* vii].) His optimism about the individual, however, should not be confused with optimism about either history's direction or any historian's capacity to foretell it. Like a work of art, a work of history is the negotiated product of a private creator and the public practices of a given society.

This does not mean that Greenblatt does not discern historical change, or that he is uninterested in describing it. Indeed, in works from *Renaissance Self-Fashioning* (1980) to *Shakespearean Negotiations* (1988), he has written about Renaissance changes in the development of both literary characters and real people. But his view of change — like his view of the individual — is more Foucauldian than Marxist. That is to say, it is not melioristic or teleological. And, like Foucault, Greenblatt is careful to point out that any one change is connected with a host of others, no one of which may simply be identified as cause or effect, progressive or regressive, repressive or enabling.

Not all of the critics trying to lead students of literature back to history are as Foucauldian as Greenblatt. Some even owe more to Marx than to Foucault. Others, like Thomas, have clearly been more influenced by Walter Benjamin, best known for essays such as "Theses on the Philosophy of History" and "The Work of Art in the Age of Mechanical Reproduction." Still others — McGann, for example — have followed the lead of Soviet critic M. M. Bakhtin, who viewed literary works in terms of discourses and dialogues between the official, legitimate voices of a society and other, more challenging or critical voices echoing popular or traditional culture. In the "polyphonic" writings of Rabelais, for instance, Bakhtin found that the profane language of Carnival and other popular festivals offsets and parodies the "legitimate" discourses representing the outlook of the king, church, and socially powerful intellectuals of the day.

Moreover, there are other reasons not to consider Foucault the single or even central influence on the new historicism. First, he critiqued the old-style historicism to such an extent that he ended up being antihistorical, or at least ahistorical, in the view of a number of new historicists. Second, his commitment to a radical remapping of the relations of power and influence, cause and effect, may have led him to adopt too cavalier an attitude toward chronology and facts. Finally, the very act of identifying and labeling *any* primary influence goes against the grain of the new historicism. Its practitioners have sought to "decenter" the study of literature, not only by overlapping it with historical studies (broadly defined to include anthropology and sociology) but also by struggling to see history from a decentered perspective. That struggle has involved recognizing (1) that the historian's cultural and historical position may not afford the best purview of a given set of events and (2) that events seldom have any single or central cause. In keeping with these principles, it may be appropriate to acknowledge Foucault as just one of several powerful, interactive intellectual forces rather than to declare him the single, master influence.

Throughout the 1980s it seemed to many that the ongoing debates about the sources of the new historicist movement, the importance of Marx or Foucault, Walter Benjamin or Mikhail Bakhtin, and the exact locations of all the complex boundaries between the new historicism and other "isms" (Marxism and poststructuralism, to name only two), were historically contingent functions of the new historicism *newness.* In the initial stages of their development, new intellectual movements are difficult to outline clearly because, like partially developed photographic images, they are themselves fuzzy and lacking in definition. They respond to disparate influences and include thinkers who represent a wide range of backgrounds; like movements that are disintegrating, they inevitably include a broad spectrum of opinions and positions. From the present vantage point, however, it seems that the inchoate quality of the new historicism is characteristic rather than a function of newness. The boundaries around the new historicism remain fuzzy, not because it hasn't reached its full maturity but because, if it is to live up to its name, it must always be subject to revision and redefinition as historical circumstances change. The fact that so many critics we label new historicist are working right at the border of Marxist, poststructuralist, cultural, postcolonial, feminist, and now even a new form of reader-response (or at least reader-oriented) criticism is evidence of the new historicism's multiple interests and motivations, rather than of its embryonic state.

New historicists themselves advocate and even stress the need to perpetually redefine categories and boundaries — whether they be disciplinary, generic, national, or racial — not because definitions are unimportant but because they are historically constructed and thus subject to revision. If new historicists like Thomas and reader-oriented critics like Steven Mailloux and Peter Rabinowitz seem to spend most of their time talking over the low wall separating their respective fields, then maybe the wall is in the wrong place. As Catherine Gallagher has suggested, the boundary between new historicists and feminists studying "people and phenomena that once seemed insignificant, indeed outside of history: women, criminals, the insane" often turns out to be shifting or even nonexistent (Veeser 43).

If the fact that new historicists all seem to be working on the border of another school should not be viewed as a symptom of the new historicism's newness (or disintegration), neither should it be viewed as evidence that new historicists are intellectual loners or divisive outriders who enjoy talking over walls to people in other fields but who share no common views among themselves. Greenblatt, McGann, and Thomas all started with the assumption that works of literature are simultaneously influenced by and influencing reality, broadly defined. Whatever their disagreements, they share a belief in referentiality — a belief that literature refers to and is referred to by things outside itself — stronger than that found in the works of formalist, poststructuralist, and even reader-response critics. They believe with Greenblatt that the "central concerns" of criticism "should prevent it from permanently sealing off one type of discourse from another or decisively separating works of art from the minds and lives of their creators and their audiences" (*Renaissance* 5).

McGann, in his introduction to *Historical Studies and Literary Criticism,* turns referentiality into a rallying cry:

> What will not be found in these essays . . . is the assumption, so common in text-centered studies of every type, that literary works are self-enclosed verbal constructs, or looped intertextual fields of autonomous signifiers and signifieds. In these essays, the question of referentiality is once again brought to the fore. (3)

In "Keats and the Historical Method in Literary Criticism," he suggests a set of basic, scholarly procedures to be followed by those who have rallied to the cry. These procedures, which he claims are "practical derivatives of the Bakhtin school," assume that historicist critics will study a literary work's "point of origin" by studying biography and bibliography. The critic must then consider the expressed intentions of the author, because, if printed, these intentions have also modified the developing history of the work. Next, the new historicist must learn the history of the work's reception, as that body of opinion has become part of the platform on which we are situated when we study the work at our own particular "point of reception." Finally, McGann urges the new historicist critic to point toward the future, toward his or her *own* audience, defining for its members the aims and limits of the critical project and injecting the analysis with a degree of self-consciousness that alone can give it credibility (*Inflections* 62).

In his introduction to a collection of new historical writings on *The New Historicism* (1989), H. Aram Veeser stresses the unity among new historicists, not by focusing on common critical procedures but, rather, by outlining five "key assumptions" that "continually reappear and bind together the avowed practitioners and even some of their critics":

1. that every expressive act is embedded in a network of material practices;
2. that every act of unmasking, critique, and opposition uses the tools it condemns and risks falling prey to the practice it exposes;
3. that literary and nonliterary texts circulate inseparably;
4. that no discourse, imaginative or archival, gives access to unchanging truths nor expresses inalterable human nature;
5. finally, . . . that a critical method and a language adequate to describe culture under capitalism participate in the economy they describe. (xi)

These same assumptions are shared by a group of historians practicing what is now commonly referred to as "the new cultural history."

Influenced by *Annales*-school historians in France, post-Althusserian Marxists, and Foucault, these historians share with their new historicist counterparts not only many of the same influences and assumptions but also the following: an interest in anthropological and sociological subjects and methods; a creative way of weaving stories and anecdotes about the past into revealing thick descriptions; a tendency to focus on nontraditional, noncanonical subjects and relations (historian Thomas Laqueur is best known for *Making Sex: Body and Gender from the Greeks to Freud* [1990]); and some of the same journals and projects.

Thus, in addition to being significantly unified by their own interests, assumptions, and procedures, new historicist literary critics have participated in a broader, interdisciplinary movement toward unification virtually unprecedented within and across academic disciplines. Their tendency to work along disciplinary borderlines, far from being evidence of their factious or fractious tendencies, has been precisely what has allowed them to engage historians in a conversation certain to revolutionize the way in which we understand the past, present, and future.

In the essay that follows, Casey Finch and Peter Bowen discuss the function of gossip, both in society in general and in Jane Austen's *Emma* in particular. Gossip, they argue, "binds communities together"; it tends to serve the community's "social agenda" and to provide a means of "surveillance and self-control" (p. 543). (For a different view of gossip in *Emma*, see Marilyn Butler's essay in the "Combining Perspectives" section of this volume, p. 597).

A discourse that "regulates the community *from within* by insinuation, rumor, threat of ostracism, and covert pressure," gossip is a "powerful form of authority because its source is nowhere and everywhere at once" (pp. 544–45). In *Emma,* gossip "exposes the uncomfortable secret that there really are no secrets." It travels fast because, to a great extent, its content "is already known; it is not news at all but part of a social agenda already recognized by the community" (p. 543). For instance, the news of Mr. Knightley's engagement to Emma spreads through the sizable village of Highbury within hours because of the extent to which their marriage was, in Finch and Bowen's view, "ideologically determined" and even "politically inevitable" (pp. 544, 543).

Austen, to be sure, does not present her gossipy women characters in a positive light; she both "genders" and "trivializes" gossip by — in Patricia Spacks's words — linking " 'loose talk with women' " (p. 545). But Austen also shows how gossip "disperse[s] and democratizes" authority, serving as a "genuinely alternative mode of communication for women, who have been historically excluded from dominant discourses" (p. 545). Furthermore, Austen chooses to tell her story in what is known as free indirect discourse, a style of writing in which a nameless, faceless, omniscient narrator tells readers what characters are thinking in their own terms and idioms. In adopting this kind of "narrative voice" — a voice "critics have rightly read as feminine" — Austen in a sense "authorizes" or affirms gossip, for "the very force of free indirect style is the force of gossip" (p. 545). After all, the business of publicizing people's innermost thoughts not only smacks of speculation but also involves spreading secrets of the most intimate kind.

Finch and Bowen subsequently turn their attention to Ian Watt's classic distinction between novels that represent the world objectively, from the outside via a third person narrator, and those that represent it subjectively, i.e., from the inside via a first-person narrator. (Following Watt, they see Austen as reconciling these antithetical modes by creating a "discreet narrator" who combines "editorial comment" with psychological representation [p. 547].) In addition to Watt's framework, however, they employ the theories of Bakhtin, who argued that discourse in the free indirect style comes off as an "utterance belonging to *someone else*," and yet, at the same time, as one "transposed into an authorial context." On this theoretical base, they build an argument that, with *Emma*, Austen turned gossip into a "model of social authority that both naturalizes and authenticates the new novelistic authority of free indirect discourse." In other words, to the extent that Austen can justify gossip by showing that its supposedly "inside" secrets are really reflections of social truths and values predominant or emerging in the "outside" world, she can suggest that her narrative style of rendering the consciousness of characters is not a form of useless voyeurism but rather — to put it in the language of Michel Foucault — one instance of the system of surveillance by which a society represents and regulates itself.

In Austen's world, that system inevitably involves questions of gender and, especially, class; as Finch and Bowen put it, "the interest a community takes in its members, specifically in mapping their identities along the axes of class and gender, transforms private matters . . . into matters of public scrutiny" (p. 551). For instance, Frank Churchill proves "worthy" of community gossip, even though he has never set foot in Highbury, because he is the prized son of Mr. Weston. Class distinctions also determine the extent to which an individual uses — and is represented by — indirect discourse. Emma, whose family is of even greater consequence in the village, uses the free indirect style to give silent expression to what she imagines others are saying about her. In other words, Emma "sees herself . . . through the gossip of her neighbors," especially insofar as she "secretly imagines the community gossip that scrutinizes her" (p. 552). Calling the novel's narrative a "narrative house of mirrors," a "collapsing structure" in which one member of the represented community can "anticipate" as well as "echo" the "voices of the community, while the community, in turn, continually violates the privacy of its members," Finch and Bowen argue that "the free indirect style reflects finally a mechanics of power by which the disciplinary agenda of a community is internalized as the private wishes of the individual."

Toward the end of their provocative essay on community gossip, a novelistic style appropriate to its representation, and the way in which societies and novelists regulate behavior, Finch and Bowen bring all these subjects together in a revealing discussion of Emma's "moment of *recognition*" (p. 553). Having long believed herself to understand the secret wishes of others — and having attempted to arrange their destinies accordingly — Emma experiences a "moment of epiphanic self-revelation" in which she comes to see that she has been vain and manipulative. But "the moment . . . she subordinates her own perspective to that of the community," Finch and Bowen argue, turns out to be the same moment in which "the novel itself can realize its own manipulations" (p. 553). Putting this another way: just when "the individual," Emma, "is brought into alignment with social imperatives," she is also brought into alignment with the novel's movement toward closure. "At the very moment" Emma, the character, "attempts to renounce matchmaking" (defined by Finch and Bowen as the result of a "desire at once to unleash stories and to close them"), *Emma*, the novel, "has made its most glorious match" (p. 555).

Finch and Bowen's essay on *Emma* exemplifies the new historicist approach to literature in any number of ways. For one thing, they approach Austen in terms of historically determined but malleable ideologies regarding gender and class, and they approach *Emma* in terms of the history of the novel — a history of evolving novelistic styles. More interested in the novel's mode of narration than in its plot structure, their essay further breaks down distinctions between literature and history by erasing the boundary between the way in which societies tell their stories on one hand (thereby representing their priorities and regulating their members) and the way in which novelists tell their stories on the other. The concept of regulating narrations or discourses, of styles of speaking in which the "mechanics of power" are constituted, owes much to the work of Foucault, one of the thinkers who has most influenced new historicist criticism. At the same time, Finch and Bowen show an awareness of Marxist thought. They employ Antonio Gramsci's concept of *hegemony* (a given society's pervasive system of assumptions, meanings, and values) to help define the way in which communities, though extensions of private selves, can overwhelm individual acts of resistance. And they employ Bakhtin's understanding of the way discourses, and in particular free indirect discourse, function within texts in what Clifford Geertz might call their "thick description" of the way in which gossip functions in *Emma*.

Ross C Murfin

THE NEW HISTORICISM:
A SELECTED BIBLIOGRAPHY

The New Historicism: Further Reading

Brantlinger, Patrick. "Cultural Studies vs. the New Historicism." *English Studies/Cultural Studies: Institutionalizing Dissent.* Ed. Isaiah Smithson and Nancy Ruff. Urbana: U of Illinois P, 1994. 43–58.

Cox, Jeffrey N., and Larry J. Reynolds, eds. *New Historical Literary Study.* Princeton: Princeton UP, 1993.

Dimock, Wai-chee. "Feminism, New Historicism, and the Reader." *American Literature* 63 (1991): 601–22.

Gallagher, Catherine, and Stephen Greenblatt. *Practicing New Historicism.* Chicago: U of Chicago P, 2000.

Howard, Jean. "The New Historicism in Renaissance Studies." *English Literary Renaissance* 16 (1986): 13–43.

Lindenberger, Herbert. *The History in Literature: On Value, Genre, Institutions.* New York: Columbia UP, 1990.

———. "Toward a New History in Literary Study." *Profession: Selected Articles from the Bulletins of the Association of Departments of English and the Association of the Departments of Foreign Languages.* New York: MLA, 1984. 16–23.

Liu, Alan. "The Power of Formalism: The New Historicism." *English Literary History* 56 (1989): 721–71.

McGann, Jerome. *The Beauty of Inflections: Literary Investigations in Historical Method and Theory.* Oxford: Clarendon, 1985.

————. *Historical Studies and Literary Criticism*. Madison: U of Wisconsin P, 1985. See especially the introduction and the essays in the following sections. "Historical Methods and Literary Interpretations" and "Biographical Contexts and the Critical Object."

Montrose, Louis Adrian. "Renaissance Literary Studies and the Subject of History." *English Literary Renaissance* 16 (1986): 5–12.

Morris, Wesley. *Toward a New Historicism*. Princeton: Princeton UP, 1972.

New Literary History 21 (1990). "History and . . ." (special issue). See especially the essays by Carolyn Porter, Rena Fraden, Clifford Geertz, and Renato Rosaldo.

Representations. This quarterly journal, printed by the University of California Press, regularly publishes new historicist studies and cultural criticism.

Thomas, Brook. "The Historical Necessity for — and Difficulties with — New Historical Analysis in Introductory Courses." *College English* 49 (1987): 509–22.

————. *The New Historicism and Other Old-Fashioned Topics*. Princeton: Princeton UP, 1991.

————. "The New Literary Historicism." *A Companion to American Thought*. Ed. Richard Wightman Fox and James T. Klappenberg. New York: Basil Blackwell, 1995.

————. "Walter Benn Michaels and the New Historicism: Where's the Difference?" *Boundary* 2.18 (1991): 118–59.

Veeser, H. Aram, ed. *The New Historicism*. New York: Routledge, 1989. See especially Veeser's introduction, Louise Montrose's "Professing the Renaissance," Catherine Gallagher's "Marxism and the New Historicism," and Frank Lentricchia's "Foucault's Legacy: A New Historicism?"

Wayne, Don E. "Power, Politics and the Shakespearean Text: Recent Criticism in England and the United States." *Shakespeare Reproduced: The Text in History and Ideology*. Ed. Jean Howard and Marion O'Connor. New York: Methuen, 1987. 47–67.

Winn, James A. "An Old Historian Looks at the New Historicism." *Comparative Studies in Society and History* 35 (1993): 859–70.

The New Historicism: Influential Examples

The new historicism has taken its present form less through the elaboration of basic theoretical postulates and more through certain influential examples. The works listed represent some of the most important contributions guiding research in this area.

Bercovitch, Sacvan. *The Rites of Assent: Transformations in the Symbolic Construction of America.* New York: Routledge, 1993.

Brown, Gillian. *Domestic Individualism: Imagining Self in Nineteenth-Century America.* Berkeley: U of California P, 1990.

Dollimore, Jonathan. *Radical Tragedy: Religion, Ideology and Power in the Drama of Shakespeare and His Contemporaries.* Brighton: Harvester, 1984.

Dollimore, Jonathan, and Alan Sinfield, eds. *Political Shakespeare: New Essays in Cultural Materialism.* Manchester: Manchester UP, 1985. This volume occupies the borderline between new historicist and cultural criticism. See especially the essays by Dollimore, Greenblatt, and Tennenhouse.

Gallagher, Catherine. *The Industrial Reformation of English Fiction.* Chicago: U of Chicago P, 1985.

Goldberg, Jonathan. *James I and the Politics of Literature.* Baltimore· Johns Hopkins UP, 1983.

Greenblatt, Stephen J. *Learning to Curse: Essays in Early Modern Culture.* New York: Routledge, 1990.

———. *Marvelous Possessions: The Wonder of the New World.* Chicago U of Chicago P, 1991.

———. *Renaissance Self-Fashioning from More to Shakespeare.* Chicago: U of Chicago P, 1980. See chapter 1 and the chapter on *Othello* titled "The Improvisation of Power."

———. *Shakespearean Negotiations: The Circulation of Social Energy in Renaissance England.* Berkeley: U of California P, 1988. See especially "The Circulation of Social Energy" and "Invisible Bullets."

Liu, Alan. *Wordsworth, the Sense of History.* Stanford: Stanford UP, 1989.

Marcus, Leah. *Puzzling Shakespeare: Local Reading and Its Discontents.* Berkeley: U of California P, 1988.

McGann, Jerome. *The Romantic Ideology.* Chicago: U of Chicago P, 1983.

Michaels, Walter Benn. *The Gold Standard and the Logic of Naturalism: American Literature at the Turn of the Century.* Berkeley: U of California P, 1987.

Montrose, Louis Adrian. " 'Shaping Fantasies': Figurations of Gender and Power in Elizabethan Culture." *Representations* 2 (1983): 61–94. One of the most influential early new historicist essays.

Mullaney, Steven. *The Place of the Stage: License, Play, and Power in Renaissance England*. Chicago: U of Chicago P, 1987.

Orgel, Stephen. *The Illusion of Power: Political Theater in the English Renaissance*. Berkeley: U of California P, 1975.

Sinfield, Alan. *Literature, Politics, and Culture in Postwar Britain*. Berkeley: U of California P, 1989.

Tennenhouse, Leonard. *Power on Display: The Politics of Shakespeare's Genres*. New York: Methuen, 1986.

Foucault and His Influence

As I point out in the introduction to the new historicism, some new historicists would question the "privileging" of Foucault implicit in this section heading ("Foucault and His Influence") and the following one ("Other Writers and Works"). They might cite the greater importance of one of those other writers or point out that to cite a central influence or a definitive cause runs against the very spirit of the movement.

Dreyfus, Hubert L., and Paul Rabinow. *Michel Foucault: Beyond Structuralism and Hermeneutics*. Chicago: U of Chicago P, 1983.

Foucault, Michel. *The Archaeology of Knowledge*. Trans. A. M. Sheridan Smith. New York: Harper, 1972.

———. *Discipline and Punish: The Birth of the Prison*. 1975. Trans. Alan Sheridan. New York: Pantheon, 1978.

———. *The History of Sexuality*. Trans. Robert Hurley. Vol. 1. New York: Pantheon, 1978.

———. *Language, Counter-Memory, Practice*. Ed. Donald F. Bouchard. Trans. Donald F. Bouchard and Sherry Simon. Ithaca: Cornell UP, 1977.

———. *The Order of Things: An Archaeology of the Human Sciences*. New York: Vintage, 1973.

———. *Politics, Philosophy, Culture*. Ed. Lawrence D. Kritzman. Trans. Alan Sheridan et al. New York: Routledge, 1988.

———. *Power/Knowledge*. Ed. Colin Gordon. Trans. Colin Gordon et al. New York: Pantheon, 1980.

———. *Technologies of the Self*. Ed. Luther H. Martin, Huck Gutman, and Patrick H. Hutton. Amherst: U of Massachusetts P, 1988.

Sheridan, Alan. *Michel Foucault: The Will to Truth*. New York: Tavistock, 1980.

Smart, Barry. *Michel Foucault*. New York: Travistock, 1985.

Other Writers and Works of Interest to New Historicist Critics

Bakhtin, M. M. *The Dialogic Imagination: Four Essays.* Ed. Michael Holquist. Trans. Caryl Emerson. Austin: U of Texas P, 1981. Bakhtin wrote many influential studies on subjects as varied as Dostoyevsky, Rabelais, and formalist criticism. But this book, in part due to Holquist's helpful introduction, is probably the best place to begin reading Bakhtin.

Benjamin, Walter. "The Work of Art in the Age of Mechanical Reproduction." 1936. *Illuminations.* Ed. Hannah Arendt. Trans. Harry Zohn. New York: Harcourt, 1968.

Fried, Michael. *Absorption and Theatricality: Painting and Beholder in the Works of Diderot.* Berkeley: U of California P, 1980.

Geertz, Clifford. *The Interpretation of Cultures.* New York: Basic, 1973.

———. *Negara: The Theatre State in Nineteenth-Century Bali.* Princeton: Princeton UP, 1980.

Goffman, Erving. *Frame Analysis.* New York: Harper, 1974.

Jameson, Fredric. *The Political Unconscious.* Ithaca: Cornell UP, 1981.

Koselleck, Reinhart. *Futures Past.* Trans. Keith Tribe. Cambridge: MIT P, 1985.

Said, Edward. *Orientalism.* New York: Columbia UP, 1978.

Turner, Victor. *The Ritual Process: Structure and Anti-Structure.* Chicago: Aldine, 1969.

Young, Robert. *White Mythologies: Writing History and the West.* New York: Routledge, 1990.

New Historicist Criticism Relating to *Emma*

Armstrong, Nancy. *Desire and Domestic Fiction: A Political History of the Novel.* New York: Oxford UP, 1987.

Dussinger, John. *In the Pride of the Moment: Encounters in Jane Austen.* Columbus: Ohio UP, 1990.

Ferguson, Frances. "Jane Austen, *Emma,* and the Impact of Form." *Modern Language Quarterly* 61.1 (2000): 157–80.

Galperin, William, ed. *Re-Reading Box Hill: Reading the Practices of Reading Everyday Life.* College Park: U of Maryland P, 2000.

Gordon, Jan B. "A-filiative Families and Subversive Reproduction: Gossip in Jane Austen." *Genre* 21.1 (1988): 5–46.

Miller, D. A. "The Late Jane Austen." *Raritan* 10 (Summer 1990): 55–79.

Poovey, Mary. *The Proper Lady and the Woman Writer: Ideology as Style in the Works of Mary Wollstonecraft, Mary Shelley, and Jane Austen.* Chicago: U of Chicago P, 1984.

A NEW HISTORICIST PERSPECTIVE

CASEY FINCH AND PETER BOWEN

"The Tittle-Tattle of Highbury": Gossip and the Free Indirect Style in *Emma*

Toward the end of *Emma,* when the news of Emma and Mr. Knightley's engagement is out, it spreads in a kind of chain reaction from Mr. Weston to Jane Fairfax,

> and Miss Bates being present, it passed, of course, to Mrs. Cole, Mrs. Perry, and Mrs. Elton, immediately afterwards. It was no more than the principals were prepared for; they had calculated from the time of its being known at Randalls, how soon it would be over Highbury; and were thinking of themselves, as the evening wonder in many a family circle, with great sagacity. (p. 369 in this volume)

It is as though this "large and populous village" (p. 25) somehow had telephone connections; within hours, indeed by sunset, the news of the forthcoming marriage is on everybody's lips. But the ability of this gossip to travel at lightning speed is only partially Austen's comment upon the smallness of the community and the idleness of its members. It is also her articulation of the mechanisms by which gossip binds communities together under a mild system of surveillance and self-control. Gossip travels fast because in a sense it is always already known; it is not news at all but part of a social agenda already recognized by the community and already unconsciously internalized by what Jane Austen — underscoring the theatricality of gossip — calls the "principals" of the marriage plot.

For the engagement of Emma Woodhouse of Hartfield and George Knightley of Donwell Abbey is by no means a "wonder," as the lovers indulgently imagine, but the politically inevitable fulfillment of the most vigorously enforced social and novelistic expectations. It is, as Austen's exact diction underscores, neither an aberration nor a convenient device for closing an otherwise unmanageable plot but an instantly recognizable "sagacity," an aspect of universal wisdom. Indeed, it is so ideologically determined and coded-in-advance that an hour is all that is required for Mr. Weston to turn the "surprise" into a recognition of the deeply familiar:

> The news was universally a surprise wherever it spread; and Mr. Weston had his five minutes share of it; but five minutes were enough to familiarize the idea to his quickness of mind. — He saw the advantages of the match, and rejoiced in them with all the constancy of his wife; but the wonder of it was very soon nothing; and by the end of an hour he was not far from believing that he had always foreseen it.
> "It is to be a secret, I conclude," said he. "These matters are always a secret, till it is found out that every body knows them." (p. 369)

Emma's engagement to Mr. Knightley constitutes a "secret" that is no secret, a surprise that is not one, precisely because it marks the moment when the inevitable is realized, when the subject is brought into perfect correspondence with the imperatives of its social environment, when the heart is lodged properly in the hearth. The very stuff of Austen's comedic vision always involves such a moment of supreme ideological triumph when political constructions are naturalized and therefore rendered invisible as such: the vicissitudes of the plot reach shimmering resolution; the characters are properly aligned along undamaged social hierarchies; the economic imperative is brought to bear on the very structure of desire.

In *Emma* gossip operates as the mechanism by which this comedic alignment of public and private spheres is enacted. As Max Gluckman suggests in his study "Gossip and Scandal," a community is "held together and maintains its values by gossiping both within cliques and in general" (308). Gossip marks an oblique mode of control, a socio-discursive practice that both defines the community of its participants — solidifying, as Patricia Spacks has it, "a group's sense of itself by heightening consciousness of 'outside' . . . and 'inside'" (5) — and regulates the community *from within* by insinuation, rumor, threat of ostracism, and covert pressure. Rather than operating through overt acts of force imposed from without upon its subjects, gossip coerces by being irresistibly assumed by its subjects, taken up and passed on in an endless system of circulation. Gossip thus naturalizes authority over the home by bringing the home under the purview of the public or, rather, by diffusing itself amongst all homes, where its power is irresistible because it seems to have no fixed, absolutely visible source. Itself never identifiably authorized — who, after all, is ever the originator of a rumor? — gossip functions as a powerful form of authority because its source is nowhere and everywhere at once. Within the novel, gossip ceases to be a matter of this or that piece of "tittle-tattle" (p. 62), this or that idle speculation, and becomes instead the very ground upon which the community is articulated, identified, and controlled.

But if gossip in *Emma* tends to operate as a hidden form of authority, at the same time the novel's gossips are often perfectly visible, and still more often visibly female. At once inheriting and renegotiating a vast tradition that links, in Spacks's words, "loose talk with women" (41), *Emma* simultaneously trivializes gossip as feminine and authorizes such discourse through the mobilization of a narrative voice that critics have rightly read as feminine. And though gossip in *Emma* never quite operates, as Jan B. Gordon argues, as an idiom potentially subversive of patriarchal authority, it nevertheless serves as a genuinely alternative mode of communication for women, who have been historically excluded from dominant discourses; in one and the same movement, gossip is dismissed as feminine "tittle-tattle" and put to use as a serious and privileged form of knowledge. The "feminine" idiom thus mobilized operates again and again, however, to reinforce what Gordon rightly calls "a recuperative, paternal authority" (40). Thrown surprisingly into relief, then, is the phenomenon of a conventionally female mode operating ultimately to reinforce patriarchal norms concerned, among other things, to trivialize gossip.

If gossip forms a mild system of surveillance and social control over the citizens of Highbury (naturalizing and "feminizing" the voice of authority by subtly disseminating it into a chattering cacophony of voices), then equally the novel's deployment of free indirect style (which Austen first brought to fruition) has the effect of naturalizing narrative authority by disseminating it among the characters. Just as the "harmless gossip" (p. 35) narrated in *Emma* forms part of a larger historical trajectory in which overt control over subjects is reformulated as a covert authority evenly spread among and within subjects, so the development in Austen's hands of free indirect style marks a crucial moment in the history of novelistic technique in which narrative authority is seemingly elided. The very force of free indirect style is the force of gossip. Both function as forms par excellence of surveillance,

and both serve ultimately to locate the subject — characterological or
political — within a seemingly benign but ultimately coercive narrative
or social matrix.

Specifically what, within *Emma*, is the relation between gossip and
the free indirect style? Within the novel's general atmospherics, the narrator maintains a mildly judgmental attitude toward the pettiness of
Highbury gossip; yet when specific differences arise among the characters, the anonymous narrator again and again sides not with the individual but with the vague chorus of gossip that permeates the community.
Ultimately, the feminine, gossipy, and supposedly low insinuations of
Highbury's small talk anticipate the high patriarchal truths the novel is
concerned to put into place with the very free indirect style that gossip
deploys. How, then, is the operation of this newly wrought narrative
technology upon the novelistic character part of the larger operation of
gossip upon the psychological subject? If, as John Bender suggests, free
indirect style creates for the reader an "illusion of entry into the consciousness of fictional characters" (177), does gossip similarly create for
a public a means of entry into the privacy of its members? Through gossip do we advance not only the community's secrets but also the community's secret mechanisms of control? How does gossip constitute a
community through a class-inflected system of exclusions and inclu-
sions, banishing some citizens even as it naturalizes others? How does
gossip as a traditionally female practice engender *Emma*'s otherwise
anonymous narrator and authorize the narrative's authority? What, in
short, is the novel's "grammar of gossip" (Spacks 165)?

It will be helpful, we think, to recall here Ian Watt's placement of
Austen within his schematization of two fundamental narrative modali-
ties of the eighteenth-century novel. Watt discerns, on the one hand, a
narrative strategy based on a Cartesian epistemology — and embodied,
for instance, in Defoe and Richardson — in which emphasis is placed
on the psychological condition of the subject, and in which the
"author" is formally absent. Novels in this tradition tend to assume
epistolary or pseudoautobiographical forms in which "the reader is
absorbed into the subjective consciousness of one or more of the characters" (296): what we know of their world can never be anything more
than what they know and tell us. And there is, on the other hand, the
narrative strategy — perhaps most perfectly embodied in Fielding —
that takes a "realistic," external approach to character, and in which the
intrusive, omniscient narrator suggests an objective, universal understanding that creates and assesses its world by the fixed, eternal standards of human nature" (296).

For Watt, Austen reconciles these antithetical modes by creating a "discreet" narrator who gives us not only the "editorial comment" of the social, omniscient author but also "much of Defoe's and Richardson's psychological closeness to the subjective world of the characters." The two modes are fused; Austen owes "her eminence in the tradition of the English novel" to the fact that she "was able to combine into a harmonious unity the advantages both of . . . the internal and of the external approaches to character" (296–97). Though Watt fails to note the term, he refers here to the free indirect style, the hybridized narrative mode first designated in French by Charles Bally in his 1912 essay "Le Style indirect libre en français moderne I et II," then in German by Etienne Lorck in his 1921 book *Die 'Erlebte Rede': Eine sprachliche Untersuchung*, and finally in Russian by V. N. Voloshinov/Mikhail Bakhtin in the 1930 *Marxism and the Philosophy of Language*.[1] Indeed, the free indirect style that Austen brought so skillfully to completion — "the technique," as Dorrit Cohn defines it, "for rendering a character's thoughts in his own idiom while maintaining the third-person reference and the basic tense of narration" (100) — marks a reconfiguration of "internal" and "external" approaches to character.

Paradoxically, the free indirect style enables the representation of a seemingly private, independent subject — able to speak his or her own mind at any time — even as it guarantees public access to any character's private thoughts. Indeed, the dual nature of each character's interiority — at once perfectly private and absolutely open to public scrutiny — is ensured by the unnameable and unlocatable nature of the narrator's voice. It is by thus keeping secret the source of community concern — for we can never know precisely who speaks in the free indirect style — that the novel makes public the private thoughts of individual characters.

Yet if for Watt this new epistemological reconciliation of the eighteenth-century "subjective" and "objective" narrative modes seems to alleviate a certain anxiety about how to narrate a world, that anxiety does not entirely disappear from Austen's novels (and from the free indirect style in general). For while Austen abandons the overtly participating narrator of, say, *Tom Jones* as well as the equally overt epistolary writers of, for instance, *Clarissa*, what is most strikingly absent from a novel like *Emma* is the explicit identification of the narration's source

---

[1]See Hamburger, Banfield, Bender, and Vološinov. Though the author of *Marxism and the Philosophy of Language* is given as V. N. Vološinov, we adopt the hybrid "Voloshinov/Bakhtin" to indicate Bakhtin's considerable role in the creation of the work, first published in Russian in Leningrad in 1930.

and purpose. The narrator of *Emma* is not simply unidentified; she is also, like any gossiper, to some degree uncertain of the very source of her information: "Emma Woodhouse, handsome, clever, and rich, with a comfortable home and happy disposition, *seemed* to unite some of the best blessings of existence; and had lived nearly twenty-one years in the world with very little to distress or vex her" (p. 23; emphasis added). *Emma* begins, then, not so much with a factual assertion as with a hermeneutic problem: to whom did Emma "seem" to unite these qualities?

In Austen's eighteenth-century predecessors, the source of authority is implicitly supplied by the narrative strategy. In the "subjective" novel, the perceiver's identity, and therefore the narrative source of knowledge, is obviously announced by the name of the first-person narrator. And in the "objective" novel, the narrator provides the source of authority by functioning as a kind of master of ceremonies and therefore as the master of the novel's truth. But in Austen no such explicitly articulated authority operates; we experience instead what Watt calls "some august and impersonal spirit of social and psychological understanding" (297) and what Alistair M. Duckworth identifies as the "oratio obliqua of the narrative discourse" (162). Traditionally, this dispersed spirit of "understanding" — this floating locus of authority — has been defined by Austen critics as irony, but the notion of irony remains strangely unhelpful. We still do not know precisely the relation of the presumably female narrator to the collectivity of gossiping characters to whom Emma seems "to unite some of the best blessings of existence." Just as there remains throughout the novel a distance between the "august and impersonal" narrator and the characters themselves, so there remains an equal distance between that narrator and her information.

Emma Woodhouse *seemed* to unite some of the best blessings of existence. To be sure, this opinion comes ultimately from the community that has observed and assessed her, a community of which the narrator may or may not be a member, but which, at any rate, she presumes to represent. But at the same time, since the absolute source of authority is elided, the narrator's knowledge cannot be equated with the community's (which, indeed, is often satirized). The narrator thus acts from the start merely as a *mediator of* privileged communal opinions, as a kind of spokesperson for her community, in short as a gossip who spreads the opinions of certain citizens about others. A new modality that reconciles the eighteenth-century novelistic antinomies, free indirect style locates narrative authority neither explicitly in the "subjective" psychological perspective of an individual nor implicitly in the "objective" law of human nature. Instead, free indirect style operates by hiding, by being neither here nor there, by functioning not as a topos of power but as a dispersed atmospherics of narrative authority. *Like* the free indirect style — but not *as* it — gossip in Highbury derives its power neither from the opinion of a single individual nor from the dictates of an identifiable institution — the police, the law courts — but from the collectivity of voices that whisper about neighbors in private rooms and across gateways. Just as the free indirect style *of* the novel functions as a form of narrative surveillance over the novel's characters, so gossip *in* the novel deploys a mild surveillance over the members of the Highbury community. Through covert insinuation rather than overt pressure, gossip delineates a circle of consensual values. Beyond this circle, and therefore excluded entirely from the purview of gossip, are those whose interactions cannot significantly affect the mechanisms of social exchange and economic production operative in the "community" thus delineated. Interestingly, then, gossip links by exclusion such otherwise incompatible citizens as, for instance, the invisible liveryman who drives the carriage containing Mr. Elton and Emma from the dinner party at Randalls, on the one hand, and Mrs. Bragge, who, according to Mrs. Elton, "moves in the first circle" of Maple Grove, on the other (pp. 242–43). For just as Mrs. Bragge's properties and activities, important as they are to Maple Grove, lie too far outside the social economy of Highbury to be of interest, so the personal lives of the working classes lie too far below the immediate interest of the community's property owners to merit notice. In *Emma*, we might call this the first of gossip's two fundamental mechanisms: it constitutes a community by separating who is and who is not crucial to whatever economic (and marital) exchanges are at stake within the novel's representations. Gossip's second fundamental mechanism concerns the establishment of a "naturally" enforced hierarchy, *within* its circle of inclusion, by which certain citizens are privileged over others. Gossip, after all, enacts and reinforces not only subtle gradations of class between such landless but eligible women as Jane Fairfax and Harriet Smith or such patriarchs as Mr. Woodhouse and Mr. Elton but also specific gender inequalities between such characters of nearly equal rank as Emma and Mr. Knightley.[2]

---

[2] Robert Martin supplies a nuanced and, for Emma, unsettling example of someone whose hard work and courtship of Harriet have brought him to the very brink of social recognition. Situated on the troubling threshold between the inconsequential and the unavoidable, he must be rendered invisible by Emma's exclusionary logic. See her speech to Harriet, beginning: "The yeomanry are precisely the order of people with whom I feel I can have nothing to do" (p. 42).

In telling the story of Emma, the novel inevitably also narrates the
story of Highbury, the civic drama of suspicious glances, mysterious
gifts, and annoying newcomers. The relation between these two stories
is entangled and obscured in the novel's description of Emma's home
and her community: "Highbury, the large and populous village almost
amounting to a town, to which Hartfield, *in spite of its separate lawn
and shrubberies and name, did really belong,* afforded her no equals"
(p. 25, emphasis added). Paradoxically both adjacent to and contained
within its village, Emma's home is encompassed by and (through the
enormous weight of its civic importance) encompasses the community.
This zoning paradox is perhaps no less than the narrative paradox of the
free indirect style. For the operations of this new narrative technology
have two curious consequences. On the one hand, the independence of
the novel's subjects is both ensured and violated by the articulation of
their private thoughts in the public space of the novel. And on the
other, the public opinion that continually constricts, controls, and,
in the end, becomes the private thoughts of individuals is itself guaranteed privacy, if only by the anonymous nature of the narrator who re-
peats it. "Somebody said . . ." (p. 203); "Somebody else believed . . ."
(p. 203); "There was a strange rumour in Highbury . . ." (p. 34) —
what is interesting about such phrases is not simply the lengths the narrator has gone to to preserve the confidentiality of her sources, but that
these anonymous comments, in many ways, serve as their own sources;
they signify a community of interest. While anyone could say these
things, only individuals with knowledge and a vested interest in Highbury in fact would.

Thus in the relation between the novel's two stories (the story of
Emma told through Highbury, and the story of Highbury told through
Emma), the articulated private thoughts that mark Emma's interiority
find their equivalent in the anonymous public voices that represent
Highbury society. This is not to say that the novel does not clearly
assign actual names, words, and thoughts to certain citizens but rather
that the abstract notion of a community of consensus — as opposed to
a genuine heterogeneity — resides in the unassigned opinions that circulate through the novel in the form of gossip. Gossip, operating as a
mode of community authority, thus comes to represent the community
itself. By acting as a gauge of community interest, gossip maps out the
community's circumference with Emma at the center, liminal characters at the borders, and more impoverished or irrelevant characters
nearly outside the scope of representation altogether.

And since those characters on the threshold of a community are, as Victor Turner suggests, "necessarily ambiguous," existing "betwixt and between the positions assigned and arrayed by law, custom, convention, and ceremonial" (95), their introduction to Highbury (and to the story itself) brings both civil hospitality and community circumspection. When the name of Mrs. Elton, née Hawkins, enters the community of Highbury, for example, less than a week passed "before she was . . . discovered to have every recommendation of person and mind" (p. 154). But while the name preceding the body in the circulation of gossip is thus welcomed, the actual person receives a more thorough examination: "Mrs. Elton was first seen at church: but though devotion might be interrupted, curiosity could not be satisfied by a bride in a pew, and it must be left for the visits in form which were then to be paid, to settle whether she were very pretty indeed, or only rather pretty, or not pretty at all" (p. 219). Here, the carefully managed passive voice has a curious effect. For the question of agency is rendered as unclear as it is perfectly comprehensible; while the precise villagers who compose Mrs. Elton's welcoming committee are left unnamed, we rightly understand them to represent the community at large, a community whose interests here concern the criterion, crucial to the patriarchally enforced marriage system the novel represents, of female attractiveness.

The interest a community takes in its members, specifically in mapping their identities along the axes of class and gender, transforms private matters of citizens and families, men and women, into matters of public scrutiny and sentiment. The paternal pride that Mr. Weston takes in his (absent) son, Frank Churchill, "naturally" becomes an instance of community pride: Mr. Weston's "fond report of him as a very fine young man had made Highbury feel a sort of pride in him too." Thus, Frank Churchill's status as a favored son of a prominent Highbury citizen (and as an eligible bachelor) is enough to make him "one of the boasts of Highbury" and a source of "common concern" (p. 32). As in Mrs. Elton's case, word of Frank Churchill precedes the entrance of his person into Highbury. But unlike the reception that attends Mrs. Elton, gossip here concerns itself with the propriety of his words rather than the appearance of his body. Frank's "highly-prized letter" written to his new mother becomes quite literally the talk of the town: "For a few days every morning visit in Highbury included some mention of the handsome letter Mrs. Weston had received" (pp. 32–33).

Highbury's adoption of individual citizens' concerns marks how deeply private acts and family correspondence are inscribed within community affairs. In fact, the principle of gossip provocatively questions the very nature of private business or, rather, the business of privacy. While the free indirect stylist blurs the narrative distinctions between objective and subjective discourse, she blurs too the proprietary difference between communities and individuals. For if the power of the community is enforced and represented by voices that seem to be everywhere and nowhere at once, the voice of the individual, the community's most private property, is represented in publicly circulating letters and interior monologues that somebody, although it is never clear who, overhears. Consider Mr. Knightley's celebrated censure of Emma for her inconsiderate comment to Miss Bates at the Box Hill party. As Mr. Knightley says, not only has Emma insulted a woman who has seen her "grow up from a period where her notice was an honour"; still more egregiously, Emma's words were heard by "others, many of whom (certainly *some*,) would be entirely guided by [Emma's] treatment of her" (p. 300). But this is really no news to Emma, who knows that she is continually being scrutinized and discussed by the community around her. She is aware, for instance, that her playful conversation with Frank Churchill

> must have had such an appearance as no English word but flirtation could very well describe. "Mr. Frank Churchill and Miss Woodhouse flirted together excessively." They were laying themselves open to that very phrase — and to having it sent off in a letter to Maple Grove by one lady, to Ireland by another. (p. 294)

Although she imagines being talked about as far away as Ireland, the force of such gossip is enhanced by the fact that Emma, in a sense, herself initiates it. Beyond simply locating the perfect "English word," Emma constructs an entire sentence to be passed on in the gossip of letters and neighborly chats. So far from being oblivious to the effect of her actions upon others, Emma sees herself completely through the gossip of her neighbors. If gossip secretly imagines the private life of others, Emma herself, at the very center of this economy of "tittletattle," secretly imagines the community gossip that scrutinizes her. What concerns Emma concerns Highbury; what involves the subject involves as well the social context by which it is inscribed — such is the very force and truth of gossip. And the compulsion by which characters in the novel concern themselves with the words and lives of others echoes the very mode of the free indirect style, a technique in which the authority and existence of the narrator derive from the fact that she reveals everyone's thoughts but her own. In *Emma,* narrative authority is neither dismissed altogether nor enacted, as Watt suggests, simply by conflating the two dominant eighteenth-century modes of narration: instead, like gossip, it operates as a general space of surveillance and knowledge.

Emma's crucial realization — tellingly rendered in free indirect style — that "with insufferable vanity had she believed herself in the secret of everybody's feelings; with unpardonable arrogance proposed to arrange everybody's destiny" (pp. 327–28) marks the moment when she subordinates her own perspective to that of the community. At the same time, though, it describes the very narrative technique of *Emma*. For even as the novelist is able to "arrange everybody's destiny," the free indirect style allows her not only the illusion of access to "everybody's feelings" but the more ideologically significant illusion of the private, autonomous subject violable by gossip and narrative technique alike. *Emma*'s agenda is clear: the heroine must renounce her manipulative tendencies so that the novel itself can realize its own manipulations.

Thus Emma's self-realization, like the news of her engagement to Mr. Knightley, constitutes a surprise that is not really a surprise at all but the acceptance of a social (and novelistic) imperative that she has already unconsciously internalized:

> A few minutes were sufficient for making her acquainted with her own heart. A mind like her's, once opening to suspicion, made rapid progress. . . . Why was it so much worse that Harriet should be in love with Mr. Knightley, than with Frank Churchill? . . . It darted through her, with the speed of an arrow, that Mr. Knightley must marry no one but herself! (p. 324)

Although Emma here believes herself to be experiencing a "clearness which had never blessed her before" (p. 324), a truth of the body that enters violently from the outside "with the speed of an arrow," her epiphany in fact marks merely an uncanny moment of *recognition:* the moment when the individual is brought into alignment with social imperatives. And the moment is therefore only seemingly dramatic; really, it is no more surprising to us than it is, upon retrospection, to Emma herself:

> How long had Mr. Knightley been so dear to her, as every feeling declared him now to be? When had his influence, such influence begun? — When had he succeeded to that place in her affection, which Frank Churchill had once, for a short period, occupied? . . . She saw that there never had been a time when she did not

consider Mr. Knightley as infinitely the superior. . . . She saw, that in persuading herself, in fancying, in acting to the contrary, she had been entirely under a delusion, totally ignorant of her own heart — and, in short, that she had never really cared for Frank Churchill at all! (p. 327)

The truth of Emma's character is obscured even as it is clarified. For if this revelation makes her "acquainted with her own heart," it does so precisely by revealing to her how "totally ignorant of her own heart" she had been until now. Free indirect style has here literally created the space of the unconscious as the natural source of Emma's inner desires, which, naturally enough, now discover themselves perfectly aligned with the overriding social imperative the novel has been at pains to establish from the start: "Mr. Knightley must marry no one but herself!"

At the level of the novel's *plot*, gossip frankly reveals the subject's "secrets," which, upon revelation, turn out to be universally known, overdetermined, and as Mr. Knightley likes his neighbors to be — public and open. But the novel's *narration* operates more covertly; the free indirect style leaves both the subject and the community seemingly autonomous of one another even as it insists on their correspondence. As the modern narrative technique par excellence, free indirect style, like gossip, has thus a dual function. On the one hand, it reveals (and constitutes) the subject as a function of public pressures even as that subject is articulated as an inviolable *autonomy* never absolutely enthralled by its social environment.[3] And, on the other, it reveals (and constitutes) the community as an extension of the private, individual character of any of its members even as that community is articulated as a hegemony impervious to any resistance a subject might wish to make.

Yet we know, for instance, from the very first narrative strokes of *Emma* that the public knowledge of gossip and the private secrets of the heart can never fail to interpenetrate, to reinforce one another. The inside and the outside; the private and the public; the subject's inner desire and political necessity — these must necessarily reach ideological as well as narrative correspondence. In the novel, these "naturally" harmonious polarities are most forcefully embodied, of course, in the ultimate marriage of Emma and Mr. Knightley, which marks the climactic moment of political, narratological, and sexual *necessity*. And if, while the story unfolds, we agree as readers temporarily to suspend our fore-

---

[3]See D. A. Miller. Our essay is greatly indebted to the spirit of Miller's work.

knowledge of such impulsions, temporarily to resist the "natural" affinities of Emma and Mr. Knightley, of the private and public realms, this complicity reveals our desire at once to postpone the inscription of the subject by its social context *and* to facilitate it. We might even call this complicity the narrative impulse within us. To the extent that we enjoy delaying the moment when the subject and its social context — as it were, Emma and Mr. Knightley — are absolutely aligned, we enjoy, too, the tensions of the story and the illusion of the autonomous self; but to the extent that we facilitate the (inevitable) moment of alignment, we enjoy the pleasure of closure, the harmonious reconciliation of self to society.

In Emma herself this dual impulse takes the form of matchmaking, an activity that marks her desire at once to unleash stories and to close them. And it is Emma's matchmaking, of course, that leads her to the series of blunders over which so many Austen critics are fond of moralizing. But while critics — along with Mr. Knightley — chastise Emma, few remember at the same time that the novel itself is unashamedly in the business of matchmaking. Few remember that at the very moment when Emma attempts to renounce matchmaking *Emma* has made its most glorious match.[4] And when Emma renounces her tendency thus to manipulate others, foregoing her pretensions to penetrate into "everybody's feelings" (p. 327), she renounces at the same time her tendency, like gossip's, to penetrate the lives of others and to transform them into narrative. When at the beginning of the novel Mr. Knightley chastises Emma for meddling in the affairs of Miss Taylor and Mr. Weston, his point, of course, is well taken; or rather, by the *end* of the novel, we are made to feel how "natural" and "just" his position is. For Emma is an uneven novelist at best. She tends to lose control of her characters' destinies, and she is just as likely to botch a marriage plot as to bring one to successful conclusion. It is, after all, to the public, anonymous narrator of *Emma* that the privilege of absolute manipulation belongs. And, indeed, the novel as a whole performs the very tasks for which it reproaches its main character. If Emma herself resists marriage and meddles, instead, in making marriages for others, the novel is sure to humiliate her for her matchmaking and to install her — despite

---

[4]Though Emma upbraids herself for attempting to "arrange every body's destiny," she renews her scheming when the Westons have a daughter: "She had been decided in wishing for a Miss Weston. She would not acknowledge that it was with any view of making a match for her, hereafter, with either of Isabella's sons; but she was convinced that a daughter would suit both father and mother best" (p. 363).

her initial objections — within a marriage whose recommendations are unexceptionable.

And after all, the match between herself and Mr. Knightley is imperative; as Mrs. Weston ruminates: "It was in every respect so proper, suitable, and unexceptionable a connexion, and in one respect, one point of the highest importance, so peculiarly eligible, so singularly fortunate, that now it seemed as if Emma could not safely have attached herself to any other creature" (p. 368). In this passage, free indirect style functions specifically to disguise the ideological imperatives of the novel as the autonomous ideation of one of its characters. The authority for approving good marriages — marriages in which landed families are untainted by the "stain of illegitimacy" (p. 379) — is naturalized and made to seem as though it issued from a subject wholly free and autonomous. And though Mrs. Elton, for instance, may begrudge the match of Emma and Mr. Knightley, her thoughts, as they are reproduced in the free indirect style, turn out to be limited and inconsequential. The free indirect style may well recognize certain resistances to the novel's political impulsions, but it will always do so in order to render them palpably illegitimate; for while this new narrative technology seems to reveal a democracy of independent and differing opinions, individuals' thoughts are finally judged against the overriding social imperatives. When, for example, Emma realizes that "Mr. Knightley must marry no one but herself" (p. 324), we recall that this revelation echoes and reverses her earlier desire that "Mr. Knightley must never marry" at all (p. 188), a command that marks her concern (really the entire novel's concern) for the larger problem of family inheritance.

Concomitantly, the community is construed as the outcome of the natural desires of its individual citizens. Through "the perfect happiness of the union" embodied in Emma's marriage to Mr. Knightley (as well as the other marriages consecrated at the novel's end), "the wishes, the hopes, the confidence, the predictions of the small band of true friends who witnessed the ceremony, were fully answered" (p. 381). Here, in its last sentence, the novel articulates the norms of the community — the rules according to which a farmer, like Robert Martin, must marry a tradesman's daughter, like Harriet Smith, and according to which George Knightley of Donwell Abbey must marry Emma Woodhouse of Hartfield — as the natural realization of its citizens' desires. For though it is but a "small band of true friends who witnessed the ceremony," it operates both as a synecdoche and as a metonymy of the community as a whole, a community at once heterogeneous (since it gathers within its scope, for instance, both Harriet Smith and Mr.

Knightley) and monolithic (since resistances to its impulsions are neu-
tralized by the novel's end).

What has been enacted is a new and formidable technology of
truth. In the passage on Miss Taylor's wedding to Mr. Weston, for
instance, the joke on Mr. Woodhouse is that he obtusely refuses to
believe what is indisputably true. The finicky Mr. Woodhouse hoped to
dissuade the gathering from eating the wedding cake, and to this end
he had secured the opinion of Mr. Perry, the apothecary who reluc-
tantly "could not but acknowledge, (though it seemed rather against
the bias of inclination,) that wedding-cake might certainly disagree
with many — perhaps with most people, unless taken moderately"
(p. 34). In order to align public tastes with his own, Mr. Woodhouse
must mask his private opinions in the guise of medical authority; he
must reinforce his personal whims with impersonal — here scientific —
truths. "But still," we are told, "the cake was eaten." And what is more,
it was eaten by the Perry children themselves: "There was a strange
rumour in Highbury of all the little Perrys being seen with a slice of
Mrs. Weston's wedding-cake in their hands: but Mr. Woodhouse would
never believe it" (p. 34). What this novel of rumors clearly satirizes here
is not simply Mr. Woodhouse's feeble attempts to justify his private
idiosyncrasies by recourse to public (medical) authority but his in-
credulity toward the authority of rumor itself, his refusal to accept what
must clearly be true. Here the truth of the invisible narrator (located literally nowhere) and the truth of Highbury gossip (located absolutely
everywhere) are completely aligned. Almost total authority — a near
epistemological hegemony — is staged and enacted because its agency
is either elided altogether or spread so thinly that it cannot ever be
named as such. Ultimately, the irresistible force of public opinion
expresses itself by anonymity, by an authority that is everywhere apparent but whose source is nowhere to be found.

WORKS CITED

Banfield, Ann. *Unspeakable Sentences: Narration and Representation
in the Language of Fiction*. Boston: Routledge, 1982.

Bender, John. *Imagining the Penitentiary: Fiction and the Architecture
of Mind in Eighteenth-Century England*. Chicago: U of Chicago P,
1987.

Cohn, Dorrit. *Transparent Minds: Narrative Modes for Presenting
Consciousness in Fiction*. Princeton: Princeton UP, 1978.

Duckworth, Alistair M. *The Improvement of the Estate: A Study of Jane Austen's Novels.* 1971. Baltimore: Johns Hopkins UP, 1994.

Gordon, Jan B. "A-filiative Families and Subversive Reproduction: Gossip in Jane Austen." *Genre* 21.1 (1988): 5–46.

Gluckman, Max. "Gossip and Scandal." *Current Anthropology* 4.3 (1963): 307–16.

Hamburger, Käte. *The Logic of Literature.* Trans. Marilynn J. Rose. 2nd ed. Bloomington: Indiana UP, 1973.

Miller, D. A. "Secret Subjects, Open Secrets." *The Novel and the Police.* Berkeley: U of California P, 1988.

Spacks, Patricia Meyer. *Gossip.* New York: Knopf, 1985.

Turner, Victor. *The Ritual Process: Structure and Anti-Structure.* Chicago: Aldine, 1969.

Vološinov, V. N. *Marxism and the Philosophy of Language.* 1973. Trans. Ladislaw Matejka and I. R. Titunik. Cambridge, MA: Harvard UP, 1986.

Watt, Ian. *The Rise of the Novel.* Berkeley: U of California P, 1957.

Feminist Criticism
and
Emma

WHAT IS FEMINIST CRITICISM?

Feminist criticism comes in many forms, and feminist critics have a variety of goals. Some have been interested in rediscovering the works of women writers overlooked by a masculine-dominated culture. Others have revisited books by male authors and reviewed them from a woman's point of view to understand how they both reflect and shape the attitudes that have held women back. A number of contemporary feminists have turned to topics as various as women in postcolonial societies, women's autobiographical writings, lesbians and literature, womanliness as masquerade, and the role of film and other popular media in the construction of the feminine gender.

Until a few years ago, however, feminist thought tended to be classified not according to topic but, rather, according to country of origin. This practice reflected the fact that, during the 1970s and early 1980s, French, American, and British feminists wrote from somewhat different perspectives.

French feminists tended to focus their attention on language, analyzing the ways in which meaning is produced. They concluded that language as we commonly think of it is a decidedly male realm. Drawing on the ideas of the psychoanalytic philosopher Jacques Lacan, they reminded us that language is a realm of public discourse. A child enters the linguistic realm just as it comes to grasp its separateness from its mother, just about the time that boys identify with their father, the family representative of culture. The language learned reflects a binary logic that opposes such terms as active/passive, masculine/feminine, sun/moon, father/mother, head/heart, son/daughter, intelligent/sensitive, brother/sister, form/matter, phallus/vagina, reason/emotion. Because this logic tends to group with masculinity such qualities as light, thought, and activity, French feminists said that the structure of language is phallocentric: it privileges the phallus and, more generally, masculinity by associating them with things and values more appreciated by the (masculine-dominated) culture. Moreover, French feminists suggested, "masculine desire dominates speech and posits woman as an idealized fantasy-fulfillment for the incurable emotional lack caused by separation from the mother" (Jones, "Inscribing" 83).

French feminists associated language with separation from the mother. Its distinctions, they argued, represent the world from the male point of view. Language systematically forces women to choose: either they can imagine and represent themselves as men imagine and represent them (in which case they may speak, but will speak as men) or they can choose "silence," becoming in the process "the invisible and unheard sex" (Jones, "Inscribing" 83).

But some influential French feminists maintained that language only *seems* to give women such a narrow range of choices. There is another possibility, namely, that women can develop a *feminine* language. In various ways, early French feminists such as Annie Leclerc, Xavière Gauthier, and Marguerite Duras suggested that there is something that may be called *l'écriture féminine:* women's writing. More recently, Julia Kristeva has said that feminine language is "semiotic," not "symbolic." Rather than rigidly opposing and ranking elements of reality, rather than symbolizing one thing but not another in terms of a third, feminine language is rhythmic and unifying. If from the male perspective it seems fluid to the point of being chaotic, that is a fault of the male perspective.

According to Kristeva, feminine language is derived from the pre-oedipal period of fusion between mother and child. Associated with the maternal, feminine language is not only a threat to culture, which is patriarchal, but also a medium through which women may be creative in new ways. But Kristeva paired her central, liberating claim — that truly feminist innovation in all fields requires an understanding of the relation between maternity and feminine creation — with a warning. A feminist language that refuses to participate in "masculine" discourse, that places its future entirely in a feminine, semiotic discourse, risks being politically marginalized by men. That is to say, it risks being relegated to the outskirts (pun intended) of what is considered socially and politically significant.

Kristeva, who associated feminine writing with the female body, was joined in her views by other leading French feminists. Hélène Cixous, for instance, also posited an essential connection between the woman's body, whose sexual pleasure has been repressed and denied expression, and women's writing. "Write your self. Your body must be heard," Cixous urged; once they learn to write their bodies, women will not only realize their sexuality but enter history and move toward a future based on a "feminine" economy of giving rather than the "masculine" economy of hoarding (Cixous 880). For Luce Irigaray, women's sexual pleasure (jouissance) cannot be expressed by the dominant, ordered, "logical," masculine language. Irigaray explored the connection between women's sexuality and women's language through the following analogy: as women's jouissance is more multiple than men's unitary, phallic pleasure ("woman has sex organs just about everywhere"), so "feminine" language is more diffusive than its "masculine" counterpart. ("That is undoubtedly the reason . . . her language . . . goes off in all directions and . . . he is unable to discern the coherence," Irigaray writes [This Sex 101–03].)

Cixous's and Irigaray's emphasis on feminine writing as an expression of the female body drew criticism from other French feminists. Many argued that an emphasis on the body either reduces "the feminine" to a biological essence or elevates it in a way that shifts the valuation of masculine and feminine but retains the binary categories. For Christine Fauré, Irigaray's celebration of women's difference failed to address the issue of masculine dominance, and a Marxist-feminist, Catherine Clément, warned that "poetic" descriptions of what constitutes the feminine will not challenge that dominance in the realm of production. The boys will still make the toys, and decide who gets to use them. In her effort to redefine women as political rather than as sexual beings, Monique Wittig called for the abolition of the sexual categories that Cixous and Irigaray retained and revalued as they celebrated women's writing.

American feminist critics of the 1970s and early 1980s shared with French critics both an interest in and a cautious distrust of the concept of feminine writing. Annette Kolodny, for instance, worried that the "richness and variety of women's writing" will be missed if we see in it only its "feminine mode" or "style" ("Some Notes" 78). And yet Kolodny herself proceeded, in the same essay, to point out that women *have* had their own style, which includes reflexive constructions ("she found herself crying") and particular, recurring themes (clothing and self-fashioning are mentioned by Kolodny; other American feminists have focused on madness, disease, and the demonic).

Interested as they became in the "French" subject of feminine style, American feminist critics began by analyzing literary texts rather than philosophizing abstractly about language. Many reviewed the great works by male writers, embarking on a revisionist rereading of literary tradition. These critics examined the portrayals of women characters, exposing the patriarchal ideology implicit in such works and showing how clearly this tradition of systematic masculine dominance is inscribed in our literary tradition. Kate Millett, Carolyn Heilbrun, and Judith Fetterley, among many others, created this model for American feminist criticism, a model that Elaine Showalter came to call "the feminist critique" of "male-constructed literary history" ("Poetics" 128).

Meanwhile another group of critics including Sandra Gilbert, Susan Gubar, Patricia Meyer Spacks, and Showalter herself created a somewhat different model. Whereas feminists writing "feminist critique" analyzed works by men, practitioners of what Showalter used to refer to as "gynocriticism" studied the writings of those women who, against all odds, produced what she calls "a literature of their own." In *The Female Imagination* (1975), Spacks examined the female literary tradition to find out how great women writers across the ages have felt, perceived themselves, and imagined reality. Gilbert and Gubar, in *The Madwoman in the Attic* (1979), concerned themselves with well-known women writers of the nineteenth century, but they too found that general concerns, images, and themes recur, because the authors that they wrote about lived "in a culture whose fundamental definitions of literary authority" were "both overtly and covertly patriarchal" (45–46).

If one of the purposes of gynocriticism was to (re)study well-known women authors, another was to rediscover women's history and culture, particularly women's communities that nurtured female creativity. Still another related purpose was to discover neglected or forgotten women writers and thus to forge an alternative literary tradition, a canon that better represents the female perspective by better representing the literary works that have been written by women. Showalter, in

A Literature of Their Own (1977), admirably began to fulfill this purpose, providing a remarkably comprehensive overview of women's writing through three of its phases. She defined these as the "Feminine, Feminist, and Female" phases, phases during which women first imitated a masculine tradition (1840–80), then protested against its standards and values (1880–1920), and finally advocated their own autonomous, female perspective (1920 to the present).

With the recovery of a body of women's texts, attention returned to a question raised in 1978 by Lillian Robinson: Shouldn't feminist criticism need to formulate a theory of its own practice? Won't reliance on theoretical assumptions, categories, and strategies developed by men and associated with nonfeminist schools of thought prevent feminism from being accepted as equivalent to these other critical discourses? Not all American feminists came to believe that a special or unifying theory of feminist practice was urgently needed; Showalter's historical approach to women's culture allowed a feminist critic to use theories based on nonfeminist disciplines. Kolodny advocated a "playful pluralism" that encompasses a variety of critical schools and methods. But Jane Marcus and others responded that if feminists adopt too wide a range of approaches, they may relax the tensions between feminists and the educational establishment necessary for political activism.

The question of whether feminism weakens or fortifies itself by emphasizing its separateness — and by developing unity through separateness — was one of several areas of debate within American feminism during the 1970s and early 1980s. Another area of disagreement touched on earlier, between feminists who stress universal feminine attributes (the feminine imagination, feminine writing) and those who focus on the political conditions experienced by certain groups of women at certain times in history, paralleled a larger distinction between American feminist critics and their British counterparts.

While it gradually became customary to refer to an Anglo-American tradition of feminist criticism, British feminists tended to distinguish themselves from what they saw as an American overemphasis on texts linking women across boundaries and decades and an underemphasis on popular art and culture. They regarded their own critical practice as more political than that of North American feminists, whom they sometimes faulted for being uninterested in historical detail. They joined such American critics as Myra Jehlen in suggesting that a continuing preoccupation with women writers may bring about the dangerous result of placing women's texts outside the history that conditions them.

British feminists felt that the American opposition to male stereo-types that denigrate women often leads to counterstereotypes of femi-nine virtue that ignore real differences of race, class, and culture among women. In addition, they argued that American celebrations of individ-ual heroines falsely suggest that powerful individuals may be immune to repressive conditions and may even imply that *any* individual can go through life unconditioned by the culture and ideology in which she or he lives.

Similarly, the American endeavor to recover women's history — for example, by emphasizing that women developed their own strategies to gain power within their sphere — was seen by British feminists like Judith Newton and Deborah Rosenfelt as an endeavor that "mystifies" male oppression, disguising it as something that has created for women a special world of opportunities. More important from the British standpoint, the universalizing and "essentializing" tendencies in both American practice and French theory disguise women's oppression by highlighting sexual difference, suggesting that a dominant system is impervious to political change. By contrast, British feminist theory emphasized an engagement with historical process in order to promote social change.

By now the French, American, and British approaches have so thor-oughly critiqued, influenced, and assimilated one another that the work of most Western practitioners is no longer easily identifiable along national boundary lines. Instead, it tends to be characterized according to whether the category of *woman* is the major focus in the exploration of gender and gender oppression or, alternatively, whether the interest in sexual difference encompasses an interest in other differences that also define identity. The latter paradigm encompasses the work of femi-nists of color, Third World (preferably called postcolonial) feminists, and lesbian feminists, many of whom have asked whether the universal category of woman constructed by certain French and North American predecessors is appropriate to describe women in minority groups or non-Western cultures.

These feminists stress that, while all women are female, they are something else as well (such as African American, lesbian, Muslim Pak-istani). This "something else" is precisely what makes them, their prob-lems, and their goals different from those of other women. As Armit Wilson has pointed out, Asian women living in Britain are expected by their families and communities to preserve Asian cultural traditions;

thus, the expression of personal identity through clothing involves a much more serious infraction of cultural rules than it does for a Western woman. Gloria Anzaldúa has spoken personally and eloquently about the experience of many women on the margins of Eurocentric North American culture. "I am a border woman," she writes in *Borderlands: La Frontera = The New Mestiza* (1987). "I grew up between two cultures, the Mexican (with a heavy Indian influence) and the Anglo. . . . Living on the borders and in margins, keeping intact one's shifting and multiple identity and integrity is like trying to swim in a new element, an 'alien' element" (i).

Instead of being divisive and isolating, this evolution of feminism into femin*isms* has fostered a more inclusive, global perspective. The era of recovering women's texts — especially texts by white Western women — has been succeeded by a new era in which the goal is to recover entire cultures of women. Two important figures of this new era are Trinh T. Minh-ha and Gayatri Spivak. Spivak, in works such as *In Other Worlds: Essays in Cultural Politics* (1987) and *Outside in the Teaching Machine* (1993), has shown how political independence (generally looked upon by metropolitan Westerners as a simple and beneficial historical and political reversal) has complex implications for "subaltern" or subproletarian women.

The understanding of woman not as a single, deterministic category but rather as the nexus of diverse experiences has led some white, Western, "majority" feminists like Jane Tompkins and Nancy K. Miller to advocate and practice "personal" or "autobiographical" criticism. Once reluctant to inject themselves into their analyses for fear of being labeled idiosyncratic, impressionistic, and subjective by men, some feminists are now openly skeptical of the claims to reason, logic, and objectivity that have been made in the past by male critics. With the advent of more personal feminist critical styles has come a powerful new interest in women's autobiographical writings.

Shari Benstock, who has written personal criticism in her book *Textualizing the Feminine* (1991), was one of the first feminists to argue that traditional autobiography is a gendered, "masculinist" genre. Its established conventions, feminists have recently pointed out, call for a life-plot that turns on action, triumph through conflict, intellectual self-discovery, and often public renown. The body, reproduction, children, and intimate interpersonal relationships are generally well in the background and often absent. Arguing that the lived experiences of women and men differ — women's lives, for instance, are often characterized by interruption and deferral — Leigh Gilmore has developed a theory of women's self-representation in her book *Autobiographics: A Feminist Theory of Self-Representation* (1994).

Autobiographics and personal criticism are only two of a number of recent developments in contemporary feminist criticism. Others alluded to in the first paragraph of this introduction — lesbian studies, performance or "masquerade" theory, and studies of the role played by film and various other "technologies" in shaping gender today — are so prominent in contemporary *gender* criticism that they are discussed in a separate introduction (see "What Is Gender Criticism?" pp. 425–40 in this volume). Although that introduction will outline several of the differences between the feminist and gender approaches, the fact of this overlap should remind us that categories obscure similarities even as they help us make distinctions. Feminist criticism is, after all, a form of gender criticism, and gender criticism as we have come to know it could never have developed without feminist criticism.

Devoney Looser begins the essay that follows by asking "Is Jane Austen a feminist?" She proceeds by asserting that the "answer depends not only on how one understands her novels but also how one defines feminism." If feminism is primarily concerned with "how women are limited and devalued within a culture," then Austen — and *Emma* — can indeed be said to be feminist (p. 577). In proceeding to demonstrate Austen's concern with the limitations on and devaluation of women, Looser shows how *Emma* explores the potential of a countervailing force: what its protagonist refers to as "the duty of woman by woman" (p. 191) but also women's friendships and, more generally, what Looser calls "equitable relationships among women" (p. 579).

In reflecting on women's relationships with one another, the novel considers those "companionate relationships" involving a "wealthier mistress" and her "humble companion," who "was usually single and economically dependent, descended from a gentleman whose fortune had turned or was apportioned to an eldest son." The companion — a woman such as Harriet Smith — "entertained or assisted her wealthier mistress, performing unpaid and nonmenial tasks. The companion served as a confidante or offered a hand at cards. In return, the mistress-employer introduced the companion into 'good' society and provided requisite leisure activities" (p. 580).

Unfortunately, the relationship between mistress and companion sometimes mirrored that between husband and wife (which, in

Austen's time, commonly involved the exercise of autocratic power by the former over the latter). For example, "Emma uses her prerogative as a patroness to assume masculine and powerful roles over Miss Taylor and Harriet" (pp. 580–81). (For a different view of Emma's abuse of her power over other women see Beth Fowkes Tobin's "Aiding Impoverished Gentlewomen" ["What Is Marxist Criticism?" pp. 473–87]). Austen's novel, Looser goes on to argue, "functions as a critique" of this sort of "female/female paternalism, exposing in the process the exploitable structure of companionate relationships; it reveals the ways powerful women wield influence over fellow females, by uncovering" the "mistakes" made by its protagonist and by other insensitive characters, especially Mrs. Elton (p. 581). Thus, while *Emma* may not go so far as to reject male/female paternalism, it certainly does reject it as a model of relationships between women.

Responding to the charge by some feminists that Austen endorsed class distinctions — and that *Emma* ultimately fails "to envisage a female community across social barriers" — Looser admits that Austen "steers a course between the protofeminist community imagined by Mary Astell (1666–1731) and the conservative female paternalism offered by Hannah More (1745–1833)," not to mention by the highly restrictive conduct manuals of Austen's day (p. 582). But, she insists,

> *Emma*'s implicit criticisms of both revolutionary and conservative female philosophies place [the novel] in the liberal feminist category. . . . Accepting much of the political and economic structure around her, Austen seeks to shift the ways women function within it. In *Emma*, she chooses not to represent sisterhood within or across social levels, but she exposes the hypocrisy and potential damage of hierarchical female/female paternalism. (p. 582)

To show the gap between Austen's "liberal feminism" and the radicalism of a Mary Astell, Looser discusses a work of fiction influenced by Astell's ideas: Sarah Scott's *Millenium Hall* (1762), about a "female utopia in which single upper-class women choose to live together and perform charitable works" (pp. 582–83). Austen's novels, in contrast, suggest that women living without men would "not *necessarily* treat other women any better than men would" (p. 583). Her women characters, Looser argues, are fully "capable of profound cruelty toward one another," and her "novels illustrate with painstaking detail the ways that unscrupulous women compete in a society configured to advance the legal and economic interests of men." Indeed, they may be at their most feminist in revealing "the limits of women's alliances with each other in a patriarchal culture," for, in doing so, they "also imply more positive possibilities of relationships for women" (p. 583).

To show the gap between Austen's liberal feminism and the "conservative female paternalism" of a Hannah More, Looser contrasts *Emma* with More's novel *Coelebs in Search of a Wife* (1808), which "follows its eponymous, worthy, and priggish hero [Coelebs] as he searches for the right woman, ruling out one after another for flaws of various kinds" (p. 584). (In comparing Austen's novel with More's, Looser remarks that *Emma* "could be retitled *Emma in Search of Husbands for Other Women* or *Emma Not in Search of a Husband* [p. 584].) Looser then contrasts More's patronage of a working-class poet, Ann Yearsley, with Emma's patronage of Harriet Smith. Yearsley came to resent More, who "believed strongly that class hierarchy reflected a natural and divine order" (p. 585) and who, though she may have helped Yearsley improve as a poet, also controlled the money her protégée earned, doling it out as she saw fit to her and to her children.

Austen's Emma and her protégée Harriet, Looser argues, "appear headed for a Hannah More/Ann Yearsley-like clash" insofar as "Emma's belief that she can control Harriet Smith's rise parallels More's approach to Yearsley" (p. 586). But in the last analysis — as a result of Emma's evolving understanding of "the duty of woman by woman" and the replacement of Emma by the Martin sisters as equitable patron-companions — a potentially destructive, control-based conflict and crisis is avoided. Thus Hannah More's destructive patronage relationship with Ann Yearsley, in Looser's view, ends up being more comparable to Mrs. Elton's patronage of Jane Fairfax than to the Emma-Harriet relationship.

Looser's approach to Austen's *Emma* is an example of contemporary feminist criticism that has clear antecedents in the early examples discussed in this introduction. Its focus on women writers, relationships between such writers and communities of women, and the role played by those relationships and communities in the development of "women's literature" owes an obvious debt to so-called gynocriticism. But the author's interest in woman-woman patronage, its similarity to husband-wife relationships, and, therefore, the way in which "female/female paternalism" can and did mirror patriarchal oppression is entirely contemporary.

Positioning herself at the boundary between feminist and gender criticism (whose practitioners would argue that oppressive dominance is no more "essentially" masculine than nurturing is feminine), Looser also proves herself a contemporary feminist through the interest she takes in economic relationships, "nonliterary" documents (e.g., conduct manuals), and changing cultural practices (involving patronage but also friendship). "The Duty of Woman by Woman" thus reflects the need contemporary feminists feel to frame their arguments in terms of issues and contexts the boundaries of which might narrowly be viewed as woman-centered economic relationships (e.g., the one between Hannah More and Ann Yearsley) but that in fact define human relationships across time — relationships that are still evolving today.

Ross C Murfin

FEMINIST CRITICISM: A SELECTED BIBLIOGRAPHY

French Feminist Theory

Cixous, Hélène. "The Laugh of the Medusa." Trans. Keith Cohen and Paula Cohen. *Signs* 1 (1976): 875–94.

Cixous, Hélène, and Catherine Clément. *The Newly Born Woman*. Trans. Betsy Wing. Minneapolis: U of Minnesota P, 1986.

Feminist Readings: French Texts/American Contexts. Spec. issue of *Yale French Studies* 62 (1981).

French Feminist Theory. Spec. issue of *Signs* 7.1 (1981).

Irigaray, Luce. *An Ethics of Sexual Difference*. Trans. Carolyn Burke and Gillian C. Gill. Ithaca: Cornell UP, 1993.

———. *This Sex Which Is Not One*. Trans. Catherine Porter. Ithaca: Cornell UP, 1985.

Jardine, Alice A. *Gynesis: Configurations of Woman and Modernity*. Ithaca: Cornell UP, 1985.

Jenson, Deborah, ed. *"Coming to Writing" and Other Essays* (essays by Hélène Cixous). Trans. Sarah Cornell. Cambridge: Harvard UP, 1991.

Jones, Ann Rosalind. "Inscribing Femininity: French Theories of the Feminine." *Making a Difference: Feminist Literary Criticism*. Ed. Gayle Green and Coppélia Kahn. London: Methuen, 1985. 80–112.

———. "Writing the Body: Toward an Understanding of *L'Écriture féminine*." Showalter, *New Feminist Criticism* 361–77.

Kristeva, Julia. *Desire in Language: A Semiotic Approach to Literature and Art*. Ed. Leon S. Roudiez. Trans. Thomas Gora, Alice Jardine, and Leon S. Roudiez. New York: Columbia UP, 1980.

Marks, Elaine, and Isabelle de Courtivron, eds. *New French Feminisms: An Anthology.* Amherst: U of Massachusetts P, 1980.

Moi, Toril, ed. *French Feminist Thought: A Reader.* Oxford: Basil Blackwell, 1987.

Spivak, Gayatri Chakravorty. "French Feminism in an International Frame." *Yale French Studies* 62 (1981): 154–84.

Stanton, Donna C. "Language and Revolution: The Franco-American Dis-Connection." *The Future of Difference.* Ed. Hester Eisenstein and Alice Jardine. Boston: G. K. Hall, 1980. 73–87.

Wittig, Monique. *Les Guérillères.* 1969. Trans. David Le Vay. New York: Avon, 1973.

Feminist Theory: Classic Texts, General Approaches, Collections

Abel, Elizabeth, and Emily K. Abel, eds. *The "Signs" Reader: Women, Gender, and Scholarship.* Chicago: U of Chicago P, 1983.

Barrett, Michèle, and Anne Phillips. *Destabilizing Theory: Contemporary Feminist Debates.* Stanford: Stanford UP, 1992.

Beauvoir, Simone de. *The Second Sex.* 1949. Trans. and ed. H. M. Parshley. New York: Vintage, 1974.

Benstock, Shari, ed. *Feminist Issues in Literary Scholarship.* Bloomington: Indiana UP, 1987.

de Lauretis, Teresa, ed. *Feminist Studies/Critical Studies.* Bloomington: Indiana UP, 1986.

Fetterley, Judith. *The Resisting Reader: A Feminist Approach to American Fiction.* Bloomington: Indiana UP, 1978.

Fuss, Diana. *Essentially Speaking: Feminism, Nature and Difference.* New York: Routledge, 1989.

Gallop, Jane. *Around 1981: Academic Feminist Critical Theory.* New York: Routledge, 1992.

Greer, Germaine. *The Female Eunuch.* New York: McGraw, 1971.

Herndl, Diana Price, and Robyn Warhol, eds. *Feminisms: An Anthology of Literary Theory and Criticism.* New Brunswick: Rutgers UP, 1991.

hooks, bell. *Feminist Theory: From Margin to Center.* Boston: South End, 1984.

Keohane, Nannerl O., Michelle Z. Rosaldo, and Barbara C. Gelpi, eds. *Feminist Theory: A Critique of Ideology.* Chicago: U of Chicago P, 1982.

Kolodny, Annette. "Dancing Through the Minefield: Some Observations on the Theory, Practice, and Politics of a Feminist Literary Criticism." Showalter, *New Feminist Criticism* 144–67.

———. "Some Notes on Defining a 'Feminist Literary Criticism.'" *Critical Inquiry* 2 (1975): 75–92.

Lovell, Terry, ed. *British Feminist Thought: A Reader.* Oxford: Basil Blackwell, 1990.

Malson, Micheline, et al., eds. *Feminist Theory in Practice and Process.* Chicago: U of Chicago P, 1986.

Meese, Elizabeth. *Crossing the Double-Cross: The Practice of Feminist Criticism.* Chapel Hill: U of North Carolina P, 1986.

Millett, Kate. *Sexual Politics.* Garden City: Doubleday, 1970.

Rich, Adrienne. *On Lies, Secrets, and Silence: Selected Prose, 1966–1979.* New York: Norton, 1979.

Showalter, Elaine, ed. *The New Feminist Criticism: Essays on Women, Literature, and Theory.* New York: Pantheon, 1985.

———. "Toward a Feminist Poetics." *The New Feminist Criticism* 125–43.

———. "Women's Time, Women's Space: Writing the History of Feminist Criticism." *Tulsa Studies in Women's Literature* 3 (1984): 29–43. Rpt. in Benstock, *Feminist Issues in Literary Scholarship.* 30–44.

Stimpson, Catherine R. "Feminist Criticism." *Redrawing the Boundaries: The Transformation of English and American Literary Studies.* Ed. Stephen Greenblatt and Giles Gunn. New York: MLA, 1992. 251–70.

———. *Where the Meanings Are: Feminism and Cultural Spaces.* New York: Methuen, 1988.

Weed, Elizabeth, ed. *Coming to Terms: Feminism, Theory, Politics.* New York: Routledge, 1989.

Woolf, Virginia. *A Room of One's Own.* New York: Harcourt, 1929.

Women's Writing and Creativity

Abel, Elizabeth, ed. *Writing and Sexual Difference.* Chicago: U of Chicago P, 1982.

Abel, Elizabeth, Marianne Hirsch, and Elizabeth Langland, eds. *The Voyage In: Fictions of Female Development.* Hanover: UP of New England, 1983.

Auerbach, Nina. *Communities of Women: An Idea in Fiction.* Cambridge: Harvard UP, 1978.

Benstock, Shari. "Reading the Signs of Women's Writing." *Tulsa Studies in Women's Literature* 4 (1985): 5–15.

Diehl, Joanne Feit. "Come Slowly Eden: An Exploration of Women Writers and Their Muse." *Signs* 3 (1978): 572–87.

DuPlessis, Rachel Blau. *The Pink Guitar: Writing as Feminist Practice.* New York: Routledge, 1990.

Finke, Laurie. *Feminist Theory, Women's Writing.* Ithaca: Cornell UP, 1992.

Gilbert, Sandra M., and Susan Gubar. *The Madwoman in the Attic: The Woman Writer and the Nineteenth-Century Literary Imagination.* New Haven: Yale UP, 1979.

Homans, Margaret. *Bearing the Word: Language and Female Experience in Nineteenth-Century Women's Writing.* Chicago: U of Chicago P, 1986.

Jacobus, Mary, ed. *Women Writing and Writing about Women.* New York: Barnes, 1979.

Miller, Nancy K., ed. *The Poetics of Gender.* New York: Columbia UP, 1986.

———. *Subject to Change: Reading Feminist Writing.* New York: Columbia UP, 1988.

Montefiore, Janet. "Feminine Identity and the Poetic Tradition." *Feminist Review* 13 (1983): 69–94.

Newton, Judith Lowder. *Women, Power and Subversion: Social Strategies in British Fiction, 1778–1860.* Athens: U of Georgia P, 1981.

Poovey, Mary. *The Proper Lady and the Woman Writer: Ideology as Style in the Works of Mary Wollstonecraft, Mary Shelley, and Jane Austen.* Chicago: U of Chicago P, 1984.

Showalter, Elaine. *Daughters of Decadence: Women Writers of the Fin de Siècle.* New Brunswick: Rutgers UP, 1993.

———. *A Literature of Their Own: British Women Novelists from Brontë to Lessing.* Princeton: Princeton UP, 1977.

———. "Women Who Write Are Women." *New York Times Book Review* I (December 16, 1984): 31–33.

Women's History/Women's Studies

Bridenthal, Renate, et al., ed. *Becoming Visible: Women in European History.* Rev. ed. Boston: Houghton Mifflin, 1998.

Donovan, Josephine. "Feminism and Aesthetics." *Critical Inquiry* 3 (1977): 605–8.

Farnham, Christie, ed. *The Impact of Feminist Research in the Academy*. Bloomington: Indiana UP, 1987.

Kelly, Joan. *Women, History & Theory: The Essays of Joan Kelly* Chicago: U of Chicago P, 1984.

McConnell-Ginet, Sally, et al., eds. *Woman and Language in Literature and Society*. New York: Praeger, 1980.

Mitchell, Juliet, and Ann Oakley, eds. *The Rights and Wrongs of Women*. London: Penguin, 1976.

Riley, Denise. *"Am I That Name?": Feminism and the Category of "Women" in History*. Minneapolis: U of Minnesota P, 1988.

Rowbotham, Sheila. *Woman's Consciousness, Man's World*. Harmondsworth, UK: Penguin, 1973.

Spacks, Patricia Meyer. *The Female Imagination*. New York: Knopf, 1975.

Feminisms and Sexualities

Snitow, Ann, Christine Stansell, and Sharon Thompson, eds. *Powers of Desire: The Politics of Sexuality*. New York: Monthly Review P, 1983.

Vance, Carole S., ed. *Pleasure and Danger: Exploring Female Sexuality*. Boston: Routledge, 1984.

Feminism, Race, Class, and Nationality

Anzaldúa, Gloria. *Borderlands: La Frontera = The New Mestiza*. San Francisco: Spinsters/Aunt Lute, 1987.

Christian, Barbara. *Black Feminist Criticism: Perspectives on Black Women Writers*. New York: Pergamon, 1985.

Collins, Patricia Hill. *Black Feminist Thought: Knowledge, Consciousness, and the Politics of Empowerment*. Boston: Hyman, 1990.

hooks, bell. *Ain't I a Woman?: Black Women and Feminism*. Boston: South End, 1981.

———. *Black Looks: Race and Representation*. Boston: South End, 1992.

Mitchell, Juliet. *Woman's Estate*. New York: Pantheon, 1971.

Moraga, Cherrie, and Gloria Anzaldúa, eds. *This Bridge Called My Back: Writings by Radical Women of Color*. New York: Kitchen Table, 1981.

Newton, Judith, and Deborah Rosenfelt, eds. *Feminist Criticism and Social Change: Sex, Class, and Race in Literature and Culture*. New York: Methuen, 1985.

Newton, Judith L., et al., eds. *Sex and Class in Women's History.* London: Routledge, 1983.

Pryse, Marjorie, and Hortense Spillers, eds. *Conjuring: Black Women, Fiction, and Literary Tradition.* Bloomington: Indiana UP, 1985.

Robinson, Lillian S. *Sex, Class, and Culture.* 1978. New York: Methuen, 1986.

Smith, Barbara. "Towards a Black Feminist Criticism." Showalter, *New Feminist Criticism* 168–85.

Feminism and Postcoloniality

Emberley, Julia. *Thresholds of Difference: Feminist Critique, Native Women's Writings, Postcolonial Theory.* Toronto: U of Toronto P, 1993.

Minh-ha, Trinh, T. *Woman, Native, Other: Writing Postcoloniality and Feminism.* Bloomington: Indiana UP, 1989.

Mohanty, Chandra Talpade, Ann Russo, and Lourdes Torres, eds. *Third World Women and the Politics of Feminism.* Bloomington: Indiana UP, 1991.

Schipper, Mineke, ed. *Unheard Words: Women and Literature in Africa, the Arab World, Asia, the Caribbean, and Latin America.* London: Allison, 1985.

Spivak, Gayatri Chakravorty. *In Other Worlds: Essays in Cultural Politics.* New York: Methuen, 1987.

———. *Outside in the Teaching Machine.* New York: Routledge, 1993.

Wilson, Armit. *Finding a Voice: Asian Women in Britain.* 1979. London: Virago, 1980.

Women's Self-Representation and Personal Criticism

Benstock, Shari, ed. *The Private Self: Theory and Practice of Women's Autobiographical Writings.* Chapel Hill: U of North Carolina P, 1988.

Brodski, Bella, and Celeste Schenck, eds. *Life/Lines: Theorizing Women's Autobiography.* Ithaca: Cornell UP, 1988.

Gilmore, Leigh. *Autobiographics: A Feminist Theory of Self-Representation.* Ithaca: Cornell UP, 1994.

Miller, Nancy K. *Getting Personal: Feminist Occasions and Other Autobiographical Acts.* New York: Routledge, 1991.

Feminism and Other Critical Approaches

Armstrong, Nancy, ed. *Literature as Women's History I.* Spec. issue of *Genre* 19–20 (1986–87).

Barrett, Michèle. *Women's Oppression Today: Problems in Marxist Feminist Analysis.* London: Verso, 1980.

Belsey, Catherine, and Jane Moore, eds. *The Feminist Reader: Essays in Gender and the Politics of Literary Criticism.* New York: Basil Blackwell, 1989.

Benjamin, Jessica. *The Bonds of Love: Psychoanalysis, Feminism, and the Problem of Domination.* New York: Pantheon, 1988.

Benstock, Shari. *Textualizing the Feminine: On the Limits of Genre.* Norman: U of Oklahoma P, 1991.

Butler, Judith, and Joan W. Scott, eds. *Feminists Theorize the Political.* New York: Routledge, 1992.

de Lauretis, Teresa. *Alice Doesn't: Feminism, Semiotics, Cinema.* Bloomington: Indiana UP, 1986.

de Lauretis, Teresa, and Stephen Heath. *The Cinematic Apparatus.* London: Macmillan, 1980.

Delphy, Christine. *Close to Home: A Materialist Analysis of Women's Oppression.* Trans. and ed. Diana Leonard. Amherst: U of Massachusetts P, 1984.

Dimock, Wai-chee. "Feminism, New Historicism, and the Reader." *American Literature* 63 (1991): 601–22.

Doane, Mary Ann. *Re-vision: Essays in Feminist Film Criticism.* Frederick: University Publications of America, 1984.

Felman, Shoshana, ed. *Literature and Psychoanalysis: The Questions of Reading: Otherwise.* Baltimore: Johns Hopkins UP, 1982.

———. "Women and Madness: The Critical Fallacy." *Diacritics* 5 (1975): 2–10.

Feminist Studies. Spec. issue on feminism and deconstruction, 14 (1988).

Gallop, Jane. *The Daughter's Seduction: Feminism and Psychoanalysis.* Ithaca: Cornell UP, 1982.

Gilligan, Carol. *In a Different Voice: Psychological Theory and Women's Development.* Cambridge: Harvard UP, 1982.

Hartsock, Nancy C. M. *Money, Sex, and Power: Toward a Feminist Historical Materialism.* Boston: Northeastern UP, 1985.

Kaplan, Cora. *Sea Changes: Essays on Culture and Feminism.* London: Verso, 1986.

Meese, Elizabeth, and Alice Parker, eds. *The Difference Within: Feminism and Critical Theory.* Philadelphia: John Benjamins, 1989.

Modleski, Tania. *Feminism without Women: Culture and Criticism in a "Postfeminist" Age.* New York: Routledge, 1991.

Mulvey, Laura. *Visual and Other Pleasures.* Bloomington: Indiana UP, 1989.

Newton, Judith Lowder. "History as Usual? Feminism and the New Historicism." *The New Historicism.* Ed. H. Aram Veeser. New York: Routledge, 1989. 152–67.

Nicholson, Linda J., ed. *Feminism/Postmodernism.* New York: Routledge, 1990.

Penley, Constance, ed. *Feminism and Film Theory.* New York: Routledge, 1988.

Riviere, Joan. "Womanliness as a Masquerade." *The International Journal of Psycho-Analysis* 10 (1929): 303–13. Rpt. in *Formations of Fantasy.* Ed. Victor Burgin, James Donald, and Cora Kaplan. New York: Methuen, 1986. 35–44.

Rose, Jacqueline. Introduction II. *Feminine Sexuality: Jacques Lacan and the Ecole Freudienne.* Ed. Juliet Mitchell and Rose. Trans. Rose. New York: Norton, 1983.

Sargent, Lydia, ed. *Women and Revolution: A Discussion of the Unhappy Marriage of Marxism and Feminism.* Montreal: Black Rose, 1981.

Weedon, Chris. *Feminist Practice and Poststructuralist Theory.* New York: Basil Blackwell, 1987.

Feminist Criticism Relating to *Emma*

Auerbach, Nina. *Communities of Women: An Idea in Fiction.* Cambridge: Harvard UP, 1978.

Booth, Wayne. "Emma, *Emma,* and the Question of Feminism." *Persuasions* 5 (1983): 29–40.

Gilbert, Sandra M., and Susan Gubar, *The Madwoman in the Attic: The Woman Writer and the Nineteenth-Century Literary Imagination.* New Haven: Yale UP, 1979.

Johnson, Claudia L. *Jane Austen: Women, Politics, and the Novel.* Chicago: U of Chicago P, 1988.

Kaplan, Deborah. *Jane Austen Among Women.* Baltimore: Johns Hopkins UP, 1992.

Kirkham, Margaret. *Jane Austen, Feminism and Fiction.* 1983. Rpt. with new pref. London and Atlantic Highlands, NJ: Athlone, 1997.

Looser, Devoney, ed. *Jane Austen and Discourses of Feminism*. New York: St. Martin's, 1995.

Moffat, Wendy. "Identifying with *Emma*; Some Problems for the Feminist Reader." *College English* 53.1 (1991): 45–58.

O'Farrell, Mary Ann. "Jane Austen's Friendship." *Janeites: Austen's Disciples and Devotees*. Ed. Deidre Lynch. Princeton: Princeton UP, 2000. 45–62.

Poovey, Mary. *The Proper Lady and the Woman Writer: Ideology as Style in the Works of Mary Wollstonecraft, Mary Shelley, and Jane Austen*. Chicago: U of Chicago P, 1984.

Smith, Leroy W. *Jane Austen and the Drama of Women*. New York: St. Martin's, 1983.

Stewart, Maaja A. *Domestic Realities and Imperial Fictions: Jane Austen's Novels in Eighteenth-Century Contexts*. Athens: U of Georgia P, 1993.

Sulloway, Alison G. *Jane Austen and the Province of Womanhood*. Philadelphia: U of Pennsylvania P, 1989.

Trumpener, Katie. "The Virago Jane Austen." *Janeites: Austen's Disciples and Devotees*. Ed. Deidre Lynch. Princeton: Princeton UP, 2000. 140–65.

A FEMINIST PERSPECTIVE

DEVONEY LOOSER

"The Duty of Woman by Woman": Reforming Feminism in *Emma*

Is Jane Austen a feminist? That answer depends not only on how one understands her novels but on how one defines feminism. Should Austen be measured against today's feminist politics and practices? Or should she be compared to contemporaries who criticized women's status in late-eighteenth- and early-nineteenth-century Britain — a time when the word *feminism* did not yet exist in the English language? (It first appeared in 1851 and was not widely used in the sense we now understand until the 1880s.) If we define feminism broadly as a movement attending to how women are limited and devalued within a culture, then Austen's novels surely participate. When feminism is defined more specifically as a movement to eradicate gender, race, class, and

sexual prejudice and to agitate for change, it is harder to justify so labeling Austen. She was not in the vanguard of social justice movements by
the standards of her time. Critics continue to argue about Austen's relationship to feminism, demonstrating no promise of an easy resolution.
Many agree that feminist literary critical approaches to Austen have
productively shifted the terms on which her novels are read, providing
an "invigorating new approach" (Stovel 236). It has become a critical
duty to investigate how Austen's fiction responds to, incorporates, or
extends the range of feminist ideas available in her time.

"THE DUTY OF WOMAN BY WOMAN"

The word duty appears more than twenty times and is an important
concept in Austen's *Emma*. Mr. Knightley expresses concern that Frank
Churchill has not done his duty because he postpones a visit to his
father and new wife. Emma Woodhouse worries about doing her duty
by her protégée Harriet Smith after Harriet refuses Robert Martin's
proposal. Jane Fairfax is only too aware that it may be her duty to
become a governess. In these instances duty signifies obligation, but
the nature of the obligation varies (Frank's is filial, Jane's one of economic necessity). When Emma reflects on her behavior at the Coles's
party we encounter another context for the term:

> [T]here were two points on which she was not quite easy. She
> doubted whether she had not transgressed the *duty of woman by
> woman,* in betraying her suspicions of Jane Fairfax's feelings to
> Frank Churchill. It was hardly right. . . . The other circumstance
> of regret related also to Jane Fairfax; and there she had no doubt.
> She did unfeignedly and unequivocally regret the inferiority of her
> own playing and singing. (p. 191 in this volume; emphasis added)

Emma has "no doubt" about regretting the inferiority of her talents in
comparison to Jane's, but she has to resort to pseudo-double negatives
("doubted whether she had not") even to conceive of her conversational
betrayal of Jane as a personal failing. Emma dislikes being thought inferior to Jane more than she regrets gossiping about her in potentially
reputation-destroying terms. Emma's faults are revealed through her
half-hearted self-recriminations, and readers begin to see how she abuses
her social power over other women. Emma's reflections not only reveal
her flaws; they point the way to the novel's embedded feminist concerns.
The duty of woman by woman has rarely been seen as a central
theme of *Emma,* perhaps because, while Emma performs her duty to her

hypochondriacal father, she fails almost everyone else. Viewing the novel as about women's duty to women is also complicated by Mr. Knightley's role. Emma's shortcomings in the performance of her duty are first pointed out by him, and he emerges as the most trustworthy arbiter of her behavior. The older women with whom Emma is intimate — her sister Isabella and former governess Mrs. Weston — are of little help in guiding her (Todd, *Women's* 276–80; Reid-Walsh 109). The female community fails to help her grow. *Emma* would seem to offer a patriarchal tale: an older, wiser male berates, corrects, and improves a flawed female whom he reshapes in his own image until she is lovable enough — perfected enough — to marry. They then live dutifully in "perfect happiness" (p. 381). There is, of course, much more to *Emma* than this caricature suggests; the novel is never merely a patriarchal tale.

Emma's most egregious failures of duty lie in her mistreatment of fellow females, most notably her manipulation of Harriet, her jealousy toward and backstabbing of Jane, and her cruel sarcasm directed against Miss Bates on Box Hill. Emma comes to see each of these behaviors as wrong, which readers are led to believe is a sign of her growth. But is Emma's realization of her womanly duty a feminist awakening, a discovery of the indignities to which dependant women are subject, coupled with an awareness of her own culpable part in their exploitation? Or is the novel's ending a capitulation to dominant ideologies of ideal femininity that insist women be modest, kind, and certainly not meddlers? Although not unequivocally feminist by today's standards, Austen's descriptions of women's relationships imply a reformist feminism in her own time; they engage both conservative and revolutionary views of women's role. While the novel does not seek to break down received gender and class boundaries, it does encourage more equitable relations among women; and though, as Ruth Perry has shown, the novel's generic investment in the marriage plot "interrupts" Emma's friendship with women — and particularly Jane Fairfax, who seems a natural "sister" — it also offers "testimonies to the pleasures of women's friendship" (189).

In Austen's day, women's friendships were structured to include greater degrees of intimacy and influence, and one kind of friendship involved "someone who has the power to act on one's behalf, for one's protection or advancement" (Wiltshire 85). Although it may seem odd to call patronage "friendship," the concepts were commonly linked if not always approved. Maria Edgeworth's novel *Patronage* (1814) explores the evils of influence and the virtues of independence. Furthermore, patronage was not only a transaction between men.

Women's patronage to women was so prevalent as to be virtually institutionalized, as Betty Rizzo's *Companions Without Vows: Relationships
Among Eighteenth-Century British Women* argues. The companionate
relationship of patroness and humble companion "mirrored the marriage relationship and was often identified with it" (Rizzo 1). A humble
companion was usually single and economically dependent, descended
from a gentleman whose fortune had turned or was apportioned to an
eldest son. She entertained or assisted her wealthier mistress, performing unpaid and nonmenial tasks. The companion served as a confidante
or offered a hand at cards. In return, the mistress-employer introduced
the companion into "good" society and provided requisite leisure activities. A companion was useful to her patroness for both formal and
informal outings that would be considered improper if conducted
alone. For privileged women, who were relegated to relatively powerless positions vis-à-vis their husbands and fathers — a condition Emma
successfully but atypically evades — a companion could mitigate the
restrictions imposed even on elite women.

As Emma had "very early foreseen," Harriet would be "useful"
as "a walking companion"; she would be "a valuable addition to
[Emma's] privileges" (p. 39) in perambulations beyond the grounds of
Hartfield. Emma's understanding of Harriet as "useful" was a logical
outcome of companionate relationships that stressed form over substance. Harriet was "the *something* which [Emma's] home required";
Emma required "*a* Harriet Smith" (p. 39; emphasis added). Emma
"never saw [Harriet] as a person but as a blank page to be filled in," as
Jacqueline Reid-Walsh notes (113). Searching for a young woman to
"improve" and "form" (p. 37) was not unusual in someone of Emma's
position. Humble companions offered an opportunity for wealthy
women to use their economic and social privilege: "The autonomous
mistress had the same powers over her companion that the husband
had over his wife. She could choose either to exercise those powers
autocratically . . . or to work out an equitable relationship such as she
herself would have liked to experience in her dealings with men" (Rizzo
1–2). Just so does Emma open the question of how she will exercise her
powers. Choosing Harriet was to her mind "a very kind undertaking;
highly becoming her own situation in life, her leisure, and powers"
(p. 38). But as usual Emma is deceiving herself; hers is an autocratic
gesture because she is using Harriet to further her own views, plans,
and projects. It can hardly be suspected that Emma would wish to be
treated by Mr. Knightley as she herself treats Harriet.

As Rizzo briefly indicates, Emma uses her prerogative as a patroness to assume masculine and powerful roles over Miss Taylor and Harriet (8–9). Emma has long been seen by critics as masculine in her moral life and expression of privilege, but using Rizzo's framework, we can see that Emma sets out to perform a typically *female* (though not feminine) action. The role of a patron who improved or formed single females could not be undertaken by unrelated males; their access to unmarried women was strictly limited for reasons of sexual propriety. Emma's wish to mold Harriet takes its cue from the patroness's accepted and even encouraged role in preparing younger, less wealthy female companions for marriage. The idea of twenty-one-year-old (spoiled, undisciplined) Emma becoming a prenuptial guide to (illegitimate, giggling) eighteen-year-old Harriet may seem ludicrous, but even the skeptical Mr. Knightley at first concedes that Emma has improved Harriet when he mistakenly believes that Robert Martin is about to take Harriet out of Emma's hands. As Mr. Knightley tells Emma, Harriet "really does you credit" (p. 63), a compliment he rescinds when he learns that Emma has dissuaded her from accepting the proposal. Emma's actions where Harriet is concerned do neither of them any credit, although there is — conveniently — no long-lasting damage.

The novel has been taken to task by some feminists for its taming of its spirited protagonist by marrying her off, but I argue that it also serves as a corrective to certain kinds of same-sex exploitation. *Emma* functions as a critique of what I call female/female paternalism, exposing in the process the exploitable structure of companionate relationships; it reveals the ways powerful women wield influence over fellow females, by uncovering its protagonist's mistakes which, we will see, are repeated and exaggerated in Mrs. Elton's behavior. The novel also implicitly warns readers about how women of modest means may be (mis)treated by their more powerful female mentors. Austen did not espouse the revolutionary idea of a feminist sisterhood whereby women from different social levels would work together for their collective betterment. Instead *Emma* shows possibilities for establishing greater fairness within existing female friendships.

EMMA, SISTERHOOD, AND THE LIMITS OF FEMALE/FEMALE PATERNALISM

As Wayne Booth argues, "Jane Austen never . . . talks about 'all women' or 'all men,' and she makes fun of those who do" (33). Though Booth overstates the case, *Emma* does suggest that gentlewomen should use social class and economic status rather than sex to determine the kind of treatment they owe each other: their "duty." Then they should gauge educational achievement and moral character to determine appropriate levels of intimacy. Many feminists today rightly find the novel's acceptance of social ranking as troubling as its failure to envisage a female community across social barriers. *Emma*, however, indirectly responds to its own era's political commentary on sisterhood. Redefining the duty of woman by woman, Austen steers a course between the protofeminist community imagined by Mary Astell (1666–1731) and the conservative female paternalism offered by Hannah More (1745–1833). *Emma*'s implicit criticisms of both revolutionary and conservative female philosophies place it in the liberal feminist category to which recent scholars assign Austen (Johnson, Kirkham, Sulloway). Accepting much of the political and economic structure around her, Austen seeks to shift the ways women function within it. In *Emma*, she chooses not to represent sisterhood within or across social levels, but she exposes the hypocrisy and potential damage of hierarchical female/female paternalism.

In order to analyze how Austen redefines the duty of woman by woman, it will be useful to consider how duty is conceived in earlier writings. Womanly duty was addressed by many eighteenth-century conduct books, the forerunners of today's self-help and etiquette manuals. Guides to behavior concerned themselves with "the whole duty of woman" (the title of a 1696 conduct book), a phrase invoked throughout the century. A woman's whole duty involved exhibiting proper ways of "speaking, looking, walking, imagining, thinking" (Goreau 10). Discretion, modesty, and silence were recommended; the proper education of girls was widely debated (11). The recommendations of conservative writers centered on how women should behave in the company of men. Feminist writers of the time responded with their own arguments, countering dominant conceptions of femininity and arguing for educational opportunities for girls that went beyond fashioning them into submissive, ornamental wives. Some imagined how women might bolster their status and protection by allying with other women.

Mary Astell made the radical proposal in 1696 that wealthy single women's unused dowries be pooled to create female Protestant nunneries, where unmarried women could establish communities of mutual support (Todd, *Dictionary* 32). Her idea found expression in a later work of fiction, Sarah Scott's *Millenium Hall* (1762), a female utopia in which single upper-class women choose to live together and perform charitable works. Astell influenced British feminist writers of the 1790s, whose ideas circulated in the wake of the French Revolution but waned in popularity as violence escalated and anti-Jacobin repression became the order of the day. She may have influenced Austen (Sulloway 55–61). We might speculate that Austen was familiar with the writings of Astell and Scott and perhaps even sympathized with communal living arrangements for "spinsters" of means. There are, however, counterindications that Austen did not share Astell's and Scott's idealism about female communities. Austen's fictional depictions suggest that, in her view, elite women would not *necessarily* treat other women any better than men would. Astell and Scott envision a sisterhood that Austen may have questioned.

Austen viewed herself as an important part of a community of women, as Deborah Kaplan and Ruth Perry have argued, but Austen's female community was a chosen one, primarily made up of family members. She rarely, in life or in fiction, expressed the belief that women were or must be the blind supporters of all women as a group or even of women within their own class.[1] Her fictional female characters demonstrate, on the contrary, that she believed women to be capable of profound cruelty toward one another. It is difficult to imagine Augusta Elton, the female "villain" of *Emma*, as worthy of Emma's or of readers' support. Mrs. Elton's function as unsuccessful spoiler is echoed in *Northanger Abbey*'s Isabella Thorpe, *Pride and Prejudice*'s Lady Catherine de Bourgh, *Sense and Sensibility*'s Lucy Steele, and *Mansfield Park*'s Mary Crawford. All relish opportunities to foreclose other women's chances for happiness in favor of their own self-serving plans. Austen's novels illustrate with painstaking detail the ways that unscrupulous women compete in a society configured to advance the legal and economic interests of men. They show the limits of women's alliances with each other in a patriarchal culture, but, in so doing, also imply more positive possibilities of relationships for women.

Austen left scanty evidence about her estimations of early feminist writers such as Astell, Mary Wollstonecraft, and Mary Hays, but she provides direct and cutting commentary on conservative writer and philosopher Hannah More, who has been called "hardly a friend to her own sex" (Sulloway 33). More — a prolific and financially successful author — wrote conduct books, political propaganda, and works of

---

[1]She did, however, express sisterly sympathy for Caroline, Princess of Wales, the estranged and ill-treated wife of the Prince Regent: "Poor woman, I shall support her as long as I can, because she *is* a Woman, & because I hate her Husband" (*Letters*, 208).

religious devotion. Austen disliked More's fellow Evangelicals because of their affected piety, but she attended to More's writings. Discussions of More and Austen have usually centered on *Mansfield Park,* a novel many suspect was influenced by More. Austen's assessments of More may also have prompted the representations of female female relationships in *Emma.*

More's only fictional work was titled *Coelebs in Search of a Wife* (1808). Because More disdained novels as immoral, she came under attack for hypocrisy in writing one. Nevertheless, *Coelebs* was popular with readers. It earned £2,000 within its first year, and thirty editions of one thousand copies each were sold before her death in 1834 (Jones 193). (*Emma,* by way of contrast, was issued in late December 1815 with a print run of 2,000; 539 copies, still unsold in 1820, were remaindered, and no further edition appeared until 1833 [Gilson 68–69].) The novel follows its eponymous, worthy, and priggish hero as he searches for the right woman, ruling out one after another for flaws of various kinds. The women whom he does not choose serve as warnings for readers. Austen ridicules More's novel in a revision she made to a short work in her juvenilia and in a letter to her sister Cassandra. In *Catharine,* Austen's sensible heroine is accused by her severe, scrutinizing maiden aunt of behaving impudently, despite having been given *Coelebs* to read, which presumably should have molded her differently. In a letter written before reading More's novel, Austen tells her sister that "the only merit [the title of the novel] could have, was in the name of Caleb, which has an honest, unpretending sound; but in Coelebs, there is pedantry & affectation. — Is it written only to Classical Scholars?" (172). Austen then cheekily proclaims that when she reads *Coelebs* she is certain to be delighted as much as other people, but until then she will dislike it.

Although *Emma* and *Coelebs* have few direct similarities, *Emma* could be retitled *Emma in Search of Husbands for Other Women* or *Emma Not in Search of a Husband.* As Austen's only published novel with a woman's name as its title, *Emma* diametrically opposes *Coelebs* by centering on a flawed single female, rather than a flawless single male. Emma is not on a marriage quest for herself — an act considered acceptable in a male but horrifying in a female, who must remain passive until chosen. She is on a marriage quest on behalf of others. Austen's reversal of More's plot amuses for biographical reasons. More, like Austen, never married. From the age of twenty-two, More was betrothed, but her fiancé refused to marry her after six years of engagement. As a result of the humiliating experience, More vowed never to marry and later turned down a proposal in order to make good on her vow. *Emma* makes an indirect comment on the sophistry of an author like More, an unmarried woman who moralizes about and offers expertise on how to attract a husband. To counter the advice of More and those like her, Emma is given precisely the qualities that they would have women guard against: intelligence, confidence, wit, and even some arrogance. This feature alone has led some critics to suggest that Austen's novels are feminist because her heroines "grow into a moral independence which public opinion of the day would probably have denied them" (Lenta 31). Defying convention, Emma has the audacity to proclaim (like More) that she will never marry because she has no economic or social inducements to do so. But then, despite her professed desire to avoid marriage in favor of seeking marriage for others who lack her advantages, Emma finds a worthy husband.

If *Emma* is in many respects the anti-*Coelebs*, Emma is by no means the anti-More. In addition to their mutual vows to remain single, the fictional Emma and the author More share a fault. Both intervene in other women's lives. In her fiction and conduct books, More indirectly encroaches by preaching to women about how to catch husbands; Emma herself does this directly through her matchmaking. The similarities are more striking when we compare an unpleasant episode in More's life to that of the fictional Emma. Hannah More was committed to "patronage of genius, especially female genius," which was regarded in her circle as a "duty and privilege" (Jones 73). More chose protégées, as Emma did, and with at least one disastrous outcome. That episode has an interesting bearing on *Emma*. More's most notable experiment with a companionate relationship was with a working class poet, Ann Yearsley, in 1784–85. Yearsley, a poor Bristol milkwoman with a husband and five children, was "discovered" as a poetic genius, and More became her patron. In some ways, Yearsley was an odd choice for More. More believed strongly that class hierarchy reflected a natural and divine order — that the poor should not be ambitious and that their reward for accepting a humble lot on earth would be joy in heaven. More never intended that Yearsley would abandon her station in life to write poetry. Nevertheless, More spent thirteen months teaching Yearsley the rules of composition, translating and correcting her poems, and writing more than 1,000 pages of letters appealing for subscriptions to Yearsley's first book (Jones 74). More created a reputation and a following for the milkwoman poet.

An argument between the two occurred when the book was published and had considerable success, earning proceeds of £360. More

and her set formed a trust to control the money, with plans to dole it
out to Yearsley and her children as they saw fit. Yearsley felt that the
money belonged to her and resented More's interference. Their falling
out was bitter. Of being denied control of the book's profits, Yearsley
wrote, "I felt as a mother deemed unworthy of the tuition and care of
her family" (qtd. in Jones 75). More resigned from the trust, but the
matter was not resolved. Yearsley published vindictive criticisms of
More, dredging up More's failed engagement, as well as accusing her of
financial impropriety. More did not publish or publicly speak in her
defense, but she talked angrily for years about the matter (Jones
75–76). The More/Yearsley episode offered one of the most celebrated
failures of companionate relationships, of female/female paternalism.

EMMA, JANE, AND MRS. ELTON

Emma and Harriet appear headed for a Hannah More/Ann Yearsley-
like clash. Emma teaches Harriet social aspirations far beyond those
conventionally expected of her. As a result, Harriet might have ended
up with the man whom Emma belatedly realizes she desires for herself.
Despite our doubts as readers that Mr. Knightley could prefer Harriet
to Emma, Emma fears that a match between Harriet and Mr. Knightley
is "far, very far, from impossible" (p. 328). The potential tussle is over a
bachelor rather than a book or an authorial reputation, but Emma's
belief that she can control Harriet Smith's rise parallels More's approach to Yearsley. Both More and Emma create monsters in their own
images (on *Emma* as *Frankenstein,* see Todd, *Women's* 288). Emma
and Harriet's relationship more than once suggests impending catastro-
phe because Harriet is too socially and educationally disadvantaged to
fulfill Emma's dreams for her. Jane has much more to recommend her,
by birth and accomplishments, as almost everyone but Emma acknowledges. Even the otherwise dull Isabella remarks that Jane would make
"a delightful companion for Emma" (p. 99). Jane is "exactly Emma's
age," as well as "so very accomplished and superior" (p. 99). Jane
makes a promising humble companion precisely because she is not too
humble (as is Harriet) and because she can offer substantial rather than
functional companionship. Whereas Harriet brings Emma flattery and
fawning, Jane would carry more solid qualities to a friendship, despite
her often described coldness and reserve.

At the novel's opening Jane has just left the patronage of the Campbells, whose daughter seems to have engaged Jane in an ideal compan-

ionate relationship. That relationship is curtailed when Miss Campbell becomes Mrs. Dixon and moves to Ireland, but all of the information we have (Emma's inappropriate speculations notwithstanding) points to an equitable friendship. Mrs. Dixon is referred to repeatedly as Jane's "very particular friend" (p. 169). We can only assume that as Miss Campbell she had a role in throwing together Frank Churchill and Jane, perhaps even fulfilling the matchmaking function that Emma imagines for herself. The qualities that most recommend Jane as a companion in other's eyes are precisely the problem for Emma. As Emma remarks about Jane's association with Miss Campbell, there is a "misery of having a very particular friend always at hand, to do every thing better than one does oneself!" (p. 169). Emma avoids this misery by refusing to make Jane her very particular friend.

Jane Fairfax is Emma's "equal friend, sanctioned by society and the novel," as Todd argues. Their friendship never develops because the novel "laughingly dispatches friend Jane to Yorkshire and sends Emma home" (*Women's* 275), but not before Emma recognizes her loss:

> Had she followed Mr. Knightley's known wishes, in paying that attention to Miss Fairfax, which was every way her due; had she tried to know her better; had she done her part towards intimacy; had she endeavoured to find a friend there instead of in Harriet Smith; she must, in all probability, have been spared from every pain which pressed on her now. — Birth, abilities, and education, had been equally marking one as an associate for her, to be received with gratitude; and the other — what was she? (p. 333)

Emma comes to see herself as Jane's worst evil, particularly because of her gossiping and speculation about Mr. Dixon, but it is Mrs. Elton who contributes more substantially to Jane's discomfort. Mrs. Elton is not worried about Jane's superior accomplishments overshadowing her own because, already safely married, she wrongly imagines her own station to be well beyond any Jane could aspire to. Mrs. Elton also conveniently gives up music so that she no longer need compete with a pianist of Jane's abilities, another privilege of the patroness.

Mrs. Elton — the novel's gravest warning against female/female paternalism — attempts to out-Emma Emma by taking on the more worthy Jane as her companion. Mrs. Elton's patronage of Jane is immediately linked to her rivalry with Emma, although the narrator perhaps ironically claims otherwise: "Mrs. Elton took a great fancy to Jane Fairfax; and from the first. Not merely when a state of warfare with one young lady might be supposed to recommend the other, but from the very first; and she was not satisfied with expressing a natural and reasonable admiration — but without solicitation, or plea, or privilege, she must be wanting to assist and befriend her" (p. 228). The rub in Mrs. Elton's decision to take Jane under wing is that her intervention has not been solicited; there has been no request for assistance. Mrs. Elton has no familial or community privilege to justify the position she assumes over Jane. Her "knight-errantry" (p. 228) bears no resemblance to Mr. Knightley's chivalrous behavior. Mrs. Elton resolves that Jane, her timid but delightful "inferior," must not remain in "retirement, such obscurity, so thrown away" (p. 229). Emma tries to check Mrs. Elton's enthusiasm, reminding her of Jane's other connections, but Mrs. Elton wants to "set the example" and pairs herself with Emma as the village patronesses. Mrs. Elton's usurpation of the community's protecting role and Emma's social superiority are equally condemned. Emma and Mrs. Elton never form an alliance to rescue Jane. Mrs. Elton alone becomes the "very active patroness of Jane Fairfax" (p. 230). Jane is represented as a social pawn, though "[c]ould she have chosen with whom to associate, she would not have chosen" Mrs. Elton (p. 231).

Mrs. Elton is Emma's nemesis but she is also a sign of what Emma — if unrepentant — could become. Emma shares some of Mrs. Elton faults: a "vain woman, extremely well satisfied with herself, and thinking much of her own importance; . . . she meant to shine and be very superior" (p. 220). Like Emma, Mrs. Elton "had been the best of her own set" where she formed ideas of herself as a potential patron, pretending to the social position of her sister, the superior Mrs. Suckling (p. 221). If Mrs. Elton selects a more class-appropriate and deserving humble companion in Jane than Emma does in Harriet, she more egregiously oversteps her boundaries as patron in her attempted machinations. Mrs. Elton's finding employment for Jane as a governess poses as a selfless act. It is, however, an attempt to force an unwanted agenda on Jane and to prove to her new community (and to her beloved Maple Grove relatives) that she has power in Highbury. The cruel extent of her coercion appears through Miss Bates's gratitude:

> Yes, our good Mrs. Elton. The most indefatigable, true friend. She would not take a denial. She would not let Jane say, "No;" for when Jane first heard of it . . . she was quite decided against accepting the offer . . . nothing should induce her to enter into any engagement at present — and so she told Mrs. Elton over and over again . . . but that good Mrs. Elton, whose judgement never fails her, saw farther than I did. It is not every body that would have stood out in such a kind way as she did, and refuse to take

Jane's answer; but she positively declared she would *not* write any
such denial yesterday, as Jane wished her; she would wait — and,
sure enough, yesterday evening it was all settled that Jane should
go. (pp. 303–04)

Jane moves from a refusal to an acceptance of Mrs. Elton's proposed
post because of Frank Churchill's inaction. Nevertheless, Mrs. Elton
stands as the consummate version of the patroness as bully. Emma
makes wrongheaded plans for the malleable Harriet, but Harriet
unquestioningly goes along with them, where the wiser and more self-
possessed Jane resists. Harriet warns readers of the dangers of a too
pliable disposition; Jane shows us the quandaries an economically dependent woman faces with the wrong patron. Patronage exists by definition because of economic inequalities, but *Emma* implies that in an
equitable companionate relationship economic privilege must be coun-
terbalanced or complemented by accomplishments and merit. Each
party must bring something of value to the patronage exchange, and
each should respect the gifts and desires of the other, or the result will
inevitably be exploitation and unhappiness on one or both sides.

HARRIET AND THE MARTIN SISTERS

As I have been arguing, *Emma* shows us that Austen's vision of
woman's duty to woman involves a recognition of compatibility at
social and educational levels. Jane should have been Emma's companion, but the novel suggests that Harriet, too, deserved a more suitable
one. The Martin sisters hover in the background as Harriet's class-
appropriate female companions. They are much her superiors in talents
if not in rank, and they promise to educate her to the level she can most
reasonably aspire to — marriage to a sensible young yeoman, the Mr.
Knightley of his class. The Martins are worthy people, but the free indirect style that Austen uses to describe them communicates Emma's
snobbery and misplaced bias:

They were a family of the name of Martin, whom Emma well
knew by character, as renting a large farm of Mr. Knightley, and
residing in the parish of Donwell — very creditably she
believed — she knew Mr. Knightley thought highly of them —
but they must be coarse and unpolished, and very unfit to be the
intimates of a girl who wanted only a little more knowledge and
elegance to be quite perfect. (p. 37)

The Martin sisters are fitting female companions for Harriet. Like Emma, they do their part to befriend her, improve her, and ready her for marriage. Robert Martin's letter proposing marriage arrives, appropriately, in a package from his sister Elizabeth. Elizabeth's package includes "two songs which she had lent . . . to copy," reinforcing the memory of their musical evenings together and mutual improvement (p. 57). When Emma insists that Harriet give up their acquaintance, Harriet replies (with a tellingly imperfect command of English grammar): "I shall always have a great regard for the Miss Martins, especially Elizabeth, and should be very sorry to give them up, for they are quite as well educated as me" (p. 43). Emma finds Robert Martin's letter surpasses her expectations and suspects it must have been written by his sisters. She is wrong, but her mistake confirms their superior talents. Their role in Harriet's affective life is significant. When, coaxed by Emma, she rejects Mr. Martin, she worries at once about his sisters' response: " 'Now he has got my letter,' said she softly. 'I wonder what they are all doing — whether his sisters know — if he is unhappy, they will be unhappy too. I hope he will not mind it so very much' " (p. 62).

The Martin sisters show themselves to be well versed where duty is concerned. Elizabeth Martin is not perfect; resentful, she at first ignores Harriet Smith during their chance encounter at Ford's, but then politeness and perhaps fond memories assert themselves. As Harriet tells it:

> ". . . presently she came forward — came quite up to me, and asked me how I did, and seemed ready to shake hands, if I would. She did not do any of it in the same way that she used; I could see she was altered; but, however, she seemed to *try* to be very friendly, and we shook hands, and stood talking some time; but I know no more what I said — I was in such a tremble! — I remember she said she was sorry we never met now; which I thought almost too kind! Dear, Miss Woodhouse, I was absolutely miserable! . . . and yet, you know, there was a sort of satisfaction in seeing him behave so pleasantly and so kindly. And Elizabeth, too. Oh! Miss Woodhouse, do talk to me and make me comfortable again." (p. 152)

Later, when the Martins reestablish formal contact with Harriet, it is Elizabeth who carries it out. She calls on Harriet at Mrs. Goddard's, a visit that Emma tells Harriet she must return. Emma engineers a shamefully brief meeting to communicate no more than a "formal acquaintance," despite the fact that "there was something in it which her own heart could not approve — something of ingratitude, merely glossed over" (p. 157). Emma's good-heartedness falters, but the Martins rise to the occasion.

Although the visit to the Martin women began "doubtingly, if not coolly," a familiar subject brought on "a warmer manner" that indicated readiness "to return to the same good understanding" (p. 158). They "were just growing again like themselves" when Emma's carriage returned and called for Harriet, an unmistakable sign:

> The style of the visit, and the shortness of it, were then felt to be decisive. Fourteen minutes to be given to those with whom she had thankfully passed six weeks not six months ago! — Emma could not but picture it all, and feel how justly they might resent, how naturally Harriet must suffer. It was a bad business. She would have given a great deal, or endured a great deal, to have had the Martins in a higher rank of life. They were so deserving, that a *little* higher should have been enough: but as it was, how could she have done otherwise? — Impossible! — She could not repent. (p. 158).

Robert Martin is eventually received at Hartfield, showing Emma's newfound expansiveness when it comes to class, but her friendship with Harriet sinks naturally to a "calmer sort of goodwill" (p. 380). Harriet will not return to being on intimate terms, which has less to do with matrimony than with their being mismatched as friends. Emma's lessons ready her to become a better wife and enable her to look for a more fair-minded husband, but they also teach her to be a better woman to deserving women. Rather than approaching close relationships as an opportunity for exploitation or exerting her will, Emma learns to value them as exchanges to be upheld.

It has been a critical commonplace to imagine a life for Emma beyond the ending of the novel. Will Emma and Mr. Knightley enjoy a more equitable marriage than most, as his move from Donwell to Hartfield implies? Will the married Emma steer clear of authoritarian female/female paternalism? Edmund Wilson suspects that Emma will continue to dominate women, to choose another special project, despite her failures with Harriet (202). Marianne Hirsch sees Emma as unlikely to have children (44). In a recent sequel to the novel, Emma Tennant considers the possibility — contemplated in literary criticism since the 1950s — that Emma Woodhouse has lesbian tendencies. All of these imaginist enterprises put us in a position similar to Emma's — grafting our critical desires onto fictional women. There is little harm involved in such speculation in literary criticism, but one of *Emma's* warnings is the danger of this behavior in life. In Austen's world, a powerful woman with her own agenda may — if she is not careful — shirk her duty to other women, a duty that entails neither unquestioning support nor rigid paternalism. *Emma* promotes tendencies to respect other women equitably but only if they have proved through education, status, and behavior that they are worthy of such treatment. Today we may see Austen's lessons about women's duty as too individually focused or too limited in scope to offer a model for feminist practice, but in her own time she implicitly argued for greater fairness among women within the existing social, political, and economic order.

WORKS CITED

Austen, Jane. *Jane Austen's Letters.* Ed. Deirdre Le Faye. 3rd ed. Oxford: Oxford UP, 1995.

Booth, Wayne. "Emma, *Emma,* and the Question of Feminism." *Persuasions* 5 (1983): 29–40.

Gilson, David. *A Bibliography of Jane Austen.* Oxford: Clarendon, 1982.

Goreau, Angeline. *The Whole Duty of a Woman: Female Writers of Seventeenth-Century England.* Garden City, NY: Doubleday, 1985.

Hirsch, Marianne. "Female Family Romances and the 'Old Dream of Symmetry'." *Literature and Psychology* 32.4 (1986): 37–47.

Johnson, Claudia L. *Jane Austen: Women, Politics, and the Novel.* Chicago: U of Chicago P, 1988.

Jones, M. G. *Hannah More.* New York: Greenwood, 1968.

Kaplan, Deborah. *Jane Austen Among Women.* Baltimore: Johns Hopkins UP, 1992.

Kirkham, Margaret. *Jane Austen, Feminism, and Fiction.* 2nd ed. London: Athlone, 1997.

Lenta, Margaret. "Jane Austen's Feminism: An Original Response to Convention." *Critical Quarterly* 23.3 (Autumn 1981): 27–36.

Perry, Ruth. "Interrupted Friendships in Jane Austen's *Emma.*" *Tulsa Studies in Women's Literature* 5.2 (1986): 185–202.

Reid-Walsh, Jacqueline. "Governess or Governor?: The Mentor/Pupil Relation in Emma." *Persuasions* 13 (1991): 108–17.

Rizzo, Betty. *Companions Without Vows: Relationships Among Eighteenth-Century British Women.* Athens: U of Georgia P, 1994.

Stovel, Bruce. "Further Reading." *Cambridge Companion to Jane Austen*. Ed. Edward Copeland and Juliet McMaster. Cambridge: Cambridge UP, 1997. 227-43.

Sulloway, Alison. *Jane Austen and the Province of Womanhood.* Philadelphia: U of Pennsylvania P, 1989.

Tennant, Emma. *Emma in Love*. London: Fourth Estate, 1997.

Todd, Janet, ed. *A Dictionary of British and American Women Writers 1660–1800*. Totowa, NJ: Rowman and Allanheld, 1985.

———. *Women's Friendship in Literature*. New York: Columbia UP, 1980.

The Whole Duty of a Woman. 1696. London, 1708.

Wilson, Edmund. *Classics and Commercials: A Literary Chronicle of the Forties*. New York: Farrar, Straus and Company, 1950.

Wiltshire, John. "The World of Emma." *Critical Review* 27 (1985): 84–97.

Combining Perspectives on
Emma

So far, this volume's emphasis has been on mapping out and demonstrating the broad outlines of particular contemporary critical approaches. In presenting this final essay by Marilyn Butler, the emphasis is reversed; the intention is to demonstrate the permeability of such approaches, as well as their use alongside more traditional critical methods, implicitly suggesting how supposedly disparate assumptions can be held simultaneously and how diverse rhetorical conventions can mix, merge, and metamorphose. To put it simply, Butler's essay allows us to see how one can draw on the insights of *several* critical traditions (in effect, combining perspectives) to present a view of a work unavailable from any one window, any single critical perspective.

Butler begins her multiperspectival analysis by suggesting that Jane Austen's fiction presents more interpretive difficulties in "urban post-industrial societies, where marriage has lost most of its ritual resonance," than in places like Japan, India, and Nigeria, where the social rules of courtship are still well-understood. In our society, the value of marriage has become largely "personal"; marital life can provide the pleasure of regular and good sexual relations, of children, and of "emotional security" (p. 598 in this volume). In Austen's world, by contrast, sex seems to have little to do with marriage (as Butler points out, "Mr. Knightley's proposal . . . could hardly be couched less erotically" [p. 598]), and emotional security is less important than social stability.

Because our world so differs from the one Austen represents, the pleasure of reading one of her "courtship plots" is, for us, "more abstract" than that of reading a modern romance. The plot of *Emma,* according to Butler, provides us with the pleasure of watching a "Mozartian" formal dance, for courtship was *like* a formal dance in Austen's day (p. 598). Its purpose was not to reenforce and reward true love, or, in modern critical terminology, to inscribe heterosexual marriage as a societal norm. "The novel," Butler writes, "has a self-conscious design that operates to decenter Emma's love life, and to help us to see it as part of a wider scheme" (p. 599).

Having turned her attention to the novel's narrative design, Butler subsequently argues that, in spite of its formal structure and the social conventions it represents approvingly, *Emma* is by no means an entirely conventional novel. For instance, Austen renders dialogue far more naturalistically than did contemporary novelists of manners. Taking hints from such Gothic novelists as Ann Radcliffe and William Godwin, she represents a new kind of interior monologue — what Butler terms " 'inner free speech' " (p. 600).

In making her argument for the novel's unconventional narrative features, Butler concedes that Austen conventionally affords men (and members of the gentry) more sophisticated habits of audible and inner speech. And yet, she goes on to argue, "Highbury . . . is a community where the majority of 'people of note' are first- or second-generation gentry, if gentry at all" (p. 601), and where some of the older families (including the Woodhouses) face challenges to their dominance. Emma believes in social hierarchy and speaks from her privileged role in it, but because that hierarchy is in flux, her "voice [is] supplanted" (in spite of what Butler calls its "insidious involvement with the authorial voice") as the narrative progresses and as "dialogue voices unlike Emma's gain ground" (p. 602). Indeed, Butler argues, our "ability to read Highbury" (already hampered by our difficulty in understanding its outdated rules of courtship and marriage) depends upon our ability to figure out that Emma is an "unreliable narrator" (p. 602).

By contrast, Harriet Smith provides rich and reliable accounts of "subgroups normally beneath the snobbish Emma's attention" (p. 602): the teachers at Mrs. Goddard's school, for example, or the Martins of Abbey Mill Farm. Harriet reports conversations about conversations, registering shifts in tone and speech patterns that distinguish between subgroups, and ultimately provides a "news-chain . . . stitching the community together" (p. 603). The text thus "begins to democratize itself" as "Harriet opens up some of Highbury's margins and subcultures" (p. 603). Meanwhile, Emma — by contrast — provides us with an opinion of Miss Bates that is not only contradicted by "the general one" but that fails to "square with the 'reality' acted out in the second volume, where by personality, style, and force of example this commonplace woman is shown holding a key role in the community" (p. 605).

Butler goes on to differentiate the novel's "male and female modes of distributing news" (p. 605) (written vs. oral distributions) and various critical hypotheses regarding gossip, some of which specifically associate gossip with women but others of which do not tie it so tightly to gender, arguing instead that it binds small groups — or cliques — of talkers together. Austen's own theory of gossip, Butler suggests, would fall within this second category. *Emma*, she argues, "fails to anticipate the modern feminist premise that masculine and feminine discourses necessarily contend with one another" (p. 606) and, indeed, reflects Austen's historically grounded view of gossip, which associated it with "traditional agricultural communities" (p. 607) and with an artlessness that, though it didn't guarantee truth-telling, at least limited and moderated falsehood. (For a different view of gossip, see Casey Finch and Peter Bowen's "'The Tittle-Tattle of Highbury': Gossip and the Free Indirect Style in *Emma*" ["What Is the New Historicism?" pp. 543–58].)

Austen hardly celebrates gossip in *Emma*, but she does acknowledge its legitimate social role as one of the many and diverse languages that coexist within, and that help form, a given community. Butler views this acknowledgment much in the way she views Austen's naturalistic rendering of dialogue — or the "supplanting" of Emma's narrative, first by Harriet's more inclusive reportage and then, more significantly, by Miss Bates's rambling but seldom inconsequential discourse. She writes: "to promote oral language — gossip, dialect, slang — into written culture makes a democratizing gesture. . . . The commitment to record popular speech" implies "some claim for its positive value" (pp. 607–08).

As a passage like the above-quoted one may suggest, Butler's approach to Austen's *Emma* is truly one that mixes the best insights of various contemporary critical theories with those of older, more traditional approaches. Her interest in the novel's formal, dancelike structure is rooted in formalism — in the New Criticism and, more specifically, in Neo-Aristotelian criticism. (For definitions of critical and theoretical terms, see the glossary on pp. 615–34.) Formalist methods allow her to decenter the novel's love story and focus not only on plot structure but also on the role of secondary characters such as Miss Bates and Mrs. Elton. At the same time, her emphasis on *Emma*'s "democratizing tendencies" grows out of her awareness of a wide range of contemporary critical approaches. (In considering gossip, for example, Butler makes use of the theories of anthropologists such as Max Gluckman, new historicists indebted to Michel Foucault, and feminist critics such as Patricia Meyer Spacks. But she is finally no more beholden to these various theories than she is to Marxist criticism, with which she shares an interest in the role class distinctions play in social reality and its fictional representation.)

The stress Butler places on the role of cultural norms and practices (such as courtship) in fiction is also consistent with that of contemporary cultural criticism, even as her focus on the contemporary reader's reaction to it is consistent with that of narratology and, especially, of reader-response criticism. But, again, her emphasis on the value of interpretation that is informed by specific historical knowledge connects her to a long and rich tradition of traditional scholarship upon which contemporary approaches are grounded. (Examples of this emphasis include her use of biographical criticism, backward references to Shakespeare and Mozart, and comparisons between Austen and contemporary writers including Burney, Cobbett, Edgeworth, Hamilton, West, Wordsworth, and Young.)

Combining as she does critical perspectives represented in this volume with others that are not, Butler mixes approaches in a way that is typical of much contemporary scholarship. In doing so, she creates a critical whole that is greater than the sum of its parts.

Ross C Murfin

COMBINING PERSPECTIVES

MARILYN BUTLER

Introduction to *Emma*

Jane Austen's novels are as obsessive about marriage as they are repressive about sex. *Emma* begins on the wedding day of Emma's much-loved governess Miss Taylor, and ends a year later on Emma's own wedding day. By this time all the young unmarried women with speaking parts — Augusta Hawkins, Harriet Smith, Jane Fairfax —

have also been to the altar, or are on the point of getting there. On the face of it, the concern with love is just what makes any Austen novel likeable, accessible, among the friendliest of classics. Where *Emma* is concerned, it's also where the puzzles of this teasing novel begin.

The courtship plot is standard not only in eighteenth-century stage comedy and most novels, but in much popular culture worldwide. All societies have their rites of passage such as puberty and parenthood; men the world over exchange young women for money or land or in pursuit of dynastic alliances. No wonder then that Jane Austen's novels, generally taken in the British Isles as the most parochial of great novels, have readers in Japan, India, and Nigeria who can easily identify with their essential subject-matter. Austen's art naturally presents more problems in urban postindustrial societies, where marriage has lost most of its ritual resonance, and the positive ideas connected with it tend to be personal — a good sexual relationship, parenthood, emotional security within the nuclear family.

Austen is famous for on the whole omitting the language of lovers. Though Emma on Box Hill conducts a conversation with Frank Churchill that "no English word but flirtation could very well describe" (p. 294 in this volume), her interchanges with Mr Knightley resemble those of a pupil with a teacher or a young sister with an older brother — until, that is, they ask one another if they *are* brother and sister, and agree that this is not the case. When at last the moment for Mr. Knightley's proposal arrives, it could hardly be couched less erotically: "the subject . . . was in plain, unaffected gentleman-like English, . . . how to be able to ask her to marry him, without attacking the happiness of her father" (p. 354).

If marriage in Austen's fiction comes across emotionally low-keyed, why do readers continue to experience so much pleasure when the heroine accepts the right man? Or is our interest in fact distributed generally through the text, so that the pleasure is more abstract, more a question of completing a pattern, than of close identification with the heroine? Perhaps the happiest interpretation of *Emma* makes it a Mozartian formal dance, like *Così fan tutte* or *The Marriage of Figaro*. The just-married Westons at Randalls can be seen as the presiding geniuses, the instigators of merry-making in the whole community for the year that follows. The village couples are Emma and George Knightley and their protégés and "doubles" (who in Beaumarchais and Mozart would be servants), Harriet Smith and Robert Martin. The fortunes of these two pairs of lovers are intertwined, since Emma and Knightley have each taken a dislike, motivated by pique or envy, to their own partner's confidant and favorite, rather as Oberon and Titania quarrel over a favorite in *A Midsummer Night's Dream*. The novel has a self-conscious design that operates to decenter Emma's love life, and to help us to see it as part of a wider scheme. The three volumes each have eighteen chapters, plus a short nineteenth chapter in the third volume telling us of the three remaining weddings — Harriet's in September, Emma's in October, Jane's still to come in November. Even with their intertwining, the Emma/Knightley plot and the Harriet/Martin plot take the center of the stage only for part of the first half of volume I, and for most of the second half of volume III, so that in all they occupy less than a third of the action. From the halfway point of the first volume to half way through the third, our attention is deflected on to two couples essentially strangers to Highbury: the romantic, at times conventionally literary conspirators, Jane Fairfax and Frank Churchill, and the satirized and worldly young marrieds, the Eltons. Looked at this way, *Emma* comes to resemble one of Shakespeare's multiplotted comedies, *Twelfth Night*, *Much Ado About Nothing*, or *As You Like It*. Highbury becomes a version of Illyria or the Forest of Arden, a pastoral place to which the more worldly or tarnished couples of the middle sequences come to be made whole if they can.

Though Austen is much more loyal to the courtship plot than leading contemporaries such as Frances Burney, Elizabeth Inchbald, Mary Wollstonecraft, and Maria Edgeworth, she also teases us during much of *Emma* with a series of delusory or aborted love affairs — Robert and Harriet, Harriet and Elton, Elton and Emma, Frank and Emma — while the one reciprocal romance, between Frank and Jane, remains hidden from view. These disappointments are multiplied by Emma's blunders until some situations belong virtually to farce, as when the newly married Mr. Elton finds himself in the same room "with the woman he had just married, the woman he had wanted to marry, and the woman whom he had been expected to marry" (p. 220). Even though there will be an unusually large crop of weddings before we are through, directly involving ten leading characters, any erotic pleasure the reader might be expected to derive is short, since each wedding comes suddenly, denying us the usual anticipation. This is of a piece with another oddity in Austen's handling of romance, her unwillingness to show us the heroine reciprocally in love. Of all Austen's leading women, Emma is by far the freest agent. She comes nearer than the others to speaking as a critic of marriage, when she observes that a well-off young woman may be more independent as a spinster than as a wife: "I believe few married women are half as much mistress of their husband's house, as I am of Hartfield . . ." (p. 84). In *Emma* Austen does most to release herself from the narrow preoccupation with romantic love that her plots seem to hold out to the reader.

Emma is highly conventional, then, but in an unconventional way. It relies on tropes traditional to stage comedy, but also experiments with recently introduced fictional techniques. *Emma* represents a departure from Austen's earlier novels in the extreme naturalism with which it renders talk as a means of realizing a local community. But it also seems to borrow from the Gothic tradition, from Ann Radcliffe or from William Godwin, a new type of interior monologue, a more continuous and more intimate access to the heroine's consciousness. To take the second first, *Emma* has been praised in the twentieth century as a pioneering achievement in the technique known as "inner free speech." This method of narration remains conveniently third person, as though an omniscient author tells the story, but frequently appears to merge with the consciousness of the heroine, and to characterize her thoughts. Comic, endearing, very believable, Emma betrays herself, while also drawing us insidiously into her partial and misleading view of the world.

"Inner free speech" contributes greatly to the novel. Yet not even *Pride and Prejudice* relies as much on talk as Emma does, or uses it with such conscious sophistication. In his computerized study of Austen's dialogue, John Burrows has proved her exceptionally fine ear in distinguishing each speaker by his or her idiolect from every other, while at the same time grouping her speakers as types. Principal characters in all the novels are in effect privileged by Austen, and share her authorial speech characteristics: short periods, controlled syntax, an abstract vocabulary, but also a high proportion of information, concisely delivered, and a decisiveness, notably expressed in judgments of other people's behavior. A larger group of characters, most of the comic figures, display linguistic incompetence: incomplete sentences, irrelevance, a lack of selectivity as to what to report, and a lack of judgment on people or on matters of taste (e.g., literature, musical execution, and ability to draw).

Burrows's analyses show, among other things, that in Austen's fiction privileged speech habits are associated with masculinity (all eligible men throughout the novels have them), but not confined to men: all the heroines (with some allowances for the immaturity of Catherine Morland and Fanny Price) talk in this style, and so do their favorite women friends. Irrationality and ingenuousness, like compulsive talking, are stereotypical feminine traits, and most of Austen's foolish speakers are women. But a man may join this group, a point illustrated in *Emma* by Mr. Woodhouse, and by Mr. Elton when under the influence of Mr. Weston's good wine. Again, we might expect these two groups to divide along lines of class, since speech competence is much influenced by formal education; but Austen seems to go out of her way to allow exceptional men (such as Robert Martin) as well as a larger group of women into her privileged class. Though these are not his words, the general impression left by Burrows's study could be that Austen depicts her world as "patriarchal," that is governed by an educated order and governed by men, while open to meritorious individuals from below.

Just who qualifies as a speaker is a perplexing question apparently unique to *Emma*. Oliver MacDonagh has remarked on the striking discrepancy in this novel, between characters who are given names (about ninety, an immense number in Austen's supposedly minimalist world) and characters who are given voices. Only sixteen individuals, Mac-Donagh points out, speak in the style we would nowadays print within quotation marks. Of the sixteen, three (old Mrs. Bates, Mrs. Ford and Mrs. Cole) are heard from directly on only one occasion apiece. The effective speaking parts are really thirteen: three Knightleys, two Westons, two Woodhouses, two Eltons, Miss Bates, Jane Fairfax, Frank Churchill and Harriet Smith — an unusually low number. Yet there is an intermediate group which MacDonagh estimates at thirty-five strong, of characters heard from at one or more removes, through the predilection of "Highbury gossips" to relay what their friends have said to them. MacDonagh praises the technical virtuosity which enables Austen in her role of Highbury's anthropologist so economically to "thicken" our impression of a "large and populous village almost amounting to a town" (p. 25). Thanks to techniques available to the novelist, hers is a portrait that goes beyond even the statistically documented works of the nonfictional travellers of the time, Arthur Young and William Cobbett, in the nicety with which it registers social diversity and fluidity.

Highbury, clearly the main topic of the novel's long central section, is a community where the majority of "people of note" are first- or second-generation gentry, if gentry at all. The novel charts the mechanisms whereby the social elite is able to redefine itself. Everyone with a claim to have "made it" in effect competes with the others for social prestige and a share in community leadership — except Mr Knightley, who, as hereditary owner of all the land in Highbury except the Woodhouses' Hartfield, has an unassailable preeminence. Emma herself does not recognize the recent changes and their threat to her position. Her "disposition to think a little too well of herself" (p. 24) extends to her notion of her own and her father's local prestige. Because of Mr. Woodhouse's nervous self-protectiveness, they are reduced to a very small circle of "old friends" — or, as Emma thinks of Mrs. Bates, Miss Bates, and Mrs. Goddard, their usual guests in the autumn of Miss Taylor's departure, three prosing old women (p. 36). So rarely do the Woodhouses drive out to make visits that Emma is in danger of being left off the guest list of the Coles' great dinner party for the neighborhood elect.

Emma's insistence on a village hierarchy based on "old family" shapes her world anachronistically the way she would like it to be: she is a self-interested and hence thoroughly unreliable narrator. So our ability to read Highbury depends on our willingness to see Emma's voice supplanted, in spite of its insidious involvement with the authorial voice. Halfway through the first volume, the text indeed begins to democratize itself; through the dialogue voices unlike Emma's gain ground. Emma, born and brought up in Highbury, has long since accustomed herself to its lingua franca, a warmer, more desultory, more amiable language than her own. It is spoken by her father, whom she cossets and manages. Harriet Smith fills the vacancy in their domestic circle, a girl who shares most of Mr. Woodhouse's characteristics, from physical timidity to habits of speech. Each flatters Emma with the same lack of discrimination, and each incessantly quotes the words of others, though Harriet plainly has the better memory. Mr. Woodhouse's favourite source is Mr. Perry, who as the community's doctor is one of the town's tireless talkers and relayers of talk. But Mr. Woodhouse also opens doors on parts of the house and of the community that no one else reaches, the servants' quarters, for example, and the nursery. Meanwhile Harriet peoples Highbury with descriptions of subgroups normally beneath the snobbish Emma's attention. In her gushing description of what might be termed the Elton fan club, Mrs. Goddard's routine, kindly school with its three unmarried teachers and its older girls, Harriet's contemporaries, comes startlingly to life (p. 71).

Harriet's account of the Martins' little world at Abbey Mill Farm is a glimpse of a pastoral idyll outside Austen's usual register. She recalls hot days, moonlit walks, pet animals, a motherly Mrs. Martin, and a young man who arranged for her to hear his shepherd's son singing. The Martins are also givers of gifts: a "pretty little Welsh cow" is only called Harriet's, but Mrs. Goddard and the three school teachers get a real goose to eat when she goes back at the end of the holiday. Life on the Martins' farm is an idealized rustic version of Highbury life, prosperous, comfortable, affectionate, and leisured enough for culture. But Harriet's account is less characteristic of the novel than other speeches in which Harriet appears unconsciously to uncover the way the village's social mechanisms work. Her best report, a discursive tour de force, features Mr. Elton and the lovestruck Miss Nash, who is Harriet's immediate source (p. 71). In this account of Mr. Elton's trip to London, Harriet reports to Emma a conversation with Miss Nash in which Miss Nash reported a conversation with Mr. Perry, who reported a conversation with Mr. Elton — who of course half betrayed, but meaningfully abstained from reporting, the conversation in which he got the commission from Emma to have her portrait of Harriet framed. The passage registers shifts in tone, as it passes from being an intimate tête-à-tête between two women, regular confidantes, to a less confidential yet still somewhat collusive conversation between a man and a woman, again old acquaintances, to the masculine jocularities of Perry with Elton. We can pick up on the extent to which subgroups are distinguished by their different speech patterns, yet also notice that their common involvement in the news chain has the effect of stitching the community together.

Harriet opens up only some of Highbury's margins and subcultures; the center of the village has to wait for the conversational input of Miss Bates. This queen among Highbury talkers is twice described in volume I, and once mimicked by Emma, but we do not hear her speak until Emma makes a long-delayed visit to the Bateses at home in the opening chapter of volume II. From that point, Miss Bates mounts a powerful challenge to the tight little hegemony Emma has made out of the two outlying gentleman's households, Hartfield and Randalls. While the novel used those locations, most scenes occurred indoors between two or three characters. Sociability in the long middle section, however, is more likely to consist of chance meetings at the center of the village, where the key interiors are the Bateses' first-floor rooms, Mrs. Ford's shop across the main street, and the Crown Inn, "a hop, step, and jump" away (p. 164). The second volume's great set pieces occur in the ninth and tenth chapters. In chapter IX Harriet is in Mrs. Ford's shop, dithering; Emma has walked to the door, and is pleasurably observing the scene in the street. It is deservedly the most-quoted sentence in the novel:

> Much could not be hoped from the traffic of even the busiest part of Highbury; — Mr. Perry walking hastily by, Mr. William Cox letting himself in at the office door, Mr. Cole's carriage horses

returning from exercise, or a stray letter-boy on an obstinate mule, were the liveliest objects she could presume to expect; and when her eyes fell only on the butcher with his tray, a tidy old woman travelling homewards from shop with her full basket, two curs quarrelling over a dirty bone, and a string of dawdling children round the baker's little bow-window eyeing the gingerbread, she knew she had no reason to complain, and was amused enough; quite enough still to stand at the door. (p. 192)

Austen allows the brisk and active Emma her Keatsian moment of negative capability, a moment which in effect allows her to glimpse all sorts of village lives, even the curs', which coexist with her own. A few moments more, and (in chapter X) Miss Bates has drawn them into her small and densely cluttered sitting room, in which four visitors and three residents now compete for space with the new piano. It is the "crowd in a little room" normally abominated by the fastidious Emma. Yet on this occasion everyone inside is entertained by a dialogue, conducted by Miss Bates at the window and Mr. Knightley in the street below, a conversation both about gift giving and the pragmatic objections to gift giving, mounted by Mr. Knightley's housekeeper Mrs. Hodges and his steward William Larkins. Knightley takes on new dimensions as an employer and as a citizen in this short and funny exchange. The Donwell Abbey cooking apples stand for a homely habitual kindness which bonds the villagers in their daily lives, and has little in common with the expensive and mystifying present of the piano.

Emma's early remarks about Miss Bates are dismissive — and insensitive since she does not reflect that she is complaining of her to Harriet, who is a younger version of Miss Bates. Emma has to grant that her opinion is not the general one and herself supplies the reasons: "Poverty certainly has not contracted her mind: I really believe, if she had only a shilling in the world, she would be very likely to give away sixpence of it" (p. 85). Miss Bates pays charitable visits to John Abdy, her late father's clerk for twenty-seven years, and receives visits, gifts, and services from Mr. Knightley, the Woodhouses, the Westons, the Coles, the Eltons and even sharp-tongued Mrs. Wallis, the pastrycook's wife. In this way she does something for the whole community, much as Wordsworth's Old Cumberland Beggar does:

But deem not this man useless . . .
    the Villagers in him
Behold a record which together binds

Past deeds and offices of charity
Else unremembered, and so keeps alive
The kindly mood in hearts which lapse of years,
And that half-wisdom half-experience gives,
Make slow to feel. . . .
Where'er the aged Beggar takes his rounds,
The mild necessity of use compels
To acts of love; and habit does the work
Of reason. . . .   (ll. 67, 80–86, 90–93)

Emma's clever, superficial jokes fail to square with the "reality" acted out in the second volume, where by personality, style, and force of example this commonplace woman is shown holding a key role in the community.

Miss Bates's "tittle-tattle" is a collage: a disorderly local bulletin, a series of declarations of generalized goodwill, and material barely informative at all, such as "I said to my mother, Upon my word ma'am —." Her voice dominates many Highbury events, including the first half of the ball at the Crown; even Mr. Knightley, who is capable of using masculine volume to talk her down, conforms to her agenda and joins in the exchange of tittle-tattle. They compete, and she wins, as the messenger who brings the news of Mr. Elton's engagement. Distinct male and female modes of distributing news are identified in the novel, somewhat analogous to the stereotypical styles of speech. Active men, riding or walking about — Knightley, Weston, Churchill, Perry, Martin, and Cole — commonly perform the simple labor of carrying the news from one point to another. Equally masculine, as efficient, and more impersonal, the Post Office carries Frank's letters to Jane. The cabal of three (Knightley, Emma, Mrs. Weston) sitting usually at Randalls, which has two women, but an analytical masculine style, meets to discuss the news, which is a specialized way of sorting it out. But Mrs. Cole, Mrs. Perry, Mrs. Goddard, Mrs. Elton, the ladies convening in the Bateses' sitting-room, are alternative powers in the village to these other powers. They receive news both written and oral. They distribute it as the staple ingredient of companionable talk.

Recent anthropological work on systems of oral communication such as gossip can be very suggestive for *Emma*. Three contending hypotheses all work well for different aspects of the novel. One is Patricia Spacks's suggestion, in her lively literary study, *Gossip*, that gossip is a feminized alternative discourse, which tends to undercut dominant masculine discursive norms. Spacks draws on examples from many periods and cultures to show that gossip has commonly been associated with women and found threatening by men. She defends it against its detractors by citing Carol Gilligan's argument in her *In a Different Voice,* which argues that women adopt a discourse which stresses affection, cooperation, and sociability, by contrast with the more individualistic, assertive, and rational male vernacular. Spacks in this book does not discuss *Emma;* but Austen's portrayal of the speech-patterns of Harriet, Miss Bates and Mr. Woodhouse coincides with her and Gilligan's perception of a distinctive female language and subculture, operating as a bonding force within society.

A second view of gossip, which does not tie it so specifically to women, is given by the anthropologist Max Gluckman. He suggests that a community is "partly held together and maintains its values by gossiping and scandalizing both, within cliques and in general" (308). Again, Gluckman's proposition seems anticipated by Austen. *Emma* uncovers with great particularity mechanisms (such as the role of Miss Bates) through which gossip performs its task of bonding. Gluckman's significant additional phrase, "within cliques and in general," picks up the multiplicity of small subsets of talkers, illustrated in Highbury by the young women at Mrs. Goddard's school. Austen may outdo Gluckman in the imaginativeness and detail with which she genders Highbury gossip. On the other hand her text fails to anticipate the modern feminist premise, that masculine and feminine discourses necessarily contend with one another. Miss Bates' activities are not presented as if they subvert Knightley's power; nor do they challenge patriarchal norms. What Austen offers more impassively in the equivocal figure of Miss Bates — a fool if a holy fool — is indeed an alternative principle, but in the evenhanded spirit of this unusually open novel.

A third, more pessimistic, view of gossip draws on the work of the French sociologist of knowledge, Michel Foucault. In some of his more specialized studies of specialized discourses, those on madness, sexuality, and penology, Foucault shows how knowledge and culture provide the media through which power operates in society. Since the 1970s some of Foucault's followers have added gossip to this list of the modern world's mechanisms of constraint and social discipline. In an article on *Emma* [included in this volume] Casey Finch and Peter Bowen contest the more benign interpretation of gossip advanced by the Spacks school, and maintain instead a much severer theory in which gossip, supposedly a feminine mode, actually operates "to reinforce patriarchal norms" (p. 545).

At this point, we might ask what Austen herself might have thought gossip did. In fact, just as Austen's treatment of courtship is conditioned by a rich existing literature of courtship, so her treatment of Highbury is conditioned by a rich existing literature of localities, going back at the very least to the circle of John Aubrey in the late seventeenth century, and meticulously concerned with data about manners, customs, and speech-practices. While it is true, as Spacks observes, that gossip has generally been associated with women, it is also felt to be especially characteristic of villages, traditional agricultural communities where the population is fairly static and relationships have been partly pre-determined by family traditions, caste, and custom. Village life, and to varying degrees the role of gossip in it, figured largely in poetry from the last quarter of the eighteenth century and on into the nineteenth, while novels of domestic life in village settings were perhaps the most fashionable of all types of novel by the time Jane Austen took up her pen in the early 1790s. Austen owned Jane West's *A Gossip's Story* (1796), and almost certainly borrowed elements from its plot and setting, particularly in *Sense and Sensibility*. West's novel, narrated by a character with the self-explanatory name of Mrs. Prudentia Homespun, has plainly been itself deeply influenced by Hannah More's immensely widely read *Village Dialogues* (from 1793), tracts in which village characters spiritedly debate the great public issues of the French revolutionary years.

By the 1790s the representation of the English village is much more likely than not to have a political agenda. Hannah More, Jane West, and after them Maria Edgeworth, in *Castle Rackrent* (1800), and Elizabeth Hamilton, in *Cottagers of Glenburnie* (1808), all see the village as the natural home of customary wisdom, kindliness, commonsense, and Christian values, in an implied contrast with the shallowness and materialism of the town. But, though village talk lets this Burkean heritage shine through, it also expresses more disturbing possibilities. The voices of the many produce an effect which is multivocal, hence often discordant, confused, or anarchic. This is why Hamilton sends an educated woman, Mrs. Mason, to tell her Glenburnie hostess when and how to dust, make beds, introduce order into her home, and thus discipline her ungoverned children.

The "rules" on gossip and orality in written culture at this time are plainly contradictory. To some degree gossip is a derogatory term; even while it is being defended, it is also being contained. Yet it is at least equally true that to promote oral language — gossip, dialect, slang —

into written culture makes a democratizing gesture, as the controversy on the question of orality versus authority strongly suggests (Butler, Smith). The commitment to record popular speech at all is almost always accompanied by some claim for its positive value.

Gossiping in villages is generally then a benign or essentially innocent activity; its high-life equivalents, scandal and intrigue, are almost invariably destructive. "Tittle-tattle" of these kinds forms a staple linguistic medium of modern urban society's self-representation, from the Jonsonian comedy of humors, through Restoration and eighteenth-century stage comedy, and on into the late eighteenth-century novel of (for instance) Frances Burney and Choderlos de Laclos. While the notion of village talk stubbornly retains vestiges of idealism respecting communitarian and familial values, scandal and intrigue (which can be political as well as sexual) hint at popular paranoia about small, closed systems of government, a world of secret alliances and enmities, ambition, envy, and corruption.

The themes of gossip and of scandal are confused in some modern criticism of novels such as Austen's, but they do not seem to have been conflated at the time: gossip is too much a factor of village life, scandal of town life. True, Emma launches an outrageous calumny against Jane, for which she has no evidence: that Jane is having an affair with her best friend's husband. Emma certainly is embarrassed afterwards that Frank has shared her scandalous allegation with Jane. But another novelist would have been likelier to show the story damaging Jane, in her prospects either of marriage or of becoming a governess. Meanwhile Jane is in fact conducting an intrigue, her nine-month-old secret engagement with Frank. Both Knightley brothers begin to suspect something of this, John when he quizzes her about walking to the Post Office in the rain, and George when he detects a secret understanding between the couple. So far, this would look like a classic case, the surveillance of an erring female by two male authority-figures. But what George finally has to say about Jane's transgression is the mild, almost feminine observation that the social law is broken if we are not frank and open with our neighbors. We could read this as the masculine arm of the law finally handing over jurisdiction to the voluntary feminine code (which is supported on this occasion by Emma). We could notice the signs that Jane can be fairly safely left to her conscience, that internalized Big Sister. We could conclude that Austen never takes social control so seriously as a threat to the individual as many of her contemporaries do.

In *Emma* Frank is the character most seriously under investigation by Mr. Knightley, Emma, and Mrs. Weston. His letters get chapters to themselves; they are read, and read again; Knightley actually delays his proposal to Emma until he has added his opinion to Emma's reading of the last one. The puzzle we are left with is what all these regular sessions by (in effect) Highbury's informal magistracy really amount to. Frank is plainly found guilty of neglecting his father, Highbury, and his new stepmother, and of using Emma as a stalking horse while he conducts his affair with Jane. He betrayed Emma's confidences to Jane, traduced Jane to Emma, and tormented Jane by his pretended flirtation, which on Box Hill must have looked seriously meant. Mrs. Weston, mildest of the three judges, urges all along that no one should condemn Frank until they fully understand his circumstances. Yet when all circumstances are understood, his behavior looks more selfish and hurtful than anyone has suspected.

Because they are often liars, Frank and Jane do not define the external world in a fully usable way. Mrs. Elton contributes a more precise model of another world, and a better basis for comparisons with Highbury. She views the village on her arrival as a backward country place, which she can remake by teaching it her new suburban manners. Her strongest card is to be genuinely insensitive to Emma's Tory notion of hierarchy, which reserves leadership of the locality to the squire. Mrs. Elton downgrades Mr. Knightley by referring to him as "Knightley," and one by one does the same to the village's three gentry women. She cannot easily think of the two of these who lack independent incomes, the ex-governess Mrs. Weston and the future governess Jane Fairfax, as gentlewomen at all. Her insistent omission of "Miss" before Jane's name could sound like easy familiarity at Maple Grove, but in more traditional Highbury it makes Jane a social inferior. She addresses even Emma as a country mouse who will be glad to be chaperoned at Bath by Mrs. Jeffereys, the former Clara Partridge.

Emerging from the prosperous trading class, Mrs. Elton sees money and an acquaintance with the moneyed as the determinants of social prestige. Possessions are the outward signs of success, but they must be new and fashionable, expensive rather than innately valuable. Mrs. Elton herself always wears or carries something identifiable as the latest accessory — beads, a fringe, a purple and gold reticule. She walks into the Hartfield dinner party in her honour "as elegant as lace and pearls could make her," and dresses for Donwell in the paraphernalia of a stage gypsy (pp. 236, 284). All summer her formal status as a bride indeed allows her to lead, and she exploits the situation by setting out to give Highbury a more modish program of social activities. A very superior party, with candles and unbroken packs on the card tables, is to be one way she means to set an example; another, a musical club, meeting weekly under the leadership of herself and Emma. Frank Churchill, restlessly moving about the village, measuring its interiors to see how many couples they might hold, becomes unwittingly a partner in a joint project, to adapt some of the larger village properties to a more urban use. In the first half of the third volume these new amusements follow one another in succession: the ball at the Crown, the picnic at Donwell Abbey, the outing to Box Hill. Something disagreeable happens at all three gatherings, always involving one or more of the strangers: the Eltons' snub to Harriet at the ball, the bad temper and discomposure of Mrs. Elton, Frank's contretemps with Jane at Donwell, Frank's flirtation with Emma on Box Hill, which distresses both Miss Bates and Jane.

It is only in retrospect, in the second half of this final volume, that we discover how Frank and Mrs. Elton have been joined in another project — the struggle to possess Jane Fairfax. With her habitual reticence, Jane is almost a heroine under a spell, and her captors are both of them strangers to Highbury, who emerge in the final stages of the novel as unpleasant, at times threatening figures, in spite of Frank's apparent charm. Mrs. Elton, originally from Bristol, British home port of the African slave trade, is bent on selling Jane in the governess market for the best price she can get. Mrs. Bragg, a cousin of Mr. Suckling's, would be an ideal employer. "Wax candles in the school-room! You may imagine how desirable!" (p. 242). Mrs. Smallridge seems to have nothing so particular to recommend her, yet "except the Sucklings and Bragges, there is not such another nursery establishment, so liberal and elegant, in all Mrs. Elton's acquaintance" (p. 304). Miss Bates, reporting this, has perfectly caught Mrs. Elton's consumerist tone and vocabulary, another strong sign of her growing influence. As Mrs. Elton has negotiated on Jane's behalf in Maple Grove circles, she has priced Jane's distinctions — her education, intelligence, musicality — in buyers' language.

Emma has engrossed twentieth-century critics. Minor characters, especially those viewed externally in the comic "humors" tradition, do not rate by comparison. One critic remarks that Miss Bates's speeches will not sustain a complex reading (unlike Emma's thoughts), and even that they are passages to skim (Armstrong 155). It is equally noticeable that Mrs. Elton, for earlier critics one of the novel's achievements, receives much less attention by the middle of the twentieth century. Yet Mrs. Elton, like Miss Bates, plays a crucial part in the symbolic action, the plot's movement to confront the troubling spectres it has raised — the mechanics, the inevitability, the pain of social change. Mrs. Elton has gained a great deal of ground in the course of the novel. Thanks to Mrs. Churchill's sudden death, Jane escapes becoming her protegée/ property, but to judge by Miss Bates's wheedling apologies for this disappointment, the Elton influence in that household remains powerful. The fact is that she fits into the circle of the Coleses, Coxes, and Perrys more snugly than Emma can. She has emerged as a natural leader in the prosperous little commercial town nineteenth-century Highbury is becoming. It is true that she fails in her audacious bid to clinch the year's victories by acting as hostess at Donwell Abbey, but we are given signs that she has established some ascendancy over central Highbury, and if this is the case the town we have just got to know is already a fading impression. The bloom on Miss Bates's innocence may have gone for ever.

Can Emma hope, on marrying Mr Knightley, to take up all the customary perquisites of an old-style squire's wife? Will she really, as she once threatened, "drop" Harriet now that she is the wife of a mere tenant farmer? She might get away with scaling down the evenings with the Bateses and Mrs. Goddard, as her father fails and dies. An exchange of hospitality, not too often, with the Coleses would be tolerable, especially if she had her husband's agreement that they would not attend a musical evening at the Vicarage more than twice a year. This would have been the future the old Emma might have planned, but it does not square with George Knightley's much more open social habits. In particular, the Martins' farm, at the end of Donwell Abbey's lime walk, looks likely to become part of Emma's domestic existence, as it already is of her husband's. By the closing chapters, the way we see the map of Highbury has shifted a second time, out on to the village's agricultural fringe. Some readers might conclude that Highbury is about to be led again from its old feudal base, though under Knightley's conciliatory leadership. But it is equally on the cards that two Highburys are emerging, as the traditional county gentry begins to draw away from the new moneyed order that recruits new members year by year.

With the group of women of Highbury she created, Austen had many ties. She mostly lived in one of two much smaller southern English villages, Steventon as a gentlewoman and Chawton as a poor gentlewoman, though with rich connections. Like Miss Bates, she was the dependant daughter of a clergyman. In the year she finished *Emma,* when she was forty, Austen also completed a decade living essentially as the companion of her widowed mother. In her letters she was beginning to express increasing sympathy with two women of Chawton, Miss Benn and Mrs. Stent, who also shared the Bates women's position; the thought of growing with age more and more like them was not to be taken lightly, even if Emma, younger and richer, is able to brush aside its horrors. Austen might, like Jane Fairfax, have gone to work as a governess, but for the brothers who chipped in with housing and pocket money. Then, from 1811, the money she began to make from her novels transformed her situation. The fact remains that Austen knew what only Emma and Mrs. Elton in her novel have escaped knowing, real financial insecurity, and the apparent certainty of becoming a member of that populous and much-ridiculed category, the poor old maid.

This is why we have to look for Austen herself not merely in the person of Emma (Austenian though she is in her wit and her imaginativeness), but in the group whose lives, taken together, illustrate what social change means for educated women. Austen's art is always much less concerned with the direct expression of attitudes, emotions, experiences, than with elaborate displacements through which a great range of thought, feeling, and minute observation is being quietly registered. By displaying the humanity of her fools and gossips, Austen escapes the doctrinaire tendencies of so many of her contemporaries, and works her best surprises.

WORKS CITED

Armstrong, Nancy. *Desire and Domestic Fiction.* Oxford: Oxford UP, 1987.

Burrows, John. *Computation into Criticism: Jane Austen's Language.* Oxford: Oxford UP, 1986.

Butler, Marilyn. *Burke, Godwin and the Revolution Controversy.* Cambridge: Cambridge UP, 1984.

Finch, Casey, and Peter Bowen. " 'The Tittle-Tattle of Highbury': Gossip and the Free Indirect Style in *Emma.*" *Representations* 31 (1990): 1–18.

Gilligan, Carol. *In a Different Voice.* Cambridge: Harvard UP, 1981.

Gluckman, Max. "Gossip and Scandal." *Current Anthropology* 4 (1963): 307–16.

MacDonagh, Oliver. *Jane Austen: Real and Imagined Worlds.* New Haven: Yale UP, 1991.

Smith, Olivia. *The Politics of Language.* Oxford: Oxford UP, 1984.

Spacks, Patricia. *Gossip.* New York: Knopf, 1985.

Wordsworth, William. "The Old Cumberland Beggar." *Lyrical Ballads.* 2nd ed. 2 vols. London, 1800.

Glossary of Critical
and Theoretical Terms

ABSENCE The idea, advanced by French theorist Jacques Derrida, that authors are not present in texts and that meaning arises in the absence of any authority guaranteeing the correctness of any one interpretation.
See **Presence and Absence** for a more complete discussion.

AFFECTIVE FALLACY *See* **New Criticism; Reader-Response Criticism.**

BASE *See* **Marxist Criticism.**

CANON A term used since the fourth century to refer to those books of the Bible that the Christian church accepts as being Holy Scripture — that is, divinely inspired. Books outside the canon (noncanonical books) are referred to as *apocryphal. Canon* has also been used to refer to the Saints Canon, the group of people officially recognized by the Catholic Church as saints. More recently, it has been employed to refer to the body of works generally attributed by scholars to a particular author (for example, the Shakespearean canon is currently believed to consist of thirty-seven plays that scholars feel can be definitively attributed to him). Works sometimes attributed to an author, but whose authorship is disputed or otherwise uncertain, are called apocryphal. *Canon* may also refer more generally to those literary works that are "privileged," or given special status, by a culture. Works we tend to think of as classics or as "Great Books"— texts that are repeatedly reprinted in anthologies of literature — may be said to constitute the canon.

Note: The following definitions are adapted and/or abridged versions of ones found in *The Bedford Glossary of Critical and Literary Terms,* by Ross C Murfin and Supryia M. Ray (© Bedford Books 1997).

Contemporary **Marxist, feminist,** minority, and **postcolonial** critics have argued that, for political reasons, many excellent works never enter the canon. Canonized works, they claim, are those that reflect — and respect — the culture's dominant ideology or perform some socially acceptable or even necessary form of "cultural work." Attempts have been made to broaden or redefine the canon by discovering valuable texts, or versions of texts, that were repressed or ignored for political reasons. These have been published both in traditional and in nontraditional anthologies. The most outspoken critics of the canon, especially certain critics practicing **cultural criticism,** have called into question the whole concept of canon or "canonicity." Privileging no form of artistic expression, these critics treat cartoons, comics, and soap operas with the same cogency and respect they accord novels, poems, and plays.

CHICAGO SCHOOL Originally a group of literary critics associated with the University of Chicago; other critics who have followed in their footsteps have also been referred to as Chicago School critics or, more simply, as Chicago Critics. In 1952, the original group of Chicago Critics collectively published a landmark book entitled *Critics and Criticism,* which outlined their thinking about both practical criticism (a type of literary criticism) and the general history of criticism.

Chicago School critics typically examine works on an individual basis (as do practical critics and objective critics). They view the text in terms of its form, or shaping principle, and the way in which that form is articulated in the work's structure. They also, however, consider the relationship between individual works and broadly defined categories of works, or **genres.** Because they combine an historical interest in schools of criticism and literary genres with a practical or objective focus on the internal structure and relations of elements within individual works, the Chicago School critics are sometimes said to be **Neo-Aristotelian** critics. The approach of the Chicago critics has also been called formalist insofar as it involves analyzing works on an individual basis; it is important to note, however, that the Chicago critics' interest in historical matters is decidedly not formalist. Influential Chicago critics include such figures as R. S. Crane, Elder Olson, and Wayne Booth.

CULTURAL CRITICISM, CULTURAL STUDIES *See* "What Is Cultural Criticism?" pp. 488–508.

DECONSTRUCTION Deconstruction involves the close reading of **texts** in order to demonstrate that any given text has irreconcilably contradictory meanings, rather than being a unified, logical whole. As J. Hillis Miller, the preeminent American deconstructor, has explained in an essay entitled "Stevens' Rock and Criticism as Cure" (1976), "Deconstruction is not a dismantling of the structure of a text, but a demonstration that it has already dismantled itself. Its apparently solid ground is no rock but thin air."

Deconstruction was both created and has been profoundly influenced by the French philosopher of language Jacques Derrida. Derrida, who coined the term *deconstruction,* argues that in Western culture, people tend to think and express their thoughts in terms of *binary oppositions.* Something is white but not black, masculine and therefore not feminine, a cause rather than an effect. Other common and mutually exclusive pairs include beginning/end, conscious/unconscious, **presence/absence,** and speech/writing. Derrida suggests these oppositions are hierarchies in miniature, containing one term that Western culture views as positive or superior and another considered negative or inferior, even if only slightly so. Through deconstruction, Derrida aims to erase the boundary between binary oppositions — and to do so in such a way that the hierarchy implied by the oppositions is thrown into question.

Although its ultimate aim may be to criticize Western logic, deconstruction arose as a response to **structuralism** and to **formalism.** Structuralists believed that all elements of human culture, including literature, may be understood as parts of a system of signs. Derrida did not believe that structuralists could explain the laws governing human signification and thus provide the key to understanding the form and meaning of everything from an African village to Greek myth to a literary text. He also rejected the structuralist belief that texts have identifiable "centers" of meaning, a belief structuralists shared with formalists.

Formalist critics, such as the **New Critics,** assume that a work of literature is a freestanding, self-contained object whose meaning can be found in the complex network of relations between its parts (allusions, images, rhythms, sounds, etc.). Deconstructors, by contrast, see works in terms of their *undecidability.* They reject the formalist view that a work of literary art is demonstrably unified from beginning to end, in one certain way, or that it is organized around a single center that ultimately can be identified. As a result, deconstructors see texts as more radically heterogeneous than do formalists. Formalists ultimately make sense of the ambiguities they find in a given text, arguing that every ambiguity serves a definite, meaningful — and demonstrable — literary function. Undecidability, by contrast, is never reduced, let alone mastered. Though a deconstructive reading can reveal the incompatible possibilities generated by the text, it is impossible for the reader to decide among them.

DIALECTIC Originally developed by Greek philosophers, mainly Socrates and Plato (in *The Republic* and *Phaedrus* [c. 360 BC]), a form and method of logical argumentation that typically addresses conflicting ideas or positions. When used in the plural, dialectics refer to any mode of argumentation that attempts to resolve the contradictions between opposing ideas.

The German philosopher G. W. F. Hegel described dialectic as a process whereby a *thesis,* when countered by an *antithesis,* leads to the *synthesis* of a new idea. Karl Marx and Friedrich Engels, adapting Hegel's idealist theory, used the phrase *dialectical materialism* to discuss the way in which a revolutionary class war might lead to the synthesis of a new socioeconomic order.

In literary criticism, *dialectic* typically refers to the oppositional ideas and/or mediatory reasoning that pervade and unify a given work or group of works. Critics may thus speak of the dialectic of head and heart (reason and passion) in William Shakespeare's plays. The American **Marxist critic** Fredric Jameson has coined the phrase "dialectical criticism" to refer to a Marxist critical approach that synthesizes **structuralist** and **poststructuralist** methodologies.

DIALOGIC *See* **Discourse.**

DISCOURSE Used specifically, (1) the thoughts, statements, or dialogue of individuals, especially of characters in a literary work; (2) the words in, or text of, a **narrative** as opposed to its story line; or (3) a "strand" within a given narrative that argues a certain point or defends a given value system. Discourse of the first type is sometimes categorized as *direct* or *indirect*. Direct discourse relates the thoughts and utterances of individuals and literary characters to the reader unfiltered by a third-person narrator. ("Take me home this instant!" she insisted.) Indirect discourse (also referred to as free indirect discourse) is more impersonal, involving the reportage of thoughts, statements, or dialogue by a third-person narrator. (She told him to take her home immediately.)

More generally, *discourse* refers to the language in which a subject or area of knowledge is discussed or a certain kind of business is transacted. Human knowledge is collected and structured in discourses. Theology and medicine are defined by their discourses, as are politics, sexuality, and literary criticism.

Contemporary literary critics have maintained that society is generally made up of a number of different discourses or *discourse communities,* one or more of which may be dominant or serve the dominant ideology. Each discourse has its own vocabulary, concepts, and rules — knowledge of which constitutes power. The psychoanalyst and **psychoanalytic critic** Jacques Lacan has treated the unconscious as a form of discourse, the patterns of which are repeated in literature. **Cultural critics,** following Soviet critic Mikhail Bakhtin, use the word *dialogic* to discuss the dialogue between discourses that takes place within language or, more specifically, a literary text. Some **poststructuralists** have used *discourse* in lieu of **text** to refer to any verbal structure whether literary or not.

FEMINIST CRITICISM *See* "What Is Feminist Criticism?" pp. 559–77.

FIGURE, FIGURE OF SPEECH *See* **Trope.**

FORMALISM A general term covering several similar types of literary criticism that arose in the 1920s and 1930s, flourished during the 1940s and 1950s, and are still in evidence today. Formalists see the literary work as an object in its own right. Thus, they tend to devote their attention to its intrinsic nature, concentrating their analyses on the interplay and relationships between the text's essential verbal elements. They study the form of the work (as opposed to its content), although form to a formalist can connote anything from **genre** (for example, one may speak of "the sonnet form") to grammatical or rhetorical structure to the "emotional imperative" that engenders the work's (more mechanical) structure. No matter which connotation of form pertains, however, formalists seek to be objective in their analysis, focusing on the work itself and eschewing external considerations. They pay particular attention to literary devices used in the work and to the patterns these devices establish.

Formalism developed largely in reaction to the practice of interpreting literary **texts** by relating them to "extrinsic" issues, such as the historical circumstances and politics of the era in which the work was written, its philosophical or theological milieu, or the experiences and frame of mind of its author. Although the term *formalism* was coined by critics to disparage the movement, it is now used simply as a descriptive term.

Formalists have generally suggested that everyday language, which serves simply to communicate information, is stale and unimaginative. They argue that "literariness" has the capacity to overturn common and expected patterns (of grammar, of storyline), thereby rejuvenating language. Such novel uses of language supposedly enable readers to experience not only language but also the world in an entirely new way.

A number of schools of criticism have adopted a formalist orientation, or at least make use of formalist concepts. The **New Criticism,** an American approach to literature that reached its height in the 1940s and 1950s, is perhaps the most famous type of formalism. But Russian formalism was the first major formalist movement; after the Stalinist regime suppressed it in the early 1930s, the Prague Linguistic Circle adopted its analytical methods. The **Chicago School** has also been classified as formalist insofar as the Chicago critics examined and analyzed works on an individual basis; their interest in historical material, on the other hand, was clearly not formalist.

Another sort of formalism, namely **Neo-Aristotelian criticism,** coexisted (but often quarreled) with the New Criticism. Centered at the University of Chicago, and practiced by such critics as R. S. Crane, Wayne Booth, and Sheldon Sacks, Neo-Aristotelian criticism derived from Aristotle's *Poetics* an appreciation for plot and the belief that, in a successful novel, plot and such other elements of fiction as characters, themes, and language would cohere to form an integrated work. The "structural" analysis of the Chicago School came into conflict, first, with the "textural" analysis of the New Critics and, later, with the theories of **reader-response** and **deconstructive** critics, who, in variously insisting on the indeterminacy of the literary text, opposed what they saw as authoritarian in the Neo-Aristotelian method.

GAPS When used by **reader-response critics** familiar with the theories of Wolfgang Iser, the term refers to "blanks" in **texts** that must be filled in by readers. A gap may be said to exist whenever and wherever a reader perceives something to be missing between words, sentences, paragraphs, stanzas, or chapters. Readers respond to gaps actively and creatively, explaining apparent inconsistencies in point of view, accounting for jumps in chronology, speculatively supplying information missing from plots, and resolving problems or issues left ambiguous or "indeterminate" in the text.

Reader-response critics sometimes speak as if a gap actually exists in a text; a gap, of course, is to some extent a product of readers' perceptions. One reader may find a given text to be riddled with gaps while another reader may view that text as comparatively consistent and complete; different readers may find different gaps in the same text. Furthermore, they may fill in the gaps they find in different ways, which is why, a reader-response critic might argue, works are interpreted in different ways.

Although the concept of the gap has been used mainly by reader-response critics, it has also been used by critics taking other theoretical approaches. Practitioners of **deconstruction** might use *gap* when explaining that every text contains opposing and even contradictory **discourses** that cannot be reconciled. **Marxist critics** have used the term gap to speak of everything from the gap that opens up between economic **base** and cultural **superstructure** to two kinds of conflicts or contradictions found in literary texts. The first of these conflicts or contradictions, they would argue, results from the fact that even realistic texts reflect an **ideology,** within which there are inevitably subjects and attitudes that cannot be represented or even recognized. As a result, readers at the edge or outside of that ideology perceive that something is missing. The second kind of conflict or contradiction within a text results from the fact that works do more than reflect ideology; they are also fictions that, consciously or unconsciously, distance themselves from that ideology.

GAY AND LESBIAN CRITICISM Sometimes referred to as *queer theory*, an approach to literature currently viewed as a form of **gender criticism.** *See* **Gender Criticism.**

GENDER CRITICISM *See* "What Is Gender Criticism?" pp. 425–40.

GENRE From the French *genre* for "kind" or "type," the classification of literary works on the basis of their content, form, or technique. The term also refers to individual classifications. For centuries works have been grouped and associated according to a number of classificatory schemes and distinctions, such as prose/poem/fiction/drama/lyric, and the traditional classical divisions: comedy/tragedy/lyric/pastoral/epic/satire. More recently, Northrop Frye has suggested that all literary works may be grouped with one of four sets of archetypal myths that are in turn associated with the four seasons; for Frye, the four main genre classifications are comedy (spring), romance (summer), tragedy (fall), and satire (winter). Many more specific genre categories exist as well, such as autobiography, the essay, the Gothic novel, the picaresque novel, the sentimental novel. Current usage is thus broad enough to permit varieties of a given genre (such as the novel) as well as the novel in general to be legitimately denoted by the term *genre.*

Traditional thinking about genre has been revised and even roundly criticized by contemporary critics. For example, the prose/poem dichotomy has been largely discarded in favor of a lyric/drama/fiction (or narrative) scheme. The more general idea that works of imaginative literature can be solidly and satisfactorily classified according to set, specific categories has also come under attack in recent times.

HEGEMONY Most commonly, one nation's dominance or dominant influence over another. The term was adopted (and adapted) by the Italian **Marxist critic** Antonio Gramsci to refer to the process of consensus formation and to the pervasive system of assumptions, meanings, and values — the web of **ideologies,** in other words — that shape the way things look, what they mean, and therefore what reality is for the majority of people within a given culture. Although Gramsci viewed hegemony as being powerful and persuasive, he did not believe that extant systems were immune to change; rather, he encouraged people to resist prevailing ideologies, to form a new consensus, and thereby to alter hegemony.

Hegemony is a term commonly used by **cultural critics** as well as by Marxist critics.

IDEOLOGY A set of beliefs underlying the customs, habits, and practices common to a given social group. To members of that group, the beliefs seem obviously true, natural, and even universally applicable. They may seem just as obviously arbitrary, idiosyncratic, and even false to those who adhere to another ideology. Within a society, several ideologies may coexist; one or more of these may be dominant.

Ideologies may be forcefully imposed or willingly subscribed to. Their component beliefs may be held consciously or unconsciously. In either case, they come to form what Johanna M. Smith has called "the unexamined ground of our experience." Ideology governs our perceptions, judgments, and prejudices — our sense of what is acceptable, normal, and deviant. Ideology may cause a revolution; it may also allow discrimination and even exploitation.

Ideologies are of special interest to politically oriented critics of literature because of the way in which authors reflect or resist prevailing views in their texts. Some **Marxist critics** have argued that literary texts reflect and reproduce the ideologies that produced them; most, however, have shown how ideologies are riven with contradictions that works of literature manage to expose and widen. Other Marxist critics have focused on the way in which texts themselves are characterized by gaps, conflicts, and contradictions between their ideological and anti-ideological functions.

Fredric Jameson, an American Marxist critic, argues that all thought is ideological, but that ideological thought that knows itself as such stands the chance of seeing through and transcending ideology.

Not all of the politically oriented critics interested in ideology have been Marxists. Certain non-Marxist **feminist critics** have addressed the question of ideology by seeking to expose (and thereby call into question) the patriarchal ideology mirrored or inscribed in works written by men — even men who have sought to counter sexism and break down sexual stereotypes. **New historicists** have been interested in demonstrating the ideological underpinnings not only of literary representations but also of our interpretations of them.

IMAGINARY ORDER *See* **Psychological Criticism and Psychoanalytic Criticism.**

IMPLIED READER *See* **Reader-Response Criticism.**

INTENTIONAL FALLACY *See* **New Criticism.**

INTERTEXTUALITY The condition of interconnectedness among texts, or the concept that any text is an amalgam of others, either because it exhibits signs of influence or because its language inevitably contains common points of reference with other texts through such things as allusion, quotation, genre, stylistic features, and even revisions. The critic Julia Kristeva, who popularized and is often credited with coining this term, views any given work as part of a larger fabric of literary **discourse,** part of a continuum including the future as well as the past. Other critics have argued for an even broader use and understanding of the term *intertextuality*, maintaining that literary history per se is too narrow a context within which to read and understand a literary text. When understood this way, *intertextuality* could be used by a **new historicist** or **cultural critic** to refer to the significant interconnectedness between a literary text and contemporary, nonliterary discussions of the issues represented in the literary text. Or it could be used by a **poststructuralist** to suggest that a work of literature can only be recognized and read within a vast field of signs and **tropes** that is like a text and that makes any single text self-contradictory and **undecidable.**

MARXIST CRITICISM *See* "What Is Marxist Criticism?" pp. 456–73.

METAPHOR A **figure of speech** (more specifically a **trope**) that associates two unlike things; the representation of one thing by another. The image (or activity or concept) used to represent or "figure" something else is known as the **vehicle** of the metaphor; the thing represented is called the **tenor.** For instance, in the sentence "That child is a mouse," the child is the tenor, whereas the mouse is the vehicle. The image of a mouse is being used to represent the child, perhaps to emphasize his or her timidity.

Metaphor should be distinguished from **simile,** another figure of speech with which it is sometimes confused. Similes compare two unlike things by using a connective word such as *like* or *as.* Metaphors use no connective word to make their comparison. Furthermore, critics ranging from Aristotle to I. A. Richards have argued that metaphors equate the vehicle with the tenor instead of simply comparing the two.

This identification of vehicle and tenor can provide much additional meaning. For instance, instead of saying, "Last night I read a book," we might say, "Last night I plowed through a book." "Plowed through" (or the activity of plowing) is the vehicle of our metaphor; "read" (or the act of reading) is the tenor, the thing being figured. (As this example shows, neither vehicle nor tenor need be a noun; metaphors may employ other parts of speech.) The increment in meaning through metaphor is fairly obvious. Our audience knows not only *that* we read but also *how* we read, because to read a book in the way that a plow rips through earth is surely to read in a relentless, unreflective way. Note that in the sentence above, a new metaphor —"rips through"— has been used to explain an old one. This serves (which is a metaphor) as an example of just how thick (another metaphor) language is with metaphors!

Metaphors may be classified as *direct* or *implied.* A direct metaphor, such as "That child is a mouse" (or "He is such a doormat!"), specifies both tenor and vehicle. An implied metaphor, by contrast, mentions only the vehicle; the tenor is implied by the context of the sentence or passage. For instance, in the sentence "Last night I plowed through a book" (or "She sliced through traffic"), the tenor — the act of reading (or driving) — can be inferred.

Traditionally, metaphor has been viewed as the principal trope. Other figures of speech include simile, **symbol,** personification, allegory, **metonymy,** synecdoche, and conceit. **Deconstructors** have questioned the distinction between metaphor and metonymy.

METONYMY A **figure of speech** (more specifically a **trope**), in which one thing is represented by another that is commonly and often physically associated with it. To refer to a writer's handwriting as his or her "hand" is to use a metonymic figure.

Like other figures of speech (such as **metaphor**), metonymy involves the replacement of one word or phrase by another; thus, a monarch might be referred to as "the crown." As narrowly defined by certain contemporary critics, particularly those associated with **deconstruction,** the **vehicle** of a metonym is arbitrarily, not intrinsically, associated with the **tenor.** (There is no special, intrinsic likeness between a crown and a monarch; it's just that crowns traditionally sit on monarchs' heads and not on the heads of university professors.)

More broadly, metonym and metonymy have been used by recent critics to refer to a wide range of figures. **Structuralists** such as Roman Jakobson, who emphasized the difference between metonymy and metaphor, have recently been challenged by deconstructors, who have further argued that *all* figuration is arbitrary. Deconstructors such as Paul de Man and J. Hillis Miller have questioned the "privilege" granted to metaphor and the metaphor/metonymy distinction or "opposition," suggesting instead that all metaphors are really metonyms.

MODERNISM *See* **Postmodernism.**

NARRATIVE A story or a telling of a story, or an account of a situation or events. Narratives may be fictional or true; they may be written in prose or verse. Some critics use the term even more generally, Brook Thomas, a **new historicist**, has critiqued "narratives of human history that neglect the role human labor has played."

NARRATOLOGY The analysis of the **structural** components of a **narrative**, the way in which those components interrelate, and the relationship between this complex of elements and the narrative's basic story line. Narratology incorporates techniques developed by other critics, most notably Russian **formalists** and French **structuralists**, applying in addition numerous traditional methods of analyzing narrative fiction (for instance, those methods outlined in the "Showing as Telling" chapter of Wayne Booth's *The Rhetoric of Fiction* [1961]). Narratologists treat narratives as explicitly, intentionally, and meticulously constructed systems rather than as simple or natural vehicles for an author's representation of life. They seek to analyze and explain how authors transform a chronologically organized story line into a literary plot. (Story is the raw material from which plot is selectively arranged and constructed.)

Narratologists pay particular attention to such elements as point of view; the relations among story, teller, and audience; and the levels and types of **discourse** used in narratives. Certain narratologists concentrate on the question of whether any narrative can actually be neutral (like a clear pane of glass through which some subject is objectively seen) and on how the practices of a given culture influence the shape, content, and impact of "historical" narratives. Mieke Bal's *Narratology: Introduction to the Theory of Narrative* (1980) is a standard introduction to the narratological approach.

NEO-ARISTOTELIAN CRITICISM *See* Chicago School, Formalism.

NEW CRITICISM, THE A type of **formalist** literary criticism that reached its height during the 1940s and 1950s, and that received its name from John Crowe Ransom's 1941 book *The New Criticism*. New Critics treat a work of literary art as if it were a self-contained, self-referential object. Rather than basing their interpretations of a **text** on the reader's response, the author's stated intentions, or parallels between the text and historical contexts (such as the author's life), New Critics perform a close reading of the text, concentrating on the internal relationships that give it its own distinctive character or form. New Critics emphasize that the structure of a work should not be divorced from meaning, viewing the two as constituting a quasi-organic unity. Special attention is paid to repetition, particularly of images or symbols, but also of sound effects and rhythms in poetry. New critics especially appreciate the use of literary devices, such as irony and paradox, to achieve a balance or reconciliation between dissimilar, even conflicting, elements in a text.

Because of the importance placed on close textual analysis and the stress on the text as a carefully crafted, orderly object containing observable formal patterns, the New Criticism has sometimes been called an "objective" approach to literature. New Critics are more likely than certain other critics to believe and say that the meaning of a text can be known objectively. For instance, **reader-response critics** see meaning as a function either of each reader's experience or of the norms that govern a particular interpretive community, and **deconstructors** argue that texts mean opposite things at the same time.

The foundations of the New Criticism were laid in books and essays written during the 1920s and 1930s by I. A. Richards (*Practical Criticism* [1929]), William Empson (*Seven Types of Ambiguity* [1930]), and T. S. Eliot ("The Function of Criticism" [1933]). The approach was significantly developed later, however, by a group of American poets and critics, including R. P. Blackmur, Cleanth Brooks, John Crowe Ransom, Allen Tate, Robert Penn Warren, and William K. Wimsatt. Although we associate the New Criticism with certain principles and terms (such as the *affective fallacy* — the notion that the reader's response is relevant to the meaning of a work — and the *intentional fallacy* — the notion that the author's intention determines the work's meaning — the New Critics were trying to make a cultural statement rather than to establish a critical dogma. Generally Southern, religious, and culturally conservative, they advocated the inherent value of literary works (particularly of literary works regarded as beautiful art objects) because they were sick of the growing ugliness of modern life and contemporary events. Some recent theorists even link the rising popularity after World War II of the New Criticism (and other types of formalist literary criticism such as the **Chicago School**) to American isolationism. These critics tend to view the formalist tendency to isolate literature from biography and history as symptomatic of American fatigue with wider involvements. Whatever the source of the New Criticism's popularity (or the reason for its eventual decline), its practitioners and the textbooks they wrote were so influential in American academia that the approach became standard in college and even high school curricula through the 1960s and well into the 1970s.

NEW HISTORICISM, THE *See* "What Is The New Historicism?" pp. 524–43.

POSTCOLONIAL CRITICISM, POSTCOLONIAL STUDIES A type of **cultural criticism**, *postcolonial criticism* usually involves the analysis of literary texts produced in countries and cultures that have come under the control of European colonial powers at some point in their history. Alternatively, it can refer to the analysis of texts written about colonized places by writers hailing from the colonizing culture. In *Orientalism* (1978), Edward Said, a pioneer of postcolonial criticism and studies, has focused on the way in which the colonizing First World has invented false images and myths of the Third (postcolonial) World, stereotypical images and myths that have conveniently justified Western exploitation and domination of Eastern and Middle Eastern cultures and peoples. In an essay entitled "Postcolonial Criticism" (1992), Homi K. Bhabha has shown how certain cultures (mis)represent other cultures, thereby extending their political and social domination in the modern world order.

Postcolonial studies, a type of **cultural studies**, refers more broadly to the study of cultural groups, practices, and **discourses** — including but not limited to literary discourses — in the colonized world. The term *postcolonial* is usually used broadly to refer to the study of works written at any point after colonization first occurred in a given country, although it is sometimes used more specifically to refer to the analysis of texts and other cultural discourses that emerged after the end of the colonial period (after the success of liberation and independence movements). Among **feminist critics**, the postcolonial perspective has inspired an attempt to recover whole cultures of women heretofore ignored or marginalized, women who speak not only from colonized places but also from the colonizing places to which many of them fled.

Postcolonial criticism has been influenced by Marxist thought, by the work of Michel Foucault — whose theories about the power of discourses have influenced **the new historicism** — and by **deconstruction,** which has challenged not only hierarchical, binary oppositions such as West/East and North/South but also the notions of superiority associated with the first term of each opposition.

POSTMODERNISM A term referring to certain radically experimental works of literature and art produced after World War II. *Postmodernism* is distinguished from *modernism,* which generally refers to the revolution in art and literature that occurred during the period 1910–1930, particularly following the disillusioning experience of World War I. The postmodern era, with its potential for mass destruction and its shocking history of genocide, has evoked a continuing disillusionment similar to that widely experienced during the modern period. Much of postmodernist writing reveals and highlights the alienation of individuals and the meaninglessness of human existence. Postmodernists frequently stress that humans desperately (and ultimately unsuccessfully) cling to illusions of security to conceal and forget the void on which their lives are perched.

Not surprisingly, postmodernists have shared with their modernist precursors the goal of breaking away from traditions (including certain modernist traditions, which, over time, had become institutionalized and conventional to some degree) through experimentation with new literary devices, forms, and styles. While preserving the spirit and even some of the themes of modernist literature (such as the alienation of humanity and historical discontinuity), postmodernists have rejected the order that a number of modernists attempted to instill in their work through patterns of allusion, symbol, and myth. They have also taken some of the meanings and methods found in modernist works to extremes that most modernists would have deplored. For instance, whereas modernists such as T. S. Eliot perceived the world as fragmented and represented that fragmentation through poetic language, many also viewed art as a potentially integrating, restorative force, a hedge against the cacophony and chaos that postmodernist works often imitate (or even celebrate) but do not attempt to counter or correct.

Because postmodernist works frequently combine aspects of diverse **genres,** they can be difficult to classify — at least according to traditional schemes of classification. Postmodernists, revolting against a certain modernist tendency toward elitist "high art," have also generally made a concerted effort to appeal to popular culture. Cartoons, music, "pop art," and television have thus become acceptable and even common media for postmodernist artistic expression. Postmodernist literary developments include such genres as the Absurd, the antinovel, concrete poetry, and other forms of avant-garde poetry written in free verse and challenging the **ideological** assumptions of contemporary society. What postmodernist theater, fiction, and poetry have in common is the view (explicit or implicit) that literary language is its own reality, not a means of representing reality.

Postmodernist critical schools include **deconstruction,** whose practitioners explore the **undecidability** of texts, and **cultural criticism,** which erases the boundary between "high" and "low" culture. The foremost theorist of postmodernism is Jean-François Lyotard, best known for his book *La Condition Postmoderne* (*The Postmodern Condition*) (1979).

POSTSTRUCTURALISM The general attempt to contest and subvert **structuralism** and to formulate new theories regarding interpretation and meaning, initiated particularly by **deconstructors** but also associated with certain aspects and practitioners of **psychoanalytic, Marxist, cultural, feminist,** and **gender criticism.** Poststructuralism, which arose in the late 1960s, includes such a wide variety of perspectives that no unified poststructuralist theory can be identified. Rather, poststructuralists are distinguished from other contemporary critics by their opposition to structuralism and by certain concepts they embrace.

Structuralists typically believe that meaning(s) in a text, as well as the meaning of a text, can be determined with reference to the system of signification — the "codes" and conventions that governed the text's production and that operate in its reception. Poststructuralists reject the possibility of such "determinate" knowledge. They believe that signification is an interminable and intricate web of associations that continually defers a determinate assessment of meaning. The numerous possible meanings of any word lead to contradictions and ultimately to the dissemination of meaning itself. Thus, poststructuralists contend that texts contradict not only structuralist accounts of them but also themselves.

To elaborate, poststructuralists have suggested that structuralism rests on a number of distinctions — between signifier and signified, self and language (or **text**), texts and other texts, and text and world — that are overly simplistic, if not patently inaccurate, and they have made a concerted effort to discredit these oppositions. For instance, poststructuralists have viewed the self as the subject, as well as the user, of language, claiming that although we may speak through and shape language, it also shapes and speaks through us. In addition, poststructuralists have demonstrated that in the grand scheme of signification, all "signifieds" are also signifiers, for each word exists in a complex web of language and has such a variety of denotations and connotations that no one meaning can be said to be final, stable, and invulnerable to reconsideration and substitution. Signification is unstable and indeterminate, and thus so is meaning. Poststructuralists, who have generally followed their structuralist predecessors in rejecting the traditional concept of the literary "work" (as the work of an individual and purposeful author) in favor of the impersonal "text," have gone structuralists one better by treating texts as "intertexts": crisscrossed strands within the infinitely larger text called language, that weblike system of denotation, connotation, and signification in which the individual text is inscribed and read and through which its myriad possible meanings are ascribed and assigned. (Poststructuralist **psychoanalytic critic** Julia Kristeva coined the term **intertextuality** to refer to the fact that a text is a "mosaic" of preexisting texts whose meanings it reworks and transforms.)

Although poststructuralism has drawn from numerous critical perspectives developed in Europe and in North America, it relies most heavily on the work of French theorists, especially Jacques Derrida, Kristeva, Jacques Lacan, Michel

Foucault, and Roland Barthes. Derrida's 1966 paper "Structure, Sign and Play in the Discourse of the Human Sciences" inaugurated poststructuralism as a coherent challenge to structuralism. Derrida rejected the structuralist presupposition that texts (or other structures) have self-referential centers that govern their language (or signifying system) without being in any way determined, governed, co-opted, or problematized by that language (or signifying system). Having rejected the structuralist concept of a self-referential center, Derrida also rejected its corollary: that a text's meaning is thereby rendered determinable (capable of being determined) as well as determinate (fixed and reliably correct). Lacan, Kristeva, Foucault, and Barthes have all, in diverse ways, arrived at similarly "antifoundational" conclusions, positing that no foundation or "center" exists that can ensure correct interpretation.

Poststructuralism continues to flourish today. In fact, one might reasonably say that poststructuralism serves as the overall paradigm for many of the most prominent contemporary critical perspectives. Approaches ranging from **reader-response criticism** to **the new historicism** assume the "antifoundationalist" bias of poststructuralism. Many approaches also incorporate the poststructuralist position that texts do not have clear and definite meanings, an argument pushed to the extreme by those poststructuralists identified with deconstruction. But unlike deconstructors, who argue that the process of signification itself produces irreconcilable contradictions, contemporary critics oriented toward other poststructuralist approaches (**discourse** analysis or Lacanian psychoanalytic theory, for instance) maintain that texts do have real meanings underlying their apparent or "manifest" meanings (which often contradict or cancel out one another). These underlying meanings have been distorted, disguised, or repressed for psychological or **ideological** reasons but can be discovered through poststructuralist ways of reading.

PRESENCE AND ABSENCE Words given a special literary application by French theorist of **deconstruction** Jacques Derrida when he used them to make a distinction between speech and writing. An individual speaking words must actually be present at the time they are heard, Derrida pointed out, whereas an individual writing words is absent at the time they are read. Derrida, who associates presence with *logos* (the creating spoken Word of a present God who "In the beginning" said "Let there be light"), argued that the Western concept of language is *logocentric*. That is, it is grounded in "the metaphysics of presence," the belief that any linguistic system has a basic foundation (what Derrida terms an "ultimate referent"), making possible an identifiable and correct meaning or meanings for any potential statement that can be made within that system. Far from supporting this common Western view of language as logocentric, however, Derrida argues that presence is not an "ultimate referent" and that it does not guarantee determinable (capable of being determined) — much less determinate (fixed and reliably correct) — meaning. Derrida in fact calls into question the "privileging" of speech and presence over writing and absence in Western thought.

PSYCHOLOGICAL CRITICISM AND PSYCHOANALYTIC CRITICISM *Psychological criticism,* which emerged in the first half of the nineteenth century, is a type of literary criticism that explores and analyzes literature in general and specific literary texts in terms of mental processes. Psychological critics generally focus on the mental processes of the author, analyzing works with an eye to their authors' personalities. Some psychological critics also use literary works to reconstruct and understand the personalities of authors — or to understand their individual modes of consciousness and thinking.

Psychoanalytic criticism stands in stark contrast to psychological criticism. Although a type of psychological criticism, it is actually better known and more widely practiced than its "parent" approach. Psychoanalytic criticism originated in the work of Austrian psychoanalyst Sigmund Freud, who pioneered the technique of psychoanalysis. Freud developed a language that described, a model that explained, a theory that encompassed human psychology. His theories are directly and indirectly concerned with the nature of the unconscious mind.

The psychoanalytic approach to literature not only rests on the theories of Freud, it may even be said to have *begun* with Freud, who wrote literary criticism as well as psychoanalytic theory. Probably because of Freud's characterization of the artist's mind as "one urged on by instincts that are too clamorous," psychoanalytic criticism written before 1950 tended to psychoanalyze the individual author. Literary works were read — sometimes unconvincingly — as fantasies that allowed authors to indulge repressed wishes, to protect themselves from deep-seated anxieties, or both.

After 1950, psychoanalytic critics began to emphasize the ways in which authors create works that appeal to readers' repressed wishes and fantasies. Consequently, they shifted their focus away from the author's psyche toward the psychology of the reader and the text. Norman Holland's theories, concerned more with the reader than with the text, helped to establish **reader-response criticism**. Critics influenced by D. W. Winnicott, an *object-relations theorist*, have questioned the tendency to see reader/text as an either/or construct; instead, they have seen reader and text (or audience and play) in terms of a relationship taking place in what Winnicott calls a "transitional" or "potential space" — space in which **binary oppositions** like real/illusory and **objective/subjective** have little or no meaning.

Jacques Lacan, another post-Freudian psychoanalytic theorist, focused on language and language-related issues. Lacan treats the unconscious as a language; consequently, he views the dream not as Freud did (that is, as a form and symptom of repression) but rather as a form of discourse. Thus we may study dreams psychoanalytically in order to learn about literature, even as we may study literature in order to learn more about the unconscious. Lacan also revised Freud's concept of the Oedipus complex, which involves the childhood wish to displace the parent of one's own sex and take his or her place in the affections of the parent of the opposite sex, by relating it to the issue of language. He argues that the preoedipal stage is also a preverbal or "mirror stage," a stage he associates with the *Imaginary Order.* He associates the subsequent oedipal stage — which roughly coincides with the child's entry into language — with what he calls the *Symbolic Order,* in which words are not the things they stand for but, rather, are stand-ins or substitutes for those things. The Imaginary Order and the Symbolic Order are two of Lacan's three orders of subjectivity, the third being *The Real,* which involves intractable and substantial things or states that cannot be imagined, symbolized, or known directly (such as death).

QUEER THEORY *See* **Gay and Lesbian Criticism, Gender Criticism.**

READER-RESPONSE CRITICISM A critical approach encompassing various approaches to literature that explore and seek to explain the diversity (and often divergence) of readers' responses to literary works.

Louise Rosenblatt is often credited with pioneering the approaches in *Literature as Exploration* (1938). In a 1969 essay entitled "Towards a Transactional Theory of Reading," she summed up her position as follows: "a poem is what the reader lives through under the guidance of the text and experiences as relevant to the text." Recognizing that many critics would reject this definition, Rosenblatt wrote: "The idea that a *poem* presupposes a *reader* actively involved with a *text* is particularly shocking to those seeking to emphasize the objectivity of their interpretations." Rosenblatt implicitly and generally refers to formalists (the most influential of whom are the **New Critics**) when she speaks of supposedly objective interpreters shocked by the notion that a *"poem"* is cooperatively produced by a *"reader"* and a *"text."* Formalists spoke of "the poem itself," the "concrete work of art," the "real poem." They had no interest in what a work of literature makes a reader "live through." In fact, in *The Verbal Icon* (1954), William K. Wimsatt and Monroe C. Beardsley used the term **affective fallacy** to define as erroneous the very idea that a reader's response is relevant to the meaning of a literary work.

Stanley Fish, whose early work is seen by some as marking the true beginning of contemporary reader-response criticism, also took issue with the tenets of formalism. In "Literature in the Reader: Affective Stylistics" (1970), he argued that any school of criticism that sees a literary work as an object, claiming to describe what it is and never what it does, misconstrues the very essence of literature and reading. Literature exists and signifies when it is read, Fish suggests, and its force is an affective force. Furthermore, reading is a temporal process, not a spatial one as formalists assume when they step back and survey the literary work as if it were an object spread out before them. The German critic Wolfgang Iser has described that process in his books *The Implied Reader: Patterns of Communication in Prose Fiction from Bunyan to Beckett* (1974) and *The Act of Reading: A Theory of Aesthetic Response* (1976). Iser argues that texts contain **gaps** (or blanks) that powerfully affect the reader, who must explain them, connect what they separate, and create in his or her mind aspects of a work that aren't *in* the text but that the text incites.

With the redefinition of literature as something that only exists meaningfully in the mind of the reader, with the redefinition of the literary work as a catalyst of mental events, comes a redefinition of the reader. No longer is the reader the passive recipient of those ideas that an author has planted in a text. "The reader is *active*," Rosenblatt had insisted. Fish makes the same point in "Literature in the Reader": "reading is . . . something you *do*." Iser, in focusing critical interest on the gaps in texts, on the blanks that readers have to fill in, similarly redefines the reader as an active maker of meaning. Other reader-response critics define the reader differently. Wayne Booth uses the phrase *the implied reader* to mean the reader "created by the work." Like Booth, Iser employs the term *the implied reader,* but he also uses *the educated reader* when he refers to what Fish calls the "intended reader."

Since the mid-1970s, reader-response criticism has evolved into a variety of new forms. Subjectivists like David Bleich, Norman Holland, and Robert Crosman have viewed the reader's response not as one "guided" by the text but rather as one motivated by deep-seated, personal, psychological needs. Holland has suggested that, when we read, we find our own "identity theme" in the text using "the literary work to symbolize and finally to replicate ourselves. We work out through the text our own characteristic patterns of desire." Even Fish has moved away from reader-response criticism as he had initially helped define it, focusing on "interpretive strategies" held in common by "interpretive communities" — such as the one comprised by American college students reading a novel as a class assignment.

Fish's shift in focus is in many ways typical of changes that have taken place within the field of reader-response criticism — a field that, because of those changes, is increasingly being referred to as *reader-oriented criticism*. Recent reader-oriented critics, responding to Fish's emphasis on interpretive communities and also to the historically oriented perception theory of Hans Robert Jauss, have studied the way a given reading public's "horizons of expectations" change over time. Many of these contemporary critics view themselves as reader-oriented critics and as practitioners of some other critical approach as well. Certain **feminist** and **gender critics** with an interest in reader response have asked whether there is such a thing as "reading like a woman." Reading-oriented **new historicsts** have looked at the way in which racism affects and is affected by reading and, more generally, the way in which politics can affect reading practices and outcomes. **Gay and lesbian critics,** such as Wayne Koestenbaum, have argued that sexualities have been similarly constructed within and by social **discourses** and that there may even be a homosexual way of reading.

REAL, THE *See* **Psychological Criticism and Psychoanalytic Criticism.**

SEMIOLOGY Another word for **semiotics,** created by Swiss linguist Ferdinand de Saussure in his 1915 book *Course in General Linguistics.*

SEMIOTICS A term coined by Charles Sanders Peirce to refer to the study of signs, sign systems, and the way meaning is derived from them. **Structuralist** anthropologists, psychoanalysts, and literary critics developed semiotics during the decades following 1950, but much of the pioneering work had been done at the turn of the century by Peirce and by the founder of modern linguistics, Ferdinand de Saussure.

To a semiotician, a sign is not simply a direct means of communication, such as a stop sign or a restaurant sign or language itself. Rather, signs encompass body language (crossed arms, slouching), ways of greeting and parting (handshakes, hugs, waves), artifacts, and even articles of clothing. A sign is anything that conveys information to others who understand it based upon a system of codes and conventions that they have consciously learned or unconsciously internalized as members of a certain culture. Semioticians have often used concepts derived specifically from linguistics, which focuses on language, to analyze all types of signs.

Although Saussure viewed linguistics as a division of semiotics (semiotics, after all, involves the study of all signs, not just linguistic ones), much semiotic theory rests on Saussure's linguistic terms, concepts, and distinctions. Semioticians subscribe to Saussure's basic concept of the linguistic sign as containing a *signifier* (a linguistic "sound image" used to represent some more abstract concept) and *signified* (the abstract concept being represented). They have also found generally useful his notion that the relationship between signifiers and signified is arbitrary; that is, no intrinsic or natural relationship exists between them, and meanings we derive from signifiers are grounded in the differences among signifiers themselves. Particularly useful are Saussure's concept of the *phoneme* (the smallest basic speech sound or unit of pronunciation) and his idea that phonemes exist in two kinds of relationships: diachronic and synchronic.

A phoneme has a diachronic, or "horizontal," relationship with those other phonemes that precede and follow it (as the words appear, left to right, on this page) in a particular usage, utterance, or **narrative** — what Saussure called *parole* (French for "word"). A phoneme has a synchronic, or "vertical," relationship with the entire system of language within which individual usages, utterances, or narratives have meaning — what Saussure called *langue* (French for "tongue," as in "native tongue," meaning language) *An* means what it means in English because those of us who speak the language are plugged in to the same system (think of it as a computer network where different individuals access the same information in the same way at a given time). A principal tenet of semiotics is that signs, like words, are not significant in themselves, but instead have meaning only in relation to other signs and the entire system of signs, or *langue*. Meaning is not inherent in the signs themselves, but is derived from the differences among signs.

Given that semiotic theory underlies structuralism, it is not surprising that many semioticians have taken a broad, structuralist approach to signs, studying a variety of phenomena ranging from rites of passage to methods of preparing and consuming food to understand the cultural codes and conventions they reveal. Because of the broad-based applicability of semiotics, furthermore, structuralist anthropologists such as Claude Lévi-Strauss, literary critics such as Roland Barthes, and **psychoanalytic theorists** such as Jacques Lacan and Julia Kristeva, have made use of semiotic theories and practices. Kristeva, who is generally considered a pioneer of feminism (although she eschews the feminist label), has argued that there is such a thing as *feminine language* and that it is semiotic, not **symbolic** in nature. She thus employs both terms in an unusual way, using *semiotic* to refer to language that is rhythmic, unifying, and fluid, and *symbolic* to refer to the more rigid associations redefined in the Western **canon**. The affinity between semiotics and structuralist literary criticism derives from the emphasis placed on *langue*, or system. Structuralist critics were reacting against **formalists** and their method of focusing on individual words as if meanings did not depend on anything external to the text.

See also **Symbolic Order; Structuralism.**

SIMILE *See* **Metaphor; Trope.**

STRUCTURALISM A theory of humankind whose proponents attempted to show systematically, even scientifically, that all elements of human culture, including literature, may be understood as parts of a system of **signs.** Critic Robert Scholes has described structuralism as a reaction to " 'modernist' alienation and despair."

European structuralists such as Roman Jakobson, Claude Lévi-Strauss, and Roland Barthes (before his shift toward poststructuralism) attempted to develop a **semiology,** or **semiotics** (science of signs). Barthes, among others, sought to recover literature and even language from the isolation in which they had been studied and to show that the laws that govern them govern all signs, from road signs to articles of clothing.

Structuralism was heavily influenced by linguistics, especially by the pioneering work of linguist Ferdinand de Saussure. Particularly useful to structuralists were Saussure's concept of the *phoneme* (the smallest basic speech sound or unit of pronunciation) and his idea that phonemes exist in two kinds of relationships: diachronic and synchronic. A phoneme has a diachronic, or "horizontal," relationship with those other phonemes that precede and follow it (as the words appear, left to right, on this page) in a particular usage, utterance, or narrative — what Saussure called *parole* (French for "word"). A phoneme has a synchronic, or "vertical," relationship with the entire system of language within which individual usages, utterances, or narratives have meaning — what Saussure called *langue* (French for "tongue," as in "native tongue," meaning language). *An* means what it means in English because those of us who speak the language are plugged in to the same system (think of it as a computer network where different individuals can access the same information in the same way at a given time).

Following Saussure, Lévi-Strauss, an anthropologist, studied hundreds of myths, breaking them into their smallest meaningful units, which he called "mythemes." Removing each from its diachronic relations with other mythemes in a single myth (such as the myth of Oedipus and his mother), he vertically aligned those mythemes that he found to be homologous (structurally correspondent). He then studied the relationships within as well as between vertically aligned columns, in an attempt to understand scientifically, through ratios and proportions, those thoughts and processes that humankind has shared, both at one particular time and across time. Whether Lévi-Strauss was studying the structure of myths or the structure of villages, he looked for recurring, common elements that transcended the differences within and among cultures.

Structuralists followed Saussure in preferring to think about the overriding *langue* or language of myth, in which each mytheme and mytheme-constituted myth fits meaningfully, rather than about isolated individual *paroles,* or narratives. Structuralists also followed Saussure's lead in believing that sign systems must be understood in terms of binary oppositions (a proposition later disputed by poststructuralist Jacques Derrida). In analyzing myths and texts to find basic structures, structuralists found that opposite terms modulate until they are finally resolved or reconciled by some intermediary third term. Thus a structuralist reading of Milton's *Paradise Lost* (1667) might show that the war between God and the rebellious angels becomes a rift between God and sinful, fallen man, a rift that is healed by the Son of God, the mediating third term.

Although structuralism was largely a European phenomenon in its origin and development, it was influenced by American thinkers as well. Noam Chomsky, for instance, who powerfully influenced structuralism through works such as *Reflections on Language* (1975), identified and distinguished between "surface structures" and "deep structures" in language and linguistic literatures, including texts.

SYMBOL Something that, although it is of interest in its own right, stands for or suggests something larger and more complex — often an idea or a range of interrelated ideas, attitudes, and practices.

Within a given culture, some things are understood to be symbols: the flag of the United States is an obvious example, as are the five intertwined Olympic rings. More subtle cultural symbols might be the river as a symbol of time and the journey as a symbol of life and its manifold experiences. Instead of appropriating symbols generally used and understood within their culture, writers often create their own symbols by setting up a complex but identifiable web of associations in their works. As a result, one object, image, person, place, or action suggests others, and may ultimately suggest a range of ideas.

A symbol may thus be defined as a **metaphor** in which the **vehicle** — the image, activity, or concept used to represent something else — represents many related things (or **tenors**), or is broadly suggestive. The urn in Keats's "Ode on a Grecian Urn" (1820) suggests many interrelated concepts, including art, truth, beauty, and timelessness.

Symbols have been of particular interest to **formalists,** who study how meanings emerge from the complex, patterned relationships among images in a work, and **psychoanalytic critics,** who are interested in how individual authors and the larger culture both disguise and reveal unconscious fears and desires through symbols. Recently, French **feminist critics** have also focused on the symbolic. They have suggested that, as wide-ranging as it seems, symbolic language is ultimately rigid and restrictive. They favor **semiotic** language and writing — writing that neither opposes nor hierarchically ranks qualities or elements of reality nor symbolizes one thing but not another in terms of a third — contending that semiotic language is at once more fluid, rhythmic, unifying, and feminine.

SYMBOLIC ORDER *See* **Psychological Criticism and Psychoanalytic Criticism; Symbol.**

TENOR *See* **Metaphor; Metonymy; Symbol.**

TEXT From the Latin *texere,* meaning "to weave," a term that may be defined in a number of ways. Some critics restrict its use to the written word, although they may apply the term to objects ranging from a poem to the words in a book to a book itself to a biblical passage used in a sermon to a written transcript of an oral statement or interview. Other critics include nonwritten material in the designation text, as long as that material has been isolated for analysis.

French **structuralist** critics took issue with the traditional view of literary compositions as "works" with a form intentionally imposed by the author and a meaning identifiable through analysis of the author's use of language. These critics argued that literary compositions are texts rather than works, texts being the product of a social institution they called *écriture* (writing). By identifying compositions as texts rather than works, structuralists denied them the personalized character attributed to works wrought by a particular, unique author. Structuralists believed not only that a text was essentially impersonal, the confluence of certain preexisting attributes of the social institution of writing, but that any interpretation of the text should result from an impersonal *lecture* (reading). This *lecture* included reading with an active awareness of how the linguistic system functions.

The French writer and theorist Roland Barthes, a structuralist who later turned toward **poststructuralism,** distinguished text from *work* in a different way, characterizing a text as open and a work as closed. According to Barthes, works are bounded entities, conventionally classified in the **canon,** whereas texts engage readers in an ongoing relationship of interpretation and reinterpretation. Barthes further divided texts into two categories: *lisible* (readerly) and *scriptible* (writerly). Texts that are *lisible* depend more heavily on convention, making their interpretation easier and more predictable. Texts that are *scriptible* are generally experimental, flouting or seriously modifying traditional rules. Such texts cannot be interpreted according to standard conventions.

 TROPE One of the two major divisions of **figures of speech** (the other being *rhetorical figures*). Trope comes from a word that literally means "turning"; to trope (with figures of speech) is, figuratively speaking, to turn or twist some word or phrase to make it mean something else. **Metaphor, metonymy, simile,** personification, and synecdoche are sometimes referred to as the principal tropes.

 UNDECIDABILITY *See* **Deconstruction.**

 VEHICLE *See* **Metaphor, Metonymy, Symbol.**

About the Contributors

THE VOLUME EDITOR

Alistair M. Duckworth is the T. Walter Herbert Commemorative Term Professor of English at the University of Florida, Gainesville. He is the author of *The Improvement of the Estate: A Study of Jane Austen's Novels* (1971; 1994), and *"Howards End": E. M. Forster's House of Fiction* (1992). His *Case Study Edition* of *Howards End* appeared in 1997. In 1999 he received a teaching award from SAADE (South Atlantic Association of Departments of English).

THE CRITICS

Claudia L. Johnson is professor of English at Princeton University. She is the author of *Jane Austen: Women, Politics, and the Novel* (1988) and *Equivocal Beings: Politics, Gender, and Sentimentality in the 1790s: Wollstonecraft, Radcliffe, Burney, Austen* (1995). In 1998 her Norton Critical Edition of *Mansfield Park* appeared. She is currently at work on a study of cults and legends of Jane Austen.

Beth Fowkes Tobin is professor of English at Arizona State University at Tempe. She is the author of *Superintending the Poor: Charitable Ladies and Paternal Landlords in British Fiction, 1770–1860* (1993) and *Picturing Imperial Power: Colonial Subjects in Eighteenth-Century British Painting* (1999). She is also the editor of *History, Gender, and Eighteenth-Century Literature* (1994).

Paul Delany is professor of English at Simon Fraser University, Burnaby, B.C., Canada. He is the author of numerous studies of modern English literature, including books on D. H. Lawrence (1978) and Rupert Brooke (1987). His book on the economics of English literature since 1875 is forthcoming from Palgrave Press; he is also working on a biography of the photographer Bill Brandt.

Casey Finch's "'Hooked and Buttoned Together': Victorian Underwear and Representations of the Female Body," a chapter from his dissertation on the formation of the unconscious in the Victorian period, appeared in *Victorian Studies* (1991). In 1992 his *Harming Others*, a book of verse, was published. His translation of *The Complete Works of the Pearl-Poet* appeared in 1993. Casey Finch died tragically in 1994.

Peter Bowen is currently senior editor of *Filmmaker Magazine* and editorial director at Sundance Channel. He coauthored with Casey Finch "The Solitary Companionship of 'L' Allegro' and 'Il Penseroso,'" *Milton Studies* (1991), and contributed "AIDS 101" to *Writing AIDS: Gay Literature, Language, and Analysis* (1993). He continues to write for various periodicals, including *Art Forum* and *The Independent*.

Devoney Looser teaches at Louisiana State University, Baton Rouge. She serves on the board of directors of the Jane Austen Society of North America. She is the author of *British Women Writers and the Writing of History, 1670–1820* (2000), the editor of *Jane Austen and Discourses of Feminism* (1995), and the coeditor of *Generations: Feminist Academics in Dialogue* (1997).

Marilyn Butler is the rector of Exeter College, Oxford, and the author of *Jane Austen and the War of Ideas* (1975), which was reissued in 1987 with a new introduction. Among her other books are *Maria Edgeworth: A Literary Biography* (1972), *Peacock Displayed* (1979), and *Romantics, Rebels, and Reactionaries: English Literature and Its Background, 1760–1830* (1985). She is general editor of the Cambridge Series in Romanticism, and in the 1990s she produced scholarly editions of women writers including Wollstonecraft, Edgeworth, Austen, and Mary Shelley.

THE SERIES EDITOR

Ross C Murfin, general editor of the *Case Studies in Contemporary Criticism* and volume editor of Conrad's *Heart of Darkness* and Hawthorne's *The Scarlet Letter* in the series, is provost and vice president for Academic Affairs at Southern Methodist University. He has taught at the University of Miami, Yale University, and the University of Virginia and has published scholarly studies of Joseph Conrad, Thomas Hardy, and D. H. Lawrence.

(continued from p. iv)

Claudia L. Johnson, "'Not at all what a man should be!': Remaking English Manhood in *Emma*" is a revised version of the chapter that appeared in *Equivocal Beings* by Claudia L. Johnson (Chicago: University of Chicago Press, 1995), pp. 191–203. Copyright © 1995 University of Chicago Press.

Beth Fowkes Tobin, "Aiding Impoverished Gentlewomen: Power and Class in *Emma*" is a revised version of the essay that appeared in *Criticism* 30 (Fall 1988): 413–31. Copyright © 1988 Wayne State University Press.

Paul Delany, "'A Sort of Notch in the Donwell Estate': Intersections of Status and Class in *Emma*" is a revised version of the essay that appeared in *Eighteenth-Century Fiction* 12.4 (July 2000): 533–48. Copyright © 2000 and reprinted by permission of *Eighteenth-Century Fiction*.

Casey Finch and Peter Bowen, "'The Tittle-Tattle of Highbury': Gossip and the Free Indirect Style in *Emma*" is a revised version of the essay that appeared in *Representations* No. 31, Summer 1990, pp. 1–18. Reprinted by permission. Copyright © 1990 by Regents of the University of California.

Devoney Looser, "'The Duty of Woman by Woman': Reforming Feminism in *Emma*." Copyright © 2002 Bedford/St. Martin's.

Marilyn Butler, "Introduction to *Emma*" is a revised version of the introduction that appeared in the Everyman's Library edition of *Emma* by Jane Austen (New York: Knopf, 1991), pp. v–xxxiii. Reprinted by permission. Copyright © 1991 the Everyman's Library.